I AM MARY

THE MOST PERFECT WOMAN EVER CREATED

THE MOTHER OF JESUS CHRIST

I AM MARY

VIRGIN THEN NOW & FOREVER

COMPILED EDITED AND WRITTEN

BY

FARRAN VERNON "HANK" HELMICK

iUniverse, Inc.
Bloomington

I AM MARY
VIRGIN THEN NOW AND FOREVER

Illustrated by Jeanne Lobel and Robert Licher

This is a work of fiction. All of the characters, names, incidents, organizations, and dialogue in this novel are either the products of the author's imagination or are used fictitiously.

iUniverse books may be ordered through booksellers or by contacting:

iUniverse
1663 Liberty Drive
Bloomington, IN 47403
www.iuniverse.com
1-800-Authors (1-800-288-4677)

ISBN: 978-1-4502-9651-9 (sc)
ISBN: 978-1-4502-9652-6 (ebk)

Printed in the United States of America

iUniverse rev. date: 08/22/2011

Contents

Dedication

My thanks to my deceased wife Barbara Lee Spillane Helmick and her mother Ethel M. Buboltz [also deceased] who were the first to encourage by bumbling efforts to become a writer. No reflection on them, but I am still bumbling. My special thanks to Lois Jean Anderson Helmick, my recently departed wife, who for eighteen years was my patient sounding board and critic. I owe special thanks to my deceased sister Hope Helmick Davis; who held my hand through my first book. Her help and encouragement saw me through many frustrating years of learning and development.

My love to my daughters Theresa Anne Pogue and Kristine Mary Woodruff, whose constant support, typing and critiques were most helpful.

Special thanks to Journalist Barbara Starbeck, her proofing and suggestions enabled me to finish and publish this book.

Synopsis

THE GREATEST LOVE STORY EVER WRITTEN

I Am Mary is a fictional autobiography based on the private revelations of Mother Mary and Jesus Christ to the mystics: Saint Mary of Agreda, Saint Bridgett of Sweden, and Venerable Anne Catherine Emmerick. The story dictated by Mary is without a doubt the Greatest Love Story Ever Written. Mary's love for her Son, Jesus the Christ, is without par in the history of the world. God the Son created his own mother at the beginning of time with all perfection at his disposal. Once created, God the Son continued to add to her perfection throughout her entire life. His love for her is without human description. Mary's love for her Divine Son would have ruptured her heart if God the Father, the Son, and the Holy Ghost had not taken her to her just reward in her seventieth year. Mary had not only the love of a mother for her perfect human son, but she had the love for her Son who was the Son of God the Father Almighty.

In addition to Mary's own words, I leaned heavily on the Holy Bible, the teachings of the Roman Catholic Church, Catholic tradition, and the Apocryphal book of Mary to fill in the story. The story flowers to life by use of the first person. I found the style and presentation of the original documents to be archaic, stilted, wordy, passive throughout, and difficult to read. I edited them to my own liking in the hope of making them more interesting and easier to read. I trust you will agree.

The New Testament, in my opinion, portrays Jesus the man very well, but there is little interaction between Jesus as true Man and Jesus as true God. This story unravels the hidden, supernatural world of Jesus and Mary. I wrote the First Chapter in the third person to relate the story of Mary's family background. The fictional autobiography starts in Chapter Two with Mary's Immaculate Conception.

The mystical stories of the Saints entranced me and I caught myself pondering over the mystery of Jesus, being true God and true Man and how this relationship actually co-existed. With no ready answer, I found it easy to believe in the mystical realm of Jesus, true God, while he lived on earth as true Man. *However, man can no more pierce the mystery of Jesus, true God and true Man than he can divine the mystery of the Holy Trinity.* We will not understand these mysteries until we pass-over and see God face to face in the Beatific Vision.

Mary dictated the story of her life in the seventeenth century to Saint Mary of Agreda. The same century that Jesus told Saint Margaret Mary Alacoque [1647-1690] that the end of the world was slowly approaching, while in 1938 he said to Saint Maria Faustina Kowalska, "For the dreadful day of my Justice is imminent." Jesus desires, *because of his great mercy in these end times,* to make known the infinite mercy of the Immaculate Heart of Mary his mother and Co-redemptorist, so that a sinful world may have recourse to her benevolent intercession.

The autobiography, Mary's words according to Saint Mary of Agreda, in portraying Mary's life reveals her innermost feelings of love, devotion, and sacrifice to the Triune God and her fellow pilgrims. Mary's words are powerful, vivifying, deeply spiritual and meditative. The Virgin Mary's spellbinding story will capture you heart and soul and will bond you to Mary and her Son Jesus Christ forever.

If you appreciate this book please say a prayer for me.

Farran V. Hank Helmick

Forward

I Am Mary is a fictional autobiography of the life of Mary, the Mother of Jesus Christ, the only Son of God the Father. The teachings of the Roman Catholic Church, Catholic tradition, private revelation, and the apocryphal books [not included in the Bible] are the basis of my story. The Church reveals very little about the private lives of Mary and Jesus. However, there have been many private revelations about Mary since her death. The private visions and revelations of Venerable Anne Catherine Emmerick, an Augustinian nun, Saint Bridgette of Sweden, and Saint Mary of Agreda are the primary sources for this history. Mary of Agreda wrote a four-volume story of Mary's life, as dictated to her by Mother Mary; she named her work The City of God. Anne Catherine Emmerich had visions most of her life based on the lives of our Blessed Lord and Mother Mary, from which Clemens Brentano wrote four-journals on "The Life of Jesus Christ." Saint Bridgette claimed to have had visions and conversations with the Lord Jesus and Mother Mary. One of her important contributions was "The Magnificent Promises" which honors the passion of Jesus.

To the uninitiated, the extremes of devotion as portrayed in this story may appear far-fetched, perhaps even touching on fanaticism. Most Roman Catholics; however, will recognize and appreciate the utter commitment to God that certain individuals are capable of rendering. In the Roman Catholic Faith, we call them Saints. Not saints in the ordinary sense that they are, so to speak, in a State of Grace, but Saints in the sense that they lived extraordinarily heroic lives of sacrifice and devotion to the Holy Trinity. These heroic virtues; however, are not restricted to their religious orders. My primary sources of information are mystics intimately involved in their Catholic faith.

Saint Mary of Agreda was the Mother Superior of the Convent of the Immaculate Conception located in the town of Agreda, Spain. She was born in 1602 in Agreda. In 1617 she entered the convent of Discalced Franciscan Nuns in the Convent of the Immaculate Conception in Agreda. In 1625 she was chosen abbess, and except for one short intermission was re-elected every three-years, until she died in 1665. She became the confidant of important officials and even of King Philip IV of Spain. The fame of her prudence and foresight soon spread and God granted Mary the gift of bilocation. According to Mary, Jesus ordered her to write the story of Mother Mary as dictated to her by his mother.

It appears that God prefers women for private revelation; however, he seems to have chosen mostly men to reveal the great public truths of the Bible and to attend to the public teaching. There are thirty-three Saints selected as Doctors of the Church. Three of them are women. Humility, great piety, love, and deep faith are the requisites of God's special messengers. Women, as a rule, seem to be more inclined to these virtues than men.

Venerable Anne Catherine Emmerick was a nun in the Augustinian Convent of Agnetenberg at Dulman, Germany. Sister Anne subsisted almost entirely on water and the Holy Eucharist toward the end of her life. God granted her the gift of seeing past, present, and future, and her peers considered her a mystic. From 1812, until the year of her death in 1824, she bore the stigmata of Christ.

Saint Bridgette of Sweden was born in 1303. Her parents married her to a most holy young man and they had eight children. One of whom, Katherine, like her mother, was also canonized a Saint. St.

Bridgette had many revelations. When her husband died in 1343; Bridgette, as instructed by Jesus, opened the Religious Order of Our Most Holy Savior [now commonly known as the Bridgettines]. Saint Bridgette died in 1373. The Pope canonized her in 1391, and in 1396 he declared Saint Bridgette, "The Patron Saint of Sweden."

In all ages, God, in His Infinite Wisdom, has inspired His elect to heights of great holiness. In each generation there has been a saintly person blessed with the outward signs of Christ's suffering; the Holy Stigmata of Jesus Christ. The last notable person so blessed was Padre Pio of Pietrelcina, Italy. He was a monk in the Capuchin Order of San Giovanni Rotondo, Italy. Blessed with the power of bilocation, Padre Pio could also see into the hearts of those he was confessing. For fifty years, he bore the Stigmata of Christ. He was born in 1887 and died in 1968 at the age of eighty-one. Through God, Padre Pio performed hundreds of miracles. Pope John Paul II canonized Padre Pio on June 16, 2002 as a Saint for our times.

Most Roman Catholics know of the miracles at Fatima and the story of the three children to whom Mother Mary appeared in 1917. The Catholic Church has already declared that two of the children, Jacinta and Francesco, are "Blessed." I am sure the Church, since the death of Sister Lucy, will in time, canonize the three as saints.

The Catholic Church has tacitly and indirectly authorized, The City of God, as spiritual reading for members of the Catholic faith. Popes innocent XI, Alexander VIII, Clement IX, Benedict XIII, and Benedict XIV declared this book authentic, and worthy of devout perusal and free from error in faith and morals. Pope Pious IX in 1862 and the Great Congress of Malines the following year, declared Saint Bridget's revelations as Blessed. Blessed Anne Catherine Emmerick bore the stigmata of Christ and was renowned as a prophet, and visionary. Cardinal Gibbons, Archbishops Gross, Gechan, Elder, Bishop Toebbe, and many others recommended Anne's book, as suitable for Catholic reading when it was published.

It is worthy to note that the mystics did not always agree on many of the circumstances about which they wrote regarding the lives of Mary and Jesus. I believe; however, that each writer managed to more than adequately fill in much unknown information of the personal lives of Mary and Jesus not mentioned in the Gospels. They wrote down the events revealed to them to the best of their understanding. Give a hundred people a dictated or video of a particular subject and then ask them to write down what they say and heard and I am sure you will have a hundred variations.

The Church will never give full approval to such writings since that in actuality would be an addition to the Deposit of Faith left by Christ. None of these writings can ever have the same importance or authority of the Bible.

The decree of the Congregation for the Propagation of the Faith, A.A.S., 58, 1186 [approved by Pope Paul VI on October 14, 1966] states that the Nihil Obstat and Imprimatur are no longer required on publications that deal with private revelations, provided they contain nothing contrary to faith and morals. I wish to manifest my unconditional submission to the final and official judgment of the Magisterium of the Church, regarding any events presently under investigation regarding that of which I have written or compiled.

An immense domain of truth remains outside the range of natural, human-knowledge. History bears out that God, for his own reasons, often grants to his friend's higher insights into some of his supernatural truths. I believe God certainly intended his revelations to his Saints to be an additional source of meditation for his people.

The writers of the New Testament did not dwell on the personal lives of Mary and Jesus. The primary concern of the New Testament was and is, the new and everlasting Covenant established by Jesus Christ. After Christ's Ascension, Mary, the mother of Jesus, was the obvious person for the

Apostles to turn to for spiritual guidance. At Christ's direction, as he hung on the cross, Mary became our Mother, and the Mother of the Church. It is conceivable that after Christ's Ascension that Mary, as Queen of Heaven and Earth, could easily have assumed a leadership role over the sometimes confused and distraught disciples of the Church. However, Mary, ever the humble advocate of the Lord, knew how Jesus Christ intended the Church to function. Jesus' words to Peter established Simon as the first leader [Pope] of His Church on earth, and the Apostles were to be the first officials [Bishops]. For did Jesus not say,

"Blest are you Simon, son of Jonah! No mere man has revealed this to you, but my heavenly Father. I, for my part, declare to you, you are 'Rock', and on this Rock I will build my Church, and the jaws of death shall not prevail against it. I will entrust you with the keys of the Kingdom of Heaven. Whatever you declare bound on earth shall be bound in heaven; whatever you declare loosed on earth shall be loosed in heaven [Jn.16, 18-19]."

For Mary to assume an active leadership would obviously have been contrary to God's plans. The Hebrew's religious structure was the pattern used for the organization of the Roman Catholic Church. This is not a mere coincidence. After all, the composition of the Hebrew religion is that with which the Apostles were the most familiar. Mary's role as *spiritual advisor* to the leaders of the Church required a great deal of tact and humility. After all, it was the role of the Apostles, as the first Bishops, to make all decisions concerning the establishment of the Church. Mary, ever humble, always remained in the background. She led the Apostles by answering their frequent questions and making suggestions when appropriate. The writing of the first Gospels was a result of Mary's guiding hand. Mary downplayed her role ever concentrating on the Lord, not on herself. Mary knew that in her role as Jesus' mother, she was not to be the center of attention. The message that was to be proclaimed to the world was the Passion of Jesus, not his childhood. Likewise, Mary's life, while dear to all of us, also had to take a back seat to the message of the Gospels.

Mary, as Queen of Heaven, the Earth, and the Universe, has an essential role in the salvation of the human race. Throughout history, Mary has always appeared when the Church has floundered, torn with schism and disunity. Her most recent, notable appearance, approved by the Church as appropriate for meditation, was at Fatima, Portugal. God's role for Mary is that of a protective mother in heaven, to whom we can all turn. In the last hundred and fifty years, she has appeared repeatedly warning us of God's great displeasure with the sins of His people.

In the end times, Mary's function, through the power of God, is to defeat Satan and crush his head beneath her heel [Gen: 3, 15]. Some authorities believe that we are indeed in the end times. Before Vatican II, the Church seemed to concentrate on the theme of the "punishments of God," and more people were in "awe" and had a healthy "fear" or "respect" of the Lord. After Vatican II, the pendulum swung to the far left and today people are more enraptured with the "Humanity" of Jesus. Consequently, less and less people have any "awe" of God, let alone "respect" for the "Holy Eucharist." The Holy Tabernacle with its precious repository, in some Dioceses, has even been relegated to a side room or niche. In these Churches, I personally do not feel the presence of the Lord. It is the same feeling I have when I am inside the church of another denomination. Without the physical presence of Jesus Christ, to me, it becomes "just" another "hall." In 1999, the Bishops of the United States agreed that so far the *biggest mistake* they had made in the post conciliar period was their "recommendation" that "The *Tabernacle* should be removed from the central altar."

The Humanity of Christ is quite evident today, which is certainly a good thing in itself. However, on the "flip" side of the coin, with the erosion of the "fear of the Lord" many people have little conception of Jesus as a Divine Person. Consequently, statistician's today claim that eighty percent of Catholics do not believe in the real presence of Jesus Christ in the Holy Eucharist. I believe this figure to be highly exaggerated. To be a Christian, we must believe that Jesus Christ is "True God and True Man." We must believe that at the priest's words at the "Consecration" the bread and wine "actually", by the power of the Holy Spirit and the blessed hands of the priest, becomes the "Real Presence," the "Body and Blood" of Jesus Christ.

Jesus was not only "human" when He roamed the earth, but He was also "Divine." As True God, it is only logical to presume that there were many supernatural episodes in his life; supernatural events other than those we are familiar with; i.e.: his healing of the sick, raising the dead, and feeding the multitudes. It is obvious that Jesus deliberately avoided making a show of his miraculous powers. A perfect example is found when Jesus told Thomas,

**"Have you come to believe because you have seen me?
Blessed are those who have not seen and have believed." [John: 24-29]**

Jesus did not want people to believe in him, because he could heal them, but because He was truly God; and that through their faith in him; they could gain eternal life.

This story deals with many miraculous events surrounding Saint Anne, Mother Mary, and John the Baptist, Jesus Christ, and many others. In expressing Mary's words, where possible, throughout the story, I have used the dialogue attributed to Our Lady by her confidants, instead of fabricating fictional dialogue.

In my research, I was utterly amazed with the importance of the role women have played in God's scheme of things. In today's society, women demand equality with men in every *occupation*, including the *Priesthood*, although this would be contrary to the *Deposit of Faith*. Women were certainly not equal to men in biblical times due to the laws of their society. However, in their roles as mothers and religious, they were, and are, as God intended, certainly equal to men in every way. In my humble opinion, God meant for women and men to compliment one another. He did not intend for them to compete with one another. I believe the debate has to center on the *role* that God intended for women, not the *role*, women have decided is their due. However, it is not the purpose of this forward to debate that sensitive issue.

It is worthy to note that the ancestral women from Jesus' line of descendents received vast treasures of glory, trust, and confidence from God himself. In many instances, it was the women that received God's confidence, not the men. In [Mathew: 1, 1-17] the genealogy of Jesus is listed—all men. However, when one studies the history of the women of his lineage, we discover an additional treasure of God's ancestors, the holy, saintly women: Emorun the mother of Ismeria, Ismeria, the mother of Anne; Anne, the mother of Mary; Mary, the Mother of Jesus Christ.

It is true that Hebrew Law considered a woman a minor, an irresponsible person. A husband could refuse to honor a contract that she entered into. Her testimony was not accepted in court, and, as a general rule, she did not inherit from her father, or from her husband. However, she did have rights. Since she was so vulnerable, the law protected her. The wife's entire maintenance fell upon the husband, who was to house, feed and clothe her according to her status and his means. If she were not properly cared for, she could call on her father for justice, who could rebuke his son in law. However, this was seldom necessary. The Jewish husbands liked to see their wives well dressed, and adorned with jewelry. A good wife provided fine wheat-flour, honey, and oil in abundance. The respect that children gave their parents obviously included the mother. The wife used her personal earnings as she saw fit, even if the husband was the sole guardian of the household's common property.

The duties that began with, "Thou Shalt" did not apply to the women. The women did not have to recite the Shema Israel, or be present at the reading of the law, wear phylacteries, and fringed clothing, or live in a tent at the Feast of the Tabernacles. However, the rabbis added, "Before all the commandments of the Torah, men and women are upon the same footing, therefore the women were not denied these duties. The rabbis even advised the women to know the Law well, so that they might instruct their sons, and urge their husbands to the fulfillment of their religious obligations.

In the small kingdom of the home, the wife was queen. Then, as in all other eras, she was well aware of that fact. The wife produced nearly everything the Hebrews used at home. Her importance in a Jewish home was all the greater, since among the Jews, as among other nations of antiquity, the wife spun and wove the cloth and made their clothes. She carried on her head all the water, which they drank, cooked with, and bathed in. It was the wife, who ground the grain, made their daily bread, cooked their meals, cleaned their clothes and their home, raised their children, and was their first teacher of the laws of God. It was she that pressed the olives for the oil they needed for their lamps, and she who prepared the *very pure oil* for the Sabbath, and made sure the lamp did not go out. The Hebrew woman was quite necessary to their husbands, just as women have been, and will always be to men of every age.

Many of the prophets and rabbis of antiquity took their revenge on the women, because they were so bound to the so-called "weaker sex". They made many snide remarks about women in the Old Testament that puts them down severely. However, not all doctors of the law shared these sentiments. The Rabbi Gamaliel was quoted as saying, "An emperor said to the Wise Man, "Thy God is a thief; to make the woman he had to steal a rib from the sleeping Adam."

The wise doctor was at a loss for words, but his daughter told him. "Let me take care of this." She went to see the Emperor and said to him, "We call for justice."

"Indeed? What for?"

"Thieves got into our house in the night: they have taken away a silver ewer and they have left a gold one in its place."

"Ha, ha," laughed the Emperor, "I wish I could have burglars like that every night."

"Well," she replied, "that is what our God did: He took a mere rib from Adam, but in exchange, He gave him a wife."

Other rabbis; however, praised women's penetrating intelligence, their ardor for work, their steadfastness and their kind hearts. The Holy Scriptures advocates respect for women. Did not Adam, the first man, cry out and say, "Here at last is bone that comes from my bone, and flesh that comes from my flesh." God commanded that a man should leave his father and mother and instead cling to his wife, so that the two become "one flesh." The proverbs state that, "A good wife is treasure found," and "Wisdom is shown in the form of a woman." The Bible offers many examples of women admirable for their courage, their magnanimity, their long-suffering fortitude, and their greatness of spirit. The Bible parades a beautiful array of women, i.e.: from Deborah to the mother of Maccabees, from Ruth to Judith to Esther, and from Emorun to Mary. There necessarily had to be a long succession of most unusual holy women to prepare for the birth of Mary.

God, 'in His Mind's Eye" had imagined a new Eve, a spotless maiden of Zion, who would redeem the first Eve's sin of tempting Adam. In order to fulfill the divine plan, the women God chose were wondrously holy. God gave these women special gifts to strengthen, and prepare them for the important task that he had in store for them. God gave secrets to some of the women. Many times their spouses did not share in these secrets. God gave women the special gift of bringing and nurturing life into the world. Throughout the ages, women have stayed home and taken care of their children. In the nineteenth century, men worked twelve to fourteen hours a day. It was the women that raised the children, nurtured them, and taught them the morals and ethics, by which they would live, and by which they would usually die. In the last half of the twentieth century, all of this changed. Women no longer stayed home. Women no longer were there to love, nurture, and teach their children about God's laws, and the laws of society. Today, we have but to look about and see the result of the woman's absence from the home. Women are special; God made them that way.

In the writings of the mystics, in their abject humility, they commented repeatedly of how unworthy they were to write their respective documents. If they were unworthy, I can only guess as to which rung on the totem pole this leaves me? My only claim of qualification to compile and write this work is that through prayer I asked permission of Mother Mary to write it. In time I forgot all about the request. A month or so later my wife and I attended a nine day novena to the Divine Mercy; the program was presented by a very holy couple at the Sacred Heart Parish in Prescott, AZ. At the end of the novena, the couple asked if anyone wished to come forward for a personal blessing. I had never been one to respond to this type of an appeal, but suddenly I said to my wife Lois, "Let's go forward and get a blessing?"

She replied, "And ask for what?"

I paused and then said, "We will ask them to bless our marriage."

So off we went. Lois was prayed over by the man, and I was prayed over by the lady. They, and several good parishioners, laid their hands on our heads. The lady praying over me suddenly stopped and exclaimed, "There is a halo over your head, which means that God has something special for you to do."

I was speechless. I could not think of a thing to which God could be referring. Amazingly, Lois had a similar experience. We were puzzled, awed, and humbled by their revelations. At 2; 00 AM the following morning, I abruptly awoke and sat up. I realized that our experience had been a message from Mother Mary in response to my query for a sign from her. I figured Lois' message was that she was going to read all my writings and give me help and support; which she did faithfully. She never told me what her actual message was.

In a most dramatic way, Mother Mary did give me a sign, as I had asked her to do. However, she did not promise me a best seller nor did she teach me how to spell. Only you, the reader, can render that decision.

My father converted to the Catholic faith when I was very young. He converted prior to my parent's divorce when I was eight-years old. I attended Church with him only once. I went to Notre Dame in Paris, France during WWII with a friend when I was twenty-years old. As a child, I remember there was a lot of loose gossip [mostly gutter-type nonsense] about the Catholic Church among us confused children. Our group of boys [at about age twelve] was made up of fellows with parents who ranged from non-believers, to believers of the Jewish faith, to believers as Baptists, Catholics, Methodists and other non denominational religions. Mother Mary's name came up several times, usually in a derogatory manner, as did the name of Jesus. I remember stating that if I were God that I would create the mother of my Son as the most perfect person that could possibly be conceived. God did do so without any help from me. Today, I believe that I didn't just come up with that statement out of thin air. At age twenty-two when I joined the Catholic Church, I chose Michael as my Baptismal name to give me strength, and I chose Thomas to keep me from ever doubting my faith. I am a sinner like all mankind, but I can honestly say that since my conversion, I have never doubted the validity of the Catholic Faith. I thank Saint Thomas for his help, and I thank St Michael for the strength he has given me—not that I have always been a perfect Catholic.

A final note: We should all base our faith on the Scriptures and the Traditions of the Church. I add that any revelations contained herein that go beyond the foundations of Scripture and Tradition should be accepted only with human faith. I sincerely hope this book will be entertaining, and provide the reader with food for thought. I trust it will emphasize the fact that Jesus was True Man, and True God, and as such, He was Divine and did many miraculous things never mentioned in the Scriptures. Perhaps this book will satisfy some of your curiosity and the questions that so many of us have hungered for concerning the private lives and habits of the two most important humans ever born, Jesus Christ, the only Son of God, and Mary, the Mother of Jesus Christ, the Mother of God.

Farran Vernon Michael Thomas Hank Helmick

I Am Mary

I Am Mary the unworthy mother of Jesus Christ, the only Son of God the Father Almighty. He is the Emmanuel promised by Isaiah 7:-14. The Messiah waited on so anxiously for hundreds of years by the Hebrews, the chosen people of God. In every generation, Jewish mothers had prayed that their daughter would be the one selected to be the mother of God. However, it was not by random selection that God chose me as his spouse. I was perfectly conceived in the *Mind's Eye* of the Triune God, even before the Angels, the Heavens, and the Earth were created.

If no one is worthy to enter the gates of heaven except by the power of God {Matt: 19, 23-25}, think how much more unworthy would be the one chosen to be the Mother of God? However, by God's divine plan, **"I Am the Immaculate Conception."** Since my role was to be the mother of Jesus Christ, the new Adam and Redeemer, I was destined to be the new Eve and Co-redemptorist. God conceived me without Original Sin, since nothing unclean would be a suitable vessel in which to birth the Son of God. I had earned no merit whatsoever, when God planned and added many blessings to my soul before my birth. Unbeknownst to me; however, God made me so perfect that in the "Laws of Probability and Chance" there was little likelihood that I would sin, even though I, a created creature was also "fully subject" to "Free Will." However, without the scourge of "Concupiscence" and considering all the gifts given me at birth, I am sure the Son of God was not concerned, for since he was perfect, he could not allow his mother to be imperfect. He had created a *Perfect Vessel* in which to birth his *Perfect Son.* I was not aware of these advantages; however, and even if I had been, I would still have spent much anguish, in the dread that I might somehow sin and offend my God and Creator.

My Son and I were very close. No parent and child, husband and wife, or any of God's creatures were ever as close spiritually as my Son and I were. When he was happy, I was happy. When he hurt, I hurt. God allowed me to suffer in a mystical way, during my Son's Passion. I suffered the same mental, physical and spiritual pain, which he suffered. I am the New Eve and my Son is the New Adam. I did not tell my life's story to the different seers to obtain prestige for myself, but did so in obedience to my Son. I am ever subject to his Divine Wishes.

The Holy Spirit inspired my cousin Elizabeth and me to recite the Magnificat, when I visited her during her pregnancy. By God's blessing, she had conceived a child in her old age destined to be the **Precursor** of the coming of my Son. Elizabeth greeted me with the words,

"Blessed are you among women and blessed is the fruit of your womb. Whence is it that the mother of my Lord should come to me? For at the moment the sound of your greeting came to my ears, the infant in my womb leaped for joy. Blessed are you who have believed, for all the things promised you by the Lord shall be accomplished." In turn, I replied,

"My soul magnifies the greatness of the Lord, and my spirit rejoices in God my savior. He, who is mighty, has looked upon the lowliness of his handmaid. For behold, henceforth, all generations shall call me blessed, for he who is mighty has done great things for me, and holy is his name. His mercy is from age to age to those who fear him. He has shown the might of his arm and dispersed the arrogant of mind and heart. He has put down the rulers of the world and lifted up the lowly. The hungry he has filled with good things and the rich he has sent empty away. He has given aid to Israel his servant mindful of his mercy according to his promise to our fathers and to Abraham and to his posterity forever. Amen!"

Through me, my Son intends to save many souls who would otherwise be lost. My Son sent Saint Michael and me to Fatima, Portugal in 1917. We announced the end of World War I, and warned the world of the great evil of the Russian Empire and the possible event of World War II, if people did not change their ways. At Garabandal, Spain, in 1961, I warned the world again of another schism that would take place since humankind ignored the warnings of Fatima, and had instead chosen to worship the gods of power, wealth, and permissiveness. In spite of Pope John Paul 11's consecration of me to the World and to Russia in 1984, there simply have not been enough prayers to complete the conversion of Russia. Prayers have brought down the Berlin Wall, and have led to the demise of the Communist Dictatorship. Many more prayers are needed; however, to complete their conversion, and stay the evil of worldwide communism and secular humanism. Time is running out. My Son is much offended.

Only the prayers of the faithful have stayed the hand of an avenging God. Pray, make many sacrifices, visit the Blessed Sacrament frequently, and give the Holy Eucharist the honor due your Creator. God will grant your requests if you pray with sincerity. Think on the passion of Jesus and he will be with you always as will I, his devoted mother. Ask of me and I will lay your requests at the feet of my Divine Son. Honor me, live good lives as my Son wishes, and I will lead you to the feet of my Son at the hour of your death. We are all the children of God and he loves each one of us individually. Remember that God created the race of man to be with Him in heaven for eternity. Do not allow the temporary pleasures of this world to rob you of the next. I, your mother, will pray for you always. Pray the Rosary every day for peace, the conversion of the Russian people, and for the poor souls in Purgatory. In these end times, God has released his great mercy upon the world. So, if you are willing to listen, take heed.

Your Loving Mother

MARY

Chapter One

The Grandparents of Jesus Christ

Azor the father of Zadok, Zadok became the father of Achim, Achim the father of Eliud, Eliud the father of Eleazar. Eleazar became the father of Matthan, Matthan the father of Jacob, Jacob the father of Joseph, the husband of Mary. Of her was born Jesus who is called the Messiah.
[Matt: 1, 14-16]

The small caravan paused on a bluff overlooking their destination. Eliud helped Ismeria down from her Muscat Ass saying, "Let's take a short break in the shadow of the aqueduct." It had been a grueling trek. Behind them lay the serpentine, Jordan River, measuring only sixty-five miles between the Sea of Galilee and the Salt Sea. It writhed like a snake, even flowing north at times. They had avoided, as much as possible, the winding two hundred-mile long watercourse. The engineering of the Hill-Road would have been limited, for a thick jungle, known as the Es-Zor, edged the waterway. Instead the Hill Road followed a series of springs that formed a string of oases. The most famous was the Oases of Jericho. Now, only two miles south of them lay their destination, the monastery of Qumran. The cult of Qumran was the least of three major groups, the Sadducees, the Pharisees, and the Essenes that vied for dominance of a long list of more than 30 cults that made up the Jewish faith.

"It's hotter here," Eliud commented, "but once we get inside the buildings at Qumran, you will be quite comfortable." The family members of the caravan gratefully sought the shade of the huge aqueduct that cast a welcome shade below its sound of running water.

"You know I don't mind the heat of the desert, Eliud. I know it is stark and hot, but I always have a feeling of being at home here. Qumran is so serene, and the sound of the water in the aqueduct above us seems to whisper to me 'You're home, you're home."

The monks had built their monastery on the ruined foundations of an Israeli fortress abandoned in 67 BC. The travelers gazed curiously at the serene outlying Essene community that sprawled along the foot of the cliffs. The splotches of green gardens looked like a patch work quilt from the distance. Members of the Essene cult, other than the monks, lived in caves and small houses along their path, and below the community center were more caves, tents, and homes of a more solid construction. These extended another two miles before they merged with an agricultural complex at En Feskbah. A short distance to the east laid the torpid, dead waters of the Salt Sea often referred to as the "Sea of the Plain." The community of Khirbet Qumran was nestled between towering limestone cliffs on a marly terrace.

Over the eons, the Wadi Qumran had slashed a deep gorge, which in turn created the Dead Sea. The Sea, which was actually an inland lake, was fifty miles long by eleven wide, and its water was saturated with six times the salt content of an ocean. Throughout history, the lake had accumulated many other names among them, the Lake of Lot, the Lake of Palestine, and the Sea of Sodom. Its water is heavy and oily; and plant and animal life could not survive in its depths. Unknown to local residents the sea lay 1286 feet below sea level, the lowest point on earth, and its greatest depth was 1300 feet.

The welcome patches of green eased the traveler's sand-weary eyes. In the distance, a cow lowed, and a calf gamboled awkwardly to its mother's side. The heifer immediately began to suckle and nudge its mother's udder impatiently with its eager moist nose. Young shepherds, attending their scattered flocks of fat-tailed sheep and lop-eared goats, eyed them curiously as they wended their weary way to the haven of Khirbet Qumran. The travelers rode the beautiful Muscat Ass, a big, strong beast that could go their five and twenty miles a day with ease. They had journeyed from Nazareth to Magdala following the well-traveled Lake Road south to the Jordan River route. Crossing the Jordan, a few miles below Philoteria, they had taken the road on the western bank of the Jordan. From Beth Hoglah they had entered the Judean Wilderness, where the road was more of a path than a trail. Due west of Qumran across the jagged Judean Wilderness; no more than fifteen miles, as the crow flies, lay Jerusalem, the capital city of the Hebrews. The ancient city of Jericho was a mere eight miles north of Khirbet Qumran, which lay on the western shore of the Dead Sea.

The monks of the Qumran cult shared their resources with one another. They shared pottery made in a kiln from within the fortified site of Qumran. They built an irrigation system and shared in the stores of food and water furnished from the storehouses from within the compound. In the scriptorium, they wrote biblical and sectarian scrolls common to their sect. The famous Dead Sea Scrolls came from the work of these monks. To the traveler's left, a Roman-style water aqueduct ran directly to the northern end of the compound and emptied into spacious cisterns located within the walled-in structure. Each day the Elders refilled the cisterns and then allowed the excess water to follow its self made streambed on down the valley satisfying the needs of the small farms located below the monk's facilities.

* * *

The monks made the travelers welcome as they entered Qumran. The holy men led them past the huge water cisterns and the scriptorium, and then assigned them quarters near the Great Assembly Hall, located at the southern end of the monastery. The following morning, according to custom, no one spoke until after they had purified themselves in a ritualistic bath in cold water, and said their morning prayers. The monks fasted daily until noon. The monks and their guests would then partake of a Spartan meal. After prayers, the two guests were ushered to the quarters of one of the leaders of the Essenes. Entering a small room, the travelers, Ismeria and her husband Eliud, approached a metal grating set in the wall. Archos sat within a small cubical much like a confessional. The aged holy man was one of a council of three priests who stood for the three priestly families. By virtue of his age and wisdom; however; Archos was considered the Superior of the Essenians. There were twelve additional laymen rulers, who represented the twelve tribes of Israel. These fifteen men governed the community under strict rules, particularly for the Sabbath. The monks even refrained from relieving themselves on the Sabbath, lest the waste profane God's holy day.

The Essenians of Khirbet Qumran were a remarkable pious cult who could trace their ancestry back to Moses and his brother Aaron. The Essenians were a messianic cult, whose members prayed constantly for the coming of the Messiah. They fervently believed that their lineage was destined to produce the "Vessel of the Promise." A female of their sect would deliver the Messiah into the world. The Essenians were a strict moralistic cult of Hebrews that practiced a faith that was in some ways similar to the teachings of Christ. They treated the breaking of the common bread as a holy act. The ritual was similar to the Holy Eucharist, which would later be shared by the first Christians, but lacked the sacrifice and divinity of Jesus Christ and the presence and action of the Holy Spirit. The Essene office of "overseer" paralleled the later Christian office of bishop, and they spoke of their mode of life as "The Way". The monks were celibate and had to swear an oath pledging piety toward God, honesty with fellow Essenes, and secrecy regarding the group's teachings. For example, their esoteric doctrine of the naming of angels, the rules of their order, and of course their hoard of silver, was sacrosanct. The initiates to the monastic order were bathed regularly in flowing water, which in some ways paralleled John the Baptist's rite of baptism.

The couple prostrated themselves before the holy man. Archos was dressed in a simple, spotlessly clean, white tunic, the same as worn by all the monks. He blessed the couple, but before they could explain their mission, he stated firmly, "You must have patience, my children. God has spoken. As I told your parents, and their parents before them, you and your ancestors bear only female descendents. The rod of Aaron sprouted when you, Ismeria, came of marriageable age. However, once married the sign of the Promise was not found on Sobe, your first child."

Ismeria could hardly contain herself and she exclaimed, "You do not understand, oh most Holy One. Sobe was born thirteen long years ago, and when we expressed our concern a year ago, you promised us consolation if we persevered in prayer and sacrifice. I had a vision a few nights ago. In the vision, I saw an angel writing on the wall. When I awoke, I told Eliud of my dream, and he replied that he had the same dream. When we checked the wall, we found the letter "M" written there."

Archos fell to his knees in the small cell and exclaimed, "Blessed is the Lord our God. Blessed is his Holy Name. The holy vessel that is to carry the mother of the Messiah may soon be born." Rising, he blessed them, and added in a voice gruff with emotion, "Notify me when the baby is to be born. I must see this child with my own eyes."

The interview was short and to the point. The religious order did not waste the Lord's time with the entertainment of guests. Male guests were allowed to join the Essenes in their daily worship of the Lord in their great hall, but women were simply not welcome in their man's world unless they were involved in some direct manner with the coming of the Messiah. Archos loved the young couple, but he contained his innermost feelings, for nothing must interrupt his devotion to the Lord and his prayers for the coming of the Messiah.

Ismeria was well aware of rules of the religious order, but she would have dearly loved to have stayed for a week or so. She loved the serenity of Qumran and welcomed the short respite that she had in quite prayer in the holy atmosphere of her surroundings. She did not look forward to the discomfort of her return trip to her home in Galilee, but she was so enraptured with the reason for the journey that the hardships she faced did not daunt her.

The next day from his rooftop, Archos watched his visitor's departure with great affection. The specks that were Ismeria and Eliud, and their small caravan, slowly faded into the stark desert that surrounded the walls of their monastic order. The land was bleak and lifeless to the untrained eye. The desert was cold and desolate in the winter, and arid and stifling in the summer. Yet, the desert held a beauty all its own, and to Archos this was home, and he was more than content. He knew that while the desert looked lifeless, it actually teemed with microscopic life, in addition to ants, locusts, scorpions, centipedes, bees, wasps, and a myriad of insects, including beetles, and the ubiquitous flies. A favorite, and even a pet of many Palestinians, was the protected, harmless colubrine snake. However, hidden in the forests and the stark hills there also lurked deadly adders, and cobras. The forests and terrain of the Ghor Plain offered an adequate food chain to insure the survival of many species of wild life. A variety of larger animals included, jackals, foxes, and hyenas with their harsh, nerve-racking call that sounded like an insane human laugh. They also shared the desert wasteland and the forests of the Ghor. Their natural prey was the wild ass, the sleek gazelle, the Arabian oryx, the fallow deer, and the Nubian ibex. The carnivorous animals also supplanted their diet from the herds provided them by humans, vast herds of as many as ten-thousand sheep, goats and even a stray donkey was fair game, which kept the lonely shepherds ever on the alert. Prowling Palestine were also wolves, leopards, lynx, bears, and lions, who roared their mastery of the animal kingdom. However, lurking in the wilderness and in the deep reaches of Palestine was a predator far worse than the savage beasts. Desperate men, cutthroats, robbers, outlawed Essenes and Zealots, and even the dreaded Sicarii, lurked in the hidden recesses of the land making travel safe only to those who traveled in well-armed caravans.

Archos knew that when the rains finally came, the arid land would flower into a beautiful garden of minute, desert flowers whose beauty was breathtaking. Nodding his head with satisfaction, Archos ascended to his room from an outside staircase. He knelt before a small stone altar upon which lay the rod of Aaron and a beautiful chalice seemingly made of a single precious stone. In the chalice lay a small piece of the original Ark of the Covenant. A portion salvaged by the priestly Zadoks when the Babylonian, Nebuchadnezzar sacked Jerusalem and took the Hebrews into exile. The ninth day of Ab, [July] the fifth month of the Hebrew calendar 587 BC had been the day the temple was razed and the first day of the Hebrew's exile. This date was set aside for mourning in the land of Israel.

Eliud was of the tribe of Levi. He was wealthy and owned vast herds and property, but as Archos knew, they kept little for themselves giving all their profits to the needy. The couple lived in Sepphoris, the capital of Galilee, and also owned land in the lush valley of Zebulon where they spent their winters. Over many generations, other Essenians not within the fold at Qumran had accepted the Hasmonian rule of the priesthood and supported not only the Essenians of Qumran, but supported the temple in Jerusalem as well.

Archos, and his exiled followers, were not happy with this state of affairs, but accepted as God's will that which they could not control. The leader believed, deep in his heart that one day the rule of a Zadok priest would again prevail. Archos was a man of deep moral convictions and firmly believed that their cause was just. Yet, while it appeared that the Messiah would be born from an Essenian woman, it did not appear that she would be from one of the strict sects of the Essenians, but from those Essenians who worshiped at the defiled temple in Jerusalem. He had no answer for this strange paradox, but with his usual humility, he accepted that which he could not control or understand.

Nine months later, Archos, equipped with a vast store of medicinal herbs and his healing gemstones, for which his people were famous, and in spite of his advanced age of seventy winters, made the long trek to Sepphoris. Assisted by her neighbors, Ismeria delivered the Child of the Promise right on schedule. Eliud named the child Anne, and Archos was the first to hold Ismeria's baby in his arms. On the child's stomach, just as it had been with Ismeria, he beheld the sign of the promise, a well-defined "M". The prophet gave the child his blessing and a few days later, before he departed for his arduous journey back to Qumran, he wondered aloud,

"Can it be possible that by the grace of God, I have seen the vessel that shall carry the mother of our Messiah? Perhaps I may yet witness this wonderful event if it is God's will. Yet, I feel my years, and my work is nearly done." He could see Ismeria in the courtyard bustling about her oven, and behind her from atop a roof; a pair of rock doves bobbed and weaved cooing lovingly to one another. Archos looked down at the glistening cleanliness of his feet with wry amusement; Every time he stepped outside and returned to the house; Eliud rushed in and washed his feet. Eliud and Ismeria, he knew were descendents from a fine old family of the House of Levi. He remembered with fondness

Emorun, the deceased mother of Ismeria. He had espoused her to Stolanus of the House of Levi. Both families were Essenians; Emorun had also been born with the Mark of the Promise. The Essenian leader firmly believed that someday from this family, the Messiah would descend. When—only God knew. The eminent chastity and mortification of the parents had been passed down to their children. Eliud and Ismeria gave liberally to the poor, and prayed constantly for the coming of the Messiah. They and their ancestors, for generations before them, had set the perfect example for their fellow Hebrews. In his heart, Archos sensed that after hundreds of years of waiting, the long vigil was nearly over. He gave a sigh of satisfaction, and then heaved another sigh of resignation. Tomorrow he must leave for Qumran. His reason told him he must, but his aging body protested at the thought. Perhaps this would be his last trip from the monastery?

From this family tree of Essenians, many of the Messiah's future disciples would descend, for Ismeria's sisters were also "cooperating vessels" of the Promise. Ismeria's older sister Emerentia had married a Levite by the name of Aphras; they became the parents of Elizabeth. She was to marry Zachariah, and they would procreate a child destined to become known as John the Baptist, the Precursor of the Christ.

* * *

Five years sped by too quickly for Ismeria to keep track. She was ecstatically happy. However, her joy was constrained, for the Essene's life was devoted to constant prayer for the coming of the Messiah. Anne was not a beautiful child, but compared to most, she was tall, stately, and quite pretty. She was extraordinarily pious and innocent. However, today was a special day. On the one hand Ismeria was wonderfully happy and fulfilled, for her daughter had been accepted to serve the Lord in the holy Temple in Jerusalem. On the other hand, she was desolate, for now she had to give up her child. However, true to her calling, she controlled her feelings. She called out, "Anne, where are you? We must join the caravan soon."

She found Anne kneeling in her room. Only the wealthy could afford to have a separate room for their children. In spite of the fact that they had a beautiful home and furnishings, they lived an austere and simple life. The room was not large, but overly sized for one small child. Anne's delicate furniture, the simple bed, chair, table, and clothing chest had been fashioned by a master artisan. The tiled floor was made of soft rose marble. The walls were finished with plaster and inlaid with beautiful pastoral mosaics. Hand-woven rugs and wall tapestries, made in Persia, added richness to the decor. The room was spotlessly clean and neat. Pausing at the door, Ismeria's heart went out to her daughter. It was ten years ago to the day that she and Eliud had made the decision that if God granted them a child, they would consecrate the baby to serve in the temple when she reached her fifth year. Sobe, her first daughter, was already nineteen, but she had not been the Child of Promise; Sobe had not been born with the sign. Today, as they had promised, they were taking Anne to the Jewish Temple in Jerusalem. She would be completely isolated from them for many years; her heart was heavy in spite of the honor accorded the family.

Anne looked up with childlike innocence and stated gravely, "I will miss you, mother, but you know that I must go. I must serve the Lord our God."

Restraining a sob, Ismeria hugged her and exclaimed, "Yes, I know, my dear, but that does not mean I will not miss you. Always remember that your father and I love you and that you will always be safe in the hands of the Lord."

Anne squared her back, and replied, "I will pray for you and father every day. Now we must go," she announced solemnly.

Many years would pass before Anne would return to the home of her parents. Their home was in Sepphoris, only four miles from Nazareth. Sepphoris, the capital of Galilee, was a city of over thirty thousand people of mixed races; only about one-fourth was Jews.

Ismeria was daydreaming and exclaimed aloud, "Goodness, it is hard to believe that Anne is finally coming home after serving twelve years in the Holy Temple." Ismeria hurried to put the final touch to her daughter's room, for the excited sounds of the large gathering outside announced her arrival. Much had happened in twelve years "Come, Maraha," she said to her four-year old granddaughter, as she flicked imaginary dust from the spotless clothes chest. She set a bowl of flowers in the middle of the table, and looked around with approval. She was happy. Again, she had her entire flock with her. Sobe was there with her young son Eliud, and her daughter Mary Solome. Ismeria was at peace with herself. The entire family had assembled and tents and pavilions had been set up for their convenience. Unlike the Essenians at Qumran, there would be a gala celebration. Normally the local Essenians, while they ate well, still managed to live an austere life. However, their celebrations were festive, with music and dancing, and vast quantities of food and wine. The more conservative Essenians; however, ate little and gathered to discuss the Lord and the coming of the Messiah.

* * *

A scant year later Ismeria lay on her deathbed with her family gathered about. A few months before in March, a terrible storm had struck the land. In a single day, a vicious khamsin, a hot, dry wind from the desert, the evil twin of the dreaded African simoom, filled the sky for a week with a thick grayness. The wind was so dry and hot that it sucked the moisture from every living plant and left them drooping lifelessly from their stems. Many wild creatures were left mere shadows of their former robustness and health. Domestic animal herds were left decimated, only the most hardy surviving the life sucking winds. The water holes and small streams evaporated and the fish were baked to a hard mummy-like shell of their former selves. Small children and the elderly were sucked dry of life's essence. The Khamsin laid much of Palestine dry and arid for months to come. Much of Galilee; however, had survived the worst of the devastation. It was as though the hand of God had sheltered them, for all around Galilee's fields was a vast wasteland. However, the fine sand had penetrated Ismeria's lungs and she lay dying. Before she could speak, she was seized by a racking cough. Anne ran to her, cradled her in her arms, and wiped the blood from her mouth. Reluctantly, at Ismeria's direction, Anne and Eliud, Ismeria's husband propped her up with pillows so she could speak. Smiling faintly, the dying woman called her family to her side. One by one she gave each one her parting legacy of her love and advice. Pulling herself up with her last strength, Ismeria placed her hands on Anne's head, the dying woman instructed them all. "Anne will be your mistress. You will obey her in all things. She is the "Vessel of the Promise."

Anne had grown into a tall, poised, young woman of obvious quality and breeding. There was no murmuring from the family. Only welcome smiles, amidst their constrained grief for their dying mistress. There were others outside; however, shirttail relatives so to speak, who lived on the largess of the family and murmured about most things, who were not happy with Ismeria's instructions. Waving the others outside, Ismeria pulled Anne down by her side and stated firmly, "You are the "Vessel of the Promise." You have the Mark of the Promise on your stomach. You must marry. Consult with the prophet Archos. As with all the women of our family, he will select a husband for you so the prophecy may be fulfilled." Anne bowed her head in submission. So it had always been. So it would be now.

Soon after Ismeria's death, Eliud moved his family to the valley of Zebulon in lower Galilee. There were other families in the valley among them the family of Nathan from whom a man by the name of Joachim descended. Nathan lived in the town of Nazareth.

Anne had her own house in Bethlehem, a suburb of Sepphoris, not to be confused with the Bethlehem located south of Jerusalem. She was a chaste, humble, and lovely maiden. She had always led a virtuous, holy and contemplative life. A most diligent and industrious person, she had attained perfection in both the active and the contemplative life. In addition, God had granted Anne an infused knowledge, which surpassed all that which she had learned in the Temple of Jerusalem. Anne was unexcelled in her infused virtues of faith, hope and love. Equipped with these gifts, Anne continued to pray for the coming of the Messiah.

In spite of her promise to her mother, several years went by and Anne had still not married. Archos sent her word that God would call her when he was ready, so Anne waited in patience and trust. In the interim, Anne prayed constantly for the coming of the Messias. In addition, she begged that the Almighty obtain for her in matrimony a husband who would help her observe the ancient law and testament. The day after Anne's twenty-fourth birthday, God chose to speak to her through his archangel Gabriel. While she was in prayer, the angel appeared to the young maiden; Anne's room was suddenly flooded with a brilliant light. She looked up and before her stood the Archangel Gabriel resplendent in some of his glory. In spite of her awe, she felt interiorly enlightened and at peace; Anne prostrated herself in utter humility, for she knew she was in the presence of God's messenger.

Gabriel announced to her, "Servant of God, the Most High gives you His Blessing. His Majesty has heard your petitions and He wishes you to persevere and to continue to clamor for the coming of the Redeemer. It is God's will that you accept Joachim ben Mathat as your spouse, for he is a man of upright heart and acceptable to the Lord. In his company, you will be able to persevere in the observance of his law and in his service. Continue your prayers and supplications and do not be solicitous for anything else, for the Lord will see them fulfilled. Continue to pray for the Messiah, be joyful in the Lord, for he is your salvation." With these words, Gabriel disappeared.

That same night, unknown to Anne, Gabriel spoke to Joachim in his sleep. "Joachim, you are blessed by the right hand of the Most High. Persevere in your desires and live according to rectitude and perfection. It is the will of the "Almighty" that you receive Anne ben Eliud as your spouse, for she is blessed of the Lord. Give thanks to his Majesty, because he has given her into your charge, take care of her and esteem her as a pledge of the Most High."

Over the years, Anne had had many suitors, but none of them had been to her liking. Now, by the will of the Lord, she was to marry Joachim ben Mathat, Anne had never met Joachim, but she had knowledge of his family. Although she had her instructions from the Lord, she still could not ignore her duty to her mother, nor could she ignore the just authority of Archos. Thus, it was those five years after her mother's death, Anne, accompanied by her father, and a small party of armed men, Eliud, proceeded to Qumran to consult with the superior of the Essenes.

Archos helped rule the Essenes for over ninety years. In spite of his advanced age, Archos was firm and decisive when Anne came to him. "You will marry Joachim, of the House of David." Anne looked up at the seamed face framed in the iron grill of the little cell housing the Superior. Her veiled features could not contain the beauty of her soul and Archos was touched with her simple humility. Since her vision with Gabriel; however, Anne had been curious and she asked, "I most humbly accept God's decision, but I have always been taught that we could only marry a man from among the Levites of the tribe of Aaron?"

"Archos replied patiently; "Remember the words of the Prophet Isaiah my, Child. It is prophesied by Isaiah [Is: 11, 1] that the Messiah will come from the House of David. Jesse was the father of

King David and Isaiah prophesied, "But a shoot shall sprout from the stump of Jesse, and from his roots a bud shall bloom." Her curiosity satisfied, Anne then related to Archos her experience with the angel Gabriel. He smiled and replied, "I have also been so informed my, daughter. Your obedience to your mother's instructions and your honoring the authority of my office has been well received by the Lord. Go in peace, Daughter. If only I could be present when the next vessel of the Promise is delivered," he added wistfully. However, just my knowing that the line of succession is to continue is sufficient." Archos gave Anne his blessing; he watched her depart with joy and satisfaction in his heart. He wondered; however, how many more "Vessels of the Promise" were destined before the coming of the Messiah?

During her long journey back to Sepphoris, Anne had much to think about. She had never met Joachim. However, that was immaterial. Ordinarily she would have had a choice. Jewish women did have the right to refuse to marry the person picked for them, if they had a valid reason. However, Anne had no such desire, since God Himself had picked her spouse. Even with God, Anne still had a choice. She had her free will, which, if she opted to not marry Joachim, by his own rule, God would not overrule, otherwise, "free will", would be meaningless. Anne knew that Joachim's family also lived in the valley of Zebulon.

After explaining to her father all that happened to her, she had asked him, "How well do you know Joachim ben Mathat?

Her father was a somber man, but he had a good sense of humor and he replied teasingly,

"Joachim is but a runt of a man. He has a cousin; however, the son of Jacob. He is a very handsome young man who is just coming of age. His name is Joseph."

Anne laughed and retorted, "You must have your fun. For your information I have seen Joseph, He is indeed handsome, but he is still a child. He is a gentle, kind person, and some of his own family thinks he is strange, because he has time for nothing but prayer."

Suddenly serious, Eliud stated, "There is nothing strange about Joseph, he has been touched by God. His family is well off. They live in a two-story house just outside Bethlehem in Judah. Seriously; however, my dear, daughter, Joachim is indeed short, but he is a lean, broad-shouldered man. While he is not particularly handsome, he is a pleasant looking man. As you know, he is also an Essenian and is devoted to praying for the coming of the Messiah. He is much older than you are, Anne, but there is something very special about Joachim. I believe you each have much in common. Both of you are true Israelites, both of you pray constantly for the coming of the Messiah, and you both constantly purify yourselves to prepare for the coming of the Messiah."

In her heart, Anne felt relieved. God had answered her prayers. Joachim was a holy man that would honor her devotion to the Lord. Together they could deluge the heavens with their petitions for the coming of the Messiah.

Joachim wasted no time in making his intentions known. He was both pleased and surprised at the cordial welcome he received from Anne's father. Joachim and Anne's courtship was brief. Both parties were quite reserved when they first met. The couple retired to an adjoining room, and deliberated in private over their intentions. They consulted one another on the subject, and while they both regarded their marriage as blessed by God, yet neither told the other of their experience with Gabriel. When they were decided, which in their case was a foregone conclusion; they stated so to their parents. Their parents then haggled and dickered in good tradition over the wedding arrangements. A scribe scrupulously wrote down the terms of their contract word for word. Anne and Joachim stated their intentions before the priest in the synagogue, who then prayed in the sanctuary before the rolls of the law, which completed the ceremony. They were married in Nazareth on the fifteenth of the following month. The wedding celebration lasted for two full weeks.

Joachim was a poor man and had little to offer Anne in the way of comforts. Joachim's home was most humble and common. Anne; however, had been raised in the best of homes. As she entered Joachim's humble abode; however, she never wavered. Having spent twelve years in the temple, she was hardened to the harsh disciplines of temple life and she never allowed the dirt floors of her new home to bother her. Anne's father, Eliud, was a rich man and she herself was well off. All that had been hers; however, except for her dowry, was now the property of her husband. Anne was pleased to find that Mathat, Joachim's father, like her own father, gave to anyone that asked for help. Joachim and Anne followed the example of their parents. In their new home in Nazareth, the couple continued to subject themselves to the severe usage and disciplines of the Essenians. There was very little feasting or grand entertainment in their homes. When their families got together, which they did frequently, it was to converse of God with all sincerity and earnestness.

In spite of their desire to propagate, Joachim and Anne had no issue for year after year. Coming home early one day, Joachim found Anne weeping and praying for the child she so desperately wanted. He could read the despair in her voice; taking her in his arms he said, "I know just how you feel, who was it this time, your sister or that alligator-mouthed neighbor of ours?"

Going to a wash basin, Anne rinsed her face in cold water and replied, "It was just a bad day, Joachim. Everyone I talked to today, threw it up to me that I am still barren. Rachel had nerve to ask me, "What terrible sin did you commit to be so cursed by God?" Then my sister Emerenta came in with her six children and while she did not say anything, her oldest asked me why I did not have any children. Emerenta shushed her, but I could tell by her actions that she must have been talking in front of the children about my condition. Then Naomi, your dear cousin, had to add one of her not so subtle remarks. I guess it was just too much all at one time."

"I wonder how they would feel, if they wanted children and could not conceive one?" Joachim mused thoughtfully. "My husband," Anne said laying her hands in his, "do you really believe that we are being punished by God for something that we have done?"

"You know as well as I, Anne that many Hebrews believes a couple is cursed if they do not have children. However, I do not believe that God does such things. I know others who are barren and they have done nothing wrong of which, I am aware. Some of our animals are barren from time to time. They can hardly sin. Since you have not conceived, it has to be God's design that the time has not yet come. You have the Mark of the Promise, so your must not despair. Remember that Abraham and Sarah conceived when they were extremely old, for nothing is impossible to God. We must have patience, and continue to pray for the coming of the Messias. In case we have done something to offend the Lord, we must pray more and offer up many sacrifices."

Anne came to Joachim and said, "As usual, my husband, you have the right words to salve my feelings and bolster my confidence. We will continue to pray and ask for guidance for that which our Lord will be pleased as an offering to encourage him to bring to fruition our prayers and petitions[Matt: 18, 19-20]."

In spite of their lack of issue; however, Joachim and Anne had prospered financially, and again, emulating their parents, they divided the rents and incomes of their estate into three parts. The first and best portion they offered to the Temple of Jerusalem for the worship of the Lord; the second best portion, they distributed to the poor. The third they retained for their own use. The more they gave, the more they prospered. Over the years, Anne had subjected and conformed herself in all things to the will of Joachim; and that man of God, with equal emulation of humility, had sought to conform to the desires of his spouse, holy Anne.

Joachim and Anne lived together in perfect charity. Not once did they experience a time, during which either one ceased to seek the same thing as the other. They enjoyed God's unseen presence in holy awe. God had communicated to Anne the most exalted graces and infused sciences, which, unknown to her, would prepare her for the happy destiny of becoming the mother of the one, who was to be the Mother of God. As God is perfect, it was natural to expect that He should choose a worthy mother of his pure creation, God the Son from the beginning of time created and selected the woman to be his Mother and named her Mary. She was destined to be superior to all creatures and inferior only to the Trinity.

A week later, Anne was mechanically doing her chores. Nearly twenty years had passed since she had moved into Joachim's humble home. They still lived outside of Nazareth, but they now lived in a home similar in good taste to that of her father. Like her father, they now had vast herds and still divided their plenty into three parts. She hummed a psalm in praise of the Lord God Jehovah. Joachim had many men working for him, and because of the need to care for his laborers, they maintained a kitchen staff to feed them. Anne had a staff of four servants to care for the home and the needs of the workers. The well to do, as was the custom, usually gave their relatives first choice of any jobs available in their homes. Naomi was such a one, a cousin on her husband's side of the family. Naomi never failed to criticize Anne for her sterility, when the opportunity presented itself. Today was no exception. Naomi was busy in the courtyard making bread and placing the slabs of dough on the walls of a kiln.

Seeing Anne approaching, Naomi nudged a piece of firewood into the path of her preoccupied mistress. Anne was carrying a basket of leeks; catching her foot on the wood Anne stumbled and her load went flying. Naomi leaped to her assistance to steady her, Anne exclaimed, "Goodness, where did that wood come from?"

Naomi said with contempt, "You would believe, since you have been cursed with no children that the good Lord would think that was sufficient punishment for your sins?"

"If it is punishment, Naomi, I accept it as such. Now, I believe your bread is burning."

With a cry of dismay, Naomi ran to the kiln. Removing the burnt bread, she muttered aloud for all to hear, "God's wrath upon this house is spilling over."

Anne held her peace, but Naomi's words cut like a knife. Her family, friends, and neighbors had been reproaching her for years for her barrenness. Joachim's support the previous week had helped her a great deal. She did indeed have the Mark of the Promise. Encouraged by Archos, she firmly believed she would deliver a child that would eventually lead to the birth of the Messiah. Perhaps she might actually bear the mother of the Messiah? The benefits of the Messias could certainly not be denied her, if this were true? She sighed in humble resignation. In spite of their lack of children, and because of their individual visions, Anne's and Joachim's faith never wavered. Unknown to them; however, God afflicted them only in order to strengthen them for the grace that awaited them. In their patience and submission, they tearfully prepared themselves for the honor bestowed upon them. Still thinking they had somehow displeased the Lord, the couple only tried the harder to please him with their continual prayers and sacrifices.

Joachim had been gone for nearly a week. He was more moody than was Anne, and she knew her husband often went off alone into the wilderness or to one of his farms to pray. Anne was concerned, but not worried. Joachim, wishing seclusion had gone to a remote farm of his located near Jerusalem. He often went there when troubled, or when he wished to commune quietly with his Lord. He fasted, and prayed, and begged, and pleaded with the Lord to give him some sign as to what his will was. He never doubted for a second that a child would someday be born to his wife, in spite of his own advanced age. Even Anne's age would be an obstacle since she was at an age where few women gave birth.

God was well pleased with Joachim and with Anne. They had ever been faithful and had prayed unceasingly night and day for the promised child. Their prayers and sacrifices made possible the final decision of the Lord to answer their long awaited prayers. In a dream, Joachim saw Anne as a child serving the Lord in the holy temple in Jerusalem. When he awoke he returned to Nazareth and hurried to see Anne. He met with her and explained his absence, "Anne, after our talk last week, I have been doing some serious meditating. After a week of prayer and fasting, I had a dream. I saw you as a child in the service of the Lord in the Holy Temple. I do not believe it is something that we have done to offend God. Rather, I believe that it is something that we have not done. I believe God is expecting much more from us, than we have offered Him. The Lord chose you to serve him when you were a child. If he wished you to serve in the temple, would he not expect our daughter to do the same? I believe that before she is to be born, we must pledge our child to God's service in the Jewish Holy Temple in Jerusalem." There was no doubt in either of their minds that the child would be a girl.

Annie listened intently. She remembered parting from her mother at age five. It had been harder on her mother than on her. After her mother had told her of their plans to send her to the temple, her Guardian Angel had explained to her that it was God's will that she serve in the temple. Knowing that God willed it so; Anne had gone willingly, even eagerly. It would be the same with her, as with her mother, she would have to make the sacrifice of giving up her child to the Lord. With quiet resignation she replied, "We must make a vow to the Lord our God that our child will be consecrated to his service in the Temple of Jerusalem."

Unknown to either, the Holy Spirit had ordained that before Mary's birth, Anne and Joachim would have to consecrate their daughter to the Lord. God knew, that after she was born, because of the grace and sweetness engendered by the child, it would be impossible for them to part with her. Therefore, God ordained that Mary was to be raised and educated in the holy Temple.

After she and Joachim had made their fateful decision, Anne had a distasteful chore to do. The day before Naomi had requested to go to a feast. This was not permissible in the strict discipline of the Essenes.

Anne refused to give her permission and Naomi upbraided her unmercifully saying, "You are a harsh and bitter woman. You deserve to be sterile. Even your husband abandons you."

Anne had suffered her servant's reproaches for years, suffering them in humility and offering up her pain as a sacrifice. This was different. When Naomi no longer wished to live by the discipline of the Essenians, Anne knew she had no recourse. Writing a letter to accompany her, the mistress of the house sent Naomi back to her parents with more than adequate gifts and remuneration for her services.

For another year, Joachim and Anne persevered in near continual prayer. It was near the end of Hesvan [November] that Joachim received his call. Inspired by God's Angel in a dream, Joachim got up the next morning and prepared to go to the Temple in Jerusalem. He selected the best goats and kids of his flock and accompanied by his drovers he set off at once. At God's direction, he was to make offerings for the coming of the Messiah.

Before he left, Joachim sat Anne down and said to her. "The Lord himself has requested that I make my offerings at the Holy Temple." Joachim's face was animated with hope and trust, and he added, "God has heard our prayers. Pray for our deliverance. I have a good feeling about this trip."

Anne's heart went out to him; his golden years had been kind. Now sixty-four, his face was unlined, and his snow-white beard, and hair, and his erect bearing gave him an aura of dignity. He had developed into quite a handsome man, and Anne knew that the years had been kind to her as well. Now forty-four, her hair was still jet black, and she could have passed for thirty. Age had added maturity and, while she had been pretty as a young woman, she was now a strikingly beautiful woman. Anne watched Joachim go with a peaceful feeling; perhaps this was the time they had been waiting for? She would pray for his success until he came back.

Joachim entered the temple humbly, but with a lilt in his step and a confidence, he had not felt in years. The other worshipers and even the priests themselves had often ridiculed him in the past over his lack of an heir. As he headed confidently for the altar, Isachar, an inferior priest, intercepted him. He snapped at him, "Joachim, why do you insist on coming to make offerings and sacrifices, which are not pleasing to the Lord since you are a worthless creature? Do not annoy our God with your offerings and sacrifices which are offensive to him."

The white-haired, Joachim, stared at him in a state of shock. He had been so sure, had the Lord himself not sent him here? He was crushed and shamed in front of the people; humbled and confused, he addressed the Lord in love and supplication, "My, Lord and my, God, "at your command, I have come to your temple. The priest that takes your place loathes me. I humbly acknowledge that my sins have earned me this rebuke. Let it be done to me according to thy will, but do not cast away your servant."

With hanging head, Joachim fled the precincts of the temple. To hide his shame, Joachim fled to his farm located outside the city walls. There for several days, Joachim cried out to the Lord in this manner, "I supplicate your infinite goodness to look upon the affliction of my soul and the soul of Anne your servant. If I am not worthy, at least do not despise the pleas of my humble spouse. Lord God of Abraham, Isaac, and Jacob do not hide your kindness from us. The priests number me among the reprobate and the outcasts in my offerings, because you have given me no heir. If it is your pleasure to yield to my prayers and grant us a child, I will offer this holy child to your Holy Temple in perpetual service. Look down from your throne and upon this vile dust, and raise me up in order that it may magnify and adore you. Not my will, Lord, but your will be done."

Anne was in deep prayer when the angel Gabriel in a blaze of glorious light came to her in a vision. Joachim had just fled to his farm outside Jerusalem and had begun to bombard heaven with his tearful prayers and reproaches. Gabriel told Anne that her prayers for a child, accompanied by the intense prayers from Joachim were most pleasing to the Lord.

Recognizing the will of God and that of her husband Joachim, Anne prayed with humble subjection and a new confidence, "My, God, my, Lord, my, Creator, Master of the Universe, I will pray even though I am but dust and ashes proclaiming my need and my affliction. Lord, God, infinite being, create Joachim and me worthy of your blessing. I wish to offer an oblation pleasing and acceptable in your eyes. If you will grant us our petition for a child, I, Anne, from this moment sanctify and offer this child for your service in the Holy Temple. If it please thee, Lord, look upon this lowly and impoverished creature, and your servant Joachim, and grant us our prayers and may all things be resolved in your divine will."

The angels presented the prayers of Anne and Joachim before the throne of the Holy Trinity. The Triune God accepted them, and then they made their will known to their angels. "We have found great pleasure in Anne and Joachim. They have found grace in our eyes. They have been faithful and constant in their trials. In simplicity and uprightness their souls are acceptable and pleasing to us."

Turning to the archangel Gabriel, God said, "Gabriel, take tidings of joy for them and the whole human race. Announce in our condescension, we have looked upon them and found them pleasing. Promise them that by the favor of our right hand, they will receive the Fruit of Benediction, and that Anne shall conceive a daughter, to whom "We" give the name of Mary."

Thrice blessed Anne had again immersed herself in prayer and divine contemplation of the mystery of the Incarnation, which having been previously filled with a high understanding and a specially infused light, she prayed for the hastening of the coming of the Redeemer saying, "Most high, King and, Lord of all Creation, I, a most vile and despicable creature, and yet the work of thy hands, desire at the price of the life which you have given me, to urge you to hasten in your mercy the time of our salvation. Remember oh, Lord, the mercies of old shown to your people, wherein you have promised your Onlybegotten Son, and may this promise of infinite kindness unbend you."

Suddenly, the holy archangel Gabriel, more resplendent than the sun, appeared to Anne in human form and said to her, "Anne, servant of God, I am a messenger from the Lord. He has heard your petitions, for he is ever near to those who expect his salvation. If God delays in hearing your prayers, it is in order to allow you to prepare yourself in order to receive more than you ask and desire. Prayer and thanksgiving open the treasures of the Lord, and incline him to lavish them in mercy to those who ask. You and Joachim have prayed long for the coming of the Messiah. Consequently, you will give birth to a most holy child, whose name shall be Mary. This child shall be the pure "Vessel of the Promise", blessed before all other women, filled with the Holy Ghost, and she shall bring forth the long awaited Messias. In her shall be fulfilled the prophecies of your ancestors. God's angels will advise Joachim that he is to have a daughter, who shall be blessed and fortunate, but he is not to know the child will be the mother of the Redeemer. Go to the Temple of God to give thanks to the Most High for having been so highly favored. In four days you shall meet Joachim under the Golden Gate."

The Holy Ghost strengthened Anne, so that she would not faint away with admiration and joy, thus she was able to receive the news with incomprehensible joy. Rising, Anne hastened to prepare for the journey to Jerusalem. There she knew she would find Joachim, as the angel had instructed her.

Three days later, Gabriel descended from the empyrean heavens and placed Joachim in a miraculous sleep. In this dream state Gabriel told him, "Just and upright, man, the Almighty from his Sovereign Throne has taken note of your desires; moved by your sighs and prayers he has made you fortunate on earth. Your spouse Anne shall conceive and bear a daughter, who shall be "blessed" among women. The Lord himself has chosen for her a name. Her name is to be Mary. From her childhood, let her be consecrated to the temple and in it to God, as you have promised. She shall be elect, exalted, powerful, and full of the Holy Ghost. Because of Anne's sterility, her conception shall be miraculous. Praise the Lord, Joachim, for this benefit and magnify him. You shall go to give thanks in the Temple of Jerusalem on the Sabbath, and in testimony of the truth of this joyful message; you shall meet your wife Anne under the Golden Gate."

The priests had recently thrown Joachim out of the temple, troubled; he told the angel his fears.

"Fear not," the angel assured him, "the priests have already been advised of your coming."

Joachim awoke, and filled with great joy he dropped to his knees and with his heart brimming, he poured forth his soul to the Most High. Full of love and gratitude, he praised God for his inscrutable judgments. Remembering his instructions, Joachim hurriedly gathered his best animals for an offering and rushed to do the bidding of the angel. It was Thursday, and Joachim had the entire day to prepare for his return to the temple. According to the Law of Moses, no one could walk more than six stadia, a little less than one mile on the Sabbath. He also would have to transport his sacrifice to the temple on Friday during the day, in order not to violate the Sabbath that began at dark. Two priests met Joachim as he entered the temple, divinely inspired; they took charge of his animals.

When Joachim returned to the temple on the Sabbath, he found the two priests were eagerly awaiting his arrival. In spite of the fact that it was the Sabbath, they rushed out and assisted him with his offering. They slaughtered and burned his sacrifice at the customary place in the temple. Suddenly, a beam of light descended upon Joachim and the officiating priest. The bystanders were amazed when two priests rushed forward and led Joachim into the sanctuary before an altar of incense. The priests laid incense on the altar, and when it miraculously kindled itself, they retired in awe leaving Joachim standing alone before the altar. He fell to his knees, arms outstretched, while the offering slowly consumed itself. Heady incense filled the room; Joachim fell into ecstasy, and remained there all morning praying.

Just before noon, an angel, unseen by the others, appeared before him and spoke, "Anne will conceive an immaculate child who will be greatly blessed by the Lord. Do not grieve over Anne's sterility. This is not a reproach to you or her, but a blessing, for that which Anne will conceive should not be from either of you, but through you both, a fruit from God, the culminating point of the blessing given to Abraham."

Joachim did not understand the words of the angel. The messenger of God led Joachim to the altar behind which was the curtain concealing the Holy of Holies. He held up a shining ball that reflected like a mirror. Joachim instinctively breathed on it and pictures appeared in the globe that enlightened Joachim of all that had transpired, except of course, the fact that Mary was to bear the Messiah.

"The angel continued, "As you can see, Anne shall conceive through you, but will remain just as unsullied by you as the ball." The angel then anointed Joachim's forehead with the tip of his thumb and forefinger, then gave him something to drink from a glittering chalice that freed him from all sensuality. He then led Joachim from the holy place and told him, "You shall not reveal anything about this Holy Mystery to anyone."

Upon saying this, the angel left Joachim and he fell to the floor like one stupefied. The priests entered the Sanctuary and led the dazed Joachim out with reverence and fear reflected on their faces. They gave him water and tended to his needs until he came to himself. Joachim's face glowed and he looked like he had returned to the bloom of his youth. Later, the priest Simeon led Joachim to the subterranean passage that ran under the temple and under the Golden Gate. Here he left Joachim at the entrance. The enraptured man went on alone entering a narrowing, gradually widening and descending passageway. Soon he emerged into where the daylight and pillars twined with foliage lined the passage. The green and gold decorations of the walls sparkled in the rosy light that emanated from above.

Anne, accompanied by two maidservants, entered the temple. They carried with them a sacrificial offering of doves. As they proceeded to the Women's Court several devout women joined them. The priest offered up the turtledoves, and the Prophetess Anna, her former teacher at the temple, led Anne to the opposite end of the passageway that led to the Golden Gate. It was Saturday, the Hebrew Sabbath, the seventh day. At exactly noon, according to Jewish Law, all Jewish men throughout the world stopped and faced Jerusalem and recited the Shema Israel. If in Jerusalem, they faced the temple, or if they were in the temple, they faced the Holy of Holies and likewise prayed the Shema Israel.

At noon, Anne met Joachim under the Golden Gate exactly as God had foretold. Together they faced the temple and recited the Shema Israel in union with all of Israel. When finished they turned and embraced each other in spiritual ecstasy, and they became luminous. Humans had never before achieved such a supernatural purity of soul. The heavens opened and hosts of angels surrounded them; some of the angels were carrying a luminous tower. The tower descended and vanished between Joachim and Anne. A glorious, brilliant light immediately encompassed them, and all heaven rejoiced at their divine union. At the exact moment of their embrace, the Immaculate Conception of Mary took place in a supernatural manner. *This same type of conception would have been the lot of Adam and Eve, and their progeny, if it had not been for their sin in the Garden of Eden.*

A host of priests met Anne and Joachim as they exited the Golden Gate passageway. Divine services were then held under the open sky, in order not to interfere with the ritual Sabbath devotions. They stayed that night at the home of the priest Simeon, also a former teacher of Anne's. The next day they returned to Nazareth. On the long trek home, Anne and Joachim had much to talk about and had much time to pray and give thanks. While they talked freely of Anne's conception, mindful of their angel's instructions, neither one ever spoke to the other about their individual revelations from Almighty God.

Mary was conceived on the seventh day; the same day as the angels, Because of the fact that Mary was conceived on Saturday, the Holy Spirit consecrated Saturdays to Mary. Mary's conception, which fell on the eighth day of Kislev, is celebrated by the Church as a Feast Day on December eighth. God infused Mary's soul into her most pure, perfect body. Mary was more perfect in God's eyes than all those he had created, or will ever create throughout the eternities.

At the infusion of Mary's soul, God granted Anne a singular favor. Anne had a vision of his Majesty, in which, having given her special gifts of grace and enlightenment, he disposed her with special blessings of his own sweetness. God cleansed her body and soul. He sanctified her body and elevated her soul and spirit to such a degree that thenceforward she never lost sight of him, a gift normally reserved for the angels.

At the same time God said to her, "I am the God of Abraham, Isaac, and Jacob; my blessing and my eternal light is with you. I created man to make him the inheritor of my glory and participator of my Divinity. I lavished gifts upon him, which he had not earned, and raised him to a high state of perfection; but he listened to the serpent and lost all. Because of *My Infinite Mercy*, I promised man I would send my Onlybegotten Son as their Redeemer. The gates of heaven are closed. I have listened to the cries and prayers of my people, and the laments of the Patriarchs detained in Limbo. The time has come for the Eternal Word, to become man, to be born of a woman, who shall be Mother and Virgin, immaculate, pure, blessed and holy above all creatures. Of her, my chosen and only one, I make you her mother."

Anne heard with profound humility the voice of the Most High and with a submissive heart she replied, "Lord God, eternal, I have charged myself as a creature unworthy of such mercies and benefits. What shall this lowest of creatures do in your presence? Your own Essence and your own greatness alone can I offer in thanksgiving. Do with me; oh, Lord, as you will. I give myself entirely to you. I know that I am not worthy to be the slave of her who is to be the Mother of the Onlybegotten, let alone have her as my daughter. I throw myself at your feet; you are a kind Father, and all-powerful God. Justify me oh, Lord, of the dignity you bestow upon me."

God caught Anne up in an ecstasy, and she was favored with the highest understanding of the laws of nature, and of the written, and the evangelical precepts. Anne learned how she was to be united with the divine nature in the eternal Word; and how the Messiah's humanity was to be elevated to the being of God, and she learned other mysteries, which were to be fulfilled in the Incarnation of the divine Word. By these gifts of knowledge and grace, God prepared Anne for the birth of her most holy daughter, Mary, the Mother of God-Virgin Then, Now, and Forever

I Am Mary

I Am Mary, the Immaculate Conception: It is a truth that I was conceived without Original Sin and not in sin. God conceived me under the Golden Gate in one golden, supernatural moment. My

Son Jesus had joined my father and mother in a marriage more chaste and pure than any other was, or any that shall ever exist. God extinguished all sensuality in my parents. Thus, my body was formed through divine charity and free of all corruption of the flesh.

In God lies the preservation of all things, or their annihilation, for without him they would return to the non-existence from which they were drawn. However, since he has created the universe for his glory and for the glory of the Incarnate Word, he has from the beginning opened the paths and prearranged the ways by which the same Word should lower himself to assume human flesh and live among men. Then, through him, humankind might ascend toward God, know him, fear him, seek him, serve him, love him, praise him, and enjoy him eternally. In the heavens, prior to my conception and before the beginning of time, the Holy Trinity discussed among themselves the advent of my creation.

They said, "Now is the time to begin the work of our pleasure and to call into existence that pure Creature and soul, which is to find grace in our eyes above all the rest. Let us furnish her with the richest gifts and let us deposit in her the great treasure of our grace. We called into existence many others, which we know will be ungrateful and rebellious to our wishes. They will frustrate our intention in that they will conserve themselves in the unhappy state of their first parents. Since it is not proper that our will should be entirely frustrated, let us therefore create this being in entire sanctity and perfection. Thus, the disorder of the first sin shall have no part of her. Let her be a most special image and likeness of our Divinity and let her be in our presence for all eternity, the culmination of our good will and pleasure. The seed of the serpent shall have no part in Mary, for we will exempt her from the ordinary law of creation. I, the Onlybegotten Son will descend from heaven into her womb and in it vest myself from her substance with human nature."

"Thus, on earth, the Incarnate Word shall have a Mother without a father; as in heaven, he has a Father without a mother. At no time shall the dragon boast of being superior to the woman, whom God the Son will obey as his true mother. This dignity of being free from sin is due and corresponds to that of being Mother of the Word, and it is in itself even more estimable and useful. The human flesh, from which he is to assume form, must be free from sin. Since he is to redeem the sinners in his flesh, he must not be under the necessity of redeeming his own flesh, like that of sinners. Being united to the Divinity, his humanity is to be the price of Redemption, wherefore, it must before all be preserved from sin."

"She is to be a daughter of the first man; but in the order of grace, she is to be singularly free and exempt from fault; and in the order of nature, she is to be perfect, and to be formed according to a special providence. The Incarnate Word is to be the Teacher of humility and holiness. Toward this end, he is to endure labors, confounding the vanity and deceitful fallacies of mortals by choosing for himself sufferings as the treasure most estimable in our eyes. We wish that she, who is to be his Mother, experience the same labors and difficulties as he. She will be singularly distinguished in patience, admirable in sufferings, and that she, in union with the Onlybegotten Son, will offer the acceptable sacrifices of sorrow to us for her greater glory."

Informed of these blessings, the holy angels prostrated themselves before the royal throne of the most Holy Trinity. They avowed their eagerness to obey the divine mandate. Each offered their services and so it was that the Lord God of Hosts at my conception assigned one thousand holy angels as my companions, friends, advisors and protectors.

CONCEIVED WITHOUT SIN
MARY
THE MOTHER OF GOD

Chapter Two

The Immaculate Conception

A great sign appeared in the sky, a woman clothed with the sun, with the moon under her feet, and on her head was a crown of twelve stars. [Rev: 12, 1]

I Am Mary, the **Immaculately Conceived** daughter of Saint Anne and Saint Joachim, the mother of **Jesus Christ**, the only **Son of God**. My Son ordained many years ago that I make known to the faithful the history of my life. In obedience, I related in visions the story of my life to various persons throughout the ages. Their facts; however, sometimes conflicted with the writings of other visionaries, because the customs and mores of their own era heavily influenced their own interpretation. When I spoke to the visionaries as Jesus ordained, *no pride or bragging was possible in the telling of my attributes*, because I am *blessed* in heaven.

My conception took place under the Golden Gate in the holy temple of Jerusalem on the eighth day of December on the seventh day of the week in a wonderfully supernatural manner. There, the Holy Spirit caught up in spiritual ecstasy my mother, Anne, who was forty-four years of age and quite sterile. The Divinity made her aware of his presence in a most exalted manner. The Holy Ghost moved her interiorly with a joy and a devotion altogether above the ordinary. The Church has set the eighth day of December as a Feast Day to honor me.

I was conceived when my father, Joachim, was sixty-six years old. God's angels purged him of all sensuality, so that my creation was supernatural. The Holy Spirit created me to be a spouse worthy of and fit to carry in my sacred womb the Son of God. My soul took God longer to create than it took him to create the angels, and the universe. The Omnipotent God, who is infinite and rich without limit, adorned and prepared me for these dignities. He made me more agreeable than the sunrise, more beautiful than the moon, more exquisite and admirable than the sun and without equal among all things created. No saint, nor any seraphim, nor can any of them combined ever reach, nor can human tongue ever manifest, the depth of God's graces and gifts to me. Before my conception, God called his angels together and showed them the perfection of my soul.

The angels prostrated themselves in adoration and Saint Michael spoke for them and stated, "Oh great, and Omnipotent One, we acknowledge ourselves subject to this most perfect of all your creations. May we be granted an increase in purity and perfection in order to be more worthy guardians and servants of Mary?"

At the moment of the creation and infusion of my soul, the blessed Trinity stated, as recorded by Moses at that time concerning man. "Let us make Mary to our image and likeness to be our true daughter and spouse and a mother of the Onlybegotten of the Father." God's first three gifts to me were *faith, hope and charity*, which all relate directly to God. I immediately began to practice these virtues as soon as I was conceived. In addition, I received, *without any merit of my own*, the gift of reason. I was no larger than a honeybee in my mother's womb, immediately however, I prostrated myself before God in thanksgiving. Miraculously, I suddenly found myself before the throne of God. He was pleased with my offering. Unknown to me at the time, my acts merited more than the accumulated acts of all the saints in the highest state of perfection and sanctity. I recognized at once all the gifts given me by my Creator, although, the knowledge that I would someday be the Mother of his Divine Son was not then revealed to me.

At this instant of my conception, I understood the immutable being of God, and in him all creation. I saw the rise of the angels and the fall of Lucifer, the first state of Adam and Eve in all their innocence, their deception, and their fall from grace. I knew the nature of the heavens, the stars, the planets, and the elements. I saw limbo, purgatory and hell, and understood their nature and God's divine plan. At my conception, God assigned one thousand angels as my guardians, and I, as my first order to them, enjoined my angels to join with me in constant canticles of praise to the Most High. This, I informed them, was to be the unending service they were to render to me during the term of my mortal life. God ordained by the power of his right hand, although, I was hardly big enough to be distinguishable that in my perceiving the fall of man and the gravity of the offense against the Highest God that I shed tears of sorrow in the womb of my mother.

Perhaps this experience might give you an insight into the unique qualities of the soul with which our God has created for each of us. The soul is indestructibly unique; the body is flesh; however, and will go the way of all flesh until the end times and the final resurrection. However, the soul, as long as God so wills, will never perish. Mystically, even at death, our senses will not be lost to us when our souls separate from our bodies, which, the poor souls in purgatory and hell soon learn to their dismay.

While all of these events were happening to me, at a pace only made possible by Almighty God; my mother, Holy Anne, was wrapped in exalted ecstasy. She was enlightened with a deep intelligence of the most hidden mysteries, and praised God with new canticles of joy. These lasted all her life, but were especially greater during the nine months she bore me in her womb.

At my conception, I knew my parents in God, before I saw them in the body. I, at once, exercised the virtues of love and reverence of a daughter, acknowledging them as the secondary cause of my natural being. Anne was sterile before my conception, and after my birth she was to remain sterile the rest of her life. My mother was a Holy Vessel in the genealogical succession of the Messiah. Anne knew I was to be the Holy Mother of God, but never once did she reveal this information to me or to anyone else during her lifetime. My father, until he lay on his deathbed, did not know that I was to be the Blessed Mother of Jesus. Only then did God reveal to him my special blessing.

At my Conception, God showered so many gifts on me, in such an overpowering measure, that they exceeded the combined gifts of all of the saints throughout the ages. Human tongue cannot even begin to manifest them. It was impossible for me to exercise all of them at once, especially from the womb of my mother. Therefore, I concentrated on the three theological virtues, *faith, hope, and charity*. Because of God's gifts, I was wiser, more prudent, more enlightened, and more capable of comprehending God and all his works, than all the creatures have been or ever will be in eternity, except of course for my most Divine Son.

Lucifer soon took note of the gathering of the holy Hebrew women about my mother, as well as the heavenly aura that enveloped us. Lucifer well knew the prophecy that a woman would grind him beneath her heel. Consequently, when he saw all of the attention given Anne and her coming baby, he tried to find out what was going on. However, because of my angels, he could not penetrate that which was happening. Frustrated, he raged ferociously. As planned by God; however, he could not learn that my mother was to give birth to the future Mother of the Messiah. In his malice against all things that were close to God, Lucifer was particularly enraged at his own weakness in resisting the angelic force that stood between him and my mother. Satan, in his arrogance, was determined to find and take the life of the woman, who was to be the mother of the Messiah. He concluded that anyone this close to the Lord was a threat to his supremacy, so began a campaign to terrorize my mother.

Lucifer assembled his black angels, and decided to use his angelic powers to collapse Joachim's house on the heads of the family and kill them all. However, the power of my angelic princes frustrated his efforts. Consequently, throughout my mother's pregnancy, he tried to tempt her with many suggestions, misgivings, and doubts about the truth of her pregnancy. However, my mother was invincible and resisted these onslaughts with humble fortitude, patience, and constant prayers and faith in God. For, besides the protection abundantly merited by her past life, the angelic princes assigned to guard me also defended mother. Unsuccessful in his efforts, Satan decided to incite some workers to accomplish his attempts to collapse the house and kill my mother.

At this time, builders were at work on my father's home. Four months had passed since my conception, and the winter had been a severe one. Surging water had undermined certain portions of the house, and damaged the roof. However, try as he might, Lucifer could not, by his own power, destroy the house. Had he known that one thousand angels guarded me and the house, perhaps he would have abandoned the plan. Satan chose Joash and David, two of the laborers repairing the building, as his most vulnerable targets. Night after night, the black angels plied the two men with sensual thoughts. They whispered in their ears, and the men's own wicked thoughts were used to seduce them to Satan's will. Their whimsical thoughts conjured up fantasies of the flesh, which soon had both men comparing notes and lusting for the fleshpots ran by the Greeks in nearby Sepphoris, the capital of Galilee. They approached Abiel, their master, and asked for time off, but Abiel was used to their useless ways and would have none of it.

That night the black angels played upon the men's natural inclination for evil. They intensified their lustful thoughts with constant whisperings and suggestions. At last, fully aroused, David woke Joash and suggested. "Let us remove the support to the work platform tonight. We never work on the platforms, and when Abiel tries to use them tomorrow, they will collapse and the work will stop for awhile."

After dark, the two men stealthily removed a key support near the bottom of the square built frame made of poles. They hid the pole and went back to bed dreaming of their lustful pursuits. However, my thousand angels made me fully aware of their nefarious plans. I immediately prayed to my Creator for his assistance, and that very night God answered my prayers. Thus, did I begin my relationship with my Creator. Before I made any important decision throughout my life, I first consulted his Majesty, asking his advice, permission and benediction.

In a dream that same night, God's angels made Abiel aware of the plans of the two wastrels. He awoke fully alert. Troubled by the dream and unable to sleep, he went to the spot and found a support had been removed just as he had dreamed. With a grim smile, he hurried into town.

The next day during their morning meal David and Joash were in high spirits and ate heartily. Abiel commented, "You two seem in fine fettle today. I have just the job for you."

David glanced at his partner with a knowing look and said with a smirk, "We had a great night's sleep, Master; nothing would be too hard for us to do."

Later, as work was about to begin, Abiel called the two men to him. He pointed to the platform from which the support had been removed and said, "You men deserve a promotion. You two will work the top of the platform and repair the roof. I'll be back in a little while to check on your work."

Joash glanced at David and his face reflected his alarm and he stuttered, "I'm, I'm not well this morning, Abiel, it must have been something I ate; please hold me excused."

Abiel turned to David and said, I guess that leaves it up to you, David. Hop up there and let us get on with the job."

The color drained from the plotter's face and he suddenly grabbed his foot and cried out. "I turned my ankle on the way here, Master. I could never climb up there, please assign me to another job."

With a grim smile, Abiel replied, "It looks like your little scheme has trapped the two of you. He turned to his other workers and said, "See that they get a helping hand to the top of the platform. A dozen, willing, burly workers seized the two men and began to load them onto the platform.

Joash screamed, "The support has been removed, it was all David's idea, He wanted to go to Sepphoris."

From inside the building four Elders from Sepphoris stepped into view. The Chief Elder stated grimly, "We have heard enough, Abiel. We will deal with your would be badmen."

With a moan of fear David fell to his knees and begged, "Mercy, oh Elders. We meant no harm. We just wanted some time off."

"That is well and good, David. We will see that you both get a month off to mend the error of your ways. It should take about that long for your welts to heal." So speaking, the men were bound and taken to town to face trial for their misdeeds."

Lucifer was beside himself with rage, but he was far from defeated. Already, he was planning another way to accomplish his will.

Nearly every day my mother's friends dropped in for daily prayers and as a group, they often performed community services. Sobe, my mother's older sister, was a frequent visitor. Sobe had given birth to a daughter whom she had named Mary Solome; she in turn would marry a man named Zebedee. Zebedee would flourish, by the grace of God, and was destined to fish the waters of the Sea of Galilee.

Oma, another friend, was married to Nabal, a wealthy herdsman. Among her friends were Hannah, Nathonia, Theano, and Moselle, her closest neighbors. Elizabeth, whose mother was Emerentia, the sister of Ismeria my grandmother, was near the same age as my mother, and they had become intimate friends. Elizabeth was married to a priest named Zachariah, and was well off. Each year, Elizabeth made frequent treks to their summer home in Galilee, in order to get away from the heat of Judea. Each year the High Priests worked for a full month at the Jewish Temple and then returned to their homes until their next tour of duty. With few exceptions, the priests had secondary jobs to support their families during their time without income.

Blest with the gift of reason, and the use of my senses, I was able to distinguish each person's identity by the sound of their voices. I also learned their traits of character evidenced by their words and deeds, as well as from vivid word-pictures painted by my angels. Because of a special gift of God, I was able to communicate with my angels, who do not communicate the same as humans. Angel's conversations were more like instant knowledge, unlike the laborious speech of men. By God-given insight, I instinctively knew that Zebedee's future sons would someday be Apostles of the Messiah, and that Elizabeth would be the mother of John the Baptist, the "Herald" of the coming of the Messiah. Even knowing this, I still was not aware, that it was I that was to be the Mother of the Messiah.

My mother lived mentally in a spiritual world all her own. Showered with gifts and perfected by the Lord God himself, Anne was a living saint. Her immediate family and friends no longer taunted her since my conception, and now turned to her for every little thing. This situation created extra work for mother's servant Sara, who bitterly resented having to wait on so many visitors. She was lazy and of a devious disposition. When Lucifer recognized her bad traits, he began a relentless attack on her weak nature.

Oma had pressed her friendship upon my mother, although she was often petty and deceitful, and not the type of person that Anne would have favored as a friend. Mother; however, being the perfect image of God, tolerated and loved her just as she was. Xnoir, one of my angels informed me, that the correct name of Oma's husband was Abdul, and that while he pretended to be a converted Jew, he had never given himself to the Lord. Nabal was actually a Bedouin and had been raised a pagan. His real name was Abdul ben Kareem. His father was a notorious desert bandit who haunted the Judean Wilderness. Abdul, a former bandit himself, but a reluctant one, had changed his name to conceal his identity. By accepting circumcision and pretending to be a convert to Judaism, Nabal had opened many influential doors. In time; he had become a wealthy man. Oma had also ingratiated herself with Moselle and Hannah. It was not a sound relationship, and I prayed for them constantly.

I knew that it was God's plan that I not remain idle, even in my mother's womb, for even an instant, but to be always engaged in works pleasing to him. At first, I began to compose songs of gratitude in my heart and mind, for it was right and proper that the first fruits of my activity should be devoted to that Object which made all things possible. I was not to be less than all the angels and humans created. The angelic spirits made supernatural use of their God-given faculties, and although I was superior to them in every way, since I was created as their Queen and Lady, I seldom used my supernatural powers, and then only with the permission of God. I left such actions to those created for such activities. The name and office of "Mother of God and that of Queen"; however, excelled that of servants, for to none of the angels had the *Word* said,

"*Thou shalt be my Mother* [Hebrews: 1-5], nor could any one of them say to him,
"*Thou art my Son*".

I alone, by the Grace of God, could claim this commerce and relationship, although God, as yet, had not revealed this fact to me. At my Conception, I saw the essential Glory, but I did not see the Beatific Vision in all its glory. My vision was inferior to the Beatific, but was superior to all the visions and revelations, which had been granted other creatures, with the exception of the Clear Vision of the blessed in heaven, and, of course later, those of my holy Son. In addition to my prayers and constant exaltation of my Creator, I also joined my prayers with those of my mother. When I learned of the misdeeds of some of my mother's friends, my angels and I prayed for them constantly.

The morning following the revelation of Joash and David's scheming, Oma was ushered into my Mother's sitting room by Sara. The two had instinctively recognized a kindred spirit and had developed a close relationship. "Mistress," Sara greeted her cordially, "what brings you here so early?"

"Oh, Sara," she moaned embracing her warmly; "I must see Anne and ask for her advice. I am in the most difficult of situations. I have just learned that Nabal's father is coming to visit us."

"But, Oma why should that be so distressing"?

"He is a bloodthirsty desert man, Sara. He does not know that Nabal has embraced the Jewish faith. I am afraid of what he might do?"

"Then why tell him, Oma? What he does not know will not hurt him," she added smugly.

"Oh, Sara, you are so naïve. You know Jews dress differently. Nabal would have to change his entire appearance. He would not be able to wear his fringed garments or his tallith. When the men pray every morning, noon and night, the Law of Moses requires them to wear their phylacteries on their forehead and left arm for all to see. Even our doorway would reveal that we are Jewish, because t attached to the right side of our door and gatepost are the cylindrical boxes containing the Commandments of God. You know he cannot eliminate any of these things and remain a Hebrew."

Sara hugged her sympathetically, but pointed out, "You do indeed have a problem, Oma, but why do you think my mistress can help you?"

A knock sounded at the door. Sara murmured her irritation and went to attend her duties; Oma seated herself in the most comfortable chair in the room. With a gush of fresh air, Hannah and Moselle swept into the room where Sara respectfully seated them.

She excused Anne by explaining, "My mistress sends her respects. She will be delayed for a few moments."

Instead of leaving the room; however, Sara busied herself at the table at the end of the long room hoping to join in the conversation if given half a chance. Sara was on excellent terms with both women. However, she was not welcome in their homes as she was with Oma. To them, she was a servant, and beneath their station. However, when Anne was absent from the room, Oma was often included in their conversations.

From my angels and my mother, I knew these women to be terrible gossips. Behind her back, they attacked my mother unmercifully. Unknown to them, mother, who had been vilified for twenty years by her peers for her barrenness, was fully aware of their duplicity and prayed for them constantly, asking Almighty God to forgive and cure their wicked behavior. Before my conception, I knew mother had suffered terribly from the criticism of her friends, her servants, and even from her own family. Now their reproaches could hurt her no longer, except in the sense of the hurt they gave her God. I added my prayers to hers for these misguided women.

"My," Hannah said to Oma, "you certainly have a long face today. Is there something wrong?" Without hesitation Oma replied, "Of course not, Moselle, just a touch of the humors." She cast her eyes down not wishing them to pursue the subject. Moselle and Hannah would be the last people in Israel that she would trust with her problem. If she confided in them, in the space of one sun, every person in Sepphoris would know all the details.

My mother suddenly swept into the room like a fresh breath of sunshine. The guests rose and greeted her with respect. In Anne's presence, it was difficult not to realize that she exuded a marked quality of wholesomeness and spirituality. She suggested, "Ladies, unless you are tired from your walk this morning, I have prepared baskets for the poor of Sepphoris. Would you like to join me in almsgiving?" Since my Conception, Anne had suddenly gained the respect due her station. Yet, mother had always been active in the giving of alms and tending to the sick. The women eagerly accepted her invitation for they loved to be seen giving alms.

It was a beautiful day, the laborers were busily working, and the grain in the fields was ripening beneath the benevolent sun. A slight breeze was blowing and helped dispel the increasing heat of the sun.

Oma quickly maneuvered herself to a place beside my mother, and the others led the way into town. In a desperate voice, Oma pleaded her case with Anne and asked, "What am I to do, Anne?" Kareem is a violent man. I am afraid for Nabal's life."

"Have you prayed to Almighty God to help you, Oma?"

"Oh yes, Mistress, I have prayed the entire month of Adar. However, God has not answered my prayers, and Kareem will be here tomorrow. With a God-given insight Anne looked her in the eye and asked gently, "Oma, the question is, to what god did you pray to? You certainly did not pray to the Lord God of the Israelites."

Oma gasped. Overwhelmed, she stopped and stared at Anne with incredulous eyes. Unaware, Moselle and Hannah continued walking and gossiping. "You know!" Her voice tinged with awe,

Oma exclaimed fearfully, "Abdul will kill me!" Realizing she had used Nabal's former name, her face blanched and she dropped to her knees sobbing hysterically.

Anne knelt and clasped Oma protectively in her arms, I could hear the young girl's heart racing erratically, and I could tell she was utterly confused and terrified. Anne comforted and reassured her, and then asked, "Will you pray with me to the One True God, Oma? If he answers your prayers, perhaps then, you will truly believe, and give up your idols and amend your life?"

Oma gulped down her amazement, sobbed, and replied, "Yes! Oh yes! If he spares my Abdul, I will honor him all the days of my life and never cease praising his Glory."

"Then let us pray." Raising Oma to her feet, my mother faced toward Jerusalem and holding out her arms in supplication, she led the distraught girl into a prayer that lasted for half an hour. Hannah and Moselle had stopped and were looking back impatiently, but they had the grace not to intrude; they sought shelter from the sun in the shade of an Olive tree. Thanks to my guardian angels, I could hear their every word, and even the sound of the evergreen leaves of the olive tree as they clattered in the light breeze.

Moselle complained, "That Oma, she will do anything to be alone with Anne. I wonder why they are praying?"

Hannah sniffed and replied, "She did seem rather upset this morning. Perhaps," she mused, "if we talk to Sara, we might find out what is going on, the two are thick as thieves?"

Moselle grumbled, "There Anne goes praying again. She reminds me of the rich Pharisees that stand on the corner in town wearing their exaggerated tassels and phylacteries praying and giving out alms for all to see. What has she done that is so special?"

Hannah sneered and agreed, "She was supposed to be sterile for twenty years. If you ask me, Joachim is the one that is sterile, which makes one wonder, just how did she get pregnant?" She looked meaningfully to her companion.

My angels and I began to pray for these foolish girls. I could tell that the prayers of mother gave Oma a comfort that she had never before experienced. The distraught girl stopped crying, and Anne wiped her tear-streaked face. Grasping her by the arms, she looked into her eyes and said, "Now your problem is in God's capable hands. I will return home with you this evening and you can introduce me to your father-in-law when he comes tomorrow. "

"Oh no, Anne you must not." Oma cried out in genuine protest, which surprised even her. She had not realized how much my mother had come to mean to her. "Kareem is a most wicked man; the fact that you are a woman will mean nothing to him."

Anne smiled reassuringly and told her, "Have faith, Oma. God is with us." Unknown to her, my thousand angels and I were also sending up continuous prayers to the Lord our God.

It was the third hour the following morning when Kareem finally made his appearance. My angels reported his every move. The morning sun had already dispelled the chill of the morning and gave promise of a beautiful spring day. The sun was a welcome relief from the winter's rainy season. Kareem paused on a hillock and surveyed the estate with approving eyes. It was true then; Abdul had done well for himself. On his left was a handsome orchard of olive trees, and on his right endless rows of ground-hugging, leafing, grape-vines that stretched away to the end of the walled off enclosure two hundred yards away. Grapes, he knew, were often trained to hug the ground in order to catch the all important "dew" that made possible the lush grapes that were indispensable to the Hebrew economy. Guard towers made of stone rose menacingly from the middle of each enclosure. Near harvest-time, guards manned the towers to discourage would be thieves. He nodded his head in tacit approval.

Kareem was a typical Arab in size and stature. He stood no more than five foot, six inches tall, and was slim and wiry. His hair was jet black in spite of his advanced years, and his finely chiseled features were graced with an aquiline nose. His eyes were piercing and he exuded a masculine aura. Kareem's face; however, looked drawn, and his eyes were pinched with pain. It gave him the look of the desert hawk, poised, ready to strike at a second's notice. Instead of a donkey or an ass, he rode a shining black stallion. In his long-flowing burnoose, he cut a striking figure.

Kareem had recently learned through his "brotherhood of thieves" that his son Abdul had changed his name and was doing well. When so advised, he had smiled with wry amusement. Leave it to Abdul to get ahead. He had always been the wily one, quick of mind, cunning, clever, and manipulative. Had his son not manipulated him into giving him the money to make his own way separate from Kareem's band of thieves? "They would be partners," Abdul had pleaded. His son had favored his mother in looks and in disposition; he simply did not have the stomach to be a highwayman. Finally, Kareem had given in. However, he knew that his son had been raised a thief, and a thief he would always be, just as Kareem's father had been a thief, and his father before him. Ahead, on a knoll, loomed a huge walled in manor house set back from the main road. On the distant hills, Kareem noted flocks of sheep and goats grazing peacefully, watchfully tended by their shepherds. All about him were fields of ripening wheat and some barley fields were already being harvested. He had been amazed with the amount of flax grown in the area. Its sky-blue flowers carpeted field after field. When he inquired, he had learned that Sepphoris was the center for the Weaver's Guild, and they had wisely located their shops near the raw source of their business.

Guards eyed his progress warily from atop stone towers in the ripening grain fields. Precisely terraced fields met his keen gaze, as he observed the rolling hills from atop a knoll. In the spring, for a few wonderful weeks the pastures and hills, which were dotted with small patches of oak and terebinth trees, were rife with blood-red anemones, vivid yellow crocuses, tulips, hyacinths, wild gladioli, a variety of narcissus, and a multitude of other wild flowers. At this time of year, all of Israel was as picturesque as a beautiful flower garden, Galilee; however, received the most rain, had the best soil, and was truly a land flowing with milk and honey. It had been many years since Kareem had seen such lush verdure and his desert-starved eyes drank in the beauty like those of a thirsty camel.

Pausing at the huge gate to the courtyard of his son's home, the Bedouin stopped abruptly. His mouth fell open. No! This could not be! On the right side of the doorway was a cylindrical case, the distinguishing mark of the home of a Jew. Then he smiled; he had the wrong house. That ignorant lout in Sepphoris had given him the wrong directions. Returning to the main road he hailed the first passerby and inquired the location of the home of Nabal. The man glared at the Gentile scornfully, and instead of answering simply pointed to the house he had just left and continued on his way. Kareem stared at the house as the obvious sank in, his son was a Jew. His heart sank with the thought, riding slowly toward the house; his hand fondled the hilt of his sword. Anger swept over him in waves. He felt sick, nauseated, then the blood began to pound at his temples. Dismounting, his fist hammered on the gate, and he ground out between clinched teeth,

"A Jew! A damned stinking Jew. I'll see him dead first."

The ponderous door swung open and an armed servant looked at him inquiringly, choking back his anger the Bedouin growled, "I am Kareem, I have come to see Nabal." Perhaps it was the wrong Nabal? After all, Nabal was a common enough name.

However, the servant bowed low, eyeing the pagan distastefully, but managed to say, "May God's blessings be with, Kareem. Enter, my master is expecting you."

Kareem's anger purged his last hope, and again, he absentmindedly caressed the worn handle of his sword. Numbly, he followed the servant, but his eyes were ever on the alert. Kareem took in his surroundings with a sense of awe. Truly, his son had done well. This was the home of a rich man, not just a well-to-do-farmer. Passing through a large atrium, the servant led him into a room, where he could make out two women awaiting him. The servant bowed and slipped away as Kareem's eyes slowly adjusted to the dim interior, and he recognized Oma.

"Welcome to the home of your son, Abba. His home is your home." Her voice was firm, and he was surprised. Oma had always been terrified of him; her poise was completely unexpected, even to herself and she said graciously, "Nabal will be with us shortly, Abba, please be seated and allow me to wash your feet?"

Kareem looked at her suspiciously. She was dressed in the Jewish style, and the anger swelled up in him like a freshet in the spring. His eyes swung to Oma's companion, she was so striking that he could not tear his eyes from her. The woman's presence seemed to dominate the room. She was noble, dignified, and emanated a strange aura that seemed to sooth his rage. The woman wore no veil and her features were serene and firm. He shifted his feet uncomfortably, suddenly, he felt ill at ease. Then he started to get angry, why all this concern about a mere woman? She was no different than any other woman. Women were mere chattels made for the pleasure of men, and subject to their slightest whim. Before he could object; however, Oma swept forward, and taking him by the arm, led him to a Roman style armchair. A servant came with a bowl and a pitcher of water. Waving the servant to one side, Oma dropped to her knees and began washing her father-in-law's dusty feet. When finished, she dried and perfumed them and placed on his feet a pair of silken slippers, rising, she quickly poured him a goblet of wine, and placed a bowl of fruit at his elbow. Kareem numbly took the wine, and sipped automatically, his pleased palate found the wine to his liking. Nabal lived well indeed. All the while, Oma's friend just stood there looking at him with a pleasant smile tugging at the corners of her mouth.

Oma stepped back and exclaimed, "Excuse me, Abba; allow me to present my good friend Anne, the wife of Joachim.

Suddenly Kareem found himself on his feet. He bowed low and murmured, "It is indeed a pleasure. Your presence is like the morning sunrise." His anger suddenly gone, he found it was indeed a pleasure. Kareem had never before acknowledged a woman so politely in his entire life. What was going on here? He sat down gingerly, and Nabal chose that moment to enter the room.

Abdul's knees were literally knocking, and he had a knot in the pit of his stomach. It had taken all his nerve to face his father. What would he think? What was worse—what would he do? Abdul was terrified. He went up to his father and fell on his knees before him and exclaimed, "Abba!" He could say no more, and he dropped his head afraid to look his father in the face.

Kareem saw a stranger kneeling before him. The man was a Jew from head to toe. Nabal's hair fell luxuriously down his shoulders, and loose ringlets of hair dangled at his temples. His black beard was trimmed, his aquiline nose, and fine features were so like his mother's. Nabal was an extremely handsome man. Kareem noted the tassels on his cloak, there was no doubt about it, his son was a Jew. Anger blinded him; acting instinctively Kareem raised his hand in anger to strike his son. Suddenly, his eyes caught those of my mother. His arm froze in mid-air. Slowly, he felt the anger drain from him and his arm sagged lamely at his side.

Startled, Nabal looked up and saw the upraised arm and his face blanched. Oma stifled a scream, but seeing the by-play between Kareem and Anne, she suddenly relaxed, and I knew that she was remembering the promise made by my mother. Kareem grabbed Nabal by both ears, in a choked voice he exclaimed, "Your Syrian forefathers are turning in their graves. How could you, my son, how could you become a Jew?"

The fear gradually subsided in Nabal's eyes and he stated firmly, "I had no intention of really becoming a Hebrew, Father. However, in order to fit in with the people here, I found it expedient to pretend to become a Jew. I could not tell anyone that I was the son of Kareem the bandit, so I changed my name. Joachim, Anne's husband, became my friend and mentor. He convinced me that the old gods of the Syrians were nothing but mud and stone. You yourself, Father, never believed in the Syrian gods, so I did not have a false belief to overcome. Once I became convinced that the gods of the Syrians were indeed false, it was easy for me to accept the Hebrew religion even if I did not believe in their God. There were many advantages for me to convert to Judaism. Oma has secretly continued her practice of worshiping idols, but they never meant anymore to me than did the God of the Israelites. However, when you sent word you were coming, I was terrified that you would not accept my conversion even if it were a sham. Since then; however, I have had much time to think. I first had to face up to the fact that I had become a Jew under false pretenses. However, after meditating, praying and fasting all week in the Jewish tradition, I was amazed to learn that I truly believe that the God of the Israelites is the one and only God. With the money you gave me, I did not have to cheat or steal to become successful. I have a natural God-given aptitude for business. If you want to kill me for becoming a Hebrew, I will not resist? I am prepared to die for that which I believe." His confession had surprised even Abdul, himself with his declaration of faith "even to the death." Gone was his fear, and he looked his father in the eye as fearlessly as a young lion. Then, Abdul lowered his head and bared his neck to his father.

With a sob, Kareem gathered his son into his arms and cried, "Kill you, my son? Forgive me! Flesh of my flesh, bones of my bones, it would be like killing a part of myself." With a cry of pent up relief, Oma, forgetting all propriety, stepped between the two men embracing them both and bathed them in her tears. I was overwhelmed with joy and my angels joined with me in a chorus of praises to our all merciful God. Nabal jumped up and struck a gong for his servants and when they came he ordered a feast prepared for his father, but Kareem held up his hand and stated firmly,

"I did not come here to feast, Abdul. It was my wish to see you one last time. I had also hoped to see my grandchildren, alas, you have none. Now that I find you well and happy, I must return to be buried with my forefathers, the physicians cannot cure my ailment."

Nabal jumped to his feet with a cry of dismay, "Abba, allow me to send for my physician, he is the finest in Galilee." Kareem began to protest, but suddenly a fierce pain gripped his stomach, and he sat up gasping for air. Clutching a cloth to his face, he wiped a bloody flux from his mouth. Kareem rose to his feet as though to leave. Without warning he doubled up, clutched his stomach, and without a word fell senseless to the floor. Nabal called to his servants, "Quickly, take my father to the east bedroom. Oma, send Theodore for the doctor."

Morning came before Kareem again opened his eyes. He looked about in wonder. He was on a bed in a spacious, luxurious bedroom, a huge fan of woven palm leaves was mysteriously moving back and forth over his bed. Hovering over him was an elderly, professional looking man that he instantly assumed to be a physician? The man spoke solicitously, "Welcome back, Kareem you have lost a lot of blood. How do you feel?"

"Like I have lost a lot of blood," the Arab growled, but with an amused glint in his eye.

The doctor smiled, "That's a good sign. Are you hungry?"

"As hungry as a starved vulture, but it is no use, when I try to eat my stomach doubles me up with pain. I find that I can drink a little goat's milk, but even that is painful."

"You have a bleeding in your stomach, Kareem. I can give you herbs that will ease your pain and allow you to eat. However, you will not be able to eat any fruit, or solid foods. It is broth for you.

"You mean you can treat the condition, Doctor?"

The physician looked down as though to compose his thoughts. "As I said, Kareem, I can ease your pain," he replied evasively.

With a grunt, Kareem sat up on the edge of the bed, steadied himself, and replied calmly, "I know what you mean, Doctor. My physician has already told me that I am dying, and that there was nothing he could do for me. It seems I have a growth that is eating my stomach and there is no treatment."

The doctor nodded glumly. "I can actually feel the growth through the stomach wall. For now, we can control the pain, but later we can do very little." He put his hand on Kareem's shoulder sympathetically and said, "I wish I had better news."

"I have lived with pain all my life, Doctor. How much time do I have?"

"Your condition can drag out for several weeks, but you are strong and it could linger for as long as six months."

"Do not tell my son, Doctor. I wish to be a burden to no man."

Nabal spoke up from behind him, but with a catch in his throat, "It's a little late for that, Abba. With my resources, you certainly will be no burden. My new religion teaches us, "Honor thy Father and thy Mother". Would you have me dishonor my God as well as my father?"

Kareem thought, what kind of God must this Hebrew God be? Abdul had never been brave, but for this strange, unseen God, his son had become as fearless as a lion, willing even to die for his belief. Kareem cleared his throat and stated dourly, "This God of yours seems to have done well by you my, son. Tell me, does he have a rule for thieves?"

"Indeed he does, Abba, He teaches, "Thou Shalt Not Steal."

"Then how can he abide either you or me? We come from a long line of thieves."

Nabal hastened to explain, "Our God is a forgiving God, if we sin and are truly sorry, he forgives us, but we must do much penance. We pray, give alms and often fast for days at a time to express our sorrow." Kareem looked at his son long and hard. He hardly knew him. When Abdul had left home, he had still been a beardless youth.

That evening, Kareem joined Nabal at his evening meal, and he listened respectfully as his son gave thanks before eating. Nabal had spent the afternoon answering his many questions about this strange, unseen God of the Hebrews. The Bedouin was impressed with the cleanliness of his son's home, and the personal hygiene of all of its inhabitants. Oma and Anne personally served the men and then ate their own meal in a side alcove. Kareem's curiosity was insatiable, Nabal spent the entire week with his father answering his questions; when he did not know the answer, he called on Joachim for assistance. Kareem was impressed with Joachim. When they met, awe enveloped him similar to that which he had felt when he had first seen Anne.

Unknown to all of them, my angels and I were storming heaven for a healing of Kareem, body and soul, subject to God's holy will.

When alone with Joachim one day, Kareem finally got up the nerve to ask, "Joachim, I have been a sinful man. My family has been a family of brigands for generations. With what you have taught me, I feel great sorrow and regret for all that I have done, but how could I ever atone for so much?" He paused, his voice trembling, "Many of the men I attacked," he added soberly "died of their injuries." Joachim answered, "Both you and your son must reimburse those from whom you have stolen, and add a fifth more as penance. For those unfortunates that you killed you must do much penance, give much alms and fast and beg the Lord for forgiveness. If you know the wives and children of those you have slain, you must see that their needs are taken care of."

"Ah, yes of course," Kareem responded with a sigh. "The money that I have hidden away shall go to those I have robbed and the widows and orphans of those I have slain, but I do not have enough to cover my lifetime of plunder, nor do I have the slightest idea of who most of them are."

When Nabal was informed of his father's wishes, he came to him and exclaimed, "Worry not, my father, as you know, I did not wish to be a thief, and the few people that I have stolen from will be fully repaid. Your blood is my blood, and your debts are my debts. When I left your home, I told you that your money was an investment. Half of all that I possess is yours. We have more than enough money to reimburse those you have robbed and killed. I also pledge that from this day forward that I will emulate Joachim in that I will give the first third of the fruits of my labor to the holy temple, the next third to the poor and the rest I will retain for my family."

Kareem hung his head in complete submission and a tear leaked down his cheek. He asked in a humble voice, "Is it possible, Joachim, that I can become a follower of your Jewish God before I die? Nothing would please me more than to honor and worship the God of the Hebrews?

Joachim was pleased and answered, "I am overjoyed, Kareem but I do not have that authority. I will have to discuss the matter with the rabbis and the priests."

That night after their supper when Joachim and Anne were preparing to leave, Kareem rose and asked, "Before you leave, Joachim would you give me your blessing, and if I dare ask, may I have the blessing of your venerable wife Anne," and he bowed to her.

Joachim blessed Kareem and the thief felt peace steal over him like a warm blanket. When Anne approached and laid her hands on his head, heat radiated from her hands like the warm rays of the sun. My angels and I added our blessings to my mother's, with a moan of sheer joy, Kareem fell to his knees, and kissed Anne's feet.

The next morning a southwestern balmy breeze from the warm waters of the Great Sea tickled the chimes on Joachim's porch creating a pleasant harmony. The Hebrew was not an indoor people. Weather permitting, which was about two-thirds of the year, they ate in their courtyards and patios and even from the top of their roofs. Sleeping on the roof was so common that even the very rich slept outside. Sara had ushered mother's guests onto their pleasant terrace. Thatched palms covered the patio, which allowed some light to filter through. The courtyard was a beautiful miniature garden filled with date palms, fig trees, aromatic bushes, and a variety of flowers. Their date trees, although beautiful, could not compare to the superb date trees in the tropical forests of the Ghor in the Jordan Valley.

Oma was animatedly telling Hannah and Moselle about Kareem's desire to convert to Judaism, carefully omitting the personal details of the event. I knew that Oma was now a true believer, and as she had promised my mother, she had taken her idols and smashed them with a hammer. As soon as Oma had told her friends the reason for her joy, she immediately begged them to excuse her, since she had pledged to personally care for her father-in-law.

As the gate closed behind her, Moselle looked at Hannah and sniffed, "Did you hear that? Rumor has it, that there was a Kareem who was a bandit in the Judean Wilderness?"

Hannah looked up and exclaimed smugly, "That doesn't surprise me in the least."

Sara was miffed with Oma. Since Kareem had reentered her life, she had had very little time for her. She spoke up from her "pretended" dusting and complained, "Since Kareem came, my mistress has spent a lot of her time at Nabal's house, and one of their servants told me that Nabal's real name was Abdul ben Kareem. Do you suppose he was a bandit like his father?"

Moselle nodded knowingly and exclaimed, "It is a sin to consort with Gentiles, especially one pretending to be something he is not. I can't imagine what they are thinking of?" With a self-righteous look Moselle added, "It isn't proper that Anne expose herself to these pagans in her delicate condition.

God punished her before for her sins by keeping her barren for years. You would think that now that he has blessed her with child that she would conduct herself with more decorum?"

They could hear Anne coming from the other room, and Sara whispered in a conspiratorial voice. "Careful, I heard she fired her own relative for saying such things."

Hannah had had little to say, but Lucifer had been plying her with suggestions and she resented all the attention that everyone was giving my mother,

The two women rose to their feet respectfully, when Anne entered the room. Sara made a hasty exit. After their greetings Anne suggested, "Perhaps we could make some swaddling clothes for the poor of Sepphoris this week. I know of several families that are expecting."

Hannah, plagued by the insidious attacks of Lucifer's henchmen for weeks, was suddenly enraged and she lashed out with diabolic insolence, "You make me sick, Anne. You are always so good, always so perfect, and always the sanctimonious almsgiver. Here you are pregnant in your old age, after being sterile for twenty years." She added sneeringly. "If you are pregnant, then you must have been the sport of the demons."

Sara, who was listening, was as shocked as Moselle. Complainers and shirkers to be sure, but even they did not condone such language to my mother. Inside my mother's womb, compassion welled in my heart. Mother; however, never allowed Hannah's tirade to disturb her in the least. Meekly she bowed her head and replied kindly holding out her hand in compassion to her assailant, "Are you really that unhappy, Hannah? Anne hung her head humbly and prayed silently for her companion.

An uneasy silence hung in the room, when suddenly there was a frantic pounding on the gate. Rising to its urgency, and before Sara could react; Anne hurried to the gate. Oma burst into the courtyard and grasping Anne by the arms, she gushed excitedly, "You will never believe what has just happened?

Anne took her by the hand and invited, "Come in child, come in," and she led her to a bench.

Oma, still gasping for breath explained, "When I got home the Elders were just leaving. They are going to accept Kareem into the faith. He will be circumcised next week." She jumped up excitedly.

Anne hugged her and exclaimed, "Oh, Oma, I'm so happy for you and Nabal."

But that isn't all," Oma cried out, "The physician was also there. He checked Kareem and found him completely cured. The blessing that you and Joachim gave him last night cured him. He said he felt a warm feeling all over when he was blessed, and this morning when he got up, he said he has never felt better."

Moselle looked at Hannah accusingly and nearly shouted, "How could you malign Anne so viciously, she whom God has so obviously blessed?"

Hannah turned on her friend and hissed scathingly, "Who are you to talk? How about all those nasty things you said about her?"

Moselle started for her with murder in her eye, when Anne quietly stepped between the two and said, "See how one small fault prepares the way for another, and the second is only a just punishment for the first. Now is not the time for arguing, but God be praised, it is a time for celebrating. Sara," she told her, "run and bring Joachim here and notify our friends. We must go and celebrate with Nabal and his father, and offer up thanks to the Lord our God. Hurry, Sara you too, Moselle and Hannah, are you not Oma's friends?" The three were completely flabbergasted, Sara's mouth fell open as though to speak, then she turned and sped to do as instructed. Moselle and Hannah hung their heads shamefacedly, and mother pulled them together and said, "Now why don't you two hug and make up?"

Hannah started crying hysterically, she hugged Moselle and between sobs cried, "I don't know what got into me?" Hannah became inconsolable and sobbed uncontrollably.

Mother suggested, "It would be wise to take Hannah home, Moselle. Stay with her for awhile, she will need you when she gets control of herself."

Two days later Sara opened the door and ushered in Mother's two friends, Moselle and Hannah, They were quite subdued, and Sara could tell that Hannah had been weeping. They entered the room and sat down without their usual frivolity. Sara was also deeply troubled, and she sensed their concern. With Oma, she was quite at ease, but with Moselle and Hannah she did not take such liberties, usually she was quite reserved unless they spoke to her first. However, she stood before them and humbly said, "Before I announce you, I would like to beg your pardon for my remarks about my mistress. Oh, how could I have been so wrong about her? She is truly a holy child of God."

Moselle surprised her, jumping up she ran to Sara gathering her into her arms, and with a sob she exclaimed. "I, too, have acted rashly. I have come here this morning to beg Anne's forgiveness as has Hannah."

The three were having a good cry when Anne entered and with a little smile asked. "My goodness, ladies why so glum; we all have so much for which to be happy."

They all ran to her and began talking and apologizing at once, my mother calmed them in her cool, unruffled manner and said gently, "That issue, ladies, has been long settled. There is nothing left for me to forgive, I forgave you all long ago."

Sara's face flamed scarlet, and she exclaimed with wonder in her voice, "You knew all along. Oh, Mistress, I am so ashamed," and she tore her shawl in sorrow and threw it over her head in shame.

Anne removed the shawl and took the sobbing girl in her arms and said, "Now is not the time for sadness, but a time for all of us to rejoice. God has visited our house this day," and she reached out and drew them all to her bosom. My happiness was complete for my mother, her friends would no longer mock or deride her. However, I was happiest for her friends. They were the sinners for whom my angels and I had prayed so hard. Lying snug in my mother's womb, my angels and I began giving praise, honor, and glory to the Lord, which he so richly deserved.

Frustrated in his efforts to corrupt the friends of my mother, Satan was torn with anger and spite. He called his angelic demons together determined to rain a continual assault on the morals of the saintly Anne. My angels and I prayed for Anne continuously. Our prayers; however, were not needed, for my holy mother was impervious to Lucifer's deviltry. She resisted the Great Red Dragon's efforts with humble fortitude, patience, and prayer. Each conflict thus won by mother gave the Creator much pleasure. He rewarded her each time with more gifts of the spirit. Sensing this, the Serpent grew even more frustrated, but he never gave up trying as long as she lived, and God never ceased rewarding her for her triumphs. Oma, and Anne's other friends were also tempted, but the Heavenly Father took pity on them and enhanced their grace to block all of Satin's efforts to again tempt them to do his devilish work.

The time was rapidly drawing near for the event of my birth. My mother and father and all their friends intensified their fasting, prayers, almsgiving, and good works. In turn my angels and I prayed unceasingly for that holy day. Several times God had me brought before him, and at such times, he lavished even more gifts on my soul. Finally, God sent Saint Michael to inform me that the day of my birth was at hand. My tiny heart raced with joy, I instinctively kicked out, and I heard my mother exclaim, "Goodness, my precious little one that was certainly a joyful kick for the Lord. Something tells me I will soon be holding you in my arms. If only you knew how I have longed and yearned for this moment."

Indeed, I did know. In her privacy, Mother talked and sang to me for hours at a time. If she was not talking to me, she was talking to the Lord. During my time in her womb, I knew her every thought, word, and action. In all that time she never once committed so much as a venial sin. Before the Lord, she was beyond reproach. Before my birth, I had learned by mother's example, the value of the gifts of, faith, hope and charity given me at my conception by the Trinity. Her example remained with me all the days of my life. From the moment of my conception, I had resolved to never commit so much as a single venial sin during my tenure on earth. I could not bear even the thought of doing anything that might bring even the slightest distress to my Creator. My mother's example only enhanced this resolve.

My saintly father Joachim, also spiritually influenced me. He prayed constantly for a safe birth for me, for the health and well being of Anne, and for the coming of the Messiah. He was kind, considerate, and ever thoughtful of my mother's every need. Never once did he speak crossly to her, and he sought and respected her opinion on nearly everything that he did.

The Most High sent Saint Michael the Archangel late in the month of Av, to inform me that my birth was imminent. My love and gratitude was such that I went into a state of ecstasy; a trance I remained in until my birth. The Lord's messenger appeared to my mother at precisely that same moment. She was singing canticles of praise to the Lord, when the angel informed her that the time for my delivery was fast approaching. Her face glowing, and her heart overflowing with holy joy, Anne summoned her servant.

"Sara," my mother called, and in seconds, Sara was there, now eagerly serving her slightest whim.

"Yes, Mistress," she replied bowing before her respectfully.

"My time is near, Sara. Call Joachim and tell him to make the proper preparations."

Overjoyed, Sara ran to call Joachim.

Anne sat down and wrote messages to her sister Maraha, and to Sobe's daughter Mary Solome, and also, to the widow Enui, Elizabeth's sister. At the time, Elizabeth was with her husband in Jerusalem where he was serving his priestly term.

Joachim, as was the custom, relegated jobs to his hired help in order to keep them away from the house. On the evening before the expected birth, Joachim went to his herds in the fields nearest his home. The pasture grounds were beautifully divided off and hedged in. Anne's staff of cooks and servers provided the meals for the workers in small huts erected in the corners of the fields. From one such corner, steps led down to a small stone altar. The space around was neatly paved with triangular stones. Surrounding the little chapel were shrubs and flowers. Joachim selected his finest lambs, goats, and bullocks and sent them by his servants to the holy temple as an offering of thanksgiving to the Lord. Joachim and his nephews then spent their time in prayer before the altar, while they awaited the coming of the child.

The three women converged on our home toward evening. Upon arriving, they were ushered directly to Anne's apartment back of the fireplace. She told them that her time drew near, and they embraced my mother, congratulating her warmly, Anne intoned to herself a Psalm of praise and thanksgiving, "Praise God, the Lord, he has had pity on his people and has freed Israel. Truly, he has fulfilled the promise that he made to Adam in Paradise. The seed of the woman shall crush the serpent's head. The germ that God gave to Abraham has ripened in me. The promise made to Sara and the blossom of Aaron's rod is fulfilled in me."

Anne began shining with light. The room filled with glory, and above Anne appeared a vision of Jacob's ladder. The women attending her saw the ladder and were amazed and entranced. Sara came in at Anne's command, her eyes big as saucers; as she saw Anne singled out by God so wonderfully. Her hands shaking, Sara served the standing women a light meal of bread, fruit, and water. The three women then retired for a little rest, while my mother remained standing. Facing Jerusalem, she prayed until near midnight, then she woke her relatives. She took them into her oratory and lit the lamps filled with "very pure virgin oil", which I knew she had herself pressed from ripened olives. From a closet, she took a small box containing relics of the Patriarchs of Israel. In the box was a lock of Sarah's hair, which Anne held in the greatest reverence. Enclosed, also, were some small, finger-bones of Joseph, which Moses had brought with him out of Egypt. The women dropped to their knees before a small altar, one on each side of Anne, and Mary Solome knelt behind her. Anne began a canticle of praise recounting the story of Abraham, "The father of all who believe", and the miraculous conception of Sarah, his sterile wife. While she was praying thus, a supernatural light began to fill the chamber. The three women threw themselves onto the floor in awe and hid their faces. A dazzling light entirely enveloped Anne. The holy angels, a moment later, pressed me into the hands of my loving mother. Mother wrapped me in a warm blanket, pressed me to her heart with tears of joy streaming down her face, as the magnificent light slowly faded away.

Holding me up in front of her, my mother raised her eyes to heaven and prayed, "Oh, Lord and, Creator, with eternal thanks I offer you your bounty without any merit of mine. But, how shall I be able to treat such a child worthily?"

Interiorly, the Lord instructed my mother, "Bring the child up without any outward show of reverence, while inwardly you are to show profound veneration for the future mother of the Messias." While I often heard God's instructions to my mother, I was not privy to this conversation, since it referred to my being the Mother of God. My mother had been spared the usual labor and pains experienced by other mothers in this miraculous, *yet natural childbirth.* Anne began bathing me, and as my three relatives rose shakily to their feet, mother wrapped me in red and gray swaddling clothes. With incredulous eyes, the women received me in their arms. Weeping for joy, they sang a hymn of praise and thanks to the Lord.

My thousand angels and myriads of hosts from heaven suddenly filled the room singing heavenly praises all unseen by my relatives. My mother held me on high allowing the angels to venerate and honor me. They sang, "On the eighth day this child shall be called Mary". I was born at midnight on the twentieth-third day of Elul, the eighth day of September 21 BC. The angels then sang the Gloria and Alleluia, and while they continued their praises, Mary Solome dispatched Sara to inform Joachim of my birth.

Many wonderful events took place at my birth. Unknown to me, the Most High sent the archangel Gabriel as an envoy to bring this joyful news to the holy Fathers still retained in limbo. Gabriel descended into the deep cavern, and announced the good news to the just. He said to them, "Rejoice, the dawn of eternal felicity has commenced and the reparation of man, which God knows you have so earnestly desired and expected by the holy Patriarchs and foretold by the Prophets, has begun. She, who is to be the mother of the Messiah, has just been born. Soon you will see the salvation and the glory of the Most High." He then explained what the Omnipotent had begun to work in me in order that they might better understand the beginning of the mystery, which was to end their prolonged imprisonment. As Gabriel took his leave, Abraham and Moses led their companions in new canticles of praise honoring and praising the Blessed Trinity.

Unfortunately, there were adverse effects as well. The possessed souls in Palestine, upon my birth became perfectly furious. Dashed and tossed about, they uttered horrible cries. The devils from within called out; "We must withdraw. We must go out."

The fearful cries of the possessed confined on the Temple of Jerusalem aroused the priest Simeon. Simeon, among others, was in charge of them. One man cried out fiercely that he must get out. Simeon released him and then the devil inside him cried out, "I must go forth. A virgin is born, and many angels on earth torment us. We must go forth, and never again shall we dare possess a human being."

The demons cruelly threw the unfortunate man to the ground, and Simeon, informed about me, began to pray for the man. The demons tossed the man too and fro until at last with a shriek, the devils went out of him.

Anna, the Prophetess learned of my birth in a vision. Simeon and Anna discussed the matter between them and fell to praising the glory of God.

In the country of the three holy kings, a certain Prophetess had visions of my birth. She advised the priests that a virgin had been born whom many spirits had come down upon earth to welcome, but that other spirits were troubled. The kings also saw pictures of the event in their stars. My birth challenged the power of Satan, for God in his infinite wisdom, cast many Egyptian idols into the sea, and dashed many others to pieces.

At the precise moment of my birth, God's holy angels presented me to the Holy Trinity. A guardian angel temporarily replaced my physical body. Hosts of angels accompanied the Archangel Gabriel, who received me in his arms from my mother's hands. Then a solemn procession bore me heavenward with incomparable songs of joy. When I entered the empyrean heaven, I prostrated myself full of love before the royal throne in the presence of the Most High. For the first time, I saw the blessed Trinity in an unveiled Beatific Vision. I witnessed the joy of the entire heavenly court. The Trinity revealed to me all my gifts and graces in a supernatural manner, except for the knowledge that I was to be the Mother of God. In addition, God bestowed new graces and gifts upon me. At the same time, the Trinity instructed me in innumerable mysteries, and placed me at the right hand of the Son. When the festivities ended, the angels returned me to my mother's arms with all the pageantry accorded a princess in King Solomon's Court.

As I revealed before, God endowed me from my conception with the full use of my reason and all of my senses. After my birth; however, I saw my mother and father for the first time, as well as my thousand holy angels in all their glory. My heart brimmed over with great love and tenderness. My guardian angels had created word pictures of my parents for me while I was in the womb of my mother. Nothing; however, could take the place of my seeing them with my own God-given eyes, nor could the angels have prepared me for the vision of their own heavenly splendor.

Soon after my return from heaven, my father entered the room and knelt by my mother. Carefully taking me up in his arms from my tiny wooden cradle, he held me up to the Heavenly Father. Tears of joy flowed down his worn cheeks. Deeply moved by the sight and the feel of his own flesh and blood, my father sang a hymn of praise to God. For twenty years my father had prayed and made sacrifices for the moment of my birth. There was nothing more that he desired in this life.

Tenderly embracing me, he put me back in my cradle and murmured, "Now I am content to die."

Of course, father did not die at this time. Eight days later, early in the morning multitudes of heavenly angels in splendid array descended from on high carrying a beautiful escutcheon upon which the name ***MARY*** was engraved. Appearing before my mother they proclaimed, "Blessed Anne, your child shall be named ***MARY.*** We have brought you this name from heaven, and Divine Providence has selected and ordained that it be given to your child by you and Joachim." Mother conferred with my father, and he joyfully accepted the name.

Being the eighth day mother and father's relatives, and a multitude of friends had already gathered for the naming of the child. According to custom, mother remained in her room during the naming. She had dressed me in red and transparent white; when father came in to pick me up his face glowed with pride. Joachim had rearranged the partitions leaving a large meeting room. He had erected an altar in the middle of the room and decorated it with red and white cloths. All around the room was a row of tables laden with plates, glasses, and eating utensils, but the food was not yet present. A small basket-like-cradle stood on the altar. Joachim had shaped the cradle like a shell, weaving it in red and white, and in it, mother had placed a sky-blue coverlet.

As each guest entered the house, Joachim insisted on washing the feet of the men, and female relatives washed the feet of the women in a private room. The guests encircled the room with the women standing well back from the ceremony. Some women wore himations that wound elegantly about their body with the top portion covering their heads. Some wore pleated gowns, and dresses that looked much like the basic clothes of their male counterparts, but the women's clothes were much fuller, more feminine, and often embroidered, woven, brocaded, and quilted with intricate designs. Beautiful buckles, rings, brooches and necklaces made of gold, silver and pearls complimented the women's outfits. One wealthy woman wore a gold diadem in her hair that resembled a town fortification. The Jews; however, did not pierce their ears or noses, since it was a sin to mutilate the body. The women wore in their hair colorful ribbons made of wool and silk, and many had braided their hair into becoming fashions.

The men likewise wore jewelry, and like the women covered their heads with turbans and shawls. Heavy rings with seals were favorites of the wealthy and were often so heavy that the men sometimes wore them around their neck on a chain. Both men and women wore sandals usually made of camel's hide and worn without socks. A few wore a shoe made from jackal or hyena hide. No self-respecting Jew, even the poorest, would go barefooted except in the hallowed sanctuary of the temple where to wear shoes was considered a sacrilege.

It was easy to pick out the conservative Essenians from the celebrants, because of their plain white robes, cloaks and the absence of jewelry. They used a plain sash instead of the colorful belts of their neighbors. The garments were made of wool usually fabricated in Judea and linen made in Galilee; however, the Law forbade the mixture of the two. It was a colorful gathering with many garments dyed in various mixtures of blue, brown, crimson, yellow, white, and the much-prized purple obtained from the Phoenicians. These elegant gowns were usually adorned with dark-blue tassels hanging from the bottoms of the clothes.

In attendance were several priests from Sepphoris dressed in their sacred garments. In their midst was a high priest and he was robed more magnificently than the rest. Father entered the room with me in his arms and the guests immediately fell silent. He placed me in the hands of the high priest. The priest lifted me up and presented me to the Lord, while he recited ritual prayers from the holy scrolls. He then laid me in my cradle on the altar, and taking a pair of scissors, cut a lock of hair from each side, and from the top of my head. The priest then burned the hair in a small pan of coals. The acrid smell of burning hair tickled my nostrils and I sneezed, which caused many of my women relatives to smile and murmur their concern. The priest then took a flask of oil and anointed my five senses. With his work-roughened thumb, he pressed the ointment upon my ears, eyes, nose, mouth and finally my heart. Turning to my father the priest asked, "What will the name of this child be?"

In a ringing voice Joachim replied, "Her name is Mary."

Taking a piece of paper the priest wrote the name Mary and placed it on my chest. The hazzan from the local synagogue then led the guests in the singing of several psalms, at the end of which the priest terminated the ceremony and Enui, Elizabeth's sister, returned me to my mother.

A short while later, mother entered the room carrying me bundled up in my swaddling clothes. She and I, with my tiny spit curls of golden hair, were then the center of attention. God had created me with delicate, even features, and all the guests made a big fuss over me. Mother wore a simple, natural-wool pleated gown that reached to the floor. A simple crimson sash was gathered in at her waist. My mother was an attractive, tall, stately-looking woman with fine features. In addition, she had an aura of holiness that discouraged the eyes of any overly attentive males. Mother had embroidered her garment with beautiful vines of the grape with clusters of purple fruit artfully worked onto her gown. She had braided her hair in loose tresses in a simple but effective style. At father's command musicians began to play festive music and the women loaded the tables with a great variety of food. Mother soon returned me to my cradle and Sara became my sitter while mother attended to her guests. The guests then seated themselves around the low tables, and the celebration continued well on into the night. The gaily garlanded house and courtyard were soon filled to capacity resounding with the happy cacophony of laughter and music.

My name, like that of my Son Jesus, had been selected for me by the Divine Trinity even before the formation of the heavens or of the earth, and had been revealed to the angelic spirits before my birth. The holy angels heard a voice from the throne speaking in the person of the Father. "Our chosen One shall be called ***MARY,*** and this name is to be powerful and magnificent. Those that shall invoke it with devout affection shall receive abundant graces. Those that honor and pronounce it with reverence shall be consoled and vivified. They will find in it the remedy for their evils, treasures for their enrichment, and the light which shall guide them to Heaven. It shall be terrible against the poser of hell, it shall crush the head of the serpent, and it shall win glorious victories over the princes of hell."

My thousand guardians and a horde of angels from the Empyrean Heavens joined in our joyful celebration; however, my mother and I were the only persons that were able to see and hear their sweet and ravishing music. I was thus, first named by the Holy Trinity in Heaven on the day of my nativity, and again on earth eight days later by my parents.

According to the Law of Moses, as stated in the twelfth chapter of Leviticus [Lv. 12, 1-4], a woman who has given birth shall be deemed impure for forty days. My birthing by Anne was pure and undefiled as befit my heavenly status, and also because my mother was a sharer in my own purity. However, my mother and father were bound by the Law of Moses the same as any other Hebrew, and in spite of their holiness and purity, they, too, were subject to God's Law. A few days before her implied impurity was up; father prepared us for our trip to the Jewish Temple in Jerusalem. It was to be my first visit to the temple, and I eagerly anticipated the event praying and praising the God whom it honored. Father attached our small group to a caravan of travelers. Included in our party were my relatives Maraha and Enui. We traveled slowly, and on the forth day, when we neared the Damascus Gate, our caravan broke up, each going their separate way. Elizabeth met us at the gate in a happy reunion. She could not wait to see the new addition to the family

The Holy Temple was not the beautiful temple that Solomon had built, nor was it the second temple that the prophets Haggai and Zechariah had urged Zerubbabel to build after their return from the Babylonian exile in 538 BC. The temple Zerubbabel built was a poor imitation of that built by Solomon. The exiles were poor and only the bare essentials were included in the new structure, which was dedicated in 515 BC. However, it would satisfy the needs of the Hebrews until Herod the Great began rebuilding the temple in 20 BC, which was the temple in use during the time of the ministry of my Son. The temple Herod built was often called Herod's Temple and surpassed the beauty of the temple built by King Solomon. However, according to some the Holy Ark had been carried off by Nebuchadnezzar to Babylon when he had conquered the Israelites in 587 BC. Others have contested this claim and believe the Holy Ark was hidden beneath the temple by the priests. Yet others contend that the Ark was destroyed for the gold content. In any event, the Holy of Holies was now an empty room, which the High Priest tremblingly entered once a year on the annual Day of Atonement.

The next day my mother took me to the Women's Court, while Joseph made his sacrifice to the Lord from the Men's Court. We had no sooner taken our places, than the presiding priest, officiating in the morning daily service, sacrificed an unblemished lamb to the Lord. Then another priest came out on the steps that stood above the Court of the Men of Israel, and read the "Shema Israel" aloud, and then read a passage of the Law.

Mother presented herself to the priests at the temple on the fortieth day. Assisted by our family, mother gave the priest Simeon a one-year old unblemished lamb as a holocaust for my birth, as well as a turtledove to forgive her for all her faults, thus complying with the obligation of the Law to the very last point. Although she and I were not subject to its penalties, mother considered herself bound in the eyes of men, and of course even though I had nothing to say regarding the matter, the Law also bound me in spite of my lack of sin.

God granted Simeon, a most holy priest, the privilege to see me at my mother's presentation and on other occasions as well. Simeon looked on my mother with great favor, as with tears of humility, she pleaded with him to pray for herself and for me, and prayed that the Lord forgive us for any fault of which we might be guilty. I added my own prayers of unworthiness, and God was most pleased that we presented ourselves as sinners, and he rewarded us for our humility. Simeon began experiencing impulses of the spirit regarding the holiness of the child he held in his arms.

He asked himself, "What strange feeling is this within me? Are these the women God told me about? Perhaps this child is to be the parent of the Messiah who is to come?" Consequently, he treated us with the greatest benevolence. From the Women's Court facing the Holy of Holies, mother held me up to the Lord, and offered me to our Creator with her most devout and tender tears for she alone knew that I was to be the Mother of God. Still unaware of my destiny, I joined my prayers with hers with tears of supplication and adoration. Enui, Maraha, and Elizabeth joined in the prayers praising God and glorifying his Holy Name. Overwhelmed by the holiness and grandeur of the edifice dedicated to my God, I wished with all my heart that I might prostrate myself on the floor and kiss it.

Since I could not, I prayed, "Oh most High God, I thank you that I have been allowed to adore you in your holy temple. O Lord, I glorify and most humbly petition that I may be allowed to serve you in this your most holy of houses according to your blessed will."

Suddenly a beam of bright light shone down from heaven, it illuminated my mother and me, a sign that our prayers had been heard. In her heart mother heard a voice, which I was privileged to hear, urging her to renew her vow to consecrate me at age three to God's service in the temple. Mother replied, "Oh my, God, my life, my all, as I promised before you so magnificently blessed me with child, I renew my pledge of my daughter's service in the Temple of God."

Simeon, observing the light and the fervor of mother's prayers, began praying silently to himself for the coming of the Messiah. My angels informed me that Lucifer, the ancient serpent, had been intent on studying mother when she had so humbly submitted to all the regulations of the priests thinking she might be the bearer of the Messiah. However, when she asked the priests to intercede for her; he scornfully concluded that she was just "another" pious woman. In his arrogance, he was deceived. Satin could not conceive that anyone, who was to bear the Messiah, could be so humble. I smiled to myself; I intuitively knew that Satin's pride would be his final downfall. The Lord concealed from him that which he was not to know. He permitted Lucifer, in his desire to destroy others, to obtain knowledge only of what was necessary for his own undoing, and only so much as might serve to make him an instrument in the execution of the secret judgments of the Most High.

I Am Mary

God created my soul in all perfection as only he could. When God showed the angels my soul before my creation, they prostrated themselves in adoration of their Infinite God and pledged undying loyalty to me as their Queen and Mother. Every angel offered to attend me in person. However, the Triune God had already selected those angels he knew to be the most perfect in their love for the Son as represented in the Word and in me as the person that would give him flesh.

From each of the nine choirs, God chose one hundred angels, totaling nine hundred of the most devoted of the angels. God next chose the twelve angels mentioned in the Apocalypse as the guardians of the portals of the City. They would assist me in corporeal and visible forms, and they were to bear the emblems and escutcheons of the Redemption. He then chose from the highest ranks eighteen others who were to ascend and descend by the mystical stairs of Jacob's ladder with my messages to his Majesty and those of the Lord to me. I used them countless times, in order that at all times, the Holy Spirit would govern my actions. From the highest ranks of the Seraphim, and from those nearest to the Divinity, God appointed seventy additional angels. Their job was to communicate and converse with me in the same manner as the Angels converse with one another. These seventy angels had direct reference to the seventy years that I would spend upon earth. The sixty angels mentioned in the Canticles as guarding the chamber or couch of Solomon was included in these seventy angels.

God selected these mighty princes and captains as my guards from the highest orders of the angelic hierarchy and assigned them as my personal guardians. The sixty were the ones that distinguished themselves in the battle with Lucifer by the arms of divine grace granted them by the merits of the Incarnate Word. The other ten Seraphim, which complete the number of seventy, were also chosen from the distinguished leaders who in their opposition to the dragon had manifested a greater reverence for the Divinity and humanity of the Word, and for me, his mother. Altogether, God selected a thousand angels from the Seraphim and the lower orders of angels as my guards, friends and counselors. He assigned Saint Michael the archangel, the prince of the heavenly militia, as their leader. He also appointed the Archangel Gabriel to act as Legate and Minister of the Eternal Father in my personal affairs. However, neither of these princes would remain with me all the time. Thus did God the Father, God the Son, and God the Holy Spirit provide for the care and defense of the Mother of God, of which, at the time, I was not aware that I was to be that most fortunate of all women.

At the moment of my creation and the infusion of my soul, God filled me with graces and gifts far above those of the highest Seraphim of heaven. I was never found wanting or deprived of the light, the friendship, and love of the Creator, nor was I ever touched by the stain or darkness of original sin. God granted me a perfect justice superior to that of Adam and Eve. At the precise moment of the infusion of my soul, the Creator gave me the light of reason that corresponded to the gifts of grace that I had received. I prostrated myself before my God in gratitude and admiration, worshipping and adoring him with all my soul. God mysteriously transported me before his throne in Heaven and he accepted my offering with delight and love.

God had closed the Gates of Heaven at this time, according to the teachings of the Holy Church. Therefore, some of you might question how my body could be transported into the Empyrean Heavens'? The Heavenly Gates were to remain closed until the Messiah reopened them through his life and death, and until he himself, as Redeemer and Chief, should enter it on the day of his admirable Ascension. It is befitting that the Chief should enter before the children of Adam. If Adam had not sinned men would have ascended freely, in order to enjoy the Divinity in the Empyrean Heavens.

My dear Son, who is the Lord of virtues and graces, was responsible for presenting me to God the Father. He had exalted me from the first moment of my Immaculate Conception. I was free from the impediments of sin. Unblemished by sin, I was therefore not prevented from entering the eternal Gates of Heaven like other mortals. On the contrary, the powerful arm of my Son acted with me as being the Mistress of all virtues and as the Queen of Heaven. As I was not a slave of sin, I exercised the virtues not as a subject, but as a Mistress, without contradiction, but with sovereignty, not like the children of Adam, but like the Son of God, who was soon to become my Son.

I admonish you, my children, to strive with all your strength to imitate me in an exercise in which I persevered my entire life from the very moment of my birth. I did not omit it for a single day, no matter the cares and labors with which I might have been plagued. Every day, at dawn, I prostrated myself in the presence of the Most High and gave him thanks and praise for his Immutable Being, his infinite perfection, and for his having created me out of nothing. I acknowledged myself as his creature and the work of his hands. I blessed him, adored him, and gave him honor, magnificence, and Divinity, as the supreme Lord and Creator of myself and of all that exists. I rose up my spirit, placed it in his hands, and offered myself with profound humility and resignation to him. I asked him to dispose of me according to his will during that day and during all the days of my life, and to teach me to fulfill whatever would be to his greater pleasure. This I repeated many times during the external works of the day, and in the internal ones, I first consulted his Majesty, asking his advice, permission and benediction for all my actions.

God created every soul to understand the human frailty and the freedom of the will for good or evil. Of this knowledge, the Almighty did not deprive me, nor does he deprive anyone of it. He gives it to all to measure, in order that by its guidance, they may be filled with holy fear of falling into any fault, even the smallest. In me, this light was greater, and as my mother so succinctly pointed out,

"A small fault prepares the way for another, and the second is only a punishment for the first.

It is true that because of the blessings and graces of the Lord, sin was nigh impossible in me. But his Providence so disposed of this knowledge that my security from sin was hidden to me: I saw that as far as depended on me alone I could fall, [Free Will] and that it was only because of God's will that I was preserved. Thus, he reserved for himself his knowledge of my security, and left me in solicitude and holy fear of sinning during my pilgrimage. From the instant of my conception until my death I never lost this fear, but on the contrary grew in it as life flowed on. God also gave me humility and discretion, not to ask or to examine too closely this mystery, but to solely direct my attention toward increasing my confidence in his goodness with a view to obtain his assistance against sin.

Even the righteous person sins seven times a day. I suggest that each night you ask my Son and I to help you sift through your deeds and actions of the day in order that we might help you to detect and recognize your faults and in so doing eliminate them through prayer, fasting and almsgiving. Say your rosary every day for the Holy Father, the priests and religious, the poor souls in purgatory, and for the forgiveness of the sins of the world.

Pray! Pray! Pray!

Mary

Chapter Three

Consecrated to God

"And God said, Mary is to be a daughter of the first man; but in the order of grace she is to be singularly free and exempt from fault; and in the order of nature she is to be most perfect and to be formed according to a special providence."

For the next three years I led a quite ordinary life in that I was treated much the same as other children of my age, and I was subject to the common laws of nature the same as any baby. I never cried from mere annoyance, which is common in most children, and I was most amiable and caused trouble to no one. I was nursed by my mother the same as all children since the advent of Cain and Abel. The fact I did not cry caused no wonder, since from time to time while meditating and praying, I often wept and sighed for the sins of the world. Of course being a baby, everyone wished to hold and fondle me, but even my mother and father were inspired by God to handle and caress me with unusual restraint. However, when anyone did anything for me, I always rewarded their efforts with humble gratitude by praying and begging the Lord to reward that person. I slept very little due to my prayers, nor did I eat as much as was normal, and my parents were most solicitous that I eat and sleep more.

Often by a secret influence and a certain outward austerity, by which God wished to preserve my dignity, I discouraged guests from picking me up. However, I did have a special affinity for my cousin Elizabeth that rivaled that of my parents. Next to them, I had a filial and spiritual devotion for Elizabeth that far exceeded the feelings I had for the rest of my relatives, not that I did not dearly love them all. A few months after our presentation, just before Passover, Elizabeth came to visit for a week. Mother met her in the courtyard. It was a beautiful clear day. The sun was already caressing the hills and before long the valleys would be toasted a golden brown. The barley would soon be ripe and the farmers were sharpening their hand sickles in readiness for the harvest. Soon the reapers would ply their trade, and close behind them the gleaners would busy themselves gathering their just due according to the Law of Moses. Two beautiful fig trees in the garden, pruned in the shape of huge umbrellas, protected us with their cool shade. The thick foliage gave welcome refuge from the sun, and we were already enjoying the early crop of large, succulent, sweet figs that always preceded the usual harvest that came during the Passover. A pleasant breeze from the western sea ruffled the gray leaves of an ancient olive tree standing alone in a corner of the courtyard, all of which made the heat bearable.

After greeting my mother affectionately, Elizabeth hovered over my cradle looking at me with great tenderness. Observing my pleasant countenance, which was tempered with a serene gravity, she commented to my mother, "I recognize in this child a holiness that far transcends the ordinary. Enui told me about the miraculous events surrounding her birth. Mary has a majestic aura about her that can only be the reflection of Almighty God himself. Somehow I feel drawn to her as though our paths are star-crossed by Divine Providence."

Mother murmured tactfully with a faint smile, "Perhaps God is trying to tell you something, Elizabeth?"

Joachim, my devout father, loved to hold and caress me. I welcomed his attention, because I knew how beloved he was of God and I loved him dearly. Yet, God inspired him and all others with whom I came in contact, to approach me with an extraordinary reverence and modesty. I in turn, knew that God did not wish me to become too involved with the things of this world. In fact from the beginning, I had resolved in my mind to love naught but him, and before long, worldly things became most repugnant to me. To reject one's family; however, takes a special type of love as only those totally dedicated to the service of Almighty God can testify. Of course, there is also a proper time to declare or express that love. However, while I was prepared mentally for such dedication, I knew that in my infantile state, I was not physically equipped to meet God's expectations of me.

Mother of course nursed me and gave me the tender love, solicitude, and caressing tenderness that any baby must have. Perhaps I received even more, since I was the child that was someday to be the Mother of God, and my parents were to have me with them for such a short time.

Since I was in full possession of my faculties since my conception, I could have talked and asked for anything that I needed However, out of modesty and submission to God, I deliberately refrained from doing so, and offered up my silence to God for the sins of the world. When I made this decision, I became aware that this had been God's intention all along. He was most pleased, and unknown to me, he rewarded me with even greater gifts. When alone: however, I did speak mentally with my angels, and I prayed aloud to my Creator. At my conception, the Trinity had filled me with the light of the Lord and his mysteries. Perhaps for this very reason, and by properly using all the gifts he had given me, *I judged myself to be the least of all creatures*. I found that the more one learns of the mysteries and the glory of God, the more humble one must become. When we become fully aware of the incredible majesty of the Creator, it is then that we realize how truly insignificant we really are.

The first day mother released my arms and legs from their bindings; I grasped my parent's hands and kissed them in reverent humility. They were amazed and pleased by my gesture, and as long as I lived with them, whenever I got the opportunity, I kissed their hands. Please do not confuse my desire to give up all worldly things as a lack of love or respect for my parents. It is only by giving up all the things of this world that we can truly love and enter a complete relationship with our Lord.

I was eighteen months old when God said to me, "Daughter, it is now time for you to begin to walk and speak."

I was deeply concerned about becoming too deeply attached to my parents, and I exclaimed, "Oh my, Lord, I beseech you, consider my frailty. To avoid all risks of losing you, I would rather maintain silence all my life." My Creator reassured me that he would assist me in directing all my thoughts and words to him. He also urged me to pray constantly for the coming of the Messiah, which I eagerly attended to my every waking hour. Even if engaged in other activities, even talking, I had the God-given grace to be able to conduct at the same time my separate prayers, as well as my petitions to the Holy One. Even during my sleep my interior acts of love, and all other activities of my faculties, which were not dependent on the exterior senses, were never interrupted.

The next morning, after my mother had freed me from my bindings, and after the daily blessing, I spoke for the first time and asked, "My blessed and holy parents, may I have your personal blessing?"

Delightfully surprised, my father eagerly took me in his arms and holding me seated *throne-like* on his hands before him, he responded with his blessing, "Oh sweetness of my heart, this is truly a blessed hour. Let your words be few and well considered, and always speak with the thought to honor the Holy One who created you." I indicated I wished to get down, and Joachim obligingly set me on the floor. With amazing agility I walked for the first time to my mother and held up my arms.

With a joyful smile my mother picked me up and solemnly added her blessing, "May all your footsteps be directed toward the honor of Almighty God."

Although many children were not weaned until they were three or four-years of age, mother weaned me shortly after the blessings. For the next year and a half, I was subject to my parents love, devotion and guidance. I was prone to seldom speak, because of modesty and respect for my parents and my Lord. Mother; however, in order to get me to talk asked me one day. "Mary, it would please me greatly if you spoke to me of God and his mysteries."

Mother knew that I was God's chosen one, but she never let on, but I am sure that she knew that I must be in close communion with our Lord God. However, I demurred and asked her instead, "Dearest, Mother would it not be more seemly if you were to instruct me in the ways of the Lord?" Thus, began a beautiful mother-daughter relationship. This relationship; however, made our parting more difficult when it came time for me to be presented to the temple.

I often saw mother watching me with tears in her eyes and I could only wonder at her thoughts. I later learned that she was shedding tears of love and gratitude that I had been chosen to be the Mother of God. We spoke often of the coming of the Messiah, since after all, at God's own command; this was the subject ever on my mind, in my heart, and on my lips. Mother's face would sometimes suddenly become inflamed with ardent love. She would then innocently portray to me, in the most glowing terms of awe and reverence, a word picture of the fortunate maiden of Israel, who was to give the Messiah to the world. However, mother never once revealed to anyone the great secret of her life.

In my eagerness to display my own unworthiness in that I was the least of God's creatures, I insisted on helping mother with the housework. I was large for my age and very strong. Most two-year olds are awkward and limited in their intellect. This was not my case. I was well coordinated, and while I was not always as efficient as I would have liked, because of my size, I helped scrub and clean the house. Sometimes when I was alone, my angels would join in with great zeal and assist me in my assumed duties.

Mother was prone to dress me in the most beautiful clothes that she could afford, and my parents were not poor, although they were far from rich. However when I began to talk, I begged my mother, "My dear, Mother," I pleaded, "please dress me in a more humble manner. My preference is a plain ash-gray cloth of a cheap and coarse material."

I think mother was a bit taken back, but she studied me thoughtfully and replied firmly, "I understand your desire to humble yourself before our Lord and God, and I will yield to your request as to the form and color, but it would not be seemly for you to be dressed in cheap cloth." So we compromised and I dutifully accepted her decision.

God had revealed to me many times, how grievously the sins of men offended him. Consequently, I often retired to my room, prostrated myself on the floor and begged for mercy for the poor sinners. I practiced penance and mortification to the point that I soon taxed my bodily strength. Mother became aware of my sacrifices and firmly ordered me to refrain from the excesses of my devotions. Dutifully, I obeyed, and while I continued my prayers for the poor sinners, in obedience I learned to pray in moderation.

After my second birthday, I learned the joy of performing works of charity toward the poor. From my parents, I begged alms for the poor, and mother and I both set aside portions of our meals for them. My kind-hearted mother readily granted my petitions, both for the sake of the poor, and to satisfy my tender charity. At the same time, she wished to encourage me, the Mistress of Mercy and Charity, to learn to love and esteem the poor. Mother took me to the poorest section of town, and I was overwhelmed with compassion for the poor. The first person I encountered was a street beggar. Her clothes were filthy, and even from a distance, she stank of her dirt and poverty. Her haggard face reflected the distress of her body and soul. I gave her our food, but not as though I was conferring a benefit on her, but as though I was paying a debt due her. I kissed her hand when she eagerly took the food.

I mused to myself, "This poor woman, my sister, deserves what she needs and what I possess without deserving it."

I prayed to God to give her spiritual graces. Later in life when alone, I kissed not only the hands of the poor, but their feet as well, and if that were not possible I kissed the ground where their feet had trod. They were God's deserted children, and needed all his love that I could give them.

Mother decided to teach me to read and write by virtue of my remarkable progress, and since I would soon be consecrated to the Holy Temple I humbly submitted to their efforts, although, I had been granted infused knowledge of all things created. My angels were impressed with the wisdom and humility that I displayed to willingly listen to the teachings of all. Each day that went by, I could tell that my mother's love for me grew in leaps and bounds. As the day of my presentation to the Jewish Temple became imminent, the dread of her losing me became a haunting torment to her of mind and soul. However, I know her vow to God would be punctually fulfilled, in spite of her great love for me.

At the age of two and a half, I took upon myself the duty to prepare and dispose mother for the inevitable. I knew if she waited at the last minute to prepare that it would be much more difficult for her to make the break. I began by asking discreet questions about how she and my father had prayed and prepared themselves for twenty years for the coming of the child promised them by God. I pointed out the benefits, which they had received, and how much they were obliged to seek God's greater pleasure. "Oh, Mother," I exclaimed, "if you only knew how ardently I wish to live in the Holy Temple of my Lord and God. Only there, can I immerse myself fully into the service of the Lord. Don't you understand that by my dedication to God in his temple, I will be more your daughter than in your own house?"

It became obvious that mother was resigned to the divine will and fully intended to fulfill her promise of offering me up to the Lord. However, the natural force of her love for such a beloved treasure, joined with the full understanding of my absence from her care caused a mortal strife in her most faithful heart. There is no doubt that mother would have died in this fierce and vivid sorrow, except that the soothing hand of the Almighty comforted her so that she did not perish. She knew that I was to be the Mother of God and the grace and dignity I possessed had entirely ravished her heart, making my presence dearer to her than life itself.

However in time, mother was able to face the issue squarely and said to me, "My beloved, daughter, for many years Joachim and I longed for you. From the beginning, we knew that we would merit your company for only a short time. I do not wish to be unfaithful to my promise, nor does your father. However be patient in your desires to serve the Lord in his temple. There is time left before we must part with you to fulfill our promise. Let us cherish our remaining time together, which the Lord has so generously allowed."

We talked frequently about serving the Lord, and mother told me much about the daily routines established for the virgins serving in the temple. She also taught me various prayers and rules of our religion, especially those relating to my future tenure in the Holy Temple. This helped me a great deal in formulating how I would best be able to serve the Lord in his house. The time remaining before my birthday passed all too quickly for my parents, but I never ceased praying for that precious day to arrive. I know this sounds cold, but as I said before, the love of God so transcends all other love and considerations that it leaves one with no room for regrets when the decision is made. From the beginning, God created us for one purpose, to love, serve and live with the Creator in his heavenly abode. Because of the gifts granted me by God, I knew better than any one how important it was for me to dedicate my life to serving our Creator. God never granted any other person such gifts. A few days before my third birthday, I was favored with an Abstract Vision of the Divinity.

God said to me, "My, child, the time for your departure for the temple has arrived. We wish you to live a life dedicated and consecrated to our service."

I was overjoyed, and I responded with love and gratitude, "Most, High God of Abraham, Isaac, and Jacob, my eternal and highest Good, since I cannot praise you worthily, let it be done in the name of this humble slave by the angelic spirits. Why should you receive me into your house and service, since I do not even merit the most abject spot of the earth for my place of habitation? However since you are so urged by your own greatness, I beseech you to console my parents in their feelings of loss and grief at my parting."

At the same time mother had a vision in which the Lord spoke to her, "Anne, my devoted daughter, "It is now time for you to fulfill your promise to present Mary to the temple. It is to be done on the exact day of the third anniversary of her birth." Anne was devastated. But, as I knew he would, God consoled and comforted her by saying, "Fear not, Anne only I know the magnitude of your sacrifice. My grace shall be sufficient unto you, and I will assist you in your loneliness during the absence of your daughter."

Mother composed herself and exclaimed, "Lord, God, Master of all my being. I have pledged to your service and to the Temple my daughter, whom you, in your ineffable mercy, have given us. I return my daughter to you with heartfelt thanks for the time in which I have enjoyed her. I glorify you for having chosen me to conceive and assist in her formation. However remember God and Lord that in the keeping of your inestimable treasure I was rich. I enjoyed her company in this desert valley of tears. She was the joy of my sorrow, and the alleviation of my labors. She was the mirror for the regulation of my life, and the example of supernal perfection, which stimulated my remissness and enkindled my affections. Through Mary, I hoped for mercy and grace. I fear I will fall away from your grace if you deprive me of her. Heal, oh Lord, the wound of my heart, and deal with me not as I have deserved, but look upon me as a kind Father of Mercies, while I bring my daughter to the temple according to your command."

God was pleased with mother's prayer, and he filled her with grace to cope with the wounding of her heart. The tender words of my mother wounded my heart as well; but I knew it to be the will of the Lord to leave my parents. I was to forego their house and my people in order to follow my Creator. At this same time, my father Joachim also had a vision of the Lord and he had received the same message. In their grief, my parents huddled together comforting one another, careful not to do anything to upset me. They resolved to fulfill their obligation with humble submission and arranged for the priests to come to examine me as required by the Law. My father was grieved at the thought of losing me, but not as much as my mother, for at that time, he still did not know the high mystery of my destiny to become the Mother of God, nor did I.

Within a few days, my father had arranged for a great feast. He had engaged the services of five priests from Sepphoris and Nazareth including Elizabeth's husband Zachariah, who was a High Priest in the Temple. The priests would judge, in a sacred ceremony, if I were sufficiently mature and worthy for service in the Temple. Joachim, since this was a solemn occasion, met the priests at the entrance and personally washed their feet. The least servant in the home usually performed this courtesy. A large atrium furnished the light for the central hall of our home. In honor of the occasion, a red carpet covered the tiled floor. A table had been set up as an altar in the middle of the atrium. A red cloth covered the altar and over that was laid a white transparent veil. Upon the altar, behind an embroidered curtain, was a case of sacred writings. Also piled on the altar table were various gifts from my parents, family, and friends as a dowry for me. A kind of throne stood on the steps before the altar. Included on the altar were three ceremonial dresses cut out for me by the priests themselves, and then quickly sewn together by mother and the women present.

It was a hot day for September, but the thick walls of our home maintained a pleasant temperature. The priests entered the hall in bare feet, but only three of them proceeded with the examination. Mother and father were present with many of our relatives. The women stood back and the little girls stood at my side. I was dressed in a simple white robe for the occasion. A priest took one of the suits from the altar and explained its significance. He handed it to Elizabeth and she dressed me in a yellow, knitted robe; she then placed over my head a colored, laced bodice. Over that was placed a brownish mantle with armholes, from which lappets hung. Removing my shoes, Elizabeth replaced them with brown sandals with thick green soles. She arranged my hair with a silken crown with feathers in it. The feathers bent over toward the inside of the crown. A large square, ash-colored veil, was then placed upon my head. It appeared to be a mantle often used in time of prayer, and traveling.

Joachim then presented me to the priests. Zachariah looked at my father and commented, "If I did not know better, Joachim, I would find it difficult to believe Mary is only three. She looks to be a child of five or six?" I had grown rapidly, not only in size, but also in manners and decorum, I was slim and lithe, and my dark, natural-curly hair hung loose. Everyone commented on how beautiful I was. Compliments made me most uncomfortable. When they said such things, I offered up devout prayers lest I fall into the sin of vanity. Father laughed proudly and assured the priest of my age.

Zachariah explained the duties and disciplines of the temple to me. He then proceeded to ask me questions regarding these duties. Afterwards, he said, "In consecrating you to God, your mother and father vowed that you would give up wine, vinegar, grapes and figs. What do you think of this, and what other sacrifice do you wish to freely add to those? Think it over and tell us later after you eat." My angels hovered over me during the questioning, directing and assisting me in all things. The priests were more than satisfied with my answers. They were particularly pleased with the naïve wisdom that I displayed, and mother and father wept with pride and joy. After a lengthy questioning by the priests, I was then dressed in the second outfit. It was sky blue, and had a blue mantle, but of a lighter hue. Over this, she placed a rich, white bodice of silk, which fell in folds, something like the consecrated veil of a nun. In addition, Elizabeth placed a close-fitting wreath of colored flower buds made of silk and intermixed with small green leaves. Zachariah placed a white veil, gathered at the top like a cap, over my face. It was caught with three clasps, one below the other by means of which the veil could be raised upon the head either one third, or one half, or even the whole. Elizabeth carefully explained the use of the veil to me, for it was part of the ritual of eating and answering questions.

Zachariah then led me to the table of honor, seated me between two priests, and took his place across from me. Father had used flagstone to pave a large section of the courtyard over which he had erected a huge grape arbor. In the middle of the arbor was an extremely long wooden table with benches for seats. Scattered about the garden additional tables had been set up and all were loaded with food. The rainy season was upon us, but while a bit chilly; the sun warmed the protected patio and the festive party. Women did not usually eat with the men. However, since I was the guest of honor, I was treated differently. The priests on each side of me practiced me in many points upon the use of the veil, which I appreciated.

Zachariah, since I was eating so little, reminded me that I could still partake of everything on the table, and they all took turns trying to tempt me to eat and plying me with various questions to see just how I would react. I had a weakness for vinegar; however, I tasted sparingly of only a few dishes, none of which my parents had vowed that I was to give up. I would have willingly given up eating entirely for the privilege of serving the Lord in his Temple. I answered all their questions with simplicity and wisdom, and I could tell they were impressed.

After the meal, Zachariah led me to the altar. Assisted by Elizabeth, one of the priests clothed me anew. One priest explained the signification of each garment, and spoke of spiritual things. These robes were the most beautiful of all. The robe had a violet-blue bodice. Over it, the priest placed a vest embroidered in colors. He fastened the vest to the back, which caught to the plaited shirt, which fell below in a point. Over this, Elizabeth placed a violet mantle, full and magnificent, made much like a chasuble. It had five rows of gold embroidery buttoning down the front. The priest then placed a large colored veil on my head, which glanced from white to violet to blue. Upon this veil rested a crown, closed on top by five clasps. It was a thin, broad circlet lined with gold, and the upper edge spread into points tipped with little balls. A network of silk covered the outside. Five perfect pearls embedded in small roses rose from the center. The five points also were of silk and were surmounted by a ball. My breast piece fastened from behind, and yet, it had cords in front as if for lacing. A cross band secured my mantle and in turn, a button with a long shank prevented it from pressing upon the breast ornament. It closed again under the bodice and fell behind the arms in folds. I did not resent these fancy clothes, for I knew that this was what God wanted of me.

Surrounded by little girls all dressed in white, I was then placed on the steps before the altar. I said to the priests, "In answer to your question, I have decided to give up fish, meat, milk, and all fruits except berries. I would also prefer to sleep on the floor, and to get up and pray three times each night." Father was deeply moved when he heard this, taking me up in his arms he wept as he said to me, "My dear child that is far too much. If you lead such a hard life, I will never see you again."

However, Zachariah looked at me with approval and ruled, "I insist that you pray only once during the night, like the other girls, and you should allow yourself other relaxation as well, and you shall eat fish on all the great feast days. Many of the poorer virgins enter the temple without a dowry," he went on to explain. "On this account, and with their parent's consent, they engage to wash the blood-speckled robes of the priests and the rough woolen cloths. This you will not be called upon to do, since your parents are able to maintain you at the temple." When I heard this, I responded firmly,

"If I am deemed worthy, honorable priests, I would willingly do such work."

Zachariah was surprised, and in admiration gave me his personal blessing.

Throughout the examinations, under the guidance and inspiration of my angels, I had remained perfectly recollected and serious. Now deeply moved, mother caught me up in her arms, and pressing me to her heart, kissed me tenderly. Father, with tears in his eyes, joined in respectfully caressing me. The head priest said to my parents, "She is not only the holiest, but the most strikingly beautiful and lovable child that I have ever interviewed." At this speech, father broke down again sobbing uncontrollably.

In the final ceremony, Zachariah and his fellow priests blessed me, as I sat on my little altar throne. Zachariah stood before me, while the two priests stood on either side of me. They all held sacred scrolls in their hands and each in turn prayed over me. Zachariah gave me his final blessing, and as he finished a ray of sunshine from the atrium opening fell upon me and enhanced my features.

At the same time, unknown to me, Zachariah received an interior assurance, a heavenly monition that I was the chosen Vessel of the Mystery. He never once divulged this heavenly message to anyone, not even his wife Elizabeth. From it, he had received a ray that had appeared figuratively in me. Zachariah took my hand, I stood up, and he led me to my parents; the ceremony was over. Mother caught me to her breast and kissed me, but father—deeply affected—reverenced me, and only took my hand. Elizabeth kissed me with much more gaiety than my mother did, for she was a more serious, practical, moderate, and self-possessed woman. The priests took me again to the altar and disrobed me down to my original dress. They then led me forth clothed in my simple white frock and presented me to our guests.

The next day everyone began busily packing for our trip to Jerusalem. I felt like I was floating on a cloud. My every wish was coming true. Mother made me several fine ceremonial dresses for my reception at the Temple, and she carefully packed them for the journey. Finally one morning, as dawn broke, we began our journey. Mother had dressed me warmly because it was the rainy season, and no matter the elements, we had to be in Jerusalem in time for the presentation. We set out with two donkeys loaded down with our supplies, as well as several beasts loaded with gifts for my dowry. In addition, we each had a large, nearly-white, Muscat ass for riding. All of our relatives and close friends accompanied us, which formed a sizable party. They helped father care for our live sacrifices, a herd of unblemished sheep, goats, and two beautiful oxen, which father intended to offer up to the Lord through the priests at the temple.

It was not a particularly pleasant trip, for the cold fogs in the mornings chilled us to the marrow. I; however, traveled in a golden haze of happiness. At last, I was on the way to my Father's House. There I could serve my Creator to my hearts content, there I could give him my every waking moment, and even in my sleep I would be secure in God's Holy Temple.

Knowing my parents growing unhappiness, since each step we took, in effect, took me further from them; I frequently nuzzled my mother and kissed her frequently. Father was like a lost soul. Repeatedly, I heard him mutter forlornly, "My dear, child, I will never see you again," and tears would run down his cheeks. When he did, I always went up to him and asked him to carry me. There, safe in his strong arms, I felt secure, and he was comforted for the moment. I made over him much more than ever before. During our stopovers, I made a point to spend as much time with him as possible. Mother carried me much of the way, to which I did not object, because I knew it was her way of holding on to me for as long as she could, She was relieved periodically by father. We all felt the need from time to time to get down and walk, and of course, I insisted on walking along with them up and down the tortuous trails until exhaustion forced me into their protective arms. At last just ahead, I could see the three and a half miles of the high fortified-walls that encircled the City of David. The walls; however, were not noticeable because of the splendor of Jerusalem, the City of God, which was dominated by the newly constructed, magnificent, golden-domed Temple of the Israelites.

We had followed the Ridge Road to Jerusalem and as we neared the city, we all stopped and gaped in awe at our first glimpse of the new temple. Across the way, bordering the east wall of the city stood the glorious, nearly-finished, Temple of Jerusalem. In the sunshine, the temple sparkled like a gorgeous diadem. Its golden spikes soared to a height of 165 feet and its walls had been built of perfectly carved and fitted white marble stones, which were then covered with gold plates. The temple hurt my eyes to look directly at it. King Herod the Great had begun the rebuilding of the temple in 20 BC to find favor with the Hebrews. It was necessary for Herod to specially train one-thousand priests as masons and carpenters to construct the temple itself. By law, no laymen were allowed to touch the sacred building materials. In addition, Herod imported the very best of masons and architects from Phoenicia and beyond. Altogether more than ten thousand workers were required to build the temple complex. As Solomon had done before him, Herod used only the finest materials; cedar from Lebanon, the purest of gold, and the finest of limestone and marble.

As we passed through the Damascus Gate, we passed the customhouse where the Roman tax collectors collected duty on all merchandise leaving or entering the city. After entering the city, Elizabeth and Zachariah led us proudly through the streets of Jerusalem. Zachariah, because of his rank, maintained a house in Jerusalem. There he made us welcome and served us refreshments. That evening, we attended a reception and feast in our honor, all paid for by Zachariah. He spared no expense, and I met one of my cousins, a delightful, young girl by the name of Veronica. I sensed a special holiness about her, and unknown to me, we would later become fast friends. I also met Susanna, whose place I was taking in the Temple, and I was impressed with her graciousness and holy wisdom. Susanna had just turned fifteen, and her parents had quickly espoused her to a fine, upright young man. Instinctively, I knew that she would someday be a follower of the Messiah.

The following morning, father went on ahead to take his animal offering to the Temple. I felt uncomfortable in receiving so much attention. However, the Jewish customs dictated otherwise. Mother dressed me in a lovely sky-blue robe with garlands of flowers set around my arms and neck. Three girls carrying flowers and candles escorted me. Then twenty young girls of our party, all relatives, fell in behind us playing music on harps, flutes, and tambourines. The girls were all dressed in white, embroidered with gold, and each wore bluish mantles, and they were all gaily decorated with garlands and flowers twined about their arms. Unlike our first trip to Jerusalem, we processed gaily through the winding streets of the City of God in a beautiful joyful procession, which was the custom. From all sides, I heard many exclamations of how pretty we all were, and how beautiful and holy I looked; I was kept busy with prayers of humility, knowing full well my own unworthiness.

Actually, except for the people attracted by our music and procession, the residential streets of Jerusalem were quiet. However, outside the city gates, vendors busily plied their wares to prospective clients. The harvesting of the year's crop was complete. The markets inside the town were also spilling over with melons, leeks, corn, dried figs, dates, barley, wheat, olives, olive oil, wine, and for sacrifices countless doves and lambs. There were manufactured goods such as, tools, shoes, jewelry, scents, wool and linen cloth, and a myriad of trade goods from even as far away as China and India. To prevent gouging there had been established positive tariffs fixing the prices for the entire region. The local Sanhedrin appointed market inspectors equipped with wide-ranging powers to maintain order. In direct competition to the vendors were the downtown business centers. Similar businesses were usually subject to guilds and banded together, thus creating the Street of Bakers, the Street of Potters, etc. There were over four hundred synagogues in Jerusalem, and many were congregated, one beside another, on the same streets. The synagogues often served as inns to attract travelers.

A half-hour later, from the upper city we crossed the busy Tyropean Bridge, which spanned the deep Tyropean Valley between King Herod's fortified palace and the temple. Below us, the houses clung tenaciously to the steep hills like mud dauber's-nests plastered on a rock wall. The Central Valley below, often called the Valley of Cheese Makers, was a bewildering maze of unpaved alleys and courtyards. Here the common people lived, the backbone of their traditional culture. I noted with surprise that many of the Hebrew men of the city were clean-shaven and some even wore their hair quite short in the Roman style. The women were cosmopolitan and coifed their hair in the latest styles. The causeway led us directly through the eastern gate that opened onto the Temple Mount. Towering above us loomed the spectacular Jewish Golden Temple and just to the northwest was the forbidding Fortress of Antonia. Six hundred Roman Soldiers made their home there and they guarded everything of importance in the city. Jerusalem was an occupied city, and one had only to look about to see the evidence of their menacing presence.

Father explained to me that the temple plan was similar to Solomon's first temple. Before Herod the Great began to build the temple, he had directed his architect to re-read chapters forty to forty-three of Ezekiel. In these, the prophet describes the future temple with extraordinary exactitude; the Israeli Temple of Jerusalem was restored in full glory. The architects first cleared the old temple mount and then doubled its original size to an area roughly one-thousand by fifteen-hundred feet. The entire area was girded by a huge retaining wall built of fitted stones fifteen-feet long by thirteen-feet thick. The entire area was paved with white limestone. The newly trained priests under the supervision of the architects rebuilt the sanctuary itself in only eighteen months. Like a busy colony of ants, we could see hundreds of workers swarming over the temple mount, the construction sites roped off from the multitudes of priests, Levites, and worshipers.

The city wall towered high above us, creating an aura of indestructibility. Herod the Great began rebuilding the temple in 20 BC, and its completion was still decades away. I knew by a God-given insight and by constant God-given instructions from my angels, for only God the Father knows the future that the temple would not be completed until 64 AD, only to meet it's fate by the Roman Titus in 70 AD. This knowledge saddened me. The majesty of the new temple, however, so overwhelmed me that I had little time to dwell on the matter. The king, aiming at a sense of the colossal constructed the temple in the Graeco-Roman style. Many compared the temple, with its colonnades, capitals, and triangular pediments, as being even more magnificent than the Egyptian monuments. Around the roof of the temple ran a finely carved marble balustrade, covered with gold. Gleaming golden spikes arose from atop the balustrade to prevent birds from perching on it. When I had first seen it from afar, the golden spikes looked like sparkling snow.

The Golden Gate pierced the immense outer wall leading directly to the temple complex. The gate opened into a deep covered passage closed by double gates at each end. Altogether there were four gates on the western side, one of which serviced the Tyropean Bridge; two on the south, a single heavily fortified gate on the north, and two on the east. Before we entered the temple area through the Golden Gate father picked me up and carried me the rest of the way. The priest artisans had decorated the gate with beautiful carvings of grapevines, ears of wheat, and flowers. We had arrived just in time for the opening of the famous Nicanor Gate that led into the Men's Court. Twenty Levites struggled with its immense weight and it opened with a rumbling, grinding noise. The heavy Nicanor Gate was made entirely of decorated bronze. However, King Herod had the rest of the gates plated with solid silver and gold. It was amazing how much work had been completed, and yet, they had just begun the real work of the supporting buildings and porticos.

We passed through the Portals of God into a rectangular court. Father explained everything to me as he carried me through the gate. This area was the thirty-five acre Court of the Gentiles and anyone, even sinners and Gentiles could not enter with dirty shoes, or have "unclean" money on one's person. All along the walls, I could see the groundwork laid for many porticos. Those under construction were beautiful and the most prominent portico was to be the eastern one named Solomon's Porch. It was to have a triple row of two hundred and sixty eight pillars thirty-six feet high, and from that area, there was a magnificent view of the Mount of Olives and the Kidron Valley. The southernmost porch, named the Royal Porch, had three aisles with the central one rising to a height of ninety-two feet on splendid Corinthian columns. Its inspiration was Greek, and it was worthy of its origin.

The Court of the Gentiles was already completed; it was filling quickly with a multitude of people through its many entrances. Sellers of doves and sparrows for the sacrifices were already shrilly hawking their wares. Moneychangers at the entrances were busily exchanging ritually clean coins for the pagan "unclean" money and doctors of the law throughout the court could be heard loudly proclaiming their viewpoints before interested spectators. The multitude created a din that gradually turned into a muted roar. The court was similar to the Roman Forum and the Greek Agora. It was forbidden to carry a stick inside the Temple area, to spit, wear dirty shoes, or have unclean money on one's person. The bleating and lowing of bewildered beasts added to the din. Rising up like a golden crown in the end of this daily circus stood the sanctuary itself running from east to west and standing several yards higher than the Court of the Gentiles. The ascent of each level of the temple was gained each time by a flight of stairs indicated the increasing holiness of each level. Fifteen steps extended from the Court of the Gentiles to the outer wall of the Sanctuary. Here set against a balustrade, were repeated inscriptions found in various languages that solemnly forbade the pagans to go any farther. The signs boldly stated,

> **No foreigner is allowed within the balustrades and embankment above the sanctuary. Anyone who is taken shall be killed, and he alone shall be answerable for his death.**

Only Jews could enter the temple areas from the Courtyard of the Gentiles. The gates were all magnificent; however, one was outstandingly beautiful and was appropriately named the Beautiful Gate. Father left us here to enter the Men's Court. Women could not enter the Men's Court. Likewise, only women had the right to enter the Women's Court, a room sixty-five yards long and quite wide. In the court were thirteen receptacles for offerings, which were commonly called the "Trumpets" because of the shape of their mouths. The Jews donated their shekels in these receptacles for the expenses of the temple. These gifts even included wood and incense given as thank-offerings. At the four-corners of the court were four chambers "little courts" in various stages of construction, which were to be used by the Nazarites and the healed lepers. There were to be storage chambers for wood, wine, and the oil used on the altar.

From the western side of the Women's Court a splendid flight of fifteen low curved steps, already completed, led up to the Court of the Men, also called the Court of the Israelites. The gate that opened into it was particularly magnificent; it was the famous Nicanor Gate, which I described earlier. An immensely wealthy Alexandrian Jew had given the gate to the temple because of a vow that he had made during a shipwreck. This court was long and narrow, some five yards wide and sixty-five yards long. I had to smile because the real purpose was to separate the men from the women during the services, and thus to mark the superiority of the male in religious matters. My angels informed me that the Men's Court became most crowded during the great celebrations. Although, the segregation was necessary, according to the tradition of the times; the men, compared to the women, paid dearly in their cramped court.

Raised above the court by only three steps, and divided from it by a thin balustrade was the Court of the Priests, the beginning of the truly sacred area. It was from the little flight of steps in the middle of the balustrade that the high priest blessed the people. This was the last enclosure and it was very large, some sixty-five yards by ninety: at the far end of it stood the completed sacred building with its lofty colonnade, soaring pediment, and high above, the gold spikes of its roof. I later learned that on the north and south of this court various covered halls were planned. In particular, was to be the famous Hall of Cut Stone in which the Sanhedrin were to meet, and in one, already enclosed, was the spring, from which the water for the ritual ablutions was drawn. Additional halls were to be built, which were to be used for storing wood and incense. There were partially completed stables for the sacrificial animals—and there was one completed room appropriately named The Slaughterhouse.

In my duties, I came near this place often to pick up the bloody uniforms of the priests that I had volunteered to wash. The stench was nauseating, and I sometimes held my breath.

Many times I would see the Great Laver that stood in the courtyard. It was an immense brass basin of water used by the priests for ritual washing, and for the altar of burnt offering. The altar was an enormous square block, thirteen feet high and forty-seven feet long. It was made of uncut stone. The altar's four corners rose in horns and a system of gutters carried off the blood of the sacrifices. The priests tied the sacrificial animals to eight cedar posts to await the sacrificial knife. The bewildered animals were later, either led docilely or dragged up the ramp to the altar. The priests next placed the slaughtered animals on marble tables and cut them into pieces. The entrails and refuse were thrown into the blazing fire. It was not a pleasant sight and the heavy smell of incense could not overcome the acrid smell of burning flesh, blood, and the stink of burning bile from the entrails. My angels described many of these scenes to me, since I could not see everything that was taking place.

I will not dwell on the pathetic animals, for I knew that God did not wish holocausts but desired contrite hearts. The temple itself rose in awesome splendor beyond the Court of the Priests. It stood another twelve steps higher, fifty feet higher than the level of the Court of Gentiles. The priest artisans had built the temple of white marble and covered the slabs with thick gold. A porch ran across the front of the Holy Temple. The thick walls of the temple abruptly cut off the outside noise as the priests entered the temple. The pious silence filled them with reverential awe. The priests left the immense front doors of the sanctuary open during the day. The gates were made of cedar covered with gold and above them hung a beautiful golden vine. A magnificent Babylonian tapestry of purple, blue, and crimson veiled the entrance. The tapestry was embroidered with gold and depicted the heavens.

In spite of the grandeur of the temple, like Solomon, I knew it was folly to believe that God could be contained in a dusty, veiled space. Even the heavens and the heavens above the heavens could not contain Him. So how could a mere temple, even if it was the most lavish temple in the realm of the Great Sea, the center of the world to the Israelites, with its thousands of priests, and its bloody and bloodless sacrifices, contain that which is not containable?

As I entered the court, I prayed with deepest humility, "Oh my, Lord and my, God, I give myself to you with all my mind, and with all my heart, and all my soul, do with me as you will." Unknown to me at the time, my parents also inwardly offered me up to our Creator. I did hear my mother say to Elizabeth,

"Now does the Vessel of the Promise enter the temple!"

I alone; however, perceived that the Holy Spirit welcomed me and accepted my offering for he said to me, "Come my, beloved, my, spouse, come into my temple where I wish you to offer me praise and worship."

Walking west, we then crossed to the Women's Court, also enclosed in ornate columns, which was bounded by fifteen curved steps leading up to the great bronze Nicanor Gate. Inside the gate, I could see the Court of Men, also called the Court of Israel where the men assembled for the Temple services. Jewish law forbade women to enter the Court of Men. From where I stood, I could see a low balustrade separated the men's court from the Court of Priests and Levites who served in the temple. In the center of this court, I later discovered, was the great horned altar of sacrifice with a long ramp leading to the top.

Dominating the entire complex was the majestic sanctuary itself, which rose fifty feet above the Court of Gentiles, and was located at the rear of the Court of Priests. It was built of perfectly chiseled and fitted white-marble stones covered with heavy gold, and of course, as I explained before, golden spikes rose from the roof too a dizzying height of 165 feet. I had heard my father say that there was so much gold covering the building that no one was able to look directly at it in bright sunlight.

My parents were to make the formal offering of me to God while I stood on the fifteen steps. A priest led and stood me on the first step, and I asked him if I could speak to my parents. With his permission, I knelt before my mother and father and with tears of keen love and gratitude I kissed their hands and asked for their prayers and permission for me to join the temple virgins. Mother's eyes clouded with tears, but tears ran unashamedly down my father's cheeks, as they laid their hands on my head and solemnly pronounced the words by which they gave me to the Lord. While they spoke a priest clipped a few locks of my hair, which he then burned in pan of incense, and the young girls of our party sang these words of Psalm 44,

> **"Thou art beautiful—therefore hath God blessed thee forever—Hearken, oh daughter, and see, and incline thy ear, and forget thy people and thy father's house. And the King shall greatly desire thy beauty; for he is the Lord thy God. Therefore shall people praise thee forever: yea, forever and ever."**

Father pressed me to his heart and said weeping, "Remember my soul before God."

Mother hugged and kissed me and murmured in my ear, "Oh my precious gift from God. I give you back to him where you shall belong to the ages. Forget not your loving parents." Placing their hands on my head, they then each blessed me. Their love and sincerity affected me deeply.

After the tender blessing of my parents I turned and unfalteringly climbed the fifteen steps. I did not look back. A priest tried to assist me up the steps, but filled with resolution and dignity I declined his offer. My holy fervor and joy was unbounded and was obvious to all. Many people were visibly affected by my ardor, but, but my single, unswerving goal was to hurry, hurry, to serve the Lord. Two priests met me at the top of the stairs and led me up to the gallery. From there, I could see the Holy Place. While incense burned on the altar, they read some prayers over me, which officially consecrated me to the Jewish Temple and God's service. As they did, my thousand angels and a multitude of angels from Heaven filled the temple, played music, and sang a heavenly chorus of the glories of God. Only I could see and hear the angels, but the entire temple took on a holier atmosphere, which the people sensed and they avidly participated in the services.

Then the priests removed my garlands, took the candle I carried and placed a brown veil over my head. They conducted me to a hall in which ten girls in the service of the temple welcomed me by throwing flowers before my path. It was a most humbling scene. The priest then presented me to the Prophetess Anna, who was to be my head teacher. I liked her immediately. I sensed in her a holiness that could only be from that of the Lord himself.

As the priests left, my parents and relatives came in to say goodbye. Weeping, my father took me in his arms and asked again, "My, child pray to God for my soul!"

Mother embraced me and I could feel her steel herself as she tried to keep from breaking down, but mother was made of sterner stuff than my father and she had courageously resigned herself to do the will of God. As she turned and walked away, I heard her say to Cousin Elizabeth,

"The Ark of the Covenant is now in God's Temple."

As they left, I knelt humbly before my teacher Anna and asked for her blessing and forbearance for the trouble I would be to her. I then, as was the custom, greeted each of the ten girls and embraced them, I asked if I could be their servant, and I urged them to instruct and command me. Some of the girls then asked me questions, for they also had a say whether they were willing to have me among them. Once satisfied, the girls then performed a dance with teams of girls who swayed in expressive movements of the entire body, which was expressive of our Jewish character. The older girls provided the dance music, playing harps, flutes, triangles, chimes, lyres, and some instruments with which I was not familiar.

I learned that Noeme, who was the sister of Lazarus's mother, was to be one of my teachers. The family of Lazarus was quite wealthy and they were distant relatives of my mother. Anna then led our group of virgins to another room where we were furnished a meal, and then Noeme, who proved to be in charge of our group of virgins, took me to my little cell that was to be my simple home during my stay in the temple. It was a place of retirement, especially selected for the first-born daughters of the royal tribe of Judah, and the sacerdotal tribe of Levi.

Telling me to rest, Noeme left, and I looked around with interest. My room was high up, with a view over the Holy Place and the inner temple containing the Holy of Holies. The holy place stood on a higher level at the top of twelve steps. I soon learned that the colonnade of the Jerusalem Temple was ninety-eight feet high and a hundred and forty-seven feet wide. There was a porch across the front of the temple, and it was above this porch that King Herod had wished to place an eagle made of gold. This action provoked a furious riot, because in the eyes of the Jews the graven image defiled the holy place. As soon as one passed through the entrance the noise died away, and even the skeptic could feel the divine presence of God.

The great door of the sanctuary was a cedar door covered with gold. Above it was a golden vine, which the Romans made fun of and claimed, "Bacchus is the real God of Israel." This door was open throughout the day, but a magnificent curtain embroidered in the Babylonian manner hid its opening. Only the Officiating Priest, whose turn it was, had the right once a year when celebrating the Rite of Penance, to draw the veil aside and enter the Inner Sanctum.

The Sanctum was the focus of the attention, the expectation, and the thoughts of the faithful. The main room itself was a simple gallery paneled with cedar and cypress, and surrounded by rooms. There were three stories of them, offices and lodgings, thirty in all. The nave; however, was divided in two by another curtain, a second veil of the temple, as it were; or rather a system of overlapping curtains that frustrated any impious eye. The first room, well lit by grilled windows, was called the hekal. A table stood inside the hekal upon which was maintained the twelve loaves of shew-bread, and a gold-covered incense altar, where incense was placed twice a day. In addition there was a golden menorah, a seven branched candelabrum lit by seven lamps that burned only the purest of olive oil. The curtained off Inner Sanctum, which lay beyond the hekal was almost dark, and ever silent, it was called the Debir. The Debir was the most sacred place in the temple. Traditionally the Hebrews called it the Qadosh Hagedoshim, the Holy of Holies. The sanctuary in Herod's Temple had always been empty. The Babylonian King Nebuchadnezzar, in 586 BC, captured Jerusalem, destroyed Solomon's Temple, and carried off the Ark of the Covenant, which had been housed in the Inner Sanctum. The very absence of objects now symbolized the intangible, invisible person of God Consequently, once a year; the high priest entered the empty sanctum of Herod's Temple, stood face to face with the invisible presence of God, and offered incense on the Day of Atonement.

My little cell was quite plain, which suited me perfectly. Its only furniture was a lamp, a low round table, and a rolled-up mat, which was to serve as my bed. As soon as I was alone, I prostrated myself on the floor and kissed it, for to me it was holy ground, God's Temple. I considered myself unworthy of treading upon its holy floors. I turned to my angels and prayed, "Messengers of the Almighty, faithful friends, I beseech you to remain with me in this temple of my Lord and to remind me of all that I should do. Please instruct me and direct me so that in all things I may fulfill the will of God."

I then prayed to God, "Infinite and eternal, Lord, if trouble and persecutions suffered in patience are precious in your sight, do not consent that I be deprived of so rich a treasure and pledge of your love. But give the rewards of these tribulations to those who deserve them better than I." God was pleased with my prayer and I petitioned him. "Oh my, Lord and, God, may I take in your presence the vows of chastity, poverty, obedience, and perpetual enclosure in the temple?"

The Lord answered me, "My chosen, one, you do not yet understand why it is impossible for you to fulfill all your desires. The vow of chastity I permit and wish you to make. In addition, from this moment forward, I want you to renounce earthly riches. It is my will that you observe whatever pertains to the other vows as if you had made them. You indeed will be allowed to suffer and labor for love of me during your life; however, you will not know in advance how this will happen."

I eagerly thanked and answered him with all the fervor of my soul, "Before, you my, sweetness, my, life, my, hope, I most humbly pledge to you my vow of chastity, and renounce all affection for earthly riches. I humbly resolve to obey all creatures because of my love of you."

I had no sooner finished speaking than the Seraphim closest to the Lord, at his instruction, illumined my senses with an effulgent light, which filled me with grace and beauty. Then they robed me in a mantle of most exquisite splendor and girded me with a cincture of vary-colored and transparent stones of flashing brilliancy, which adorned me beyond human comprehension. The stones signified my immaculate purity, and the various heroic virtues of my soul. The angels then placed on me, a necklace of inestimable and entrancing beauty, which contained three large stones symbolic of the three great virtues of faith, hope and charity. The necklace rested upon my breast as if indicating the seat of these precious stones. They next adorned my fingers with seven rings of rare beauty, whereby the Holy Ghost wished to proclaim that he had enriched me with his holy gifts in a most eminent degree. In addition, the Holy Trinity crowned my head with an imperial diadem made of inestimable material, set with the most precious stones constituting me thereby as his spouse and as the Empress of Heaven.

In testimony, whereof the white and refulgent vestments were emblazoned with letters or figures of the finest and the most shining gold, proclaiming: "Mary, Daughter of the eternal Father, Spouse of the Holy Ghost, and Mother of the true Light."

I was not allowed to fully comprehend this statement; but the angels understood it, and while lost in wonder and praise of the Author, were assisting in this new and strange ceremony. Finally, the Most High spoke to me, "Mary, you shall be our spouse, our beloved and chosen one among all creatures for all eternity; the angels shall serve you and all the nations and generations shall call you Blessed,"

Thus attired in the court dress of the Divinity, was celebrated a more glorious and marvelous espousal than ever could enter the mind of the highest Cherubim and Seraphim. For the Holy Spirit had accepted me as his sole and only spouse and conferred upon me the highest dignity that can befall a creature. He deposited within me his own Divinity in the person of the Word, and with it, all the treasures of grace befitting such eminence.

However, I was puzzled by his words and I pointed out, "My most, High King and incomprehensible God, who are you, and who am I that you condescend to look upon me, I am dust, and unworthy of such mercy? In you, Lord, as in a clear mirror seeing your Immutable Being, I behold and understand without error my lowliness and vileness. Yet, I am lost in astonishment that your Infinite Majesty should stoop to so lowly a creature. In your sight, I merit only oblivion and the contempt of all creation. How can this deed exalt and magnify my Creator? I accept you, oh my, King and my, Lord, and my, spouse, and I offer myself as your slave. Please do not allow my eyes to look upon any other creature, nor allow my faculties and senses to attend upon anything besides you and whatever your

Majesty shall direct. You alone are my spouse and my beloved, and I am only for you, who are the Immutable and Eternal Good."

The Most High received with ineffable pleasure my consent to enter the new espousal with all my soul. God then lavished upon me, as his true spouse and Mistress of all creation, all the treasures of his grace and power. He then instructed me to ask for whatever I desired and assuring me that nothing would ever be denied me. My heart leapt for joy and I begged him with burning fervor, "Oh my, Lord and my, God, I humbly beseech you to send the Redeemer to the world so that all men might know Him. Please bless my parents with grace and console the poor and the afflicted in their troubles." Then my beautiful vision faded away, and I fell happily on my face and prayed until I slept from sheer exhaustion. When I awoke for my nightly prayers, I found that someone had placed me on my sleeping mat and had covered me with a blanket. As I dropped to my knees and began my prayers, tears of happiness scalded down my cheeks and I had never before felt so at peace, and at the same time, so completely humble.

IN THE HOLY TEMPLE OF GOD

Early the next morning, Anna came for me, and I asked her, "Anna, my beloved teacher, if you would be so kind, please give to the poor, all my clothes, money, and personal belongings, which my mother has left for me. I wish to retain only those items that are necessary for my duties in the temple."

"My dear, child," Anna replied, "you must realize that if I do as you request that the other girls will have spending money and you will have none."

"Oh yes, blessed, Anna I know," I replied, "Please treat me as one who is destitute and poor."

I could tell Anna was pleased, because her entire face lit up, but she seldom displayed much emotion. However, she was ever kind and serene. Her face seemed to glow with an inner light, as though being completely one with the Lord. Anna replied softly, "It shall be done as you request, little, One. Now we must go to Simeon the priest. He is the superintendent of the temple. He will advise you of the "Rule of Life" that you will observe while you are here."

When presented to Simeon, I dropped to my knees and remained there with my eyes cast down while he was speaking, the priest was quite old and had spent his entire life in the temple, as had Anna the Prophetess. They were both wonderful examples of what God had intended for all of his people, but of which few had taken advantage. Simeon, like Anna, was exceedingly thin from fasting. Simeon had a firm, but kindly face seamed with wrinkles, but an aura of holiness emanated from his person. He instructed me briefly and to the point. "Pray always for the Temple of the Lord, for his people, and for the coming of the Messiah. Retire to sleep at eight o'clock and rise at dawn to praise the Lord until nine. During the day, as your teacher directs, engage in manual work and study the Scriptures. Take exercise before meals, and in all things be humble, courteous, and obedient."

I asked for his blessing and kissed his hand and Anna's. Rising, I was dismissed by Simeon and followed Anna to begin my new existence of work, prayer, fasting, and devotion to the Lord our God. Anna, like all the temple women, was dressed in a simple white gown, long and full, and girdled at the waist with a simple rope-sash. Like the rest of the children, I wore a coarsely woven striped dress, blue and white, embroidered with saffron flowers. The first day, Noeme supervised me closely. She walked me through the temple routine relative to the virgins and the following day she simply observed. Satisfied, the third day she allowed me to work along with the other girls. I was skillful far beyond my years, so I had no trouble whatsoever. My first job each day was to help wash the priest's white robes used during the bloody, sacrificial services in the Temple. We had daily chores to do, including the cleaning and washing of our own clothes, the daily maintenance of our rooms and workrooms, and assisting in the temple services.

Whenever I completed my work before the others, I jumped in and assisted the other girls with their work. We also did embroidery work, in which I was most proficient; in addition, we did ornamental work. The hardest work was the washing of the heavy, cumbersome, blood-soaked clothes of the sacrificial priests, and the heavy metal vessels used in the daily services. My hands were rubbed raw the first day. In time my hands toughened and I no longer had any problem. The first few days; however, Anna came and carefully tended my needs by rubbing a soothing, healing salve on my hands.

I asked Anna, "Oh blessed, Anna, will the promised Child be born soon? Oh, if I could only see that Child; if only I am living when he is born!"

Anna looked at me kindly and replied, "Think how old I am and how long I have waited for that child dear, Mary. And you—you are still so young!"

I shed many tears of longing for the promised Savior. I quickly learned that while a few of the maidens had no such allusions that they would be the Mother of the Messiah, most of them lived, worked, dreamed, and had the highest hopes that they would be that most fortunate of mothers. The other girls like me, because of their religious training at home, were already dedicated to the Lord. Upon reaching marriageable age, the virgins would be given by their parents in marriage to a carefully selected, pious young man. Among the more enlightened Israelites was the secret hope that from such a virgin dedicated to God, the Messiah would be born.

To each of my companions, I was always sincerely kind, friendly and humble. We spun, sewed, mended and washed the vestments of the priests. We took lessons on Holy Scripture, sang in choirs, and participated in the daily ceremonies of the temple. I never had a problem with any of the girls, and for this, I was extremely humble and pleased; however, I did not know that the Evil One was monitoring my every move. Seeing how diligent I was in my duties and how close to God I had become, he plotted to destroy my faith through the actions of these same virgins.

Because of my infused mystical knowledge, I always had a remarkable advanced understanding of the Scriptures. Now that I was required to read them daily, I spent many pleasant hours dwelling and meditating on them, especially on those inspired prophecies pertaining to the coming of the Redeemer of mankind in human form. I often turned to my angels and spoke to them of these wonders. I asked them profound questions, and with their help, I gradually pieced together many of the significant scriptural references to the mysteries of Christ's life, such as these three:

The Promise of his Incarnation: "The Desired of all nations shall come rejoice greatly, O daughter of Zion, shout for joy: behold, the King will come to thee, the just and Savior."

The Nativity: "Behold a virgin shall conceive and bear a Son."

His Apostolate: "He is poor, he will teach us his way. 'I will open my mouth in parables. Behold, I myself will seek my sheep, and I will feed my sheep. I will save my flock."

After mediating on these prophesies, filled with awe, I said to my angels, "My princes and lords, is it possible that the Creator himself is to be born of a creature and shall call her mother? That the Omnipotent and the Infinite, he that has made the heavens and is not encompassed by them, should be enclosed in the womb of a woman, and should be clothed with limited human nature? Is he that is vested in beauty, the elements, the heavens, and the angels to become subject to suffering? Is it possible that a woman endowed with our human nature should be so fortunate as to be able to call him Son? Will he, who is uncreated, who created the whole universe, and who made her out of nothing, call her mother? Oh unheard of wonder! If the Author himself would not have declared it, how could earthly frailty conceive a thing so magnificent? Oh miracle of His miracles; oh the happy eyes that shall see it and the happy times that shall merit it."

I spent many happy hours contemplating these and many other prophecies in the Old Testament. I discussed them with my angels and they enlightened me on many points that I had not considered, but never once did they tell me that it was I that was to be that most fortunate of mothers. As I prayed, often with tears in my eyes, a supernatural light often surrounded me.

My first six months went by like a blur. I was then honored by a vision from my Lord, and he said to me, "My beloved and chosen one, I love you with an infinite love, and I desire of you what is most pleasing in my eyes. Hence, I wish that you dispose yourself for tribulations and sorrows for love of me. You are aware my, daughter, of the hidden treasure, which is contained in hardships and tribulations, so much dreaded by the blind ignorance of mortals. It is not unknown to you that my Onlybegotten Son, when he shall clothe himself in human nature, shall teach the way of the cross as well in words as in deeds. He shall leave it as a heritage to my chosen ones. My Son shall choose it for himself and establish upon it the law of grace, making humility and patience in suffering the foundation, the firmness, and excellence of that law. For this is best suited to the present condition of human nature, and much more so, after it has been depraved and evilly inclined by so many sins. It is also conformable to my equity and providence that the mortals should attain and merit for themselves the crown of glory through hardships and the cross, since my Onlybegotten Son is to merit it by the same means of human flesh. Therefore, my spouse, you will understand that having chosen you by my right hand for my delight, and having enriched you with my gifts, it would not be just that my grace should be idle in your heart, nor be excluded from the inheritance of my elect. Hence, I wish that you dispose yourself for tribulations and sorrows for love of me."

I was now three and a half years of age, but you must not forget that from birth I had the complete use of my reason, infused knowledge of all things, as well as being the recipient of numberless gifts from my Creator. I was more than mature enough to handle God's declaration, and I fully expected and hoped that I was to suffer trials and tribulations. I replied with all the fervor of my soul, "I wish only to choose suffering unto death for love of you."

Pleased by my response, the Lord continued, "I accept your desires. As a beginning of that fulfillment, I announce to you that your father Joachim must pass from this mortal to eternal life. His death will happen shortly, and he will pass away in peace and be placed among the saints in Limbo, to await the Redemption of mankind."

I loved my father with a holy love, and I could only feel keen sorrow and compassion. I offered up a fervent prayer for him. "Please, my loving and kind God, do you give my father grace, and in his transit through death defend Joachim against the demon especially in his last moments. In order to oblige your Majesty, I offer to suffer all that you may ordain for the glory of his soul." God assured me that he would assist my father in his last moments. After the vision, I concentrated my prayers for the welfare of my father, and the consolation of my mother and the rest of the family.

Eight days before my father's death, the Lord returned and informed me the day and hour that he would die. I asked my twelve angels, led by Xnoir, to go to my father and console him, since I, myself could not be present. In the meantime, I spent every possible moment praying for his soul. On his final day, I dispatched the rest of my angels to help him, I asked the Lord in his Infinite Mercy to allow Joachim to see my angels.

My request was approved and in addition, unknown to me, the Lord instructed my angels to say to Joachim, "Man of God, in order that the pain and sorrow of natural death may be relieved by the joy of the spirit, the Almighty wishes you to know now that your daughter Mary is to be the happy

Mother of the Messiah! Since you leave to the world a daughter through whom God will restore it, do you part from it in the joy of your soul, and may the Lord bless you."

Mother stood at the foot of the bed, and she also heard this message. At that same moment, Joachim lost his power of speech, and he began his agony in conflict between joy at this great news and the pains of death. Cradled in my mother's arms, he silently made many fervent acts of love, faith, humility, and thanksgiving. The prayers of my sainted mother joined his in a joint act of faith, which was most pleasing to our Lord and God. In this holy and supernatural setting, my father died a most holy death at the age of sixty-nine and one-half-years. Upon his death, my angels carried his soul to Limbo where he joined the ranks of the Patriarchs. God allowed Joachim to share with them the happy tidings that from his child Mary; the Redeemer of the world would soon be born. There was great rejoicing and jubilant praising of the Lord, in which my angels were most happy to participate.

When my angels returned they told me of my father's death, and I begged God to console my mother. Little did I know that this sorrowful day was to be just the beginning of my sufferings for my Lord and my God?

After Joachim's death, my mother sent notification to the Prophetess Anna the news of his death. She asked Anna to break the news to me gently, to which Anna readily agreed; I listened to Anna thankfully, concealing my own knowledge of the affair. I took myself at once into the temple, reiterating my sacrifices of praise, humility, and patience. When finished, I again requested my angels to concur and assist me in blessing God.

Unknown to me, The Most High, who in his infinite wisdom dispenses and regulates the welfare of his beloved ones according to weight and measure, resolved to exercise me with some afflictions adapted to my age and state of childhood. Although I was always great in grace, he wished by this means to increase my glory. God had filled me with grace and wisdom; nevertheless, it was befitting that I should also learn by experience. Thus, by actual suffering, which only experience can bring to its ultimate perfection, could I advance and understand better the science of suffering, I had enjoyed the delights of the Most High during the brief span of my three and a half years. I had reveled in his caresses, the tender love of my parents, and in the temple, I had enjoyed the love of my teachers and of the priests.

Now it was time for me to experience the good that I possessed in another light and from a different viewpoint. I had to learn by the practice of those virtues, which arise from comparison between the state of favors and caresses, with the state of dereliction, aridity, and tribulation. God, from the moment of my conception, had given me the privilege to behold the visions of my Lord on a regular basis; In addition, my thousand angels had been my constant companions, counselors and advisors. A week later, following my father's death, I awoke to a most somber scene. My usual communication with my Lord was gone. In addition, none of my angels were visibly present, nor could I hear their voices. There was not any doubt in my mind that my angels were still with me, but now like all humans, I could not see or hear them. In spite of my loss, I never lost faith that my angels were present and still willing to do my bidding. However, I could no longer see or seek their counsel, nor enjoy their excellent and heavenly presence. I felt entirely forsaken and left alone in sudden darkness occasioned by the absence of my Beloved and my Holy Angels.

I was greatly surprised, for the Lord, although he had prepared me for coming tribulations, had not specified their nature. My innocent heart entertained no conclusions except as were conformable to my own humility and incomparable love. I accepted all according to this same light of reasoning. In my humility, I could only assume that I had not merited the further presence and possession of my Creator; perhaps, because of my negligence and ingratitude? In my inflamed and thwarted love,

I sighed and yearned after my lost Love with such great and loving affection and sorrow that I have no words to express them.

I turned with my whole soul to the Lord in this ***dark night of my soul*** and I said to him, "Highest, God and, Lord of all creation, infinite in bounty and rich in mercies, I confess, my, Lord, that such a vile creature cannot merit your favors. My soul in utmost sorrow reproaches itself with its own ingratitude, and with the loss of your friendship. If my ingratitude had eclipsed the Sun, which vivified, animated and illumined me, and if I have been remiss in giving thanks for your great benefits, I acknowledge, my, Lord and, Shepherd, the sin of my great negligence. If like an ignorant and simple little sheep, I did not know how to be thankful and do what is most acceptable in your eyes, I humbly beg your pardon. I prostrate myself on the earth. My soul wastes away in bitterness, bewailing your absence. Since you are my soul's sweetest life, only you can restore its drooping life. To whom shall I go in your absence? Where shall I turn my eyes without having light to direct them? Who shall console me when all is affliction? Who shall preserve me from death, when there is no life left?"

I had returned to my small cell to pray. The four walls seemed to close in on me. The flickering olive-oil lamp sputtered and cast grotesque shadows on the dim walls. I looked about, bewildered and all alone. Without my angels and the vision of my Lord, everything was so drab and uninviting. My little cell seemed to have shrunk into a cheerless, stone prison. I could not; I must not, allow myself to be depressed by such thoughts.

Having finishing my prayer to my God, I complained to my angels, "Celestial Princes, ambassadors of the great and Highest King and most faithful friends of my soul, why have you also left me? Why do you deprive me of your sweet countenances and deny me your conversation? However, I do not wonder my, Lords, at your displeasure, if through my unthankfulness I have merited falling into the disgrace of you, and my Creator. Lights of the heavens, enlighten me in my ignorance in this matter, and if I am at fault, correct me and obtain again for me the pardon of my Lord. Most noble, courtiers of the celestial Jerusalem, have pity on my sorrow and dereliction. Tell me, I pray you, where is my Beloved? Tell me where I can find him without wandering about, and without going through the gathering of all the creatures? But woe to me, for you do not answer, though you are so courteous and well know the hiding-place of my spouse, since he never withdraws his face and beauty from your sight." However, my four walls were silent, and not one cheerful angel appeared to me.

Then I turned my pleas to all of creation and cried out, "Oh sweet death in the absence of life! Oh sorrowful life in the absence of my very soul and of my beloved! What shall I do? Where shall I turn? How can I live, yet how can I die? Since my life is wanting, what force sustains me? Oh all you creatures that with your ever renewed existence and perfection's, give me such tokens of my Lord, attend and see whether there is a sorrow like unto my sorrow?"

However, I found no peace; I was in the realm known as **"The Dark Night of the Soul",** which all those close to God must experience to truly find him, for there is no easy road to perfection. For many days, I sought to approach the Lord in tears and loving supplications, but to no avail. However, the Most High Lord, my beloved spouse, who before had allowed me to possess him, did not now allow me to enjoy him as before. Yet, inflamed by my ardor for him, I managed to give him even more of myself. My ardor created so much love in the Lord's heart that he heaped even more hidden graces on me. These, in turn inspired me to love him ever better, and caused me to seek him with even greater diligence to prove my fiery love. In so doing, I suffered more spiritual torments and anxieties than all the saints put together. I believed I had fallen into disgrace, because of my own faults. Only the Lord could estimate or know what, and how great was the grief of my burning heart, which had grown to love so much. The weighing of my grief belongs to God alone. I was left by God to bask in the overwhelming anxiety and fear of having lost him, in order that I might feel it to the fullest extent.

To compensate, I plunged myself into Scripture studies. To facilitate my infused knowledge, and my God-given gift of a deep understanding of the Scriptures, I spent hours on contemplating the coming of the Messiah through the inspired prophecies. I paid particular attention to the prophets, Isaiah, Jeremiah and the Psalms, which dealt on the mysteries of the Messiah and the laws of grace. My knowledge and wisdom of the Scriptures was noticed by my instructors and teachers, Leone, Anna, Simeon, and the other priests. At this same time Beezelbub, "The Lord of Flies" also noted my progress and was back to his usual games.

The great dragon, the ancient serpent was ever watchful of all that had transpired. In particular, Satan was upset that I was setting heroic works and examples for all those about me, especially the other temple children. In his restless fury, he called a conference of the infernal leaders in order to consult about the matter with the higher powers of hell. The underground cavern was ablaze with light from the many fires. It was hot, and most disagreeable, and from an adjoining cave could be heard the sounds of souls being tormented.

Lucifer addressed his cohorts as follows, "The great triumph we have obtained in the world by the possession of so many souls, who are altogether subject to our wills, may be undone and counteracted by a mere girl. We cannot make light of such a danger, for we have been warned since our creation, and even afterward we heard the sentence confirmed against us that the woman shall crush our head [Gen: 3-15]. Therefore, we must be watchful and discard all carelessness. I have told you of the child, which was born of Anne and is growing in age, and wisdom. At the same time, she is distinguishing herself in virtue. I have paid careful attention to her actions and movements. In this child, I have not been able to discover any effects of the seeds of malice, which begin to show themselves to humans at the dawn of reason. This usually signals the activity of the passions in the rest of the children of Adam. This girl is always composed and most perfect in all that she does. I have been unable to incline or induce her to fall into the slightest human imperfection, which are so natural in the other children. On this account, I fear, lest she be the one chosen as the mother of him who is to become Man."

He paced up and down, and being spirit, was totally unaffected by the poisonous gaseous bellowing up about him. He spoke without conviction, "Even with these facts, I cannot convince myself that she is the chosen one; for she was born as the rest of women and subject to the common laws of nature. Her parents offered up the usual prayers and sacrifices in atonement for all their sins. However, even if she is not the one chosen as our enemy, her childhood points to great things and her exquisite virtues and holiness give promise later of still greater things. I cannot bear the prudence and the discretion with which she acts in all her affairs. Her wisdom enrages me, her modesty irritates me, her humility annihilates and oppresses me, and her entire behavior provokes me to unbearable wrath. I abhor her, more than all the rest of the children of Adam. There is in her a special problem, which often makes it impossible for me to approach her. If I assail her with suggestions, she does not admit them, and all my efforts in her regard, up until now, have been entirely fruitless. Hence, it is important for us all that we find a remedy. We must make the greatest exertions, lest our power be ruined. I desire the destruction of this soul more than all the combined souls of the world. Tell me then, my loyal friends, with what means, and by what contrivances must we deal with her? I offer high and liberal rewards to any one who shall accomplish her downfall."

The matter was thoroughly debated in that diabolic setting, convoked solely for my ruin, and one of the chiefs of the horrible council suggested, "Our, Chief and, Lord, do not allow yourself to be tormented by such a small matter. Such a weak little maiden cannot be as invincible and powerful as our combined strength. You have deceived Eve, dragging her down from her high position, and through her, you were able to conquer her head, Adam. Then why should you not be able to overcome this woman, a mere descendant born after the first fall? Promise yourself such a victory, and in order to obtain it, we will persist in tempting her. If necessary, we will even yield some of our greatness and haughtiness in the hope of finally deceiving her. If that does not suffice, we will try to destroy her honor, or her life."

Other demons added their advice and said to Lucifer, "By experience we know, oh powerful Chief, having caused the downfall of many souls, the most effective method is to make use of other creatures, and by these means we often succeed where we would otherwise fail. In these manners then, let us plan and contrive the ruin of this child, after first establishing the best time and most favorable opportunity. Above all, it is necessary that we apply all our sagacity and astuteness to make her lose grace by some insignificant venial sin. As soon as this mainstay and bulwark of the just is lost to her, we can persecute and ensnare her in her loneliness. Then there will be no one to snatch her from our grasp and we can exert ourselves to reduce her to despair of all remedy."

In response Lucifer expressed his thanks and said, "I command and exhort you, my comrades, to accompany me in this arduous enterprise. I myself will lead the fight against this girl, and any issue that may be forthcoming." So saying he appointed the most astute in malice among them to be his constant companions.

I continued to languish and grieve for my great loss, and it was thus that the infernal squadron found me. However, when they rushed forward to begin their temptations, the divine power that overshadowed me from my conception tempered the assaults of Lucifer and his cohorts. God did not allow the demons to approach overly close to me, nor execute all that Lucifer had planned. However, by the permission of God, the hellish host excited in my faculties many suggestions and various thoughts of the highest iniquity and malice; for the Lord did not judge temptation to be alien to me as the Mother of Grace. He intended that like all humans, I was to be tempted in all things. However, it was never God's intention that I ever sin in such temptations, for I was to be like my Son, who would never commit the slightest sin.

It is impossible for me to describe how much this new conflict caused me to suffer; suddenly, the demons assailed me with filthy suggestions that were completely alien to the ineffable purity and nobility of my heavenly mind. My heart was innocent and pure, and when the ancient serpent perceived the affliction and tears his temptations caused me, he imagined that he had on this account power over me. Blinded by his own pride, and not knowing the secrets of heaven, he gleefully urged on his followers and exhorted them, "Let us persecute her now, let us persecute her even more. Already it seems we are gaining our end, for she appears sorrowful, which is an opening for us to spread despair."

In this mistaken conviction, the imps of hell suggested new thoughts of dejection and despair, and assailed me with the most horrible thoughts. But their temptations were all in vain, for their efforts only gained for me more exalted virtues. I was superior to their infernal battery and interiorly I was unchanged. In my innocence, it was impossible for me to understand their terrible suggestions. These temptations; however, did allow me to exercise my incomparable virtues and allowed my flames of divine love to ascend even higher in the eyes of my God.

None of this seemed to daunt the dragon. Although Lucifer could see my courage and constancy, and even feel the force of divine assistance, he knew nothing of the hidden wisdom and prudence bestowed upon me by my most benevolent God. My adornments were fortitude, and my vestments were purity and charity, which served as my helmet. The serpent, unclean, proud, and blinded anew in his fury could not look upon me without being utterly confused. Therefore, he resolved to take my life, and his horde of malignant spirits began to exert their utmost powers toward this end. Try as they would; however, they had no more success than they had had with their temptations.

God; however, did not subject me to the sight of any of Lucifer's imps from hell. However, I was aware of his presence throughout my entire life, for he never gave up trying to seduce me to his will. Later, I found out how attentive the Lord had been in protecting me from Lucifer's onslaughts. The dragon lashed into a fury all the minions of hell against me, and exerted his indignation and wrath as he never done before in an attempt to establish his dominion over me. However, God neutralized his infernal power and astuteness. Remember, my children, how much greater is Satan's pride and arrogance, than his strength. He is actually very weak and helpless, in spite of his high-flown pretensions, for God had limited his power upon earth. Lucifer should learn to expect no great triumphs over me; as a little child, for I crushed his head, and sent him back to hell conquered in all things. Altogether vanquished, his pride still would not allow him to acknowledge what he could not do, nor will he ever acknowledge the little he knows, since from the second of his conception, in his ignorance, he has been unwilling to accept human beings, as the King and Queen of Heaven. Satan, defeated by the very instrument that he despised most, a mere human child in all its natural weakness, could never admit his defeat. Oh how evident is his ignorance as regards men. Men, by imitating my Son and me, can take advantage of the protection of the Most High and seek our intercession. When man turns to God, Lucifer is rendered completely powerless.

Satan, and his minions, sought to incite me to commit even the slightest venial sin in thought, word, or deed. Yet, while I sometimes wept, and I suffered from the strain of the constant pounding of Satan's black forces, I never once lost my inner union with God. I never ceased my prayers, saying to him, "Now, Oh my most high, God, while I am in tribulation be with me. I call to you with my whole heart and seek your justification. Let my prayers come to your ears; now that I suffer such violence, will you answer for me? You, my Lord and Father, are my strength, my refuge, and because of your holy name, you will deliver me from danger. You will lead me the sure way and nourish me as your daughter." God was with me, although in complete silence, and I raised my spirit on high, battled with, resisted, and conquered Satan to the inexpressible delight of the Lord. In so doing, I earned even greater merit in the eyes of my Creator.

Several years sped by and Satan never gave up his attacks on my faith and morality. It was then that he tried the same tactics on me that he had tried with my mother, but in dealing with innocent, naive children, he met with far more success. His weapons as usual were envy, pride and covetousness.

My ten companions were Esther, Jael, Jessica, Mara, Beulah, Daniela, Davida, Hagar, Jane, and Erlinda. The wealthier families paid the girl's expenses at the temple. Beulah, Davida, and Hagar were three outstanding, but very poor girls, well versed in piety and holiness, and for that reason, the temple paid for their keep. Esther, Jael, Jessica, and Mara were from extremely wealthy parents and had formed their own little snobbish click. They were strong in their opinions and the rest of us girls, eager to please, made ourselves as agreeable as possible and we neither accepted, nor fought against the four self-appointed leaders. We just did our work, asking nothing for ourselves, but were most eager to serve and please. At first the girls all accepted me, I was most amiable and friendly, but not intrusive. I threw myself into my work body and soul, and only wished to please my peers and my God. When I helped them, they were appreciative and I could tell that my teachers were pleased with my efforts.

The four wealthy girls were the easiest for Satan to inflame. He worked on their envy and jealously. These girls, in the pride and conceit of their hearts, each thought that God would choose them to bear the Messiah. Jael was the strongest minded and was from, not only an extremely wealthy family, but also a Herodian family with direct ties to Herod himself. She was six years old when she entered the temple and her parents had pampered and spoiled her. Her mother; however, convinced her beautiful daughter that she was to be the mother of the Messiah. Reassured by her mother and bolstered by her own conceit, she became more pliable and agreed to become a Temple Virgin. Being rich; however, she did not choose to wash the bloody sacrificial robes or the utensils used for the temple services. These selfish girls did not comprehend the significance of my desire to serve all the others. At first, they enjoyed my catering to their every whim and caprice. Especially did they enjoy my doing my own work and much of their own. It became a habit after awhile to take advantage of my willingness to serve. It was then that the eternal serpent began his campaign to bring about my downfall.

Arrogant and self indulgent, Jael was easy to corrupt. Satan, by his insidious suggestions, pointed out how the teachers seemed to favor me because of my devotion to my work. It was not hard for him to convince Jael, and her companions, of the injustice of such favor. Heedless and little experienced in spiritual ways, the four girls allowed their envy to grow into an interior resentment against me, and the evil spirits soon fanned their envy into a smoldering anger. Beulah, who was a tiny little thing, was having trouble one morning with the washing of a robe, and I asked, "Dear, Beulah, allow me to help you with that. It is so big and heavy for one person.

Jael, her petulant lip protruding, stepped between us, gave me a push, and exclaimed sarcastically, "You little hypocrite! Who do you think you are fooling with this goody-goody act of yours?"

Emboldened by Jael's accusation, Jessica, tall, slim, and haughty, sniffed disdainfully, looked down on me with a majestic air, and exclaimed, "You little sneak! You are always scheming to obtain the favor of our teachers and the priests. You think to discredit us with your holier then thou attitude."

Mara and Esther and pushed their way into the little circle and both confronted me belligerently. The chubby-cheeked Mara hissed at me, her small close-set eyes twin-beacons of hate, "You are the most useless thing, I have ever seen. Yes, worthless! You can't even speak properly with your crude Galilean dialect."

Esther, the fourth member of the quartet, completely dominated by her three friends, was emboldened by their actions. Slight of build, her pointed chin quivered anxiously, but gathering courage from her friend's boldness, she gave me a half-heated push.

Looking about, I saw nothing but anger and hatred on their faces. I was completely dumbfounded by their vehement outburst; however, I replied humbly and calmly, "My friends and my mistresses, you are right in saying, that I am the least and the most imperfect among you. My sisters, being older and better informed than I, please pardon me my faults and teach me in my ignorance. Direct me, therefore that I may succeed in doing better and act according to your pleasure."

"Our pleasure," sneered Jael, glaring at me eye to eye, "is to have you out of this temple and back in that Godless Galilee where you came from."

Davida and Hagar stepped forward and Davida protested, "Jael, how could you say such things, Mary has been so good to all of us."

Jael turned on her and snarled in her face, "You miserable excuse for a Holy Virgin. The only job your father can get is shoveling manure in my father's stables. If you cross me, I will have my parents run him out of town."

Davida's usually strong features suddenly crumbled. The three girls, born in poverty, were stunned with Jael's outburst. They knew what the moneyed class could do; expulsion from the temple was a public disgrace.

Filled with compassion for Davida and her friends, I broke in and pleaded, "I beseech you my, friends; do not deny me your good will, which, though I am so imperfect, I sincerely wish to merit.

I love you and reverence you as a servant, and I will obey you in all things. Command me then, and tell me what you wish of me?"

In spite of my sincerity, I did not soften their hardened hearts. The poorer girls were too intimidated to be of any help and the rest of the temple virgins were bewildered and clung together fearfully. Violence had never been part of their environment, and they were like sheep without a shepherd. Because of my humility, Lucifer became even more infuriated and used my own words to incite the spoiled rich girls to even worse offenses. As the days passed, Jael by threats, intimidation, and convincing arguments, influenced the rest of the girls to insult and to repeatedly lay violent hands on me. Once Jael assumed control, even my former friends joined in the pecking order, and I had not a friend among the girls. The evil one even tried to influence Jael to kill me, but unknown to me, the Lord did not permit the execution of such malevolent suggestions. The worst they were able to inflict upon me were their constant insults and blows.

This persecution went on for months without coming to the attention of our teachers. I took these occasions as wonderful opportunities to exercise all my virtues of charity and humility, yielding good for evil, blessings for curses, and prayers for blasphemies, I fulfilled in all things the most perfect and the highest requirements of the divine law. I exercised the most exalted virtues, by praying for God's creatures that were persecuting me. I excited the admiration of the angels, by humiliating myself, as if I was the vilest of mortals and deserved such treatment. In all these things, I surpassed the conceptions of men and the highest merits of the Seraphim. During this time, I gained incomparable merits in the sight of the Almighty

The day came when the schemers conspired to provoke me to do something rash. They then intended to accuse me before the priests and have me expelled. They formed a circle about me and herded me into an isolated room. Concealed from prying eyes, they began their usual insults and bullying tactics. When they struck me, I accepted their blows humbly and my only reaction was one of kindness and humility. However, when they found me unmovable, they began to over-react and lost control of themselves. They screamed their hatred for me and made such a commotion that the entire temple resounded with the uproar. Several priests burst into the room and demanded severely who was to blame for this commotion. I remained meekly silent, but the other girls all began talking at once blaming me. One priest exclaimed impatiently, "Enough of this childishness!" You," he said to Jael, who was obviously the oldest, "tell me what has happened here."

Looking crestfallen, Jael cast down her insolent eyes as though reluctant to tell on a comrade, then, she looked at me accusingly and claimed, "It is Mary of Nazareth who makes us quarrel," and she pointed at me with a triumphant gleam in her eyes. "She irritates and provokes everyone so much that there can be no peace among us unless she leaves the temple. When we allow her to have her own way, she becomes overbearing, but if we correct her, she makes fun of us by pretending to be humble, and then starts another quarrel."

The priest took me to the head priest Simeon. Simeon's face was grave as the charges against me were tolled off. He looked at me sadly as though I had broken his heart. He called me to him; his kindly eyes filled with pain, and exclaimed sadly, "Mary, your conduct shocks me. You are the one postulant of whom I never expected to hear such serious charges. What do you have to say for yourself?"

I replied solemnly, "I regret that I have been such a burden to my classmates. I promise to amend my ways."

Simeon's face sagged, as though disappointed with my reply, and he stated firmly, "Such conduct, Mary is never tolerated in the temple. I must warn you, any further occurrences will be just cause for your dismissal from the temple."

I was deeply hurt by his ultimatum, and I answered him through my tears, "My Masters, thank you for correcting and teaching me, the most imperfect and despicable of creatures. However, I beseech you, forgive me and direct me so that I may reform and henceforth please the Lord and my companions. With the grace of the Lord, I will resolve this anew and will commence from today."

After Simeon dismissed me, I went straight to the other girls and prostrated myself at their feet and pleaded, "I beg of you, my, sisters please forgive me and pardon my faults. I will try ever harder to please you." However, the girls led by the obstinate Jael, although I did my level best to please them in every conceivable manner, treated me even worse than before. I spent many hours on my knees praying to God for help in overcoming my faults.

A week later the Lord spoke to Simeon in his sleep. "My servant Mary is pleasing in my eyes. She is entirely innocent of anything, of which she is accused," and at that same moment the Lord enlightened my head teacher Anna. That morning after consulting with one another, Anna and Simeon sent Noeme to bring me before them. As Noeme led me away, Jael shot me a malevolent look of triumph. In my innocent heart, this summons spelled disaster. Simeon had warned me, and now he had no choice but to return me to my parents in disgrace. With each step, I offered up a litany of my many failings. Anna met me at the door. I could see Simeon seated on a massive, throne-like chair at the end of the room. The cold, cheerless walls seemed to crowd in on me, as I walked the endless length of the room. I dropped to my knees before him; my eyes cast down in humility.

The high priest reached down and taking my hands stood me up and exclaimed his eyes dewy with emotion, "We have brought you here to beg your most humble pardon for believing the false accusations of your companions. What can we do to make amends?"

I fell on my knees before them and begged, "Oh my master and my mistress please do not consider me unworthy of being scolded," and I kissed their hands and feet and asked for their blessing, which was quickly forthcoming.

Thereafter, God restrained both the devil and my companions from persecuting me. The girls of my cell later received a severe dressing down from Simeon, and they became quite restrained in their treatment of me. However that did not prevent them from being nasty from time to time, but they no longer dared strike me, or pull anymore of their devilish tricks. Beulah, Davida, and Hagar soon got over their fear of Jael and her companions and one by one apologized for their actions. I prayed for all of them constantly.

For ten years, the Lord denied me his presence and the presence of his Angels. He did have mercy on me a few times by allowing the veil to fall from his face for a brief relief of my terrible yearning for my Lord and my God. However, it was not often that he dispensed this favor, but when he did, he did it with less lavishness and tenderness than in the first few years of my childhood. This, he ordained that I might by actual exercise of all perfection, be made worthy for the dignity to which I was destined. God wished me to suffer according to the common order of other creatures. Therefore, he withdrew the vision of his Majesty. One of the few times that the Lord broke his silence was when I had reached the age of twelve years. I had enjoyed nine wonderfully holy years serving my God and I wanted nothing else. I loved my family and prayed for the soul of my father. Every night I remembered my mother, my cousin Elizabeth, and the rest of the members of my family in my prayers. I did miss and love them so very much. However, I felt it was my destiny to spend my life serving God in his Holy Temple.

My prayers for my mother were interrupted late one night, when my holy angels, without manifesting themselves, spoke to me as follows, "Mary, the life of your holy mother Anne is soon to end as ordained by the Most High. His Majesty has resolved to free her from the prison of her mortal body and bring her labors to a happy fulfillment."

My heart spilled over with love and compassion for my mother at this unexpected news. I prostrated myself in the presence of the Most High. I poured forth a fervent prayer for the happy death of my mother. I prayed, "King, of the ages, invisible and eternal Lord, immortal and almighty creator of the Universe, although I am but dust and ashes, and although I must confess that I am in debt to your greatness, I must speak to my Lord. I pour out before you my heart, believing, oh my, God that you would not despise my mother, who has always confessed your Holy Name. Dismiss, oh, Lord in peace your servant, who has with invincible faith and confidence desired to fulfill your divine pleasure. Let her issue victoriously and triumphantly from the hostile combat and enter the portal of your holy chosen ones. Allow your powerful arm to strengthen my mother at the close of her mortal career. Let that same right hand, which has helped her to walk in the path of perfection, assist her and let her enter into the peace of your friendship and grace, since she has always sought after it with an upright heart."

The Blessed Lord did not respond in words to my petition, but his answer was a marvelous favor shown to me and to my mother. That same night his Majesty commanded my guardian angels to carry me bodily to the sickbed of my mother. One angel remained in my stead assuming my mortal body as a substitute for mine. In the twinkling of an eye, I suddenly found myself in my mother's bedroom. She was alone, as God had planned. The sole oil lamp flickered, casting soft shadows on my mother's lovely, but drawn face. My mother's eyes widened with joy at my sudden appearance. I kissed the hand that she graciously extended, and said to her, "My, mother and, mistress, blessed be God; for the Most High is your light and your strength. In spite of my obligation to the temple, his angels brought me here to receive your last blessing. May I then receive it, mother, from your hand?"

Holy Anne with overflowing heart gave me her blessing, and thanked the Lord for the great favors conferred upon her. For known to her alone was the secret that I, one day, would become the Mother of God. I then turned to my mother and comforted her against the approach of death. Among many other things, I said to her, "Mother, beloved of my soul, it is necessary that we pass through the portal of death to the eternal life which we expect. Bitter and painful is the passage, but also profitable. The divine Goodness instituted our passing as the portal to our security and rest. It satisfies by itself for the negligence and shortcomings of the creature in fulfilling its duties to God. Accept death, mother, through it pay the common debt with joy of spirit, and depart in confidence to the company of the holy Patriarchs, the Prophets, the just, and the friends of God who were our ancestors. There wait with them for the beatitude, which the Most High will send to us through our Savior and his Redemption. The certainty of this hope will be your consolation until we attain to the full possession of that which we expect."

I took my mother tenderly in my arms, and she in maternal tenderness replied, "Mary, my beloved daughter, fulfill now your obligation by not forgetting me in the presence of our Lord God and creator and reminding him of the need I have of his protection in this hour. Remember what you owe me, for having conceived you and bore you in my womb for nine months. I nourished you at my breast and have always held you in my heart. Beseech the Lord, my daughter that he extends a hand of mercy toward me, his useless creature. I beg to receive his blessing in this hour of my death. I place my confidence in his holy name. Do not leave me, my beloved, before you have closed my eyes."

Mother smiled her lovely smile and caressed my cheek. The lamp seemed to spotlight her relaxing features, and she said with a tear in her eye. "You will be left an orphan and without the protection of a man; but you will live under the guardianship of the Most High. Confide in the mercies, which he has shown of old. Daughter, of my heart, walk in the path of the justifications of the Lord. Ask his Majesty to govern your aspirations and your powers, and to be your teacher in the holy law. Do not leave the temple before choosing your state of life. Listen to the sound advice of the priests of the temple, and continue to pray to the Lord that he disposes of your affairs according to his own pleasure. Pray that if it be his will to give you a spouse that he be of the tribe of Juda, and of the House of David." She continued, but more weakly, and I knew she was sinking fast,

"The possessions of your father Joachim are held in the capable hands of Zachariah, which, when the time comes will be returned to you and your spouse. Share with the poor with whom you have always dealt so generously. Keep your secret hidden within your bosom and ask the Omnipotent One without ceasing to show his mercy by sending his salvation and redemption through his promised Messiah. Ask and beseech his infinite bounty to be your protection, and may his blessing come over you together with mine."

Throughout my mother's last words, I could feel the life fleeing her body. After her last words, mother settled back in my arms with a satisfied sigh. With her eyes fixed on my face, God took her into the next life. With a little sigh, she fell heavy in my arms. I held her close, kissing her tears away. My grief knew no bounds, but at the same time, I was happy for I knew she was in the hands of the Lord. A little later, wiping my face free of tears, I laid her out in the burial position and closed the eyes of my blessed mother for the last time.

I prayed and recited the kaddish for the soul of my mother. After I finished, my angels returned and restored me to my place in the temple. The Most High did not try to impede my natural grief and filial love, which comes naturally with the death of a treasured one. I felt alone. Anne's passing left me with an empty feeling, but one governed by the graces given me by my Lord. I gave praise to God for the infinite mercies, which he had given my mother both in life and in death. My sweet complaints due to the absence of my Lord; however, went on unabated.

Unknown to me at the time, I could not appreciate the full extent of the consolation afforded my mother in having me present at her death. Mother was fully aware of my special place in God's plans. My own exalted dignity was known to her, and she carried in her heart that information to the grave, for had she not promised the Lord to never divulge the secret? My mother died in my arms which fulfilled all her mortal desires. Her life ended more happily than that of all the mortals up to that hour. She died, not so much in the fullness of years, as in the fullness of merits. Her most holy soul was placed by the angels in the bosom of Abraham, where she was recognized and reverenced by all the souls of the Patriarchs, the Prophets, and the just, who were all assembled in that place patiently awaiting the coming of the Redeemer.

God had naturally endowed my mother with a great and generous heart. In addition, he blessed her with a clear and aspiring intellect. She was fervent, and at the same time full of tranquility and peace. Her countenance was equable and composed. The Most High selected and set her apart from all other women, for she was to be my mother, and I in turn, was to become the Mother of God. Anne is the grandmother and my father Joachim is the grandfather of Jesus Christ, the Onlybegotten Son of God. This dignity in itself included much perfection for both my mother and my father. Mother lived fifty-six perfect years. Because of her having such a daughter, and of her being the grandmother of the Word made Man, all the nations may call her the most fortunate and blessed Saint Anne. With mother's death, I was now an orphan; but I was not alone. I was in good hands; I was the Espoused of God.

After my angels carried me back to my cell in the temple, I suffered a keen sense of loneliness. I spent my every spare moment praying and thanking the Lord for such a perfect mother, and for his having showered so many graces on my parents in life and in death. I sensed that the day of the clear vision of the Divinity was fast approaching. The nearness of the invisible fire inflamed my heart, which illumines, but does not consume. Emboldened by these sensations, I questioned my angels asking them, "My, friends and, lords, my most faithful and vigilant sentinels, tell me what hour is it of my ***dark night of the soul?*** When will the bright light of the day arise in which my eyes shall again see the Sun of Justice, which illumines them and gives life to my affections and my soul?"

When the news of my mother's death reached the temple, Simeon and Anna sent for me to notify me of her passing. With great solicitude, compassion, and love, they informed me of my mother's death. I never let on of my special blessing of being present at her death, but my natural grief spilled over and more than satisfied them of my expected reaction. Anna excused me from my duties for three days and I did not protest. I gladly accepted the time to offer up prayers for my mother and my father as well. They were now together in Limbo patiently awaiting the coming of the Messiah, who would open the gates of heaven as promised in the prophesies. It was while I was praying that a timid knock came to my door. It was Jael. She stood framed in the doorway, a stunning picture of a beautiful young Jewess, suddenly all grown up.

She dropped to her knees, and with tears flowing down her cheeks and she begged, "Please forgive me, Mary for having treated you so badly. I have come to offer you my condolences for the loss of your mother."

I raised her to her feet, and replied huskily, "There is nothing to forgive, Jael, we all make mistakes. Please come in and I will tell you about my mother, Perhaps you would join me in prayer for her soul?"

My prayers that night were filled with sorrow for my mother, but I was filled with joy with the melting of the heart of Jael, she, who had persecuted me so mercilessly, she whose soul was so dear to my Lord. One by one, my tormentors came to offer me condolences, and to beg forgiveness. My Lord was indeed all good and all merciful in my time of need; my cup was indeed full and overflowing.

A few days later, I was delighted when, for the first time in years, my angels again became visible to me. My little, drab cell was suddenly aflame with ethereal light and brilliant celestial beings. Xnoir explained to me, "Lady, your beloved is not absent when, for your good, he tarries and conceals himself, for he desires to be sought after. He wished that you sow in tears and so gather afterwards the sweet fruits of sorrow."

Then gradually, by a series of mystical experiences, God endowed my already pure soul with new gifts. He tranquilized my spirit in order to withdraw me from my present state and raise me to a position where I could enjoy new and different favors. To do so, I had to be renewed. This concerned in particular an increase of my affections and sentiments of love and virtues, which the Lord desired in me. At last, after his long concealment, having raised me to a still higher spiritual plane, he again manifested himself to me in an exalted vision, which more than amply rewarded me for all my suffering and loving anxiety.

Overwhelmed with joy, I prayed, "Oh infinite, Goodness and, Wisdom purify my heart and renew it so that it may be humble, penitent and pleasing in your sight. If I have not borne the insignificant troubles and the death of my parents as I should, and if I have in anything erred from that which is pleasing to you, perfect my faculties and all my works."

To my most humble prayer the Lord responded, "My, spouse and my, dove, the grief for the death of your parents, and the sorrow occasioned by other troubles is the natural effect of human nature and no fault. Because you have conformed yourself to the dispositions of my Providence in all things, you have merited anew my graces and my blessings. I am the one that distributes the true light. By my wisdom, I cause tranquility, and I set bounds to the storms, in order that my power and my glory may be exalted. Therefore, the soul is able to steer more securely with experience and hasten more expeditiously through the violent waves of tribulation arriving at the secure harbor of my friendship and grace. Thus, the soul obliges me by the fullness of merit, to receive it with so much the greater favor. This, my, beloved, is the admirable course of my wisdom and for this reason I concealed myself for ten years from your sight. For from you, I see what is most holy and most perfect. Serve me then, my beautiful one; for I am your spouse, your God of infinite mercy, and whose name is admirable in the diversity and variety of my great works."

From this vision, God renovated and made me God-like. I was filled with the new science of the Divinity, and of the hidden sacraments of the King, I confessed, adored, and praised him with incessant canticles using the flights of my newly pacified and tranquilized spirit, and by the like increase of my humility and my other virtues.

Thus, did I live out my next year following my thirteenth birthday. Several of my companions had been betrothed and left the temple to prepare for their coming marriages. Each left hoping that they would be selected as the one chosen to bring the Messiah into the world. As for myself, I honestly did not believe myself a fit person to be the Mother of God, so I never prayed for this honor. I did pray that I would live to the time of his birth, perchance, I might be allowed to be the unworthy handmaid of the one chosen to be the Mother of God?"

As I grew older, I withdrew as much as possible from the conversation and presence of my companions. I gave all that I had to the poor, reserving for myself only the scanty food and clothing necessary to perform my duties in the temple. My companions had long since grown out of their petty childishness. This particular day Jael again sought me out, her face was radiant, but I could also detect an inner peace, which had not been there before. She stood before me humbly, a most beautiful person, of body and soul. I noted that no longer were we eye to eye. It was I now that looked down upon Jael, who was of average height. I was aware that I had reached full maturity, and I expected that soon the temple officials would have to make a determination as to my future. I yearned to serve only God in the temple as a lifetime Temple Virgin. However, there was the distinct possibility that I would be betrothed, and consequently have to leave the temple.

Jael grasped my hands and exclaimed, "Oh, Mary, I could not leave without saying goodbye. Have you ever been able to forgive me for having been such a liar and trouble maker?"

I clasped her to my bosom and told her. "Dear, Jael, I told you before there is nothing to forgive. I never felt offended, only grateful to you for giving me the opportunity to suffer for my God. Now tell me your good news, it is bursting out all over you."

Jael stepped back and surveyed me soberly and remarked, "Mary, out of everyone in the temple, you have always been the one closest to God, I had always hoped that I would be the one chosen to be the Mother of the Messiah. However, if I have learned anything while I have been here, it is the knowledge that I am not worthy to be that fortunate person. Mary, I believe if anyone has ever deserved that honor—it is you," and she grabbed my hand and kissed it. I was embarrassed to be considered worthy of such an honor, and I was relieved, when, her face animated with excitement she gushed," "Oh, Mary, I have been espoused to a wonderful young man, and I leave tomorrow morning. Thank you, for just being you, you will never know how much your example has influenced my spiritual growth. I just wish I could be more like you." Dropping to her knees, she asked me humbly, "May I have your blessing before I take your leave?"

I took her hand and my heart went out to her. Jael was the most beautiful girl I had ever seen. My angels described to me how her happiness animated her natural beauty giving her a special glow that enhanced her long black hair, her finely chiseled features, and her flashing black eyes. I announced to her soberly, "Who am I, Jael, to bless anyone? However, everyone's blessing is a thing to be treasured. You have my blessing and my wish for happiness for you and your betrothed. If you wish to continue to grow in your relationship with our Creator, I suggest that every morning you open your heart and consecrate yourself to our Lord and God. Pray, '*Almighty God, I give myself to you, do with me as you will.*' Then try your utmost to live up to those sentiments. If you are sincere, God will help you."

Tears came to her eyes, and rising, she kissed me on the cheek and exclaimed, "Oh, Mary, I will, I will! God love and keep you. Pray for me, Mary," and overcome with emotion, she spun about, and dashed away before I could say more.

I was happy for Jael; she had indeed grown up. If my example had helped her, I was glad, that she had thought so, but of course she could have picked anyone else as an example and done much better. Her words about the Messiah bothered me. That I could be the Mother of God was of course nothing but utter nonsense. God would certainly choose someone much more worthy than I am. However, if I could be fortunate enough to be that fortunate person's handmaid, I would be in seventh heaven. When I returned to my cell that evening, I gave thanks to God for Jael's coming marriage, and prayed that he would help her on her pilgrimage.

I spent much time praying, and I frequently and devoutly pondered what I might do to please God, in order that He would deign to give me his grace. I studied the law of God and all of the precepts of the Divine Law, and I kept two laws with particular care, namely:

"Thou shalt love the Lord thy God with they whole heart, thy whole mind, and thy whole soul."

"Thou shalt love thy neighbor as thyself."

I used to rise in the middle of the night, and with as much longing and will and love as I could muster I begged Almighty God to give me the grace to observe these two precepts. In addition, I used to pray these seven petitions every night.

SEVEN PETITIONS

1. I prayed for grace to fulfill the precepts of charity: to love God with all my heart.
2. I prayed for grace to love my neighbor according to God's will and pleasure, and that he should make me love all that he himself loves.
3. I prayed that God make me avoid and flee all that he avoids.
4. I prayed for humility, patience, kindness, gentleness, and all virtues by which I might become pleasing in God's sight.
5. I prayed that God might let me see the time when that most holy virgin of virgins would be born, who was to give birth to the Son of God. I prayed that he preserve my eyes that I might see her; my ears that I might hear her; my tongue that I might praise her; my hands that I might work for her; my feet that I might walk as her servant; and my knees that I might kneel and adore the Son of God sitting in her lap.
6. I prayed for the grace of obeying the orders and rules of the High Priests of the temple.
7. I prayed that God should preserve the temple and all his people for his service.

Over the years, the Lord, in his kindness did with me that which a musician does with his harp. The musician sets and tunes all the strings so that they give forth a sweet and harmonious melody, and then he sings while playing on it. Thus God brought into harmony with his will, my heart, soul, mind, and all the senses and actions of my body. During this training period, my angels sometimes carried me to the bosom of God the Father. There I received such consolation and joy, such bliss and well being, and such love and sweetness that I no longer remembered that I had ever been born into this world. Besides, I was in such close intimacy with God and his angels that it seemed to me as though I had always existed in that true glory. Then, when I had stayed there long enough to please

God, he gave me back to the angels, and they carried me back to the spot where I had begun to pray. When I found myself on earth again, and recalled where I had been, this memory inflamed me with such a love of God that I embraced and kissed the ground, the stones, and other created things out of love for him who had created them. After such an experience, it seemed to me that I should be the handmaid of all the temple-women, and I wished to be subjected to all creatures out of love for their supreme Father.

One night, early in my career in the temple, while I was meditating on never being deprived of God's grace; I arose desiring something to console my soul and decided to read the Scriptures. When I opened the book, the first thing I saw was this passage of Isaiah: "Behold a virgin shall conceive and bear a son." I understood from this that the Son of God was going to choose a virgin to be his mother. In my childish enthusiasm, I resolved in my heart to offer myself to her as a handmaid and always to serve her and never to leave her, even if I had to travel all over the world with her [Is: 8, 14].

It may seem that God simply dumped graces on me without my having earned them. I assure you, that it was not that easy. After the gifts I received at my conception, I received from God no grace, no gift, and no virtue, without having first exerted great labor, from continual prayer, ardent desire, profound devotion, many tears, and many afflictions. God's gift of the grace of sanctification by which I was sanctified in the womb of my mother, as well as his gifts of faith, hope and charity, which was accompanied by the gift of reason were the only exceptions. With the gift of reason; however, as I said before, when I was no bigger than a bumblebee in my mother's womb, I turned on my face and adored my Creator. This action was so pleasing to the Lord, that I immediately merited the gifts with which he had chosen to bless me. I was always saying, thinking, and doing that which was pleasing to God in as far as I knew how and was able to perform.

I assure you that no grace descends into the soul except through prayer and mortification of the body. God, himself, comes into the soul, but only after we have given him all that we can give by our own efforts, *no matter how small that may be.* He bears with him such exalted gifts that it seems as though the soul faints away, loses its memory, and forgets that it has ever said or done anything pleasing to God. The more one becomes aware of the goodness of the Lord, the more the soul is able to recognize how truly insignificant the soul is in the presence of the awesome majesty of the Creator.

What must the soul do then? The soul must give fervent praises and thanks to God for these graces. In addition, the soul must consider itself unworthy of the divine gifts, and the soul must weep and give thanksgiving after receiving God's gifts. When the soul humiliates itself even more after receiving God's gifts, the Lord is moved to give still greater gifts You must all pray with fervor and devotion for your salvation and for that of others, *because God wants those who have—to help those who have not.*

When I first entered the temple, the Lord celebrated his solemn espousal with me, as I mentioned before. He had granted my requests of chastity, but had refused my plea to remain in the temple throughout my entire life. I had been but a child in years, but an adult in supreme wisdom, which I had received from the hand of the Most High and put to practical use throughout my service in the temple. I had withdrawn myself from all human intercourse, relinquishing entirely all worldly interest and attention, or love and desire of creatures. The pure and chaste love of the highest Good entirely transformed me. I never failed my Lord in all the trials and tribulations with which he beset me. I was in this state when without any explanation the Lord said to me in a vision,

"Mary, now that you are of marriageable age, it is my desire that you take an earthly spouse and husband."

For the first time, I was speechless before by Lord. I had been living secure in the possession of God Himself as my Spouse. My astonishment at this command left me floundering. The trial in my mind was greater than that of Abraham and Isaac, since my love for my inviolate chastity far exceeded the love that Abraham had for his son Isaac. However, I suspended such a judgment and preserved in calmness my hope and belief more perfectly than had Abraham.

Hoping against hope, I answered the Lord, "Eternal, God and incomprehensible, Majesty, Creator of heaven and earth and of all things contained therein. You oh, Lord, who weighs the winds, sets bounds to the sea, and subjects all creation to your will, can dispose of me, your worthless servant, according to your pleasure without allowing me to fail in that which I have promised to you. If it is not displeasing to you, my good, Lord, I confirm and ratify anew my desire to remain chaste during all my life and to have only you for my Lord and Spouse. Since my only duty as a creature is to obey you, please my, Spouse according to your Providence, may I escape from this predicament in which your holy love places me?"

There was some uneasiness in me as far as my inferior nature was concerned, as evidenced by my reply, and although I felt some sadness, it did not hinder me from practicing the most heroic obedience, and resigning myself entirely into the hand of the Lord. The Lord answered me, "Mary, let not your heart be disturbed, for your resignation is acceptable to me. My powerful arm is not subject to laws; by my disposition that which will happen is most proper for you."

Consoled by this vague promise from my Lord, I recovered from my vision and returned to my ordinary state. The divine command and promise left me between doubt and hope. Unknown to me, God intended that I should multiply my tearful sentiments of love, confidence, faith, humility, obedience, my purest chastity, and my many other virtues impossible to enumerate. I did not disappoint him, for I applied myself at once to vigilant prayer, evidenced by my complete resignation, prudent sighs and solicitude.

That same night God spoke to the high priest Simeon, and commanded him to arrange for the marriage of Mary, the daughter of Joachim and Anne of Nazareth since he regarded her with special care and love.

Simeon asked the Lord, "What is your will oh, Lord, as to the person whom the maiden Mary is to marry and give herself as spouse?"

God answered, "Call together the other priests and learned persons; tell them that Mary is an orphan and that she does not desire to be married. The Hebrew custom; however, dictates that the first born maidens are not to leave the temple without being provided for. Therefore, it is proper she be married to whoever seems good to them.

Thus it was decided that I, Mary, be married. The obedient priest Simeon hastened to do God's will. The days for me to remain in the temple were numbered.

I Am Mary

In spite of my honored position as the future Mother of God, it was necessary that I undergo the hardships of infancy the same as other children. I felt hunger, thirst, sleepiness, and other infirmities. As a daughter of Adam, I was subject to normal, accidental necessities and feeling the discomfort of such experiences. Perhaps it was even worse for me since I had the full use of my reason. However that same use of my reason, also helped me to endure and offer up these experiences as sin-offerings. Even my Son, Jesus, would be subject to these same inconveniences.

Hunger and thirst affected me more painfully than it affected other children, because of my exquisite composition; the want of nourishment was more dangerous to me. I bore it with patience, if food was given to me at unseasonable times or in excess. However, in spite of the presence and the heavenly conversations with my angels at night, I did not suffer from want of sleep.

When I was bound and wrapped painfully tight in swaddling clothes, it gave me a great cause for joy, for I understood by divine light that the Incarnate Lord was to suffer a cruel death, and was to be bound most shamefully. When alone, and unbound, I often placed myself in the shape of a cross, praying in imitation of him. By divine revelation, I learned that one I would consider beloved was to die in that position, although I did not know then, that the Crucified was to be my Son. In all the difficulties which I underwent, after I was born into the world, I was resigned and contented, for I never lost sight of one consideration which I desire you always to keep in mind. It is that you ponder in your mind and in your soul the truths which I saw. Thus, you may form a correct judgment of all things, giving to each that esteem and value that which is its due. In this regard, the children of Adam are ordinarily full of error and blindness, but I desire that you, my children, share it not with them.

Keep in mind that all the living is born destined for death, but ignorant of the time allowed them. You know for certain; however, that the term of life is short that eternity is without end and that in this life *only you* can harvest that which will yield life or death eternal. In this dangerous pilgrimage of life, God has ordained that no one shall know for certain whether he is worthy of God's love or hate. [Eccl: 9, 1] However, if he uses his reason rightly, this uncertainty will urge him to seek with all his powers the friendship of that same Lord.

From my infancy, the Holy Spirit was perfectly with me. As I grew, it filled me so completely as to leave no room for any sin to enter, and such was God's will. God gave me the gift of reason at my Immaculate Conception, and at once the angels presented me to my Creator. I turned to him with unspeakable love and desired him with my whole heart. I vowed in my heart to observe virginity if it was pleasing to him, and to possess nothing in the world. However, if God willed otherwise, his will not mine be done. I committed my will absolutely to him.

My, children remember that to suffer and to be afflicted, fault notwithstanding, is a benefit of which one cannot be worthy without the great mercy of the Almighty: Moreover, to be allowed to suffer for one's sins is not only a mercy, but is demanded by justice. Behold; however, the great insanity of today's children desiring and seeking after thrills, the sating of senses, and in sleeplessly striving to avoid that which is painful, or that which includes any hardship or trouble. The greatest benefit would be for mankind to seek tribulations diligently even when unmerited, yet, most people strives by all means to avoid them, even when merited, even though they cannot be happy and blessed without having undergone such suffering.

The souls of mankind are like gold that is untouched by the furnace-heat, the iron by the file, the grain by the grinding stone, or the grapes by the winepress; each are useless and will not attain the end for which they were created unless they are tried and refined. Why then will mortals continue to deceive themselves by expecting, in spite of their sins, to become pure and worthy of enjoying God, without the trials of the furnace, or the file of sorrows? If they were incapable and unworthy of attaining to the crown and reward of the infinite and eternal Good when innocent, how can they attain it when they are in darkness and disgrace before the Almighty? In addition to this, the sons of perdition are exerting all their powers to remain unworthy and hostile to God and they evade the crosses and afflictions which are the paths left open for their returning to their God. They reject the light of the intellect, which is the means of recognizing the deceptiveness of visible things. They refuse the nourishment of the just, which is the only means of grace, and the price of glory. Above all, they repudiate the legitimate inheritance selected by my Son and Lord for himself and for all his elect, since he was born and lived continually in afflictions and died upon the cross.

By such standards my, children, you must measure the value of suffering, which the worldly will not understand. Since they are unworthy of heavenly knowledge, they despise it in proportion to their ignorance. Rejoice and congratulate thyself in your suffering whenever the Almighty deigns to send you any, hasten to meet it and welcome it as one of his Blessings and pledges of his glorious love. You must fortify your heart with magnanimity and constancy. You will then be prepared to bear an occasion of suffering with the same equanimity, as you do the prosperous and agreeable things. Be not filled with sadness in executing that which you have promised in gladness, for the Lord loves those that are equally ready to give as to receive. Sacrifice your heart and all your faculties as a holocaust of patience. Chant in new hymns of praise and joy the justification of the Most High, whenever in your pilgrimage, he signalizes and distinguishes you as his own with the signs of his friendship, which are no other than the tribulations and trials of suffering.

My, children, choose the better part by being among the lowly and the forgotten ones of this world. I was mother of the God-man, himself, and on that account Mistress of all creation, ruling conjointly with my Son. My Son; however, was very much despised by men, and I was virtually unknown. If this doctrine were not most valuable and secure, we would not have taught it by word and example. This is the light, which shines in the darkness [John: 1, 7], loved by the elect and abhorred by the reprobate.

PRAY FOR SINNERS

Mary

Chapter Four

The Annunciation

"Behold a virgin shall conceive and bear a son, and shall name him Immanuel. [Isaiah: 7, 14]

On September 8, 7 BC, on my fourteenth birthday, as God had commanded, Simeon assembled before the Holy of Holies, the eligible bachelors from the tribe of Judah. There God would select the man, who was to be my spouse. These men were all from the House of David. One young man in particular, a handsome, wealthy, and pious young man from the region of Bethlehem was convinced that, I was going to be the Mother of the Messiah, and he desperately desired to be my spouse. The sweet odor of my virtue and nobility, the awaremess of my beauty, my possessions, my modesty, and my position as being the firstborn in my family was known to all of them, and each man coveted the happiness of meriting me as their spouse.

Through my angels, I learned that on the outskirts of the crowd was an older and thoroughly devout-man, whom I knew to be distantly related to me. His name was Joseph ben Jacob. God had blessed Joseph with incomparable modesty and gravity. Joseph was a darkly handsome man of pleasant countenance, a man chaste in thought and conduct, and most saintly in all his inclinations. He had often visited my parents before and after my becoming a Temple Virgin. I remembered them talking sympathetically about his plight, because of the way his family treated him. In perfect humility, I never looked upon the face of any man, except the face of my beloved father and Joseph my spouse, during my entire life, for I saved the adoration of my eyes for my God and my God alone. By a gift from God, I knew all people by their souls. In true humility, which was common for women, I always kept my eyes downcast never looking into the eyes or face of those people with whom I came in contact.

Joseph was the third of six brothers. His parents owned a large mansion near Bethlehem that ancient birthplace of David. In the front of the house was a large courtyard, and garden. In the courtyard was a stone springhouse. It was centered in the courtyard and had faucets shaped like animal heads from which waters gushed forth. Walls enclosed the garden, which had covered walks, shaded and lined by trees and shrubs. The upper deck of the house was circular with a broad gallery running around it protected with high parapets. Joseph, his brothers, and their tutor occupied the top floor and slept on sleeping mats. Joseph's parents were very holy and it was not until they immersed themselves in social activities that they gradually drifted from the true faith. Eventually they left the boys to the care of their teacher. At this point in their lives Joseph's parents were neither good nor bad, they simply had submitted to the secularism of the era, as so many people have done in the present age. As the spigots suggested, Hellenism had overly influenced them.

From the time Joseph was quite young, he was different from his brothers. He was quite talented and learned quickly. He was simple in his tastes, gentle, pious, and not ambitious in worldly things.

Because he was different, his brothers played all kinds of tricks on him and in general, he became everyone's whipping boy. Each youth had their own little garden, and Joseph's brothers would steal into his plot and pull up his plants and stomp on them. They all treated him roughly, but he bore all their pranks patiently. He often prayed alone and they would sneak up behind him, kick him, and then run away. However, he was too absorbed in God to take notice of them. He never sought revenge, but simply tried to find a secluded spot where they could not torment him. At the age of twelve, Joseph took a vow of chastity, giving himself entirely to Almighty God.

Joseph's parents were not pleased with him. Because of his talents, they wanted him to prepare himself for an important place in the world. Joseph: however, shunned worldly things, and often, spent time with his friends, my grandparents Eliud and Ismeria. He was also a close friend of my father Joachim. While visiting with them, he shared their beliefs and devotions and they, no doubt helped shape his character. While away from home, Joseph worked with a noted carpenter and began to learn a trade. Joseph's bother's harassment went so far that finally at thirteen, he left home. In Lebona, he found work with another carpenter. The parents of Joseph feared he had been kidnapped, but his brothers soon found him, and he was again persecuted. Again he fled, moving to Thanach and there continued his carpentry work. He lived a very pious and humble life, and after my parents were married, he visited them frequently until their deaths. I had known and loved Joseph when I was a child, and I had fond memories of him.

While we led a most sheltered life in the temple, we could not help but overhear much of what was happening in our small nation. I had learned that Joseph's parents had died when he was twenty and due to Joseph's earnest prayers for their souls, they had both died in a state of grace. Through mismanagement, the beautiful mansion was soon lost to the family and his brothers each went their own way. Two of his brothers still lived in Bethlehem. Their fortunes; however, had been drastically reduced. Joseph was completely reserved with women and lived an austere, pious, and chaste life praying constantly for the coming of the Messiah. So it was that Simeon suddenly summoned Joseph to Jerusalem, who at age thirty-three wore a full, well-trimmed, black beard.

When Joseph presented himself, I was to later learn, he asked the priest, "Why am I here, Simeon? You have known me for years, and you well know that I have taken a vow of chastity in order to devote my life to Almighty God."

Simeon took him by the arm and led him off to one side. He looked at Joseph fondly, but declared in a firm voice, "It is not always for us to decide such things, my friend, Joseph. It is by the command of God himself that I have convened this gathering of eligible bachelors from the House of David. It is he, who will decide whether you are to remain single or not."

Joseph hung his head and responded humbly, "Then, Simeon, let God's will be done." At Joseph's declaration of humility, God suddenly filled his heart with more veneration and esteem for me than that of all the other suitors

No sooner had the eligible bachelors been accounted for, than the Golden Doors was opened and the daily sacrifice was offered up by Simeon and his fellow priests. Then Simeon gathered the young men about him and declared, "You have been summoned here by the Divine Will of Almighty God. Mary of Nazareth has been a Holy Virgin of this temple for over ten years. It would not be proper for her to leave the temple unspoken for since she is an orphan, born of noble lineage, and is a first born daughter. Therefore, God, in his infinite wisdom will select the spouse of this maiden. I will place in each of your hands a dry stick, with the command that each ask his Majesty with a lively faith, to single out the one whom he has chosen as the spouse of Mary."

During the selection process, I was alone in my little room, busily praying that the Lord would remember my desire to lead a life of chastity. Yet, I prayed that God's will be done, not my own. A dried-up dogwood branch was handed each suitor, each man eagerly did as instructed. However, each in turn was disappointed, for their branches did not blossom. Finally, my angels told me, the only man not tested was Joseph. Was this the man that, I was to marry? If so, God had picked well, for Joseph's reputation was without blemish. With unhesitating step, Joseph reverently laid his branch on the altar and a hush settled over the room. The dead stick instantly grew and blossomed into a beautiful flower. At that moment, interiorly, I saw a dove of purest white and resplendent with admirable light, descend and rest on the head of Joseph.

At the same time God spoke to Joseph in his heart saying, "Joseph, my servant, Mary shall be your spouse; accept her with attentive reverence for she is acceptable in my eyes. Just and pure in soul and body, you shall do all that she shall say to you."

Suddenly, the rich young man from Bethlehem, with a cry of dismay, fled the hall weeping bitterly. I later learned that he hurried to Mount Carmel where, since the days of Elias, hermits had dwelt. He took up his abode on the mount and there spent his days in prayer for the coming of the Messiah.

Simeon then came for me, and another priest led the dazed Joseph by the arm. Simeon carefully unveiled my face, which, when uncovered, shone like the sun, and I was more resplendent than the moon. My countenance was more beautiful that of an angel, and as God wished, I was incomparable in the charm of my beauty, nobility and grace. It was there, in the holy setting of God's Temple that I agreed to accept Joseph that most chaste and holy of all men, to be my spouse. Simeon, the high priest, responsible to God, and responsible to see that when I left the temple that I was properly cared for, set the date for our betrothal.

God had ordained our marriage, which would seem to forgo the necessity for the meeting of our families to decide on the matter. However, true to tradition, we met the next week on a Wednesday, as the full moon was thought to bring good luck, and assembled in a public hall arranged for by Simeon. He had called upon the high priest Zachariah, Elizabeth's husband, and my closest relatives, to represent my interests. Jewish law recognized rights and obligations during the betrothal that were almost the same as those of marriage. During the betrothal, a letter of divorcement could not put a betrothed woman aside, and she was considered a widow, if a betrothed man died before the actual marriage. Children were legitimate if they were born during the betrothal. A betrothed woman suspected of unfaithfulness, in order to prove her innocence, had to drink a horrible mixture in which the main ingredient was dirt from the temple floor. The woman was guilty if she vomited or became ill. A man in similar circumstances; however, was never condemned because his act did not have any affect upon his family. A man or woman; however, if caught in adultery with a married or a betrothed person were both put to death. These laws; however, had been tempered with the advent of Hellenism and were not always enforced.

Both my parents and Joseph's parents were dead. My estate would in essence comprise a positive dowry that parents often gave their daughters, commonly called the silluhim. Often there was much haggling over the price of the mohar, which is the dowry given to the bride by the groom. However, Zachariah, believing that under the circumstances, Joseph might not be prepared to pay the dowry, privately offered to advance him the fifty shekels of silver, which was the common amount accepted by most families. This money would ordinarily have gone to my father, but now instead would go into my estate. Surprisingly, Joseph had the fifty shekels as well as an additional fifty shekels as one of his gifts to me, which is called the mattan. As usual, God had provided.

When the matter of the money had been settled, Joseph and I met, again. Following Jewish custom, Joseph came for me and took me to a private room. It was here that the prospective bride and groom often met for the first time, while in an adjoining room their parents decided their future.

Once alone we both became very shy and I sat down nervously on the edge of a chair. While my intended was bashful, he was not tongue tied, and as soon as we were alone, he said most eloquently, "My dear, Betrothed, though I judge myself unworthy even of your company, I give thanks to the Lord for having chosen me as your intended. Please assist me to make a proper return in serving him with an upright heart. Therefore, consider me your servant. By the true love that I have for you, I beg you to put up with my deficiencies in the domestic duties which as a worthy husband I should know how to perform. Just tell me what you want, so that I may do it."

I replied humbly, "Master, I am fortunate that the Lord has chosen you for my husband and that he has thus shown me he wishes me to serve you. However, if you allow me, I will speak to you from my heart of that which is most dear to me?"

God inflamed Joseph's sincere heart with grace and love, and he replied, "Speak dear, Lady, I am your humble servant."

I had never spoken to or been alone with a man since I entered the temple. Due to my training and natural inclinations, I was quite shy, even more so than Joseph. I felt a deep respect and reverence for Joseph and I asked my guardian angels, visible only to me, to gather close to give me courage. As they clustered about me, I spoke earnestly from my heart, "My dear, Joseph, our Creator has manifested his mercy in choosing us to serve him together. I consider myself more indebted to him than all other creatures, for while meriting less, I have received from his hand more than they do. As a child, he made his divine light known to me. Consequently, I consecrated myself to God by a solemn vow of perpetual chastity in body and soul. I am his, and I acknowledge him as my spouse and Lord with the firm resolve of preserving my chastity for him. I beseech you my, master, to help me in fulfilling this vow. In all other things, I will be your servant, working willingly for you all my life. My dear, Joseph, yield to this resolution, and I implore you to make a similar one. By so offering ourselves as a sacrifice to God, He may accept us, and bestow on us the eternal reward for which we hope."

As I spoke, Joseph's face blossomed with joy and with true supernatural love, he responded enthusiastically, "My heart rejoices in hearing your most welcome feelings in this matter. I did not tell you my thoughts before knowing your own. Please understand that I also consider myself under great obligation to the Lord. Very early in my life, the Lord called me by his enlightenment to love him with an upright heart. At age twelve, I also made a promise to serve our Creator in perpetual chastity. I gladly ratify this vow, and in the presence of God, I promise to help you as far as I can in serving him and loving him according to your desire. With his grace, I will be your faithful servant and companion, and I beg you to accept my chaste love and to consider me your brother."

At this moment, God filled us both with heavenly joy and consolation. In addition, he gave to Joseph new purity and complete command over his natural inclinations, so that he might lovingly serve me without any trace of sensual desire. In my case, this was not necessary, since my previous gifts from God precluded any such desires. We both dropped to our knees and privately I asked my guardian angels to join us in giving thanks to God for allowing us to serve him in perpetual chastity. Unknown to us this chastity would often be a theme in the preaching of our son Jesus the Christ and led some people into heresy long after we were all gone to our reward. It also carried over into the eventual chastity of the priests of the Roman Catholic Church and many religious orders of brothers and sisters.

After a respectful length of time, we rejoined the group and Joseph said to them all, "I am happy to announce that the lovely maiden, Mary, has consented to become my bride." The priests and scribes wrote down the terms of the marriage agreement and all parties signed the document. I was now seated on a throne-like chair and all my maiden friends clustered about me excitedly, for it was now the time when the prospective groom offered his future bride a collection of gifts, which was called the mattan. Joseph's gifts were rather like a dower, much like the silluhim given the bride by her parents, for these gifts belonged to the bride if she were left a widow.

Joseph left for awhile and when he returned he and his friends were loaded down with his mattan gifts for me. His first gift was a beautiful cedar chest, which he had made with his own master-crafted hands; practical kitchen utensils filled the chest. There were stools and other items as well. He climaxed his gifts with a beautiful handcrafted leather purse containing fifty silver shekels. This ended the ceremony and we all returned to our residences.

My heart was heavy; I now had to leave the holy temple, which had been my home for eleven years. My inclinations had been to serve God in his house for the remainder of my days. I took leave of the priests, asking for their blessings, and those of my instructors, and my companions, begging their pardon for my deficiencies. Joseph had no desire to return to Bethlehem, the city of his birth. Having no property or family there, he deemed it proper for us to live in Galilee, the home of my parents. There, surrounded by my friends and relatives, Joseph felt I would be happier than being an alien in a strange town.

Now properly espoused, our company set out gaily for Nazareth. Elizabeth and Zachariah accompanied us, and in the company of friends and other members of our family, we merrily made the trip from Jerusalem to Nazareth. It was normally a three-or four day trip to Nazareth from Jerusalem, but we were in no hurry so we took four days. Joseph and I had not had time to discuss my estate and that first evening at the inn, where we had stopped for the night, I asked him, "With your permission, my, espoused, it would please me greatly if you dispose of my property in Galilee as quickly as possible?" I wished to spare Joseph any embarrassment, since I knew that in true Hebrew tradition according to Jesus, the son of Sirach, who wrote in 175 BC, "It is a shame for a man to be kept by his wife." However, I soon learned that this humble man Joseph had no such scruples. We both knew that God did not wish us to be rich. We were to live a simple life of poverty and good example, giving our excess to the poor. With Joseph's permission, I intended that he dispose of my property and distribute the proceeds to the poor. Included in my estate was a small house near Nazareth in which my parents had begun their lives together. I asked Joseph if this were satisfactory with him?

Joseph replied, "My, Lady, nothing would please me more, but you must remember that as a humble carpenter, I cannot provide the luxuries with which you may be accustomed."

I smiled with the thought, Joseph had no idea of the modest circumstances under which I had lived most of my young life and I answered, "Have no fear, Joseph, I will be your dutiful wife and will share with you that with which the good Lord sees fit to provide." Consequently, Joseph and Zachariah engaged in long conversations regarding my estate and the matters were settled by the time we reached Nazareth. Instead of taking me to the manor home of my parents, Zachariah led us to the small house in which Anne and my father Joachim had begun their lives together. I remembered very little about Nazareth, so it was all new and exciting to me. Zachariah had a crude key that fit a large two-door entrance that opened onto the courtyard. I remembered the ancient olive tree that gave generous shade during the heat of summer, and its fruit that provided both food and lamp oil for our family. A small stable took up the far end of the courtyard, which was paved with cobblestones and was to be the home of our milk goat, a Muscat ass, and some fowl. It included a small area for storage.

Joseph eyed the courtyard with approval and he exclaimed, "This is perfect. At the far end, I can build a shelter from the sun. The shed and courtyard will provide an excellent carpenter's shop." The courtyard had also been paved with rock and channeled to outside gutters. This was indeed a blessing since the water from our daily personal washing, the washing of clothes, and the rain could turn a dirt courtyard into a bed of mud. Washing clothes was nothing new to me, but milking a goat would be a new challenge. Our toilet was also at the far end of the courtyard, which was in itself a blessing. Each month a dung keeper would service the toilet and would haul the refuse to a dump.

We entered the house through a very low and very narrow door. We all entered the house poking and prying into everything like a bunch of excited school children. The dwelling of oven-dried brick was standard for most Jewish homes. From the courtyard stairs led to the roof. There were two small sheds on the roof. They were made of loosely woven sticks and were used to both sleep and work from during the heat of the summer. Iron-straps fastened the outer doors, instead of the usual leather ones. It was a sound, well-built house, and more than adequate for our needs. In the center of the ceiling there was a small hole that served to allow the smoke from the olive oil lamps and the braziers to escape. I was pleased with the well-constructed clay-oven in the courtyard, which my father had constructed.

Our heat in the winter would come from a small charcoal brazier in the main room. The very poor could seldom afford to fuel the braziers, unless one was ill, or it was exceedingly cold. In the middle of the floor of the communal room, which would also serve as an inside kitchen and dining room was a small fireplace, built on a raised hearth. This in itself was unusual for very few homes had such a luxury. The ceilings had been constructed of small saplings and interwoven branches and all had been plastered with thick layers of clay. On the roof lay a small stone roller with a wooden hub type handle to keep the roof rolled down tight as protection against the rain. Around the roof, as required in the scriptures, a parapet had been built to avoid accidents and also, when sleeping, to allow one a modicum of privacy.

As we toured the house, my thoughts were full of my parents who had been so happy together in this very house. It was obvious that over the years they had made few improvements before building their new home in which I had been born. It was not just a house, it had the feel of a home, and I was more than content.

The very first day Joseph unpacked his tools, set up his workshop, and went into the streets announcing to his friends and relatives that his services as a carpenter were available. Until our wedding, he would live with his cousin Maraha. Elizabeth stayed with me for a week as my mentor and companion, and under her expert instructions, I soon mastered the duties of a homemaker, which included milking the goat, which I had not learned at the temple She joyfully joined in with me as I unpacked my mattan presents. We needed very little; a charcoal brazier, three oil lamps, two of them were oval and one large one was round. The pots, utensils and jars for food storage necessary in order to set up housekeeping. Many of the items needed, Joseph had made for us. The beautiful chest Joseph had made for me would be more than adequate for our meager personal belongings. Elizabeth and I slept on the floor on a pad of mats until Joseph had time to build beds for us, which he insisted upon. We often sat on the chest and Joseph made stools benches and a few chairs and one couch for our guests and us to sit on.

Because there were no windows in the small homes one lamp was kept burning day and night. This also gave the family a ready source of fire. Joseph and I each had a small clay lamp in our bedrooms, each lamp had two holes. In one was a wick of flax of hemp for the light and the other was for filling the lamp with oil. Each lamp had a handle or ear with which to pick it up to move it or to light one's way. Joseph erected a pedestal to sit the main lamp on and it had seven holes in it in imitation of a menorah. We also had small portable stoves with two holes in which twisted bundles of straw and grass were burnt to offset the worst rigors of winter. The houses all had. Before long the house had taken on the odor of rancid olive oil, which was typical of most of the Jewish homes.

Each morning after our morning meal, Joseph would enter, bow to me politely, and ask me what he could do for me that day. Elizabeth was enchanted with his shy, humble manner, and when he was not present, she was prone to tease me about him. Within a week, our little home was as furnished as it was ever going to be. Joseph had made two very simple beds and Elizabeth had presented us with a pair of handsome blankets that she had woven herself. Elizabeth's parents had been well off and as the wife of a high priest; she was used to finer furnishings. The average family; however, slept on mats on the floor and they used their cloaks as blankets. The beds and blankets were the only real luxuries in which Joseph and I indulged, other than simple partitions to create separate bedrooms in which we could maintain our privacy.

In Israel, the husband was the Lord and Master of his home. Even as Joseph's espoused, I was obligated to heed his every wish. I had no desire to engage in any business matters whatsoever. In regards to my wishes, Joseph had quickly disposed of my inheritance, and as we had discussed, he gave one-third to the temple, one-third to the poor, retaining for us the remaining third. I later learned he had also given our share to the poor after providing for the establishment of our home and other future contingencies. In so doing, he had purchased a milk goat and an ass to provide transportation for our necessary trips to Jerusalem to observe the holy days of our faith.

At the end of the first week, Joseph and I again had a discussion. He was troubled. God had made known to him how very special I was to him and he complained, "My Lady, it is not proper that you should serve me, and constantly ask my permission in the running of your household. It would please me greatly if you would allow me to serve you and attend to all your worldly needs."

I did not wish to go against the wishes of my intended; however, my station in life was to be that of an ordinary housewife, and as such, I would be subject to his every need, except for that one act, which we together had offered up to God. I stated firmly, "Joseph, the one thing we should not do is to make our coming marriage a sham. I am to be your wife, and as such, I must perform the duties of a homemaker the same as any Hebrew woman. Our faith recognizes the husband as the provider and master of the home. In good conscience, I cannot change the natural order, nor should you. Even though we have not taken the final vow of marriage, I expect to obey your every wish, but I do beg your permission to help the poor at every opportunity."

Joseph was not one to make hasty decisions. He sat there with his head lowered for a moment, and then he replied. "You are wise indeed, Mary. I agree with your decision, be advised that my every intent and effort shall be to serve and provide for you and the poor to the utmost of my ability."

That very night I had a vision of the Lord in which he said, "My most beloved, Spouse and chosen, one, behold how faithful I am to my promises with those who love me. Respond therefore to my fidelity by observing all the laws of a spouse. Be perfect, as I am perfect in holiness and purity, and let the company of my servant Joseph, whom I have given you guide you. Obey him as you should and listen to his advice."

I responded, "Most high, Lord, I praise and magnify you for your admirable disposition and providence in my regard, even though I am unworthy and so poor a creature. I desire to obey you and please you as one having greater obligation to you than any other creature. Bestow upon me, my, Lord, your divine favor, in order that I may attend to the duties of the state, in which you have placed me. I pray that you will assist me in all things, never allow me to err so that your pleasure will govern my every action. With it, I will strive to obey and serve your servant Joseph in the manner in which you, my, Lord and, Maker, command."

On such heavenly beginnings was my home and subsequent courtship founded. Joseph was very wise in his decisions and he was beloved by all. My friends dropped in from time to time and Elizabeth, who was my mother's age, was like a mother to me. Unfortunately, after a brief week she had to return to Jerusalem with Zachariah for his turn at his priestly duties. I parted with Elizabeth with regret. She had arranged for Mary Salome, my aunt, to live with me and act as my chaperon and companion. I never allowed myself the luxury of many close friends, but of course, Elizabeth and Mary Solome came to be much more to me than just friends. Elizabeth had been a friend and mentor, even a second mother, and I knew it was God's will that she go, before I became too enamored of earthly ties.

Elizabeth was a most holy woman and during that week, we worked and prayed daily together, and when our friends dropped in, we did much of the same. We had our times of levity, but we were all primarily concerned with doing God's work on earth and seriously applied ourselves in that vein. When Joseph was paid, we ate well and when he was in between jobs we prayed, helped our neighbors, and did charitable work. Later, Elizabeth, from time to time, sent us food and money, or we would have gone hungry, since we gave to the poor all that which we did not need for that day. Our neighbors often came bearing gifts of food because they also shared in, and appreciated our generosity. After Elizabeth left, Mary Solome became the close relative and friend that I had never had.

Joseph was eager to help anyone in need, and often worked for little or no wages, which sometimes compounded our financial problems. As usual, in return for his labor, there was much bartering and exchange of goods or services. The pay for Joseph's first job was a pound of salt brought all the way from the Dead Sea located a week's journey to the south of us.

I soon learned that my espoused was not just a carpenter, but was a master carpenter. Fortunately, the little town of Nazareth, and the many small neighboring communities, usually provided sufficient work for a carpenter. Sepphoris, the capital of Galilee was only four miles distant and if local work was not available, Joseph readily found work there. However, he prudently worked through the Carpenter's guild in Sepphoris and worked through the established carpenters. Since Nazareth only had a population of about a hundred families, we were again fortunate that he had no local competition. As did all carpenters when they became apprentices, Joseph had made his own tools with the exception, of course, of the metal parts that had to be fashioned by a blacksmith. He had manufactured his own planes, axes, adzes, chisels, hatchets, knives, squares, hammers, clamps, bow saws, and bow drills. His tools were all works of art, for these were the tools of his trade, and each worthy apprentice fashioned his tools with all the skill and love he possessed. Joseph sometimes stuck a curled shaving behind his ear when he was away from home announcing to all, that here was a master carpenter.

Joseph made regular trips to the forest to purchase and cut timber and then hauled it back to his workshop on the back of his Muscat ass. He performed a wide-variety of work including, the building of houses, the manufacture of jambs and lintels for masons, and the erection of arbors. He also made wheels, and did repair work that was beyond the ability of ordinary laborers. He built storage chests, measures for grain, kneading troughs, kitchen utensils, stools, chairs, tables, supports for straw pallets, and the occasional bed. Joseph received a wide-variety of work from the local farmers. He repaired their plows, and fashioned new plowshares from sycamore, which was Joseph's first choice, because of its proof against the worm, and when properly treated it was hard enough with which to plow. Wood was more economical than using iron plates to face the plowshare. All of this Joseph explained to me, as he and I learned to love, pray, and to share our lives with one another.

I was kept just as busy as Joseph, since I maintained the house, cooked the meals, and washed the clothes for Joseph, Mary Salome and me. Even in our era the old adage passed down from our ancestors held true. "A man works from sun to sun, while a women's work is never done." In the courtyard was a millstone set in the ground, and nearly everyday I spent an hour turning the upper stone on the lower to grind the grain to make our daily bread. Every day, except the Sabbath, I had to knead dough and when it had risen, place it in our oven to cook. We were most fortunate; for the very poor had to use the town's communal oven. When my friends came, we often busied ourselves holding the distaff and spindle as we weaved, wove and sewed, and made enough clothes and coverlets for our families. We often prayed and sang praises to God while we worked. Each day I milked the goat. From the soured goat's milk, I churned the milk in gourds, pressed the curds, made my own cheese, and we drank the buttermilk. Each evening when the three blasts from the ram's horn summoned the men in from the fields, Joseph walked into town to attend the synagogue services. The synagogue was perched on a small hillock, which overlooked the rest of the town. On the Sabbath all work stopped, and most of the men, women, and children attended the services.

Each morning when the water-warden gave a signal, I joined with the women at the city well, which we shared with our neighbors, and drew up enough water for our daily needs. The day I washed clothes; however, and the day before the Sabbath, I had to make several trips, and the water-warden allowed each household sufficient water to satisfy their needs. I learned to deftly balance the heavy water jugs on my head. I appreciated Mary Salome's help at such moments. Many of the women were prone to gossip, while waiting their turn at the well. However, I chose my companions carefully and Mary and I avoided all such idle talk.

The Sabbath was the Lord's Day. It was a most holy day, and the Hebrew Law forbade work of any kind. The Law included cooking, so food had to be prepared in advance. I had to purchase olive oil, both for cooking and for our lamps. However, twice a year, our tree would yield its rich harvest of olives, and I would be able to shake the ripened olives from the tree. Then using the oil press made for me by Joseph, I would make my own lamp and cooking oil. Olive oil had many uses. The oil, when mixed with wine, served as a remedy for many ailments. Oil was a soothing balm for baby's skin, and it was also a bodily cleansing agent. Our common drink was sour vinegar and only at special events did we did enjoy a taste of wine.

Contrary to many of our contemporaries, we did not live to eat, but only ate enough to live. The three of us fasted several days a week, offering our sacrifice for the sins of the world. Mary Salome was a most holy person. Noticing that I was not looking well, she admonished me, "Mary, you must take better care of yourself. You are not getting enough sleep, nor are you eating enough to maintain your good health." She held up a small polished bronze mirror and I could see that my face was haggard, and there were dark circles under my eyes.

I nodded solemnly, "You are right as usual, Cousin. I promise you, I will eat enough to maintain my health. However, as far as sleep is concerned, I have not slept more than four hours a night since I first became a Temple Virgin. As you know, I pray most of the night, and shall continue to do so. The Blessed Lord wants our prayers so badly."

Mary was a little older than I was, but she was a well organized and a disciplined person. If I had allowed, she would soon have taken over the running of my household. In spite of the fact that they were very well off, both she and her parents, now deceased, were humble Essenes and very much devoted to God. Mary Salome had several servants, but only because her husband's and her endeavors created the need for more employees. However, when she lived with me, she did her share of the work, and we were both dedicated to charitable work and prayer.

Because of his goodness and holiness, my espoused Joseph was an easy man to love. Joseph, in turn, could see the heavenly light, which shone from my countenance enhancing the calmness, beauty, and majestic features with which God had blessed me. Joseph's admiration, love and reverence for me greatly increased every day as God intended. Never did I ask Joseph for anything that I did not receive. Nor did I ever ask him for anything that was not pleasing to God. The vision of my beloved Creator was ever before me, and my thousand angles never left my side unless I delegated them a task. There was ever a constant stream of angels scaling and descending Jacob's ladder on their journeys between their Maker and me.

Neither Joseph nor I developed a passionate, all consuming love for one another. Rather, we shared a spiritual love such as the Saints share in their heavenly abode. Each day I thanked the Lord for having granted me the privilege to be the spouse of Joseph, and Joseph never ceased thanking the Lord for choosing him to be my guardian. God did not allow our prayers and good works to go unrewarded. It was my privilege to see God change many souls overnight into God-fearing people, and see him fulfill needs of many of the poor. Mary Salome learned that one of our cousins Leah was in a state of serious sin and she urged her to come to me for help. When first we met, God opened her eyes to the holiness he had wrought in me. Leah was so impressed that she fell to her knees and confessed her sin outright. When she left, she promised faithfully to avoid the near-occasion of her sin.

I only had a few close friends and family during the so-called "hidden years" in Nazareth. We were always so busy maintaining our home and helping the poor that it gave us little time to for a social life outside the home. The emanation from the perfection God had created in me often filled my friends and acquaintances with a mysterious joy. God influenced many to turn from sin from just being in my presence, and like Leah, they quickly amended their lives. This does not mean that I did not encounter many persons during this period. The poor, the homeless, the sick, and the dying were all my friends and I gave them whatever time it took for me to render them aid and comfort. God's divine influence affected all those with whom I came in contact. Consequently, many of these persons began fawning over me and overwhelmed me with their gratitude and attention. I implored the Lord that in the future that I would prefer that all such mortals would ignore me. God graciously answered my prayers by preventing those persons from communicating their admiration and from seeking me out.

I did not hear from Elizabeth after she returned to Jerusalem with Zachariah. I gave the matter little thought, for I had never maintained a close contact with anyone because of my lengthy stay in the Holy Temple of God. However, I did learn about the marvelous events that took place in Jerusalem from my holy angels.

The Conception of John

Zachariah was an important high priest, and he and his wife Elizabeth were regarded with extraordinary veneration from the fact of both having descended in a direct line from the race of Aaron. However, recently, there had been idle talk about the fact that God had not blessed them with children. Zachariah and Elizabeth were both self-conscious about their inability to conceive. For twenty-years they prayed that God would bless them with a child. If it had not been for Zachariah's obvious holiness, high position, and family background, he would not have been able to maintain his priestly position. The Hebrew was a superstitious race; they believed that if a couple was not blessed with children; it was because of their sins. Until now, no one had dared, or even suggested that this was the problem with Zachariah.

Unlike Simeon, who was a permanent priest in the temple, Zachariah served in the holy temple only twice a year. Once every twenty-four weeks his class of the priesthood, of which there were twenty-four, reported to Jerusalem to officiate and run the temple for a week. He lived in a small community by the name of Jutta, a Levitical city, northwest of Hebron. On Thursday evening at dinner, he said to Elizabeth and his assembled relatives,

"You all know how I dread going to the temple, because people are beginning to question why Elizabeth and I are not with issue. However, in spite of my fears, I feel something of great import is going to happen to us very soon."

Before his departure, the good priest and his spouse prayed long and hard begging God for a child. Armed with his confidence that something remarkable was soon to happen, Zachariah and Elizabeth left Monday morning for their home in Jerusalem. He did not have to report to the temple until Friday for his tour of duty that would begin with the Sabbath. It took a thousand priests and Levites to manage the temple for one week. However, this was the Feast of Booths and all eighteen thousand priests and Levites had poured into Jerusalem to take care of the huge masses of Jews congregated to celebrate the festival, the happiest of all the feasts. However, Zachariah and his fellow priests, all from the clan of Abia, were in charge. Elizabeth and Zachariah, in preparation for his coming duties, spent the balance of the week praying in the temple to prepare Zachariah spiritually for his work and also begging God to put an end to their shame.

On Friday afternoon, the priests, of the clan of Abia, drew lots for control of the "thirteen offices", so as to determine who would prepare, who would clean, who would burn the incense, sound the trumpets, bless the people and so on. The on-duty priests also undertook the control of the courts, the management of the temple's goods, and even the judgment of the cases of open crime discovered within the sacred precincts. The more favored class's turns of office coincided with the great feasts. In the month of Tishri, [during the last half of September and the first half of October] fell the feasts of Rosh Hashanah, Yom Kippur, Succoth, and the Festival of Booths. On this occasion, the duty of 'burner of incense' fell to Zachariah, who was one of the two hundred chief priests in Israel.

When the first star appeared that evening, close to the ninth hour, blasts from the shofar, the ram's horn, blared calling all the people to come celebrate the Sabbath of the Lord. Trumpets then sounded and the service began. At last Zachariah's turn came and he went into the sanctuary just outside the entrance to the Holy of Holies. Once inside, Zachariah turned suddenly to the other priests and told them he wished to be alone. Complying with his wishes the other priests left. The elderly priest then entered the room just outside the Holy of Holies. Zachariah placed on the gold altar, lighted by the all-gold candelabra, the Tables of the Law and then kindled the incense. Just to the right of the altar a dazzling light suddenly appeared and began to descend. Frightened, Zachariah, stepped back, but then sank to his knees in reverential awe.

A brilliant angel appeared and said to him, "Do not be afraid, Zachariah, your prayers have been heard. Your wife Elizabeth will bear you a son, and you shall name him John. You will have joy and gladness, and many will rejoice at his birth, for he will be great in the sight of the Lord. He will drink neither wine nor strong drink. God will fill John with the Holy Spirit, while still in his mother's womb. He will lead many of the children of Israel to the Lord their God. He will go before him in the spirit and power of Elijah to turn the hearts of fathers toward their children and the disobedient to the understanding of the righteous, to prepare a people fit for the Lord."

Then Zachariah, who was completely dumfounded, managed to speak and replied, "But this is not possible? For I am an old man, and my wife is well past her child bearing years."

The angel answered him sternly saying; "I am Gabriel, who stands before God. I was sent to bring you good news; however, because you did not believe my words, which will be fulfilled in their proper time, you will be speechless until the day these things take place."

In the meantime, the people outside were becoming anxious because of Zachariah's long absence. His fellow priests could see the smoke from the incense rising above the curtain, and they were ready to enter when Zachariah stepped out. His countenance was radiant and when they quizzed him; he was unable to speak. He signaled for a tablet, and he wrote down the startling events. He wrote a message telling Elizabeth what had happened, for he knew she was praying in the Court of Women. Later, he was amazed to learn that Elizabeth also had a vision at the same moment that he had. When Zachariah's tour of duty was completed, the couple returned to their home in Jutta. Zachariah and Elizabeth conceived John shortly after in the natural manner. Joy filled their hearts and they prayed constantly praying and thanking God for his great blessing.

After her conception, Elizabeth went into seclusion for five months; she cut herself off from all outside activity. She spent her time in prayer giving thanks to God for this special blessing. "It is little enough that I can do," she told Zachariah, "to give proper thanks to he who has taken away my disgrace." She gave little thought to anyone, even me whom she considered as a daughter. Elizabeth immersed herself completely in thankfulness to her God.

THE IMMACULATE CONCEPTION

Several months later, completely unknown to me, the time appointed for the Incarnation of God's Son was drawing near. In genuine humility, all I had ever dreamed or hoped for was to be the handmaiden of the fortunate person selected to be the mother of the Messiah. I never dreamed that such a widely expected event could directly involve me. Nine days preceding this decisive turning point in history, according to my custom, I arose at midnight to praise the Lord, as the Holy Ghost had taught me. I prostrated myself on the floor in the shape of the cross.

My Creator rose me up in ecstasy and revealed to me, "I Am, Who Am! It is I who created the universe purely out of my overflowing love." So saying, he infused in my mind a thorough and profound knowledge of his Creation. God showed me all that he had made on the first day of creation. I learned that God had created me, and all humankind, of low earthly matter, and I humbled myself before my God. "Pray constantly," he said, "for the union of the Divinity with human nature is now due."

Deeply moved, I exclaimed, "Oh eternal, God, the sins of man are increasing—how shall we merit the blessing of which we become daily more unworthy? If, perhaps I am a hindrance to such a limitless benefit, oh my, beloved, let me perish rather than impede your will!" I again prostrated myself on the floor in the form of a cross and began praying for the Redemption."

On each of the following six nights, I received the infused knowledge of the various works of God on the corresponding days of Creation. Then, he gave me comprehension and power over the elements of nature, such as the stars, winds, waters, minerals, plants and animals. However, since I cherished the value of sacrifice and suffering, and being ever humble before the Lord, I was never able to justify the use of such power for my own use. He next showed me the creation and fall of man. By my participation in God's love and mercy for sinning humanity, but unknown to me, God was preparing me to become the "Mother of Mercy" and the "Advocate of Sinners." God next revealed to me the new Law of Grace and the healing blessings, which he was going to pour on men through the Sacraments of his holy Church. I wept when he showed me how many souls would ungratefully reject the salvation, which the Redeemer was to offer them through his death.

I prayed fervently for all men and when I finished, the Holy Trinity said, "We promise you, our Spouse that the Son of God will soon be sent into the world."

The seventh night, God came to me again, and I heard him say, "Our chosen, dove, we wish to accept you anew as our bride, and therefore, we wish to adorn you worthily."

Before I could express my sincere, modest objections, two Seraphim proceeded to vest me with a beautiful white robe and bejeweled girdle, a golden-hair clasp, sandals, bracelets, rings, earrings, and a necklace. Each symbolized the various virtues that adorned my God-given spotless soul.

On the eighth night, I heard the voice of God saying, "Come, my chosen, one, come to me, I am he that raises the humble and fills the poor with riches. You have me for a friend. Since you have found grace in my eyes, ask of me what you desire, and I shall not reject your petition even if it be for a part of my Kingdom."

Most humbly I replied, "Oh, Lord, I do not ask for a part of your Kingdom on my own behalf, but I ask for the whole of it all for the race of men who are my brothers. Therefore, I humbly beseech you to send us our Redeemer."

The Lord answered me, "I desire what you seek, daughter. It shall be done as you ask."

I was afire with love and gratitude; I prayed unceasingly, except for the performance of my wifely duties, until the following midnight, the ninth day, when again the Lord called me to him. After revealing to me the entire harmonious constitution of the universe, God said to me, "My chosen, dove, I have created all creatures which you have beheld in all their variety and beauty, solely for the love of men, for the elect congregation of the faithful. You, my, spouse, have found grace in my sight, and therefore I make you Mistress of all these goods, so that if you are a loyal spouse, you may dispose of them as you desire."

The angels then placed a symbolic crown on my head, which bore the inscription, "Mother of God." However, God did not allow me to see these words. In spite of all these honors, I continued to humble and debase myself in my own self. All the heavenly spirits duly revered and honored me, much to my distress. However, at the same time knowing this was God's will, I humbly received the honors. Yet, I could not help but wonder why I, such a lowly person, should be accorded such honors? Lastly, the Lord renewed and increased the unique beauty of my pure soul, so that my entire being dazzlingly reflected God's own divine light evaluation. The more God gave me, the better I was able to discern my lowliness in comparison to the awesome majesty of my Creator. Therefore, I did not allow my mind, my eyes, and my heart to be elated. On the contrary, the higher God raised me up, the lowlier were my thoughts concerning my own worth. I did not have a suspicion of anything great or admirable in myself. In my heart and soul, as reflected in God's eyes, my humility was so genuine and so deep that even after all these honors, the mere thought of my being chosen to be the Mother of the Messiah simply had not and could not enter my Immaculate Heart. God had done his work well. God created me perfectly, and all the glory for this was God's, and is God's alone.

On the night of the 24th of March, the ninth day of Tishri, I retired as was my custom and slept for about four hours. Mary Salome was asleep in the other bedroom. Rising, it was now the 25th of March, the most important date in the history of humankind, I lit the branched lamp in its small alcove. Then I donned a long, white, woolen garment, such as was customary to wear during prayer. I placed a girdle about my waist, and donned an ivory-white veil over my head. My love for God burned in my heart even more intensely than before, and every day my soul was enkindled with new fervor and longing. Consequently, I had withdrawn even more to myself and spent much time at prayer. On the twenty-forth, I knew not why, I thought I would die and my heart would burst with love and longing, but God's Providence comforted me. He filled my soul with the firm hope that the Savior would soon descend from heaven. However, on the other hand, my humility made me fear lest my presence in the world might perhaps delay his coming. I was afraid that my lips might say or my ears might hear something against God, or my eyes see something evil. Even in my silence, I was timid and very anxious that I might be silent when I should rather speak. When I was thus troubled in heart, I committed all my hopes in God.

On the evening preceding this, at God's bidding, the Archangel Gabriel presented himself before the throne of God. The Blessed Trinity instructed him in the exact words with which he was to carry out his mission. God then announced to all the angels in Heaven that at last the time for man's Redemption had come. All the celestial beings were filled with joy and thanksgiving and they sang,

"Holy, Holy, Holy, art thou, Lord God."

Joseph had purchased a rush mat for my stone floor and I prostrated myself upon it in the shape of a cross, which habit I had developed in the Holy Temple. I begged the Lord that he might deign to allow me live long enough to see his Mother with my eyes, serve her with my hands, bow my head before her in reverence, and place myself completely at her service.

I began to meditate on the great power of God, how all the angels and all creatures serve him, and how indescribable and immense is his glory. While marveling over all of this, I suddenly perceived three wonderful things: I saw a star, but not like those that shine in the sky. It was a light greater and even brighter than the sun, yet unlike any light in this world. Then I inhaled a scent, but not one that comes from plants or anything of that nature. An utterly sweet and almost ineffable scent completely filled my soul and made me thrill with joy. Then I heard a voice, but not a human voice; suddenly the Archangel Gabriel appeared before me in the form of a most beautiful youth, yet not one of flesh and blood. He came in an effulgence of light and glory, and his feet hovered above the floor. I rose to my knees and would have bowed humbly and reverently to him, but he stopped me. Instead, he bowed profoundly before me. I was used to seeing my angels, so his appearance did not frighten me. God had given me one thousand guardian angels, and Gabriel was their leader, although he did not remain with me daily, as did my other angels. Even now my angels welcomed my visitor with profound respect, for Gabriel was a great Prince of Heaven.

With a benign smile, Gabriel greeted me. "Hail, full of grace, the Lord is with you. Blessed are you among women."

The angel's words troubled me, but I was not afraid. In my unworthiness, it was extremely difficult for me to accept such compliments, except humbly of course, since I realized this greeting came from Almighty God. From the midst of this light, I heard a voice say,

"You are to give birth to my Son!"

The voice then added, "Know in truth that I want others to have for you the reverence, which for love of me, you did want to have for someone else. I want you to be my Son's mother and giver, so that you will not only have him, but you will also be able to give him to whomever you wish."

The implication of God's words filled me with holy awe, so that I could hardly hold myself up. My angels steadied me and gave me strength. Then Gabriel spoke, "Do not be afraid, Mary, for you have found grace with God. Behold, you shall conceive in your womb, and shall bring forth a Son. You shall name him Jesus. He shall be great and shall be called the Son of the Most High. The Lord God will give him the throne of David, his father, and he shall be king over the House of Jacob forever. Of his Kingdom there shall be no end."

I slowly began to grasp the full significance of this tremendous grace. I raised my head to God and in all humbleness begged him for his help in such a crucial moment. My intuition told me that God, in order to test my faith, hope and charity in mystery, had at this moment purposefully left me without any other aid than the basic resources of my own human nature. I did not consider myself worthy. How could it happen that my unworthy self should become the Mother of God? Interiorly I mentioned to the Lord my vow of perpetual chastity and the mystical espousal that he had celebrated with me.

I asked the Archangel Gabriel, "How can this happen that I conceive and bear; since I know not, and have vowed before God never to know, man?"

Gabriel promptly answered me, "My Lady, it is easy for the divine power to make you a mother without the co-operation of man. The Holy Spirit shall come upon you, and the power of the Most

High shall overshadow you. Heaven and earth shall call this Child "The Son of God". Let it be known that your kinswoman Elizabeth has conceived a son in her sterile years; she who was barren is now in her sixth month. "The angel then stated in unison with my unsaid thoughts, "For nothing is impossible with God."

"He that can make Elizabeth conceive can bring it about that you, my, Lady, can be the mother of his Son. In addition, God has enhanced your virginity. To the Son, whom you shall bear, God will give the throne of his father David and his reign shall be everlasting in the house of Jacob. I remind you, my, Lady, of the prophecy of Isaiah [Is: 7-14] "that a virgin shall conceive and shall bear a son, whose name shall be Emmanuel, meaning God is with us." In you, God will fulfill Isaiah's infallible prophecy. In [Ex: 3-2], Moses saw a bush burning without its being consumed by the fire; this signified that the two natures divine and human are to be united in such a manner that the latter is not consumed by the divine, and that the mother of the Messiah shall give birth without violation of her virginal purity. Remember, also, Lady, the promise of the eternal God to the Patriarch Abraham that after the captivity of his posterity for four generations, they should return to this land. The mysterious signification of which, was that in this the fourth generation, the Incarnate God is to rescue the whole human race of Adam through your cooperation from the oppression of the devil. [Gen: 15-16]

Four generations: 1. Adam, without a mother or father: 2. Eve, without a mother, 3. Our own births from a mother and father: 4. And Jesus, from a mother without a father.]

It was revealed to me that the ladder which Jacob saw in his sleep was an express figure of the royal way, which the Eternal Word was to open up and by which the mortals are to ascend to heaven and the angels to descend to earth. To this earth the Onlybegotten of the Father shall lower himself in order to converse with men and communicate to them the treasures of his Divinity, imparting to them his virtues and his immutable and eternal perfections [Gen: 28-12].

The ambassador of heaven so instructed me in order that I might overcome any hesitancy that I might have; however, I, as the Queen of the Angels, exceeded them in wisdom, prudence and in all, sanctity. Therefore, I deliberately withheld my answer in order to comply in accordance with that of the divine will. Thus, would it be worthy of the greatest of all the mysteries and sacraments of the divine power. I reflected that upon my answer depended the pledge of the most blessed Trinity. This included the fulfillment of his promises and prophecies, and the most pleasing and acceptable of all sacrifices. The opening of the Gates of Paradise, his victory and triumph over hell, the redemption of the entire human race, the satisfaction of the divine justice, and the foundation of the new law of grace. It also meant the glorification of man, the rejoicing of the angels, and many other things connected with the Incarnation of the Onlybegotten of the Father, and his assuming the form of servant in my virginal womb. Almighty God entrusted all these mysterious to me, a humble maiden, and then awaited my decision.

Upon hearing these words and without any doubts whatsoever that what he said was true, I suddenly felt in my heart an exceedingly fervent desire to be the Mother of God. I prostrated myself upon the floor and then rising to my knees, with my hands joined, I worshipped God and my soul cried forth with love and I exclaimed," Behold the handmaid of the Lord. Let it be done to me according to your word."

A celestial light suddenly filled the room, dissolving the ceiling and revealing the heavens. In a dazzling beam, I could see the Blessed Trinity. The Holy Spirit appeared in a winged form, and masses of flame shot out like wings on his right and left. Then three intense rays flashed and darted into my right side, and I became suffused with a glorious, glowing light.

I had never before experienced such bliss and joy in my soul! Then, in that moment of ecstasy, God the Father gave me his Son. As I spoke my acceptance, the grace of the Holy Spirit overwhelmed me, I instantly conceived the Redeemer of the world in my womb, and Jesus became flesh in my purified body. God had created me perfectly in order that an unclean vessel would not defile his Son. An inexpressible rapture filled my soul and my whole body. I humbled myself in every way for I knew that the one whom I bore in my womb was the Almighty. His work done, the Archangel Gabriel left in the blink of an eye. As he vanished, a rain of white rose petals fell on and around me, but I was oblivious to everything. At this same moment, I was rapt in a marvelous vision in which the Holy Trinity revealed to me the mystery of the hypostatic union of the divine and human natures in the Person of the Eternal Word. They then confirmed me in the title and rights as the "Mother of God." The future mysteries of the life and death of my Son, the Redeemer of the human race, were then shown to me in a vision.

I was lost in humility and burning love. I adored the Lord and gave him my most fervent thanks for thus being favored, as well as thanking the Lord for the entire human race. I offered myself as a willing sacrifice in the rearing and service of my Son throughout his life on earth. In order that I might be guided in all my actions as becomes the Mother of God, I prayed for new graces and light.

The Lord answered me, "My, dove, do not fear, for I will assist you and guide you in all things necessary for the service of my only begotten Son."

It was a beautiful spring morning and dawn was just breaking. The blue flowers of the flax plant covered the gentle rolling hills of Galilee. On this day, Almighty God consecrated to himself a pure and humble Jewish girl of Nazareth that he himself had created for this very purpose. In so doing, he created a new sanctuary and fulfilled in me the words of the Prophet King,

"The Most High hath sanctified his own tabernacle. God is in the midst thereof."

Only the heavenly spirits and I witnessed this great mystery, a mystery of which the rest of the world was ignorant. However, at this magic hour the Lord infused into the hearts of some of the just men on earth a new feeling of extraordinary joy and inspiration, though each one thought he and he alone experienced this inner renewal of spirit. Throughout the whole of nature, there was a remarkable stir and movement on that blessed morning when Nature's God became man.

I finally came back to myself after having been in a state of ecstasy for hours. My first action was to kneel humbly and offer profound adoration of the Word Incarnate within my womb. Then after a long interval, I rose, in my new role as the Mother of God. I went to my little altar and for the first time, I remained standing while I prayed. Dawn was nearly breaking when with a little sigh of joy; I went up to the roof where it was cool and lay down on a mat, completely exhausted of body and spirit.

The visitation

I awoke the next morning to the gentle sounds of doves cooing. Through the lattice of woven branches above me, I could see a fleecy layer of high cirrus clouds. A pleasant cool breeze stirred the air, and from the village, I could hear the sound of a baby crying. I just lay there for a moment. As often happened, a flock of birds suddenly flocked about me greeting me with their lively movements. As if wishing to congratulate me, they divided into harmonious choirs, chirped and sang sweetly to me. In their beaks, they gathered flowers and dropped them in my hands. I told them to join me in praise and thanks to our Creator for bringing the Redeemer into the world; they bowed their heads and joined me in my morning prayers.

The strident call of a rooster announcing the new day startled me from my reverie. With a start, I realized it was time to get up. I jumped up, my mind was churning with the magnitude of the blessing the Almighty had bestowed upon me. I dropped to my knees, as I did each morning, and prayed, "My, Lord and my, God, I give you my mind, my heart and my soul. Do with me as you will." After dressing, I again knelt in quick prayer, and rising, hastened to perform my wifely duties. My first responsibility was to prepare the morning meal. Not for a moment did I believe that I should break the news of my divine pregnancy to Joseph or to Mary Salome. I would have known if God wished me to reveal this miraculous event. Since I realized I was not to tell anyone, I feared lest my glowing countenance and mien should betray me.

After our breakfast, Joseph thanked God for our food, and said to me, "My dear, Mary you seem to glow with an inner fire. What is so special about today?" His face reflected his love and devotion.

Mary Salome joined in and added, "You are right, Joseph, I have never seen Mary look lovelier."

With downcast eyes, I responded with all honesty, "Why should I not glow, my friends, God has given me everything. In addition, in a vision last night, the Archangel Gabriel informed me that my cousin Elizabeth is going to have a baby. She is in her sixth month."

Joseph exclaimed, "God be praised, but, how can this be? Elizabeth is an old woman well past her child-bearing years."

"It is a miraculous conception, Joseph. Do you not remember Abraham and Sarah? All things are possible to God. Their child will be special in the eyes of the Lord. Mary Salome was awe-stricken for she had witnessed a phenomenon far beyond her ability to comprehend. I asked them, "Will you both join with me in thanksgiving to our Lord and God for this blessing to our family and for a special intention granted me, for which I have prayed for many years?"

As we prayed, I interiorly asked my guardian angels to join us in our divine praises to our Creator. I knew that in addition to our prayers for Elizabeth and Zachariah, even if he did not know what my special intention was that they both should participate in praising God for his benevolent mercy in sending his only Son to be our Lord and Redeemer. Elizabeth was now much older than my mother was, when I was born. In true submission, I asked Joseph. "With your permission, Joseph, may we hasten to Elizabeth? She is fifty nine years old, and she will need my help."

During my absence, Mary Salome decided to return to her home. After taking me to Jutta, where Zachariah lived, Joseph would return and continue with his carpentry work and maintain the house. Joseph began at once to load the ass for our journey. I prepared some provisions consisting of some fruit, bread and a few smoked fish. Just before we left, I dropped to the floor on my knees before Joseph and asked for his blessing. Despite his protests, I insisted, and within an hour, accompanied by my thousand invisible guardian angels, we set out on the road to Jerusalem. From there, we would proceed to Jutta.

Before we left my angels appeared to me and said, "Now our, Lady, you are the true Ark of the Covenant. We wish to obey you as true servants of the supreme Lord, whose mother you are." Indeed they already served me, for whenever I ate alone; they served me my modest meals, and would have done my housework had I allowed them. It was God's will that I visit Elizabeth, for he had informed me that their son would be a great prophet and forerunner of the Messiah. It was God's will that the Redeemer, held secure in my womb, was to sanctify Elizabeth and John upon his arrival.

I felt much too alive to consider riding, and I begged Joseph to allow me to walk for awhile. Always solicitous of my welfare, Joseph gave in with good grace. The dew had been unusually heavy that morning. I slipped off my sandals and walked along the edge of the path in a patch of dew-heavy grass enjoying the chilled water on my bare feet. Everything was gloriously green and fresh, and

I breathed in the pure, cool air with the greatest of pleasure. As I walked along swishing my feet through the wet grass, I fantasized what my Son and Elizabeth's son would be like. All too soon the trail gave way to the usual rock-strewn course and upon Joseph's expressed concern for my wellbeing; I obediently put on my sandals and mounted our beast of burden. My joy was brimming over, and once mounted my daydreams quickly gave way to a litany glorifying the Holy Trinity.

It was a four days journey to Zachariah's home. I often dismounted, and urged Joseph to ride the Muscat ass, but he stubbornly refused my offer. It felt good to dismount and walk occasionally, for after awhile riding became just as tiring as walking. It was late March, and the winter had given way to a glorious spring. The rolling hills all around us were in bloom with the blue blossoms of the versatile flax plant. As we moved along grain fields took their place, interspersed with orchards of olive trees and grapevines. Herds of goats and sheep dotted the hillsides and altogether, in spite of the rough going, I thoroughly enjoyed the trip. Already a few farmers were sowing their spring crop, and we sometimes stopped for a rest and talked with those not too busy. I often conversed and prayed silently with my angels, and Joseph and I had long talks about the coming of the Messiah. I was able to provide him with an entirely new understanding and love of God, and I realized that the Word Incarnate was giving him unusual graces.

Our first innkeeper was most kind and gracious, and I had many opportunities to visit the poor and the sick, who we frequently encountered along the route. The second night, the innkeeper was rude and overbearing, but we gave him our blessings and just as we were ready to leave, I learned that his daughter was ill with a bad fever. I attended to her needs and prayed over her asking my Son to heal her. Suddenly, healed by my Son's good graces, she sat up and asked for something to eat. We were gone before the surly innkeeper knew what had happened; however, in gratitude the innkeeper amended his churlish ways. The roads were not jammed with people, but we were always passing those heading into Galilee. We passed several long caravans, and I veiled myself from the course men who sometimes worked as drovers. Their language was often crude and expressive as they herded their charges along the Damascus Road.

We soon climbed the winding road to the ridge known as the Saddle of Benjamin where the beautiful hills and valleys of Galilee gave way to the rough, rock-strewn Judean Hills. My heart yearned to revisit the temple in Jerusalem and there give glory to God for his blessings. In the distance, the Temple of the Lord beckoned enticingly, but we did not stop. It gleamed like a golden diadem and Joseph and I sang the praises of God as long as the dome was within sight. At last, about two leagues from Jerusalem, we spied Jutta, the Levitical City where many priestly families lived. As we neared the home of Zachariah, Joseph hurried ahead to announce our visit. I had never visited Elizabeth in her home in Jutta, but had visited them at their residence in Jerusalem and their summer home near Nazareth. Their house was located in the middle of a lovely garden on an isolated slope. It was a home worthy of a high priest of Israel.

As Joseph came up to the house, he called out, "The Lord be with you and fill your souls with divine grace."

Elizabeth had been sitting in the garden eagerly awaiting our arrival. The Lord himself had forewarned her of our coming. However, I soon learned the mystery of the Incarnation had not yet been revealed to her. Elizabeth, in spite of her condition, sprang up eagerly to greet me. Being younger in years, and considering Elizabeth's condition, I hastened to her, saying," The Lord be with you, my dearest, cousin."

We met near a fountain and clasped hands affectionately. My cousin was nearly as tall as I was, and in spite of her advanced years, she had a sweet face and small, delicate features. With her gray hair, she was regal looking, a fit companion for her tall, handsome husband. Suddenly, I became suffused with a mystic light, and a bright ray went forth from me to Elizabeth, which had an extraordinary effect on her as she replied, "May the same Lord reward you for having come in order to give me this pleasure."

Taking my hand, my cousin led me to the house where she again welcomed me and invited me to enter. Once inside Elizabeth and I cast all pretenses aside and threw our arms around each other and remained for some time in a warm embrace. My heart went out to Elizabeth, and I said warmly, "May God save you, my dearest, cousin, and his Divine Light give you grace and life."

The soul of Elizabeth was flooded with the Holy Spirit when I spoke to her. The Holy Spirit revealed to her the mystery of the Incarnation, my unique dignity, and her own son's sanctification. John had already attained a state of great natural perfection, a state much greater than that of other children. All this was due to the miracle of the conception by his sterile mother, and because of the intention of the Most High to make him the depository of greater sanctity than all other men, except my Son. John's soul; however, still carried the stain of original sin, the sin, which he had contracted in the same manner as the other children of Adam, the first and common father of the human race. Upon the sound of my greeting, my Son conferred the light of his grace and justification upon John. He wished John, in his office of Precursor and Baptist, to be as distinguished in purity, as I was.

The Holy Ghost looked upon the child in the womb of Elizabeth and gave the child perfect use of reason. He enlightened the baby with his divine light so that the child might prepare himself with the foreknowledge of the blessings he was about to receive. The baby in Elizabeth's womb immediately did so, praising and glorifying Almighty God. God then sanctified John from original sin, made him an adopted Son of God, and filled him with the most abundant graces of the Holy Ghost. With the plentitude of all his gifts; his faculties were sanctified, subjected and subordinated to reason, thus verifying in himself what the archangel Gabriel had said to Zachariah that his son would be filled with the Holy Spirit from the womb of his mother [Luke: 1, 12-17]. The fortunate child was able to look through the walls of our maternal wombs as through clear glass upon the Incarnate Word lying in my womb. Joyfully he leapt to a kneeling position. John beheld his Redeemer in my most holy womb as if my Son was enclosed in a chamber made of the purest crystal, and he adored him. Elizabeth felt John's leap of jubilation, and this indwelling of the Holy Spirit inspired the beginning of the Magnificat, which was the name given the dialogue between Elizabeth and me. John performed many other acts of virtue during this meeting. He exercised faith, hope, charity, worship, gratitude, humility, devotion, and all the other virtues possible to him there. John began at once to merit and grew in sanctity without ever losing it, and without ever ceasing to exercise it with all the vigor of grace.

At this same moment, Elizabeth also saw my virginal purity and the great dignity conferred upon me by my Lord and God. I was absorbed in a vision of the Divinity and of the mysteries operated by it through my most Holy Son. Elizabeth saw me filled with the majesty of our Creator, and like her son, saw the Incarnate Word in my womb. John was the third person for whom my Son made a special petition to his Father in Heaven. The first had been for me upon his Incarnation, and the second had been for Joseph, his foster father.

Upon hearing my voice, John leapt to his knees rapt in joy and began worshipping my Son. Elizabeth looked at me reverently and stepping back a little in awe, lifted her hands, and exclaimed with an expression of deep humility, happiness, and inspiration,

"Blessed are you among women, and blessed is the fruit of your womb. How have I deserved that the mother of my Lord should come to me? For behold, the moment the sound of your greeting came to my ears, the babe in my womb leapt for joy. Blessed is she who has believed, because all things promised her by the Lord, will be accomplished."

Inspired by the Holy Spirit, an extraordinary joy filled my heart, which caused me to speak words about God that I myself did not devise. Crossing my hands on my breast, I raised my eyes to heaven and spoke the words inscribed in my heart by the Holy Spirit,

"My soul magnifies the Lord, and my spirit rejoices in God my Savior. He has regarded the lowliness of his handmaid, and behold, henceforth, all generations shall call me blessed. For he who is mighty has done great things for me and holy is his name. His mercy is from generation to generation, for those who fear him. He has shown the might of his arm, and he has scattered the proud in the conceit of their hearts. He has put down the mighty from their thrones, and has exalted the lowly. He has filled the hungry with good things, and the rich he has sent empty away. He has received Israel, his servant; being mindful of his mercy; as he spoke to our fathers, to Abraham and to his posterity forever. Amen."

These inspired words were firmly etched in our minds, and Elizabeth and I never forgot them, and they later become known as the Magnificat. John and his mother, being the first to hear this sweet canticle from our lips were the first to understand it. Elizabeth and I, in the next three months, had many hours to discuss and explore the depths of these words. We shared the secret of my pregnancy, and while we privately discussed my Son at great length, neither of us divulged the information to our spouses. Elizabeth was concerned about the fact that I was not yet married, and together we determined that I was in the hands of God. When God wished this situation resolved, he would show us the way.

Immediately after we spoke our inspired words, Elizabeth exclaimed, "Oh, Mary, the fervor of the Holy Spirit is in me."

I replied, "Indeed, my dear, cousin. The grace of God is with us both," and we praised God's Holy Name. Then Elizabeth offered herself, her family, and her house for my service, asking me to take as a quiet retreat, the room, which she herself was accustomed to use as an oratory for her prayers. The room I accepted with gratitude, but I explained to my cousin, "I am not here to be served, Elizabeth, but to serve. I will be your personal maid, for that is the purpose of my visit." When she started to protest I insisted, and to change the subject, I asked her if there was one favor she would grant?

She eagerly responded, "Anything, my dear, Mary, anything you wish."

The only thing I had been concerned about was my prayer time, and I need not have been concerned, every day Elizabeth prayed for hours to our Lord.

In the garden, Joseph greeted Zachariah with great respect. Zachariah responded by writing his greetings on a tablet, and proceeded to write and explain all that had happened to him. After awhile the two came inside to greet me. I asked Zachariah for his blessing, which he gave to me silently, while placing his hands on my head.

After a few days rest, Joseph returned to Nazareth to take care of the needs of his many customers. Elizabeth and I began a relationship that in some ways was closer than that with which I had with my own mother. After all, I had known my mother only as a child and not as an adult. Of course, even then I had the full use of reason, and while Elizabeth and I were extremely close, there was only one Anne, my saintly mother, and no one could ever take her place. I remember the day well when Elizabeth asked me,

"Mary, may I presume to ask you for a great favor?"

"You have but to ask and it is yours, my dear, cousin." I replied.

"Would it be too much of an imposition to ask you to sew and prepare the swaddling clothes and coverlets in which my son is to be wrapped?"

I was overjoyed to comply with her requests in order to exercise myself in complete obedience to my cousin. I wished to serve her as her lowliest handmaid, for in obedience and humility I was destined to surpass all creatures. Elizabeth and I had quickly begun a great and sweet competition, which I found out later, was most pleasing to our Lord and wonderful in the sight of the angels. Elizabeth, knowing I was the Mother of God, wanted to serve me in every way possible. I, in turn, wished only to serve her in her time of need. The mistress of the house had requested that her family and her friends were to serve me at every opportunity. I had come to serve Elizabeth as a personal maid and companion. I knew, in her advanced age that Elizabeth needed and would appreciate my support. It was up to me to meet and divert the anxieties of my cousin and I said to her,

"My dear, cousin, during all my life I have found my consolation in taking orders and in serving others. It is not good that your love should deprive me of this comfort. I feel since I am the younger one, it is proper that I serve not only you, as my mother, but I should serve all in the house as a servant as long as I am in your company."

Elizabeth replied, "My beloved, lady, it would be more proper if I obey you, and that you command and direct me in all things. This I ask in all justice, for if you, the Mistress, wish to exercise humility, I on my part owe worship and reverence to my God and Lord, whom you bear in your virginal womb. I know that your dignity is worthy of all honor and reverence."

I quietly countered with the facts of the situation, "My Son did not choose me for his mother, in order that I might receive reverence as mistress. His Kingdom is not of this world. He desires to serve and suffer for all humankind in order to teach obedience and humility to mortals while condemning fastidiousness and pride. Since his Majesty teaches me this, and the Highest calls himself the ignominy of men, how can I, who am but his slave and do not merit the company of creatures, consent that you serve me?"

However, Elizabeth still persisted and argued, "My, mistress and, protectress, this is true for those who do not know the sacrament which is enclosed in you. But I, having been informed by the Lord, will be very blamable in his eyes if I do not give the reverence due to him as God, and to you as his mother; in serving both of you as a slave serves his masters."

To this I responded, "My dear, sister, this reverence which you owe and desire to give is due the Lord, whom I bear within my womb, for he is the true and highest Good and Redeemer. However, as far as I am concerned, I am only a mere creature and the lowliest among them. By his divine enlightenment you shall give unto God what is due to him, and allow me to perform that, which my Son desires of me, namely to serve and be below all. This I ask of you for my consolation and in the name of the Lord, whom I bear within me.

It was in such blessed and happy contentions that Elizabeth and I spent some of our time together. However, the divine prudence invested in me caused me such alertness and ingenuity in matters concerning humility and obedience that I never failed to devise methods to extract commands from my associates and then humbly obey them. In spite of our vigilant pursuit for humility; however, neither of us lost sight of the presence of the Lord in my womb. God had entrusted this knowledge to only the two of us. The high respect I rendered the Lord was such as befitted the mother and mistress of all virtue and grace, and Elizabeth, no less enlightened by the Holy Spirit, was just as respectful. Directed by his divine light, she wisely yielded to my wishes and obeyed me in whatever way she could, and reverenced my dignity. In so doing, she also reverenced her Creator. She never requested that I do anything except to comply with my wishes, and only then after she had asked permission and pardon of the Lord, at the same time never ordering anything by direct command. It took a great deal of tact and diplomacy for me to remain the humble servant of the least of Elizabeth's household. However, only by serving would I be able to set the example for all humanity, as desired by my Lord and Creator.

Simply by being present in the house of my cousin was I able to assist a neighbor of Elizabeth's. Her name was Ruth, but when I met her she had none of the attributes of her namesake. She was wont to come and listen to the conversation of the family of Elizabeth. Ruth lived a licentious life, far from honorable. When she heard the nice things being said about me, she spoke of me with some curiosity,

"Who is this stranger that has come as a guest of our neighbors, and who gives herself such holy airs?" Setting action to her question, she concealed herself in such a manner that she was able to observe me quite closely. Of course, my angels informed me of this fact; at once, I began praying for her soul. Her eyes scrutinized my manner of dress and my countenance. Her manner was impertinent and presumptuous; but far different was the effect, for she returned home with a wounded heart. In gazing upon my holiness, the Lord had transformed Ruth into a new woman. Ruth's inclinations were altogether changed, and without knowing by what efficacious influence the change came about, she felt its power and began to shed abundant floods of tears in deep-felt sorrow for her sins. God had removed the scales from Ruth's eyes, enabling her to see my virginal purity. My purity freed her from the sensual habits and inclinations of her former life. Then God made me aware of what had happened and in my office as Advocate of Sinners, I received her with maternal kindness, admonished her, and instructed her in virtue. When I left the home of Zachariah, I left Ruth, strengthened and confirmed in perseverance in her new life.

It was not long before I found ways to help Elizabeth's relatives, who had also come to assist her in much the same way as I had done with my companions in the temple. Several times a day, I happily swept out Elizabeth's oratory, helped the others wash the dishes and performed as many menial tasks as possible. I concealed my efforts from Elizabeth so as not to upset her. Fortunately, I had time to myself, and with the Blessed Lord in my womb, I passed many hours ravished and elevated above the floor in divine contemplation, and was blessed with one vision after another. I had many conversations with my angels, and a month to the day after my arrival, I spoke to them about my love for the Divinity,

"Heavenly Spirits, my guardians and companions, Ambassadors of the Most High and Luminaries of his Divinity, come and strengthen my heart, which is captured and wounded by his divine love. The limitations of my heart sorely afflict me. In spite of the obligations, which dictate its desires, I am unable to properly respond. Let us talk of the wonders of my divine Spouse; let us discuss the beauty of my Lord, and of my beloved Son! Let my heart find relief in uniting its inmost aspirations to your own, my friends and companions. For you know the secrets of my Treasure, which the Lord has deposited within me in the narrowness of so fragile and constrained a vase. Great are these sacraments and admirable these mysteries; and I contemplate them with sweet affection, but their supernal greatness overwhelms me. The profundity and the greatness of my love overpowers me, even while they inflame my heart. In the ardor of my soul, I cannot rest satisfied, and I find no repose; for my desires surpass all that I can accomplish and my obligations are greater than my desires. I am dissatisfied with myself, because I do not exert myself as much as I desire. I do not accomplish as much as I should, and I find myself continually falling short and vanquished by the greatness of the returns that are due. I am fallen sick with love, my living, Seraphim; open to me your bosoms, whence the beauty of my God is flashed forth, in order that the splendors of his light and visions of his loveliness may replenish the life, which wastes away in his love."

My angels responded, "Mother, of our Creator and our, Mistress, you possess truly the Almighty and our highest Good. Since you have him so closely bound to you and are his true spouse and mother, rejoice in him and keep him with you for all eternity. You are the spouse and the mother of the God of love. You carry in you, Jesus, the only cause and fountain of life; no one shall live with him as you our Queen and Mistress. However, do not seek to find repose in a love so inflamed; for your state and condition of a *pilgrim* does not permit your love to attain the repose of perfect consummation, nor will it cease to aspire to new and greater increase of merit and triumph. Your obligations to God surpass without comparison those of all the nations. These obligations will increase and grow so continually that even your vastly inflamed love will never equal its object. God is eternal and infinite, without measure in his perfection, and you shall always be happily vanquished by his greatness, for no one can comprehend it. Only God can love himself in the measure in which he deserves to be loved, and you oh, Lady, shall eternally find in him more to desire and more to love since that is required by the essence of his greatness and of our beatitude."

Each evening Elizabeth joined me in the oratory. Standing facing each other with our arms crossed on our chests, we recited the Magnificat together. Sometimes we spent nearly the entire night together in prayer. Usually I would sleep until midnight and then rise and pray until morning, I know that on several occasions Elizabeth merited seeing me in ecstasy, when I was raised above the floor and radiant with supernatural splendor and beauty. God so lavished his glory upon me that Elizabeth could not have looked upon my face, nor remained alive in my presence, if God had not strengthened her by his divine power. I know that she often would come when I was praying, careful not to disturb me, and prostrate herself and adore the Incarnate Word in my most holy, virginal womb. We often ate our evening meal in their lovely garden during the early summer months. Then we would take a walk through the surrounding fields and hills before retiring for the night, but we all arose before sunrise.

As Elizabeth's time drew near she become most anxious and pleaded with me, "Cousin, dear, lady, on account of the respect and consideration with which I am bound to serve you, I have not until now dared to speak of my desire and the sorrow in my heart, Give me now your permission to make my desires known?"

I replied kindly, "Speak my dear, Elizabeth, who has a better right?"

She responded, "You are the living Temple of God's glory, the Ark of the Testament, containing the manna, which is the food of the angels. His Majesty has enriched me without any merit on my part by allowing me to entertain you both in my home, the Treasure of heaven and her, whom he has chosen as his mother among all women. I justly fear that I displease you and the fruit of your womb by my sins, and that you will forsake me, withdrawing the happiness of serving you and remaining with you all the rest of my life. Call your intended Joseph and live with him here as my masters. I will serve you with affectionate readiness of heart. I beseech you not to despise my humble petition."

I listened with love and sympathy and replied, "Dearest, friend, of my soul, your holy wishes is acceptable in the eyes of the Lord. I also thank you from the bottom of my heart; but in all our undertakings it is also necessary that we conform to the divine will and entirely subject ourselves to it."

Elizabeth replied plaintively, "Please, dear, cousin, at least stay with me until after my son's birth. Let me see my child in your arms; Let me behold my child in your arms where the God, who made and preserves heaven and earth, is likewise to rest. Do not deny this consolation to me, or this great happiness to my son."

I felt obligated to Joseph to return to Nazareth, but as usual left my life in the hands of the Blessed Lord, and I prudently replied, "Nothing would please me more, my dear, Elizabeth, but I have obligations to my husband, and the will of my Lord always comes first. Let us both pray to the Lord and subject ourselves to his divine will."

Elizabeth readily agreed and that very night the Lord placed me in ecstasy where I was enlightened anew concerning the mysterious life and the dignity of John the Precursor, and he also informed me of the great sanctity of my cousin Elizabeth. God advised me that Elizabeth only had a short time to live, and that Zachariah would die before her. I begged the Lord to fulfill Elizabeth's wishes regarding her son, but in my God-given wisdom I knew it was not advisable according to the will of the Most High to recommend Elizabeth's other request.

The Lord then said, "My, dove, it is my pleasure that you assist and console my servant Elizabeth at her childbirth, which is to happen eight days hence. At his birth, you shall offer to me my servant John in pleasing sacrifice; and continue, my beloved, to pray to me for the salvation of souls. After John is circumcised, return to your home in Nazareth."

While Elizabeth united her prayers with mine, the Lord revealed to her, that her confinement was near at hand and informed her of many other things to relieve and console her for her anxiety.

After our prayers, I conferred with Elizabeth and she asked anxiously, "My, lady, pray tell me whether I shall have the happiness of your assistance at my impending confinement?"

I answered, "My beloved, cousin, the Most High has heard our prayers and deigned to command me to assist on that occasion. This I will do, not only remaining till then, but also until the circumcision of your child, which will take place in sixteen days." Elizabeth was happy and began at once to prepare not only for the pending birth, but also for my departure, since it was necessary for her to send word to Nazareth as to when Joseph was to come for me.

During my stay with Elizabeth, I was to witness many instances where my holy sanctity influenced and changed the souls of many of those with whom I came in contact. One of Elizabeth's friends, by the name of Rachel, was of a most perverse inclination. She was restless, subject to anger, and accustomed to swear and curse. With all of these vices and disorders, she was always shrewd enough to make herself agreeable to Elizabeth and Zachariah. For fourteen years many devils surrounded and accompanied her without let up in order to make certain of her soul. However, these spirits could not come into my presence. The virtue emanating from my person always tormented them, and their torment was especially bad, because I carried the Redeemer in my womb. The woman found peace and solace only in my presence. Consequently, she became most attracted to me, and she sought to be in my presence. While she had many bad inclinations, she also had a very good one. Rachel had a natural kindness and compassion for the needy and the poor, and was always ready to do them good.

I saw and understood Rachel's need and I watched over and prayed for her with the eye of a mother. I begged the Lord to give her release and he replied, "The Company and the interference with the soul of this woman is a just punishment for her sins. However, for you, I grant her pardon, remedy, and salvation."

I immediately commanded the demons to leave Rachel and not dare disturb or molest her henceforth. They yielded, not able to resist the sway of their Queen, and they fled in the highest consternation. They later conferred about it with astonishment and indignation saying, "Who is this woman that exerts such dominion over us. Where does she get such strange powers, which enables her to perform all that she wishes?" The demons then plotted even worse maladies against Rachel, but I, who had crushed their heads, sent them back to their abode in the earth never to return [Gen: 3, 15].

I admonished Rachel, "The demons have been taken from you by the power of the Lord; however, unless you amend your life many more will come to take their place and you will be worse off than before." Rachel fell at my feet bathed in tears, and I instructed her in the ways of the Lord and in a short time, she changed into a woman of kind and gentle disposition. I am happy to report, she persevered and remained humbly thankful and lived a holy life.

I was most fortunate, for many persons who merely came into my presence, were justified and enlightened by the grace of God. The Creator often gave me the power to penetrate the secrets of hearts, and I would know the remedy needed to correct their faults. Sometimes, but not always, the Lord manifested to me the final end of those I met, advising me which were chosen and which were reprobate, predestined for happiness or foreknown as damned. At the sight of the chosen ones, my heart burst forth in canticles of praise. For the just and predestined, I bestowed upon them many blessings, which I still do from heaven, and the Lord looks upon these blessings with beneficence. God granted me the justification of many that I found in sin. For the reprobates, I wept bitterly and humiliated myself in the presence of the Most High for the loss of that *image and work* of the Divinity. My entire being was of one aflame with divine love, which never rested in the hope of accomplishing great things.

God found favor with Elizabeth. She grew in the knowledge and understanding of the mysteries of the Incarnation, by being in the constant presence of my Son and me. This great matron advanced in all manner of sanctity, as a sponge draws water from its source. As these mysteries that became known to her by the divine light, Elizabeth sealed up in her bosom, being a most faithful depository and prudent secretary of that which was confided to her. Only with Zachariah and her son John did she later converse to some extant concerning these events. In all things, she acted as a courageous, wise and very holy woman. As for myself, I had moments that troubled me. God endowed me, a mere creature, with more knowledge of his world than all the rest of the human race put together. I knew why the Messiah had to come, and why it was necessary for him to die, yet I was his mother, and even if God had made me perfect in his image, I was still a mother with all the protective instincts of motherhood.

A week before Elizabeth was due, I again conferred with my angels, and as they often did, they become visible to me in human form. They often appeared before me as exquisitely-beautiful, teenagers. I was troubled and I complained and asked them, "My, lords, servants of the Most High, my heart is pierced and torn by arrows of grief, when I meditate on what the sacred Scriptures say of my most Holy Son, or what Isaiah and Jeremiah wrote concerning the bitter pains and torments in store for him. Solomon says that they shall condemn him to a most ignominious death and the Prophets always speak in weighty and superlative terms of his Passion and death, which are all to be fulfilled in him. Oh only if I could live at the time of his death in order to offer myself to die instead of the Author of my life. My soul is sorely afflicted in the consideration of these infallible truths and that my God and my Lord should come forth from my womb only in order to suffer. Who will guard and defend him against his enemies? How, my heavenly princes, can I induce the eternal Father to divert the rigor of his Justice upon me, and relieve my innocent Son from punishment, he, who is without guilt? Well do I know that in order to satisfy the Infinite God for the offenses of men the satisfaction of the Incarnate God is required. However, by his first act my most holy Son has merited more than the entire human race can lose by its offenses. Since this is sufficient, tell me, is it not possible that I die in order to relieve him from his death and torments? My humble desires will not be annoying to my God, and my anxieties will not be displeasing to him. *Yet, what am I saying? Moreover, to what lengths do sorrow and love drive me, since I must be subject in all things to the divine will and its perfect fulfillment?* [Gen: 22, 2] [Wis: 2, 20]

My angel friends comforted me, reminding me of the reasonableness and propriety of the death of Christ for the salvation of the human race, which of course I already knew. However, no one, except a mother can understand the anguish I felt when I contemplated the future, ignominious death of my Son. So deep and exalted were some of our discussions that neither can the human tongue describe, nor our capacities comprehend them in this life. When we shall enjoy the Lord, we shall see what we cannot at present conceive. From this little which I have said, our piety can help us to draw conclusions in regards to things even greater.

The day had arrived for the rising of the morning star that was to precede the clear Sun of Justice and announce the wished-for day of the law of grace. [John: 5, 35] The time was suitable to the Most High for the appearance of his Prophet in the world. John was greater than any prophet was, since it was he who was to point out with his finger the Lamb of God. [John: 1, 15] The Lord had revealed to John in his mother's womb when he was to commence his mortal career among men. The Incarnate Word, when Elizabeth and I first met, had given John the perfect use of his reason and knowledge of the divine science. John knew, therefore that he was to arrive at the port of a cursed and dangerous land. He knew he had to make his *pilgrim walk* in a world full of evils and snares. John had doubts of wishing to enter such a world, but at the same time, the will of his Creator was by far the most compelling, and John overcame his fear of leaving the protection of the maternal womb and prayed,

"Bestow, Lord, your blessing for my passage into the world."

Elizabeth did not call for me to be present at the birth of her son. Her reverence for my dignity, and for the fruit within my womb, prudently withheld her from asking, what, in her opinion, might not be regarded as befitting. When I heard she was in labor, I sent her the coverings and swaddling clothes that I had made for the baby. With only moderate pains on the part of his mother, the child was born, perfect and complete. Elizabeth insisted on personally wrapping her son in the clothes I sent her, and I knew she kept and maintained them as holy relics the rest of her life, as did her heirs. When all was in order, Elizabeth sent for me. She desperately desired that I hold her child in my arms and bless him, as I had promised, and as God had so ordained. Inwardly, the child showed me every reverence, for he was well aware of the privilege granted him by the Lord. He prayed and performed acts of fervent thanksgiving, humility, love and reverence of God and me, his spiritual, Virgin Mother. God caught me up in a secret ecstasy, as I took John in my arms. I silently spoke this prayer, which only God could hear, and which, at the same time, God divinely revealed to Elizabeth.

"Highest, Lord and, Father, all holy and powerful, accept in your honor this offering and seasonable fruit of your most holy Son and my Lord. Your Onlybegotten Son, by sanctification rescued John from the effects of sin and from the power of your ancient enemies. Receive this morning's sacrifice and infuse into this child the blessings of your Holy Spirit in order that he may be a faithful minister to you and to your Son." As I spoke, I was aware of the many blessings with which the Lord was enriching his Precursor.

God revealed my prayer to Elizabeth when she saw me holding up her child in blessing. At that moment, Elizabeth and I formed a sweet tie of affection that has never waned. The baby snuggled in my bosom, and my arms ached for the touch of my own child, soon to be born. The child manifested the joy of his spirit, and he clung to me and sought my caresses and I knew he desired to remain with me, for while Elizabeth was his mother of the flesh, I was his mother of the spirit. I refrained from kissing him, although I dearly wished to do so, but I preserved my chaste lips intact for my most holy Son. I also did not look directly into his face focusing all of my attention to the holiness of his soul. My prudence and modesty in the use of my eyes did not allow me the joy of photographing his face in my memory, and later, I would scarcely have known him by sight, although his soul was indelibly impressed in my heart. My eyes were for the Lord and the Lord alone. I refrained from looking directly on the face of any person, which was also a custom of the women of Israel, for a woman was expected to drop her eyes modestly when meeting those strange to her. The only exception I had made to this was with Joseph, which I knew was according to God's wishes.

Once the birth of the high priest's child became known, all the relations and acquaintances gathered to congratulate Zachariah and Elizabeth, for his house was rich, noble and honored in the whole province. Their piety had attracted the hearts of all that knew them. The fact that Elizabeth was sterile and childless was common knowledge. Because of Elizabeth's advanced age, everyone looked upon the birth of the child rather as a miracle than as a natural event. Unfortunately, the noble priest remained mute and was still not able to manifest his joy by word of mouth, since the hour of his miraculous cure had not yet arrived. However, Zachariah showed his joy in other ways, and he was full of affectionate gratitude and silent praise for the rare blessing, which he had now witnessed with his own eyes.

Soon after the birth of her child, Elizabeth said to me, "My Mistress and Mother to be of the Creator, I know you must leave soon and I will be deprived of your loving help and protection. I beg you to furnish me with some good counsel, which will help me to conduct all my actions to the greater pleasure of the Most High. You bear him who is the corrector of the wise and the fountain of light. Through him, you can do all. Let some of the rays which illumine your pure soul fall upon me, in order that I may be enlightened in the paths of justice, until I arrive at the vision of the God of gods in Zion."

These words of my dear cousin moved me to tender compassion and I replied, "The Lord has advised me that your sojourn on this earth will soon come to an end, and your dear husband Zachariah will precede you in the near future, but fear not, for the Most High will take care of your child. The Lord has selected you for the fulfillment of most exalted mysteries. He has condescended to enlighten you concerning them and wishes that I should open to you my heart, which I have done. I will not forget the devoted kindness with which you have treated me; and from my most holy Son and Lord, I hope you shall receive a plentiful reward. The extreme mercy of the Most High in favoring us more than all other creatures with his knowledge and light ought to incite us to make up by our thankfulness for the blind ingratitude of mortals, who are so far removed from acknowledging and praising their Creator. This shall be our task that we keep our hearts free and unhindered in our advance toward the last end. Avoid all earthly things in order to be void of earthly hindrances. You must hope in the coming of the Lord, so that when he arrives you may answer his call joyfully and not with convulsive violence at the thought of leaving your body and all earthly things."

"As long as your husband lives, seek to love, serve and obey him with especial earnestness. Look upon your miraculous child as a continual sacrifice to his Creator, for he shall be a great Prophet, and in the spirit of Elijah, he shall defend the honor of the Most High and exalt his name. My most holy Son, who has chosen him for his Precursor and for the harbinger of his coming, will favor him with the special gifts of his right hand He will make him great and wonderful among the nations, manifesting to the world his great sanctity [Matt: 11, 9]."

"See that the holy name of God and the Lord of Abraham, Isaac and Jacob be honored and reverenced by all your house and family. Above all, be anxiously careful to relieve the needs of the poor as far as is possible. Enrich them with the temporal goods so lavishly given to you by your God. Show a like generosity to the needy, knowing that these earthly goods are more theirs than yours, since we are the children of the heavenly Father to whom all things belong. Follow your plans of even greater charity since Zachariah has given this work into your hands. With this permission, you can be even more generous. Confirm all the tasks imposed upon you by the Lord, and with all your fellow human beings practice kindness, humility and patience in the joy of your soul. Pray also for me, that his Majesty may govern and guide me worthily to preserve the Sacrament confided by his goodness to so lowly and poor a servant as me."

Elizabeth was lost in the exalted teachings and sentiments of these heavenly doctrines, and God made her mute by the force of the spiritual light that he infused into her. When she could speak, she replied, "My, Mistress and, Queen of the Universe, speech fails me in alternate sorrow and consolation. May the Lord, who is the enrichier of our poverty, return to you the favor you show me? I beseech you, who are the fountain of all my help and the source of all my blessings, to obtain for me the grace to fulfill your counsels and to bear the great sorrow of losing your company, and that of my Lord who you carry within your holy womb."

We then began planning for the baby's circumcision. The naming of a child was an important Jewish tradition, and called for the gathering of the entire family. Under the miraculous circumstances of the birth and the high position of Zachariah and Elizabeth, a huge gathering of friends and relatives assembled on the eighth day after the birth of their child. Since Zachariah could not speak it was necessary for Elizabeth to preside at the meeting. Elizabeth exhibited such evident signs of the sanctification of her soul that all of her relatives and friends commented on the change. Consequently, they all accorded her the greatest respect and reverence. In her countenance, she exhibited a kind of effulgence, which was the reflection of the Divinity in whose presence she had been living, and it made her mysteriously attractive.

In my modesty, I had not wished to attend the naming of the child. However, once Elizabeth made her wishes known, my humility compelled me to comply. I attended, but I begged the Most High not to make known any of my great privileges, lest I bring the approval and veneration of others. In this, the Lord heeded my wishes. The family suggested many different names from the long lineage of their ancestors, but they could not come to a common agreement. Finally after much discussion and haggling they turned to Elizabeth and asked, "What shall the name of the child be?"

Elizabeth answered, "My son must be named John."

The family drowned out her voice with loud protests. Indignantly, Zachariah's brother rose and stated, "This cannot be—no one in our family has ever been named John."

Elizabeth countered firmly, "Nevertheless, the child will be called John."

The brother said plaintively, "The names of our illustrious forefathers have always been preferred in order to inspire their namesakes to imitate their virtues." He turned to Zachariah for support and stated, "Zachariah, you must tell us. What will the child be named?"

Unable to speak, Zachariah signaled for a pen and declared God's will by writing on his tablet, "His name is John.

I saw that it was time that I made God's will known. I loosed Zachariah's tongue with a silent command, by ordering his dumbness to leave. The proper time had come for the high priest to bless and thank the Lord. At my mental command, Zachariah was freed from his affliction, and to the astonishment and fear of all present, he began to speak.

What I have stated here is not contrary to the Gospel narrative. The angel had declared that Zachariah would remain mute until the child was born. God, when he reveals any decree of his will, infallible as it is, does not always reveal the means or the manner of their fulfillment. Thus, had the Archangel Gabriel, announced to Zachariah the punishment of his unbelief. Gabriel; however, did not tell him how he was to be released from his punishment, although God had foreseen and decreed that I was to free him of his affliction.

No sooner had I released his tongue than Zachariah, inspired by the Holy Spirit, broke forth into the divine canticle of the Benedictus in which he embodied all of the highest mysteries, which the ancient prophets had foretold in a more profuse manner concerning the Divinity. I will not attempt to explain the deep meaning of these prophecies.

In a beautiful baritone Zachariah chanted, "Blessed be the Lord God of Israel; because he hath visited and wrought the redemption of his people: He hath raised up a horn of salvation to us, in the house of David his servant. In addition, he has spoken by the mouth of his holy prophets, who are from the beginning salvation from our enemies, and from the hands of all that hate us: To perform mercy to our fathers, and to remember his holy testament, the oath, which he swore to Abraham our father that he would grant to us in holiness and in justice before him, all our days. That being delivered from the hand of our enemies, we may serve him without fear. In addition, you Child, shall be called the Prophet of the Highest: for you shall go before the face of the Lord to prepare his ways:

To give knowledge of salvation to his people: unto the remission of their sins: Through the bowels of the mercy of our God, in which the Orient from on high has visited us: To enlighten them that sit in darkness, and in the shadow of death; to direct our feet into the way of peace."

Much more clearly than I can explain, Zachariah perceived these mysteries in their depth and expressed them in his prophecies. Some of those present were also enlightened, becoming aware that the time of the Messiah was at hand.

Full of wonder, John's brother exclaimed, "Who shall this child be, since the hand of the Most High is in him so marvelous and powerful?"

The priest then circumcised and officially named John in accordance with the letter of the Law. The report of these wonders spread throughout all the mountains of Judea.

I Am Mary

My, children, I once asked Saint Elizabeth of Schoenau, "Do you know why God selected me to be the Mother of God," and, I answered my own question?" Because I believed in him and because I had completely humbled myself."

I had subjected myself completely to God's wishes, when Simeon explained that God had ordained my marriage. However, I was deeply concerned because of my vow of chastity, and I flooded heaven with a multitude of prayers accompanied with my sincere tears and sighs. God finally appeared and consoled me. Even then, still distraught, I appealed to my angels. They also consoled and counseled me to be at peace with myself.

They said, "For sooner will the heavens and the earth fail, than the fulfillment of God's promises. You may trust securely in his Word." I bowed to their wisdom, and I asked them to convey to the Lord my complete subjection to that which his divine-pleasure should ordain in my regard. Actually, I never doubted the promises that the Lord had made regarding my pledge and desire for perpetual chastity. I knew he would honor his promises. However, in my limited experience, marriage would mean the end of my chastity, and my espousal with the Lord God. It was not doubt on my part, but a complete lack of comprehension. In spite of this fact, I still subjected myself to God's Will.

His majesty had commanded me to enter into the state of matrimony. At the same time, he concealed from me the conditions dependent upon entering it. My subjection to his Will was highly pleasing to God. Matrimony, I later learned, was required in order that my pregnancy might be respectable in the eyes of the world. Lucifer, his demons, and the world were at first to remain ignorant of this great mystery until Jesus chose to reveal his divinity. Lucifer thought I might be the woman of the prophecies, because of my total innocence. Consequently, the demons persecuted me until I entered the married state. Then their fury was somewhat appeased. They did not think it compatible that a married woman could also be the Mother of God.

I wish you to understand, my children that because I did not know the mystery concealed from me by the Lord, the prospect of me being espoused to any man was the greatest sorrow and affliction, which until then I had ever experienced. If the Lord had not given me some kind of confidence, although it was only obscure and undetermined, I would have lost my life in this suffering. However, from this event, perhaps you have learned how complete must be the resignation of the creature to the will of the Most High. It must restrict any shortsighted judgment and guard against scrutinizing the secrets of Majesty so exalted and mysterious. Whenever the soul seeks to scrutinize the decrees of his wisdom and satisfy itself before it obeys and believes, let it be convinced that it defrauds the Creator of his glory and honor, and at the same time loses for itself the merits of its own good works.

Some people throughout history have questioned whether I was married or merely betrothed to Joseph before; the Holy Spirit impregnated me. Holy Scripture cannot be wrong. It says;

"Now this is how the birth of Jesus Christ came about. When his mother Mary was *betrothed* to Joseph, *but before they lived together*, she conceived a child through the Holy Spirit. *Joseph, her husband*, since he was a righteous man, yet unwilling to expose her to shame, decided to divorce her quietly [Matt: 1, 18-20]."

Some people have questioned why God impregnated me when I was only betrothed. In the eyes of the Hebrews, betrothal was just as binding as marriage, and either, required a letter of divorce. Only Joseph could have exposed me, and of course, the Lord enlightened him accordingly.

During my betrothal, I lived in the house in Nazareth left me by my parents through Zachariah. I was properly chaperoned by my cousin Mary Salome. During this period, Joseph lived in Nazareth with his cousin. We both lived with the same perfection as I had lived in the temple; for in changing our state of life, neither of us altered our sentiments or our desire and anxiety to love and serve God. On the contrary, I added to my attentiveness lest my new obligations should hinder me in God's service. On this account God favored me, and disposed and accommodated powerfully all things in conformity to my desires. The Lord will do the same for all men, if on their part they communicate. However, in this modern day and age, people blame everyone but themselves for their problems. They especially blame the state of matrimony, and their lot in life, deceiving only themselves. For it is in their seeking and preferring the vain and superfluous things of this world that they lose sight of the sweetness of the Lord.

One point I would like to make clear. My attitude towards Zachariah was different from that toward Elizabeth. The Most High holds all priests in high esteem. If he finds them of the right disposition, he exalts and fills them with his Spirit. This was true with Zachariah, and it is true with many priests today. Good examples are Pope John Paul II and Mother Theresa, and I am sure that in your personal experiences, you have met that holy priest or holy person that leaves little doubt in your mind that God has filled them with his Holy Spirit. The Holy Spirit used me as the instrument by which he communicated his gifts to Elizabeth, Zachariah and John. I saluted Elizabeth in such a manner that at the same time, I demonstrated a certain authority by exerting my power [through God] over the original sin of her son. At my words this sin was forgiven him, which was the will of God. The Holy Ghost at the same time filled John and his mother with his spirit. Since I had not contracted original sin and was exempt from it, I possessed dominion over it on this occasion. Therefore, the Lord desired that, in order to free John from the slavery and chains of sin that I should command over it as one who was never subject to its bondage.

I did not salute Zachariah in an authoritative manner, but I prayed for him, observing the reverence and decorum due to his position and dignity and my modesty. I would not have commanded the tongue of the priest loosed, or the original sin of his son absolved, not even mentally and secretly, if the Most High had not enjoined it upon me.

I leave you with a last thought. Remember: God has no need of our foresight. He is superior to all creatures, and seeks only the subjugation of our will, since a creature cannot give him counsel, but only obedience and praise. Although you may not always know why God ordains or allows certain things to happen in the world around us, we must resign ourselves entirely to his protection and confide in the firmness of his promises. I earnestly implore you,

Live Good Lives.

Mary

Chapter Five

The Birth of Christ

"And you Bethlehem, land of Judah, are by no means least among the rulers of Judah; since from you shall come a ruler, who is to shepherd my people Israel." [Matt: 2, 6]

Joseph arrived for me the day after the circumcision of John. He was late because the work he was doing had to be completed before he could leave Nazareth. My husband was met with indescribable reverence and devotion by Elizabeth and Zachariah; for now the holy priest also knew that Joseph was the guardian of the sacramental treasure of heaven, though this was not yet known to Joseph himself.

I met him with discreet jubilation, and kneeling at his feet, I asked, "My espoused, may I have your blessing, and I most humbly beg your pardon for having deprived you of my presence?" I knew that I was not guilty of any fault, since I had simply conformed to the will of God with the express permission of my intended. By this act of humility; however, I wished to repay my promised one for not being able to continue our courtship.

Joseph replied with tears in his eyes, "Now that I see you again, my, intended, I delight in your presence. I am relieved of all pain caused by your absence," and he gave me his wholehearted blessing. Two days later, we left my cousin's home with many a tear shed by Elizabeth. John hung on to my fingertips as though to forcibly make me stay. I blessed him and noting the deference accorded me by Zachariah, I realized that the Lord had revealed to him the mystery I contained in my womb.

"Mistress," he said, "praise and bless eternally your Maker who in his infinite mercy has chosen you among all his creatures as his Mother, and as the sole keeper of all his great blessings and sacraments. Be mindful of me, your servant, before our Lord and God. May he lead me in peace through this exile to the security of the eternal peace, for which we hope. May I, through you, merit the vision of his divinity, which is the glory of the Saints? Remember also, oh,lady, my house and family and especially my son John, and pray to the Most High for your people."

I knelt before the good priest and in profound humility asked, "May I have your blessing before we leave?"

Zachariah hesitated and instead asked me, "Nay, Mary, It is you that should bless me."

However, my humility would not allow me to do this, and I begged the good priest until he relented and said, "May the right arm of the Almighty and true God assist and deliver you always. May the dew of the heavens and the fruits of the earth grace God's unfailing protection? Let him give you an abundance of bread and wine, and allow the nations to serve you and the generations to honor you, since you are the Tabernacle of God. You are the Mistress of your brethren, and allow the sons of your mothers kneel in your presence. God will bless and honor those who honor you, and he will curse those who do not bless and extol you. In you, let all nations know their God through you, and let the name of the Most High of Jacob be glorified."

I then asked the holy priest, "I beg you, oh most holy, priest, to forgive me the faults I have committed while in your home." Zachariah was touched by my humble plea. Forever afterward, he bore hidden within him the memory of the mysteries God revealed to him concerning me. Only once did he ever allude to his knowledge of this matter. That was when, at a meeting of the temple priests, they congratulated him on the birth of his son, and moved by an excess of joy, he told them, "I firmly believe that the Most High has visited us and has already sent us the promised Messiah who will redeem his people." Afterwards; however, no matter how pressed, he refused to explain his statement.

Simeon, who was present at the time and heard these words, was seized with great joy of spirit and by divine impulse exclaimed, "Let not, oh Lord God of Israel, thy servant to depart from this valley of misery before he has seen your salvation and the Redeemer of his people?"

Leaving Zachariah in tears, I turned to Elizabeth who by this time was nearly beside herself with grief at the thought of now losing the source whence so many blessings had flowed and were yet to flow. She was barely able to speak and I said, "My beloved, cousin, do not grieve so much over my departure, since the charity of the Most High, in whom I truly love you, knows no distance of time or place. Short is the time of our bodily separation, since all the days of human life are so fleeting. God will remain in your heart and console you."

Prudently, I said no more, but instead knelt at her feet and asked for her blessing and her pardon for what might have been disagreeable in our relationship. She protested, but I would not yield until I received her blessing. In turn I had to bless her, and then picking up John I bestowed upon him many mysterious blessings.

Suddenly, by divine dispensation, John spoke to me in a natural infantile voice: "You are the Mother of God himself, the Queen of all salvation, and the keeper of the ineffable Treasure of heaven, my help and protection. Grant me your blessing, and may your intercession and favor never leave me." Three times John kissed my hand, and silently adored the Incarnate Word in my virginal womb, and then John asked him for his benediction and grace. The Infant God in my womb manifested his pleasure and benevolence toward his Precursor. God granted me the privilege to witness all that took place between them. Joseph now approached with our donkey and with John trying futilely to cling to my fingers, we took our final leave.

Notwithstanding the ease and lightness of my pregnancy, I found the trip home unduly fatiguing. However, I made no use whatsoever of my special gifts to ease the burden of our journey. It was natural that my condition should soon become noticeable. Yet, in regards to my pregnancy, God had given me no intimation of his will. How long would it be before Joseph took notice? In spite of my concern, I did not attempt to conceal that which God had wrought in me. Unknown to either of us, God had ordained that the event should come about in such a way as to increase his glory and the merits of both Joseph and me. In view of my condition, I began to look on Joseph with greater tenderness and compassion. Once he found out, I had no doubt he would take it very hard. I besought his Majesty to fill the heart of my intended with patience and wisdom, and to assist him with grace that he might react according to divine pleasure. The more I dwelled on the subject, the more convinced I became that it would occasion him great grief to see me pregnant.

Our first night of travel saw us to an inn and there I observed a young maiden that had fallen under the spell of the evil one. The young girl was very ill and her friends were taking her to Jerusalem to seek spiritual help at the Jewish Temple for the unknown malady. God revealed to me that this woman had led a most virtuous life and thus had attracted the attention of Lucifer, who knew her character and her advanced virtues. He began an attack on her as he always does with the friends of God since all such are his declared enemies. He finally caused her to commit some minor sin. Once he had his foot in the door, he tempted her with despondent thoughts and disorderly grief at her fall. Soon he gained entrance into her soul, and he and many demons had taken possession of her.

Lucifer, when he had first seen me portrayed in heaven as the woman clothed with the sun, had conceived a great hatred against all virtuous women. For this reason, he exerted all his arrogance and tyranny against the body and soul of this hapless woman. Moved with motherly pity, I begged my most holy Son to give health of body and soul to the unfortunate woman. Perceiving that the Divine Will was inclined to mercy, I used my power as Queen and commanded the demons to instantly leave this unfortunate woman banishing them to the infernal depths, their lawful and appropriate dwelling. My command was so powerful that Lucifer and his companions hurled themselves into the infernal darkness.

The girl, freed of her slavery, was seized with wonder. She instinctively felt drawn to me and looked upon me with especial veneration and love. In so doing, she merited two other favors. First, God filled her with a most sincere sorrow for her sins. Secondly, he erased the evil effects and traces of the demonical possession under which she had suffered.

She spoke to me and said, "I feel the goodness in you, and I know that I have you to thank for my deliverance from the evil one."

I explained to her that she must be careful or a worse fate could befall her, and instructed her to persevere, and I could tell my words went directly to her heart. Her friends attributed her cure to their promise to take her to the temple and offer up a gift for her. I encouraged them all to go to the temple and offer up fasting, sacrifice and thanksgiving for her cure.

Lucifer was furious when he found himself and his demons back in hell. He exclaimed, "Who is this puny woman that commands us and oppresses us with so much power? What new surprise is this, and how can my pride stand it? We must hold a council and see how we can unite to destroy her."

The following night, Joseph and I came to another hostelry whose master was a man of bad habits and character. God ordained that he should receive Joseph and me with good will and marks of kindness. Consequently, he was most pleasant and rendered more courtesy and good services than he was accustomed to show to others. I recognized the true state of his heart and prayed for him, which justified his soul and caused him to change his life. From that time on, the man lived a good life and his inn prospered. In addition, our chance meetings sanctified those that we met along the way, who were of proper disposition.

It was good to get home. Joseph applied himself to his carpentry work, and Mary Salome returned and helped me set my house in order cleaning it from top to bottom. Unknown to Mary Salome, my angels often assisted us. They now vied with me in humility, and were anxious to serve and honor me by taking part in these humble occupations.

While we were still traveling, Lucifer, and his demons, began plotting my demise. They were still reeling from their chastisement that took place at the Incarnation of the Word. Lucifer and all hell had felt the power of the right arm of the Almighty, which had hurled them to the deepest of the infernal regions. There they remained overwhelmed for some days until the Lord in his admirable Providence allowed them to come forth from this captivity, the cause of which they did not know. However, Lucifer had no sooner become comfortable in the body of the girl he had possessed, than

I had again hurled him into the depths of hell, grinding him beneath my heel. Lucifer raged at such humiliation from a mere woman. He led his demons and scoured the earth from end to end for three months seeking the woman clothed with the Sun they had seen in a vision when God had tested their loyalties at the instance of their creation.

Confused, and very much aggrieved, Lucifer called together all his infernal hosts, without excusing or permitting a single one of the demons to be absent. From a place of vantage, he spoke to them, "You all know, my subjects, with what great anxiety I have attempted to destroy the power of the Almighty. I have sought to avenge myself ever since God cast us out from his dwelling and deprived us of our might. Although I cannot do anything to injure him, I have spared no time or exertion in extending my dominion over humankind whom he loves. By my own strength, I have peopled my reign and many nations and tribes obey and follow me. Every day, I deceive innumerable souls, depriving them of the knowledge and possession of God, in order that they may not enjoy the happiness which we have lost. I ensnare them to make them suffer the same eternal pains, which we must suffer. On them, will I wreak my vengeance, since they so easily follow my teachings and guidance? However, all this is of small consequence to me in the face of the sudden overthrow, which we have just experienced. Since God first hurled us from heaven nothing, so powerful and ruinous has happened to us. I must acknowledge that my power, as well as yours, has met a serious setback. This new and extraordinary defeat must have some new cause, and our weakness, I fear, may be the beginning of our ruin."

"This matter will require renewed diligence, for my fury is unquenchable and my vengeance remains insatiable. I, myself, have scoured the whole earth, observed all its inhabitants with great care, and yet I have found nothing notable. I have watched and persecuted all the virtuous and perfect women who are of the race of her whom we saw in heaven, and whom I expected to meet among them. However, I found no sign of her having yet been born. I have not found one who possesses the marks of the one who is to be the Mother of the Messias."

"A maiden whom I feared, because of her great virtues and whom I persecuted in the temple is already married. Therefore, she cannot be the one we look for, since Isaiah says, "She is to be a virgin [Is:7, 14]. Nevertheless, I fear and detest this maiden, since such a virtuous woman might give birth to the Mother of the Messiah or to some great prophet. To this hour, I have not been able to overcome her in anything, and of her life I understand less than that of all the others. She has always valiantly resisted me, as she eludes my memory; or remembering her, I cannot approach her. I have not yet been able to decide whether these difficulties are miraculous, or arise from my forgetfulness, or whether they are simply the consequences of the contempt in which I hold such an insignificant maiden."

"However, I will reconsider this matter, for recently, we could not resist the power of her command. This certainly requires satisfaction, and she merits my wrath solely because of what she has shown herself to be on these occasions. I resolve to persecute her and overcome her, and do you, yourselves, assist me in this enterprise with all your strength and malice? Those who will distinguish themselves in this conquest shall receive great rewards at my hands."

The entire infernal rabble, which had listened attentively to Lucifer, praised and approved his intentions and assured him, "Do not worry over this woman, since your power is so great and you rule with strength over the entire world [John: 14, 30]. She can be easily overcome and you shall not be without your triumphs over her.

The praise soothed Lucifer and he ground out, "Here is what we will do." I will send seven legions of my minions to tempt the woman in each of the seven capital sins. This time we will not fail. No one can possibly stand before such power."

The Lord concealed from these enemies the dignity he had bestowed upon me, as well as the wonderful manner of my pregnancy, and my virginal integrity before and after the birth of my Son. God effectively concealed it by simply giving me a husband. The fallen angels were to be deceived until the moment of my Son's death. Only then would they understand that they had been deceived. If they had known before, they would have done anything to prevent the noble sacrifice of my Son, even exposing Jesus to the world that Christ was and is the true God.

Aware of their plotting, my human Son rose up in my defense and prayed to his heavenly Father, "Father, I ask you to renew your favors and graces in my mother; in order that she may have added strength and crush the head of the ancient serpent. I pray that she will humiliate and overcome his designs and all his powers, and that she come forth victorious over hell to the glory and praise of Almighty God."

God answered his Son, by allowing me to see my most holy Son in my virginal womb. In this vision, God granted me a plentitude of graces and unspeakable gifts, and he illumined me anew with additional light of wisdom. I recognized the highest and the most hidden mysteries impossible for me to describe, and then my Son said to me, "My, mother, Lucifer has designs on your soul. You will be sorely tempted by seven legions of his evil followers. I; however, will be with you in battle. I wish to confound these enemies before I appear in the world. The demons are convinced that the redemption of the world is near. They hope, before this happens, to ruin all souls. I trust this victory to your fidelity and love. You are to battle in my name, against this dragon and ancient serpent."

When I learned that my most holy Son wished me to defend the honor of the Most High, I was inflamed with divine love and filled with invincible fortitude. Consequently, if each one of the demons had been an entire hell and filled with the fury of all its inmates, compared to the incomparable strength that God had given me, they would only have been as insignificant as a few weak ants. I replied to the Lord "My, Lord and my, God, from whom I have received my being and all the grace and light which I possess. I belong entirely to you. Do with your servant what shall be to your greater glory and pleasure. For if you are in me and me in you, who shall be powerful enough to resist your will? I will be the instrument of your almighty arm; give me your strength and come with me, and let us go forth to battle against the dragon and all his followers."

In order to do battle, Lucifer brought with him seven legions with their seven principal leaders, who, after their fall from heaven, he had appointed to tempt men to the seven capital sins. [Rev: 12] The battle began while I was occupied in prayer. The first legion of demons began by tempting me to the *sin of pride.* They tried to cause changes in my natural passions and inclinations in the manner in which the demons had been successful with other mortals. They thought that I was infected the same way as other people with passions disordered by sin. The demons; however, repelled by the fragrance of my virtues and holiness, could not come as close to me as they wished. This tormented them more than the fire, which consumes them. Their rage was so great that ignoring their pains they lashed themselves into furious and ungovernable wrath in their obstinate endeavors to approach nearer to me and exert upon me their cursed and damnable influence.

This attack took place over a period of several weeks with little let up on the part of the demons. This was not a battlefield of swords and banners flying, this was a battlefield of good versus evil, the same as it had been when the Archangel Michael and his good angels defeated Lucifer and his evil angels in the battle for heaven. God left me all alone; leaving me only my natural forces with which to do combat against Satan's countless demons. The demons presented themselves before me in the most horrid masks and told me the most wicked of lies. I did not allow myself to be moved by the demons whatsoever. I showed no fear or emotion on my face for them to read, for I needed to give an example to those who would honor me as their heavenly Queen.

I despised them with an invincible and magnanimous heart. This kind of battle is a battle of virtues, and Christians do not resort to extremes of noise and excitement. I fought them in all tranquility, in outward and inward peace, and modesty. My lack of Original Sin kept my faculties from disorder, as in the rest of the children of Adam. Therefore, the arrows of these enemies, as David says, were like those of little children, and their armories were like those without ammunition. Only to themselves were they harmful, for their weaknesses only brought confusion and pain upon themselves.

The demons next assumed corporeal shapes of the most horrible and dreadful kind; and began to emit fearful howls. They, pretending to rush upon me, roaring with terrible voices, and threatened me with destruction. They shook the earth and the house, and by other furious assaults sought to frighten and disturb me, so that at least in this, or in making me desist from my prayers, they might seem victorious. However, I was not disturbed in the least, although in order to do this battle, the Lord had left me entirely to the resources of my own faith and virtue. God had, "for the time being," suspended the effects of the other favors and privileges, which I was wont to enjoy at other times. The Most High did so, in order that my triumph might be more glorious and honorable. Besides this, there are other reasons God has in allowing a soul to be tempted in this manner. However, his judgments are unsearchable and unknowable [Rom: 11, 33-34]. At times I repeated those powerful words of Saint Michael, *"Who is like unto Go that lives in the highest and looks upon the humble in heaven and upon the earth?"* Finally, by repeating these words, I routed the demons that opposed me.

The demons returned immediately, presenting themselves to me as resplendent angels and tried to convince me that they came from God in order to congratulate and praise me. However, they quickly gave themselves away when they promised to select me as the Mother of God. For did I not carry the Son of God himself within my womb. I now prostrated myself on the floor, withdrew entirely within myself, and quietly and firmly continued to pray and adore the Lord, which act drove the demons back into hell.

Next, the second legion of demons tried to tempt me to *avarice* by offering me great wealth in gold and jewels. They told me that God wanted me to distribute it to the poor; since it was far better that a holy person like me should have these riches than to leave them to be misused by wicked sinners. I, who carried the wealth of the universe in my womb, did not argue with the devils. I merely prayed these words of the Psalmist:

"I have acquired for my heritage and for my riches the keeping of your testimonies and your laws my Lord."

Then the third group of devils sought to tempt me to *impurity*. I, who had pledged my entire life to chastity in the Lord, was not even affronted. Instead, I renewed my vow of chastity with great fervor and merit. My merits drove the demons from my presence like an arrow shot from a bow.

The fourth group then did all they could to provoke me to *anger*. They posed as some women whom I knew, shouted outrageous insults and threats at me, and stole items from the house that I sorely needed to maintain my household. However, I saw through their tricks and I utterly disregarded them. The next day one of the devils took on the appearance of a woman in Nazareth and told an easily influenced neighbor that I had criticized and slandered her. The deceived woman, who often lost her temper, hastened to insult me to my face.

I listened to her quietly as she poured forth all of her anger and then I said, "Come, Jane, and have some fruit and cheese with me and we will talk." I spoke with her in a kind and humble manner and her heart softened. She realized she had been deceived, and she apologized. I pointed out to her the dangers of allowing the devil to stir her up to such anger. Jane was quite poor and had had much to suffer. The death of small children was all too common in Israel, and Jane had lost two of her three children. I gave her some food and as she went away she blessed and begged me for forgiveness.

When the fourth legion failed, Lucifer sent his fifth legion to tempt me with *gluttony*. They failed miserably and quickly ceased their efforts. Then Lucifer sent his demons to seduce me with *envy.* The demons pointed out that God had bestowed many natural blessings and spiritual favors on others, but which had been denied me. Inwardly, I had to smile. I, who had been given so much. My numberless gifts were unknown to the demons, so they plied me with their usual guile, which had no effect whatsoever. The following week they induced several prosperous people to call on me. They bragged of their happiness at being rich, well off, and fortunate in worldly things.

To each, I said much the same thing, "You indeed have many blessings from our Lord. Be sure to thank him for all you have and use it well, forgetting not the poor and needy. As for myself, I judge myself quite unworthy of such favors."

When all else failed, Satan sent his last legion to try to tempt me to *idleness* by making me tired and dejected, suggesting that I postpone my prayers and good deeds on account of weariness, so that I might do them all the better after I had rested. Then they sent an endless cycle of people to my door to take up my time in order to prevent my prayers and to hinder me from doing my acts of charity. However, I acted prudently and did not allow them to keep me from my prayers and good works.

Lucifer was enraged and the following week, he himself, strove with all his might to hurt my Child and me. However, by displaying humble faith before his onslaught, I thwarted his plans. Satan feared that anyone born of me would naturally become a great enemy of his. Therefore, seeking to terrify me, he assumed the form of a horrifying monster, and rushed at me, howling and shooting forth fire and fumes from his mouth. The stench of hell was disgusting. I saw, heard, and smelled him, but I remained seated and unmoved as if he were nothing but a gnat.

Unsuccessful, he then tried to poison my mind. For days, the father of all lies recited every falsehood and heresy known to history concerning God and his truths. To each of his charges, I firmly proclaimed the various truths opposed to these errors and then sang hymns of praise to almighty God. Concerned for the human race with the deceit of his lies, I prayed to the Lord to prevent the devils from spreading such false teachings so freely throughout the world. Consequently, the Creator did in fact set *narrower limits* to the demon's activities.

In one last attempt, Lucifer stirred up a bitter quarrel over petty things among my neighbors by taking on the appearance of a woman known and respected by them all. She convinced them that I was the true source of all their troubles. The first thing, I knew about it was when the entire group came and pounded on my gate. They were all angry and worked up, and they accused me as an instigator of their problems. I calmly invited them to come in and I sat them down in the cool of the patio and served them cool drinks and fruit.

Then I said, "I humbly and patiently beg you all to forgive me if I have offended you." Then I took each charge they had made against one another and proved to them that none of them had done anything to offend the others. They all left with apologies. Then with God's permission, I commanded the defeated black angels to return to hell. As a reward the Lord himself appeared to me with all my angels and honored me, and I joyfully and modestly praised the Author of all good.

I was now beginning my fifth month of pregnancy. One day as I was coming out the backdoor, Joseph saw me and started to speak. Suddenly, a stricken look fell over his face, as though for the first time he noticed the evident change in my condition, which of course, I had never attempted to conceal.

He mumbled something and busied himself with the piece of wood he was working on. I could see that he was deeply troubled. I later learned that seeing me so large, he could no longer deny that which he had seen, and had seen so clearly several times before. However, because he loved me so dearly, he had refused to accept the proof of his own eyes. Now, even his kind heart could no longer reject that which was so obvious. Even yet; however, this holy and just man could not render judgment against me, and he agonized over the matter hour after hour, day after day. That which gave him the greatest pain, was the dread of being obliged to deliver me over to the authorities as an adulterer, for which, according to the Law of Moses, I could be stoned. He had no sooner thought this, than he rejected the thought as unworthy of him and me. I truly felt sorry for Joseph. I had not volunteered any explanation, and because of his love for me, he refused to embarrass me by broaching such a delicate subject.

I prayed for him constantly, and Joseph likewise turned to the Lord in frequent and fervent prayer saying, "Most High, God, my grief is almost killing me! My reason proclaims Mary blameless, while my senses accuse her. What shall I do? Nothing I have seen in her could occasion any doubt in her modesty and her extraordinary virtue. Yet, at the same time, I cannot deny that she is pregnant. Why does she conceal this matter from me? In love and loyalty, I find I must withhold my judgment. Receive my tears as an acceptable sacrifice. I cannot believe that Mary has offended you. If I believed that Mary had any guilt in causing this condition, I would die of sorrow. Is there perhaps some mystery beneath it that I cannot fathom? Please, Lord, govern my mind and my heart."

I knew all of Joseph's sufferings, since by the light of my divine science, God allowed me to penetrate into his interior thoughts. Intense compassion for him filled my heart. However, I felt obliged to keep God's secret to myself until he gave me permission to reveal it to anyone. With wisdom and confidence, I resigned the entire matter into the hands of the Divine Providence. I tried to make it up to Joseph by serving him with even more attention and devotion. All the while, the Word Incarnate in my womb was growing in health, gracefulness and loveliness.

My intended, on the other hand, was so troubled in mind and heart that he began wasting away before my very eyes. Dropping to my knees before him, I exclaimed with deep concern, "My dear, Joseph, "I know you are troubled, but you must take more rest and eat your food. Look, see the nice meal I have prepared for you." However, Joseph, in his sorrow, was inconsolable. Mary Salome also made every attempt to relieve him of his anxiety, although she had no idea of the cause of his depression. In my concern, I prayed fervently to the Lord to bring peace of mind to my unhappy espoused.

For two more months Joseph bore his tribulation patiently and nobly, but finally he came to the sad conclusion that the best thing for him to do was to graciously absent himself from my presence and decided to do so that very night at midnight. After packing a small bundle of clothes, he prayed to God. "Oh, Lord, I find no other way to restore my peace. I do not believe my wife an adulterous. Yet, I must leave and from afar take care of her needs. Do not forsake me my, Lord." Joseph prostrated himself on the ground and made a vow to go to the temple in Jerusalem and offer up a sacrifice in order that God might help and protect me. Then, mentally exhausted, Joseph lay down to rest before his trip.

I knew Joseph's intentions, and I addressed myself exclusively to my most holy Son in my womb, "I beseech you, Lord and God of my soul, although I am but dust and ashes, may I speak of that which cannot be hidden from you? I must not be remiss in assisting my spouse, for I see him overwhelmed by the tribulation you have sent him. If I have found grace in your eyes, I beg you to console your servant Joseph and do not permit him to carry out this decision and leave me?"

The Lord answered me, "My dearest, dove, I shall presently visit my servant Joseph at his cousin's home in Nazareth and console him. My angel shall reveal the mystery, which is now unknown to him. You may then discuss openly all I have done with you. I will fill him with my Spirit, and he will assist you in all that will happen." Greatly relieved I began a litany praising the glories of our Creator.

The Lord in his mercy sent the Archangel Gabriel that very night to Joseph while he slept. While Joseph did not see the angel distinctly, he heard an inner voice say to him, "Do not be afraid, Joseph, son of David, to take Mary as your wife, for that which is begotten in her is of the Holy Spirit. She shall bring forth a Son, and you shall name him Jesus, for he shall save his people from their sins."

Joseph awoke the next morning with the overwhelming realization that I was actually the Mother of the Messiah. Joy engulfed Joseph's heart. However, he was overwhelmed with sorrow for having doubted me in the slightest. Joseph prostrated himself on the floor and humbly gave thanks to God for having revealed this mystery to him. Then he began to recriminate for all that had happened and he exclaimed aloud, "Oh my beloved, how could I, your unworthy slave, have dared to doubt your faithfulness? How is it that I have not kissed the ground that your feet touched? Woe is me—all my thoughts were open to her sight, also that I intended to leave her! Oh my, Lord and, God, give me strength to ask her forgiveness, so that for her sake, you may pardon my great fault."

Shedding tears of repentance Joseph ran to my little home in Nazareth; entering, while I was praying in my room, he began to scrub the floors upon which I had walked, and to do other chores, which I normally did. He resolved henceforth to be my servant in all things.

When he knew that I was finished with my morning prayers and meditations, he knocked on my door as he always did. Upon my invitation, Joseph entered my oratory and threw himself on his knees before me with the deepest reverence saying, "Betrothed, Mother of the Eternal Word, I beseech you to pardon my audacity. Great was my presumption in deciding to leave you instead of serving you as the Mother of my Lord. However, you know that I did so in ignorance. Now I consecrate my heart and my whole life to your service. I will not rise from my knees until I have obtained your pardon and your blessing."

I raised Joseph to his feet and knelt before him, saying, "I should ask for your forgiveness for the sorrow and bitterness which I have caused you, Joseph. As much as I wanted to, I could not on my own account give you any information about the Holy Sacrament hidden within me by the power of the Almighty. I will always be your faithful servant. However, the Lord made me his mother in order that I should be the servant of all and your slave. It was not his intention that I be served, but that I serve, for such is my duty."

Joseph raised me to my feet, and when he did the Holy Spirit overwhelmed me. Suddenly, I was aflame and transfigured in a mystical ecstasy. I began to recite the Magnificat. Joseph, seeing me thus surrounded by a bright radiance of heavenly light, fell to his knees with profound humility and reverence, and adored the Lord in my womb. God looked upon Joseph with kindly favor, accepted him as his foster father, and spiritually changed Joseph into a new man. I noted the change in him at once, for he began to act toward me with much greater reverence. Whenever he passed me or spoke to me alone, he respectfully genuflected and he no longer wished me to serve him, clean the house or wash the dishes. Of course I protested, so he resorted to doing these things for me while I meditated in my oratory. In all humility, I appealed to the Lord.

Consequently, Joseph's guardian angel was sent to him with these instructions. "Exteriorly, allow Mary to serve you, and interiorly treat her with the highest reverence. Always worship *in her* the Lord of all creation. It is his will and his mother's *to serve and not to be served,* in order to teach the world the value of humility." Thereafter, Joseph allowed me to do my own work, for which I was most grateful to him and to the Lord. However, he approached me the next day and stated, "It is not proper that we delay our wedding any further. Would you please set the earliest day possible for our nuptials?"

I was quite relieved at his foresight for people would talk and I did not wish to bring discredit to my Son or to my espoused. I set the middle of the month as our wedding day, and immediately set about making the proper arrangements, as did Joseph. I immediately asked Mary Salome to take charge of the wedding. She promptly sent out invitations to all our friends and family, and began work on my trousseau.

Elizabeth and Zachariah, who were to represent my parents, brought me a beautiful wedding dress. In my sincere modesty, I declined to wear the gown, until, in a vision; God explained to me that as the Mother of his Son, he wished me to be accorded every honor since I was to be the Mother of God. He wished me to conform to the custom of the times. Then to please the Lord, I turned myself over joyfully to the dressmakers, and the hairdressers, who descended upon me at four AM on the morning before the wedding and began to outfit me in my lavish gown.

I bathed privately, and then my angels outfitted me with a colored, woolen under-garment with no sleeves. As previously stated, I did not wish any person to see my body, so the Lord provided me with angelic bridesmaids, which no one questioned. They then encircled my arms with white-woolen fillets. The white collar ornamented with jewels and pearls rose to my neck. Over this, I wore a blue gown, embroidered with large red, white and yellow roses and green leaves. The gown was full and concealed my condition perfectly, as God had planned. Tassels fringed the dress's lower border. Over this was a scapular of white-and gold flowered silk, set over my breast with pearls and shining stones. It also was fringed with tassels, and balls, and covered the front opening of the dress, and. it was only about one half an ell wide. Over this costume fell a long, sky-blue mantle fastened at the neck by an ornament, and over it was a white ruffle of silk dots. The mantle fell back from the shoulders, forming a large fold on the sides, and it hung behind in a pointed train with flowers of gold embroidered around the edge. The hairdresser then parted my hair on top of my head, divided the hair into numerous strands, and then interwove them with white silk strips, inlaid with pearls. It formed a large net that fell over my shoulders and down my back to the middle of the mantle. When she finished, it looked like a web. My angelic hairdresser then rolled in the ends of my hair, which she then edged with gems and pearls.

She next placed on my head a wreath of white, raw silk closed on top with three bands of the same, meeting in a tuft. On this rested a crown about the breadth of my hand. It was set with many colored jewels. A gold ball was perched atop three arched pieces that rose from the circlet. In my left hand, I carried a little garland of red and white roses made of silk. In my right, I carried a beautiful candlestick covered with gold. The handle had knobs above and below the grip, similar to a scepter. The stem began to swell out in the middle and ended in a little dish upon which burned a white flame.

On my feet, they placed a pair of embroidered sandals about two fingers in thickness. They were green and gave me the appearance of standing upon sods. Two straps, white and gold, went over my foot and held the shoes in place. The usual wedding clothing of Jewish women enveloped them closely. It gave them a wrapped appearance. However, my wedding dress was more on the Roman style, although I was far from being an authority in such matters. Elizabeth, inspired by God, and knowing that I was bearing the Son of God, had tactfully designed a full-bodied wedding dress that did not accentuate my body. If anyone noticed my condition, they tactfully chose not to mention the fact. After all, it was not that unusual for a betrothed couple to conceive a child before the actual wedding took place.

On a Wednesday, the fifteenth day of the month, Joseph and his entourage came for me at my home, as was the custom. They sang love songs and made merry on their short trip from Nazareth to my small home. Joseph was darkly handsome, and my angels informed me that his face glowed with a holy happiness. My espoused was of average height and weight, and he wore a full-black beard that he kept closely trimmed, except for the traditional curls about his ears. He was dressed in a long, blue coat fastened from the breast down with loops and buttons. Lacing edged the coat's wide sleeves, and a broad cuff turned up at the wrist, which served as pockets. Around his neck was a brown collar upon which lay a white stole, and upon his breast hung two white bands. Joseph stopped short when he saw me. My face was modestly downcast, but my angels let me know that his face flamed with reverent love and devotion.

My betrothed was seeing me at my best. I was a Galilean, and our people were prone to be taller and fairer than the average Hebrew. They, for the most part, were shorter and much darker of skin and hair. God had graced me with auburn hair, finely arched dark eyebrows, and a high forehead. My eyes were downcast, and were thick with dark lashes, my nose was straight, but delicate and tastefully long, God had given me a lovely mouth and a pointed chin. I was slim and taller than most Jewish girls, but perhaps average for a Galilean. I felt most self-conscience in my rich attire.

In spite of the short notice, Joseph's friends, my temple friends, my relatives, some of my teachers, and the entire population of Nazareth had formed an immense wedding party. Joseph had prudently set aside money for this momentous occasion. My cousin Lazarus, his sister Martha, and their two younger sisters, both named Mary, were present. As I stated, when Joseph approached and saw me in all my finery, he stopped short in awe. God had ordained that Joseph, by my mere presence and conversation, would be infused in a holy awe and reverence greater than words could ever suffice to describe. A divine light, which shone from my face, wrought in Joseph a reflection of the perpetual vision, granted me of my indescribable and always visible Majesty. Because my association and conversation with God had been so much more extended and intimate than that of Moses descending from the mountain, God had bestowed this honor upon me.

Joseph's best friend Jeremiah, acted as master of ceremonies and he quickly formed our group into a procession. As was tradition, my husky, male relatives carried me on a litter. My ten maids of honor, all dressed in white and carrying bouquets of beautiful flowers, gathered around me excitedly. We then paraded through the streets of Nazareth dancing to the music of the lyres and harps, and the tambourines and cymbals. Everyone was dressed in their best, and our colorful wedding party swept through the gate of Nazareth. The maidens sang verses from the Song of Songs, including,

"Who is this that makes her way up by the desert road, erect as a column of smoke, all myrrh and incense, and those sweet scents the perfumer knows."

Upon our arrival at the banquet hall, my litter bearers carried me to a raised platform in the center of the room upon, where a canopy [the huppah] had been erected. Interwoven into the latticework of the canopy were garlands of red and white roses. Once seated in this queen-like setting, our families and friends then led the guests in traditional blessings to express their wishes for the happiness and fruitfulness of our marriage. The father of the bride usually welcomed the bridegroom into the family by proclaiming, "This day you are my son in law." The blessings were the actual wedding ceremony, and Zachariah climaxed the event by rendering his priestly blessing for our family. Then, acting in place of my father, he stated to Joseph for all to hear, "This day you are my son," and he clasped Joseph to his breast.

This act completed the wedding ceremony and after the congratulations, I withdrew with my friends into a side room that was set aside for that purpose. Our guests played games and danced the rest of the evening, and of course, as the bridegroom, Joseph participated. However, my friends and I, as also was the custom, did not join in, but remained in our side room.

The next morning began a day of feasting and rejoicing. The young played various games of skill, and the young women danced amidst the beds of flowers of the beautiful gardens attached to the pavilion. Wine flowed freely during the festivities. Joseph served his guests a huge banquet that evening, the men and women eating separately according to custom. The presentation of gifts came after the dinner, and one by one the guests came forward and laid their gifts at my feet. I held up each gift and everyone oohed and awed. I thanked each person for his or her thoughtfulness and generosity. Most of the gifts were practical, since this was the beginning of housekeeping for Joseph and me. The gift-giving completed the bride then usually sang love songs to her beloved; however, Joseph and I sang songs of our fidelity and devotion to one another, and to our Creator. In so doing, we avoided the explicit love verses from the Song of Songs. This; however, according to custom, did not discourage the guests from singing exotic love songs.

They sang, "A kiss from those lips," and "Wine cannot ravish the senses like that embrace," all of which caused me to blush and made me most uncomfortable.

The guests now all threw grain down in front of Joseph and I, and one couple broke a pomegranate at our feet, both old fertility rites. Next, a vase full of scent was broken, and the sweet smell of myrrh wafted through the pavilion. With a great shout, our guests began the feast again, and this time the men and women joined one another at the tables and everyone drank and ate a great deal.

Later that evening, Joseph came for me and took me to a private room, it was customary that sometime during the evening's celebration that the groom takes his wife away and in the side room consummates their marriage. Of course Joseph and I had settled this issue many months before and when we retired to the room we spent our time in humble prayer giving thanks to our Creator for his many blessings and praising and glorifying him for sending his only Son into the world. Two hours later, we rejoined the festivities and the celebration went on for two full weeks.

When our guests had departed, there came the cleaning up of the mess they had left behind which took Joseph, our friends, and me two days to put into order. Once completed, Joseph then took me to our home outside Nazareth and for the first time, we entered the house as man and wife. He took up residence in another partitioned off room, which also served as his oratory. I was relieved that the ordeal for Joseph was over, and he could now concentrate his efforts as the head of the household. We easily fell into a daily routine of prayer, and work and my chaperone cousin, Mary Salome, returned to her family where she was soon to marry Zebedee, a fisherman. I wove and presented her with a set of swaddling clothes for her hope chest as a parting gift in thanksgiving for all her assistance and support.

It was not long before Joseph began to come into my room to talk to me during the day. Joseph was privileged many times to see me in a state of ecstasy raised above the ground, or when I was conversing with my angels. He would often find me lying prostrate on the floor in the form of a cross. At such times he often heard heavenly melodies and detected a marvelous fragrance, which filled him with deep spiritual joy.

I always dressed conservatively, and most of my clothes I dyed a light gray. Underneath, I wore a white cotton tunic. Like most of my Hebrew brethren, I kept myself spotlessly clean and washed my hands many times a day. I ate sparingly and took no meat, although sometimes, I did prepare meat for Joseph. Both of us ate cooked vegetables, bread, fruit, fish and cheese.

Joseph and I prayed together everyday. We read and discussed the various prophecies in Holy Scripture concerning the Messiah, especially that which related to his birth. However, out of consideration for Joseph, I did not dwell on the Redeemer's sufferings and death. Joseph's eyes would often fill with tears of joy, when he was moved by my words

One day he exclaimed with wonder, "Is it really possible that I shall see my God in your arms, and hear him speak and touch him? It is incredible for me to contemplate that he will live with us, and that I shall sit at the same table, and eat and talk with him. I do not deserve this good fortune, which no one could ever deserve. Oh how I regret that I am so poor!"

I consoled my spouse and said, "Joseph, you must remember that the Lord is coming to redeem the world and to guide men on the path to life eternal, by means of humility and poverty. In these two virtues, he wishes to be born, to live, and to die, in order to break the chains of greed and pride in the hearts of men. That is why he chose our poor and humble home. He does not want us to be rich in passing goods, which are but vanity and which darken the understanding."

Joseph asked me to instruct him in the various virtues, touched deeply I did so with humility and conscientiousness. I led him in such a manner as to lead him in choosing the proper conclusions. The most important thing I taught him was to make his daily labor more a practice of virtue instead of mere manual work. I taught him to make each stroke of the saw and each hammering of the nail an offering to God, thus making his entire day a day of prayer. Joseph was used to charging a set amount for his work, although his fees were much less, than those fixed by his competitors. Although we both performed work for others, we decided to refrain from demanding any wages or setting a price on our labor. We began working for charity, or to supply a need, instead of gain. We left our pay up to our employers and accepted it as freely given alms rather than as an earned reward. Consequently, we often found ourselves so poor that we even lacked the necessities, since we were extremely generous to the poor, and there were few persons in Nazareth that did not meet that description. We never stocked food, and what we had was never in our home long enough to spoil. Yet, when I needed money, food, or clothing for some unfortunate, the Lord always provided me with the means to relieve their needs.

I blessed the Lord for our poverty, which was a source of profound spiritual consolation to me. However, heeding the needs of my husband, I asked God to supply Joseph with adequate food to sustain him. The Lord heard my prayers, and, as he often did when I needed material goods for some charitable cause, he moved one of our neighbors, or a client to bring us gifts of food or the money owed us sufficient to fulfill our needs. My cousin Elizabeth sent us gifts frequently, as did Mary Salome and the family of Lazarus. In return, as an acknowledgment, I always sent them articles made by my own hands. On a few rare occasions, at God's suggestion, I would ask the birds to bring us food and they would cheerfully respond by bringing me fish, fruit, or bread in their beaks. They would alight and drop the food in my hand. Often they were content to remain on my hand and would sing me their own unique, beautiful song. Joseph always marveled when this happened and when the birds flew away, he would drop to his knees and offer up thanksgiving to the Lord.

Of course, we both fasted regularly as an offering to the Lord, Once; however, after such a fast, we found ourselves without funds or food, and for an additional two days we had nothing to eat. I was concerned for I was in my eighth month and I asked Joseph what we should do. Taking my hand, we knelt together, and he said. "Let us thank God for this privation and ask him for his help. When we arose from our prayers some time later, we were overjoyed to find that my angels had prepared our table and set on it fresh bread, fish, fruit, and a wonderfully sweet and nourishing jelly. We wept tears of gratitude and sang hymns of praise before we allowed ourselves the pleasure of sitting and partaking of this heavenly food.

I had all in readiness for the coming of my Son. I had made swaddling clothes, blankets, and all the items necessary for attending to the needs of a baby. When working on these clothes for my Son,

I worked on my knees, and often shed tears of devotion and love. As I lovingly folded the last of his little clothes away, I murmured aloud, "My sweetest, Love, when shall my eyes enjoy the light of your divine face? When shall I, as your mother, receive my beloved's tender kiss? However, how shall I, a poor insignificant nothing, ever be able to treat you worthily? Look graciously upon me and let me take part in all the labors of your life, since you are my Son and my Lord?"

At that moment, Joseph entered the house, and I said to him. "All is in readiness for the coming of our Son. However, I am not sure how we should treat my Son once he has been delivered into this world?" Again, Joseph relied entirely on the Lord and said, "Let us put this matter before the Lord, my, spouse, for I have no knowledge of such things." Then as we knelt in prayer we both heard a voice saying. "I have come from Heaven to earth in order to exalt humility and discredit pride, to honor poverty and scorn riches, to destroy vanity and establish truth, and to enhance the value of labor. Therefore, it is my will that exteriorly; you treat me according to the humble position, which I have assumed. Treat me as if I were your natural child, and interiorly love and revere me as the Man-God, Son of my Eternal Father."

The next day Joseph hurried home from the market place, and from his manner I could tell that he was upset. "What is it Joseph, what troubles you so?" Looking miserable, he dropped down heavily on a bench and resting his face on his hands, he replied, "It is the worst of news, Mary. The Romans have issued an edict for a census that pertains to the head of each family in Israel. I must return to Bethlehem, the city of my birth, to register and pay their taxes. You are too far along in your pregnancy for me to ask you to go with me to Bethlehem, for I fear to place you in such risk. I would be heartbroken if the severity of the trip should cause you to miscarry. Due to my poverty, I cannot provide for you adequately." He uncovered his face and as tears of anguish ran down his cheeks, he exclaimed, "But, how can I ever leave you when the Child is soon to be delivered? Please pray that I may not have to be separated from you, for my heart would not have a moment's peace away from you."

My heart went out to Joseph, he was so distressed, and I replied, "Do not be alarmed, my, husband, for all that happens to us is ordained by God. Do you not remember that which the Prophet Micah prophesied? And I quoted, "But you Bethlehem-Ephrathah, too small to be among the clans of Judah. From you shall come forth for me, one who is to be ruler in Israel; whose origin is of old, from ancient times [Micah: 5, 1]."

"Yes, Mary, I am familiar with this prophecy," Joseph responded. However, I am concerned for the Lord has commissioned me as your guardian and that of the Child. If the delivery should happen along the way, amid inconveniences, which I could not alleviate, I would be heartbroken. I pray, Mary that you present my fears before the Lord and ask him to grant me my desire of not being separated from you and that I have his permission to take you with me to Bethlehem."

My husband's wish was my command, and although I knew that the Lord positively wished his Son to be born in Bethlehem, this fact I could not reveal without betraying the trust of he who had entrusted this information to me. I presented to the Lord the fervent wishes of Joseph and he replied at once, "My dearest, dove, yield to the wishes of my servant Joseph. Accompany him on the journey. I shall be with you, and I shall assist you with paternal love in the tribulations, which you shall suffer, for my sake. Do not fear since this is my will."

Then, in my presence, God gave my guardian angels a new and special precept. They were to serve me during this journey with particular care and solicitude. As befitted the magnificent mysteries that were soon to be transacted, God assigned, as my guard of honor, an additional nine thousand angels led by Saint Michael and Saint Gabriel. Knowing that King Herod would persecute me, the Lord renewed and strengthened me. Thus prepared, I advised Joseph of God's decision.

Relieved, my spouse exclaimed, "My, Lady, source of my happiness and good fortune, the only cause of grief now will be traveling in the middle of winter, since I do not have the means to procure the conveniences to alleviate the hardships of the journey. However, in Bethlehem, we shall find relations, acquaintances and friends of my family who will make our stay more pleasant and there you can rest from the exertions of the trip. However, the Lord has sent his angels to me and has instructed me to take no conveniences, but only the barest of necessities. I am also to take a little she-ass of one year, which has not yet foaled besides our beast, which you are to ride. We are to allow this creature to run at large, and then follow the road that it takes."

I said nothing to discourage Joseph's plans, for I knew what God had already ordained regarding the birth of his Son. Instead I said, "My, spouse, Mary Salome has a beast you described, and I am sure she will let us have her. According to God's will, we will make this journey as poor people in the name of the Lord, for the Most High will not despise poverty, which he comes to seek with so much love. Relying on his protection, we will proceed with confidence."

We entrusted our home to the care of Mahara, Joseph's cousin, who had been so good to us. Closing the door I dropped to my knees before my husband and asked for his blessing. He strenuously objected because of my dignity, but I remained adamant in my humility and prevailed upon him to render his blessing. He did so with great timidity and reverence and then cast himself at my feet in a flood of tears asking me to present him anew to my most holy Son, and obtain for him divine pardon and grace.

Thus, we began our journey, poor and humble in the eyes of the world. However, we did not walk alone, poor or despised, but prosperous and rich in magnificence. For hidden to the proud, we carried with us the treasure of heaven, the Deity itself. Ten thousand angels, more refulgent than many suns, marched along as my retinue, their human forms visible to us both. In their joy, they composed new songs in honor of the Lord, and in my honor. Deeply concerned for my health, Joseph shortened each day's journey so that it took us five days to get to Bethlehem. We experienced no darkness, since in the evenings when we were forced to walk on into the night, the holy angels spread about such effulgence that our path was as bright as day. Joseph was also privileged to enjoy their light, and their singing, and he joined in heartily."

The little she-ass ran playfully along beside us. Sometimes she dashed ahead of us, and sometimes she delayed, while eating a frozen tuft of grass. Soon; however, she would gallop past us and again take the lead. The first night the ass led us to an inn and stopped; however, the innkeeper, eyeing our obvious poverty, refused us admittance as worthless and despicable people. The second inn was not much better, for it was packed with people also summoned by the imperial edict. Again, because of our poverty, the innkeeper treated us shabbily. He treated us with less consideration than that extended to those, whose outward appearance suggested wealth and position. The innkeeper subjected us to sharp reprimands and assigned us no more than a place in a hall. We rejoiced; however, since we could add to our humility by such treatment. No matter where we ended up; however, we were always surrounded by my thousands of angels. Joseph, consoled by this knowledge was able to sleep undisturbed. While he slept, I continued my celestial colloquies with the ten thousand angels of my retinue. I gloried in being able to suffer for my Lord, and my angels and I gave glory and praise to our Creator most of the night.

I observed and knew the secrets of all those whom we passed along the way. The little she-ass had a knack for ferreting out people who seemed to need our help, and would run up to them and nuzzle them gently. By the graces given me by the Lord, I was able to penetrate the thoughts and conditions of each person. I knew if they were predestined or reprobate, whether they would persevere, fall, or again rise-up. All of which inspired me to exercise heroic virtues, and I was able to help many people.

For some, I gained the grace of perseverance, for others, I rendered them efficacious help so they could rise from their sin to grace. In others, I prayed to the Lord tearfully, as I did for the reprobate, although I did not pray as hard for them. The sick, afflicted and indigent, whom I met along the way, I consoled and assisted by asking my most holy Son to grant them comfort in their necessities and adversities. Many times, I wore myself out by these sorrows, much more so than to the rigors of the travel itself. When this happened, my angels bore me up in their arms in order that I might rest and recuperate. For the main part, I was preoccupied with the fruit of my pregnancy. The little she-ass agilely avoided the multitudes, but I still attended to the needs of the people with my prayers and petitions.

We were eventually to bypass Jerusalem, which, when we passed by, was off to the east. Our little guide acted like it was a beautiful sunny afternoon; gamboling and playing along the route, in spite of a cold wet rain that set in the second day and chilled us to the bone. I was dreadfully cold and was becoming concerned for the welfare of my son when the Lord took pity on us. Saint Gabriel took my hands and warmth spread throughout my body, which, in turn, by holding Joseph's hands, I was able to warm his entire body. Finally, late at night, we came to an isolated house where the little she-ass hesitated, so Joseph knocked and asked for shelter, without opening the door the heartless man shouted,

"I am not running an inn, be off with you."

Consequently, the little ass then led us unerringly to an out of the way stable, where we were glad to take refuge from the cold rain, now turned to sleet. The animals in the shelter showed us more courtesy and kindness than that of their masters. At the entrance of their Maker, carried within my virginal womb, they retreated in reverence to the rear of the stable. It is true that I could have commanded the winds and the storm to abate, but I would not give the order which would have deprived me of suffering in imitation of my divine Son even before he came forth into the world. The inclement weather did affect me, but Joseph did his utmost to shelter me as did the angels, especially the holy prince Michael who remained at my right side without leaving me for even a minute. Whenever the Lord permitted, he shielded me against the weather and performed many services for me.

The third night, since we were on the by-paths away from the inns, the little ass could not find shelter, so Joseph pitched the small tent he had packed. Inside, with our ten thousand angels, Saint Michael warmed us and again, while Joseph slept, I spent most of the might in prayer with my angels.

The final night that we were on the road, the little donkey led us to a large farmhouse. The farmer's wife was young and conceited and she became jealous of the fair looks my Lord had given me. She treated me coldly, but the farmer more than made up for it obviously embarrassed by her rude conduct. My son was to tell me years later that during his ministry, he found her lame and blind, and after reproaching her for her vanity and heartlessness, he healed her.

The next day was the Sabbath and we were unable to travel, so the farmer insisted that we remain there for the day. This we did, spending our time in prayer and song and even the wife thawed out a little bit and joined in our joyous songs of praise to the Lord. The farmer, before we left early the next morning, advised Joseph that Bethlehem was jammed with people because of the edict. However, Joseph turned to me and said, "Fear not, my Lady. I have many friends and relatives there and we should have no problem".

Thus, it was that we arrived in Bethlehem late in the afternoon of our sixth day of travel, but our little ass would not enter the city and ran playfully off into the hills.

It was the time of the winter solstice, and the sun was already sinking and night was fast approaching. We entered the town and wandered through the streets in search of a lodging house or inn. We went first to the homes of Joseph's two brothers. One turned him away rudely, berating him for running away when he was but a boy, and calling down God's curses upon him for being a wastrel. His other brother, swayed by greed, instead of offering hospitality to strangers, as was the Hebrew custom, had sold all the available space in his home. He added his insults to his brother's, and sent us on our way.

I suggested to Joseph that he try at the inn, hoping that if he could find a room there that it might mitigate the hurt of his brother's rejection. The inn keeper was courteous, but the inn had been full since early morning. Now concerned, Joseph wended his way through the winding streets seeking out relatives and acquaintances one after another with no success. I followed Joseph patiently through the streets listening to one lame excuse after another often accompanied with insults as well. Thus, was I able to share Joseph's indignity and unmerited shame.

While wandering about we passed the public registry, and while there Joseph inscribed our names and paid them the tax in order to comply with the edict and not be obliged to return. Finally my strength gave out, and Joseph now anxious, found me a place out of the wind. I waited patiently for him while he went from door to door of over fifty different homes, but to no avail. It was dusk when I saw the little she ass outside the city gate looking at us hopefully.

"Joseph said regretfully, "My sweetest, lady, my heart is broken with sorrow at the thought of not being able to shelter you as you deserve. I am unable to offer you any kind of protection from the weather or a place to rest, a thing rarely or never denied to even the most poor and despised of the world. The fact that heaven is thus allowing the hearts of men to be so unmoved as to refuse us a night of lodging conceals some mystery. I have been reminded by the inn keeper, Mary that outside the city walls there is a cave, which serves as a shelter for shepherds and their flocks. I used to hide there in order to get away from my brothers. Let us seek it out; perhaps it is unoccupied; we must depend on Heaven, since we receive none from men on earth."

I responded, "My, spouse and my, master, let not your kind heart be afflicted, because the ardent wishes which the love of God excites in you cannot be fulfilled. I beseech you to give thanks for the events having been disposed in this way. The place of which you speak shall be most satisfactory to me. Let your tears of sorrow turn to tears of joy, and let us lovingly embrace poverty, which is the inestimable and precious treasure of my most holy Son. He came from heaven to seek poverty, let us then afford him an occasion to practice it in the joy of our souls. Let us go gladly wherever the Lord shall guide us. Our little colt is outside waiting for us. I have a feeling she will lead us to your cave." Our holy angels accompanied us lighting the way. The little she ass led us directly to the cave. It was empty except for an ox and three sheep. The little colt made a beeline for a stall and began eating the straw. She alone had known all along our final destination.

We thanked the Lord for his mercy and entered the lodging thus provided for us, and by the radiance of the ten thousand angels, we could easily ascertain its poverty and loneliness, which we esteemed as favors and welcomed them with tears of consolation and joy. We fell on our knees and gave God thanks for this shelter, which we knew had been provided by his wisdom for his own hidden designs. I suddenly felt a fullness of joy, which entirely elevated and vivified me. I besought the Lord to bless with a liberal hand all the inhabitants of the neighboring city. I knew that our rejection by the people of Bethlehem had given occasion to the vast favors, which awaited us in this neglected cavern. The cave was formed entirely of coarse rock on two sides, and closed off on the other two with rocks and sod slabs to close out the wind and weather, a place intended merely for the shelter of beasts. Yet, the eternal Father had selected it for the shelter, birth, and dwelling-place of his only Son.

My angelic spirits, who, like a celestial militia guarding their Queen and Mistress, formed themselves into cohorts in the manner of court guards in a royal palace. They no longer concealed themselves from Joseph, but appeared to him in their visible forms. For, on this occasion, it was befitting that he should enjoy such a favor. Thus, Joseph's sorrow for not having providing for me was assuaged by his seeing our drab surroundings so beautifully adorned. God granted this blessing in order to enliven and encourage Joseph for the miraculous events about to take place that night in this forsaken stable.

I set about cleaning the cave, which was soon to serve as a royal chamber and sacred mercy seat of my Son. I did not wish to miss this opportunity for exercising my humility, for only by preparing and cleansing his temple could I express my devotion and reverence to my Lord and God.

Joseph was at once concerned and implored me, "Please my, spouse, do not deprive me of this work, which I consider to be mine alone," and he hastened to set about cleaning the floor and the corners of the cave, although, at my urging, he allowed me to assist him. My angels abashed at our eagerness for humility, speedily emulated our efforts and in short order the cave was sparkling clean and filled with a heavenly fragrance provided by the angels. Joseph then built a fire with materials he had brought with him for that purpose. It was very cold, and I was happy to warm myself by the fire. Then, I prepared our supper from the meager supplies left in our saddlebags, while Joseph stabled our Muscat ass, the little she-ass and the other animals off in one corner. He fed them some hay that he found in the cave, and they were contentedly munching away as we also ate our rations. I knew my time was quite near, and the impending mystery of my divine delivery took up all my thoughts. I was only able to eat out of obedience to my spouse.

After our meal, we gave thanks to the Lord, and after having spent a short time in prayer and conferring about the mysteries of the Incarnate Word, I suddenly felt the approach of the most blessed birth. God did not plan for Joseph to be present at the birth. The hour being quite late, I requested Joseph to prepare our sleeping pallets. He immediately prepared a couch for me in a manger. Joseph used our articles of clothing and the material available to make me as comfortable as possible. Leaving me in the portion of cave, thus furnished; he retired to a corner near the entrance where he began to pray. The Holy Spirit immediately enveloped Joseph into a state of ecstasy. During his rapture, God showed Joseph all that was to happen that night. I did not awaken him until after Jesus was born. The sleep that my spouse enjoyed that night was more exalted and blessed than that of Adam in paradise.

I heard a voice call me, which strongly and sweetly raised me above all created things and caused me to feel new effects of divine power; for this was one of the most singular and admirable ecstasies of my entire life. God filled me with new enlightenment and divine influences, until I reached a clear vision of the Divinity. The veil fell, and I saw intuitively the Godhead itself in such glory and plentitude of insight, as all the capacity of men and angels could not describe or fully understand. All the knowledge of the Divinity and humanity of my most holy Son, which I had ever received in former visions were renewed, and moreover other secrets of the inexhaustible archives of the bosom of God were revealed to me. Words are insufficient for me to properly express that which I was privileged to witness. The Most High then announced to me the time and manner of his Son's coming into this world. I prostrated myself before the throne of his Divinity. I gave him glory, thanks, and praise for myself and for all creatures, such as was befitting the ineffable mercy and condescension of his divine love. With profound humility, as one who understood the greatness of this new sacrament, I asked the Lord for new light and grace in order to be able to worthily undertake the service, worship, and the rearing up of the Word made flesh, he, to whom I was soon to give birth, to bear in my arms, and to nurse with my virginal milk.

I held myself totally unworthy of the office of being the Mother of God, and so I prudently and humbly pondered this weighty matter. However, because I did humble myself and acknowledge my nothingness in the presence of the Almighty, his Majesty raised me up and confirmed anew upon me the title of Mother of God by saying,

"My most humble, spouse, I command you to exercise the office of the Mother of God. You are to be my legitimate and true mother. You shall treat me as the Son of the Eternal Father, and at the same time the Son of your womb. All of this I entrust to you, the most perfect of all mothers. I remained in this ecstasy and Beatific Vision for over an hour preceding my delivery. When I regained my senses, I felt and actually saw the body of the infant God begin to move in my virginal womb, as my Son freed himself from the place he had occupied the last nine months. His movements did not cause me any pain or hardship, as happens during the childbirths of the other daughters of Adam and Eve. Instead, it filled me with incomparable joy and delight causing in my body such exalted and divine effects that they exceeded all thoughts of men. God so spiritualized my body with the beauty of heaven that I no longer seemed a human and earthly creature. My countenance emitted rays of light like a sun colored pink; inflamed with fervent love, I shone in indescribable majesty.

I knelt in the manger, my eyes raised to heaven, my hands joined and folded at my breast, and I was entirely immersed in God. In this position, and at the end of my heavenly rapture, I gave to the world the Onlybegotten Son of the Father and of my flesh, our Savior Jesus, ***true God and true man.*** It was midnight on a Sunday, in the year of the creation of the world five thousand one hundred and ninety nine [5199], which is the date given in the Roman Catholic Church. In common terms, it happened on midnight on a Sunday in the year 6 BC. There have been errors made by the creators of calendars over the years that have led to many disputes about this date, and the dates of future events involving my Son and me.

There were many wonderful circumstances and particulars, which all the faithful have assumed to have miraculously accompanied this most divine birth. Since Joseph, our donkeys, and I were the only witnesses to these marvelous events, only I, with the permission of our Lord, can divulge them to you. At the end of my vision, which I described above, was born the Sun of Justice, the Onlybegotten Son of the Eternal Father and of my immaculate body. My Son did not divide, but penetrated the vaginal chamber as the rays of the sun penetrate the crystal shrine, lighting it up in prismatic beauty. The divine Child was born pure and disengaged, without the protecting shield called secundines, which is the manner in which other children are commonly born, and in which they are enveloped in the wombs of their mothers. I will not attempt to explain this phenomenon, it is enough to know and suppose the arm of the Almighty selected and made use of all that substantially and unavoidably belonged to natural human generation. In this manner, the Word could truly call himself conceived and engendered as a true man and born of the substance of me, his Mother ever Virgin.

Anything related or consequent upon any sin, original or actual, that could be in any way lessen or impair the dignity of me as the Queen of Heaven and as true Mother of Christ our Lord had not been formed in me. Such imperfections of sin or nature were not necessary either for the true humanity of Christ, or for his office of Redeemer or Teacher. Nor must we be ungenerous in presuming wonderful intervention of the Author of nature and grace in favor of me who was his mother. The Lord had prepared, adorned, and made me increasingly beautiful and perfect for this very purpose. The divine right hand enriched me at all times with gifts and graces and reached the utmost limits of his Omnipotence possible in regard to a mere creature.

The power of the Holy Ghost was responsible for my remaining a virgin in the conception and birth of my Son, and did not impair my true motherhood in any manner. It is true; I could have lost my virginity in a natural manner without incurring any fault. However, in that case, it would have left me without my singular prerogative of virginity. Therefore, I must conclude that in order that I should not be without it, the divine power of my most holy Son preserved it for me. Likewise, my divine Son could have been born with nature's covering or cuticle in which others are born. Yet, this was not necessary in order to be born a natural Son of God and me. Hence, he chose not to take it forth with him from my virginal and material womb. It was not just that the Incarnate Word should be subject to all the laws of the Sons of Adam. The miraculous Birth of Jesus exempted and held him free from all corruption or uncleanness of matter. This matter had been closely connected and attached to his most holy body and it was composed of my blood and substance [the afterbirth]. In a like manner it was not advisable to keep and preserve it outside of me, nor was it becoming to give it the same privileges and importance as to his divine body in coming forth from my body. God therefore decreed that the sacred covering should be appropriately disposed of within my womb by supernatural means.

My infant Son was brought forth from my virginal chamber glorious and transfigured, unencumbered by any corporal or material substance foreign to him. The divine and infinite wisdom had decreed and ordained that the glory of his most holy soul should participate in the gifts of glory in the same way as would happen later in his Transfiguration on mount Tabor in the presence of the Apostles. This miracle was not necessary in order to penetrate the virginal enclosure and to leave unimpaired my virginal integrity, for without this Transfiguration God could have brought this about by other miracles. Thus, agree the holy Doctors of the Church; who however, see no other miracle in my Son's birth than that the Child was born without impairing my virginity. God willed that I should look upon the body of my Son, the God-man, for the first time in a glorified state for two reasons. The one was in order that by this divine vision I should conceive the highest reverence for the majesty of him whom I was to treat as my Son, the true God-man. I had already been informed of my Son's two-fold nature. Therefore, when I saw my Son for the first time, God filled me with new graces corresponding to the greatness of his most holy Son. Secondly, God rewarded me because of my fidelity and holiness, and because my pure and chaste eyes had avoided all worldly things for love of my most holy Son. Thus, God permitted me to see Jesus, at the second of his birth, in all his glory, as a reward for my, humility, loyalty, and love.

Saint Michael and Saint Gabriel were my only assistants at the birth of my Son. They stood at a proper distance in human corporeal forms. At the precise moment when the Incarnate Word penetrated the virginal chamber by divine power and issued into this world they received him into their hands with ineffable reverence. In the same manner as a priest elevates the sacred host to the people for adoration, so these two celestial ministers presented to me my glorious and refulgent Son. At this precise moment my Son and I looked into one another's eyes, and in this one look I was wounded with love by the sweet Infant and was at the same time exalted and transformed in him and he spoke to me,

"Mother, become like unto me, since on this day, for the human existence, which you have today given me, I will give you another more exalted existence in grace, assimilating your existence as a mere creature to the likeness of me, who am God and Man."

Inspired, I answered him, "Lift me, elevate me, Lord, and I will run after you in the odor of your ointments," many of the hidden mysteries of the Canticles were fulfilled, when I prayed these words.

At this same time, I felt the presence of the most holy Trinity, and God the Father said "This is my beloved Son in whom I am greatly pleased and delighted."

Enlightened, I answered, "Eternal, Father and exalted, God, Lord, and, Creator of the Universe, give me anew your permission and benediction to receive in my arms the desired of nations; and teach me to fulfill as your unworthy mother and lowly slave your holy will." A voice said, "Receive your Onlybegotten Son, imitate him and rear him; and remember that you must sacrifice him when I shall demand it of you."

I replied, "Behold the creature of your hands. Adorn me with your grace so that your Son and my God receive me for his slave. If you come to my aid with your Omnipotence, I shall be faithful in his service. May you count it no presumption in your insignificant creature that I bear in my arms and nourish at my breast my own Lord and Creator."

Upon my saying this, my Son suspended the miracle of his transfiguration, and in effect created another miracle by confining himself entirely into the soul of my infant Son. As a helpless baby, I now saw him as one capable of suffering, and remaining in a kneeling position, I adored him with profound humility and reverence. The angels now laid the child in my arms, and I spoke to him and said, "My sweetest, love, light of my eyes and being of my soul; you have arrived in good hour into this world as the Sun of Justice [Malach.3, 20], in order to disperse the darkness of sin and death! True God of the true God, save your servants and let all flesh see him who shall draw upon it salvation. Make me my, Son, as you would desire me to be in your service."

Then I spoke to the Father and holding his Son up to him said, "Exalted, Creator of the Universe, here is the altar and the sacrifice acceptable in your eyes [Malachi: 3, 4]. From this hour on, oh, Lord, look upon the human race with mercy; and inasmuch as we have deserved your anger, it is now time that you be appeased in your Son and mine. Let your justice now come to rest, and let your mercy be exalted; for on this account the Word has clothed itself in the semblance of sinful flesh [Rom: 8, 3], and become a brother of mortals and sinners [Phil: 2, 7]. In this title, I recognize them as brothers and I intercede for them from my inmost soul. You, Lord, have made me the mother of your Onlybegotten Son without any merit on my part, since this dignity is above all merit of a creature. However, I partly owe to men the occasion of this incomparable good fortune; since it is on their account that I am the Mother of the Word made man and Redeemer of them all. I will not deny them my love, or remit my care and watchfulness for their salvation. Receive eternal, God, my wishes and petitions for that which is according to your pleasure and good will." I then directed my attention toward all mortals and addressed them indirectly saying,

"Be consoled you afflicted and rejoice you disconsolate, be raised up you fallen, come to rest you who are uneasy. Let the just be gladdened and the saints be rejoiced; let the heavenly spirits break out in new jubilee, let the prophets and the patriarchs of limbo draw new hope, and let all generations praise and magnify the Lord, who renews his wonders. Come, come you poor; approach you little ones without fear, for in my arms I bear the Lion made a Lamb, the Almighty become weak, the Invincible subdued. Come to draw life, hasten to obtain salvation, approach to gain eternal life, approach to gain eternal rest, since I have this for all, and it will be given to you freely and communicated to you without envy. Do not be slow and heavy of heart, you sons of men; and my, Son, oh sweetest joy of my soul, give me permission to receive from you that kiss desired by all creatures." Then, with my unblemished lips I kissed my Son in order to receive the loving caresses of the divine Child.

Holding my Son in my arms, I served as an altar and the sanctuary, where over ten thousand angels adored in visible human forms their Creator Incarnate. At the birth of the Word, God emptied heaven of its inhabitants. The entire heavenly court now joined us in our simple cave and adored their Creator in his garb and habit of a pilgrim [Phil: 2, 7]. In their concert of praise, they intoned the new canticle:

"Gloria in excelsis Deo et in terra pax hominibus bonae voluntatis." [Luke: 2, 14]

I was fifteen and the angels held me in wonder, for with the gifts of prudence, grace, humility, and beauty, given me by the Lord, I had become a worthy trustee and minister of such vast and magnificent sacraments.

It has been asked, "How many angels can be held on the head of a pin? This fills me with amusement. It would be more appropriate to ask, how was it possible for billions of holy angels in all their glory to all be present at the same time within the small confines of our humble stable carved out of the soft sandstone prevalent throughout Judea.

It was now time, to call my saintly husband Joseph, to view his new foster Son. It was proper that he should, before all other mortals, be present and experience, adore, and reverence the Word made flesh. God had chosen Joseph, above all other men, to act as the faithful warden of this great sacrament. His first sight as he recovered his senses was the divine Child I held in my arms. There, he adored him in profoundest humility; with tears of joy he kissed his Son's tiny feet in such ecstasy and admiration that the life in him would have been destroyed, if he had not been preserved by divine power. I then asked my Son for permission to rise, for I was still on my knees, and while Joseph handed me the wrappings and swaddling clothes, I clothed my Son for the first time with incomparable reverence, devotion and tenderness. I then laid him in a manger, which Joseph had arranged for him as a crib [Luke: 2, 7].

Then, according to divine ordainment, an ox from the neighboring fields ran up in great haste. He joined the other animals and our beasts of burden, which had so faithfully led and carried my Son and me from Nazareth. I commanded them to acknowledge and adore their Creator, and the humble animals fell to their knees and reverenced their God. They warmed the Child with their breath and with the blessed Lord wrapped in swaddling clothes lying between them; they shared with him the warmth of their bodies. Thus was the prophecy fulfilled that read, "The ox knows his owner, and the ass his master's crib; but Israel has not known me, and my people have not understood."

I picked my Son up and holding him before me, I said to Joseph, "My husband and my helper receive in your arms the Creator of heaven and earth. Enjoy his amiable and sweet company as a recompense for your faithful service. Take to yourself the Treasure of the eternal Father and participate in this blessing of the human race." Then, speaking interiorly to the divine Infant, I said, "Sweetest love of my soul and light of my eyes, rest in the arms of Joseph my friend and spouse. Do you converse with him and pardon me my shortcomings. Much do I feel the loss of you even for one instant, but I wish to communicate without envy the good I have received, to all that are worthy."

My most faithful husband acknowledged this blessing, and humbled himself to the dirt floor and replied, "Lady and Sovereign of the world my, spouse, how can I being unworthy, presume to hold in my arms God himself, in whose presence tremble the pillars of heaven [Job: 26, 11]? How can I, such a lowly creature, have courage to accept such an exalted favor? I am but dust and ashes, but do you, Lady, assist me in my lowliness and ask his Majesty to look upon me with clemency and make me worthy through his grace."

Trembling with discreet fear, Joseph fell on his knees to receive the Redeemer of the world in his hands. Tears of joy and delight flowed copiously from his eyes in extraordinary happiness. The divine Child looked at him caressingly, and at the same time he renewed Joseph's inmost soul with such divine efficacy as no words will suffice to explain. Joseph broke into new canticles of praise at seeing himself thus enriched with such magnificent blessings and favors. He then replaced Jesus into my arms, both of us being on our knees. At this time, we established a pattern of worship of our divine Son, for when we approached him we genuflected three times, kissed the ground, and executed heroic acts of humility, worship and reverence. Thus, did we observe all propriety in receiving or giving the Christ Child from and to one another.

"During our heavenly celebration in our humble quarters, many of the courtiers of heaven were dispatched to announce the happy news to those, who according to the divine will were properly disposed to hear it. Saint Michael appeared to the holy patriarchs in limbo and announced to them the good news that the Onlybegotten Son of God was born into the world. At my request, he spoke personally to my saintly parents Joachim and Anne. He congratulated them that I now held in my arms the Salvation of all nations; He, whose coming had been foretold by all the patriarchs and prophets [Is. 7, 14] [Is. 9, 5]. God granted this great gathering of the just; who had been banished for so long, this most consoling and joyful day. They all acknowledged this new God-man as the true Author of eternal salvation, and they composed and sang songs of adoration and worship in his praise. Joachim and Anne in turn asked Michael to ask me to worship in their name the divine Child, which I did at once.

I dispatched another messenger to Elizabeth and her son John to inform them of the good news. In spite of John's tender age, upon hearing the news, he and his mother prostrated themselves upon the ground and adored their God made man. God renewed John interiorly with a spirit more inflamed than that of Elijah, causing new admiration and jubilation in the angels themselves. They in turn asked that I adore my Son and offer him their services; all of which I did at once. Elizabeth immediately dispatched one of her domestics to Bethlehem with presents for all of us. They included money, some linen, and other items for the comfort of the Child. After the glowing report from her servant of our poverty and the feelings excited in him at our holiness and happiness, Elizabeth had a hard time to restrain herself from coming to us, but denied herself the privilege not wishing to expose John to danger. Instead, she sent us many more gifts. I selected those we needed the most and distributed the rest to the poor, for I did not wish to be deprived of the company of the poor in the days in which we would have to remain in the area.

I sent other angels to bring the news to Zachariah, Simeon, Anna, and to some other just and holy people, who were worthy to be trusted of this new mystery. All of the just were not notified, yet in all of them were wrought certain divine effects in the hour in which the Savior of the world was born. These just souls felt in their hearts a new and supernatural joy, though they were ignorant of its cause. God even renovated and enlivened the plants. The sun accelerated its course, the stars shone in greater brightness; and for the Magi Kings was formed that wonderful star which showed them the way to Bethlehem. Many trees out of season began to bloom and others to produce fruit. The Lord overthrew many heathen temples, and in others, he destroyed the idols and put their demons to flight.

Men accounted for many of these marvels in different ways, but they were far from the truth. Many of the just, who by divine impulse, suspected or believed that God had come into the world, did not knew for sure except those to whom it was revealed. Among these were Three Magi rulers of separate Oriental kingdoms. I sent angels of my guard to inform them by interior and intellectual enlightenment that the Redeemer of the human race had been born in poverty and humility. At the same time, they were inspired with the sudden desire of seeking and adoring Him. They saw the star sent them as a guide to Bethlehem and set out on a journey they knew not where.

The local shepherds, who were tending their flocks of sheep at the time of the birth of Christ, were especially blest [Luke: 2, 8]. Not only because they accepted their calling with resignation from the hand of God; but also because, being poor and humble and despised by the world, they belonged in sincerity and uprightness of heart to those Israelites, who fervently hoped and prayed for the coming of the Messiah. In effect, they resembled Jesus as they were far removed from the riches, vanity and ostentation of the world, and were far from its diabolical cunning. [John: 10, 4] Thus, it was that the Lord sent Gabriel in human form, but in great splendor to them. The shepherds were suddenly enveloped and bathed in the celestial radiance of the angel. At his appearance, the shepherds, being little versed in such visions, were filled with great fear.

The holy prince reassured them, "Do not be afraid, upright men; for I announce to you tidings of great joy. Today is born the Redeemer Christ, our Lord, in the city of David. As a sign of this truth you shall find the Infant wrapped in swaddling-clothes and placed in a manger" [Luke: 2, 10-12]. At these words there suddenly appeared a great multitude of the celestial court, who in voices of sweet harmony sang to the Most High these words,

"Glory to God in the highest, and on earth, peace to those on whom his favor rests." After repeatedly singing this refrain, so new to the world, the holy angels disappeared. All of this happened in the fourth watch of the night. By this angelic vision the humble and fortunate shepherds were filled with divine enlightenment and were unanimously impelled by a fervent longing to witness with their own eyes the Most High mystery of which they had just been informed. The angels easily made the shepherds proficient in the divine wisdom, because they were free from the arrogant wisdom of the world. Conferring among themselves and led by the star, they hastened with all speed to Bethlehem to see the wonder described to them. When the shepherds presented themselves to the cave, Joseph ushered them in and they found my infant Son lying in a manger as had been described to them. My Son looked upon them kindly, emitting from his countenance a holy aura, which wounded the sincere hearts of these humble shepherds with love. It charged them anew, and constituted in them a new state of grace and holiness and filled them with an exalted knowledge of the divine mysteries of the Incarnation and the Redemption of the human race.

As one, they prostrated themselves and adored the Word made Flesh. They presented to him their simple gifts of a sheep, a young goat and a few chickens. No longer as ignorant rustics, but now as wise and prudent men they adored him, acknowledging and magnifying him as true God and true man, and as Restorer and Redeemer of the human race. I could see into their inmost hearts, and, as the representative of my Son, I said to them,

"In view of all that you have seen and learned, I exhort you to persevere in the divine love and in the service of the Most High." In conversing with them, I was pleased with their understanding of the mysteries. They remained with us worshiping my Son until mid-day. Then giving them some food, I sent them off full of heavenly grace and consolation. The angels had tended their flocks of sheep in their absence. They returned a few times bringing simple gifts, for they were very poor. Few of the local residents believed their stories, because they considered them uncultured and ignorant people.

In the holy Temple of Jerusalem, at Christ's birth, the various writings of the Sadducees were hurled repeatedly with great force from the place they were ordinarily kept causing much dread. In Rome, across the river where a great number of Jews lived, a well of oil erupted and gushed forth, to the wonder of all the witnesses. On this night, the Emperor Augustus at the Capitol had an apparition of a rainbow upon which sat the Virgin and Child. His oracle told him, "A Child is born, and before him we must all flee." Augustus at once erected an altar and offered sacrifice to the Son of the Virgin, as the "Firstborn of God". Fear seized them all when God caused a magnificent statue of Jupiter to fall and shatter. Sacrifices were ordered to Venus and instead of the priests speaking from the idol, the devil was forced to speak and said,

"A virgin has conceived and brought forth a Son."

The pagan priests were mystified and searched their records. They found that seventy years before a prophet had visions and had stated that a Virgin should bring forth a Son. They had put the prophet aside as a fool. Now, the people remembered the story and marveled at the prophecy. In Egypt beyond Heliopolis and Memphis, there was an idol, which gave answers to all kinds of questions. God made the statue mute. To appease the idol, the king ordered his entire kingdom to offer sacrifices to the statue. Then again was the devil forced to say by the command of God,

"I have become silent; I must give place to another. The Son of the Virgin is born and a temple will be erected here to his honor."

The king had a temple erected honoring the Virgin and Child whom the idol had proclaimed. The people honored my Son and I there, unfortunately they were pagan rites. Although God had forced Lucifer to make these statements, he also clouded his mind and he had no memory of them.

For the denizens of Hell, the birth of my Son was a terrible catastrophe. It meant the "beginning of the end" for the evil one and his demonic forces. It was God's long-range plan to depose this black prince of the world. Therefore, God hid the sacrament of the coming of the Word from him until Jesus had completed his Passion on earth. Because of the malice of Lucifer, he was not only unworthy to be informed of the mysteries of the divine wisdom; but it was just that by divine Providence, the malice of this enemy should be blinded and confused. In his malice, he had brought into the world the deceit and blindness of sin and cast down the entire human race by the fall of Adam. It is necessary to take note of this historical fact, for if Lucifer had known positively that Christ was the true God, he would not later have planned and obtained his death. Instead, he would have done everything possible to prevent this from happening. For in dying, Jesus redeemed the world and opened the gates of heaven, which placed stricter limits on the devil's power on earth.

God only allowed Lucifer to know that I, a holy woman, had given birth to a Son in a forsaken cave in great poverty. God calculated to mislead the demon's pride rather than to enlighten it. God veiled the miraculous birth, the angels, the shepherds, the messages of the angels, and the guiding star from their understanding. The demons were aware of the changes in the elements, the stars, and planets, but they could not understand them. Lucifer called his demons together to discuss all these events, and concluded by saying,

"We all know the power and greatness of God, and I cannot conceive of a Son of God being born in such mean circumstances."

After the shepherds left, I judged it time to nourish my Son at my breast. I reverently asked permission of my Son. Although I knew that I was to nourish him as a true and human child, I nevertheless bore in mind that he was at the same time the true God and a great distance intervened between the infinite Being and a mere creature such as myself. Therefore, in all my future dealings with my Son, I nourished, served, and tended my Child with unremitting care, reverence, and discretion. I later learned this caused new admiration in my angels, whose celestial understanding reached not so far as to fully comprehend such heroic acts of a tender maiden. All of these mysteries are worthy of your remembrance and attention, and you cannot allow yourselves to be negligent in forgetting them or failing to acknowledge them sufficiently.

In order to assist me, all the angels of my guard remained present in visible forms from the time of the birth until two years later. I was so solicitous of my divine Son that I would not part with him to place him in the arms of my spouse, or into those of the holy princes Michael or Gabriel, except on rare occasions when I was obliged to take some nourishment or do other things. Michael and Gabriel begged me to consign the child to them during meals or when Joseph was at work. Thus, when I complied, was my Son placed in the hands of the angels, in admirable fulfillment of the words of David:

"Upon their hands they shall bear you up, lest you dash your foot against a stone [Ps: 91, 12]."

Ever watchful, I refused to take any sleep in my solicitude for my Son, except when his Majesty commanded me to do so. However, in reward for my diligence, he provided me with a new and more miraculous kind of sleep, for now, while I slept, my heart was awake, continuing or rather not interrupting the divine intelligence and contemplation of the Divinity. However, from this day on, the Lord added still another miracle, namely that I retain in my arms the power of holding and embracing my Son in the same way, as if I were awake. In this manner, I could gaze upon him with the eyes of my intellect, understanding all that my Child and I did exteriorly in the meantime. Thus, what is said in the Canticles was miraculously fulfilled, "I was sleeping, but my heart kept vigil [Songs: 5, 2B]."

I composed new canticles of praise and exaltation of the Lord, in honor of my Child, which I sang alternately with Joseph and my angels. Joseph participated in and understood many of them. His greatest joy was the favor I received from my Son. Our friends and family always referred to Jesus as the Son of Joseph, since they did not know the true nature of our relationship. With my Son's approval, I often referred to Jesus, as *our son* in Joseph's presence, which caused him immeasurable delight.

When I first learned that I was to be the Mother of the divine Word, I began to meditate upon the labors and sufferings in store for my Son. My knowledge of the Scriptures was profound, and I understood the mysteries contained therein. From the beginning, I foresaw and prepared with deep compassion for all he was to suffer in the Redemption of Man. This caused me much anguish; I suffered a private martyrdom by sharing in his passion. However, I had no knowledge of what my Lord's wishes were regarding the circumcision of his Son, although Jewish Law required the circumcision of all males on the eighth day after their birth. My Son had come to honor and confirm the law by fulfilling it. Since he had come to suffer for man, he would in no way shirk the pains of circumcision. Circumcision was a Hebrew rite instituted for cleansing the newborn children from original sin. My Son was free from this guilt, since he was free of original sin. Jesus, by submitting to the knife, would constitute the first letting of his innocent blood for the salvation of man.

Just before the eighth day, I fell on my knees and addressed the Lord, "Highest, King, Father of my Lord, I hold the true sacrifice and victim in my arms. My, Lord, I know what should be done with your Son according to the Law. However, if by my own suffering, I can rescue my Son from this pain, my heart is prepared. I am likewise ready to see him submit to circumcision, if that is your will."

The Most High answered me saying, "My, daughter and my, dove, do not let your heart be afflicted because your Son is to be subjected to the knife, and to the pains of circumcision; I have sent him into the world as an example that he may put an end to the Law of Moses by entirely fulfilling it. [Matt: 5, 17] Remember: he is my natural Son by an eternal generation, the image of my substance, equal to me in essence, majesty and glory. By thus subjecting himself to the Sacramental Law, without letting man know that he is exempt from such laws, he gains much merit. Resign yourself then to the shedding of his blood and willingly yield to me the first fruits of the eternal salvation of men."

With complete and loving obedience, I offered up my Son saying, "Supreme, Lord and, God, I offer to you this victim and host of acceptable sacrifice with all my heart. I am full of compassion and sorrow that men have offended your immense goodness in such a way as to force a God to make amends. I shall praise you eternally for looking with such infinite love upon your creatures and for preferring to refuse pardon to your own Son rather than hinder the salvation of man. I offer you the meek Lamb, who is to take away the sins of the world by his innocence. However, if it is possible to mitigate his pains caused by this knife at the expense of suffering in me, your arm is mighty to affect this exchange."

I then approached Joseph reminding him that the appointed time by the Law for the circumcision of our Son had arrived. There was no reason to advise him of God's commands, for he replied in all modesty and wisdom by saying to me. "I wish above all things to conform myself to the divine will and therefore will conform myself to the common law, even though the Incarnate Word is not subject to the Law. He has clothed himself in our humanity. As a perfect Teacher and Savior, he no doubt wishes to conform like other men in its fulfillment. When and how will you wish the circumcision to take place?"

"It shall be performed as with all children, my dear, spouse. However, I will not hand him over to another, for I shall hold him in my arms."

Joseph replied, "It shall be done as you direct, Mary. May I point out that when the holy angel informed me of this great sacrament, he also told me that your most sacred Son should be named Jesus." I answered, "This same name was revealed to me when my Son assumed flesh in my womb. It is fitting that in humble reverence that we conform to the will of the Almighty."

Joseph nodded his agreement and affirmed, "His name shall be Jesus."

While Joseph and I were talking, innumerable angels descended in human forms from on high filling the cave with dazzling light. They were clothed in shining white garments, on which were woven red embroideries of wonderful beauty. They had palms in their hands and crowns upon their heads and emitted a greater splendor than many suns. Pre-eminent in splendor were the escutcheons on their breasts, which were engraved or embossed with the name "**Jesus**" the beauty of which exceeded even that of the angels themselves. The holy angels divided into two choirs keeping their gaze fixed upon the King and Lord held in my arms. The chiefs of these heavenly cohorts were the two princes, Saint Michael and Saint Gabriel. They shone in greater splendor than the rest and they bore in their hands, as a spiritual distinction, the most holy name of Jesus written in larger letters on placards of incomparable beauty and splendor.

The two princes presented themselves to me and said, "Lady, this is the name of your Son which was written in the mind of God from all eternity. The blessed Trinity has given this name to your Onlybegotten Son as the signal of salvation of the whole human race; establishing him at the same time on the throne of David. He shall reign on it, chastise his enemies, triumph over them, and make them his footstool and pass judgment upon them. He shall raise his friends to the glory of his right hand. This is to happen at the cost of much suffering and bloodshed. Even now, he is to shed it in receiving this name, since it is that of the Savior and Redeemer. It shall be the beginning of his sufferings in obedience to the will of his eternal Father. We all are come as ministering spirits of the Most High, appointed and sent by the holy Trinity in order to serve the Onlybegotten Son of the Father and you in all the mysteries and sacraments of the law of grace. We are his guardians and shall accompany him and minister to him until he shall ascend triumphantly to the celestial Jerusalem and open the portals of heaven. Afterwards, we shall enjoy an especial accidental glory beyond that of the other blessed to which no such commission has been given."

Joseph and I witnessed all of these events, but his understanding was not as deep as mine was. God had blessed me with the wisdom to comprehend and understand the highest mysteries of the Redemption. Although Joseph understood many more mysteries than did other mortals, yet he could not penetrate them in the same way as I could. Both of us were filled with heavenly joy and admiration at the angel's words, and we extolled the Lord in new canticles of delight.

Anyone, by the Law of Moses, could perform a circumcision. Most pious Jewish mothers preferred their children be circumcised at the hands of a priest. In an era when two out of three infants died before their second birthday, a priestly circumcision was most comforting to Israeli mothers. I had no such feeling of danger to my Son, but because of the dignity of my Child, I wished a priest to administer this rite. Therefore, I requested my husband to go to Bethlehem to bring a priest to the cave.

While Joseph was making the arrangements in Bethlehem, I unpacked my carefully wrapped crystal vessel for preserving the sacred relic of the circumcision. I then prepared some linen clothes and a soothing, healing ointment made with an olive oil base. Joseph soon returned with a priest from the local synagogue. Two other officials, who were to render such assistance as was customary at the performance of the rite, accompanied him.

The rudeness of our dwelling at first astonished and somewhat disconcerted the priest. I spoke to him and welcomed him in such a manner that his constraint quickly changed to one of admiration. Without knowing the cause, the priest was moved to reverence and esteem, for when he looked upon my face and the face of my Son he was filled with devotion; he wondered at the contrast amid such poverty and in such a lowly place. The priest touched the divine flesh of my Son, and was instantly sanctified and perfected. It gave him a new existence in grace and raised him up to a state of holiness very pleasing to the Lord.

Joseph lit two candles in reverence for the sacred rite, and the priest asked me to give him the Child so that I did not have to watch the sacrifice. I hesitated; my first call was one of obedience to the priest.

But, my concern for my Son overrode this call, and I stated, "If it pleases you, Sir, I most humbly ask you to allow me to remain since I desire to be present at the performance of the rite, since I hold it in such high esteem. I assure you, I will have the courage to hold him in my arms, since I do not wish to leave him alone on such an occasion."

I breathed a sigh of relief as the priest acceded to my request promising at the same time to be most careful. Thus did I become the sacred altar on which the truths typified in the ancient sacrifice became a reality. I offered up this sacrifice myself in order that it might be acceptable to the eternal Father in all its particulars. I unwound the swaddling clothes and drew from my inner garments the linen cloth I had placed there to warm, for the cave was very cold.

The priest used his small sacrificial knife made of flint to perform his duty. As he did so, my husband, as was tradition, recited the ritual prayer, "Blessed be Jehovah the Savior. He has sanctified his well-beloved son from the womb of his mother and has written the Law in our flesh. He has signed his son with the sign of his Covenant that he may impart to him the blessings of Abraham our father."

Interiorly I felt my divine Son offer up to his Father in Heaven the sacrifice of this first shedding of his most Precious Blood as a pledge that he would one day give it all for the Redemption of mankind.

True to his human nature, my Son began to cry, and I knew he was crying as was expected of a human infant, but his tears were for the sins of man. I also wept and caught the sacred relics in the glass crystal, paid for with money sent to us by Elizabeth. With God's permission I placed a silver cap on the crystal glass, and sealed it with a single *mystical* command. I then handed it to Joseph for safekeeping. I clasped my Son to my breast stilling his cries and then tended to his cuts placing soothing salve on them. I quickly dressed him, for it was bitter cold; as I did my Son offered up to the eternal Father three sacrifices. The first was that he, being innocent and the Son of the true God assumed the condition of a sinner by subjecting himself to a rite instituted as a remedy for original sin and to a law not binding on him. The second was his willingness to suffer the pains of circumcision, which he suffered as a true and perfect man. The third was the most ardent love with which he began to shed his blood for the human race, giving thanks to the eternal Father for having given him a human nature capable of suffering for his exaltation and glory.

These prayers were accepted by the Father, and according to our way of thinking, he began to declare himself satisfied and paid for the indebtedness of humanity. God allowed me to share in all of these mysteries.

The priest now asked us, "What name will you give to this Child?"

Ever attentive to honor my spouse, I turned to Joseph and asked him, "What name shall we call our Son, Joseph?"

My spouse turned to me in like reverence and replied, "I believe it would be proper, Mary, for his sweet name to first flow from your lips."

Suddenly inspired by the Holy Spirit, we spoke in unison and stated,

"***JESUS*** is his name."

The priest announced, "The parents are unanimously agreed, and great is the name, which they give this Child:" and thereupon he inscribed it in the tablet of names, of the rest of the children born in Bethlehem. The priest was interiorly moved when he wrote the name, and he shed copious tears. He could not fully understand what was happening and he prophesied,

"I am convinced that this Child is to be a great Prophet of the Lord. Use extreme care in raising Him," and he added kindly, "please tell me in what manner may I relieve your needs."

We assured him we lacked for nothing and gave him gifts of precious wax candles and other items set aside for this purpose, and thanked him for his services. Being left alone with the Child, Joseph and I sang canticles of praise with our angels, all having been unseen by our visitors, and we adored our infant Lord and Savior now sleeping peacefully in my arms.

Our neighbor's curiosity excited by the tales of the shepherds, we began to have visitors. They came seeking gossip, but left carrying stories of the wonderful Child born to a holy man and woman in a cave. Beggars came and we gave them what we had, and later when we had given everything away, a few cursed us in our poverty for we had nothing left to give them. Then, inspired by the curious stories by those visiting our cave, people began to come in large numbers and even Joseph's friends and relatives came out of curiosity. But after seeing my Son and me, they fell to their knees and begged forgiveness for their shoddy treatment of us that memorable night. Many returned bearing gifts, and again, we were able to help our precious poor.

The people then started coming in droves. A few reminded Joseph that he had Essenian friends living nearby that he had forgotten about previously. They had helped him as a boy with his religious studies, and had fed and shielded him when he sought shelter from his brothers who loved to torment him. Three of these holy women returned to help us with the crowds. They also brought with them food and other necessaries, which they gladly helped us dispense to the poor.

A few days after the birth of Jesus, Elizabeth and Zachariah came with several asses loaded with bedding and food. We embraced and Elizabeth holding me by the shoulders said with tears streaming down her face, "Truly, you are the Mother of God." She stepped back and fell to her knees in reverential awe and I placed the Son of God in her eager arms. Tenderly she pressed him to her breast. My Son showed his pleasure and as Zachariah held the child up to God and gave him his priestly blessing, Jesus filled them both with enlightenment and grace. We laid the two babies down together; John's chubby fingers leapt out and clasped the hands of my Son tightly, as though he would never let him go.

They remained for three days, and Elizabeth and I had several long intimate talks; I described to her all that Joseph and I had experienced in Bethlehem. She wept when I told her about the star, the miraculous birth of Jesus, and the visitation of the Shepherds.

When I was finished she said, "The birth of my son John was also painless, but you have not given birth the same as other mothers. The Redeemer has certainly made a most remarkable, humble and inauspicious entry into his kingdom. Scripture has it that he has much to suffer, and I know his exit from this earth will be much more spectacular than his entry." When they left, Elizabeth gave me a large purse of money and said, "I know better than to tell you to save some of this for when you need it. So use it as you see fit for your precious poor." After they left, I asked some of Joseph's

Essenian friends to take the money and distribute it to the poor in Bethlehem. They left eagerly to carry out my request.

During the healing of my Son, I did not take him out of my arms for a single moment. My tender love is beyond all comprehension or understanding of man, as my children will tell you from all over the world. My natural love is greater than any other mother is capable of, and my supernatural love exceeds that of all the angels and saints combined. My reverence and worship of the Trinity cannot be compared with that of any other created being.

Joseph's Essenian friends came hurriedly to the cave one day obviously upset. They conferred with him and left as they came. A short time later we had three rather distinguished visitors; they were Herod's spies. Everyone knew them not so much by looks but by their insincerity and arrogant manners. Herod having heard the stories of the shepherds had sent his agents to look into the matter. Joseph invited them into our simple abode, but they observing his humility and simplicity, and our humble quarters left him with a contemptuous smile.

By the infused knowledge of Holy Scriptures and my high supernatural enlightenment, I knew that the Magi Kings of the Orient would soon come to acknowledge, honor, and adore my most holy Son as their true God. My angels advised them of my Son's birth. Joseph had no knowledge of these historic events and being discreet, I had not discussed them with him. After Jesus' wounds had healed, and moved with compassion for my welfare and that of our Son, my spouse suggested,

"Perhaps it would be prudent," he suggested, "if we moved into Bethlehem until it is time for your purification and the presentation of our Lord to the priests in the temple in Jerusalem? The shelter here is hardly adequate for you, let alone a newly born infant."

I had developed an affection for the cave on account of its humbleness and poverty, and because my divine Son had consecrated it by the mysteries of his birth and circumcision. I knew he intended to also hallow it by the mystery of the Magi's visit. Resigning myself to the will of my husband, I responded, "My Spouse and Master, I will go wherever you wish to go, arrange it as you please."

I knew that God had other plans, which I, of course, could not reveal without violating my trust. While we were thus conferring, Michael and Gabriel, who were still in attendance to our needs, advised us, "Divine Providence has ordained that three kings of the earth, coming from the Orient in search of the King of heaven, shall adore the divine Word in this very place. Angels informed the Magi of his birth, and they immediately set out on their journey. They are already on the way. Therefore, they will arrive shortly fulfilling all that the Prophets had from very ancient time's foreknown and foretold."

Joseph said to me in all humility. "Let it be done as God has ordained. But since it is his pleasure, perhaps he will afford us some protection and shelter against the inclement weather during the short time in which we shall remain here, since I fear for your health, and that of the Child."

Upon hearing this news, I began cleaning our humble quarters for the coming of the kings. In spite of my work, I held my Son in my protective arms, never setting him down for a minute unless it was a matter of necessity. Jesus often gave me the privilege to see through his humanity as through a crystal casement. Thus, was I able to perceive the hypostatic union of the Son of God with his human nature, and I witnessed the activity of his soul in interceding with the eternal Father for the human race.

Joseph often witnessed the favors and caresses which passed between my Son and me. He himself, shared in others, which our Son loved to confer upon him. Many times, whenever I had to do some work, during which I could not hold him myself; I then placed my Son into his protective arms. This happened, as for instance, when I prepared the meals, cleaned the clothes of Jesus and Joseph, or cleaned our abode. Joseph, when he held Jesus in his arms, always felt divine effects in his soul.

Jesus showed exterior signs of affection for his foster father by his pleased looks. Joseph, when he was holding his Son, received the usual tokens of affection that passed between other children and their fathers. However, Jesus always tempered these tokens with kingly majesty.

King David, among others, had prophesied the coming of the three Magi Kings. Balaam, who, having been hired by Balaac, king of the Moabites to curse the Israelites, blessed them instead [Nm: 24, 1-17]. In this blessing Balaam said that he would see the Christ Child, although not at once, and that he would behold him, although not at present; for he did not see him with his own eyes, but through the Magi, his descendents many centuries after. He said also that a star would arise unto Jacob, which was Christ, who arose to reign forever in the house of Jacob [Luke: 1, 32].

The three Magi Kings were Balthazar, King of Persia; Gaspar, King of Mesopotamia; and Melchior, King of Media; all these countries were east of Palestine. These Kings were well versed in the natural sciences, and well read in the Scriptures of the people of God. Because they were so learned, the people called them Magi. In their wisdom and knowledge, they came to believe in the coming of the Messiah. These were upright men, truthful and very just in the government of their countries. They ruled adjoining kingdoms, became mutual friends, and shared with each other the virtues and knowledge, which they had acquired. My angels informed them that the King of the Jews was to be born as *true God and true man*, and that he was the expected Messiah and Savior promised in the Scriptures and prophecies. The Lord had singled them out to seek the star, which Balaam had foretold. The angels advised them that God expected them to co-operate with the divine light and execute what it pointed out. They were all inspired and inflamed with a great love and with a desire to know the God made man, to adore him as their Creator and Redeemer, and to serve him with most perfect devotion.

The three Kings independently resolved to leave immediately and prepared gifts of gold, incense and myrrh in equal quantities. Without heeding the commotion caused among their own people, they resolved with fervent zeal and ardent love to depart for Judah immediately. They put their trust in the bright star formed by the messenger angels to lead them to the Messiah. It was a resplendent star though not so large as those of the firmament; for it was not to ascend higher than was necessary for the purpose of its formation. All three following this same star soon met and their animals and servants formed a considerable party. The star's splendor was different from that of the sun and the other stars. It's most magnificent light illumined the night like a brilliant torch, and by day, it mingled its active brilliancy with that of the sun. The star descended through many layers of aerial space and drew close to them. It astounded and inspired the kings and their servants by shedding its refulgence over them at closer range. They all broke out in praise and admiration at the inscrutable works and mysteries of the Almighty.

The star guided the Magi, until they reached Jerusalem. They entered the city openly inquiring about the Child saying, "Where is the king of the Jews, who is born? We have seen his star in the east, announcing to us his birth, and we have come to see and adore him [Matt: 2, 2-8]." The spies of King Herod, the unjust ruler, informed him of the Magi's quest. The wicked king, panic-stricken at the thought that a more legitimate claimant to the throne should have been born, felt much disturbed and outraged by this report. With him, the entire city was aroused. Herod asked his priests and scribes where the Christ was to be born, according to the Holy Scriptures?

"According to the words of the Prophet Micah [Mi: 5, 1-3], oh high lord and King, he is to be born in Bethlehem. It was written by him that thence the Ruler of Israel is to arise." Herod immediately plotted to kill this usurper and dismissed his priests. Then he secretly had the Magi brought to him in order to learn of them at what time they had seen the star as harbinger of Christ's birth. Innocent of his intentions, they informed him of what they knew, and he sent them on to

Bethlehem saying, "Go and inquire after the Infant; when you have found him, please inform me, in order that I, too, may go and adore him."

Upon leaving Jerusalem, the Magi rejoiced, for once again the star was before them hanging over the small village of Bethlehem a mere two hour journey away. The star gradually diminished in size and led them directly to the cave of the Nativity. Here Joseph met them respectfully and ushered them into the presence of the King of Kings. Even then the star preceded them constantly diminishing in size until it hovered over the head of my infant Son and bathed him in its light; whereupon the matter of which it was made completely dissolved and disappeared.

I had asked Joseph to remain at my side. The precaution of sending him away was not necessary. The angels had informed the Magi that I was yet a virgin, and that he was the true God and not a son of Joseph. God would not have allowed them to be led to the cave ignorant of such an important circumstance as his origin, and thus allowing them to adore the Child as the son of Joseph and of a mother not a virgin. These exalted and complicated mysteries deeply impressed the Magi by their sacramental character. I put on my cape and in all modesty covered my head and shoulders with my veil. I then seated myself in the middle of the cavern, holding my Son on my lap. We were ready to receive our royal guests.

The three Kings of the east in abject humility removed their turbans and their sandals at the entrance to the cave. They entered reverently and at the first sight of my Son and me, they were at first overwhelmed with wonder, in spite of the barren cave and its rough interior. I was enhanced by the light of heaven shining on my countenance, for the Lord illuminated me in all my modesty and majesty. Still more visible was the light emanating from Jesus, shedding through the cavern effulgent splendor, which made it like heaven. The Magi prostrated themselves in awe upon the earth. From this position they worshipped and adored the Infant Jesus, acknowledging him as *true God and true man*, and as the Savior of the human race. The sight of Jesus and his presence filled them with divine power, and new enlightenment. They were privileged to see the multitude of angelic spirits, who as servants and ministers of the King of kings and Lord of lords attended upon him in angelic reverence [Heb: 1, 1-4].

Arising they congratulated me as the mother of the Son of the eternal Father, and approaching they dropped before me on their knees. They sought to kiss my hand as they were accustomed to do in honoring their queens in their countries. However, I withdrew my hand and instead offered them the hand of the Redeemer of the world, saying,

"My spirit rejoices in the Lord and my soul blesses and extols him. Because among all the nations, he has called and selected you to look upon and behold that which many kings and prophets have desired in vain to see, namely, him, who is the eternal Word Incarnate [Luke: 10, 24]. Let us extol and praise his name on account of the sacraments and mysteries wrought among his people; let us kiss the earth, which he sanctifies by his real presence."

At my words, the three Magi humbled themselves again before the Lord. Interiorly, they each uttered a fervent prayer offering to the Son of God their kingdoms, themselves, their families, and all their possessions. Humbly, they begged him to rule over them and their peoples, and to bring peace and understanding to their people. Afterwards, they spoke to Joseph congratulating him and extolling his good fortune in being chosen to be the spouse of the Mother of God.

Balthazar said, "We are amazed and filled with wonder and compassion at the great poverty we behold, but beneath which is hidden the greatest mysteries of heaven and earth." After three hours, the Magi took their leave and a shepherd led them to the valley where the shepherds were still tending their sheep. There, they set up their camp. The king's servants, who had accompanied them into the cave, did not see the glories of the angels; they only saw the barren walls of the cave. They wondered at all they did see, especially marveling at our destitute and neglected condition. Although wondering, they perceived nothing of its deep mysteries, but they were all overwhelmed with the majesty of my Son.

The three kings met in a huge tent and spent the night in abundant tears and aspirations speaking of all they had seen, of the feelings and affections aroused in each, and what each had noticed for himself in the divine Child and in me, his mother. In their reveries, they remembered the dire destitution, in which they had found us and resolved to send us some gifts to show their affection, concern, and their desire to serve, since they could not do anything else for us. They sent us many presents, which they had brought with them, and others, which they obtained in town. We received these gifts with humble acknowledgement and returned their good favor with our efficacious blessings for the spiritual consolation of the three kings. I was delighted with these gifts for they enabled us to prepare for the poor and our ordinary guests, an abundant repast.

At dawn, the following day, the Kings returned to the cave in order to offer my heavenly Son the special gifts which they had provided. They prostrated themselves and in profound humility opened their treasures, as Scripture relates, and offered Jesus gold, frankincense and myrrh [Matt: 2, 11]. They consulted me regarding many mysteries, practices of faith, matters pertaining to their consciences, and to the governing of their countries. Each wished to return well instructed and capable of perfecting themselves and others in holiness. I heard them with exceeding pleasure, and I conferred interiorly with the divine Infant concerning all that they had asked, in order to answer and to properly instruct these sons of the new Law. They did not wish to leave our presence, for they had many unanswered questions, and they knew the Holy Spirit inspired all my words. However, an angel of the Lord appeared to them and told them,

"It is the will of the Lord that you should return to your country with all haste. Do not return by way of Jerusalem for King Herod would do harm to the Child."

I received the gifts from the three kings and in their name offered them to the Infant Jesus. My Son showed by signs of highest pleasure, that he accepted their gifts. They themselves became aware of the exalted and heavenly blessings with which he repaid them more than a hundredfold. According to the custom of their country, they offered me some gems of great value, but since these gifts had no mysterious signification and referred not to my Son, I returned them to the kings reserving only their gifts of gold, incense and myrrh for my Son. In order to show appreciation: however, I gave them some of the clothes in which I had wrapped my infant Son. The three kings received these relics with such reverence and esteem that they encased them in gold and precious stones in order to preserve them forever. As a proof of their value, these relics spread a copious fragrance that revealed their presence a league in circumference. However, only those who believed in the coming of God into the world were able to perceive it. Later, in their own countries, the Magi performed great miracles with these relics of our Lord Jesus Christ.

Before the Magi left, they distributed food, clothing, and money among the needy families of Bethlehem. Then, with the blessings of Joseph and me ringing in their ears, the three Magi returned home. They had no sooner begun their journey than the beautiful star reappeared to guide them safely.

After dismissing the kings, Joseph, our angels, and I created new canticles of praise of the wonders of the Most High. I remembered all that had transpired and treasured them in my bosom. The holy angels, who were witnesses of these holy mysteries, congratulated me as their Queen. They praised the fact that my most holy Son had been manifested and that men had adored his Majesty. They then sang canticles to him, magnifying his mercies wrought upon humankind.

The following day I said to Joseph, "My, Master and, spouse, the offerings, which the kings have made to our God and Child must not remain here, idle. Apply it in the service of our Son and use it according to his will. Please dispose of these gifts as belonging to my Son and to you." Joseph demurred and wished me to dispose of it. However, I insisted and said, "Since you make an excuse of humility, my master, do it then for the love of the poor, who are waiting for their share." Amicably, we then decided to divide the gifts into three parts, one destined for the Temple of Jerusalem, namely the incense and myrrh, and part of the gold. Another offering we gave to the priest, who had circumcised the Child, in order that he could use it for himself and for his synagogue in Bethlehem. The third part we distributed to the poor. In this third almsgiving, we decided to give a good portion to one of the Essene woman, who was a widow and quite poor. In addition, I confided in her some of the basic mysteries of the coming of the Magi, but did not reveal to her the hidden sacrament concerning my Son and myself.

Joy filled the heart of the poor woman. Overcome with joy, she insisted that we move in with her. The fact that it was a home of poverty made it more attractive to me. Joseph and I yielded to her entreaties and moved in while waiting the time of my purification and the presentation of my Son in the Temple. I left the cave with tender regret. God assigned a holy angel to guard the entrance of the holy cave and to this day, he is still there. The cave was never again used to house animals. However, God did not interfere with the comings and goings of men. When we moved, our angels never left our side. Our hostess received us with the greatest charity and assigned us the largest portion of her home. In preparation for my purification, I performed every heroic act of love I could conceive to honor my Son and his divine Father. My infant Son often spoke to me orally. Joseph, until after Jesus was one year of age, was not allowed to hear his words. Jesus often repeated his first words to me

"Make yourself like unto me, my, Mother and my, dove."

The Purification and Presentation

After the birth of the Incarnation of the Word, I realized the fact that God had held me exempt from actual sin and from the stain of original sin. Nor was I ignorant of the fact that my parents had conceived me mystically by the grace of the Holy Ghost. In addition, I had been brought forth from my mother's womb without labor, remaining a virgin more pure than the sun. Thus, there was no need for me, or my divine Son, to seek purification. Yet, the Law of Moses, according to Exodus, chapter thirteen, demanded the sanctification and presentation to the Lord of all the Hebrew's first-born sons. My forty days, required for purification, was fast drawing to a close, and instead of holding myself exempt from the Law, I longed with all my heart to comply with this Law of my own free will in order to humble myself before the Lord. My Son revealed to me his own desire to sacrifice and offer Himself as a living Victim to the eternal Father in thanksgiving for having formed his most pure body. Also, for having destined him as an acceptable sacrifice for the human race and for the welfare of mortals. Jesus desired that his consecration to his Father should take place in the Temple of Jerusalem, where God was adored and magnified in his house of prayer, expiation, and sacrifice.

After conferring with Joseph, we decided to be in Jerusalem on the very day appointed by the Law. Having made our preparations, we took our leave of the good woman who had so devotedly hosted us. The hidden identity of my Son had pierced her heart, and she was grief stricken at the thought of our leaving. We stopped at the cave of the Nativity, and I handed Jesus to Joseph and

I prostrated myself on that holy ground and worshiped the earth, which had been witness to such venerable mysteries.

I said, "My, master, please give me your benediction for this journey. I beseech you to allow me to perform this journey on foot and without benefit of shoes, since I am to hold in my arms the Victim, which is to be offered to the eternal Father. This ceremony is a mysterious work, and as far as possible, I should wish to perform it with all due reverence and ceremony."

My good husband distressed at my kneeling at his feet told me to arise and replied, "May the Most High Son of the eternal Father, whom I hold in my arms, give you his blessing. As for the rest it is well and good that you journey afoot to bring him to Jerusalem. However, you must not go barefoot because the weather does not permit it. I am sure your desire will be accepted by the Lord instead of the deed."

Since my husband only obeyed me, and humiliated and mortified himself in commanding me, it happened that both of us exercised humility and obedience reciprocally. I accepted humbly his command for me not to go barefooted, for he had only my best interests at heart. He had no way of knowing the wonderful qualities and composition of my virginal and perfect body, nor the other privileges conferred upon me by the divine right hand. After Joseph's blessings, and after asking for God and my Son's blessings for our journey, I wrapped Jesus carefully to shield him from the inclement weather and we set out on our trip. Joseph loaded the Muscat Ass with our temple offering and our own necessary supplies. We did not present a drab, cold appearance, for accompanying us were the ten thousand heavenly courtiers, so beautiful and shining, all visible to us in human forms. God's glorious world around us was reduced to less than a heap of dirt or mud compared to their splendor for they obliterated the sun in its brightest light and would have turned night into the brightest day. We began to sing beautiful canticles of praise to honor the divine Son of God.

The weather turned unusually severe, so that without regard for my tender Child, it's Creator, the cold and sleety blasts pierced to his shivering limbs and caused him to shake as he lay in my arms. In indignation, I finally turned to the winds and the elements, and as their Mistress, I reprimanded them for having thus persecuted their Maker.

I commanded them, "Moderate your rigor toward the Child, but not toward me." The elements obeyed my command and the cold blasts were turned into soft and balmy air for my Son, but without diminishing their ferocity toward me.

While we made our pilgrimage, the Holy Ghost enlightened Simeon, concerning the coming of my Son and his forthcoming Presentation. God also notified Anna, the holy prophetess, and advised of our suffering on our way to Jerusalem. They conferred together and then called the chief procurator of the temporal affairs of the temple. Simeon described us and then posted him at the Bethlehem road gate to intercept and receive us into his home with all benevolence and hospitality. This he did, and we were much relieved, since we had been anxious about finding a suitable lodging for our divine Son. Joseph and I then conferred about how we should handle the gifts of the Magi, to avoid a noisy demonstration the next day.

The following morning, as a stranger to most in the temple, Joseph gave the myrrh, incense and gold to the priest who usually received such gifts for the temple, but Joseph took care not to reveal himself as the donor of these gifts. We could have retained some of the money and purchased a lamb for an offering, the same offering the rich usually offered for their first-born. We chose not to do so, but instead purchased two doves, the offering of the poor [Luke: 2, 24]. Neither of us thought it fitting to depart from poverty and humility, even under the cover of such a pious and special occasion. In all things, I was to be the teacher of perfection, and my most holy Son was ever the example of holy poverty into which he was born, lived, and died.

Simeon was a just and God-fearing man and was hoping in the consolation of Israel. The Holy Spirit, who dwelt in him, had revealed that he should not taste death until he had seen the Christ, the Lord. Simeon was again divinely enlightened and made to understand more clearly the mysteries of the Incarnation and Redemption of man. This presentation, he was told, would specifically fulfill the prophecy of Isaiah, "That a Virgin should conceive and bear a Son and that from the root of Jesse a flower should blossom," namely Christ [Is: 7, 14]. He received a clear understanding of the hypostatic union of the two natures in the person of the Word, and of the mysteries of the passion and death of the Redeemer. Thus informed, Simeon was inflamed with the desire of seeing the Redeemer of the world.

The holy matron Anna was also favored with a revelation that same night, concerning many of these mysteries and great was the joy of her spirit on that account. Anna had been my teacher during my stay at the temple. She and Simeon never left the temple grounds serving in it night and day in prayer and fasting. Anna was a prophetess, daughter of Samuel, of the tribe of Aser. She had lived seven years with her husband before he died and she was now eighty years old.

The presentation of the birth of the first-born son of all Israelites was instituted by God to keep alive in the people's minds and hearts the tenth plague of the passing over of the angel of death, whereby God freed his people from the Egyptians. It had also become the hope that if the Hebrews should perpetually sanctify and offer to the Lord their first-born sons, one thus presented might prove to be the Son of God and a Child of the mother of the expected Messiah [Ex: 13, 2-10].

I prayed all night long and spoke to the Father saying, "My, Lord and, God most high, Father of my Lord, a festive day for heaven and earth will be that in which I shall bring and offer to you in the holy temple the living Host. Rich is this oblation oh, Lord, and you can in return for it, pour your mercies upon the human race. Pardon the sinners, console the afflicted, help the needy, enrich the poor, succor the weak, enlighten the blind, and stay the feet of those who have strayed away. You have given him to me as God. I return him to you as God and man. His value is infinite, and what I ask of you is much less. In opulence do I return to your holy Temple, from which I departed poor. My soul shall magnify you forever, because your divine right hand has shown itself so liberal and powerful toward me.

For the ceremony, I dressed in a light-blue robe, over which I wore a long yellow mantle and a white veil. My Son, I dressed in warm woolen swaddling clothes and wrapped him in a long sky-blue veil. We left early the next morning, my fortieth day, and set out for the temple. I could not take my eyes from the glorious temple with its golden spires flashing in the early morning sunlight. As we neared, I held Jesus up so that he could gain, for the first time as true man, an unobstructed view of his Father's House. I was amazed with the progress of the construction of the temple since I had last been here. We arrived in time to hear the shofar horns and the blare of the trumpets and the rumbling of the Golden Gate as the twenty men struggled to open the massive doors. The priests then presented the morning offering of an unblemished goat in burnt holocaust to the God of Abraham, Isaac, and Jacob.

We proceeded to the Court of the Women, where before I entered, Joseph turned over our offerings of two turtle doves and a basket of money and other donations to Noeme, my cousin, temple friend, and teacher. Prompted by Anna of our coming, she had been eagerly awaiting our arrival. I placed my Son in her arms and she was overjoyed. No longer young, Noeme had given her entire life to God, as a Temple Virgin. My Son filled her with an interior knowledge of who he was and only God's graces kept her from swooning with joy. I knelt with Jesus in my arms to offer myself to my Lord and my God. All about us was our cordon of heavenly angelic guards visible only to Joseph, my divine Son, and I. We were joined by additional angels carrying the magnificent shields bearing the name of Jesus in bold letters. They were singing wonderfully beautiful canticles of praise of my Son and the divine Trinity.

God immersed me in an intellectual vision of the most holy Trinity. In addition, I heard a voice issuing from the eternal Father, saying, "This is my beloved Son, in whom I am well pleased." At the same time, Joseph felt a new sweetness of the Holy Ghost, which filled him with joy and divine light.

The holy high-priest Simeon, moved by the Holy Spirit, also entered the temple at this time [Luke: 2, 27-30]. Approaching, where I stood with the Infant Jesus in my arms, Simeon saw us surrounded by God's holy angels in their angelic splendor. The Prophetess Anna also saw this wonderful sight, when she joined him. They approached and I placed the infant Jesus in the eager outstretched arms of Simeon.

Rising up his eyes to heaven he offered him up to the eternal Father, pronouncing at the same time these words so full of mysteries, "Now Master, you may let your servant go in peace, according to your word, for my eyes have seen your salvation which you prepared in sight of all the peoples; a light for revelation to the Gentiles, and glory for your people Israel [Luke: 2, 29-32]. Let me go now, Lord, free and in peace. For until now I have been detained in my body by my hope of seeing your promises fulfilled, and by my desire to see your Onlybegotten Son made man. Now that my eyes have seen your salvation, joined to our nature in order to give it eternal welfare according to the intention and eternal decree of your infinite wisdom and mercy, I shall now enjoy true and secure peace."

Simeon turned to me and said, "Behold this Child is set for the fall and for the resurrection of many in Israel, and for a sign which shall be contradicted. And your own soul a sword shall pierce, and out of many hearts thoughts may be revealed." He then gave his priestly blessing and the prophetess Anna acknowledged the Incarnate Word. Holding him in her arms she spoke to all in hearing distance of the mysteries of the Messiah, who were expecting the redemption of Israel. Thus, God, through his two holy servants, gave public testimony of the coming of the Redeemer to the entire world [Luke 2, 34-35].

When Simeon mentioned the sword and the sign of contradiction, which were prophetical of the passion and death of Jesus, my Son humbly bowed his head. Thereby, and by many acts of interior acts of obedience, Jesus ratified the prophecy of Simeon and accepted it as the sentence of the eternal Father pronounced by his minister. All of this I saw and understood, and I began to feel the sorrow predicted by Simeon, as if in a mirror I saw all the mysteries included in this prophecy. I saw how my holy Son was to be the *stumbling block*, the perdition of the unbelievers. I also saw the salvation of the faithful, the fall of the temple, the synagogue, and the establishment of the Church among the heathens. God allowed me to foresee the triumph he would gain over the devils and over death. A great price was to be paid for it, namely the frightful agony and death of the Cross. I foresaw the boundless opposition and contradiction, which the Lord Jesus was to sustain both personally and in his Church [John: 15, 20]. At the same time, I saw the glory and excellence of the predestined souls. Excited by Simeon's prophecies and these hidden mysteries, I performed many heroic acts of virtue, and I forgot not the least iota.

Simeon then withdrew carrying my Son into another part of the building, while Anna led me to the Temple Court. Some Levites placed a large table in front of the altar and covered it with a white cloth. Placed in the center were a cradle like container and two baskets. Simeon came and returned the Child to me and led me to the table where I placed my Son in the cradle. Then Anna led me back to the grilled women's section, in which about twenty mothers with their first-born sons awaited their turn. The temple was filled with a heavenly light for Almighty God was in attendance at his

Son's presentation, all of which was unseen by the worshipers. Above Jesus the heavens opened in all their glory before the throne of the Holy Trinity.

Simeon and his fellow priests were now dressed in their ceremonial vestments. Taking their places around the table they prayed in unison over the Child all the while offering up incense. Then Anna returned to me my offerings and Simeon again led me to the table. The priests took my gifts and placed them in their appropriate places, the doves went into the basket with the wicker top. Simeon raised the Child to heaven while his fellow priests recited prayers over them from their rolled manuscripts. Simeon then brought my Son to me and placed him again in my arms. With tears of joy running down his wrinkled cheeks, the old priest led me back to the Women's Court.

The ceremony over, I kissed Simeon's hand and again asked his parting blessing, as I also did with Anna and Naome, my former and most holy teachers. Then with my Son and Joseph, accompanied with our troupe of fourteen thousand angels we returned to our lodgings. We planned to remain there for nine days in order to satisfy our devotion at the temple. Simeon, Anna, and I had several conversations speaking of the mysteries, which filled them both with the sweetest sentiments of joy in their souls. Both were to die in the Lord a short time later, their pilgrimages on this earth finished and their reward now assured them. We lodged at the home of Simeon. God accorded me many favors, consolations and recompense for the sorrow caused by Simeon's prophecies.

We returned to Nazareth and the days sped by all too quickly. On one fortunate day, my Son spoke to me interiorly and said, "My dearest, Mother and my, dove dry your tears and let your pure heart be expanded; since it is the will of my Father that I accept the death of the Cross. I desire that you be my companion in my labors and sufferings. I long to undergo them for the souls, who are the works of my hands [Eph: 2, 10], for I made them according to my image and likeness. They now become partakers of my reign and of eternal life in triumph over my enemies, for I know that you desire to suffer in union with me."

I answered my Son, "Oh my sweetest, Love and, Son of my womb; if my accompanying you includes not only the privilege of witnessing and pitying your sufferings, but also of dying with you, so much the greater will be my relief, because it will be a greater suffering for me to live, while seeing you die." Together, we passed several days in these exercises of love and compassion. An angel then advised Joseph in a dream to flee to Egypt with all haste, as I shall relate in the next chapter.

I Am Mary

My, children, no sooner had I consented to be the Mother of God than I was rightly and truly considered the Queen and Sovereign of the world and of all creatures. Thus, I began my personal ministry. I would not be able to abide the just punishments that are to be inflicted on the guilty, if I were a Queen of Justice. Rather, I am a Queen of Mercy, intent only on commiserating and pardoning sinners. Right after the Annunciation, and the begetting of my divine Son; I began my duties as the Queen of Mercy and as related in my story, I was able to help many people with whom I came in daily contact.

I will quote that which I revealed to St. Bridget of Sweden, "I am the Queen of Heaven and the Mother of Mercy, the door through which sinners are brought to God no matter how accursed, for, if they receive nothing else through my intercession, they receive the grace of being less tempted by the devils than they would otherwise have been. No one, unless the irrevocable sentence has been pronounced" [that is the irrevocable sentence pronounced on the damned] "is so cast off by God that he will not return to him and enjoy his mercy, if he invokes my aid. I am called by all ***"Mother of Mercy"***, and truly the mercy of my Son towards men has thus made me merciful towards them.

Anyone that is so miserable that he will not invoke my aid, and is thusly damned, will therefore be miserable for all eternity."

Sister Catherine of theAugustinian Order relates the story of a woman by the name of Mary. In her youth this woman was a great sinner and in her old age remained obstinate and full of wickedness. The people drove her from the city, and Mary had to live in a cave. Half consumed by disease, she died there all alone, and the people interred her in a field like a beast. Sister Catherine considered her soul as lost and never prayed for her. One day four years later, the woman appeared to Catherine in a vision and exclaimed. "How unfortunate is my lot, Sister Catherine! You recommend the souls of all those that die to God; but on my soul alone you have no compassion."

Puzzled, Sister Catherine asked her, "Who are you?" The poor woman answered, "That poor Mary that died alone in the cave." Catherine asked, "Are you then saved?"

"I am," she replied, "but only by the mercy of the Blessed Virgin Mary. When I saw myself at the point of death, loaded with sins and abandoned by all, I remembered our Mother of Mercy and cried out, "Lady, you who are the refuge of abandoned creatures; behold me at this moment, abandoned by all. You are my only hope; you alone can help me. Have pity on me." The Blessed Virgin obtained for me the grace to make a sincere act of contrition. I died, was thus saved, and in addition my Mother has obtained for me another favor. Mother Mary obtained for me a shorter time in purgatory, if I suffered in intensity that which would have otherwise lasted for many years. I lack now only a few masses to be entirely delivered. I beg you to have them said, and in return, I promise to pray always for you to God and to Mary."

Catherine immediately complied with her request and after a few days the soul again appeared to her, shining like the sun, and exclaimed, "I thank you, Catherine: behold, I go to paradise, to sing the mercies of my God, and to pray for you."

I later spoke to Saint Mary of Agreda and in general said, "My, daughter, the doctrine and example contained in this mystery will teach us to strive after the constancy and expansion of heart. In this manner, we may prepare ourselves to accept blessings and adversity, the sweet and the bitter, with equanimity. How persistently the human heart forgets that it's Teacher and Master has first accepted sufferings, and has honored and sanctified them in his own Person."

Before I close this chapter, I must address sin and warn you of its dangers. Fortunately, because of God's divine plan, I never contracted sin during my short pilgrimage on earth.

"Oh, **sin**, how most disorderly and inhuman you are, since in order to satisfy for you to the Creator, my Son is afflicted by the very creatures, which he has made and preserves in being! You are a terrible and horrible monster, offensive to God and destructive of creatures. You turn the human race into abominations and deprive them of their greatest happiness; namely that of being friends of God. Oh, children of men, how long will you be so heavy-hearted as to love vanity and deceit? Do not be so ungrateful toward the Most High and so cruel to yourselves. Open your eyes and recognize your dangers. Do not despise the precepts of your eternal Father, and do not forget the teachings of your heavenly mother, who has brought you forth by charity. For, when the Onlybegotten Son of the Father assumed flesh in my womb, he made me Mother of all creation, and as such I love you. If it was possible and according to the will of the Most High, I would accept with pleasure and suffer all the punishments visited upon you from the time of Adam until now."

I remind you, as I told St. Bridget of Sweden, "I did not need purification like other women, because my Son, who was to be born of me, made me clean. That the Law and prophecies might be fulfilled, I chose to live according to the Law. Nor did I live like worldly parents, but humbly conversed with the humble. Nor did I wish to show anything extraordinary in me, but loved whatever was humble. On the day of the Purification, my suffering for my Son was increased. Simeon's words had pierced my heart keenly. Divinely inspired, I knew what my Son was to suffer, and what he suffered—I suffered. My suffering; however, was tempered by the consolation of the Spirit of God. Let not then this same grief leave your heart, for without tribulation few would reach Heaven."

Remember the sorrow that pierced my heart at the prophecies of Simeon, and how I remained in peace and tranquility, my heart and soul transfixed by a sword of pain. Seek ever to preserve inward peace. Have full trust in me. Whenever tribulation comes over you, fervently exclaim,

"The Lord is my light and my salvation: whom shall I fear?"

Your Mother in Heaven

Mary

Chapter Six

Land of the Pharaohs

OUR LORD SAID TO SAINT BRIDGET OF SWEDEN

"By my flight to Egypt, I showed the infirmities of my humanity and fulfilled the prophecies. I set an example to my disciples that sometimes, for the greater future glory of God, persecution is to be avoided. That I was not found by my pursuers, is proof that the counsel of my Divinity prevailed over the counsel of man; for it is not easy to fight against God."

Joseph and I decided to remain in Jerusalem for nine days following the Presentation of my Son to render fitting thanks to God. The Lord had prepared me for the Incarnation of the Word by nine days of prayer, and I had developed a special veneration for the number nine. It was also the number of months during which I had borne Jesus in my virginal womb. To honor these events, we initiated a prayer period of nine days, called a novena. We wished to present our divine Child nine days in succession to the eternal Father as an acceptable offering. We began the novena early the next day. Joseph went on to the Court of Men after dropping me off at the Court of Women. We prayed in the temple until nightfall, and I began my prayer to the Lord thusly,

"I find myself, oh, Lord, forced forward by the impetuous flood of your blessings to give you thanks. What return can I offer you, Lord? I, who have nothing. I, who have received my very existence and my life from you, and I, who have been overwhelmed by incomparable mercies and blessings from you ever since my Immaculate Conception; what thanks can I possibly render to acknowledge your immense bounty, which has kept me from the contagion of sin, and has chosen me to give human form to your Onlybegotten Son? My soul, my being, and my faculties, all have I received and continue to receive from your hands. Now; however, my heart is revived. I rejoice in possessing a gift worthy of your greatness, since I can offer you He who is one in substance with you. He, who is equal in majesty, and perfection of attributes, the mirror of your intellect, the image of your being, the fullness of your own pleasure, your only and most beloved Son."

"I offer the victim, whom I bring you, and I am sure you will receive him. Having received my Son as God, I give him back to you as *true God and true man*. No other creature or can I ever offer a greater gift, nor can your Majesty ever demand one more precious. In his name and in mine, I offer and present him to you. I am the mother of the Onlybegotten, having given him human flesh, I have made him the brother of mortals, and as he wishes to be their Redeemer and Teacher, it behooves me to be their advocate, to assume their cause and claim assistance for them. Therefore, Father of the Onlybegotten, God of mercies, I offer him to you from all my heart. With him and because of him, I beg you to pardon sinners, to open new fountains for the renewal of your wonders. This is the Lion of Judah become a Lamb, which takes away the sins of the world [Rev: 5, 5]. He is the treasure of your Divinity."

As an answer to my offering, God conceded to me new and greater privileges, and he said to me, "I am pleased with your offering my, daughter; as long as the world shall last, I grant you the privilege that whatever you ask of me concerning your clients, I shall grant to you. Even if the greatest of sinners secure for themselves your intercession, their souls shall find salvation. In the new Church and law of the Gospel, you shall be the Cooperatrix and Teacher of salvation with Christ your most holy Son."

At the end of the first day of our novena, Joseph came to get me and as we prepared to depart, Anna met us and told us sadly, "It is a time for rejoicing and a time of sorrow. As he promised, the Lord gave Simeon life until he saw the Promise. Simeon has died in his happiness and is now with his ancestors. We have prepared his body and he is ready for burial. Would you join us in honoring him at his funeral?"

Stricken to the heart, we followed Anna. She led us to where Simeon's body lay in state. His body was bound to a board with low curved sides and wrapped in strips of linen. The priests had wrapped green leaves and herbs inside the bindings. Six of his fellow priests picked up his bier and amid much wailing and other signs of grief we followed the procession to a sepulcher hewn in the side of a nearby hill not far from the temple. The funeral ceremony was quite brief. The priests buried Simeon and then rolled a heavy flat stone into its niche to seal the entrance. My friend Veronica and Zachariah were Simeon's closest relatives. Veronica, Elizabeth, Zachariah, Lazarus, and many of their relatives and friends were there and we comforted them in their sorrow. Interiorly, my Son blessed Simeon and I knew he was safe with the Patriarchs in Limbo. The holy priest Simeon carried the "good news" to those in Limbo and they all eagerly anticipated with mixed emotions that the coming Passion, death, and resurrection of my Son was at hand.

For nine days Joseph, my Son, and I, spent our days in the temple totally dedicated to our novena. For privacy, I always sought a secluded corner of the Women's Court. On the fifth day, the Deity revealed itself to me. God raised me up and the Holy Spirit filled me with special blessings. God had done this to me many times before. His power is infinite; he never gives so much as not to be able to give still more to his creatures. In this instance, he wished to prepare me for the labors that were awaiting us.

He comforted me saying, "My, Spouse and my, dove, your wishes and intentions are pleasing in my eyes and I delight in them always. Now that you have finished your nine days novena, return to Nazareth for now and be prepared to leave there on a moments notice.

I replied, "My, Lord and, Master, behold your servant with a heart prepared to die for your love if necessary. Dispose of me according to your will. This only do I ask of you, please do not allow my Son to suffer. Turn all pains and labor upon me, for I am obliged to suffer them."

I was deeply concerned and Joseph and I talked it over on our return to Nazareth. My angels were no help on shedding light on what God meant when he told me to be prepared to leave on a moment's notice. They cautioned me to be prepared to leave as God had cautioned me. Joseph and I prepared a pack for our Muscat Ass and we settled into a quiet routine much the same as our neighbors in Nazareth. We informed Mahara that we might be leaving soon and instructed her on how to care for our home in our absence.

While praying one evening, the Lord appeared to me in a vision and raised me up and the Holy Ghost filled me with special blessings. God had done this to me many times, but this time he comforted me first then said, "My, spouse and my, dove, in order to protect our Son, I will instruct Joseph to take you and our Son to Egypt for Herod is intent on destroying what he believes to be a threat to his throne. He is seeking the life of the Child."

The Lord added, "Do as Joseph instructs you in all things concerning the journey. The journey is long, dangerous and most fatiguing. You will suffer it for my sake, but **I AM,** and I will always be with you.

I was upset. In the vision, I had foreseen the hardships awaiting my Son. Shedding many tears, I went directly to my room. Joseph thought I was again grieving over the passing of Simeon, and was only concerned that I did not confide to him the cause of my affliction. That very night the angel of the Lord appeared to Joseph in his sleep and said to him, "Wake up, take the Child and Mary and fly into Egypt. Herod is seeking the Child in order to take his life]. You shall remain there until I return to give you further advice [Matt: 2, 13-14.

Joseph arose at once full of solicitude and sorrow, dressed hurriedly, and rushed to my room and knocked anxiously. I had been expecting him and listened as he exclaimed, "My, lady, God's holy angel has informed me that Herod wishes to destroy the Child. We are to flee at once to Egypt. The trip will be hard and arduous. Tell me what I need to do to make your journey as comfortable as possible."

I answered him, "My Husband, we have such great blessings of grace, it is right that we joyfully accept all afflictions. We bear with us the Creator of heaven and earth. What arms can harm us, even if it were the arms of Herod? Where our Son is there can be no desert. Let us prepare some food at once, load the Muscat Ass and depart within the hour [Job: 2, 13]."

Joseph loaded our pack and the little food we had on our faithful beast of burden. Some will ask why was it necessary for God to flee before the wickedness of men? God would contradict himself as the *Author of grace* and as *Author of nature*, if he resorted to miracles to prevent the natural course of events. God only uses miracles on special occasions, subject to his immutable will. It is necessary that we all embrace and bear with equanimity and patience the labors and difficulties of mortal life. Jesus and I were eminent masters in the practice of this doctrine. My Son began to suffer, as soon as he was born into the world. Now banished by Herod into a desert, Jesus' sufferings would continue until he died on the Cross.

In spite of our faith, Joseph and I were full of anxiety as we fled Southwest to near the road called The Way of the Sea. We had no idea where we were going, but began our journey in haste, faith, and confidence that the Lord would guide us to his planned destination. We were much relieved, for when, my ten thousand heavenly courtiers again appeared to us in human form and again changed night into brightest day for us. They did homage to my Son and encouraged us saying, "Fear not, Mary, it is the will of the Lord that we accompany and guide you on your journey. Nevertheless, it will be a hard and arduous trek and will tax your strength and your will, but be of good heart, for the Lord is with you."

I expressed my desire to stop in Bethlehem to visit the site of my Son's birth, but Xnoir said, "Our Queen and Lady, mother of our Creator, we must not go out of our way. We must hasten on our journey without delay. Herod is enraged, since the Magi Kings failed to report to him. The people have become aroused and have taken to heart the words spoken by Simeon and by Anna. Some of them have begun to say that you are the Mother of the Messiah. Others say that you know of him, and still others say that your Son is a Prophet. Consequently, Herod ordered that you be found and brought to him. If you are found, it will mean the death of your Son."

I readily yielded to the will of the Almighty, and reverenced the place of his birth from afar. As we passed well west of the sacred place, the holy angel who stood guard at the sacred cave approached us in visible form and adored the Incarnate Word in my arms. The angel comforted me, and I was not distressed that he had left the holy cave, for I knew the guardian angel had the power of bilocation. I knew that Elizabeth and her son John were in their home near Hebron, and I desperately wished to see her. However, Joseph advised the need for all haste. Instead, I asked him, "Please grant me permission then to send an angel to Elizabeth to warn her of Herod's intentions. Her son may also be in danger and she must take all precautions to protect him."

With Joseph's blessings, I dispatched an angel to carry my message to Elizabeth. She was thrilled with the news of my nearness and wished to meet me, but the angel discouraged this and she sent me her most affectionate greetings. Then Elizabeth dispatched a servant with many gifts consisting of provisions, money and material for clothing for my Son. Her servant did not overtake us until we were in Gaza, on the river Besor. Joseph had avoided the main thoroughfare that followed the course of the Great Sea. We had traveled the side roads and paths, which, after five days of hard going, we arrived in Gaza. I sent the servant back with careful instructions not to reveal our location. On his way; the Lord erased from the man all remembrance of what we had charged him to conceal, so that he retained only that part of the message that pertained to Elizabeth.

Elizabeth and Zachariah hid their son from Herod's wrath. Herod's soldiers were searching everywhere for newborn male children and only Zachariah's prominence saved them from closer investigation. Elizabeth set out with one servant and several donkeys loaded with clothing and provisions to last them for several months. Zachariah knew of a cave hidden deep in the Judean Wilderness, and he sent them there with a trusted servant. His station in life protected him from Herod's vindictiveness, but his position as a high priest of Israel demanded that he perform his priestly duties, so he had to remain in Jutta.

We stayed in Gaza for two days allowing our beast of burden and Joseph to rest, for he had pushed himself and the beast to exhaustion. From the material sent us by Elizabeth, I made cloaks for Joseph and for my Son to protect them from the rigors of the journey. I kept only enough food for our needs, and gave the rest to the sick and the poor that surrounded us, for I could not deny them their just due. In addition, Joseph and I gave them the money and the rest of the gifts Elizabeth had sent us. As for myself, I preferred to subject myself to the natural order and depend upon our own efforts.

From Gaza we did not avoid the famous caravan route known as the "Way of the Sea" because it led to Egypt. Herod's soldiers were not in Gaza, and if his soldiers followed us into a foreign country, he would do so with the risk of starting a war with Egypt. This event was not likely. The country ahead was the stark, desolate, Sinai Desert. Our angels told us our destination was Heliopolis, a distance of a hundred and eighty miles. It would take us at least another two or three weeks of walking. Joseph purchased two new goatskin water bags, which he filled with water. The next day we again set out entering the area known as Bersabe. The going became extremely rough. The sand was deep and difficult to walk in, the terrain was pristine and inhospitable, and our progress was laboriously slow. Everywhere we looked; there was nothing but sand, desert cacti, scorpions, poison snakes, and a merciless terrain. There was no shelter, other than that which Joseph was able to provide with our meager supplies. It was February and very cold. The first night we rested at the foot of a small hill seeking shelter from the merciless winds that penetrated right through our clothing. It quickly burned up our energy. Joseph formed a small shelter with the outer cloak I had made him. Our ten thousand angels formed a guard around Jesus and me, their King and Queen. We ate from the supplies we had brought with us, I nursed my Son, and then we settled down for the night. Joseph slept outside on the ground. From inside the small shelter I lay down cuddling my Son to my breast. I spent most of the night praying with my Son, and before he slept, my Son offered up to his eternal Father the hardships of our little family.

The next day we set out at the break of day. We had covered only eight miles the first day because of drifting deep sand that lay thick over much of the well-traveled trail. On the third day a storm arose, a storm of wind and rain which harassed, and blinded us by its fury. Joseph and I suffered badly, and I tried to protect Jesus by carrying him inside my cloak. In spite of my best efforts, my Child, not yet fifty days old began to shiver and tears ran down his uncomplaining cheeks. Again, the frigid weather forced me to use my power over the elements. I commanded them to not afflict their Creator, but to afford him shelter and refreshment and to wreak their vengeance upon me alone. In return for my concern for him, my Son commanded his angels to assist me and shield me against the inclement weather. They complied at once and constructed a resplendent and warm globe around Joseph and me. Several times, I was forced to command the elements to abate their fury, or we would not have survived the severe weather.

Nearly three weeks later we ran out of food and our water supply was running dangerously low. The Lord allowed us to fall into need in order that in listening to Joseph and my prayers, he might make provision for us by the use of our angels. We traveled all the next day without any food. That night, at God's command, the angels served us delicious bread, well-seasoned fruits, and a delightful drink. Then, the angels sang hymns and praises to God and we joined in with gratitude and fervor. This wilderness of Bersabe was the same desert in which Elijah, fleeing from Jezebel, was comforted by a hearth cake, brought to him by an angel in order that he might travel to Mount Horeb. When has the Lord ever failed him who hoped in his assistance?

I had much time to converse with my Child, and of course was much concerned about his welfare, and I asked him, "My Love and light of my soul, how can I diminish your labor? How can I relieve you of your hardships? What can I do to lighten the sufferings of this journey? Oh if I could but carry you, not in my arms, but in my bosom and make for you a soft couch in my heart, in order that you might rest there without fatigue!"

My sweet Son replied, "My beloved, Mother, very easily do I rest in your arms reclining on your breast. I am delighted by your affection and pleased by your words and your prayers."

Other times we conversed interiorly, and these conversations were so exalted and divine that my words cannot express them. Joseph was able to forget his hardships by sharing in many of these mysteries and consolations. However, he did not yet share in hearing his Son's voice. We had traveled all day, dusk was falling, and Joseph could not find a satisfactory place to camp nor find shelter from the merciless wind that continued to plague us. At a distance from the traveled path, Joseph suddenly spied the glimmer of a light through the darkness. In the hopes of finding shelter, he led us toward the light. Drawing near, we could make out a good-sized hut sheltered amidst the palms and dense undergrowth of a small oasis. I felt a surge of relief. We had obviously managed to cross the desert and we could not be too far from our destination. Stretched across our path was a string with bells attached. Joseph's foot struck the cord, and bells clanged a warning. Suddenly, five men, their intentions all too obvious, surrounded us. We were among a band of thieves. Their leader came up and rudely looked into the face of Jesus. He was so moved that he ordered his men to offer us no harm. He led us into his hut where he told his wife how he had been so strangely affected by the Child. One of the thieves objected so the young leader gave him forty drachmas to leave our family alone.

The people were at first shy and shamefaced, and would not look Joseph in the eye. We seated ourselves in a corner on the ground. The women brought us some little rolls, fruits, honeycombs, and something to drink. While we were eating, the women cleared out a little room for me and brought in a small tub of warm water in which to bath the Child. She took his swaddling clothes, washed them, and then hung them near the fire to dry. The hut was warm and snug after our many days on the road and I was most grateful for their hospitality.

Their young leader seemed to be most impressed with us, especially Jesus. He said to his wife, "This Hebrew Child is no ordinary child. Beg the lady to allow us to wash our leprous child in his bathing water. It may, perhaps, do our child some good."

His wife came to me, but I already knew her mission and I said, "Take the water, wash your sick child in it, and he will become cleaner than he was before being attacked by the disease." The child, named Dismas, was about three years old and his little body was stiff from the skin disease. The mother did as I instructed and wherever the water touched the body of the child, some of the leprosy fell like scales to the bottom of the tub. The mother was out of her mind with joy. She wanted to embrace my Son and I, but stretching out my hand, I stopped her and said, "Save the water so that it can be used again and again until your son is cured." I asked her, "Does the other man wish to wash his son Gestas in the water?"

The woman looked frightened when I asked about the child by name. She shrank back and shook her head negatively. It was obvious that she feared the father of Gestas.

I told the woman to dig a hole in the soft volcanic rock, pour the water into it and cover it well. We talked to her at length and I extracted a promise from her to embrace the first opportunity to escape from her present abode. The word spread quickly and soon other members of the band began to drop in and meet us. Their reverential bearing was all the more remarkable, since during the night several travelers attracted by the light, were captured and carried into the forest to an immense cave that served as a storehouse for their ill-gotten goods. A heavy thicket concealed the entrance to the cave. My angels informed me that in the cave were clothes, carpets, goats, sheep, and innumerable other items. In addition, the thieves had kidnapped several young boys; an old woman attended to their needs. I did not sleep at all, but kept close watch over my Son. Our hosts, who urged us to stay longer, supplied us with food and water, and we set out again at dawn. They now accompanied us part of the way, in order to help us avoid the snares they had set up as protection from sudden attack by the authorities.

We were now in Egypt and from the nearby jungle; we began to encounter various small animals, but it was too cold for the deadly snakes that were native to the area. Our angelic light, while not visible to humans, warded off any dangerous animals we met. Finally late that afternoon, we came to our first town by the name of Lepe in which was numerous canals and ditches, some with high dams. We came to a small river and for a small fee, two ugly, brown-complexioned, half-naked men with flat noses and protruding lips ferried us across on a small raft. The first house we came to, the occupants were so rough and ill mannered that without saying a word, Joseph led us on past the house.

This was our first Egyptian village, and we had been traveling for twenty days since leaving Gaza. We camped out that night well off the road, so as not to attract unwelcome visitors. We had given some of our food to some beggars, and yet again, we were running low on supplies. We were traveling through a rolling countryside full of pasture ground with many clumps of trees. Idols shaped like swathed dolls and fish were prevalent throughout the area. Egyptian writing underneath described their function. Most were fertility gods, and the fish idols were the gods of the local fishermen. The people in this area were short and fat and they were very active in the worshipping of their idols. That night we sought shelter in a small cattle shed and the animals graciously made way for us. We were out of water and had nothing left to eat. I was most concerned because my milk was drying up. Jesus' little face was drawn, but he never complained, but interiorly offered up his and our sufferings to his Father in heaven. God allowed us to experience every kind of human misery during our journey in order to gain merit for the race of man. In front of the shed was a well, but it was locked. Finally some shepherds came and watered their stock. They would have left us without water, but Joseph pleaded with them and they relented and gave us a little water.

The next morning we continued on our weary way. My strength was fast waning and I was deeply concerned for my Son. However, as I later told Mother Mary of Agreda; "I was not alarmed in my exile and prolonged journey, since I trusted in the Lord. He provided for us in the time of our need. Even when help was somewhat delayed; it was always at hand at a time when it would do us the most good."

That evening, completely exhausted, we hid ourselves in the edge of a forest to avoid the curious Egyptian children that still followed us from the last village. Alone at last, I dropped to my knees and called aloud to my Lord and my God for his help. With a cry of relief, Joseph pointed to a slender date tree, its top clustered with fruit. I approached the tree, held Jesus up and prayed; the tree bowed down low. Joseph helped me gather the fruit, and we ate our fill. Suddenly, near the tree, a spring began to flow from beneath a huge rock. It quickly filled a small basin and the overflow found a natural channel and flowed off onto the plain. Our faithful Muscat ass walked out into the middle of the little stream—drank deeply—and then just stood there soaking his weary hooves and dipping his muzzle into the water from time to time savoring the cool life-giving water. Gathering the unused dates, Joseph took them to the children who had found the new stream of water and were happily drinking and playing in the water. I bathed Jesus, washed his clothes and washed those of ours that we could spare, for the nights were still cold. Before dawn, Joseph filled our water skins, and we quietly departed, without waking the sleeping children so, they would return to their homes.

At each town that we entered, Jesus made use of his sovereign and divine power and drove the demons from the multitude of idols that abounded in every town, every village, and every byway. The demons were blasted forth, like lightning flashed from the clouds, and cast to the lowermost caverns of hell and darkness. The demons, although they felt the divine power, did not know from where this power came. At the same instant the idols crashed to the ground, the altars disintegrated, and the temples crumbled to ruins. Joseph knew what was taking place. He marveled at the work of his divine Son, and silently praised and extolled him in holy admiration. It was here that my divine Son revealed to me that our journey was just beginning. At his command, our angels would lead us from hamlet to hamlet and from city to city throughout Egypt. Wherever we went the idols and the temples were destroyed, and the devils plunged back into the hell of their own making. Jesus the Redeemer, by our prayers and sufferings, intended to save as many of the pagan Egyptians as were willing to heed his message; "There is but one God, there is no god before him."

The Egyptian people were astounded at these inexplicable events; although among the more learned, ever since the sojourn of Jeremiah in Egypt, an ancient tradition was current that a king of the Jews would come and that the temples of the idols would be destroyed. The common person did not know about the prophecy, and the wise men said nothing. Therefore terror and confusion was spread among them as was prophesied by Isaiah [Is: 9, 1]. In this disturbance and fear some people reflected on these events and came to Joseph and I, since we were strangers in their midst, and spoke to us fearfully of the ruin of their temples and idols.

As the Mother of Wisdom, I was delighted to enlighten these people. I spoke to them and said, "There is but one God, and he is the Creator of the heavens and of the earth, and he alone is to be adored and acknowledged as God. All others are false and deceitful gods, nothing more than wood or clay or stone or metal, which you have fashioned with your own hands. None of which have eyes, or ears, or any power with which to stop these same artisans or any other man, from destroying them at their pleasure. The oracles that give forth answers from the mouths of the idols, are either deceitful priests talking through speaking tubes or the answers of lying, deceitful demons concealed within them, who have no infinite power for there is but one true God."

The simple people were so impressed with my sincerity, my God-given sweetness, and the kindness of my instructions that the news of our arrival into Egypt soon preceded us. We soon became more than an object of idle curiosity and many people flocked to see and hear us speak. The people accepted Joseph with his sweet winning ways, and believed his teachings. Moreover, the powerful prayers of the Incarnate Word wrought a change of hearts, as well as the continued crumbling of the idols, all of which caused an incredible commotion among the people. My Son speeded the people's conversions by instilling into their mind knowledge of the true God and consequently sorrows for their sins without them knowing from where these blessings came. As we traveled through the hamlets and cities of the Egyptians, we performed many latent miracles, driving out the demons not only from the idols, but also from out of many persons possessed by them. We cured, by the power of my Son, many people who were grievously and dangerously ill. However, those persons that were cured during the six years that we were in Egypt were done so gradually in a natural manner. The time for miracles to be done openly would not happen until my Son began his ministry years later. However, many persons came to believe the doctrines that we taught on how to live a good and salutary life.

In Jerusalem, Herod was enraged when he found that the Magi Kings had tricked him. He began an investigation and as each day went by with no news of a king being born, he became obsessed with the fear that the newborn Child was a threat to his position as king. Six months after our flight to Egypt, Herod, frustrated in his efforts to uncover the truth, gave secret orders to his officers to kill all the male children in Israel less than two years of age. An edict was written ordering women with children under two years of age to assemble in Jerusalem. Unsuspecting, the mothers from all over Israel, including Jerusalem itself, Hebron, Bethlehem, Nazareth and from even as far away as the Syrian and Babylonian frontiers, trustingly brought their innocent children to Jerusalem thinking that perhaps the great king was going to reward them. Some even had two infant children. Upon their arrival in Jerusalem, Herod's soldiers separated the women and children from their husbands. The soldiers took the women and their babies to a huge fortress-like building where they suddenly found themselves placed under arrest and put in chains. They huddled together fearfully, clutching their children close to their breasts not knowing what to expect.

I saw all that happened in Bethlehem just as clearly as though I was present. Herod fully intended to murder every child under the age of two. My Son wished to offer up the murdered children as the first fruits of his own death. To do this, the children needed the use of their reason. Jesus prayed to his Father in heaven for this favor. With the use of their reason, the children could make a willing sacrifice for their Redeemer and accept their death for his glory. Thus, he would be able to reward them with the crowns of martyrdom for that which they were to suffer. God granted his Son's request. When Jesus asked the children if they would accept their deaths for God's glory, they joyfully gave themselves to the Lord for the sins of humankind offering themselves up as the first fruits of the death of Jesus. I joined my Son in his prayers and sacrifices, all the time pitying the parents of the martyred infants in their heartrending tears and sorrows for their sons. I was concerned regarding the welfare of Elizabeth, Zachariah, and their son John. I refrained from asking my Son of their welfare because I knew that if God wished me to know their fate, he would so advise me. However, the Father did take notice of my compassionate desires and informed me that Zachariah, the father of John, had died four months after my purification. My cousin Elizabeth remained hidden in her cave living under great hardship and difficulty.

I prayed for the holy priest Zachariah, and my Son informed me that his soul was safe in limbo with the Patriarchs. The Innocents, some only a few days old, were now equipped with the use of reason. The children, when advised of their fate, also received a high knowledge of God, perfect love, faith, and hope. They all eagerly offered to sacrifice themselves for the greater glory of their Redeemer. They prayed for their parents and in reward for their sufferings, obtained for them light and grace.

At the fortress, Herod and his officers seated themselves on a balcony overseeing the place of the anticipated murders. From here, no one on the outside could hear that which was about to happen. Soldiers herded the chained women, carrying their innocent babies, into the courtyard where Herod's executioners awaited them. Many of the babies were still in swaddling clothes and some came in toddling after their mothers. As soon as the door slammed shut behind them, soldiers snatched the children from their mother's clinging arms. The soldiers pierced the innocent babies little hearts and slit their throats with their swords before the eyes of their horrified mothers. A multitude of angels was present and as each child was slain, a host of angels administered to them during their sufferings. As each child died, their souls were borne triumphantly by their guardian angels to their place in limbo to await the coming of the Redeemer, who was soon destined to open the Gates of Paradise. Slaves had dug a deep hole in one corner of the courtyard. The soldiers callously hurled the dead babies into the pit, and herded the women into another hall from which a death wail rose that would have melted a heart of stone—but not Herod's.

Some people question why a benevolent God would allow such a tragedy to happen. In the sweetness of God's Providence, he gives sinners time, hoping for their conversions, as in the case of Herod. If God used his absolute power and performed miracles to prevent the course of secondary causes, the order of nature would be confounded and to a certain extent, he would *contradict* himself in his double role as *Author of grace* and as *Author of nature*. Therefore, God rarely performs public miracles. However, God does perform miracles on special occasions. We must not wonder that he should consent to the death of the innocent children that Herod murdered, for it would not have been to the children's benefit to save them through a miracle. By their death, these children gained eternal life together with an abundant reward, which vastly recompensed them for the loss of their temporal life. If they had been allowed to escape the sword and die a natural death, they would not have necessarily been saved. The works of the Lord are just and holy in all particulars, although we do not always see the reasons why they are so. However, we will come to know them in the Lord when we shall see him face to face.

We were in Egypt when Herod butchered the children. My Son and I were aware of the tragedy, for Jesus in his role, as God had comforted the children. The children's voluntary sacrifices made many miracles possible in Egypt. Our hearts bled for the *Innocents* and their mothers, and our joint suffering was balm for the sins of the human race. In answer to my concern, God advised me that John was safe in his cave in the Judean Wilderness. He and Elizabeth were suffering great hardships. With God's permission, I frequently sent my angels with gifts of food and clothing to alleviate their sufferings. All of Herod's efforts to thwart the plans of God went for naught, for who can be like unto God?

We had been wandering about the delta country for nearly a year visiting many Egyptian cities to satisfy the yearning of my Son to help alleviate the spiritual and physical misery of this pagan culture. Jesus wrought many hidden miracles and wonders during our journey. I recall in particular Hermopolis, which was called by some the City of Mercury. In it was many idols infested by powerful demons. One of them dwelt in a tree at the entrance of the city; for the neighboring inhabitants had begun to venerate the tree because of its size and beauty. A demon had seized this opportunity to erect his place of abode in the tree accepting the worship as his own. Jesus hurled the demon from his seat and cast him into hell, as we came within sight of this wondrous tree. In gratitude the tree bowed down before its Creator rejoicing in its good fortune, for even the senseless creatures testified how tyrannical the dominion of the devil is. The miraculous reverence of trees happened at other times during our sojourn in Egypt, although they have not all been recorded. The memory of this event; however, has remained for centuries, and the leaves and fruit from this tree has cured many sicknesses.

During this first year of our exile, we celebrated the first anniversaries of the Incarnation and of the Nativity of the divine Word. I began and observed these customs in Egypt, and I observed and celebrated them throughout my life. Joseph, and my Son and I, began our celebration nine days before the anniversary of these events. I invited all the angels of heaven, together with those of my guard, the guards of Jesus, and the guardian angels of Joseph to assist me in the celebration of these great mysteries and to help me to acknowledge and give worthy thanks to the Almighty. In addition, I practiced these same devotions at all the festivals, seeking to appease the divine justice and soliciting mercy for sinners. The Most High regaled Joseph and I with many graces on these days of thanksgiving. Inflamed with charity, I ended my first celebration with beautiful hymns, singing them alternately with my angels, who formed a heavenly choir. The holy angels intoned their songs; I answered them on my part in hymns sweeter to the ears of God, and more acceptable than were those of the most exalted Seraphim and heavenly choirs. For these were the echoes of his infinite virtues piercing to the very throne and judgment seat of the eternal God.

At the end of the first year of our journey, Jesus, resting in my arms, spoke to Joseph for the first time. Jesus was nearly the size of a two-year old child. He was already losing his baby look. His face was taking on the firm straight lines that would make him so distinctive, as an adult. His auburn hair was long and hung down naturally to his shoulders. Joseph and I were speaking of the infinite being of God, of his goodness and excessive love, which induced him to send his Onlybegotten Son as the Teacher and Savior of men. He clothed him in human form in order that he might converse with men and suffer the punishments of their depraved natures.

Joseph was lost in the wonder at the works of the Lord and my Son seized upon this occasion to say, "My Father, I came from heaven upon this earth in order to be the light of the world, and in order to rescue it from darkness and sin. I come to seek and know my sheep, and as a good Shepherd give them nourishment of eternal life, to teach them the way of heaven, and open its gates, which has been closed by their sins. I desire that my parents be children of the light, which they have so close at hand."

Joseph was overwhelmed. He fell on his knees before the Infant Jesus with the deepest humility and thanked him for having called him, "Father" by the very first words spoken to him. With tears of gratitude he said, "I beseech you, Lord, to enlighten me and enable me to fulfill entirely your most holy will." Although Joseph was not the natural father of Jesus, his love for him exceeded by far all the love of parents for their children, since in him grace, or even natural love, was more powerful than in others, yes—even more than that of all the parents together.

My infant Son, like other children of his age, was dressed in swaddling clothes. It was now time for me to free him from his confining wrappings. I knelt at his cradle and said to him, "Oh light of my eyes, it is time for us to change the manner in which I clothe you. Tell me if you have any preference as to how I am to dress you?" He answered in his sweet baby voice, "My mother, because of my love for man, whom I have created and have come to redeem, the swaddling clothes of my childhood have not been irksome to me. When grown, my enemies shall likewise bind and deliver me over to suffer a cruel death. I wish to possess only one garment during all my life, for I seek nothing more than what is sufficient to cover me. Although all created things are mine, because I have given them being, I turn them all over to men. In this manner, they will owe me so much the more. Thus, according to my example, men will learn to repudiate and despise all that is superfluous for natural life."

"Clothe me, mother, in a tunic of a lowly and ordinary color. This, alone will I wear, and it shall grow with me. Over this seamless garment, they shall cast lots at my death [John: 19, 24]; for even this shall not be left to my disposal, but at the disposal of others. By this, men will see that I was born and wished to live poor and destitute of visible things, which being earthy, oppress and darken the heart of man. I shall make use of only that which is sufficient to sustain my natural life, which I will afterwards yield up for man's sake. All other visible things I shall offer up to the eternal Father, renouncing them for his love. By this example, I wish to impress upon the world the doctrine that it must love poverty and not despise it; for I, who am the Lord of the entire world, entirely repudiate and reject all its possessions."

My Son's reference to his death transfixed my heart, and his doctrine and example of extreme poverty excited my admiration and urged me even more to emulate him. Seeing that he did not wish to wear footwear, I urged him, "My Son, as your mother, I have not the heart to allow you to go barefoot upon the ground at such a tender age. Permit me to provide some kind of covering to protect them. I also fear that the rough garment, which you ask of me, will wound your tender body, if you permit no linen to be worn underneath."

My Son responded, "My mother, I will permit a slight and ordinary covering for my feet until the time of my public preaching shall come. However, at the time of my ministry, I must do so with bare feet. I wish to teach many by my example of humility."

I set about fulfilling my Son's wishes. I purchased some wool in its natural and uncolored state. Then I spun it very finely and of it, I wove a one-piece garment without any seams. To accomplish this required a mysterious process of which I am not at liberty to discuss [John: 19, 23]. At my request, Jesus allowed me to dye the natural color to a more suitable hue. The garment's color was a mixture of brown and a most exquisite silver-gray. I also wove a pair of sandals of strong thread-like hemp with which I covered my Son's tiny feet. In addition, I made a half tunic, which was to serve as an undergarment.

When they were finished, I knelt at my Son's crib, and with his permission, I clothed him. He was pleased with my loving service and I set him on his feet for the first time. It had not been necessary for me to measure him, yet the tunic fitted him perfectly, and covered his feet without hindering them in walking, and the sleeves extended to the middle of his hands. The collar was cut out round, without being open at the front, and was somewhat raised around the neck adjusting itself to the throat. As I passed it over his head, the garment gracefully adjusted itself according to my wishes. Jesus never divested himself of this tunic, until his executioners themselves tore it off to scourge and later to crucify him. This garment, as well as his shoes and under garment, continually grew with him, adjusting themselves to his body as he grew. They never wore or became old or lost their newness in his over thirty years on this earth. They remained just as I had made them, and they never became soiled or filthy, but preserved their original cleanliness. Later, in Nazareth, I made Jesus a cape, which he wore over his shoulders. This cape had the same properties as the rest of his clothing, and this is the garment, which Jesus during his Ministry, laid aside in order to wash the feet of his Apostles. The cape was slightly darker than his tunic, but was made of the same material.

Once placed on his feet my Son walked freely about as though he had been doing so all along. However, until he advanced in age, he did so only in our presence. The angels were astounded at the humble and poor raiment chosen by Jesus, who clothes the heavens in light and the fields with beauty. Jesus was the most beautiful among all the sons of man. Who, but the Son of God, can be like unto God in human or divine form? When Jesus was a year and a half old, I stopped nursing him at his request, although it was quite common at the time to nurse a child until they were three years of age or more. Jesus ate sparingly after that, and his meals were quite frugal in quantity as well as in quality. At first, I fed him broth mixed with oil and some fruits or fishes. He never asked for food, but I made sure that he had two meals a day, no matter how frugal. We always took our meals together and we always waited until our Son pronounced the blessing at the beginning and gave thanks at the end.

Once he began to walk, Jesus spent long hours in my oratory praying. I was anxious to know his wishes regarding his privacy at prayer, yet I refrained from asking. However, divining my thoughts he responded to my mute appeal and said, "My Mother, enter and remain with me always in order that you may imitate me in my works. I wish that in you be modeled and exhibited the high perfection, which I desire to see accomplished in all souls. If they had not sinned, I would have endowed humankind with my most abundant and copious gifts. Since the human race has hindered this, I have chosen you as the vessel of all perfection and of the treasures of my right hand. The rest of the creatures have abused my gifts and lost. Observe me, therefore, in all my actions in order to imitate me. It was in this manner that my Son installed me as his first Disciple. From then on, there passed between us such great and hidden mysteries that God will not reveal them until the day of eternity.

At times, Jesus prostrated himself on the ground, as I was wont to do. His Father often raised him from the floor in the form of a cross as he prayed to him for the salvation of mortals. In all this, I imitated him, for to me were made manifest the interior operations of his most holy soul, just as well as I saw the exterior movements of his body. In all our activities, I nearly always enjoyed the vision of the most holy humanity and soul of my Son. In a special way, I was witness of the effects of the hypostatic and beatific union of the humanity of the Divinity. I did not always see this glory and this union substantially. I did perceive the interior acts by which his humanity reverenced, loved and magnified the Divinity to which it was united. God reserved this privilege solely for me.

On these private occasions, I often saw my Son perspire blood, for this happened many times before his agony in the garden and on the cross. At other times, I would find him refulgent with heavenly light and surrounded by angels that sang sweet hymns of praise. His works of love, praise, and worshipful gratitude, and his petitions for the human race, would take volumes to describe.

On nearing Heliopolis, we stopped overnight at a beautiful little fountain, whose cool, clean waters refreshed us immensely. I drew water from the well, we drank gratefully refreshing ourselves, and I washed my Son and then washed our clothes. Through Jesus, we performed many cures, and the people of the area readily accepted our teachings of their Creator. This fountain became a traditional place of veneration for the infidels, and pagans still gain temporal benefits there. In this manner, my Son preserves the memories of his wonders among them.

The morning we reached Heliopolis, the City of the Sun, the very portals of hell were shook. Later, the city was renamed Cairo, the grand. Jesus had performed many miracles and wonders since we entered Egypt. However, Jesus performed his principal wonders in Heliopolis. Lucifer became alarmed when such a large number of demons were driven back into hell; he left his abode to investigate the cause. Jesus had already overthrown many temples and idols in Egypt. When we entered Heliopolis, Jesus smashed to the ground and destroyed every temple and idol in the city. The utter destruction of his evil structures astounded Lucifer. In places the earth had opened and swallowed the huge temples and idols leaving utter destruction in its wake. Lucifer found nothing new except that Jesus, Joseph and I had recently entered the city. Of my Son, Lucifer took no notice, deeming him a child just like all the rest of that age, for he was unable to learn any more about him. My virtues and holiness had often vanquished Satan. Yet, Lucifer still considered a woman far too insignificant to have performed such great works. Anxiety filled Lucifer when he saw me, and he resolved anew to persecute me and to stir up his associates in wickedness against me.

Lucifer returned to hell and called a meeting of his princes of darkness. He explained all that had happened and of the utter destruction of the temples and idols in Egypt. Jesus had hurled the demons involved into hell so quickly that they had no idea that the idols and temples had been destroyed. Satan explained the problem to them and complained, "I fear the destruction of my power in Egypt, and I cannot explain why. I found only the Woman, our enemy, and while I know her power is extraordinary, I cannot presume it to be so great as to account for such destruction. We must again wage a campaign against the Woman, and I want all of you to join me in my just cause."

The demons tried to console Satan in his desperate fury and promised him victory, as if their forces were as great as their arrogance [Is: 16, 6]. Many legions of devils immediately sallied forth to where I was at the time. By defeating me, they hoped to recoup their losses and restore their dominion over the pathetic pagans of Egypt. Yet, when they attempted to approach me in order to begin their diabolic temptations, they could not come nearer to me than a distance of two thousand paces. They soon learned that this power issued forth from me. Although they struggled violently, they were paralyzed, and found themselves as if bound in strong and tormenting shackles without being able to gain a single inch toward me, for I held in my arms the omnipotence of God himself. God suddenly hurled Lucifer into the abyss of hell with all his squadrons of wicked spirits. This defeat filled the dragon with anxiety, and as the same thing had overtaken him repeatedly since the Incarnation, he began to have new misgivings, as to whether or not the Messiah was already present in the world. Since he knew nothing of the mystery, he fully expected the Messiah to come in great splendor and renown; he remained full of uncertainty. The more he inquired into the cause of his sufferings, the more was he involved in darkness and so much the less did he ascertain the true cause.

The traditions, which in many parts of Egypt kept alive the remembrance of the wonders wrought by the Incarnate Word, have given rise to differences of opinion among the sacred and other writers as to the city in which we lived during our stay in Egypt. Let it be sufficient to say that we passed through Matarieh and Memphis, often called the Babylon of Egypt, and many other cities. Our destination was Heliopolis, the "City of the Sun", and we were finally led there by our holy angels. As I stated before, Jesus destroyed all the idols and pagan temples as he entered the city. It was here that Jesus had resolved to perform great, but hidden miracles for the rescue of souls of the inhabitants of the city. The Sun of Justice and Grace had risen and now shone upon them. Following the angel's orders, Joseph purchased for a suitable price a dwelling in the most humble of neighborhoods. The angels had advised Joseph previously, and he had prudently laid aside money from the Magi gifts for that purpose. It was a poor, yet serviceable house, located in the middle of the city, which was exactly what I had hoped for.

Upon first entering our new home, I prostrated myself on the dirt floor and kissed the ground in profound humility. Joseph and I thanked the Most High for having provided us a place of rest after our long and extended journey. After our prayers, I rose, and with the aid of my angels cleaned and arranged the house borrowing suitable instruments for this purpose from our friendly neighbors. God had given us divine help many times in the desert, but now the Lord left us to our own devices. Joseph went out into the streets begging for alms. He thereby gave an example to the poor not to complain of their afflictions and all other means failing, not to be ashamed to have recourse to this expedient. In so doing, the Lord of all creation allowed himself to fall to this extreme of being obliged to beg for his sustenance, in order that he might have an occasion to return the alms a hundredfold.

Joseph had prudently packed his basic carpenter tools. In the first week, he had earned not only enough to sustain us, but was also able to construct a humble couch for me, and a small bed for our divine Son. Within a short time, he had furnished our little home with the necessities, which was all that we needed or desired. In our extreme poverty, neither of us ever regretted our much finer home in Nazareth, or pined for the help given us by our relatives and friends there. We bore our sufferings in joy and tranquility, resigning ourselves completely to the divine Providence. In our basic one-room house, Joseph set aside a separate space as a sanctuary for our Son and me. In another; he set up an oratory and sleeping place for himself. In the third, he set up his carpenter shop. The people we lived amidst were extremely poor, and they simply did not have enough money to live on. Joseph, ever mindful of their needs, performed his work at very little cost to the people. Consequently, we soon found ourselves worse off than we had been in Nazareth. I returned to my needlework to help us survive and to help our blessed poor. I was a skilled seamstress, and some pious women, who lived in the area, heartily recommended me, so that the fame of my work spread quickly.

I found that even with the extra income that we would barely be able to survive and I determined to give up my daytime prayers and to work all day on my sewing and then spend the balance of the night attending to my spiritual exercises. All of this, of course, had to be in addition to the maintaining of my home, my husband, and my Child. I united my prayers with my labors working as though only by my work could I accomplish my goals, and at the same time praying to God as though, only he could fulfill our needs.

My Infant Son was pleased with my prudence, and my resignation to our dire poverty. However, he wished to lessen the labors I had undertaken. Shortly thereafter, he spoke to me and said, "My, Mother, I wish to set up a rule for your daily life and labors."

I dropped to my knees before him and said, "My sweetest love and Lord of all my being. May it please you to direct my footsteps according to your holy will? Speak for your servant hears."

My divine Son replied, "My dearest Mother, from the time of nightfall, nine PM, you shall take some sleep and rest. From midnight until the break of dawn, you may occupy yourself in contemplation with me, and we will praise the eternal Father. Thereupon prepare the necessary food for yourself and Joseph. Afterwards give me nourishment and hold me in your arms until the third hour, you shall then place me in the arms of your husband in order to afford him some refreshment in his labors. Then retire until it is time to prepare his meal and return to your work. Since you do not have with you the sacred Scriptures, which gave you consolation, you can by your holy science, enter the doctrines of eternal life in order that you may follow me in perfect imitation. In addition, continually pray to the eternal Father for sinners."

This rule governed our life during our stay in Egypt. I nursed my Son three times a day until he was eighteen months old, for Jesus had not forbidden me to offer him nourishment at other times than the one time stipulated. As instructed, I placed my Son in the arms of his foster father each morning, not that this was the only time that he held him. This; however, was the specific time allocated him by the Divinity and had special meaning and significance This privilege made him forget all the hardships of his labors, and made his sacrifices easy and sweet in his eyes. It is impossible for me to describe the blessings that I received when I adored and caressed my Son with the tenderness of a mother. On the other hand, I had to fulfill all obligations that were due him as from a creature to its Creator. I looked upon him in his Divinity, as Son of the eternal Father, as King of Kings, and Lord of Lords, and as the Maker and Preserver of the entire universe. On the other hand, in serving and nursing him, I gave to him all the attention that he deserved as an infant. Between these two extremes, I was entirely inflamed with love, and my entire being was consumed in heroic acts of admiration, praise and affection. In the eyes of our angels, Joseph and I attained the summit of holiness and of divine pleasure.

Isaiah said that the Lord would enter Egypt upon a light cloud in order to work miracles for that Country. Isaiah in referring to me as the cloud was pointing out the humanity derived from me. A cloud that through me, the Lord intended to fertilize and water the barren land of the hearts of its inhabitants in order that they might produce the fruits of sanctity and of divine knowledge. Inspired by the power of Jesus, many Egyptians began to believe in the true God. The demons had closed the paths of eternal life and now God began to open them. However, after the Sun of Justice began to illumine Egypt, and I, the taintless cloud, began to overshadow that land, it became so fertile in holiness and grace that it gave forth abundant fruit for many centuries. Many saints and hermits, who lived there afterwards, witnessed this fact.

Many Hebrews lived in Egypt and thus knowledge of God came from as far back as the time of the Exodus. These Hebrews usually congregated in small communities separate from the rest of the city, and they had their own synagogues and worshiped the one true God. However, many Hebrews had fallen into a superstitious hodgepodge of Hebrew Scripture and pagan idolatry. They began coming to us when they heard of the wondrous Child that exuded such holiness and sanctity. Joseph and I were able to correct their errors of faith and bring them back into the fold of holiness.

As stated before, when we entered Heliopolis all the idols, altars, and temples came crashing to the ground and the evil demons were immediately plunged into the abyss. There were more idols and temples here than in all the other cities. The utter destruction and the noise and confusion caused by these events sent the people racing panic stricken through the streets seeking answers as to what was happening. As in other towns, some of the people thought to ask us as newcomers what we thought of these startling events. Fully aware of God's intentions, I spoke to them with wisdom, prudence and sweetness. In addition, my gentleness and exalted teachings filled the Hebrews with wonder, which enlightened them of the error of their ways. To let them know that my words were true, I cured some of their sick and the news of my teachings spread quickly and soon a great concourse of people gathered to see us. I consulted with my most holy Son when so many people gathered as to what further steps I should take.

He answered, "Instruct my children in the knowledge of God, teach them his true worship, and exhort them to desist from sinful life."

God had cast into hell the imps of Satan plaguing the Egyptians. God contained them there for some time giving the people an opportunity to be free to accept new ideas and philosophies. The people readily turned from sin and to God. So instructed by my Son, I served as his instrument, and he lent power to my words and miracles. I always held my infant Son in my arms when I spoke to the Egyptians. With his help, I was able to speak to each person suitable to that person's capacity for learning the doctrine of eternal life. I explained to them concerning the Divinity and made them understand that there cannot be more than one God. I taught them the several articles of faith pertaining to the Creation and Redemption of the world. I impressed upon their minds the Commandments of the Decalogue, founded upon the natural law. Then we explained to them the manner of adoring and worshipping God, and how they were to expect the regeneration of the human race.

The Egyptians knew that the demons existed, but they did not realize the evil intent of these damned creatures. I explained how and why they were the enemies of God and of men. I showed them how deeply the devils kept men in error by their idol worship and the false answers of the oracles designed to mislead them and induce men to commit the vilest abominations and how they tempted them by exciting their disorderly passions. I told them of the coming of the Redeemer, who was to overcome the demons, and that he was already in the world. I did not; however, tell them that I held that precious person in my own two arms. In order that my teachings would be more widely accepted, Joseph and I confirmed my words with great miracles, curing all sorts of people who were sick, or possessed by the devil, and who had come to us from all parts of the country.

I hesitated between two different sentiments: the one of charity which drew me to nurse the wounded with my own two hands and the other of modesty, which forbade me to touch men. To observe all propriety, my Son empowered me to cure the men by my mere words and exhortations. God; however, allowed me to cure the women and cleanse their wounds with my own hands. To assist me, God endowed Joseph with new light and the power of healing, and he joined me in the curing of the sick. As I stated before, these cures were not immediate, but were accomplished in a timely manner, so that no one could claim an out and out miracle. Soon Joseph tended to the instruction and cure of the men and I concentrated my efforts with the women. In order to tend to my poor and relieve their physical ailments, I often had to place Jesus in his crib, which went against my every motherly instinct, and in itself was a deep penance for me. According to the custom of the time, and due to my complete subjugation to my Lord and God, I never looked directly upon the face of either man or woman. Even when the wound was on a person's face, I contained my gaze to that one spot. I could not have identified a single person I served, except for the fact that I could see each person interiorly. Once I had met a person, I could identify them unerringly by their soul.

When Jesus was two years old, while he and I were at prayer together, my angels gave us a message. Herod the Great, the despot of Israel who had lived in filth and corruption, was dead. He died in agony, completely out of his mind, his body infested and eaten by worms. We were instructed to remain in Egypt, for it was still too dangerous for us to return home. That night, Joseph, in a dream, was also informed.

The next day, he said to me, "God's angel has informed me that King Herod is dead. However, we are still in danger and must remain here until conditions change for the better in Israel. Let us join together in prayer for his soul."

Because of the excessive heat in Egypt, many physical disorders were rampant among the people. The distempers of the Egyptians were widespread and epidemic. During our years in Heliopolis, pestilence often devastated the land and hearing of our message, multitudes of people came to us from all parts of the country and we sent them home cured in body and soul. Many people wished to give us gifts, but we refused all payment for our services and we continued to provide for our personal needs by the labor of our hands. The only exception I made to this practice was to accept and redistribute some items to the needy and the poor. Even then, as I had done in Nazareth, I made the donor a present made by my own hands, in return for their donation.

Of course everyone was not converted—more is the pity. Many persons were set in the ways of the abominable one, and they often confronted us in great wrath and indignation. The pagan priests were the worst. We were only able to convert a few of them, because they were so steeped in their evil ways. They came frequently at first, ranting and raving and even tried to have us arrested as blasphemers and troublemakers. However, most of the local magistrates were sympathetic to our cause. My holy Son helped us by implanting a holy reverence for God in the hearts of the magistrates. Finally, the crowds of people who wished to hear the true word of God and feel his healing hand drove the pagan priests away.

When Elizabeth's son John was four years old, his saintly mother died. Elizabeth died at peace, for her guardian angels assured her that John would be under the direct protection of God's holy angels. My angels buried Elizabeth in the desert on a rise facing Jerusalem. The Holy Spirit educated John, and every day my angels carried food to him until he was old enough to provide for himself. John grew up in the desert, living an austere life, subsisting mainly on wild honey and roasted locusts. No wine or meat of animals ever passed his lips, and scissors never touched his hair. He was the Precursor of Christ and his life was one of mortification and prayer. His only companions and playmates were the angels, the wild animals, and the birds of the air. The birds often brought him food in their beaks and loved to perch on his shoulders. John conversed with his angels as freely, as we converse with our families. John's entire life, from the moment of his sanctification by Jesus in the womb of his mother, was one of preparation for his job as the Precursor of Christ.

The years raced by quickly and before I knew it, my divine Son was six years old. He had grown in the admiration and esteem of all that came to know him, and together we had created heavenly wonders with the common people of Egypt. Jesus now began to visit the sick in their homes, seeking out the stricken ones and mysteriously comforting and consoling them. Many of the inhabitants of Heliopolis came to know him. The secret attractions of his divinity and sanctity drew toward him the hearts of all, and many people offered him gifts. These, according to the urging of his interior knowledge, he refused or accepted for distribution to the poor. The admiration caused by his wise counsels and his modest and considerate behavior caused many to extol and congratulate us as his parents for having such a Son. The people were ignorant of the mysteries and the true dignity of my Son and I, yet the Lord of creation being desirous of honoring me, permitted them to reverence me as far as was possible under the circumstances, without their learning the special reason they did so.

Many children of all ages flocked around my son, because the qualities of leadership, kindness, compassion, and wisdom evidenced by Jesus, drew admirers the same as nectar attracts bees. They came to him free of malice drawn by his heavenly light. My Son welcomed them as far as was befitting. He instilled in them the knowledge of God and of the virtues. He taught them in the way of eternal life, even more abundantly than he did with the adults, for the children were more pure of heart and more susceptible to his teachings. He won their hearts and impressed his truths so deeply upon them that afterwards, those who had this good fortune, became great and saintly men. For in the course of time, the fruit of this heavenly seed sown so early in their souls ripened and burst into flower.

I was fully aware of all that my Son did. When he and Joseph returned from one of these errands, in which he had fulfilled the will of the Father by looking after his flock, my angels and I prostrated ourselves before Jesus and gave him thanks for the benefits done to those innocents, who did not yet know him as their true God. I always asked for his blessings upon all my undertakings, as did Joseph, and I never lost an opportunity for practicing virtue with all the intensity of my love and divine grace. I sought new ways of humiliating myself, and adored the Incarnate Word by many genuflections, prostrations, and other loving and profound ceremonies as an outward token of my prudence and holiness. Even the angels were impressed with my efforts, and they exclaimed my praises among themselves.

After he began to walk, Jesus showed a more serious side of his nature, and as he grew older became more earnest in his demeanor. The tender caresses given me when he was a baby had always been tempered and measured in his dignity. Now gradually, they were withheld, for in his countenance shone forth such majesty as a reflection of his hidden Deity that if he had not mixed it with a certain sweetness and affability, reverential fear would have prevented all interaction with him. Joseph and I felt the affects of a divine power and efficacy, as well as the kindness and devotedness of a loving Father, proceeding from his countenance. Joined with this majesty and magnificence was his filial affection toward me, while on the other hand, he treated Joseph as one, who had as well the name as the duties of a father toward him. Therefore, he obeyed us both as a most devoted Son obeys his parents. In his whole behavior the Incarnate Word practiced the virtues of obedience, humility, and human kindness with such an admirable mixture of majesty and gravity that his divine wisdom shone forth in all his actions and none of his grandeur was impaired by triviality or smallness.

I alone, as far as a mere creature could, comprehended the work of my most holy Son and understood the ways of his infinite wisdom. To describe the affects of his works on my most pure and prudent soul, or how closely I imitated his ineffable sanctity, would be most difficult to relate. The souls which were converted and saved in Heliopolis and in all Egypt, the sick that were cured and the wonders wrought during our seven years stay in that country cannot be enumerated. God turned the cruelty of King Herod *to the holy innocents and to us* into a blessing for Egypt. The goodness and wisdom of God can draw from the very wickedness and evils of sin the greatest good. For if in one direction men cast away God's mercies and shut them out, he calls upon them in other directions to open their hearts and admit their blessings. The floods of the sins and ingratitude of humanity cannot quench the ardent desires of God to benefit the human race.

Jesus was seven, when God informed me that this ended the term set by the eternal Wisdom for his mysterious sojourn in Egypt. The prophecies stated that Jesus was a Nazarene. It was time for us to return to Nazareth. The prophecies were the word of God given to man spelling out the destiny of his Son. God transmitted his wishes to his holy Son in my presence, while I was in prayer with him. I saw it mirrored in his deified soul and he submitted to it in complete obedience to his Father. That very night an angel spoke to Joseph in his sleep and made known this new decree of heaven [Matt: 2, 19-23]. The Almighty set much value on the proper order in created things. Jesus was the true God, and I, his mother, the Queen of Heaven. However, God did not permit the arrangements for our return to proceed from us. The order was to come from Joseph, who was the head of our family. The Providence of God governs by natural order and he hoped to teach us this fact by example. Joseph advised us of God's will and of course we both answered that we were God's humble servants.

I knew how much it meant to Jesus to give alms to the poor, so I placed in his hands the disposal of our furniture and he joyfully gave it to his beloved poor. The house, we gave to a devout family in Heliopolis, their virtue and holiness had gained them this favor in the eyes of my Son. They could not fully appreciate the blessings of this gift, but they considered themselves indeed fortunate to occupy the same house in which we had lived for nearly six years. Abundant light and grace for their eternal salvation was their reward for their affectionate devotion.

We departed for Palestine accompanied only by our angels as we had on our journey to Egypt. I sat cross saddle, as was the custom. I seated Jesus on my lap and our Muscat Ass set off eagerly as though he knew we were on our way home. Our friends and many benefactors were sorrowful at our departure. We parted with much weeping and complaining on their part that they were losing all their consolation and refuge in our going. The inhabitants of Heliopolis felt the night of their miseries secretly setting upon their hearts at the parting of the Sun; the Sun that had dispersed and brightened its darkness [John: 1, 9]. In traversing the inhabited country, we again passed through many cities of Egypt, and everywhere we went, we scattered our graces and blessings. The news of our coming spread before us like the light, and the sick, the afflicted, and disconsolate gathered to seek us out. In his final miracles for Egypt, Jesus relieved many inhabitants in body and soul. During our journey, Jesus cured many of the sick and cast out their demons. The demons never knew who it was that hurled them back into the abyss.

I will not relate all the particular events of our journey back to Nazareth. I will sum it all up to say that anyone who came to us with greater or less devotion left our presence enlightened with truth, assisted by grace, and wounded with the love of God. The people felt a secret force, which urged and compelled them to the pursuit of virtue, and while withdrawing them from the paths of death, showed them the way of eternal life. They came to the Son, drawn to him by the Father, and they turned to the Father, sent there by the divine light of Christ's truth, which enkindled their souls with the knowledge of the true God [John: 6, 44]. Nevertheless, he concealed his real identity, since it was not yet time to reveal himself openly. However, the fire, which he came to enkindle and spread in this world, secretly and incessantly, produced its divine effects among the Egyptians. We went through much the same sufferings and privations that we had experienced in coming to Egypt. God permitted our hardships and tribulations in order to give us the occasion of merit. However, it was Jesus now, not I that ordered the angels to provide us with relief when it was necessary for our survival. Jesus allowed Joseph to hear his commands, and he saw the spirits obey and bring what was needed. This greatly encouraged and consoled Joseph in his anxiety for my Son and me. At other times my divine Child made use of his omnipotence and created all that was necessary to supply our wants from a crumb of bread or a drop of water.

When we arrived in Palestine, Joseph learned that Archelaus had succeeded Herod his father in the government of Judea [Matt: 2, 22]. The son had inherited all of his father's cruelty, so Joseph turned from our route to Jerusalem. I had hoped not only to visit the holy temple, but also to revisit the holy cave near Bethlehem where my most holy Son had been born. We passed instead through the land of the tribe of Dan and Issachar below Galilee, following the coast of the Great Sea and avoided Jerusalem entirely. It was with a great deal of satisfaction when we entered Nazareth again. It was home, be it ever so humble. The Conception of my Son, the Redeemer of the world, had taken place here. It was a most sacred and holy place.

After the birth of Jesus, when we learned we had to leave Nazareth, Joseph contacted his cousin Mahara asking her to take care of our home until our return. We found it in perfect condition, and Mahara and her family greeted us with great love and tenderness. She dearly loved me, although she did not know of my dignity. Upon entering the house, I prostrated myself in adoration of the Lord and gave him proper thanks for having brought us back safely to our home, for avoiding the wrath of Herod, and for preserving us in the dangers of our exile and our long and arduous journeys. I also gave him thanks for my Son, now grown both in years, in grace, and in virtue [Luke: 2, 40].

Taking counsel with my divine Son, I proceeded to set up a rule of life and regulate my pious practices, as I had done in whatever circumstances I found myself. Now; however, settled comfortably in my own home, I wished to include many exercises, which on our journey had been impossible. My greatest desire was to always cooperate with my most holy Son in the salvation of souls, which was the work most urgently enjoined upon me by the eternal Father. Toward this end, I directed all my practices in union with my Redeemer, and this was our constant occupation, as I will soon outline. Joseph resumed his occupation in order to earn enough to sustain us as a family. Work, which many other sons of Adam consider a punishment and a hardship, was to Joseph a great happiness. Joseph was blessed and consoled beyond all measure, for he had been chosen to labor and by his sweat, to support God himself to whom belonged Heaven and Earth and all that they contain.

To repay my devoted husband, I provided him his meals and attended to his comforts with great care and in most loving gratitude. I was obedient to him in all things and I humbled myself before him, as if I was his handmaid instead of his wife. I knew the depth of the magnitude and infiniteness of God better than any other person did, except my holy Son. This knowledge made me aware of how unworthy I was to exist, or to be allowed to walk upon this earth. I thought it just that I want in everything. In my knowledge of having been created out of nothing and therefore unable to make any return for either this benefit or, according to my estimation, for any of the others. I established in myself such a rare humility that I thought of myself as less than dust and unworthy to mingle with it. For the least favor, I gave profuse thanks to the Lord.

To some persons, I gave thanks because they conferred favors upon me, to others because they denied me favors. To others, who bore with me in patience, I acknowledged myself as indebted to them, though I filled them with the blessings of sweetness and placed myself at the feet of all. I sought ingenious means and artifices to let no instant and no occasion pass for practicing the most perfect and exalted virtues. In so doing I gained the admiration of the angels and the delight of the Most High.

I AM MARY

The Infinite Mercy, with which God blessed me, can only be measured by his Infinite Love for me. I am the Mother of Mercy and the Mother of Perseverance. I justly earned this latter title by the fact that I persevered in faith all the days of my life. Final perseverance is so great a gift of God that the Holy Council of Trent declared that perseverance is quite gratuitous on God's part and we cannot merit it. Saint Augustine states that all who seek for perseverance, may obtain it from God; and according to Father Suarez, they obtain it infallibly, but only if the person is diligent in asking for it every day of their lives. For, as Saint Bellarmin remarked,

"That which is daily required—must be asked for every day.

In order to increase my children's confidence, I will quote Saint Anselm, who sums up my gifts of Mercy and Perseverance very well. He states, "When we have recourse to our divine Mother, we may be sure of her protection. However, it is a fact that *often* we shall be heard more quickly and thus preserved, if we have recourse to Mary first, even more so than if we had called upon the name of Jesus our Savior."

This is a startling statement and requires an explanation and Saint Anselm continues,

"In calling on Jesus, he is not only **all Mercy**, but is also **all Justice**. By this very fact—while he will grant us mercy, yet, he must also **punish**. Mercy alone; however, as a gift from God, belongs to me, the Blessed Virgin as a patroness." This means that you can more easily find salvation by having recourse to me than by going to my Son. That is not because I am more powerful than my Son is to save you, *for we all know that my Son alone is our Redeemer and Savior. He alone by his merits has obtained and obtains for us Salvation.* However, when we have recourse to Jesus, we must consider him at the same time as our judge, to whom it belongs *also* to chastise ungrateful souls, therefore, the confidence necessary to be heard may fail us. However, when you come to me, I have no other office than to be compassionate as your *Mother of Mercy*. God wishes *me* to be the advocate for all sinners. My intercession of mercy for these sinners may save those who would otherwise be damned.

It is *vital* that those who call upon my name must have "***true contrition***" for their sins. I cannot help the reprobate, who has no contrition and only hopes to avoid the pains of hell. If you invoke my name and are "***truly contrite***", although you do not merit that your prayers be granted, I will supply that which you will need to save your soul. All of this is possible only because God has so decreed it, in order to honor me his Mother.

In the words of Ecclesiasticus, and those words that are applied to me by the Church on the Feast of the Immaculate Conception, *"They that work for me shall not sin. They that explain me shall have life everlasting*." I can grant you spiritual fortitude, which each person needs to resist the enemies of salvation. The book of Proverbs assures you this fortitude, for the Church applies this passage to me,

"***Strength is mine; by me kings reign.***" Meaning that by the words "***Strength is mine***" that God has bestowed this precious gift to me in order that I may dispense it to my faithful clients. By the words, ***"By me kings reign,"*** my clients, through me, are able to reign over and command their senses and passions, and thus they become worthy to reign eternally in heaven."

"In the book of Proverbs, it states that all of my clients are clothed with double garments. This means that I adorn my faithful servants with the virtues of my Son and with my own virtues. Thus clothed, they persevere in virtue. Saint Philip Neri, in his exhortations to his penitents, used to say, "My children if you desire perseverance be devout to our Blessed Lady. Venerable John Berchmans of the Society of Jesus also said, "Whoever loves Mary will have perseverance." Abbot Rupert in his commentary on the parable of the prodigal son said, "If this dissolute youth had had a mother living, he would never have abandoned the paternal roof, or at least would have returned much sooner than he did." By this he meant that if he had been one of my sons, he would either never have abandoned God, or, if he did, by my help, he would soon have returned."

"Isaiah tells us, "When a man is on the point of leaving the world hell is opened and spews forth its most terrible demons, both to tempt the soul before it leaves the body, and also to accuse it when presented before the tribunal of Jesus Christ for judgment." Isaiah also said, "Hell below was in an uproar to meet you at your coming; it stirred up the giants for you." Saint Lawrence remarked, "When Mary defends the soul, the devils dared not even accuse it knowing that the judge never condemned, and never will condemn, a soul protected by Mary."

I will close these thoughts for mediation with this anecdote of Charles, the son of Saint Bridget, who died in the army far from his mother. Bridget feared much for his salvation, because of the many temptations young men face in a military career. I saved this young man because of his love for his mother and her prayers for his soul. I assisted him at his death by suggesting to him the acts that he should make at that terrible moment. When Charles came before the throne of my Son, the devil brought two accusations against me. The first was that I had prevented him from tempting Charles at the moment of his death. The second was that I had myself presented his soul to the judge, and so saved it without even giving him the opportunity of exposing the grounds on which he had claimed the soul for his own. Without a word, my Son drove the devil away and carried Charles off to heaven.

Come to me my children; allow me to be your *"City of refuge"* for I am the refuge to all who fly to me. I am the public infirmary in which all, the sick, poor, and destitute can be received. I ask you, "In hospitals erected expressly for the poor, who have the greatest claim to admission?" Certainly it is the most infirm and those who are in the greatest need. Come to me, I am your *Mother of Perseverance*, I am *your Mother of Mercy*, pray daily for perseverance and I will grant you my mercy.

"That which is daily required—must be asked for every day."

ALL MY LOVE

Mary

Chapter Seven

The Missing Years

God Says

"I will destroy the wisdom of the wise and thwart the cleverness of the clever."

The mysteries and sacraments that passed between my Son and me, until he began, his ministry would require many chapters and many books. Because of the lack of space, I will relate only the smallest part. As I told you before, God granted me the privilege to contemplate the Holy Soul of my son. Shortly after our return from Egypt, Jesus decided to test me in the same manner that he had tested me in my childhood, and in the same manner that he has often tested the Saints throughout the history of the Church. I had grown vastly in the exercise of my love and wisdom. The power of God is infinite, and since my capacity as Queen exceeded that of all creatures, the Lord wished to raise me to *even* a higher level of holiness and merit.

God wished to form me into a disciple of such exalted knowledge that I would truly become a consummate Teacher and a living example of his own doctrines; for such was to be my office after the Ascension of my Son and Redeemer, of which I will relate later. It was befitting and necessary for the honor of my Son that the teachings of the Gospel, by which, and on which, he was to found the law of grace, should give full evidence of its efficacy and power in a mere creature. God desired that one person should exhibit all of its super eminent effects, so they would be a standard for all humankind. It later became clear that God intended that person to be me, who as the mother of Jesus stood so close to the Master and Teacher of all holiness.

Therefore, in order to implant in my heart this edifice of holiness to a height beyond all that is not God; the Father laid the foundations of trying the strength of my love. The Lord withdrew from my sight for this purpose, causing me great anguish. He hid himself from my interior sight and suspended the tokens of his most sweet affection. He did so with no explanations whatsoever. To add to my consternation, Jesus became most reserved and withdrew from my company. Many times, he retired at night and spoke but few words to me. When he did speak, he spoke with great earnestness and majesty. What affected me the most was the eclipse of the light by which I was accustomed to see reflected as in a crystal the human operations of his most pure soul. God suddenly dimmed this light so much that I could no longer distinguish them as a living copy of my own actions.

This unannounced and unexpected change was the crucible by which God tested me, for thus was my love cleansed and assayed into the purest of gold. Totally taken by surprise, I took refuge in my humility, since, from the first, I had never deemed myself worthy of the vision of the Lord. I assumed my lack of gratitude for his blessings had led to my banishment. I did not feel so much the privation of his delightful caresses, as the dread of having displeased him and of having fallen short in his service. My heart was pierced with an arrow of grief, for I was filled with such true and noble love that I could not feel less. The delight of love is founded in the pleasure and satisfaction given by the lover to the one beloved. Therefore, I could not rest when I believed my beloved was not contented or pleased.

My loving sighs of grief and anguish were highly pleasing to my Son. He was enamored anew and my tender affection wounded his heart. However, when I sought him out in order to converse with him, he continued to show exterior reserve. The application of insufficient water to the flame of a forge or a conflagration intensifies its heat. Thus, this adversity fanned my love to a more intense blaze.

I exercised myself in heroic acts of all the virtues. I humbled myself below the dust of the earth. I reverenced my Son in deepest adoration. I blessed the Father, thanking him for his admirable works and blessings and conformed myself to his wishes and pleasure. I unceasingly renewed my acts of faith, hope, and my burning love. I persevered in tearful prayers with continual sighing and longing from my inmost heart. I continuously poured forth my prayers in the presence of the Lord, and recounted my tribulation before the throne of God. Many times, I broke out in words of ineffable sweetness and loving sorrow.

I addressed myself to my holy angels and said, "Sovereign, princes and intimate friends of the highest King and my guardians, by your felicitous vision of his divine countenance and the ineffable light, I conjure you to tell me the cause of his displeasure, if such he has conceived against me? Intercede for me in his real presence, if I have offended him that through your prayers he may pardon me?

The holy angels replied, "Our, Queen and, Sovereign, dilated is your heart so that you cannot be vanquished by tribulation. No one is as able as you are to understand how near our Lord is to the afflicted, who call upon him. Without doubt, he recognizes your affection, and does not despise your loving sighs. A humble heart does not displease our king. Upon it he fixes his loving regard, and he is never unhappy about receiving the clamors of those who love Him."

I knew they would not speak more openly, but the answers of the holy angels did console and gladden my heart. I learned later that my Son hid his compassion under a severe countenance. He would sometimes delay his response to my call to his meals, or he would eat without looking at or speaking to me. On these occasions, I always managed to restrain my feelings and my tears were reserved for when I was alone. In as far as he was man, the child Jesus delighted in seeing his divine love and grace bring forth such abundant fruits in me, his Virgin Mother. The holy angels sang to him new hymns of praise for this admirable and unheard-of prodigy of virtues.

At my request, Joseph had made a simple couch for our Son replacing the cradle we had left in Egypt. I covered it with a single blanket and from that time forward, Jesus would not accept any other bed or more covering. Although he did not stretch himself out on this couch, nor use it much, he sometimes reclined in a sitting posture, resting upon his poor pillow made of wool, which I had fashioned for him.

I tried to get him to make use of a better resting-place, but he explained, "In order to teach men by my example, the only couch that I will stretch out on is that of the Cross. No one can enter eternal rest by things beloved of Babylon. To suffer is our true relief in mortal life."

I imitated him in this manner of taking rest with new earnestness and attention. It had been my custom before retiring for the night to prostrate myself before my Son as he reclined on his couch. I then asked for his pardon for not having fulfilled all my duty in serving him and for not having been sufficiently grateful for his blessings. I poured out my thanks anew, and with many tears I acknowledged him as true God and Redeemer of the world. I would not rise from the ground until my Son commanded me and gave me his blessing. In the mornings, I repeated this procedure asking my Son to impose upon me all that I was to do that day in his service. This, my Son always did with tokens of great love.

Now however, he changed his bearing and manner toward me. When I approached to reverence and adore him, he would not answer me a word. He would listen unmoved and would then command. "Leave me my, mother. I wish to be alone."

My loving heart was changed ineffably by the actions of Jesus. My Son's behavior, he that was true God and true man, changed completely. He was distant in his actions, sparing of words, and changed in all his exterior bearing. I searched my interior, investigating all the conditions, circumstances, and sequence of my actions, and racked my memory into the celestial workings of my soul and faculties. I could find no shadow of darkness, for all was light, holiness, purity and grace. Yet since I knew, as Job said that neither the heavens nor the stars are pure in the eyes of God, and since he finds fault even in the angelic spirits [Job: 25, 5], I feared lest I might have overlooked some defect. In my anxiety, I though filled with supreme wisdom, suffered agonies of love; for my love being strong as death, caused in me emulation enkindled by an unquenchable fire of suffering and tribulation. My Son looked with incomparable pleasure upon my responses to my trials. ***[The dark night of the soul]*** My Son, because of these virtues, raised me to the position of a Teacher of all the creatures. He rewarded my unwavering love and loyalty with abundant graces in addition to those, which I already possessed, including the name *Beautiful Love.*

Thirty days passed in what seemed ages for me, for I deemed it impossible to live even one moment without the beloved of my soul. In my sufferings, I forgot all the visible and created things and even my own life, accounting it all for nothing until I again found the grace and love of my most holy and divine Son. I feared that I had lost him, although I continued to possess him. No words can equal my care and solicitude, my watchfulness and diligence in trying to please my sweetest Son and the eternal Father.

At the end of thirty days, I threw myself at his feet. The heart of my Child Jesus could no longer contain itself or resist further the immense force of his love for me, his mother. He himself had suffered a delightful and wonderful violence in thus holding me in such a suspense and affliction. With tears and sighs coming from my inmost heart I said to him, "My sweetest, love and highest, good, of what account am I, but insignificant dust and ashes before your vast power? If I have not been zealous serving you as I am forced to confess my Son please chastise my negligence and pardon it. However, let me see the gladness of your face, which are my salvation and the wished for light of my life and being. I lay my poverty at your feet, mingling it with the dust, and I shall not rise until I can again look into the mirror of my soul."

Jesus looked at me with great tenderness and said, "My, mother, arise."

God instantly transformed and elevated me into a most exalted ecstasy, and I saw the Divinity by an abstractive vision. In it, the Lord received me with sweetest welcome and embraces of a Father and spouse, changing my tears into rejoicing, and my sufferings into delight. The Lord manifested great secrets to me of the scope of his new evangelical law. The Trinity, wishing to write it entirely into my pure heart, appointed and destined me as their first-born daughter and the first disciple of the Incarnate Word. They set me up as the model and pattern for all the holy Apostles, Martyrs, Doctors, Confessors, Virgins and other just of the new Church and of the law of grace, which the Incarnate Word was to establish for the Redemption of man. The twenty-forth chapter of Ecclesiasticus had attributed this to me under the figure of divine wisdom. These words of Scripture will at once lift up your hearts. You will understand and feel to what an inexplicable greatness and excellence the teaching and instruction of my Son have exalted me, his sovereign mother. The most holy Trinity decreed that I was the true Ark of the Covenant in the New Testament [Rev: 11, 19].

When I came out of my trance, I adored my most holy Son and said. "Forgive me my, Son, for my negligence that I might have been guilty of in your service?"

Jesus raised me to my feet and said, "My, Mother, I am much pleased with the affection of your heart. I wish you to dilate it and prepare it for new tokens of my love. I will fulfill the will of my Father and record in your bosom the evangelical law, which I came to teach in this world. Then, Mother, put it to practice with the perfection, which I desire."

I responded, "My, Son and, Lord, may I find grace in your eyes and will you govern my faculties in the ways of your goodness and pleasure. Speak my, Lord, for your servant hears, and will follow you to death."

From this time forward, I again began to see the holy soul of Jesus and its interior operations; and from that day on this blessing increased as well subjectively as objectively; for I continued to receive clearer and more exalted light. In my Son, I saw mirrored the whole of the new law of the Gospel. I saw all its mysteries, sacraments and doctrines, as the divine Architect of the Church had conceived it and as he had in his quality of Redeemer and Teacher, predisposed it for the benefit of man. In addition to this clear vision of this law, which was reserved for me alone, he added another kind of instruction. In his own living words, he taught and instructed me in the hidden things of his wisdom. This wisdom, I partook without deceit, and I communicated it without envy, both before and still more after the Ascension of my Son.

For me to reveal the hidden mysteries which passed between my Son and I would require volumes. During all the years of Jesus' youth until he began his preaching, he taught me all the mysteries of the Holy Scriptures, and the entire Christian Doctrine. He explained all the virtues, all the traditions of the holy Church, all the arguments against errors and sects, as well as the decrees of the holy councils. He taught me all that upholds the Church and preserves her to the end of the world, and the great mysteries of the glorious lives of all the saints. God wrote all of this in my Immaculate Heart as well as all the works of the Redeemer and Teacher in multiplying the blessings of the Church; also all that the holy Evangelists, Apostles, Prophets, and the ancient Fathers have recorded, and that which afterwards was practiced by the Saints. As well as the light vouchsafed to the Doctors, the sufferings of the Martyrs and Virgins, and all the graces which they received for bearing their sufferings and accomplishing their works of holiness. God taught me all of this and so much more, which space; however, does not allow me to enumerate. In my own way, I gave proper thanks for these gifts, which I will try to explain further on, in so far as is possible.

During this time, I never failed to fulfill all my works to the highest perfection, nor did I ever fail in what concerned the service and the bodily needs of Joseph and my Son. I provided for their food and their comforts, all the while giving proper reverence to my divine Son. I encouraged my Son to treat Joseph as his father with all due respect as such. As Jesus grew, he obeyed my instructions for him to assist his foster father and to learn his craft. Many times, as Joseph aged and grew less able, Jesus performed small hidden miracles to ease his burden.

Once settled in our home in Nazareth, we like all Jews, took on the duties of our faith. Hebrew men were obliged to present themselves before the Lord in the Jewish Temple three times a year [Ex: 23, 14]. The Israelites visited the temple on the Feast of the Tabernacles, the Feast of Weeks, or Pentecost, and the Feast of the Unleavened Breads, also called the Feast of the Pasch [Passover}, and numerous other feasts as well. Sacrificial offerings kept the priests at the holy Temple busy the year around. The women and children were not obliged to attend; however, and could go or come, according to their devotion.

I conferred upon this subject with Joseph, and he said, "My sweet, spouse, I am highly desirous of your company and that of our most holy Son at all times. I desire to offer him anew to the eternal

Father in the temple. However, it is thirty leagues to Jerusalem and I hesitate to expose you to the hardships of the journey."

Although drawn by my own piety, I did not allow myself to decide without the counsel and direction of the Incarnate Word, my Teacher. When I asked Jesus, he replied, "Let it be that two times each year Joseph will go to Jerusalem by himself, while on the third occasion, the Feast of the Pasch, we will all go together."

When Joseph made these pilgrimages alone, he made them for himself and our family in the name of the Incarnate Word. Instructed by Jesus and furnished with his graces, Joseph journeyed to the temple accompanied by the holy men of Nazareth. There, he offered to the eternal Father the gifts always reserved for such occasions. Being the substitute of my Son and I, who remained at home, praying for him, and since he offered up his prayers for his holy family, his offering was more acceptable to the eternal Father than the offerings of the whole Jewish people.

During the Feast of the Passover when Jesus and I accompanied Joseph, the journey was a most wonderful one for him and for our heavenly courtiers. Our ten thousand guardian angels processed us in human forms, seen only by us, refulgent in their beauty and full of profoundest reverence, serving their Creator and their Queen. After our return from Egypt, Jesus stated that the holy family should do all their pilgrimages by foot. In our first journeys; however, due to his age, we sometimes carried Jesus in our arms, or allowed him to ride on our Muscat Ass. This was but a brief respite; however, and in later years he insisted on making the entire journey on foot. Knowing his desire to suffer, we did not interfere and often led him by hand to ease his way. My heart ached for him, and we stopped frequently for him and dropping to my knees, I would refresh him by wiping his beautiful face with a wet cloth. As was our custom, we made our trip enjoyable by singing canticles of praise and worship to our heavenly Father.

During these journeys, we performed many heroic works of charity for the benefit of souls. We converted many to the knowledge of the Lord, freeing them from their sins, justifying them, and leading them on the way of life eternal. Since it was not yet time for the Teacher of Virtue to manifest himself, all these works were done in secret. I knew that the eternal Father enjoined such activity upon Jesus, and for the present, his good works were to remain hidden. In order to govern myself according to the dictates of the highest wisdom, I prudently consulted with my divine Child concerning all my doings on the journey such as our stopping places and lodging-houses. I knew that he pre-arranged the occasions for his admirable works, which he foresaw and foreordained in his wisdom.

Weather permitting we slept in the open fields, staying in the inns only when necessary. I attended to my Son and Master at all times, carefully watching his every action in order to imitate him in every way. I did the same when we visited the temple, often joining my prayers and petitions with those of the Incarnate Word to his divine Father. I was witness to his humble and profound reverence, by which his humanity acknowledged the gifts flowing from the Divinity. A few times, I was privileged to hear the Father say, "This is my beloved Son with whom I am well pleased; listen to him [Matt: 17, 5]."

At other times I perceived and witnessed how my Son prayed for me as his true mother; this knowledge was inexpressibly joyful to me. He prayed for the entire human race and offered up all his works and labors for these ends. In these things I accompanied, imitated and followed him at all times. When we were in the temple, the holy angels intoned hymns of sweetest harmony in honor of the Incarnate Word, and my pure heart was inflamed and blazed up in divine love. The Most High, on these occasions, showered me with new gifts and blessings, which cannot be clothed in words. By these gifts, he prepared me for the adversities, which I was to suffer.

Many times after these consolations, I saw as in a panorama all the affronts, ignominies, and sufferings awaiting my most holy Son in that same city of Jerusalem. In order that I might see all this with so much more vivid sorrow, Jesus was wont to enter upon his prayers in my presence. God filled me with the light of divine wisdom and with a divine love for God and my Son. In so doing, I was pierced with the sword of sorrow mentioned by Simeon [Luke: 2, 35]. I shed many tears in anticipation of the injuries, sufferings, and the ignominious death to be borne by my sweet Son. My soul was filled with anguish at such thoughts; for I knew that the beauty of the Son of God, greater than that of all men, was to be disfigured worse than a person eaten with leprosy [Wis: 2, 20].

I was to see all this with my own eyes and in order to lessen my sufferings. Jesus instructed me, "Dilate your Immaculate Heart my, Mother with charity for the human race and together let us offer to the eternal Father all these sufferings for the salvation of man."

Together, we made delightful offerings to the holy Trinity, applying them for the benefit of the faithful and especially for the predestined who would profit by their merits and by the Redemption through the Incarnate Word.

My words might lead you to believe that the Holy Family did nothing but pray. Nothing could be further from the truth. We fashioned with our own hands everything that we needed to maintain our standard of living. However, we did our work, and play, in such a manner as to be a prayer in itself. The poor people of Nazareth kept Joseph busy. However, they could little afford to pay for his labors. Consequently, Joseph did much of his work for little or nothing, and a few took advantage of Joseph's compassion and paid him not at all. I gave much of my embroidery work to those who frequently brought us food and gifts. Jesus' natural humanity as a young boy brought him in constant contact with the children and the people of the area. He grew tall and slender with a delicate face and throughout his life his hair fell naturally to his shoulders. Like John, his cousin, shears never touched his locks. Yet the length of his hair never varied. Jesus was not a typical dark-haired, dark-skinned Hebrew, but like many of the Nazarenes, was fair and his hair, parted in the middle, was auburn and full.

My Son soon became the favorite of the people of the village of Nazareth and the surrounding area. As he had done in Egypt, he visited the poor and the sick, always taking a bit of food or some piece of clothing to warm them. When not helping his parents he had time, not only for the children of Nazareth, but for every person there, especially for the sick and the poor. The parents of his friends were especially impressed with his good nature, good manners, and good behavior. He became the model for every family in Nazareth and when their children were naughty or not nice their parents said to them, "What will Joseph's Son say when I tell him this?"

Everyday Jesus brought me water from the well and often did so even as a full-grown man, which was unheard of amidst our neighbors. The parents sometimes gently complained to Jesus before their little ones, saying, "Tell them not to do such a thing anymore." Jesus played his role playfully and like a little child. He would beg the children affectionately to do so, and would pray with them to his Heavenly Father for strength to do better. Jesus inspired the children to acknowledge their faults, and ask their parents for forgiveness.

Family was all-important in Israel. It sometimes seemed that everyone was interrelated though usually many times removed. We had family friends scattered all over Palestine. Only an hour away lived my aunt, Mary Salome. During our trek to Egypt, she had married a man named Zebedee. They lived in the parental home of Zebedee in Ophna, which was near Sepphoris. They were the parents of James [the Greater] and John, who was born when Jesus was twelve; both were to later become Apostles of my blessed Son. They were his close friends in those early years until the family moved to Bethsaida, near the Sea of Galilee. There, they went into the fishing business.

An Essenian family related to Joachim lived in Nazareth. They were the ones that took care of our house while we were in Egypt. Mahara was married to Daniel. They had four sons, some older, and some younger than Jesus was. Their parents named them respectfully, Cleophas, James, Judas and Japhet. They, too, were playmates of Jesus, and often journeyed with us to Jerusalem during the High Holy Days.

These four brothers were, at the time of Jesus' baptism, disciples of John the Baptist. After Herod murdered John, the brothers became disciples of my Son. At the time of Jesus' baptism, Andrew and Saturnin crossed the Jordan and spent the whole day with him. They were among those disciples of John whom Jesus took with him to the marriage feast at Cana. Cleophas and Luke were the two disciples to whom Jesus appeared on the road to Emmaus. Cleophas was married and dwelt in Emmaus. His wife later joined the women of the Community.

At age eight years, Jesus went with us for the first time to celebrate the Pasch. In these visits, my Son excited attention among our friends with whom we stayed in Jerusalem, and also, among the priests and doctors at the Temple. They often spoke of the pious, intelligent Child, Joseph's extraordinary Son. Thus did the next four years speed by, with Jesus growing in stature, love and grace.

When Jesus was twelve, we formed a caravan from our friends and neighbors and again set out for Jerusalem to give worship during the Feast of the Pasch [Luke: 2, 42]. Jesus was now a tall, lithe boy and the rigors of the ninety mile journey to Jerusalem were no longer a physical problem to him. Again we traveled by foot and on the fourth day arrived in Jerusalem. The city was unusually packed. The Hebrews to give proper thanks to Yahweh, our one and only God, had assembled over eighteen thousand Levites and priests and their assistants. Jews from every section of the known world had made their pilgrimage and every guestroom in the hundreds of synagogues in Jerusalem, as well as every commercial room was packed to capacity. Many Hebrews opened their homes freely to give hospitality to the pilgrims. The pilgrim Jews had blanketed Mount Olivet and every surrounding hill and dale with pitched tents. Nearly half a million pilgrims occupied every patch of bare ground.

Thousands of sacrificial sheep, goats and bullocks thronged the byways and paths, and we passed caravan after caravan filled with the necessities of life to take care of the needs of this seething mass of humanity. As we neared the city, a muted roar from the multitude greeted our ears, which would not abate until after the feast was over and the crowds disbursed. We were to be guests in the home of Joseph's cousin Amos, located just outside the city. However, we intended to enter the city first to make sacrifice to the Lord. A holy excitement laced the air amidst the bleating of sheep and goats, the braying of donkeys, the harried cries of drovers, and the excited yelling of children as they raced in and out of throngs of people, as we neared the city. We stopped for a breather when the golden spires of the Holy Temple unfolded before us in its breathtaking splendor. The colorful tents of the people had turned the hillsides into a rolling, multi-colored carpet of canvas, with gay pennants flying from the tent poles. Everyone was dressed in their best; the men wore colorful cloaks, and the women wore gaily-decorated dresses. Most of the women had freshly coifed their hair, and they wore their best jewelry resplendent about their necks, wrists, waists and in their hair.

Well-known rich men stood on corners passing our alms, their servants blasting on trumpets so that all could hear and see. Pitiful beggars thronged the streets. The pilgrims were in an alms-giving mood, and the Jews were encouraged to spend ten percent of their income during their visits to Jerusalem and the beggars faired well. Servants blew horns to clear the way for travel sedans of the rich, and the burly servants carrying the sedans pushed their way rudely through the throngs. Roman patrols in their colorful red capes and metal helmets marched up and down the streets in a show of force. People scattered before them like quail. Patience was not one of the Roman's virtues. The

Romans had stationed soldiers in every important spot, and the authorities brought in extra soldiers each holy day. The soldiers were alert for the slightest hint of trouble, and they dealt harshly with any violations.

We spent seven heavenly days at the temple giving thanks and praise to our Creator and Master. The first and last days were the most solemn. The blood of the huge number of animals sacrificed daily filled the gutters, which flowed into the Valley of Hinnom, also known as the Valley of Gehenna. There the flies and the small carnivorous animals had their own feast. The stench of burning flesh and ashes filled the azure blue skies and tried even the strongest of stomachs. The bleating and bellowing, the stench of the disemboweled, and defecation of thousands of frightened animals fouled the air. The chanting of the priests in their rituals, the cries of exited children, the prayers of the faithful, and the shrill cries of the venders hawking their wares, created a cacophony of sounds, sights and smells that left an indelible memory of something harsh, but grand, something magnificent, but marred with its own imperfections, and something barbaric, but splendid in its intent. The rituals were all in keeping with that which the Jews sought, the sanctification and cleansing of the defiled with the sprinkling of blood and the ashes of sacrificed animals offered up to Yahweh, their one and only God. However, I knew that all this was destined to change. My Son was soon to enter the sanctuary and to offer to God *"once"* for all humanity, not the blood of goats and bulls, but his own unblemished blood in order to cleanse our consciences from dead works and to enable us to worship the living God with love and good works, not burnt offerings.

Early on the morning of the eighth day, the three of us assembled with our family and friends outside the city near the Damascus Gate, for the return home. There we divided into groups of men and women as much for reasons of decency, as well as the natural gravitation of the men seeking the company of men and the women desiring to share the trials and tribulations of their lives with other women. The men acted as guards taking up positions on each end of the column. The older children went with either parent, as the mood struck them. I was still in a state of exalted ecstasy from the holy services, and I instinctively joined the women. When Jesus did not join me I did not deem it strange, since being twelve, and in the Jewish tradition, he was no longer a boy, but a young man. As such, it was natural to assume that Jesus had preferred the company of the men. In addition, my Son, for reasons of his own, had diverted my attention from the mirror of his soul with holy and divine contemplations.

By the end of the first day, the main body of travelers had thinned out somewhat as several families turned off on the different byways that led to their homes. Families began to gather together as we traveled and when we came to the end of the first day's journey, Joseph met me at the place designated where we were to meet. Unknown to us, Jesus had remained in Jerusalem. As my state of exalted ecstasy waned, I realized that Jesus had closed his mind to me, and I was unable to merge my thoughts with his. Jesus had been obliged to use supernatural means by placing me in a state of ecstasy to elude my close supervision of his person. Without his interference, I would have no more have lost sight of him than of the sun that lighted our way. Therefore at our initial parting of the men and women, which I mentioned, my Son visited me with an abstractive vision of the Divinity, which with divine power centered and withdrew all my faculties toward my interior. I thus remained so abstracted, inflamed and deprived of my senses that I could make use of them only in as far as was necessary to pursue my way. I was entirely lost in the sweetness and consolation of the divine vision. Joseph, while he was satisfied that Jesus was with me, was also wrapped in a most exalted contemplation, which made possible his assumption concerning the whereabouts of the Child Jesus. Thus our Son had been able to withdraw himself from both of us and had remained in Jerusalem.

When I came to myself and realized that Jesus was not with us, I turned to my angels to assist me knowing that they never lost sight of the divine Trinity, yet, while they were solicitous and concerned, they could not reveal to me his whereabouts.

Joseph and I became frantic as our search among our relatives and friends failed to turn up our missing Son. Finally, Joseph turned to me with tears in his eyes and cried out, "I have failed you my, spouse. I thought Jesus was with you, but I should have checked to make sure."

I consoled him by saying, "It is no one's fault, Joseph. Yours was a natural assumption, for I also assumed that he was with you. My Son's mind is closed to me, so I have no idea of his present status."

Joseph replied, "As usual, Mary, you always know how to comfort me. Come, we must quickly return to Jerusalem. We will search along the way and if he is not found, we will have to alert all our friends and relatives in Jerusalem to help us find him."

Both of us, filled with self-reproach at our carelessness in watching over our Holy Charge, our trail weariness forgotten, set out immediately with a handful of our friends. We gathered all the torches we could find and purchased more at several inns that we came across. At dawn, we spied the golden spires of the holy Temple. The sight quickened our hearts and renewed our resolve giving fresh life to our leaden legs as we hurried through the Damascus Gate. I wanted to go our individual ways in order to cover more of the city. However, Joseph insisted that we work in pairs so we could support one another. Of course, he being my husband, and knowing he would never leave me alone in the city, I complied with his decision. I said to our loyal group, "Joseph and I will check the temple first. Jesus' love for God transcends all else. Let each pair take a portion of the city so that we can cover the entire town as thoroughly as possible. We will use the house of Amos, Joseph's cousin, as our headquarters."

My heart was beating with anticipation as we entered the temple. Surely, this was the logical place to find my Son? Where else, would I expect to find him, but in his Father's house? However, Jesus could not be found, although we searched the temple thoroughly. I called on all my old temple friends and alerted them to our problem. With feet dragging, we finally left the Temple. Joseph insisted that I return to the house of Amos, in order to eat and rest. I could not disobey my husband's instructions. Amos and his family received us with cries of sympathy, and food and wine was immediately set before us, but I could not eat. Amos hurried off to arrange for his friends and our relatives to join the search. Amos even asked the hated Romans for help on the off chance that some of them might have knowledge of his whereabouts. As Joseph wished, I lay down to rest. However, rent with grief, there was no sleep in my eyes.

I poured out my heart to my Creator, begging for his help, and then without letup called on our ten thousand angels to help me saying. "My, friends and, companions, you well know the cause of my sorrow. In my bitter affliction be my consolation and give me some information concerning my beloved Son, so that I may seek and find him. Give relief to my wounded heart, which, torn from its happiness and life, bounds from its place in search of him."

My holy angels though they never lost sight of the Creator and Redeemer, were aware that the Lord wished to furnish me this occasion of great merit, and that it was not yet time to reveal the secret to me. They soothed me, but still would not tell me where my Son was. Instead, they encouraged me to pray for help, and they joined their prayers with mine. Their evasive answers raised fresh doubts; my anxiety caused me to break out in tears and sighs of utmost grief.

Again my angels comforted me and said, "Rise, Mary, and continue your search for the treasure of heaven and earth [Luke: 15, 8]."

Unable to remain in the room any longer, I called on Joseph to resume our search. Physically refreshed, we hurried out of the house. My mind raced with all of the possibilities as to where my Son could be. My worst fear was that Archelaus, the ruler son of Herod, should have recognized in Jesus the same threat that had prompted Herod to slaughter the Innocents; he might have taken him prisoner and done him bodily harm. Yet, I knew from the Holy Scriptures, the revelations, and the knowledge revealed to me by my Son that the time for his Passion and Death had not yet come. Also, in my profoundest humility, I had misgivings that perhaps I had in some way displeased my Son, and therefore deserved that he should leave me and take up his abode in the desert as had his precursor, John.

As we looked, I prayed. "Oh my Highest, Good," I said, "you chastise me by your absence, I who did not know how to profit by your company. Why have you my, Lord enriched me with the delights of your infancy, if I am so soon to lose the assistance of your loving instruction? Since I was not worthy to retain and enjoy you as my Son, I must confess that I am obliged to thank you even for the favor of condescending to accept me as your slave. If the privilege of being your unworthy mother can be of any avail in finding you, oh Lord, permit it, and make me worthy of again finding you, so that I may go with you to the desert, to sufferings, labors, tribulations, or whatever you will. My soul desires to merit at least in part sharing your sorrows and torments to die, if I do not find you, or to live in your service and presence. Although you were austere when the Divinity hid itself from my sight, at least your amiable humanity remained, and I could still throw myself at your feet. I only have my groans left to me, now that my happiness is taken away. I have lost sight entirely of the sun, which enlightens me. Sweet love of my soul, what sighs from the inmost of my heart can I send you as messengers? I must be unworthy of your clemency, since my eyes find no traces of you."

Joseph, our friends and relatives, and I, searched every nook and cranny of the city for three whole days, and all the while I persevered in my tears and prayers. Joseph was frantic with concern for me, but knowing my state of mind he respected my needs and refrained from ordering me to eat or rest, so that the two of us sought our Son without sleeping or eating for the three days. We were past exhaustion, but persevered in our search with only our faith to strengthen us.

Only after we had returned to Nazareth did my Son enlighten me as to where he had been during those three terrifying days. When he departed, Jesus was given foresight of all that was to happen. He offered it up to his eternal Father for the benefit of souls. Jesus set out for the homes of the poor to give spiritual aid to those unfortunate inhabitants. On the way, he begged for alms. This handsome young lad begging for alms charmed the pilgrim Jews, and they were unusually generous. With so many benefactors, Jesus performed wonders of grace and light. He thus fulfilled from that time on the promise that he was to afterwards make to his Church. He stated that a person, who gives to the just and to the prophet in the name of the prophet, shall receive the reward of the just. With these alms, Jesus purchased food and water for the poor sick people and set out to console them physically and spiritually. Jesus secretly cured many of them, but not all at once. Instead, some of them took a turn for the better, and in a day or two were able to return to work. He looked into the troubled souls of others, and mentally forgave them their sins, which in many instances was the beginning of an eventual recovery. He returned each day to the poor bringing hope and comfort.

Each day, he joined the children in their Synagogue School sessions taught by the hazzans and rabbis. My twelve year old Son both surprised, and in some cases upset, the teachers to such a degree that on the third day, chagrined by his questions, and thinking to embarrass and humiliate him, they invited Jesus to a meeting of rabbis and priests of the temple. These men met in an auditorium of the temple complex, where they had decided to discuss some of the hotly debated points of Holy Scriptures. Crowds of priests and scribes packed the auditorium to listen to the learned rabbis.

Jesus presented himself to these learned gentlemen and stepped into their midst with exceeding majesty and grace. By his pleasing appearance, he awakened in the hearts of these learned men a desire to hear him speak, and they began to ask him questions. The rabbis were so entranced with his replies that they seated Jesus on a Moses Seat made of stone. The chair was much too big for him, but in his natural majesty, no one noticed. Grouped around him was assembled a notable crowd of well-known priests and teachers. Many of the priests knew Jesus, for they had watched him mature and grow in knowledge and grace over the years. His was such a strong personality that once a person met him it was not possible for them to ever forget him.

Several of the men began to question my Son about his previous analogies that he had made from nature and the arts. He answered them, "Learned, priests and scribes, blasphemous knowledge is not the proper subject for teaching in the temple; however, I will answer you because such is the will of my Father."

The priests and rabbis assumed he was talking about Joseph, and that his foster father had instructed him to respectfully respond to their questions. Jesus spoke about the law, medicine, astronomy, architecture, agriculture, and mathematics. My Son masterfully correlated these sciences with the prophecies and mysteries of the Jewish faith. He was especially learned in the mysteries of the human body, which quickly aroused the respect of the learned doctors. At first, his answers astounded those listening. Some of them were embarrassed that a mere lad of twelve was so much more knowledgeable than they were.

Gamaliel, a young but well noted authority on the Bible asked Jesus, "We assembled here today to discuss the coming of the Messiah; perhaps you have some words for us on this subject?"

Jesus hoped to awaken in them the knowledge that indeed the Messiah had already come. He had inspired Gamaliel to speak for he knew him to be a good and holy man, and hoped to enlighten him as to the true nature of his coming. Jesus' opening words were barely out of his mouth, when one elderly scholar replied pompously, "With all due respect young, man. There is no way possible for the Messiah to have come. Our Scriptures tell us that he will come in great pomp and ceremony. The Messiah will be a great leader; people will flock to him, and he will free his people from the yoke of the Romans. He will be the King of all Kings and our people will prosper and flock to God as never before. Ours indeed will be a land flowing with milk and honey."

Jesus replied, "I have heard and understand completely your argument. I have difficulty in that solution, the prophets do say that his coming shall be in great power and majesty. Isaiah says that he shall be our Law-Giver and King, who shall save his people. David says that he shall crush all his enemies {Psalms: 93, 96, 97, 99]. In addition, Daniel says that all tribes and nations shall serve him [Dan: 7, 14]. All the Prophets and Scriptures are full of similar promises manifesting his characteristics clearly and decisively enough, for all those that study them with enlightened attention. However, the doubt arises from the comparison of these with other passages in the Prophets. All prophecies must be equally true; however, their very brevity may make them seem to contradict one another. Therefore, they must agree with each other in another sense. How then shall we understand what this same Isaiah says of him that he shall come from the land of the living?

Then he asked them, "Who shall declare this generation that he shall be satiated with reproach that he shall be led like a sheep to the slaughter, and that he shall not open his mouth [Is: 53, 8] ? Jeremiah states that the enemies of the Messiah shall join hands to persecute him and mix poison with his bread, and they shall wipe out his name from the earth, although they shall not prevail in their attempt. David says that he shall be the reproach of the people and of men, and that he shall be trodden under foot, and shall be despised as a worm [Ps[s]: 22, 7-8]. Zechariah says that he shall come meek and humble seated upon an insignificant beast [Zech: 9, 9]. All the prophets say the same concerning the signs of the promised Messias."

"Hence, added Jesus, "how will it be possible to reconcile these prophecies, if we suppose that the Messias is to come with the power and majesty of arms in order to conquer all the kings and monarchs by violence and foreign bloodshed?" He then pointed out, "The prophecies stated that there would be two comings; the first to redeem man, and the second to pass judgment upon him. In the first advent, he is to overthrow the demon, hurling him from his sovereignty over souls obtained through the first sin. Therefore, the Messiah must render satisfaction to God for the whole human race. Then he must teach men, by his word and example, the way of eternal life. By the Word of God; he must teach them how they are to overcome their enemies, serve and adore their God and Redeemer; how they must correspond to the gifts and use well the blessings of his right hand. All these requirements the Messiah must fulfill in the first coming. The second coming is for the purpose of exacting an account from all men in the general judgment, by giving to each person the return for his works, good or bad, and chastising his enemies in his wrath and indignation."

Then he added, "Accordingly, when we wish to understand how his first coming shall be in power and majesty, or as David says that he shall reign from sea to sea that in his advent he shall be glorious, as said by the other Prophets. You cannot interpret all this as referring to visible and terrestrial sovereignty, with all its outward show of pomp and majesty. Instead, it refers to a spiritual reign in a new Church. This new Church will extend over all the earth with sovereign power, and riches, and grace, and virtue in opposition to the demon. By this interpretation the entire Scripture becomes clear, while in another sense its different parts cannot be made to harmonize." He asked, "The people of Israel are now in a state of bondage under the Romans, which cannot be held as proof of the Messiah not being here. Instead, as stipulated in the prophecies, it is an infallible sign that he is already come. Have you forgotten the coming of the three Magi? Those Eastern Kings who came in great majesty led by a mystical star seeking the newly born king of the Jews in order to give him gifts and render him homage? Was not the subsequent slaying of the Holy Infants throughout Israel by Herod proof that a king had been born in Bethlehem of humble estate as prophesied by the Prophets? Our patriarch Jacob commanded us to expect the Messias as soon as they should see the tribe of Juda deprived of the scepter and sovereignty of Israel [Gen: 49, 10]. You must confess that neither Juda nor any other tribe of Israel can hope to recover the crown or hold it. The same is also proved by the seventy weeks of Daniel [Dan: 9, 25]; which certainly must now be complete."

In this manner did my Son, while seeming to ask questions, educate them on things they did not know, all the while teaching with divine conviction.

Hearing their arguments refuted one by one, the scholars were at first dumbfounded. While a few seemed to understand the message some of them felt shamed, for a twelve year old boy was explaining the mysteries much better than they, and yet they were all overwhelmed with the knowledge and wisdom that Jesus displayed.

In the meantime, Joseph and I were still searching. My fears that Archelaus the King might be torturing him left me no peace. I kept wondering, could he have gone into the desert to live as had John? In spite of my fears, I never ceased my prayers for the human race. An arrow of affliction pierced my heart. In spite of my natural motherly fears, and my concern for the only Son of God, I never lost my interior or exterior peace, nor did I ever despair. I asked every woman I came across if she had seen my son, knowing the compassion women have for their own children.

One, in reply, asked me, "Is he light and of ruddy complexion, a boy out of thousands?"

I eagerly responded, "Yes! He is like the gentleness of spring and the freshness of summer."

She nodded thoughtfully, "There can be only one like him. He came by yesterday to my door for alms. I gave him some, and his grace and beauty ravished my heart.

I felt myself overcome by compassion to see a child so gracious in poverty and want." Here and there, I began to meet other people who had occasion to remember him and spoke highly of him. Guided by their insights I headed for the nearest home of a sick person I had heard of. It was there that I received my first ray of hope. Learning of his trips there, the sick man sent me on to the synagogues and finally to the Synagogue of Fishermen. The hazzan informed me that he had attended his class that morning, and that he had gone that afternoon to question the elders at the Holy Temple. I gave thanks to Almighty God and it was then my holy angels chose to enlighten me as to his whereabouts.

"Our Queen and benefactor, the hour of your consolation is nigh. Soon you will see the light of your eyes. Your Son is safe in his Father's House in the great hall. Hasten your footsteps, for the meeting will soon disburse." I told Joseph, and he was ecstatic with joy. He had kept his suffering deep within his heart. So vast was his grief that if God had not strengthened him he would have died. Strengthened with the news, we hurried to the temple. At last, we saw him.

My Son was surrounded by scholars and a myriad of holy men. As I approached, I heard them say. "This boy is a prodigy. He will go far, for the Lord God is with him." However, others were murmuring against him.

As we neared Jesus, Joseph dropped slightly behind to allow me to speak. I said with all the love of my heart and with all respect and reverence, "Son, why have you done so to us? Your father and I have searched for you for three days and three nights sorrowing all the while [Luke: 3, 48]."

Jesus replied, "Why is it you have sought me? Did you not know that I must be about my Father's business [Luke: 2, 49]?"

At first, overcome with joy, we did not understand what he meant by his statement. Nor did we hear my Son's explanation of the mission of the Messiah. The soul of my Son had been veiled from my eyes for three terrifying days and he still had not removed that veil. For the second time in my life, I had no idea of what he was thinking or doing. Several of the scholars were upset, and I feared lest they take out their anger on my Son, so Joseph and I hustled him out of the temple. We returned to the home of Amos where our friends and family joyfully welcomed us.

That evening we celebrated and gave thanks for finding our lost son. At dawn the next morning, we were on the road to Nazareth. After leaving Jerusalem behind, I dropped to my knees before my Son and asked for his blessing, which my son graciously gave to both of us. Raising me to my feet, he comforted me and the veil fell, revealing anew his most holy soul with greater depth and clearness than ever before. At once, I was able to read and perceive in the soul of my most holy Son the mysteries of his efforts during those three days in Jerusalem. I understood what had transpired during the debate with the doctors and rabbis. I learned what Jesus had said in an effort to open the eyes of the elders. He revealed many other sacramental secrets at the same time, depositing them with me as in an archive of all the treasures of the Incarnate Word.

Reading my thoughts, he remarked sorrowfully, "Unfortunately, the scholars, doctors, and rabbis did not recognize me as the Messiah. They were steeped in the arrogance and pride of their own interpretation of the coming of the Messiah. I thought there was hope for young Gamaliel. However, he was not receptive. Tradition, not love, steeped his heart, like the others. Had they been humble and meek of heart, my reasoning would have convinced them of my identity."

The fact that these knowledgeable and holy men did not have the faith to follow the teachings of my Son saddened me.

Our trip home was most gratifying. My Son converted many souls to the way of salvation on this journey, and he used me as an instrument of his wonderful works. By means of my prudent words and admonitions to those we met, Jesus enlightened the hearts of each of them. He restored health to many of the sick, which of course would not happen to them right away. He consoled the afflicted and sorrowful, and scattered grace and mercy without ever revealing his divine presence.

It says in [Luke: 2, 51] that Jesus returned to Nazareth with his parents and was subject to them. I would like to mention that the humility and obedience of my Godly Son was the admiration of the angels. The dignity and excellence of the nature God had created in me helped make this possible. Joseph and I governed my Son and disposed of him as our own. This subjection and obedience was to a certain extent a natural result of my motherhood. Yet, in order to make proper use of this maternal right and superiority, a different grace was necessary than the one by which I conceived and gave birth to my Son. The graces necessary for such ministry and office were given to me in such abundance that they overflowed into the soul of Joseph, making him worthy of being the reputed father of Jesus and the natural head of our family.

Joseph and I both tried to imitate our Son in all his actions. This was my destiny and I exerted myself most anxiously to copy them and reproduce them in my own life. My perfect response to my Son bonded me to him with chains of invincible love. My Son, thus being bound as God and as son to me his heavenly princess, gave rise to such an interchange and divine reciprocity of intense love, as surpasses all created understanding. For into the ocean of my soul entered all the vast floods of the graces and blessings of the Incarnate Word, and I never once allowed this ocean to overflow [Sir: 1, 7].

I was especially enlightened in regard to the decrees of the Holy Trinity concerning the law of grace, which was now to be established by the Incarnate Word using the power, which was given to him in the consistory of the most blessed Trinity. At the same time, I saw how the eternal Father consigned to his Son the seven-sealed books, of which Saint John speaks [Rev: 5, 1]. A seal no one in Heaven or on Earth could unseal and open, until the Lamb breaks its seals by his Passion and Death. For in this figure, God wished to establish that the secret of this book was the new law of the Gospel and the Church. I saw in spirit that by the decree of the most blessed Trinity that I was to be the first one to read and understand this book. My Son was to open it for me and reveal it all to me, and in turn I was to put it perfectly into practice. I was to be the first one to accompany the Word, and I was to occupy the first place next to him on the way to Heaven, which he was to open up for mortals. In me, as his true mother, was to be deposited this New Testament.

God the Father said, "My, spouse prepare your heart for receiving the New Testament and the Law of my Son in your soul. Receive from us the gifts of our liberality and of our love for you. In order to give us fitting thanks consider that by the disposition of our infinite wisdom, we have resolved to make you, *a mere creature*, the closest image and likeness of my Son, and thus produce in you effects and fruits worthy of his merits. Thus, in a fitting degree, you will magnify and honor his holy name. Be mindful my, beloved and chosen, daughter that a great preparation is required of you."

In my most humble manner I answered. "Eternal, Lord and mighty, God, in your real and divine presence I lie prostrate, acknowledging at the sight of your infinite being my own insignificance. I know that I am unworthy of the kindness with which you have looked upon me. I offer you the fruit of my womb, your Onlybegotten Son, and I beseech him to answer for me, his most unworthy mother. My heart is prepared and is overwhelmed with gratitude and affection for your mercies. However, if I find grace in your eyes, I will speak in your presence asking only this that you do with me whatever you wish and command, for no one is able to execute such a chore unless you yourself assist him. Oh, Lord and most high, King, if you desire from me a heart free and devoted, I now offer it to you, ready to obey you and suffer for you until death."

I felt at once new influences of the Divinity. I was being enlightened, purified, and spiritualized with such plentitude of the Holy Ghost as to exceed all that had previously happened to me, for this blessing was one of the most memorable ones that I was to ever receive. Yet, in the participation of the divine perfections there is no measure, as long as the capacity of the creature to receive them does not fail. This great gift merely disposed me for still greater ones, because the power of participation was so vast in me, and God increased it in me with each new encounter. The Divine Power, therefore, not finding in me any obstacle, set all its treasures in motion and laid them up in the secure and most faithful depository of my most stainless soul."

When I recovered from this ecstatic vision, I went directly to my Son and prostrated myself at his feet and said, "My, Lord, my, Light, my, Teacher, behold your unworthy mother prepared for the fulfillment of your wishes. Admit me anew as your disciple and servant, and make use of me as the instrument of your wisdom and power. Execute in me your pleasure and that of the Eternal Father."

My Son received me with the majesty and authority of a divine Teacher, and instructed me in most exalted mysteries. In most persuasive and powerful words, he explained to me the profoundest meanings of the works enjoined upon him by the Eternal Father in regard to the Redemption of man, the founding of the Church, and the establishment of the new Evangelical Law. He declared and reaffirmed that in the execution of these high and hidden mysteries, I was to be his companion and coadjutrix, receiving and enjoying the first-fruits of grace. Therefore, with a well-prepared heart of invincible and unhesitating constancy, I was to follow him in his labors until his death on the Cross. He added heavenly instructions that enabled me to prepare for the reception of the entire Evangelical Law, the understanding and practice of all its precepts and counsels in their highest perfection. My, Son manifested to me on this occasion other sacramental secrets concerning his works. I met all his words and intentions with profound humility, obedience, reverence, thanksgiving and my most ardent love. God molded me as the living image and stamp of his only Son, creating me so well adjusted and refined in grace that those who know me see in me another Christ by communication and privilege [Gal: 4, 4]. Thus was established a singular and divine intercourse between my Son and me. I had given him form and existence of man, while the Lord gave me the highest spiritual existence of grace, so that there was mutual correspondence and similarity of gifts.

The second end, which the Lord had in view of this work, concerned likewise the ministry of the Redeemer. The work of our Redemption was to correspond with those of the Creation of the world, and the remedy of sin was to be correlative with its entrance among men. Therefore, it was befitting that since Adam had our mother Eve, as a companion in sin that Christ our Lord, was to have me, his most pure mother as a companion and helper. I was to concur and co-operate in the Redemption; *although in Christ alone*, who is our Savior, existed the full power and adequate cause of the general Redemption. In order that this mystery might not want the proper dignity and correspondence, it is necessary that what was said by the Most High in the first formation of man be also fulfilled concerning my Son and me

"It is not good for man to be alone: I will make a suitable partner for him [Gen: 2, 18]."

The Lord did this in his Omnipotence, so that speaking of Christ, the second Adam, he could say, "This one at last, is bone of my bones, and flesh of my flesh. This one shall be called 'woman' because out of 'her man' this one has been taken [Gen: 2, 23]."

In order that I become proficient in all the mysteries of the Evangelical Law, my Son used different methods of teaching me. He used abstractive visions of the Divinity, with which during this period of eighteen years, I was frequently favored. At other times he used intellectual visions, which were more habitual though less clear. In each, I saw the entire Militant Church, with all its history from beginning of the world until the Incarnation. I also saw its lot afterwards until the end of the world, and then to eternal beatitude. These instructions were so clear, distinct, and comprehensive that I had knowledge of all the just and the saints, as well as those who were to distinguish themselves afterwards in the Church. I knew all the Apostles, Martyrs, and Patriarchs of the religious orders, the Doctors, and the Confessors and Virgins. These I knew as well as the merits and graces and the rewards to be apportioned them.

I was acquainted with all the Sacraments, which my divine Son was to establish in the Church, their efficacy, the results in those that receive them varying to the different dispositions of the recipients. God furnished me with a clear understanding of all the doctrines, which Jesus was to preach and teach of the New and Old Testaments. I knew all the hidden mysteries of these holy books under its four different ways of interpreting them; the literal, moral, allegoric and anagogic, and all that the interpreters of the Scriptures were to write in explanation. However, my understanding of all these were much more extensive and profound than theirs was. God gave all this knowledge to me, in order that I might be the teacher of the entire Church. For, after my Son's Ascension, this was to be my office. In me, God intended the new children of the Church and the faithful inspired by grace, to have a loving mother to carefully nourish them at the breasts of her doctrines as with sweetest milk, the proper food of infant children.

Besides these visions and instructions concerning Jesus and his human nature, I had two other sources of information, which I have already mentioned. The one was the reflection of my Son's most holy Soul and its interior operation, which I saw as in a mirror. In it was included a reflex image of all his knowledge of things created; so that I was informed of all the counsels of the Redeemer and Artificer of sanctity and also of all the works, which he intended to undertake and execute either by himself or by his ministers.

The other source of information was the spoken word of my Son. My Lord conversed with me about all things concerning the Church, from the greatest to the smallest including all the happenings contemporary with and bearing upon the different phases of the history of the Church. Thus, my Son imbued in me his doctrine. I was so proficient in the perfect practice of it that the excellence of my works corresponded with my immense wisdom and science. My knowledge was so clear and deep, that it comprehended everything. No creature can ever equal my knowledge, nor can anyone conceive it in its full extent either in thoughts or words. I lacked nothing that was necessary, and God added nothing that was superfluous. I never mistook one thing for another, nor had need of discourse or inquiry in order to be able to explain the most hidden mysteries of the Scriptures, whenever such explanations were necessary in the primitive Church. This knowledge was indispensable to the Apostles after the death of my Son.

I shall not detain you in further explanation of these gifts. The resemblance between my Son and I is manifest. During these eighteen years of my hidden communication with Jesus, I fed upon and digested the substance of the evangelical doctrines that I received from their author, Christ the Redeemer. Thus, when my divine Son ascended into heaven, I would be prepared for my duties as teacher of the primitive Church.

On the following December 25, Jesus was thirteen, the coming of age in the Jewish faith. The Law required that at age five the child begins his sacred studies; at ten he must set himself to learn the tradition; at thirteen he must know the whole of the Law of Yahweh and practice its requirements;

and at fifteen he must begin the perfecting of his knowledge. In perfect obedience, Jesus had attended all the necessary classes, although he knew all things. Therefore, at age thirteen, a young man had finished his schooling unless he wished to perfect his knowledge. At thirteen, a young Israelite had certainly left his childhood behind, although none of them were capable of the reasoning of Jesus before the doctors of the Law in the Holy Temple of Jerusalem.

From age thirteen a young man, as an adult, would be required to recite three times every day that famous prayer, the Shema Israel, in which every believer must declare his faith in the one God. Adults were required to fast regularly. Set days for fasting had been established, and in particular the sacred ceremony of the Day of Atonement. As an adult, Jesus would have to attend the three required Holy Days each year. He would now sit with the men in the Court of Men in the Holy Temple in Jerusalem, as well as in the synagogues. My Son, the same as all Hebrews at age thirteen, attended the religious service called the Bar Mitzvah. The priest, at the end of this ceremony, declared that Jesus was a "Son of the Law. The priest then allowed my Son to read a passage of the Law at the synagogue service amid great rejoicing. As of the coming of age, my Son now belonged to the community.

Joseph and I, according to custom, honored our Son with a party celebrating his coming of age. We invited thirty young men including Cleophas, James, Judas, Paphet, and the sons of Mahara, Joseph's cousin. Also present were the sons of Mary Salome, the daughter of Sobe, the sister of my mother Anne. Mary Salome had thirteen children, nine of whom lived, including James the Greater, and John [the beloved disciple], who were also destined to be disciples. Nathaniel, another cousin, was also present.

Joseph erected bowers over the tables and the other mothers and I festooned them with garlands of vine leaves, and ears of corn and flowers. The banquet table was decorated with corn and grape leaves. In addition, before each guest was bunches of grapes and bread. Jesus took firm charge of the banquet. His mystical prophecies held his family and friends spellbound. He told them, "When you are grown there will be a great wedding feast. The newly wedded couple will run out of wine, a prophet will turn water into wine, and lukewarm guests will become lifelong friends. Later, there be a different kind of wedding in which bread and wine will be changed into flesh as a living covenant, which will last until the end of the world. Turning to his cousin Nathaniel, he added, "I promise that I will be present at your wedding."

The group were mystified, but enthralled by their host's words. All the boys teased Nathaniel unmercifully about his foretold marriage. My Son became the natural leader of this group, for Jesus had handpicked each of them and all were to play an important role in his future ministry. Jesus was to spend much time with each of these young men, and he taught and instructed them so their development would be truly God-oriented.

For the next six years, Jesus was subject to Joseph and me. He assisted Joseph learning his trade, and in a short time was a master carpenter in his own right. Jesus, in his free time, taught and instructed his friends by word and example. Together the three of us did many acts of mercy and we fed the hungry and clothed the poor. Joseph and his foster Son refurbished and repaired many homes of widows and the poor in acts of charity. We prayed together each evening, and after Joseph retired, Jesus and I prayed together most of the night. Jesus began spending more time with his friends taking long walks with them teaching and instructing them in ways meant to strengthen their spiritual growth. Joseph was aging and less able to function as a full-time carpenter, and it was about this time that my Son began to venture further and further from home and before long he was sometimes gone for days at a time.

When I reached my thirty third birthday my body attained its full natural growth not unlike Adam and Eve who were created in that age and condition, nor unlike my Son who was destined to die at the perfect age of thirty three. By the grace of God, I was well proportioned and beautiful, so much so that I was not only the admiration of my fellow human beings, but of the angelic spirits themselves. I had grown in size and stature in perfect proportion in all parts of my body. I most strikingly resembled my divine Son in features and complexion when he later arrived at that same age; always taking into account that Christ was the most perfect Man, while I was the most perfect Woman. However, perhaps it would be more proper to state that he had chosen to resemble his genetically perfect mother, and God, his spiritually perfect Father.

While the bodies of other mortals, because of human's genetic code, ordinarily began to deteriorate and decay from this age on, my Son had favored me and from that date forward, my body never aged another day. I rendered my Son my most heartfelt and humble thanks for this great blessing. In addition, God perfectly preserved in my countenance, the image of my most holy Son

Joseph at age fifty-one was much broken and worn out as far as his body was concerned. Jesus assisted him and even at times made his work easier by use of his divine power. Joseph's continual cares his journeys and his incessant labors to support his Son and I had weakened him much more than his years. The Lord ordained this condition. God wishing to lead him on to the practice of patience and other virtues permitted him to suffer sickness and pain. I was always ready to serve him and concerned by his rapidly failing health.

I spoke to him and said, "My, Spouse and, Master, I am deeply obliged to you for the faithful labors, watchfulness and care that you have bestowed on the welfare of my Son and I. By the sweat of your brow you have supported us and in so doing you have spent your strength and the best part of your health. From the hands of the Almighty, you shall receive the reward of your works and the blessings of sweetness that you so richly deserve. However, I beseech you to rest since your body is no longer capable of sustaining your efforts. I wish that from now on that you allow me to labor in your service and provide for such sustenance as the Lord wishes us to have."

Joseph listened patiently to my plea and with abundant tears of humility replied, "I beg of you to allow me to continue forever in my labors. I desire nothing more than to die in the service of you and your divine Son." However, after I again talked with him, he finally agreed, for he knew he no longer had the strength to continue his work.

I next went to my Son and explained my actions and added, "My most holy and divine, Son, Joseph is no longer able to work and I desire to take his place as the sole provider for our family. You must now have time to lay your groundwork for your ministry. With your permission, I will work with my hands spinning, weaving and embroidering linen to earn enough to sustain us."

My Son looked at me lovingly and replied, "It shall be done as you wish and until his death, I will curtail my trips to a minimum and shall help you with the care of Joseph until he is called to his abundant reward."

JOSEPH

A common defect in all of us is that we look upon Jesus too much as our Redeemer and not sufficiently as our teacher in sufferings [Luke: 24, 26]. We all desire to reap the fruit of salvation and enter the portals of grace and glory. However, we do not with the same zeal seek to follow him on the way of the Cross by which he entered and upon which he invites us to attain eternal glory [Matt: 16, 24]. Although, as Catholics, you do not fall into such insane errors as others; for you know and profess that without exertion and labor there can be no reward or crown. We believe that it is a sacrilegious blasphemy to avail ourselves of the salvation of Christ in order to sin without remorse or restraint. Nevertheless, as far as really practicing the works inculcated by faith, some of the children of the Church differ little from the children of darkness; for they look upon difficult and painful works as unnecessary for the following of Christ and for the participation in his glory.

Let us dispense with this error in our practice and let us understand well that suffering was not only for Christ our Lord, but also for us. For if he suffered labors and death as the Redeemer of the World, he suffered them as our teacher, thereby inviting us as his friends to enter upon the way of the Cross. His nearest friends receive the greatest share of suffering, and no one can merit Heaven without the price of personal exertions. The Lord did not suffer only in order to excite our admiration, but so that we might imitate his example. He did not even allow his divinity to stand in the way of labor and suffering, but allowed sorrow and suffering to overwhelm him in proportion to his innocence and sinless ness.

God especially selected Joseph from among all the men of the world to be the foster father of my Lord and Son, Jesus the Christ. Had there been a man more perfect than he was, God would have chosen him to be the foster father of my Son. There is no doubt that Joseph was "the" perfect man upon Earth. God certainly in his almighty power, created, perfected and destined Joseph's end in proportion to his dignity. That is [according to your way of thinking], his holiness, virtues, gifts, graces and infused and natural habits were made to correspond by divine influence with the end for which he was selected. There was a certain difference in the graces given Joseph and those given to other saints. Many saints were endowed with graces and gifts that are intended not for an increase of their own sanctity, but for the advance of the service of the Most High, gifts so to speak, freely given and not dependent on the holiness of the receiver. However, in the case of Joseph, all the divine favors were productive of personal virtue and perfection; for the mysterious purpose of helping along that which was closely connected with the holiness of his own life.

The more angelic and holy he grew to be; so much the more worthy was he to be my spouse. He was a miracle of holiness. This marvelous holiness commenced with the formation of his body in the womb of his mother. In this providence, God himself interfered and secured for him an evenly tempered disposition, which made his body a blessed depository fit for the abode of an exquisite soul and well-balanced mind [Wis: 8, 19]. God, seven months after Joseph's conception, sanctified him in the womb of his mother. God had destroyed the leaven of sin in him for the whole course of his life, He received the use of his reason with this first sanctification, which consisted principally in justification from original sin, and his mother at the time felt a wonderful joy of the Holy Ghost. Without understanding entirely the mystery, she elicited great acts of virtue and believed that her Son or whomever she bore in her womb would be wonderful in the sight of God and man.

Joseph was a beautiful child, perfect of body. He caused his father Jacob, the son of Mat than, an extraordinary delight, something like that caused by the birth of John the Baptist, though the cause of it was more hidden. God perfected the use of his reason in his third year, endowed it with infused science and augmented his soul with new graces and virtues. From that time, the child began to know God as the Author of all things through faith, natural reasoning, and science, at this premature age he began the practice of the highest levels of prayer and contemplation and eagerly engaged in the exercise of the virtues proper to his youth. Joseph was already a perfect man in the use of his reason when other children at the age of seven or so first came into the use of reason. He was of kind disposition, loving, affable, sincere, and showing inclinations not only holy, but also angelic. As he aged, he grew in virtue and perfection, advancing toward his espousal with me by living an irreproachable life.

Not unlike his predecessor Joseph, the son of Jacob as described in Genesis, my spouse Joseph was also the son of a Jacob. Like his namesake, the brothers of my spouse in his youth were also jealous of their brother. They resented the talk of his marvelous birth and all the predictions that Joseph, with his special gifts, would be wonderful in the sight of God. They gave vent to their discomfort, when coupled with the fact that they recognized in their brother all the signs of such holiness, they become uncomfortable in his presence. Consequently, they played cruel pranks on him and they never ceased taunting him. In spite of all they did to him, he always forgave them, but he did make every effort to avoid them.

Over the years, his parents became quite well off, and in their rise in the Pharisaic Community, they lost sight of the God they had known so well in their youth when they had to struggle to make ends meet. Then, because of Joseph's concern and prayers for his family, God, little by little, took away their good fortune and his parents died a premature death, but one well steeped in faith and in the love of God.

When I learned that it was God's intention that I marry Joseph, I began to pray to God for him and asked, "My, Lord and my, God, I most earnestly beseech you to sanctify Joseph and inspire in him with the most chaste thoughts and desires in conformity with those of my own?"

The Lord granted my request and permitted me to see what great effects his right hand had wrought in the mind and spirit of the already chaste and spotless Joseph. Human words cannot describe the copious gifts received by Joseph. God infused into Joseph's soul the most perfect habits of all the virtues and gifts. He balanced anew all his faculties and filled him with grace, confirming it in an admirable manner. In the virtue and perfection of chastity, the holy Joseph was elevated higher than the Seraphim. The purity, which they possessed without body, Joseph possessed in his earthly body and in his mortal flesh. Never did an image or an impure thought ever engage, even for one moment, any of my future spouse's faculties. This freedom from all such imaginations and his angelic simplicity prepared him for my companionship and presence, for God had made me the most pure among all creatures, and without this excellence on his part Joseph would not have been worthy of so great a dignity and honor.

Joseph had been worthy of God's trust. His devotion and hard work had earned him merits and crowns for his life of selfless giving and sacrifice. The Lord led Joseph along the royal highway of the Cross. He loved this chaste and holy man above all other sons of men. To increase Joseph's merits and crown before his death, when his time of his meriting should come to an end, Jesus visited him in the last eight years of his life with certain sicknesses, such as fever, violent headaches, and very painful rheumatism, which greatly afflicted and weakened him. Joseph's greatest sufferings; however, were from another source. The fire of his ardent love was so vehement, so sweet, but so extremely painful that the flights and ecstasies of his most pure soul would have often burst the bounds of his body, if the Lord, who vouchsafed them, had not strengthened and comforted him against these agonies of love. In these sweet excesses, the Lord allowed him to suffer until his death. However, because of the natural weakness of his emaciated body, this exercise was the source of ineffable merits for the fortunate Joseph. These merits were earned because of the love by which these sufferings were brought about, and not just because of the sufferings occasioned.

I was a witness of all of these mysteries knowing the whole interior of the soul of my beloved spouse, and I rejoiced in the knowledge of having for my spouse a man so holy and so beloved by the Lord. I beheld and comprehended the sincerity and purity of his soul; his burning love; his exalted and heavenly thoughts; his dove-like patience and meekness in his grievous ailments and exquisite sufferings. He never complained of either these or of any of the other trials nor ever asked for any relief in his wants and necessities, for he bore all with incomparable equanimity and greatness of soul. In contemplating and weighing all these heroic virtues, I grew to look upon him with such veneration as cannot ever be properly estimated by any one. I labored with incredible joy for his support and comfort, and the greatest of his comforts was when I prepared food and fed him with my own hands.

Sometimes, overwhelmed by my love and compassion for him, I made use of my heavenly powers as Queen and Mistress of all creation. I commanded that the food, which I fed him, should impart special strength and supply new life to the body of my holy and just husband. When Joseph tasted of this food, he would say, "My, Lady and, spouse, what celestial food is this which revives and restores my strength and fills my soul with delight?"

I often served him his meals on my knees, and when he was disabled and suffering, I took off his shoes and held him in my arms. He sometimes sought to rouse himself and forestall some of my ministrations, because he did not deem it proper that I serve him. However, he could not altogether prevent them for his strength was failing fast. In these cases, he had to submit to my will, for he was too weak to function for himself. At such times, I comforted him with sweet and tender words of love and encouragement.

In his last three years, I tended to him night and day attending to his every need and my only other employment was the service and ministration due my most holy Son. Jesus often joined and assisted me in the care of his foster father, when he was not engaged in other necessary works. There was never a sick person, nor will there ever be one who was so well nursed and comforted. Great was the worth of Joseph, this man of God, for he alone deserved to have for his wife the spouse of the Holy Ghost.

However, I was not satisfied with these proofs of my devotion toward my spouse Joseph and several times I prayed to God saying, "Oh my,Lord and my, God, my debt to you is greater than that of all born of the earth. Since I have been unable to render proper return, I offer my heart for all manners of pain and suffering. I beg of you for the sanctity of Joseph, his purity, and his innocence. I thank you for having created a man so worthy of your favors, a man so full of justice and holiness, and I ask that special blessings be rained upon him."

Repeatedly, I asked my angels to give thanks to God for him, and in contemplating the glory and wisdom of the Lord as shown in Joseph, I sang new hymns of praise. On the one hand, I could see the pains and sufferings of my beloved spouse, which excited my pity and condolences. On the other hand, I was aware of his merits and the delight of the Lord in this worthy man, and how by his patience in his sufferings, Joseph pleased and glorified God.

Sometimes, when I perceived the bitterness and severity of the sufferings of Joseph, being moved by tender pity, I humbly asked permission of my beloved Son to be allowed to command the natural sources and occasions of his pains to disappear and thus put a stop to his sufferings. In such instances, he would be relieved for a day and sometimes longer. Then, his ailments according to the decree of the Almighty, again assumed their severity for the increase of his merits. I often requested my angels to console Joseph and to comfort him in his sorrows and labors, as the frail condition of his body worsened. The angels appeared to him in human form, most beautiful and shining and spoke to him of the Divinity and its infinite perfections. Then they would raise their voices in perfect harmony of celestial music, singing hymns of divine canticles by which they restored his drooping strength and inflamed the love of his purest soul. To rejoice him more, he was specially informed not only of the source of these blessings and divine favors, but of my great holiness and of my singular love and charity in conversing with him and serving him, and of many other privileges extended him by me, his spouse. All of these blessings caused such effects in Joseph, and so raised his merits before God, as no tongue can express nor any human comprehend in this life.

Joseph suffered for eight long years; and his soul's purification increased each day. As his bodily strength gradually diminished and he approached the unavoidable end, in which the stipend of death is paid by all the children of Adam [Heb: 9, 27]. In a like manner, I increased my care and solicitude, assisting and serving him with unbroken punctuality. Perceiving, that the day and hour for Joseph's departure was very near, I asked my blessed Son and Lord, "Lord, God, Most High, Son of the eternal Father and Savior of the world, by the divine light I see the hour approaching which you have decreed for the death of your servant Joseph. I beg you, by the ancient mercies and by your infinite bounty to assist him in that hour by your almighty power. May Joseph's death be as precious in your eyes, as the uprightness of his life was pleasing to you? My, Son, may he depart in peace with the certain hope of eternal reward; the reward to be given to him on the day in which you shall open the gates of heaven for all the faithful. Be mindful my, Son, of the humility and love of your servant, of his exceeding great merits and virtues, and of the fidelity and solicitude by which this just man has supported you and me by the sweat of his brow."

Jesus answered, "My, Mother, your request is pleasing to me and the merits of Joseph are acceptable in my eyes. I will assist him and will assign him a place among the princes of my people [Ps[s]: 115, 15]. I will place him so high that he will be the admiration of the angels and will cause them and all men to break forth in highest praise. No human person shall be held as high in esteem, as your spouse."

I thanked my Son profusely, and for nine days and nine nights before my husband's death, my Son and I attended to Joseph's every need. By command of the Lord, the holy angels, three times on each of the nine days, furnished celestial music mixing their hymns of praise with the benedictions of the sick man. The entire house was filled with sweet fragrance and wonderful odors. They not only comforted Joseph, but also invigorated those who came near the house.

Just before he died, being wholly inflamed with divine love because of these blessings, Joseph was wrapped in ecstasy, which lasted twenty-four hours. My Son himself supplied strength for this miraculous intercourse. In this ecstasy, Joseph saw clearly the divine Essence. He saw manifested therein, all that he had believed by faith, the incomprehensible Divinity, the mystery of the Incarnation and the Redemption, and the Militant Church with all its sacraments and mysteries. The blessed Trinity commissioned and assigned him as the messenger of our Savior to the holy Patriarchs and the Prophets of Limbo; and commanded him to prepare them for their issuing forth from the bosom of Abraham to eternal rest and happiness. I saw all of this reflected in the soul of Jesus together with all the other mysteries, just as they had been made known to Joseph, and I offered my sincerest thanks for all this to my Son.

Joseph's face shone with wonderful splendor when he issued from his ecstasy. His vision of the essence of God entirely transformed his soul. He said to me, "I beseech you, my beloved, spouse, to give me your benediction."

However, I requested my Son to bless him in my stead, which he did to Joseph's great joy, then I fell on my knees, and begged Joseph to bless me, as being my husband and family head. With divine impulse Joseph blessed me, and I kissed the hand with which he had blessed me.

I asked him, "My beloved, spouse, please salute the just ones of Limbo in my name?"

Joseph sealed his life with an act of self-abasement, and asked pardon of me for all his deficiencies in my service and love and begged me to grant him my assistance and intercession in this hour of his passing away.

He said to our Son, "My precious, Lord and, Savior, I thank you for the blessings of my very existence and my life, and being granted the privilege of being chosen to be the most unworthy spouse of your most holy mother, and being granted the honor of being allowed to be your foster father. I especially thank you for the blessings I have received during my illness."

The last words Joseph spoke to me were, "Blessed are you among all women and elect of all the creatures. Let angels and men praise you; let all the generations know, praise, and exalt your dignity. May in you be known, adored and exalted the name of the Most High through all the coming ages. May all humankind praise God forever for having created you, you who are so pleasing in his eyes and in the sight of all the blessed spirits. I hope to enjoy your sight in the heavenly fatherland."

Then he turned to Jesus in the profoundest reverence. He tried to kneel before him, but my sweetest Son, coming near, received him in his arms, and Joseph reclined his head upon the breast of the Lord. Joseph said to him, "My highest, Lord and, God, Son of the eternal Father, Creator and Redeemer of the world, give your blessing to your servant and the work of your hand. Pardon, oh most merciful king, the faults that I have committed in your service and presence. I extol and magnify you and render eternal and heartfelt thanks to you for having, in your ineffable condescension, chosen me to be the spouse of your true mother. Let your greatness and glory be my thanksgiving for all eternity."

The Redeemer of the world gave him his benediction, saying: "My, Father, rest in peace in the grace of my eternal Father and I. Notify the Prophets and Saints, who await you in Limbo, the joyful news of the approach of their redemption."

At these words of my Son, and still reclining in the arms of his Lord and Savior, the most fortunate Joseph expired with his eyes fastened on those of his foster Son and Redeemer. Jesus himself closed his eyes. At the same time, the multitude of ten thousand angels, who attended us, intoned hymns of praise in loud and harmonious voices. God desired that Joseph's death would be more the triumph of his love instead of the effects of original sin. The fire of his intense love of God had not consumed Joseph, because of assistance from God. The Lord withdrew his divine assistance. Joseph's love was greater than that of nature. His love dissolved the bonds and chains, which detained his soul to his mortal body. The separation of the soul from the body in which death consists then took place. Love then was the real cause of death of Joseph; my husband and I wept at his passing so magnificently to his reward. I was relieved that his pain and suffering was over, but I could not have wished that he did not suffer for his merit would have been so much less. My tears were a mixture of sorrow and joy. For while I would miss Joseph immensely, and for this I sorrowed deeply, it was physically and spiritually impossible for me to deeply mourn while I was in the physical and spiritual presence of my Lord, my Redeemer, my most holy Son, Jesus, the only Son of God. While my sorrow was well ordered and most perfect, it was far from being less deep than that shared by others of the human race. My love was great, so much the greater since I had been exposed for twenty-seven years of marriage to the goodness of Joseph and knew not only the rank he held among the saints, but had personally experienced that goodness for all those years. We do not lose without sorrow what we love in an ordinary manner; and so much the greater will be our sorrow for losing what we love much.

By command of the Lord, the holy angels carried Joseph's most holy soul to the gathering-place of the Patriarchs and Prophets. The souls there recognized Joseph as the foster father and intimate friend of the Redeemer. He was clothed in the splendors of incomparable grace worthy of the highest veneration. Conformably to the will and mandate of the Lord, his arrival spread unutterable joy in this countless gathering of the saints by the announcement of their immanent rescue.

My spouse having passed away, I notified our relatives and trusted them to take care of notifying other relatives and friends. As per custom, burial would take place that same day, usually within no more than eight hours. As for me, as was also the custom, I began to prepare my husband and spouse for burial, no hands but mine, and the holy angels who assisted me would touch his chaste body. My virginal eyes and pure hands had never seen nor touched the nude bodies of any man not even my husband's. To maintain the utmost propriety, God enveloped the body of Joseph in a wonderful light, which hid all except his countenance. A sweet fragrance rose from Joseph's body, a gift given other saints over the years. None; however, would ever exceed the sweet fragrance that rose from Joseph. His body remained beautiful and lifelike, having lost the gaunt look of the chronically ill. I wrapped him with cloth according to our custom, and our neighbors came eagerly to see this marvelous transformation and were all filled with admiration.

Amidst a great multitude of unseen angels, relatives, friends, and neighbors, my Son, the Redeemer of the world and I, bore the body of my sainted husband Joseph to his final resting-place. Throughout this ordeal, I kept my composure without allowing my countenance or mannerisms to reflect any unwomanly or disorderly excitement nor did my sorrow prevent me from attending to all that belonged to the service of my beloved spouse or my treasured Son. As a Queen, I behaved as a Queen, with quiet dignity and gravity. As King and Redeemer, my Son could do no less and I heard several comments on his regal and somber bearing.

After the burial, we fed our guests and later that evening as soon as the last person departed, I dropped to my knees at the feet of my Son and exclaimed, "Lord, and, Master of my whole being, my true Son, the holiness of my spouse Joseph might until now have detained you in my company, though unworthy of it. I beseech you by your own goodness not to forsake me now. Receive me anew as your servant and look upon the humble desires and longings of my heart."

The Savior of the world accepted this new offering of mine and he promised, "Fear not my beloved, mother, I will not leave you until the time when obedience to my eternal Father obliges me to do so to begin my ministry."

Joseph was sixty years of age when he died. He had done his earthly work to perfection, and had earned his reward. The manner of his death was a privilege of his singular love, for his sweet sighs of love surpassed and finally put an end to those of his sickness. Joseph's most pure and faithful heart was unavoidably consumed by the loving effects of his close union with Christ his King and me, Mary his Queen. At his death, I had completed my forty first year and Jesus was twenty-six. As I stated before, I was blessed with the body and perfect health of a thirty-three year old woman and now, with Joseph's startling appearance, many people commented on how neither Joseph nor I had seemed to age.

My husband Joseph deserves to be known and extolled by all nations and by all generations of men, since the Lord has wrought such things with no other man and to none has he shown such love. The Most High conferred certain privileges upon Saint Joseph because of his great holiness. These privileges are especially important to those who ask his intercession in a proper manner. In virtue of these special privileges, the intercession of Saint Joseph is most powerful, because he attained the virtue of purity and overcame the sensual inclinations of the flesh. He can obtain powerful help for you to escape sin and return to the friendship of God. He can increase your love and devotion to me the Mother of God. He can secure the grace of a happy death and protection for you against the demons in the hour of your death. Calling his name can inspire the demons with terror at the mere mention of his name. He can gain for you health of body and assistance in all kinds of difficulties. He can secure issue of children for you in families and can help you sell your home. Please do not insult him by burying his statue upside down in a hole in the ground. He is eager to help any that call upon him in good faith. These and many other favors God confers upon those who properly, and with good disposition, seek the intercession of my spouse. I beseech all the faithful children of the Church to be very devout to Saint Joseph and they will experience these favors in reality, if they dispose themselves, as they should in order to receive and merit them.

Some of my experiences after the death of Saint Joseph

Christian perfection is all included in the two states of life known to the Church: the active and the contemplative life. To the active life belong all the operations of the body and the senses practiced in our association with our neighbors in temporal affairs. They embrace a wide field and include the practice of the moral virtues, which constitute the perfection of our active life.

To the contemplative life belong the interior activities of the understanding and will aiming at the most noble and spiritual objects proper to the rational creature. Therefore the contemplative life is more excellent than the active, and, as it is more delightful and beautiful, it is more desirable in itself. It leads directly to God, since it consists in the deepest knowledge and love of God, and thus participates in the qualities of eternal life, which is entirely contemplative. This is demonstrated by these two lives, the two sisters Martha and Mary [Luke: 10, 41-42], the one quiet and thoughtful, the other solicitous and bustling.

The active life is more productive though in it the soul is taken up with numerous and various occupations. On the other hand, the contemplative life is most beautiful, although in the beginning not so productive, because its fruits are to be the result of prayer and merits. The combination of these two lives is the acme of Christian perfection; however this combination is very difficult. We do not see both kinds of life united in one person, but existing separated to a remarkable degree in Martha and Mary. Although the saints have labored much to attain this perfect combination, and all the teachers of spiritual life have sought to direct souls toward it; yet they always knew, that the active life, on account of the multitude of its interests and occupations concerning inferior objects, dissipates the heart and disturbs it, as the Lord tells Martha. Although those engaged in the active life may seek quiet and repose in order to raise themselves to the highest objects of contemplation, they never succeed in doing so during this kind of life without great difficulty and only for a short time, except by a special privilege of the Most High. On this account, the saints that wished to give themselves up to contemplation sought the deserts and solitude, which are more favorable to that kind of life; the other that pursued the active life and the care of souls by teaching and exhortation, set aside some of their time for retirement from exterior activity, and divided their days between contemplation and active life. By thus attending to both with perfection, they attained the merits and reward of the two kinds of life, founded on love and grace as their principal support.

I alone was able to join these two lives in a manner perfect before our Lord and God. Although I had attended my ailing spouse and supported him and my most holy Son by my labor, I did not at any time interrupt or curtail my heavenly contemplations nor was I under any necessity of seeking solitude or retirement, in order to restore the quiet and peace of my heart. After Joseph's death, I arranged my exercises to spend my time entirely in the interior activity of divine love. I perceived, by my insight into the interior of my most holy Son that such was his will. I knew now that instead of the hard labor of attending to the wants of Joseph through night and day that instead, I could now join my Majestic Son in his prayers and exalted works.

Jesus said to me. "My, mother, with the moderate nourishment necessary to feed the two of us, you will only have to labor a short time each day. Until now, out of custom and regard to Joseph, we joined with him twice daily in order to give him consoling company at mealtime. That will no longer be necessary. From now on, we shall eat but one meal a day at eventide."

From that day forward, my Son and I ate but one meal a day at about six o'clock in the evening. Many times we ate only a little bread, at other times I added fruits, herbs, or sometimes fish, and this formed the only sustenance that we allowed ourselves. When we dined with family or friends, we ate of that which our hosts placed before us, but we both ate sparingly. At our six o'clock meal, I served my Son on my knees only after asking permission thus to serve him. While I had treated my Son with all due reverence while Joseph was alive, I now practiced prostrations and genuflections much more frequently; for there was always more freedom for such actions in the presence of my holy angels, than in the presence of my spouse. Many times, I remained upon the floor until the Lord my Son commanded me to rise. I often kissed his feet, and at other times his hand. My Son was the Son of the living God and I always stood in his presence in a posture of adoration and most ardent love, awaiting his divine pleasure and intent upon imitating his interior virtues. Although I had no faults, and I was not guilty of even the least imperfection or negligence in the love and service of my most holy Son, my eyes were continually upon the works of my Master to obtain the graces necessary to assist me to greater perfection. We lived alone, without any other company than that of our ten thousand holy angels. My utter love and devotion to Jesus, moved the angels to admiration and they rendered the highest praises, for they saw themselves as inferior in wisdom and purity to me, a mere creature. I alone of all of God's creatures, made a full return for the graces that I received.

I wished to perform all the humble housework myself, and with my own hands scrub the house and arrange its poor furnishings, wash the dishes and cooking utensils, and set the rooms in order. However, my angels wishing to serve me their Queen, usually anticipated these services before I could find time to perform them. I caught them, and wishing to satisfy my humility and devotion in performing these tasks myself, I said to my angels, "Ministers of the Most High, you are such pure spirits that you reflect the light of the Divinity for my illumination, and, therefore these low and servile occupations are not suitable to your state, your nature, and your condition. These pertain to me, who besides being only of earth, is the lowest of the mortals and the least of the servants of my Lord and Son. Permit me my, friends, to perform the service to which I am bound, since I can thereby gain merits, which because of your station and dignity, you do not need. I know the value of these servile works, which the world despises, and the Lord has given me this knowledge, not in order that I may allow them to be done by others, but that I may perform them myself."

They replied, "Our, Queen and, lady, it is true that these works are valuable, as you know. However, if you do thereby earn the precious rewards of your humility, take notice that we would be deficient in obedience to the Lord if we would knowingly omit any of these works permitted us by the Most High. The merits which you lose in not performing this service, you can easily make up by the mortification of denying yourself the desire of executing them."

I responded to their arguments by pointing out, "No my, masters and sovereign, spirits, you must not look upon these works in such a light. If you consider yourselves bound to serve me as the mother of your great Lord, whose creatures you are, remember that he has raised me from the dust to this great dignity, and that therefore my debt of gratitude for this benefit is greater than yours. As my obligation is so much the greater, my return must also be greater than yours must. If you desire to serve my Son as his creatures, I likewise must serve him on this account, and I am more bound to do so because I am the mother of such a Son. Thus you will always find me more obliged than yourselves to be humble, thankful and annihilated to the very dust in his presence."

Humility is not for the proud of heart. Nor is lowly service for purple and fine linen, scrubbing and washing for costly gems and silks, nor are the precious jewels of these virtues intended indiscriminately for all men. However, if the contagion of worldly pride disgracefully enters our religious communities and our parishes, we cannot deny that such sentiments are nothing but a most shameful and reprehensible pride. If religious men and women, like worldly people, despise the benefits of such humble occupations and count them a degradation, how can you appear before the angels and me, your Queen, who esteemed as greatest honors those very works which you look upon as contemptible and dishonorable? I would rather that you look upon me as your heavenly Teacher, who is the perfect example of a holy and perfect life.

Many times, while I was engaged in harmonious prayer with my Son, our holy angels in sweet, harmonious voices sang the hymns and canticles that I had composed. I often asked them to repeat these hymns to my Son and alternated verses with them. Then, when Jesus retired to rest, or during our meals, I commanded them as the mother of the Creator, to furnish sweet music in my name. By listening, my Son yielded to the ardor of my love and veneration, with which I served him in these his final years at home before he began his ministry.

It is impossible for any mortal to worthily understand such profound secrets. The soul of my divine Son was a transparent and flawless mirror. In it, I saw reflected all the mysteries and sacraments; which the Lord, the Head and Artificer of the holy Church, the Redeemer of the human race, the Teacher of eternal salvation, and the Angel of the great council, wrought and accomplished according to the eternal decrees of the most blessed Trinity.

In the execution of this work consigned to him by the eternal Father, Christ our Lord consumed his whole earthly life and lent to it all the perfection possible to a God-man. The measure, as he approached its consummation and the full accomplishment of its sacraments, made more evident the force of his divine Wisdom and Omnipotence. Of all these mysteries, I was the eyewitness and my pure heart was their depository. In all things, I cooperated with my divine Son, as his helpmate in the works of the reparation of humankind. Accordingly, in order to understand entirely the designs of eternal Providence and the process of dispensing all the mysteries of salvation, it was necessary that I comprehend also the things hidden in the science of Christ our Redeemer. It included the works of his love and prudence, by which he prepared the efficient means of attaining his high purposes. In all these things, I co-operated with him and imitated him as my pattern and model. All the mysteries of this period, Luke sums up in a few words at the end of his second chapter. "And Jesus advanced in wisdom, and age, and grace before God and man [Luke: 2, 52]."

Among men I cooperated and grew in knowledge with the increase and progress of my Son, never remaining ignorant of anything that the Son of God and man could ever communicate to a mere creature. I perceived during these years, how my Son and true God began more and more to extend his plans, not only those of his uncreated Divinity, but of his humanity, so as to include all the mortals in his Redemption as a whole. He weighed its value in the eyes of the eternal Father, and how, in order to close the gates of hell and call men to eternal happiness, he had come down from heaven to suffer the bitterest torments and death. In spite of his sacrifices, men, instead of changing their evil ways, seemed to urge Jesus to widen the very portals of hell and cast them into the lowest abysses of the pit, which they in their blind ignorance continued to disregard.

The knowledge and contemplation of this sad fate caused great affliction and sorrow to the human nature of my holy Son; sometimes it caused him to sweat blood. Jesus knew that his merits and sacrifices would not save all humankind. Nevertheless, he understood that in all events the divine justice must be satisfied. All the offenses to the Divinity had to be made good by the punishment, which divine equity and justice had prepared from all eternity for the infidels and the thankless sinners on the day of retribution. I entered these profound secrets by my deep wisdom and joined Jesus in the sorrowful contemplation and sighs for those unfortunates. I saw my Son sweat blood many times. I shed copious tears and my heart was torn by grief, for only my Son and I could ever justly weigh, as in the scales of the sanctuary, what it meant on the one hand to see the true God and true man dying upon the cross in order to seal up the infernal regions, and on the other hand, see the hardness and blindness of mortal hearts in casting themselves headlong into the jaws of eternal death.

Sometimes, during these prolonged sorrows, a deathly weakness overcame me. The Lord preserved me by his divine intervention or my life would have ended. My devoted Son, in return for my faithful and loving compassion, would sometimes command the angels to console me and take me in their arms. At other times, he would have them sing to me in honor of the Divinity and humanity. Sometimes he would take me in his arms, and give me new celestial understanding of my exemption from this iniquitous law of sin and its effects. While reclining in his arms, the angels sang to me in admiration, and I would find myself enraptured in heavenly ecstasies, experiencing new and exquisite influences of the Divinity. At such times I was truly reclining on the left hand of the humanity, while rejoiced and caressed by the right hand of the Divinity.

During our time together, Jesus acquainted me with the deepest secrets concerning the predestination of the elect in virtue of the Redemption. My Son showed me how he applied his merits to them and efficaciously interceded for their salvation. I learned how he awarded his love and grace to the predestined according to their different dispositions. Among the predestined, I also saw those, whom the Lord in his wisdom and solicitude was to call to his Apostolate and imitation. By means of his hidden and foreordained decrees, he began to enlist them to the standard of his Cross, which they afterwards were to unfold before the world. I noted how he pursued the policy of a good general, who, planning a great battle or conquest, assigns the different duties to various parts of his army, and chooses the most courageous and well-disposed for the most arduous positions. Thus, Christ our Redeemer, in order to despoil the demon of his tyrannical possession by the power of his Godhead, as the Word assigned the dignities and offices of his courageous and strong captains and predestined them for posts of duty. All the preparations and apparatus of this war were prearranged in the divine wisdom of his most holy will and in the order in which all was to take place.

All of the foregoing was made manifest to me, and to me was given the privilege to personally know many of the predestined, especially the Apostles and disciples and a great number of those who were called to the holy Church in the primitive and later ages. Just as the divine Master had prayed and obtained for them their vocation before he called them, so I also made them the object of my prayers. Hence, in the favors and graces, which the Apostles received before hearing or seeing Jesus, and which disposed and prepared them to accept their vocation to the Apostolate, I had likewise cooperated. In proportion as the time for his public preaching drew nearer, the Lord redoubled his prayers and petitions for them and sent them greater and more efficacious inspirations. In like manner, my prayers grew to be more fervent and efficacious.

Afterwards, when they and the others had attached themselves to the Lord and we came face to face, I was wont to say of them to my Son, "These, my Son and Master, are the fruits of your prayers and of your holy desires." Then I would sing songs of praise and thanksgiving, because I saw his wishes fulfilled, and because I saw those, who were called from the beginning of the world, drawn to his following. In my prudent contemplations of these wonders, I would break out in matchless hymns of admiration and praise. I was entirely transformed and penetrated by the divine fire, which issued from my Son in order to consume the world, I exclaimed, "Oh infinite, love, oh manifestation of, goodness; why do mortals not know you; why should your tenderness be so ill repaid? The labors, sufferings, sighs, petitions and desires of you my, Son, are more precious than pearls, and all the treasures of the world. Who shall be so unhappy and so ungrateful as to despise you? Oh, children of Adam, whom can you find to die for you so many times, in order that your ignorance might be undeceived, your hardness be softened and your misfortunes relieved?"

Jesus took me in his arms, consoled me and said, "I remind you, Mother of how pleasing you are to the Father, You have merited great grace and glory for the predestined in comparison with the ingratitude and hardness of the reprobate." He then showed me his love for me, as well as that of the blessed Trinity, and how much God was pleased with my faithful correspondence and immaculate purity.

At other times, Jesus showed me what he was to do in his public preaching; how I was to cooperate with him and help him in the affairs and in the government of the new Church. He told me of Peter's denial, the unbelief of Thomas, the treachery of Judas, and other events of the future. When told about Judas, I resolved to labor zealously in order to save that treasonous disciple. Unfortunately, the perdition of Judas began by Judas despising my good will and by conceiving against me a sort of ill will and impiety. So great was the wisdom and science deposited in me that all attempts to explain them is vain, for only the knowledge of Jesus could exceed that which the holy Trinity had deposited in me, which far excelled that of the Seraphim and Cherubim.

Jesus and I used all of these supernatural gifts of grace and science in the service of mortals. A single sigh of Jesus was of incalculable value for all creatures. And mine, while not of the same value as his, since I am a mere creature, was worth more in the eyes of God than all the doings of all creation taken together. With all of my Son's petitions, tears, bloody sweat, fearful torment, and death on the Cross, and those actions which I, as the Mother of God, added to those of my divine Son as his helpmate and partaker, what can be said for the gratitude of men?

Oh ingratitude of men! Oh hardness of your carnal hearts, more than adamantine! Where is your insight? Where is your reason? Where is even the most common compassion or gratitude of human nature? Why are souls unmoved by the life and sufferings of the Lord, he who is the cause of everlasting happiness and peace in the life to come?

As the time approached when Jesus was to begin his ministry, we both increased our prayers and prayed more fervently for the future Apostles. It was during this period of several years that my Son began to absent himself from our home for two or three days at a time. By these actions, I foresaw the approach of his labors and sufferings. This began my sufferings as well, for I felt the sword of sorrow pierce my heart and soul, and I supported his efforts by my tender acts of love for my beloved. During these absences, my holy angels attended me in visible forms and I spoke to them of my sorrows, and sent them as messengers to my holy Son in order that they might bring me news of his occupations and exercises. In this manner, I was able to join my prayers with his activities.

My Son's frequent and prolonged absences brought on some severe criticism from our neighbors. They thought it scandalous that my Son left me alone for days at a time, and for having forsaken Joseph's trade as a carpenter. The town's Pharisees pilloried him harshly for his open criticism of their actions. They also objected to his seemingly idleness, while I in turn was working and supporting the family. Evidently, they had forgotten all the good works and all the prayers we had said for them. Consequently my, Son and I prayed for them all that much harder.

When my holy Son returned from one of his trips, I would prostrate myself before him and thank him for the blessings, which he had gained for sinners. I would then quickly attend to his needs serving him refreshment, for he often went two or three days without food or rest. As true man, he was also subject to suffering from lack of food and sleep. As previously described, I was not only aware of his comings and goings by my messenger angels, but also saw the results of his efforts by the reflection of his most pure soul. After his return, Jesus would then inform me of the hidden blessings communicated to many souls by new light concerning the Divinity and concerning the Redemption.

Full of this knowledge I said to him, "My, Lord, highest and true happiness of souls; I see that your most ardent love for men will not rest or be appeased until it has secured eternal salvation for them. This is the proper occupation of your charity, and the work assigned you by the eternal Father. I desire that all the mortals be attracted and correspond to your great charity. Behold me your slave oh, Lord, with a heart prepared to fulfill all your wishes. I offer you my life if necessary, in order that all creatures may submit to the longings of your most ardent love."

In my charity, I desired that humankind should give proper thanks for my Son's favors, and I participated to a most exalted degree in all the works of my Son. Jesus said to me, "My dearest, mother; the time has now come when I must submit to the will of my eternal Father. I must commence to prepare certain hearts for the reception of my light and doctrine, and give them interior notice of the opportune and foreordained time of the salvation of men. In this work, I wish you to follow and assist me. Beg my Father to send his light into the hearts of the mortals and awaken their souls that they may with upright intentions receive the message of the presence of their Savior and Teacher in the world."

From that day on, according to my Son's wishes, I accompanied him in all his excursions from the little town of Nazareth. He began to make these trips more frequently in the three years proceeding his public preaching and baptism. We made many trips in the province of Nephtali, as was prophesied by Isaiah [Is: 5, 2], during his conversations with those we met, he began to tell them that the Messiah was already in the world, and in the territory of Israel. He did so without intimating that he himself was the one to be expected. God had reserved this privilege for himself, when John would baptize Jesus in the Jordan River. In general terms, Jesus spoke of his presence as one who knows with a certainty; he performed no miracles and made no outward demonstration of his powers. However, he secretly accompanied his teachings and testimonies with interior inspirations and helps. He conferred these on the hearts of those with whom he conversed and treated. Thus, by disposing their souls by faith, he prepared them to receive him afterwards so much the more readily in person.

Jesus, by his divine wisdom, made acquaintance with such as he knew to be prepared and capable to accept the seed of truth. To the more ignorant, he spoke of the signs of the coming of the Redeemer known to all, such as the coming of the Magi, the slaughter of the Holy Innocents, and of similar events. With the more enlightened, he cited the testimonies of the Prophets, already fulfilled. He explained to them these truths with the power and force of a divine teacher. He proved to them by Scripture that the Messiah had already come to Israel, and he pointed out to them the kingdom of God and the way to reach it. He exhibited in his outward appearance much beauty; grace, peace, sweetness and gentleness of manner and of speech. In addition, since all his discourse was veiled, it was nevertheless vivid and strong, and since he added his interior help of grace; the fruits of this wonderful mode of teaching was very great. Because of his instruction, many souls abandoned the path of sin, and others began a virtuous life. Jesus instructed them all and made them capable of understanding the great mysteries and believing that the Messiah had already begun his reign.

In addition, Jesus consoled the sorrowful, relieved the oppressed, visited the sick and grief-stricken, encouraged the disheartened, gave salutary counsel to the ignorant, and assisted those in the agony of death. He secretly gave health of body to many, helped those in great distress, and at the same time led them on to the path of life and of true peace. Jesus filled with light and with powerful gifts of the Divinity all those that trustfully came to him, or heard him with devout and upright mind. It is not possible to enumerate or estimate the admirable works of the Redeemer during these three years of preparatory instruction. Jesus did all of this in a mysterious manner, so that without manifesting himself as the author of salvation, he communicated it to a vast number of souls.

In nearly all of these wonderful operations, I was present as a most faithful witness and co-worker. As all of them were manifest to me, I assisted and gave thanks for them in the name of the creatures and the mortals who were thus favored by divine bounty. I composed hymns of praise to the Almighty, and prayed for the souls as one knowing all their interior necessities. By my prayers, I gained for them new blessings and favors. I also undertook to exhort and counsel the women, drawing them to the sweet teachings of my Son and giving them intimation of the coming of the Messiah. I practiced these acts of mercy among the women, as was my place, leaving the men to the comfort of my holy Son.

We had no real following for it was not yet time to encourage a close following of my Son's doctrines. Interiorly those who would have followed my Son were encouraged to remain at home and lead a more perfect life. Our ordinary companions were our ten thousand angels, who served us as most faithful vassals and servants. Although we often returned to Nazareth, we were often in need of the ministry of these courtiers of heaven. Many nights we passed in prayer without any other shelter than that of the sky; on these occasions the angels protected and sheltered us from the inclement weather and sometimes they furnished us with food. At other times we begged for our food and refused to accept any money, or other gifts not necessary for our current nourishment. At times, we separated and the Lord visited the sick in their homes. I was able to perform my works of charity and keep informed of the workings of my most holy Son through the mediation of my angels.

I will not expand on the labors and difficulties that we encountered on these excursions, especially in the taverns, and other places of low repute, or from the obstacles, which the common enemy placed in our path. It is enough to know that the Teacher of life and I were looked upon as poor pilgrims, and that we preferred the way of suffering without evading any labor deemed advisable for our salvation. In this hidden manner, my Son and I spread the knowledge of his coming to all sorts of persons; yet, the poor were more especially the objects of my Son's blessed solicitude. The poor are more receptive of God's truths. Their minds were more free and unhampered by vain anxieties. God endowed them with more light, because they were less burdened with sin. They were likewise more humble and diligent in subjecting themselves to an upright and virtuous life. During these preparatory years, Jesus addressed himself to the humble and poor. For Jesus knew that with less show of authority, he could lead the poor to the truth. In spite of his caution, the words and good works of Jesus aroused the attention of the ancient serpent. My Son's miracles could not all be concealed, although the power by which they were done was hidden. Jesus' words and exhortations brought many sinners to penance. They amended their lives, and thus escaped the tyranny of Lucifer. Satan noticed that others advanced in virtue, and all those who listened to the Teacher of life, made a great and unheard of change.

What enraged Lucifer most was that he could not succeed in his attempts with those that were in the throes of death. Though he multiplied his cunning and malice, the entrance of my Son and I interrupted him. The power of our mere presence hurled the demons to the deepest caverns of hell. If we had been there previously visiting the sick, the demons could not enter and could exert no further influence upon the sick person, who thus died in the powerful protection of the Lord. As the dragon felt this divine power without being able to account for it, he was rent with insane rages, and anxiously sought means of counteracting the damage done to his prestige and power.

Lucifer began comparing and connecting the events since the birth of my Son, our sojourn in Egypt and his frustrating encounters with me. His fears and suspicions began to greatly trouble him. Satan feared that a vast, unknown force had established itself on the earth. Since his fall from heaven, Lucifer had most anxiously tried to ascertain when and how the divine Word would leave heaven and assume human flesh, for this wonderful work of God was what his pride and arrogance feared the most.

This anxiety induced him to convoke the many council meetings, of which I have spoken of before, and the one of which I will now speak. Since Satan could not clear the mystery for himself, he decided to again consult with those of his associates who excelled in malice and astuteness. He roared forth a tremendous bellow in the language understood by the demons and called together those who were subject to him and said, "My, ministers and, companions, you, who have always followed me in my just opposition, well know that in the first state in which we were placed by the Creator of all things, we acknowledged him as the universal source of all our being and thus also respected him. However, when he imposed upon us the command that we adore and serve the person of the Word, in the human form, which he intended to assume, we resisted his will. We knew that reverence was due him as God. Yet as he chose to unite himself to the nature of man, so ignoble and inferior to us, we could not bear to be subject to him, nor could we bear to see that he did not favor us rather than the creature of man. He not only commanded us to adore him, but also to recognize as our superior a woman, his mother a mere earthly creature. To these grievances, I took exception and you stood with me. We objected to them and resolved to deny him our obedience. Consequently, God punished us and made us to suffer the pains of our present condition. Although we are aware of these truths and acknowledge them with terror among ourselves, it will not do to confess them before men [Jas: 2, 19]. This I put as a command upon you all, in order that men may not know of our present difficulty and weakness."

"The coming into the world of this God-man and his mother shall begin our greatest ruin and torment. For this reason, I must seek with all my strength to prevent it and destroy them, even at the cost of overturning and destroying the world. You all know how invincible has been my strength until now, since such a great portion of the world obeyed my commands and is subject to my will and cunning. However, in the last few years, I have noticed on many occasions, that our powers seems to have decreased and weakened that you were oppressed and overcome, and I myself feel a superior force, which restrains and intimidates me. Several times I have searched with you through the whole world, trying to find some clue for this loss and oppression which we feel. God has promised to send a Messiah to his chosen people. If he is already in the world, then we have failed to discover him on the entire face of the earth. We see no certain signs of his coming and we perceive none of the pomp and outward show naturally attendant upon such a person. In spite of this, I have my misgivings lest the time of his coming from heaven onto this earth be already near. Therefore, we must be eager to destroy him and the woman whom he shall choose to be his mother. Whoever shall be distinguished in this work shall not complain of my thankfulness and reward. Until now I have found guilt and the effect of guilt in all men, and I have seen no such majesty and grand magnificence as would induce the Word to become man, which would oblige mortals to adore and offer him sacrifice. The certain indication of his coming and the distinguishing mark of the Messiah will no doubt be that neither sin nor its consequences, common to other children of Adam, will ever be able to touch him."

"So much the greater therefore," continued Lucifer, "is my confusion. For, if the eternal Word has not yet come into the world, I cannot understand these new experiences nor from where this strong opposition comes which overpowers us. I ask you, who drove us out and hurled us from Egypt? Who destroyed the temples and crushed the idols of that country, in which, all the inhabitants adored us? Who oppresses us now in the land of Galilee and its neighborhood, and prevents us from perverting many of the persons in danger of death? Who keeps so many souls away from sin as if they were withdrawn from our jurisdiction, and who causes so many to better their lives and begin to seek the Kingdom of God? We do not comprehend this damaging influence. However, if we allow this secret force to continue, great misfortune and torment may arise for all of us. It is necessary to put a stop to it and search anew all over the world for a great prophet or saint, who seeks our destruction. I have not been able to discover any one to whom I could ascribe such a power. The only one that comes to mind is that woman, for whom I have a great hatred, the one we persecuted in the temple and later in her house in Nazareth. Each time we were vanquished and terrified by the virtue which shields her and resists our malice. We have never been able to search her interior or come near her person. She has a Son, and when both of them attended at his father's death, none of us were able to approach the place where they were. However, they are poor and neglected. She is an unknown and helpless little woman. However, I presume without a doubt that both Son and mother must be counted among the just. For I have continually sought to draw them into the failings common to men. Yet, I have never succeeded in causing them to commit the least reprehensible of actions, which are so common and natural with other people. The Almighty conceals from me the state of these souls; this, without a doubt, argues some hidden danger for us. At times the condition of certain souls has been withheld from us, yet this is quite rare and not in the same manner as these two. Even if this man is not the Messiah, it is certain he and his mother are just and our enemies, which are just reason for persecuting and ruining them. It is especially important that we find out who they are. All of you are to follow me in this enterprise with all diligence, for I shall be your leader in our fight against them."

Lucifer, the prince of darkness, together with his countless hordes of evil spirits, issued forth from hell and spread over the whole world. They persisted in roaming through it many times, searching out in their malice and cunning all the just, tempting those they recognized as such and provoking them and other men to commit the evil deeds hatched out in their own infernal minds. However my Son in his infinite wisdom concealed our persons for many days from the haughty Lucifer. He did not permit him to see or recognize us until he went to the desert, where he desired Satan to tempt him after his long fast. Lucifer did tempt him, as I shall relate in its proper place. My Son knew this infernal meeting was to take place, for he knows all things. He prayed to his Father against the malice of the dragon and his followers. I was fully aware of Lucifer's evil counsels and saw all that passed in my divine Son and the prayers that he offered for the sake of humankind against the plotting of Lucifer. As the Coadjutrix of my Son's triumphs, I joined in the prayers and petitions of Jesus. The Most High granted all of our prayers and on this occasion my Son and I obtained immense assistance and rewards from the Father for those that battle against the demons in the name of Jesus and Mary. Consequently all those, who pronounce our names in reverence and faith, overcome their hellish enemies and precipitously repel them in virtue of our triumphs and victories. Because of these and all the other helps furnished you in the holy Church, no excuse is left for your not overcoming and vanquishing the demon.

Over the years, my Son was to suffer much from the persecution of our neighbors and former friends in Nazareth. It had been a blessing for Joseph to die before these events occurred, because he could not have not endured the final crucifixion of his Son, for he was already suffering for the uncalled for attacks on Jesus. The Pharisees called Jesus a vagrant, for they could not bear the sight of him. They told everyone that Jesus thought he was better than other people were, and that he was in conflict with the teachings of the Hebrews. They complained about his following of young people, and unfortunately as time pressed on some of these young followers came of age, married, and became the very Pharisees that were persecuting my Son.

Upon our return to Jerusalem from one of our trips my Son said to me, "It is time for us to leave Nazareth. The Pharisees have undermined all of our work here; even our friends and relatives are confused. Most of the young men who followed me have married, the Pharisees have overly influenced them, and they fail to follow my example. The people never recognize a prophet in his hometown. Our friend Lazarus has placed a cottage at our disposal near Capernaum. This site will be more convenient when I begin my ministry, for from this area I shall select my future Apostles."

We moved our meager belongings on our donkey to Capernaum. Our new home was in a small cluster of homes between Bethsaida and Capernaum. We then thoroughly cleaned our home and closed it up leaving its supervision to the care of Maraha and Daniel. Thereafter, from time to time during our travels, we would stay in our little home in Nazareth, which had meant so much to Joseph, my Son and I, as well as to my mother and father, Anne and Joachim.

On one such trip, we had left Capernaum and going through Hebron passed through the indescribably beautiful country of Gennesaret and by the hot baths of Emmaus. These baths were in a declivity of a mountain, an hour's distance further on from Magdalan in the direction of Tiberius. The meadows were covered with thick grass, and on the declivity stood the houses and tents between rows of fig trees, date palms and orange trees. The road was crowded, for a feast was in progress. Men and women in separate groups were playing games. The winners received fruits as their reward. There we saw a man known as Nathanael, also called Chased, standing among the men under a fig tree. My sensitivity to sin made me realize that he was struggling against a sensual temptation, and he was glancing over at the women's game. Instinctively Jesus cast him a warning look. Nathanael deeply moved by the glance, thought, "That man has a sharp eye." He instinctively felt that my Son was more than an ordinary man. He became conscience of his guilt, and subjected his thoughts and overcame the temptation, and from that time on he kept a stricter guard over his senses. Another man, Nephtali, known as Bartholomew, was also there, and a glance from my Son touched him as well.

There were over a hundred small towns and villages in Galilee and we spent time in them all. Jesus was fascinated with Sepphoris the capital of Galilee. All the vices of the secular world were inherent in this beautiful city, and offered my Son many opportunities to turn various people from their sinful life. King Herod held court here in his palatial palace. Sepphoris was an Alexandrian style city with more foreigners populating the city than Jews. It was the center for the flax industry. The sky-blue flowers of the flax plant in the spring, undulated in the breeze like the waves of an ocean. Galilee was a veritable garden. The region received more rain and there were many springs nestled amidst the charming valleys that were extraordinarily fertile due to the hard work and diligence of the farmers. The hills were rife with beautiful plants, leaves, blossoms and fruits. Many of the elite of Israel made their summer homes here, and there were any number of beautifully terraced gardens, estates, and castles including the one owned by King Herod.

Further south in Magdala, near the shore of the Sea of Galilee, was a beautiful castle belonging to the family of Lazarus. They also owned a large estate at Bethel as well as an estate near Capernaum. Lazarus was a distant cousin of Joseph, had become a fast friend of Jesus, and did many favors for him. He was extremely rich and was of the princely class having huge estates and castles. Lazarus had three sisters, none of them married. Martha ran his house for him. Mary was a gifted child with an ethereal air and was very close to God, but was considered a simpleton by her peers. Mary Magdalan was the youngest and the most willful and promiscuous. Upon the death of her father Zarah, Mary, at age eleven, took over one of the families castles located at Magdala. She moved to it with a large retinue of servants. She had earned a reputation for herself as a rich wastrel. Mary loved giving parties and dressed in the most modern, alluring, and revealing gowns of the time. She had her first affair at the age of nine and led a decadent, hedonistic life.

John the Baptist

While Jesus prepared himself for his ministry, and I assisted him in prayer and sacrifice, our cousin John had nearly completed his preparations as the Precursor of Christ. John had remained in the cave after the early death of Elizabeth when he was only four years old. The angels attended to his every need, and the Holy Spirit had instructed him. Each day, for a period of seven years, I sent John food by my holy angels. From his seventh year until his ninth, I sent him only bread. I understood that during the rest of his stay in the desert, it was the will of heaven that he nourish himself with roots, wild honey, and locusts, which he accordingly did until he came forth to preach. His playmates were the angels, the wild animals and the birds. The birds led John to the hives of the wild bees. The bees allowed John to eat freely without attacking him. He never took enough to suffer them any hardship. He learned to build a fire and how to roast the locusts that infested the desert area. His main diet was wild honey, roasted locusts, berries, grapes, and roots. He was as wild and free as the foxes, martins, wild boars, porcupines, jackals, and the beautiful antelopes and gazelles that frequented the edge of the desert. Lions and bears were his friends and the birds gathered food for him in their beaks and loved to sit on his shoulders. John dressed in the skins of wild animals and wore a heavy leather belt about his waist.

John's uncut hair fell to his waist and his beard was heavy and full. No razor ever touched his hair or face, and he ate neither of meat, nor drank of wine. He was fully aware from the moment of his consecration in the womb of his mother Elizabeth, by my Son Jesus, of his role in announcing the coming of the Lord as prophesied in the Pentateuch. His conversation was with the holy angels and with the Lord of all Creation. This was his sole occupation and he was never idle in the exercise of his love and of the heroic virtues, which he began in the womb of his mother. Not for one moment was grace in him unprofitable, nor did he fail in the least point of perfection possible. He had withdrawn his senses from all earthly things, which did not in any way hinder him. His senses did not serve him as windows through which the images of the deceitful vanities of the creatures are wont to bring death to the souls. Since John was so fortunate as to be visited by the divine light before he saw the light of the created sun of this world, he overlooked all that is seen by eyes of flesh, and fixed his interior gaze immovably upon the being of God and his infinite perfections.

The divine favors received by John exceed all human intelligence, and his holiness and his exalted merits, you shall understand only in the Beatific Vision and not before. I did more than just send John food, for I continuously sent him my holy angels in order to console him and inform him of the doings and mysteries of the Incarnate Word, but containing these visits to no more than once a week. These favors encouraged John to bear his solitude. Our tokens of love served to counteract the vehemence of his love, which drew him toward my Son and I and to make our absence and the want of our association bearable to him. There is no doubt that his desire for direct communication with us was a far greater pain and suffering to his soul than all the inclemency's of his habitation, his fasting, his penances, and the stark loneliness of the mountains. They would have been impossible if I had not assisted him by continually sending him my holy angels to bring messages from his beloved Lord and Savior.

The great hermit inquired into all the particulars of Jesus and me, with the anxious solicitude of a loving bridegroom. He sent us the messages of his ardent love and of the sighs that came from his inmost heart. He asked me through my messengers to send him our blessings and he asked the angels to adore and humbly reverence the Lord in his name. He never ceased to adore him in spirit and in truth from his solitude, and he asked all the angels who came to him to do the same. As a very young boy, the Creator had taught John about the mysteries of the Cross. My Son and John both slept with their spiritual crosses throughout their lives.

Jesus knew he was to accomplish his mission on earth upon a Cross. He sanctified this emblem by spiritually placing himself upon it during his prayers and in offering himself freely to die upon it. John and I did not adore the cross in itself, nor the material of which it was made, for reverence was not due to it until the works of the Redemption should have been completed upon it by the Incarnate Word. The subsequent death of Jesus Christ on a Cross, led to the current practice of the adoration of Christ's crucifix in the Roman Catholic Church.

John, the son of Zachariah and Elizabeth, was now in the prime of his life, and he received his call from the divine Trinity in the form of an ecstasy [Luke: 3, 1-2]. It was the destined and acceptable time decreed by the eternal wisdom for sending forth John, the harbinger of the Incarnate Word. The voice resounding in the desert had now come [Is: 40, 3]. It was the fifteenth year of the reign of Tiberius Caesar, under the high priests Annas and Caiaphas. Thus, in the year 27 AD, John was enlightened and prepared by the plentitude of the light and grace of the Holy Spirit. In this rapture, he obtained a deep insight into the mysteries of the Redemption, and was favored with an abstractive vision of the Divinity. John's vision transformed and changed him to a new existence of sanctity and grace. The Lord ordered him to issue forth from the desert in order to preach and prepare the way for the Incarnate Word. God instructed and filled John with grace, thus enabling him to exercise the office of a Precursor and all that pertained to it.

John, the new preacher, came from the desert clothed in camel skin, girded with a cincture of cord. His feet were bare, his features thin and his skin was parched dark by the sun like seasoned leather. John was graceful, modest, humble, and an invincible and magnanimous courage filled his soul. His heart was inflamed with the love of God and man. His words rang forth strong and forceful, piercing to the souls of his hearers like the sparks from the immutable and divine essence of the Almighty. John was gentle toward the meek, loving toward the humble, wonderful in the sight of angels and men, awful to the proud, severe to the sinners, and an object of horror to the demons. He was a preacher fit to be the instrument of the Incarnate Word, for the Hebrews were hard-hearted, thankless, and stubborn. They were a people cursed with heathen governors, and proud and avaricious priests without enlightenment; a people without prophets, without pity, and without fear of God even though they had been visited by so many calamities and chastisements for their sins. The Lord sent John to open the eyes of God's people to their miserable state, in order to prepare their hearts to know and receive their Savior and Teacher. John came to the banks of the Jordan River preaching the baptism of penance for the remission of sins and preparing the hearts for the reception of the promised Messiah.

Our final preparations for my Son's public life

The love I had for my divine Son must always remain the standard by which you must measure all my actions as well as all my emotions either of joy or sorrow during my earthly life. You cannot; however, measure the greatness of my love itself, nor can the holy angels measure it, except by the love, which they see in God by the Intuitive Vision. All you can envision or imagine is but the least portion of what my heart really contained. I loved Jesus as the Son of God, equal to him in essence and his divine attributes and perfections. I loved him as my own natural Son; a son to me as far as he was a man. He was the Saint of saints and the meritorious cause of all other holiness. He was a most dutiful Son, my most magnificent benefactor, since it was he, by his Sonship that had raised me to the highest dignity possible among creatures. He exalted me above all the treasures of his Divinity and by conferring upon me the dominion over all creation together with favors, blessings and graces, such as were never to be conferred upon any other being.

Today many scholars question where my Son received his religious training. Some go so far as to assume that he even traveled to the Far East, where, the mystics educated him. What need did my divine Son need for teachers? If you are to sincerely believe that my Son was true God and true Man, what need did he have of instructors? After all, he was the same man-God, who had come to establish his Church upon this earth, as had been pre-ordained from the beginning. How, they ask, can a man be truly a man with a free will, subject to the same trials and tribulations as other men, if he is God at the same time and fully aware of the fact that he is God? **There is no way that a mortal being can understand the mystery of how my Son could be a true man, and at the same time True God, anymore than they can understand the mystery of the divine Trinity.** Only God could create such a situation and only God can fully understand and explain it; however, no mortal mind can comprehend it.

Being a most prudent mother, I knew that the time of my sacrifice was fast approaching. We had returned to Nazareth and I was enjoying the peace and security I always felt when I was in the original home of my parents. John, the son of Zachariah and Elizabeth, was already preaching on the banks of the Jordan preparing the way for the appearance of my Son. It was soon after that God caught me up in a most exalted vision. I felt that I was being called and placed in the presence of the throne of the most blessed Trinity. From it issued a voice of wonderful power saying to me,

"Mary my, Daughter and, Spouse, offer to me your only-begotten-Son in sacrifice."

By the living power of these words came the light and intelligence of the Almighty's will. In it, I understood the decree of the Redemption of man through the Passion and Death of my most holy Son, together with all that which from now on would happen in the preaching and public life of the Savior. I felt my soul overpowered by sentiments of subjection, humility, love of God and man, and compassion and tender sorrow for all that my Son was to suffer.

I answered my, Lord "Eternal, King and omnipotent, God of infinite wisdom and goodness, all that has being outside of you exists solely for your mercy and greatness, and you are the undiminished Lord of all. Why then do you command me, an insignificant nothingness, to sacrifice and deliver over to your will the Son, whom you have given me? He is yours eternal, Father, since from all eternity before the morning star, you have engendered him. You have begotten him and shall beget him through all the eternities. I have clothed him in the form of servant in my womb. I have nourished his humanity at my breast and ministered to it as a mother. Therefore, this most holy humanity is also your property, and so am I, since I have received from you all that I am. I acknowledge that in our receiving so many infinite treasures that in order for you to bind us to you, you wish to have them returned to you as a free gift, even your Onlybegotten son.

From his hands, I received immense gifts and graces. He is the virtue of my virtue, the substance of my spirit, life of my soul and soul of my life, the sustenance of all my joy of living. It would be a sweet sacrifice, indeed, to yield him up to you who alone know his value. However, to yield him for the satisfaction of your justice into the hands of his cruel enemies at the cost of his life, more precious than all the works of creation, this indeed, most high, Lord, is a great sacrifice which you ask of me, his mother. However, *let your will not mine be done.* Let the freedom of the human race be thus brought. Let your justice and equity be satisfied. Let your infinite love become manifest. Let your name be known and magnified before all creatures. I deliver my beloved Son over into your hands. Then, like Isaac, he may be a true sacrificial lamb. I offer my Son, the fruit of my womb, in order that according to the unchangeable decree of your will, he may pay the debt contracted not by his fault, but by the fault of the children of Adam. Thus, by his death, he will fulfill all that your holy Prophets, inspired by you, have written and foretold."

This sacrifice with all that pertained to it was the greatest and the most acceptable that had ever been made to the eternal Father since the creation of the world, or that will ever be made to the end, outside that made by my own Son, the Redeemer. Mine was most intimately connected with and like to that which my Son offered. God so loved the world that he gave his only Son, so that in order that none of those who believed in him might perish. I also loved my fellow man so much that I, too, gave my only Son for the salvation of the world. If I had not given him in this manner when the eternal Father asked it of me, the salvation of men could not have been executed by this same decree. This decree was to be fulfilled on condition that my will should coincide with that of the eternal Father.

The Blessed Trinity rewarded me for having made this sacrifice. They comforted me in my sorrow by wrapping me in a heavenly vision. The Trinity raised me to a more exalted ecstasy, in which I was prepared and enlightened when the Divinity manifested itself to me by an intuitive and direct vision. In this vision, by the clear light of the essence of God, I comprehended the inclination of the Infinite God to communicate his fathomless treasures to the rational creature by means of the works of the Incarnate Word. I saw the glory that would result from these wonders to the name of the Most High. Filled with jubilation at the prospect of all these sacramental mysteries, I renewed the offering of my divine Son to the Father. God comforted me with the life-giving bread of heavenly understanding. In this manner, I could with invincible fortitude assist the Incarnate Word in the work of the Redemption as his Coadjutrix and helper, according to the disposition of infinite Wisdom and as it actually happened afterwards.

By the effects of these blessings, I was now prepared to separate from my divine Son, who had already resolved to enter upon his fast in the desert in view of his receiving his Baptism at the hands of John, who was to be the Precursor of Christ. Jesus called me to him and in tokens of sweetest love and compassion said, "My, Mother, my existence as man I derived entirely from your substance and blood, of which I have taken the form of a servant in your virginal womb. You have nursed me at your breast and taken care of me by your labors and sweat. For this reason, I acknowledge you more my mother than any other will ever acknowledge himself as the son of his mother. Give me your permission and consent toward accomplishing the will of my eternal Father. Already the time has arrived in which I must leave your sweet company and begin the work of the Redemption of man. The time of rest has ended and the hour of suffering for the rescue of the sons of Adam has arrived. I wish to perform this work of my Father with your assistance and you are to be my companion and helper in preparing for my Passion and Death of the Cross. Although, for now, I must leave you alone, my blessing, and loving, and powerful protection shall remain with you. I shall return later and claim your assistance and company in my labors; for I am to undergo them in the form of man, which you have given me."

My Son placed his arms around me and we both shed abundant tears. Yet, we both maintained a majestic composure such as befitted us in the art of suffering. I fell at the feet of my beloved Son and in ineffable sorrow and reverence replied,

"My Lord and eternal God, you are indeed my Son and in you is fulfilled all the force of love, which I have received of you. My inmost soul is laid open to the eyes of your divine wisdom. My life would amount to nothing if I could thereby save my own instead of dying for you many times. However, the will of the eternal Father, and your own, must be fulfilled. I offer my own will as a sacrifice for this fulfillment. Receive it my Son, and as Master of all my being, let it be an acceptable offering, and let your divine protection never be wanting to me. Please, I beg of you, take some food with you, or allow some to be sent to where you are going."

My Son; however, explained that this would not be befitting for the occasion, and he moved to the door. Again I fell at his holy feet, and kissed them and asked him for his blessing. My divine Master gave me his benediction and he left to begin his journey to the Jordan. He issued forth as the good Shepherd to seek his lost sheep and bring them back to the fold on his shoulders to the way of eternal life, from which they had been decoyed by deceit [Luke: 15, 5].

Once my Son left, I felt as if I was in an eclipse or under a shadow; I immersed myself in the contemplation and praise of the Trinity. I gave myself up entirely to the exercise of prayer and petition in order that the seed of the divine word and doctrine, which my Son was to plant into the hearts of men, might not be lost because of their hardness and ingratitude. By means of my infused knowledge, I knew the intentions of the Incarnate Word and therefore I resolved not to converse with any human creature, in order to imitate my Son during his fasting in the desert.

I was in close communion with Jesus through my angels, and as he traveled to the Jordan, in secret, he dispensed his ancient mercies by relieving the necessities of body and soul in many of those he encountered along the way. During his journey, he filled the heart of John with new light and joy, which changed and elevated his soul. Perceiving these new workings of grace within him, John reflected upon them full of wonder and said,

"What mystery and happiness is this? From when I first recognized the presence of my Lord, from within the womb of my mother, I have not felt such stirring of soul as now! Is it possible that the Savior of the World is near?"

Thus enlightened, God gave John an intellectual vision, wherein he perceived with great clarity the mystery of the hypostatic union of Jesus with humanity and other mysteries of the Redemption. The Lord had previously instructed John to go forth, and preach and baptize. Now, Jesus again manifested all of this to him anew in greater depth. In addition, God notified John that the Savior of the World was coming and that he was to baptize him.

When Jesus arrived at the Jordan, he joined the masses of people along the shore, asked to be baptized, and waited his turn. When John saw him; however, he recognized him as the Savior and he fell at his feet crying, "I have need of being baptized, and you Lord ask baptism of me?"

My Son answered him saying, "Suffer it to be so now; for so it becomes us to fulfill all justice {Matt: 3, 14-15].

John then baptized Jesus and when he was finished, the heavens opened and the Holy Ghost in a celestial light, together with innumerable angels, descended visibly in the form of a dove upon the head of Jesus and from a cloud the voice of the Father was heard, "This is my beloved Son, in whom I am well pleased [Matt: 3, 17]."

Many of the bystanders, those who were worthy of such a great favor, also, saw the angels and the dove settling upon the head of the Redeemer. God's words were convincing proof of the divinity of my Son. In addition, God the Father acknowledged Jesus as his Son. Without any reservation, God manifested Jesus as true God, equal to him in substance and in perfection. God the Father was the first to testify to the divinity of his Son; in order that by virtue of his testimony all the other witnesses might be ratified.

In this act of humiliation of receiving baptism, Jesus, who was without the stain of sin, offered up to the eternal Father an act of acknowledgement of the inferiority of his human nature, which he held in common with all the rest of the children of Adam. After his Resurrection, my son instituted the Sacrament of Baptism, as he made it a general law and enjoined the public ministration of it upon the Apostles. By thus humiliating himself, Jesus sought and obtained from the eternal Father a general pardon for all those who were to receive it. He freed them from the power of the demon and of sin and regenerated them to a new existence, spiritual and supernatural as adopted sons of the Most High, brethren of their Redeemer and Lord.

My Son could have begun his ministry with his baptism. Jesus; however, did not desire to commence his preaching, or to be known as our Redeemer, without first having triumphed over the sins of the world, the flesh, and the devil. He wished to give us our first lesson as a Christian and to teach us by these triumphs of Christian perfection, how we are to strengthen our weaknesses. He wishes us to discourage our common enemies by continued battle and victories. Otherwise, the fluctuations of our own wills might deliver us over to them. My Son, as God, was infinitely above the demon; in addition, Jesus, as man, was without the deceit of sin, and was supremely holy and the Master of all creation. He nevertheless wished to overcome in his human nature, by his personal justice and holiness, all the vices and their author. Therefore, he offered his most holy humanity to the buffetings of temptation, concealing his superiority from his invisible enemies. Therefore, Jesus set out to the desert to fast for forty days and forty nights, to deliberately allow the demon to tempt him. By his fasting, Jesus began to conquer and to teach us how to conquer the world. It is an established fact that the world is accustomed to forsake those whom it does not need for its earthly purpose. It does not seek those who themselves do not seek it.

My prayers were so ardent that I shed tears of blood in weeping over the sins of men. I genuflected and prostrated myself upon the ground no less than two hundred times each day. I practiced this devotion throughout my entire life, as an exterior manifestation of my humility, charity, reverence and worship of God. In the absence of my holy Son, I succeeded so successfully that because of my merits, God forgot the sins of all the mortals, who were then making themselves unworthy of the preaching and doctrine of Jesus. I was the Mediatrix. I had received the law of the holy Gospel from my Son's lips, and gained for men the blessing of being taught by my Son himself. My Son had ordered my thousand angels to attend to me in bodily forms during all the time in which he was to be absent. My angels were delighted and served me diligently with admirable and befitting reverence. While thus occupied, I did not experience the sharp pain of the absence of Jesus. When I finished my prayers; however, I immediately felt the irresistible force of my intense, chaste and sincere love for my holy Son. Consequently, I felt such an intense pain of loss that I could not have lived if it had not been for divine intervention.

I turned to my angels and said, "My Friends and Companions give me news of my cherished Son and Master. Tell me where he is, and tell him that I am dying because of the want of his life-giving presence. Inform me of his movements and omit nothing of his activities. Point out to me his footsteps in order that I may follow and imitate him."

My heavenly Spirits related to me the prayers of Jesus, and of his teachings, his visits to the poor and sick, and his other actions, so that I was able to imitate his every move. I could not send him food or fresh linens by my angels, as I usually did, since he was now on his forty day fast. When advised of this fact, I closed up my house, retired to my room, and began a forty-day fast in imitation of my Son. I separated myself from all human company. My neighbors thought that, since I had closed up the house that I had left on a trip. God favored me with almost continuous ecstasies, in which I received peerless gifts and treasures of the Divinity. All of these new graces and gifts I employed in working for the salvation of men, and my thoughts and occupations closely followed the doings of our Savior, as became the Coadjutrix of the Lord in his labors. These benefits and close association with my Son brought me an exultation of soul in the Holy Spirit, yet in the sensible parts of my being I experienced pains. These were the very pains, which I had sought and asked of our Savior, so that in union with him, I could imitate his sufferings. In my desire to follow my Redeemer in his pain, I was insatiable, and I begged the eternal Father for this privilege with incessant and burning love. God granted me my wishes to suffer with my beloved, and I endured great pains.

On his journey to the wilds of the desert, only his angels accompanied Jesus. Before beginning his trek to the desert, Jesus stooped and removed his sandals. During his long journey, his angels attended to and worshipped him singing divine praises for what he was about to undertake for the salvation of men. Finally, he came to the spot chosen for him, a desert spot among bare and beetling rocks, where there was also a cleverly concealed cavern. My Son chose this barren spot as his home during his fast [Matt: 4, 1]. He prostrated himself upon the ground in the shape of a cross in deepest humility, which rite was always a prelude to his prayers, as it was mine. He thanked the eternal Father and even thanked the desert for giving him shelter and keeping him hidden from the world. His prayers were so intense that he often sweated blood.

Many of the wild beasts came to the area just to be near him, and each in his own nature roared their welcome to him. Multitudes of birds gathered and eagerly manifested their joy with their sweet songs in his presence. For forty days and forty nights our Lord fasted and prayed as recompense to the eternal Judge for the common disorder and sin of *gluttony*. Our Savior, in order to assume the office of Preacher and Teacher, and to become our Mediator and Redeemer before the Father, vanquished all the vices of mortals. He satisfied the offenses committed through them by the exercise of the virtues contrary to them, just as he did in regard to gluttony. Although he continued this exercise throughout his life with the most ardent charity, yet during his fast he directed in a special manner all his efforts toward this purpose.

A loving father, whose sons have committed great crimes for which they are to endure the most horrible punishment, sacrifices all his possessions in order to ward off their impending fate. Therefore it is that Jesus, our most loving brother, wished to pay our debts by his love and sacrifices. In satisfaction for our *pride,* he offered his profound humility. For our *avarice*, he offered his voluntary poverty and total privation of all that was his. For our *base and lustful inclinations*, he offered penance and austerity. For our *hastiness and vengeful anger*, he offered his meekness and charity toward his enemies. For our *negligence and laziness*, he offered his ceaseless labors. For our *deceitfulness and our envy*, he offered his candid, upright sincerity, truthfulness, and the sweetness of his loving communication. In this manner, he continued to appease the just Judge and solicited pardon for us *disobedient and bastard children*. He not only obtained pardon for us, but he merited for us new graces and favors, so that we might make ourselves worthy of his company and the vision of his Father and his own inheritance for all eternity. Although he could have obtained all this for us by the most insignificant of his works, he chose to demonstrate his love so abundantly that for our *ingratitude and hardness* of heart there would be no excuse.

In order for me to keep informed of the doings of our Savior, I actually needed no other assistance other than my continual visions and revelations. However, I made use of my holy angels by sending them to my divine Son. The Lord had thus ordered it, in order that by means of these faithful messengers we both might rejoice in the thoughts and inmost hearts of one another. As I related before, when I learned that my Son was on the way to the desert, I locked up my house and remained inside so that my neighbors thought I had joined my Son on one of his journeys. I entered my oratory, and remained there for forty days and nights without ever leaving it, and I ate nothing just as my Son was doing in the desert. We both observed the same course of rigorous fasting, in all his prayers and exercises, his prostrations and genuflections; I followed my divine Son, not omitting any of them. I was careful to perform them at the same precise moment as Jesus. Whether Jesus was present or not, I knew the interior operations of the soul of my Son. All his bodily movements, which I been privileged to witness previously, I now knew by intellectual vision or through my holy angels.

While Jesus was in the desert, he made three hundred genuflections daily, which I imitated. The other portions of my time, I spent in composing hymns with my angels. By thus cooperating with Christ the Lord in his prayers and petitions, I gained the same victories over the vices, and on my part I proportionately satisfied for them by my virtues and exertions. Christ as our Redeemer, while in the desert, gained for us many blessings and abundantly paid all our debts. I, as his helper, and as the Mother of the World, lent all persons my merciful intercession and became their Mediatrix to the fullest extent possible to a mere creature.

On the thirty-fifth day of his fast, my Son, in preparation for his contest with Lucifer, directed a prayer to his Father, saying, "My Father and eternal God, I now enter into battle with the enemy in order to crush his power and humble his pride and his malice against my beloved souls. For your glory and for the benefit of souls, I submit to the daring presumption of Lucifer. I wish thereby to crush his head. Thus, when Lucifer attacks mortals by his temptations without their fault, they may find his arrogance already broken. I beseech you my, Father, to remember my battle and victory in favor of mortals assailed by the common enemy. Strengthen their weakness through my triumph, let them obtain victory; let them be encouraged by my example, and let them learn from me how to resist and overcome their enemies."

With this prayer, God allowed Lucifer to approach Jesus. Lucifer rejoiced when he found that I was not with my Son. I had defeated him many times in the past and he considered me his archenemy. Satan had never had any contest with my Son, and in my absence he counted his victory secure. However, when he observed his enemy more closely, he began to feel great fear and discouragement. Jesus had permitted the demons to remain under the false impression that he was a mere human creature though very holy and just. My divine Son wished to raise Lucifer's courage and malice for the contest. Yet, great fear and dread seized Lucifer and his demons when they saw that he manifested so much reserve and majesty, and because his actions were perfect and heroic. His behavior and actions were totally different from those of other men, whom they had tempted and easily overcome.

Awestruck, Lucifer conferred with his demons, saying, "What manner of man is this, who is so adverse to the vices by which we assail other men? If he is so forgetful of the world and has his flesh in such subjection and control, how shall we find any opening for our temptations? How shall we hope for victory, if he has deprived us of the weapons by which we wage warfare among men? We must therefore rouse ourselves with greater prowess and fierceness than we have with any other man."

Lucifer began his onslaught against Jesus on the thirty-fifth day of his fast when he was weak and weary from his ordeal. The demons would not cease their efforts until the end of my Son's fast. During this battle, my Son's heavenly entourage of angels remained hidden from the sight of the demons. In addition, from my little home in Nazareth, I joined my fasting, prayers, and sacrifices with those of my Son. I was fully aware of all that transpired and was likewise subjected to the tempter.

Lucifer assumed the shape of a man and presented himself before Jesus as a stranger who had never seen or known him before. He clothed himself in refulgent light, like that of an angel, and knowing that my Son after his long fast must be suffering great hunger said to him,

"Your fast has been most pleasing to our God." Seeking information as to who Jesus truly was, he cunningly added, "If you be the Son of God, command that these stones be made bread."

However, the Savior of the world answered him only in the words taken from the eighth chapter of Deuteronomy, "Not in bread alone does man live, but in every word that proceeds from the mouth of God."

However, Lucifer understood him to mean that God could sustain the life of man without bread or any other nourishment. Yet, while this was also the true signification of these words, our Lord included a much deeper meaning, desiring to say to Lucifer, "This man, with whom you speak, lives in the word of God, which is the divine Word, hypostatically united to his humanity." Though these words were precisely what Lucifer desired so much to know, he did not deserve to understand the words of the God-man, because Lucifer did not wish to adore him as true God.

Lucifer found himself repulsed by the force of this answer and by the hidden power which accompanied it, but desiring to show no weakness, he pressed his attack. The Lord allowed the demons to pursue their attack and even permitted the devil to carry him, bodily to Jerusalem. Lucifer then placed my Son on the highest pinnacle of the Temple of Jerusalem. Jesus could see a vast multitude of people below; however, he remained unseen by anyone. Lucifer tried to arouse in my Son the vain desire of casting himself down from this high place, so that the crowds of men, seeing him unhurt, might proclaim him as a great and wonderful man of God.

Again, using the words of Holy Scriptures, Satan said to him, "If you are the Son of God, cast yourself down, for it is written [Ps[s]: 91, 12] that he has given his angels charge over you, and in their hands they shall bear you up, lest perhaps you dash your foot against a stone [Matt: 4, 6].

The ten thousand angelic spirits guarding my Son were full of wonder that he should permit Lucifer to carry him bodily in his hands, solely for the benefit of mortal man. Innumerable demons gathered about the prince of darkness to render him assistance. The Author of Wisdom, exhibiting matchless meekness, the profoundest humility, and a majesty so superior to all the attempts of Satan, which of itself was sufficient to crush Lucifer's arrogance and to cause him torments and confusion replied, "It is also written, you shall not tempt the Lord your God [Deut: 6, 16].

Foiled again in his efforts, Lucifer attacked Jesus in still another way seeking to rouse his ambition by offering him some share in his dominion. For this purpose Jesus allowed Satan to take him to the top of a high mountain, from which could be seen many lands and he said to him with perfidious daring, "All of this I will give to you, if falling down you will adore me [Matt: 4, 9]." He offered to my Son that which he did not possess, nor ever could give, since the earth, the stars, the kingdoms, principalities, riches and treasures, all belong to the Lord, and he alone can give or withhold them when it serves and pleases him. Lucifer cannot give anything, for he has nothing, therefore all his promises are false.

The King of the heavens, the earth, and the universe answered with imperial majesty, "Be gone, Satan, for it is written, "The Lord your God you shall adore, and him only shall you serve."

By this command, Christ the Redeemer took away from Lucifer permission to further tempt him, and he hurled him and all his legions into the deepest abyss of hell. There they found themselves entirely crushed and buried in the deepest caverns, unable to move for three days. When they were permitted again to rise, seeing themselves thus vanquished and annihilated, they began to wonder whether he, who had so overwhelmed them, might not be the Incarnate Son of God. In this doubt and uncertainty they remained without being able to come to certain conviction until the death of Jesus. Hellish wrath overcame Lucifer, at his defeat, and his fury nearly consumed him.

My Son, in his triumph sang hymns of praise and thanks to his eternal Father, for having given him this triumph over the common enemy of God and man. His joyful angels carried their king back to the desert, although he could have made use of his own divine power. However, this service was due him in recompense for enduring the audacity of Lucifer in carrying to the pinnacle of the temple and to the mountaintop, the sacred humanity of my Son, in which also dwelt substantially and truly the Divinity itself. There the angels ministered to him [Matt: 4, 11]. His angels, to invigorate his body, served him with celestial food. Not only were the angels present to rejoice at this divine banquet, but also the birds of the desert came in order to contribute to the recreation of their Creator by their harmonious songs and graceful movements. In their own way the wild animals of the desert joined them, and throwing off their native wildness produced their joyful antics and sounds in acknowledgment of the victory of our Lord.

From my little house in Nazareth, I witnessed the battles of my most holy Son. I had seen them all by the divine light and by the uninterrupted messages of my angels. I repeated at the same time the same prayers of my Son. I likewise entered the conflict with the dragon, although invisibly and spiritually. From my retreat, I anathematized and crushed Lucifer and his followers, co-operating in all the doings of my Son. When I saw the dragon carrying the holy person of my divine Son from place to place by the dragon, I wept bitterly. I wept because the malice of sin reduced the King of Kings to such misusage. In honor of all of my Son's victories over the devil, I composed hymns of praise to the Divinity and the most holy humanity of Jesus. My angels set them to music and I sent them to sing and congratulate him for the blessings won for the human race. My Son, for his part, sent back the angels with words of sweet consolation and rejoicing because of his triumphs over Lucifer.

Since I had been his faithful companion throughout his trials and fasts of the desert, my Son sent me some of the celestial food and commanded the angels to present and minister the food to me. The great multitudes of birds, in an exceedingly swift flight, entered my dwelling, and sang and chirped before me in the same way as they had done for my Son. The food my Son sent, after my long and rigorous fast, strengthened me. I celebrated and gave thanks to the Almighty and humiliated myself to the very earth. My acts of virtue were so heroic and excellent that human words and conceptions cannot encompass them. You will not see the blessings gained by my Son and I in their true light until you shall rejoice in the presence of the Lord, and then glory and praise will be given for these ineffable blessings, as is due from all the human race.

I Am Mary

My, children, those of you who desire to be a disciple of my Divine Son, be advised that Jesus exercised this office of Teacher, not only at the time when he taught his holy doctrine while yet in mortal flesh, but that he continues to be the Teacher of souls to the end of the world. He admonishes, instructs and inspires souls to put into practice whatever is perfect and most holy. Nothing can be hidden from this great Master and Teacher [Heb: 4, 13]. He withdraws in disgust from those who are ungrateful and disobedient. No one must think that these withdrawals of the Most High always happen the same way as they happened to me. For the Lord withdrew from me, *not because of any fault of mine*, but out of exceeding love. However, he is accustomed to withdraw from other creatures in order to visit them with merited punishment for their many sins, outrages, ingratitude's and negligence's."

For those who have been given much, much is expected.

If you negligently repay God for his love with ingratitude and outrageous conduct, then you are fortunate indeed if God favors you with punishment *now* instead of *later*. By your punishment you can repent, after death you cannot. God is wisdom and goodness. He wishes us to love him, not only with sweetness, but also with the wisdom and knowledge of the one that loves.

I once told Mother Mary of Agreda of my desperate search for my Son in Jerusalem saying, "The Lord absented himself from me in order that by seeking him in sorrow and tears, I might find him again in joy and with abundant fruits for my soul. In my great love, the uncertainty as to the cause of his withdrawal gave me no rest until I found him. In this, I wish that you imitate me, whether you lose him through your own fault or by the dispositions of his will. For a person to lose sight of God for being tried in virtue and love is not the same as losing sight of him in punishment for sins committed. Always remember,"

"So strong are the bonds of Jesus' love that no one can burst them except through the use of their own free will."

God calls each of us to imitate him to the very best of our individual abilities. He wrote in my heart the whole Law of Grace and all the doctrine of the Gospel. When we meditate on and imitate Jesus' every action, the greatest gift God will ever bestow upon you is the enlightenment and paths of divine light that he will reveal to you. Then you can walk secure from the darkness of ignorance enveloping other people.

I wish to warn you, as a solicitous and loving mother, of the cunning of Satan for the destruction of these works of the Lord. Many watchful and relentless demons follow each soul from the very moment in which mortals begin to have the use of their reason. These demons, with incredible fury and astuteness, seek to root out the divine seed as soon as the souls raise their thoughts to the knowledge of their God and commence the practice of virtues infused by baptism. If they cannot succeed in this, they try to hinder its growth and prevent it from bringing forth fruit by engaging men in vicious, useless or trifling things. Thus, they divert their thoughts from faith and hope and from the pursuit of other virtues leading them to forget that they are Christians. Moreover, the same enemy instills into the parents a base neglectfulness and even carnal love for their own offspring. He incites the teachers to carelessness, so that the children find no support against evil in their education. Their many bad habits cause them to become depraved and spoiled losing sight of virtue and of their good inclinations and going the way of perdition.

However, God does not forget them in this danger. Through his angels and ministers, he renews in them his holy inspirations and special helps. He holds out to them the aid of the sacraments and many other inducements to keep them on the path of life. Those that walk in the way of salvation are the smaller numbers due to the vice and depraved habits imbibed and nourished in childhood. For that saying of Deuteronomy is very true: "As the days of your youth, so also shall your old age be. The demons believe that the more they can draw man into sin in his youth, the more, greater, and more frequent the sins will be in later years. With each sin the soul loses increasingly the power of resistance, and subjects itself to the demon and is urged onward from one precipice to another. By these means Lucifer has hurled into hell a great number of souls and continues to do so every day. In this manner, he has been able to spread among men forgetfulness of death, the judgment, and heaven and hell. In so doing, he is casting many nations from abyss to abyss of darkness and bestial errors, such as are contained in the heresies and false sects of the infidels and nations warring against nations.

In your temptations, I exhort you not to be troubled or afflicted very much; for if they cause you to halt in your course, they will gain a great advantage over you and they will prevent you from becoming strong in the practice of perfection. Listen therefore to the Lord alone, who desires the beauty of your soul and who is liberal in bestowing his gifts upon it. He is eager to deposit therein the treasures of his wisdom, and anxious to see you prepare yourself to receive them. Allow him to write into your heart the Evangelical Law. Let that be your continual study. Thus, you will obtain what the Most High and I desire for you, and that which each of you, by the grace of God, inherently desire.

Beware of these terrible dangers, my children, and let not the memory of the law of your God, his precepts, Commandments, the truths of the Catholic Church, and the doctrines of the Gospels to ever fail in your minds. Do not allow a single day to pass in which you do not spend time in meditating upon all these truths and urge all those who will listen to do the same. The enemy never sleeps and never ceases to labor vigilantly to obscure the understanding of souls of the divine law seeking to stop them from the practice of justification. Read your Bible every day and keep yourself abreast of the daily actions and deeds of the Church by reading good Catholic publications and newspapers.

Be not materialistically wise and clever, but meek and humble, for God says,
"I will destroy the wisdom of the wise, and thwart the cleverness of the clever."

Your Spiritual Mother in Heaven

Mary

Chapter Eight

Mother's Role in the Public Life of Jesus

**When Jesus heard that John had been arrested, He withdrew to Galilee.
He left Nazareth and went down to live in Capernaum by the sea
near the territory of Zebulon and Nephtali.
[Matt: 5, 12-13]**

Jesus, desiring to secure new testimony of his mission and divinity through the mouth of John, went directly to Bethany, where just across the Jordan his noble Precursor John was still preaching and baptizing. Jesus was drawn by John's own love to see and speak with him, for during his baptism the heart of the Precursor had become inflamed and wounded by the divine love of the Savior, which so effortlessly attracted all creatures. During the fast of Jesus in the desert, the hostile authorities in Jerusalem sent priests and Levites to John to demand of him,

"Who are you? Are you the Messiah?"

John replied, "I am not the Messiah."

"What are you then? Are you Elijah?

John replied, "I am not."

However, they persisted and asked, "Are you then the Prophet?"

He answered, "No."

Exasperated, they stated forcefully, "Just who are you then, so we can give an answer to those who sent us? What do you have to say for yourself?"

John; since his job was to announce the coming of the Messiah, replied patiently for he knew the deceit in their hearts "I am the voice of one crying out in the wilderness; make straight the way of the Lord."

His inquisitors left, but were soon replaced by some Pharisees, who continued to press him, "Why then do you baptize if you not the Messiah, or Elijah, or the Prophet?"

John answered with pity for them in his voice, "I baptize with water, but there is one among you whom you do not recognize. The one who is coming after me, whose sandal strap I am not worthy to untie."

The next day when John saw Jesus approaching him for the second time, his words were those recorded by the Evangelist and are the words made immortal in the Holy Mass of the Catholic Church when the priest holds up the Holy Eucharist and exclaims,

"Behold the Lamb of God, who takes away the sin of the world."

While John gave this testimony, he pointed to his Savior and said to those who were listening to his instructions and were receiving baptism at his hands, "This is the one of whom I said, 'A man is coming after me who ranks ahead of me, because he existed before me. I did not know him, but the reason why I came baptizing with water was that he might be made known to Israel." John added, "When I baptized Jesus, I saw the Spirit come down like a dove from the sky and remain upon him. The one who sent me to baptize with water told me, 'On whomever you see the Spirit come down and remain, he is the one who will baptize with the Holy Spirit.' Now I have seen and testified that *He* is the Son of God [John: 2, 29-34]."

From my home in Nazareth, I was well aware of all that transpired. I was deeply impressed with the faithful testimony of John in denying that he himself was the Christ. I begged the Lord to reward him The Almighty granted my prayer, and because John had refused the honors for himself, God conferred upon him the highest honor that is possible to give to a man next to that of the Redeemer. When John saw the Savior the second time, God filled him with new and best graces of the Holy Ghost. Some of the bystanders when they heard John say; "Behold the Lamb of God," were strangely moved and asked him many questions. While John informed his audience of these facts, Jesus turned away and returned to Bethabara where he was preaching in the local synagogue. My Son was to remain for ten months in Judea, while I remained in Nazareth supporting myself and uniting all my efforts and prayers with the groundwork being laid by Jesus for his public ministry.

My Son spent the next ten months in the small towns and villages of Judea. He taught the people in a veiled manner telling them that the Messiah was already in the world. He directed them on the way of salvation and induced many of them to ready themselves through John's baptism in order to prepare themselves by penance for the coming redemption. He did not bother with the Pharisees or scribes for they were not well disposed to believe that the Messiah had come. Even when the truth had been confirmed by the Lord's preaching, his miracles, and his other testimonies, the Pharisees and scribes still would not admit to such a belief, which had so clearly given witness to Christ our Lord. First, Jesus tended to the humble and the poor. My Son felt their station of life merited them being the first to be evangelized and instructed. To them he showed his mercy, not only by individual instructions, but also by his hidden favors and private miracles. Consequently, they received him as a great Prophet and a holy Man. He stirred the hearts of innumerable persons to forsake sin and to seek the kingdom of God, which was now approaching.

I remained in Nazareth keeping abreast of his every activity. In order to imitate him perfectly, I left my oratory at the same time that Jesus left John at the Jordan. Accompanied by my angels, and filled with the plenitude of wisdom and furnished with the power of Mistress of the universe, I went forth from Nazareth to the neighboring villages and performed great miracles, although in a hidden manner, just as the Incarnate Word was doing in Judea. I spoke of the advent of the Messiah without revealing who he was. I instructed many in the way of life drawing them from their sins, put flight to the demons, enlightened the erring and the ignorant, and prepared them for the Redemption by inducing them to believe in its Author. To these spiritual works of mercy, I added many bodily blessings, healing the sick, consoling the afflicted, and visiting the poor. I labored mostly among the women, yet I benefited many of the men, who if they were poor, were not deprived of my aid, and of the happiness of being visited by the Sovereign Queen of the angels and of the universe.

I returned a few times to Nazareth, but I needed very little rest or recuperation, for as I said before, I had been satiated and strengthened by the celestial food sent to me by my Son from the desert. This spiritual strength allowed me to travel afoot to many places and over great distances, and allowed me to also abstain from other nourishment. I was well aware of the activities of John while he was preaching and baptizing on the banks of the Jordan. I sent him a multitude of my angels in order to encourage, and thank him for the loyalty he had shown to my Son.

In the midst of all of these occupations, I suffered great agonies of desire to enjoy the sight and presence of Jesus. The clamors of my chaste and heavenly love also wounded my Son. Jesus had not yet proclaimed himself publicly as the Messiah and the Master of life. Now; however, was the time for doing so according to the decrees of Infinite Wisdom. Before returning to Galilee to see me and begin his mission, my Son decided to again stop off and see John. When John saw him coming, he publicly announced for all to hear,

"Behold the Lamb of God."

John made this statement in the presence of Andrew, the brother of Simon, and John, the son of Zebedee. By divine revelation the Baptist was made aware of this visit of the Lord and of his intention to now make him known to the world as the Redeemer and the true Son of the eternal Father. John's testimony referred not only to his previous identical words in regard to Christ, but also presupposed the more particular instructions which he had given to his own disciples.

It was as though he had said to them, "Here you see the Lamb of God, of whom I have spoken to you; he, who has come to Redeem the world and open the way to heaven."

Upon hearing this testimony, and moved by the interior light and grace imparted to them, Andrew and John began following Jesus and they were quickly joined by Saturnin and two nephews of Joseph of Arimathea, Aram and Themeni. However, John the Baptist had many disciples, and there were many that believed that John, in spite of his instructions to them, was the promised Messiah.

When Jesus saw some of John's disciples following him he turned and said to them, "What are you looking for?"

Andrew said to him, "Rabbi, where are you staying?"

"Come and you will see, "Jesus told them. My Son led them to a small inn in Bethabara and there they shared a meal with him. Jesus told them of his preaching mission about to begin and of his intentions to choose his disciples. Andrew mentioned some of his acquaintances, whom he thought would be suitable for his mission, including his brother Simon, and his friends Philip and Nathanael. Jesus was cordial and friendly towards these disciples of John, but they were rather humble and somewhat shy. For ten months my son traveled throughout Judea, and sent many receptive souls to John to be baptized. While Jesus found many amenable souls the Pharisees and Sadducees began to follow him and were telling the people not to listen to him. His reception was becoming more and more hostile and my son was debating whether he should withdraw to Galilee and begin his Ministry from where the people were more receptive.

Andrew and John followed my Son in consequence of John's testimony and were the first of his disciples. They stopped in Jerusalem and Jesus prayed all day in the Holy Temple offering up his coming Passion for the sins of man. While there some of John's disciples found him, they were greatly distressed. John had been arrested by King Herod and they had learned that Herod's men intended to arrest Jesus as well. Jesus knew it was time to begin his ministry and he decided to return to Galilee to avoid Herod's spies and begin his ministry from there.

Leaving there, they moved on toward Galilee, where, knowing of his pending arrival, I anxiously waited for him. In passing through the country of Gennesaret, they ran across Andrew's friend Phillip also from Bethsaida, the hometown of Andrew. When introduced to Phillip, Jesus added him as one of his followers.

Phillip immediately sought out his friend Nathanael and said to him, "We have found the one about whom Moses wrote in the law, and also from the Prophets. He is Jesus son of Joseph, from Nazareth."

Nathanael was of a bright and lively disposition and with a laugh he looked at Andrew and asked, "Can anything good come from Nazareth?"

Andrew looked at the frank and sincere Philip, and challenged him, "Come and see for yourself."

Jesus saw Nathanael coming toward him and said to John, "Here is a true Israelite. There is no duplicity in him."

Overhearing the remark Nathanael said to him, "Sir, how do you know me?"

Jesus looked at him knowingly and replied, "Before Phillip called you, I saw you under the fig tree."

Nathanael recognized Jesus and remembered the incident when he had been so lustfully tempted. Overwhelmed, the young man replied, "Rabbi, you are the Son of God, you are the King of Israel."

Jesus answered and said to him, "Do you believe because I told you that I saw you under the fig tree? You will see greater things than this. Amen, amen, I say to you, you will see the sky opened and the angels of God ascending and descending on the Son of Man."

Phillip and Nathanael joined his growing group of disciples and they were to be the first stones in the foundation of the new Church. The following day, Andrew brought his brother Simon to Jesus, and he said to him. "You are Simon, the son of Jonah. I shall name you Cephas, "Rock" [or Peter]. Jesus entered Galilee with his first five disciples for the purpose of soon beginning his public preaching. In each new disciple, he enkindled, from the moment of their joining him, a new light and fire of divine love and showered upon them the sweetness of his blessings. It is not possible to describe the labors undergone by the divine Teacher in the vocation and education of these men, in order to found upon them his Church. He sought them out with great diligence and solicitude. He urged them on frequently by the powerful and efficacious help of his grace. He enlightened their hearts and enriched them with incomparable gifts and blessings. He received them with admirable kindness. He nourished them with the sweetest milk of his doctrines, and bore with them with invincible patience. He caressed them as a most loving father caresses his tender and darling sons. Our nature is base and uncouth material for the exalted and exquisite aspirations of the Spirit. However, these Apostles were to be not only perfect disciples, but also consummate masters of perfection in the world and in the Church. The work of transforming and raising them from their rough natural state into such a heavenly and divine position by my Son's instructions and example was a vast enterprise.

Knowing of my Son's gathering of his first disciples, I gave thanks to the eternal Father for them, acknowledging and admitting them in imitation of my Son as my spiritual children, and offering them to the divine Majesty with new songs of praise and joy. On this occasion, I was favored by a new revelation of the Most High in which I was again informed of his holy and eternal decree concerning the Redemption of man, and of the manner in which it was to be executed in the preaching of his most holy Son.

God said to me, "My, daughter and my, dove, chosen out of thousands, it is necessary that you accompany and assist our Onlybegotten Son in the labors which he is about to undertake in the work of the Redemption. The time of his suffering has come and I am about to open the stores of wisdom and goodness in order to enrich men by my treasures. Through their Redeemer and Teacher, I wish to free them from the slavery of sin and of the devil. I desire to pour out the abundance of my grace upon the hearts of all the mortals who prepare themselves to know my Incarnate Son and to follow him as their head and guide upon the way of eternal salvation. I wish to rise from the dust and enrich the poor, cast down the proud, exalt the humble and enlighten the blind in the darkness of death [Is: 9, 2]. I wish to set up my friends and chosen ones and make known the greatness of my name. In the execution of this, my holy and eternal will, I wish that you, my cherished and chosen one, cooperate with my Son. Accompany him, follow and imitate him, and I will be with you in all that you shall do."

I humbly replied, "Supreme, King of the universe, from whom all creatures receive their being and preservation, although I am lower than dust and ashes, accept, oh most high Lord and God, the heart of your handmaid, which is prepared to sacrifice itself for the accomplishment of your pleasure. Fulfill in me entirely your will. I desire oh, Almighty God, if it is possible, to suffer and to die either with or instead of our most holy Son. Our Son is sinless, as well as by nature, as also by the prerogatives of the Divinity. Would it not be better that you Strike me with your sword of justice since I am closer to guilt? Is it not true that any of the acts of your Onlybegotten Son is abundantly sufficient for the Redemption, since he has already done so much for man? If it is not possible for me to die in order to save his priceless life, grant that I may pour out my life with his. However, in all of this, I submit to your will just as I am ready to obey you in following him and in sharing his labors. Please assist me with the power of your right hand, in order that I may hasten to imitate him and fulfill your pleasure and my own longings."

Having stated these sentiments, I issued forth from my vision and the Most High again commanded my angels to assist and serve me in what I was to do. It would have been sweet for me to suffer and die instead of my Son; however, God denied me that privilege, and it caused me far greater pain.

On the final leg of his journey home with his newly acquired followers, my Son began to instill in them the truths and mysteries relating to his divinity and humanity. In order for him to make himself known as the Messiah and the Redeemer of the World, who had descended from the bosom of his eternal Father to assume human flesh, it was urgently necessary to explain to them the manner of his incarnation in my blessed womb. Jesus told them the details of his holy birth. It was important that his disciples know and venerate me as a true mother and virgin together with that which relates to the hypostatic union and the Redemption. My Son inspired his disciples to regard me with the utmost reverence and love before they had ever seen me. Although all of them were divinely enlightened, it was John, who was to distinguish himself in his love for me before all the rest. From Jesus' very first words, John grew in loving esteem of my virgin holiness. The Lord selected John from the beginning, because of his chastity, love, and humility, and prepared him for greater privileges in my service. It was his simplicity of heart and purity of soul that endeared John to both my Son and me.

The new followers of my Son begged him to grant them the consolation of seeing and reverencing me. In accordance with their petition, he journeyed directly to Nazareth continuing to preach and teach publicly on the way proclaiming himself as the Master of Truth and Eternal Life. Many carried away by the force of his doctrines, and by the light and grace overflowing into their hearts began to follow him. At this time, Jesus did not perform any outward miracles, however, as he entered Galilee, he began to preach, "This is the time of fulfillment. The kingdom of God is at hand. Repent, and believe in the gospel [Mark: 2, 14-15]."

When my Son approached the house, I waited and as he entered the door, I prostrated myself on the floor adoring him, kissed his hands and feet, and asked for his blessing. My Son gave me his blessing and I gave praise of the most holy Trinity and of my Son's humanity in the most exalted and wonderful words. This I did to show his followers the honor and adoration due to him as the true God-man. I also wished to make a return for the praise he had heaped upon me in the eyes of his disciples. In addition, I wished to instruct them to the worship due to their divine master.

The profound humility and worship with which I received their master filled the disciples with new devotion and reverential awe for my divine Son. Thereafter I always served them as an example and model of true devotion, entering at once into my office as instructress and spiritual mother of the disciples of my Son by showing them how to converse with their God and Redeemer. They were drawn to me as their Queen and cast themselves on their knees before me and asked me to receive them as my sons and servants. The first to do so was John, who from that time on was distinguished in exalting and reverencing me more than all the Apostles did. I, on my part, received John with an especial love, for besides his excelling in virginal chastity; he was of a perfect, meek, and humble disposition.

I received them respectfully as our guests, serving them their meals and combined my solicitude as a mother, but with the majesty of their Queen. I served my Son on my knees. I began at once instructing the Apostles in the majesty of their Teacher and Redeemer, and of the great doctrines of the Christian faith. Later that night, after the Apostles had retired, my Son came to me as he was inclined to do, and I placed myself at his feet and humbled myself, as I had done so many times in the years gone by. My Lord lifted me up from the floor and spoke to me the words of life and eternal salvation, yet quietly and serenely. At this time he began to treat me with even greater reserve in order to afford me a chance to merit, as I mentioned before when he had departed for the desert.

I now asked Jesus for the same baptism as given by John, which he agreed to do, as he had promised before. God sent an innumerable host of angelic spirits from heaven in visible forms to add dignity to the ceremony worthy of my Son and I. Attended by the disciples, my Son baptized me with the waters of repentance, as he had been baptized by John, so that I could emulate him in all things. I heard the voice of the eternal Father saying, "This is my beloved daughter, in whom I take delight."

The Incarnate Word said, "This is my mother, much beloved, whom I have chosen and who will assist me in my works."

The Holy Ghost added, "This is my spouse, chosen from among thousands."

At this time, I felt and received such great and numerous effects of grace in my soul that no human words can describe them. God exalted me to new heights of grace and he made my holy soul more resplendent with new and exquisite beauty of heaven. I merited especial graces because of the humility with which I submitted to this baptism of repentance. By it, I accumulated blessings like to those of my divine Son, with only the difference that I received an increase of grace, which was not possible in my Son, since he was already perfect. I broke out into a canticle of praise in harmony with my angels, prostrated myself before my divine Son, and thanked him for the most efficacious graces I had received in this baptism.

The very next day, we packed our few belongings and moved to Capernaum. The fishing village stood on the northwestern shore of the Sea of Galilee near the territory of Zebulon and Nephtali. I loved the beautiful lake and the cooling off shore breezes that we often received from the lake.

Jesus had returned to Galilee in the power of the spirit. The next day, accompanied by his new followers, my Lord set out and began his evangelizing. He preached in Capernaum and the Jews were swept up into a religious frenzy with his words. News of him spread throughout the entire region, and he was welcomed wherever he went. He taught in the synagogues and he and his disciples were praised by all. Several months later, he was invited to speak at the synagogue in Nazareth where he had grown up. We went to the synagogue on the Sabbath day. Jesus stood up to read, and was handed a scroll of the prophet Isaiah. He unrolled the scroll and found the passage where it was written:

> **"The spirit of the Lord is upon me, because he has anointed me to bring glad tidings to the poor. He has sent me to proclaim liberty to captives and recovery of sight to the blind to let the oppressed go free and to proclaim a year acceptable to the Lord,"**

Rolling up the scroll, he handed it back to the hazzan and sat down. All eyes were on him and he said to them. "Today this scripture passage is fulfilled in your hearing."

The people were impressed and spoke highly of him. They were amazed at his gracious words and they asked him, "Aren't you the son of Joseph?"

Jesus said to them, "Surely you will quote me this proverb. "Physician cure yourself," and say, 'Do here in your native place the things that we have heard were done in Capernaum.' "Amen, I say to you, no prophet is accepted in his own native place. Indeed I tell you, there were many widows in Israel in the days of Elijah when the sky was closed for three and a half years and a severe famine spread over the entire land. Elijah was not sent, to any of these but only to a widow in Zarephath in the land of Sidon. Again, there were many lepers in Israel during the time of Elijah the prophet; yet only Naaman the Syrian was cleansed."

The people were filled with fury when Jesus said this; they rose up and drove him out of town to the brow of hill on which their town was built. They intended to hurl him down headlong, but my son clouded their minds, and he passed through them unscathed. My heart was broken when my old neighbors treated my Son and God so shabbily. I rejoined Jesus and we returned to Capernaum [Luke: 4, 14-30].

I joined him with my prayers from my little home, and while he did not openly perform any public cures, many hidden miracles took place. A short time after they left, I received a wedding invitation from one of Joseph's relatives. The bride was originally from Bethlehem, but now lived in Cana with her father who was a wealthy merchant. The name of the prosperous groom was Nathanael. He was the son of the daughter of Sobe, Anne's sister, and now lived in Capernaum. The news of the coming of the Redeemer into the world and of his already having a following of disciples had spread throughout Galilee and Judea. My Son secretly ordained that he and his followers be invited to the wedding feast, for he intended to begin his public ministry by sanctifying the institution of marriage. He also desired to strengthen and unite his new disciples by performing his first public miracle with them present. I sent a message and accepted their invitation.

When Jesus entered the house, he said, to the bride' father "The peace of the Lord and his light be with you." Our host made Jesus and I, and his disciples welcome. The bride's mother invited Jesus and his followers to stay in their large home. My Son gratefully accepted her invitation and he promised to help with some of the arrangements. Jesus, during the wedding celebration, wished to combine spiritual instructions with the various entertainments. Before the wedding, my Son began to exhort and instruct Nathanael concerning the perfection and holiness of his new state of life. I, in turn, withdrew with the bride and instructed her in a similar manner, admonishing her sweetly, but with the most powerful of words concerning her obligations. My Son and I were both pleased, for afterwards, the marriage couple fulfilled most perfectly the duties of their state, into which they were ushered and for which they had been strengthened by my Son and I, the Sovereigns of Heaven and Earth.

My Son had come not to disapprove of marriage, but in order to establish it anew and give it credit, sanctifying and consecrating it a Sacrament by his presence. Jesus prayed to his eternal Father to pour his blessings upon the institution of marriage for the propagation of the human race in the new Law, and to vest this state with sacramental power to sanctity all those who would receive it worthily in his holy Church. Jesus organized games for the men and presided in the distribution of prizes of various fruits. Each time he spoke to the winners, he had a word of spiritual advice that made a deep impression on them all. The women likewise joined in the games in another part of the field separate from the men.

The night before, Jesus spoke to over one hundred of the guests in the local synagogue. He spoke to them of the pleasures, which were permissible and of the caution and restraint that must accompany them. Then he spoke of the mutual obligations of a married couple, and spoke of continence and chastity and of the spirituality of marriage. After the ceremony, and after the guests had left, Jesus again gave the two of them some private instructions. From there, we all attended a banquet given by the father of the bride and after the meal, there was a dance. The young danced for her husband, and some of the lady guests joined her. The future Apostles and the married women did not participate. The atmosphere was one of restrained gaiety and good fellowship.

The next day on Wednesday, which was the middle of the month, the wedding took place. The dress and gown of the bride was reminiscent of my own wedding. The bride wore a beautiful crown heavily encrusted with jewels, which reminded me of my own crown which had been exquisite in its simplicity. We processed from the bride's home in a colorful parade of well-wishers, accompanied by young children carrying floral wreaths and musicians playing various musical instruments. The priests performed the ceremony at the entrance to the synagogue. My Son had already blessed the rings and I now presented them to the bride and groom, who exchanged rings. The chief priest lightly cut the pair's ring fingers and let two drops of blood from the groom's finger, and one drop from the bride's finger, flow into a cup filled with wine. The bride and groom each drank from the cup. The family then destroyed the cup. After the ceremony, clothes and food was distributed to the poor who had come to witness the ceremony after which the married couple returned to their home where a festival hall had been prepared.

My Son welcomed them and said to them and all the guests, "The peace of the Lord and his Light be with you." Jesus then organized another game for the men, in which he placed flowers and plants and fruits around a large table. He placed a pointer that rotated when spun by one of the young men and it would stop before one of the prizes. In this game, my Son left nothing to chance. Each prize had a definite purpose related to the character of the person spinning the pointer. Jesus presented each winner with his prize. Then he made a short and profound comment. The person Jesus spoke to was the only one able to understand his words. My Son had looked into their most secret thoughts and addressed their needs, and each individual was deeply moved.

The bridegroom won an exotic fruit and Jesus spoke about marriage, chastity, and the hundredfold fruit that purity produces. The experience moved the groom to the innermost depths of his soul. His Lord and Master presented him with his prize, and he was shook spiritually, and interiorly underwent a mystical transformation in which he was supernaturally purified from the common lusts of the flesh. At the same moment, the bride who was sitting among a group of women had a fainting spell, and had a similar experience. I held her in my arms and when she revived, the bride and groom seemed spiritually rejuvenated. The disciples, who were also playing the game with Jesus, after having eaten of the fruit, felt their predominant passions awake and a struggle for control of their passions ensued. They each resisted and conquered it and were thereby strengthened against future temptations.

After the games the guests retired to the banquet hall and the women were seated separate from the men. The groom led Jesus to the seat of honor at the head table. Then the groom, along with several of his servants, served the men, and his bride and her servants served the women. When the groom presented Jesus with the carving knife, my Son said to him, "Nathanael, I remind you of my banquet when we were children, and I predicted that I would attend your wedding."

The young man was amazed, as he remembered the incident. While he carved the meat, Jesus told the guests the story of a lamb, which, when it became separated from the flock, was slaughtered. He stated, "The flesh in being cooked was purified by fire. The carving of the parts" he added, "symbolizes the way in which my disciples have to leave behind the persons and things to which they have become attached by bonds of flesh and blood." He stated firmly, "I tell you, those who wish to follow me will have to leave their homes and families and put their passions to death. For only then can you become, through the Lamb of God, a source of spiritual food by which you can unite your fellow men with one another and with your Father in heaven."

Throughout the celebration Jesus and I spoke and conversed with the various guests, but always with the wisdom and gravity worthy of our station and with the view of enlightening the hearts of all those present. My Son and I were good listeners and responded graciously to questions asked us, but in keeping with my position as helper to Jesus, I did not interrupt the doings and sayings of my Son. I always tried to furnish an exquisite example of retirement and modesty not only for the religious, but especially for women in the secular state. In women the most precious adornment and the most charming beauty is silence, restraint and modesty, by which many vices are shut out, and by which all the virtues of a chaste and respectable woman receive their crowning glories.

During the feast, we both ate some of the food, so as not to offend our hosts, but with the greatest moderation, yet without showing outwardly the strict abstinence that we both adhered to. It was during the middle of the feast that the bride's mother confided in me that they had just ran out of wine, and she tearfully appealed to me asking what they should do. God had filled me with wisdom and knowledge concerning the works of the Redemption. Consequently, I was well informed at what time and on what occasions the Lord was to perform them. Thus, I was fully aware of the proper moment for the beginning of this public manifestation of Christ's power.

This incident had happened by divine arrangement in order to give occasion to my Son's first public miracle. Knowing this, I went to my Son and said, "They have no wine."

In keeping with Jesus treating me with more reserve, he addressed me as woman and replied, "Woman, what is this to me and to you? My hour is not yet come."

This answer, I knew, was not intended as a reproach, but contained a mystery, for I had not asked for a miracle by mere accident, but by divine light. I knew that the opportune time for the manifestation of the divine power of Jesus was at hand. The mystery hidden in his answer was to confirm the disciples in their belief of his Divinity and to show himself to all as the true God. He was saying publicly that he had not received the power to commit miracles from me his earthly mother, but instead from his heavenly Father, but requested through me as God's instrument at the opportune and befitting time. Hence Jesus infused into the minds of the Apostles a new light by which they understood the hypostatic union of his two natures, and the derivation of the human nature from me and of the divine by generation from his eternal Father.

Knowing his divine will, I said to the servants with quiet modesty, "Do whatsoever he shall say to you," and I returned to my place among the women.

Without further hesitation, my Son commanded, "Fill the empty wine jars with water." The servants complied and turned to Jesus expectantly. He blessed the jars and then stated, "Now draw off some and take it to the chief steward."

The steward was at the head of the table, a priest of the Law and he knew nothing of what had transpired at the foot of the table where Jesus sat. He tasted of the water and called out to the bridegroom in surprise saying, "Every man at first sits forth the good wine, and when all have drunk well, he serves that which is inferior, but you have kept the good wine until now." Few of the guests realized what had happened, but before the evening was over, everyone knew and everyone was awe stricken.

My Son never sought places of honor wherever he went. He practiced the doctrine which he was afterwards to teach everyone; namely, that when invited to a feast we should not seek to occupy the better places, but be satisfied with the lowest. Jesus revealed his dignity as the Redeemer when he changed the water into wine, and confirmed the disciple's faith in him. Many of those present believed that he was the true Messiah, and they followed him to the city of Capernaum. In Egypt and Judea, Jesus had wrought his miracles in secret; he now began to preach openly, declaring himself the Teacher of men. To all of these miracles, I responded with heroic acts of virtue in praise and thanksgiving to the Most High, so that his Holy name was gloriously manifested. With my heart burning, I cried to the eternal Father, asking him to dispose the hearts and souls of men for the enlightening words of the Incarnate Word and drive from them the darkness of their ignorance.

After the banquet Nathanael came to my Son and said to him, "My dear cousin, after your instructions, I feel myself dead to all carnal desires. If my bride consents I would live with her in abstinence."

A short time later the bride came to him and announced her same intentions. After a discussion with her husband, the bride and groom again came to Jesus and stated they had decided to abstain and live together as brother and sister for three years. Then they knelt before Jesus and he gladly gave them his blessing. My son often preached celibacy, and of course we both lived celibate lives. Today priests emulate Jesus and nuns offer themselves as celibate brides of Christ

From this point in time, I began to accompany my Son on most of his tours of preaching and of teaching, which I would continue to do to the very foot of the Cross. I was to be separated from him only a few times. He did absent himself from me on Mount Tabor [Matt: 17, 1-8], and when he was with the Samaritan woman [John: 4, 7-26]. I myself remained behind with certain persons to instruct and catechize them. Each time I returned to my Lord and Master proceeding on foot, just as did my divine Son and his followers. When he was fatigued, I was even more fatigued, for we all suffered arduous journeys in all sorts of weather. Sometimes my Son was constrained to relieve my weariness miraculously. At times, he even commanded me to rest myself for a few days, and at other times he gave me such a lightness of body, that I could move about without difficulty as if I were on wings.

I had the entire doctrine of the Evangelical Law written in my heart. Nevertheless, I was as solicitous and attentive as a new disciple to the preaching and doctrine of my divine Son. I instructed my angels to report to me, if necessary, his sermons whenever I was absent. I always listened to the sermons of Jesus on my knees, so that with the utmost of my powers I could show the reverence and worship due to his person and doctrine. I was aware of the interior operations of the soul of my Son, and of his continual prayers to the eternal Father for the proper disposition of the hearts of his followers, and for the growth of the seed of his doctrine into eternal life. I joined Jesus in his petitions and prayers, and securing for them the blessings of my most ardent and tearful charity. By my attention and reverence I taught and moved others to appreciate duly the teaching and instructions of the Savior of the world. I also knew the interior of those that listened to the preaching of the Lord. I knew their state of grace or sin, their vices and virtues and the capacity of men, which caused in me many wonderful effects of highest charity and other virtues. It inflamed me with zeal for the honor of Jesus. The threat that the fruits of the Redemption be lost to the souls, and the loss to the souls through sin moved me to exert myself in the most fervent prayer for their welfare. The fact that all God's creatures would not know, adore, and serve him, pierced my heart with cruel sorrow. My sorrow was in direct proportion to the unequaled knowledge and understanding I had of all these mysteries. I suffered with ineffable grief, and often shed tears of blood for those who would not allow the divine grace and virtue of the Lord to enter their souls. My suffering exceeds that beyond all measure the pains endured by all the martyrs of the world.

I treated all the followers of the Savior with incomparable prudence and wisdom, especially those whom I held in such high veneration and esteem such as the Apostles and the Disciples of Christ. As a mother, I took care of them all, and as a queen, I obtained the necessities for their bodily nourishment and comforts. Sometimes when I had no other resources, I commanded my holy angels to bring provisions for them and the women in our company. In order to assist them toward advancing in the spiritual life, I labored beyond the possibility of human understanding, not only by my continual and fervent prayers for them but by my example and my counsels. With my prayers, I nourished and strengthened them as a most prudent mother and teacher. Later, doubts, and secret temptations frequently assailed the Apostles and disciples. When this happened, I hastened to their assistance in order to enlighten and encourage them. By the power of God, they were enlightened by my wisdom, chastened by my humility, quieted by my modesty, and enriched by all the blessings that flowed from me, for I was a storehouse of gifts from the Holy Spirit.

From the very beginning some of the women from Galilee followed my Son on his journeys. Some of them had been cured of demonical possession and of other infirmities and accompanied and served Jesus, as did I. The, Divine Wisdom so ordered it, because of his desire to provide proper companions for me. I took special interest in these pious and holy women, and gathered them about me and taught and catechized them. In order to conceal my own vast knowledge, I usually used my Son's public teachings as a text for my instructions. Not all of the women followed my Son, but through my efforts, all of them received sufficient knowledge of the sacred mysteries to their conversion. I also taught them to practice the most ardent charity by visiting the sick in the infirmaries, the poor, and the imprisoned and afflicted. As an example, I nursed with my own hands the wounded, consoled the sorrowful, and gave aid to those in necessity. I was ever in dread of losing my humility, but the more I did the more praise I received and this I shunned more than a person shunning the touch of a leper. For example, when the Jews laid the healing of the deaf mute to the devil, a woman exclaimed, "Blessed is the womb that bore you and the peps that gave you suck."

When I heard these words of praise, I mentally begged my son to divert this praise from me. My Son acceded to my request in such a way, that he turned these words into a still greater, yet, at that time, a hidden praise. For the Lord answered, "Rather, blessed are they who hear the word of God and keep it [Luke: 11, 27-28]. By these words he neutralized the praise given to me as mother, but enhanced it in application to me as a saint; directing the attention of his hearers to the essential of all virtue, in which I was distinguished above all others, and most wonderful, though at the same time none of his hearer's attention was directed to this hidden signification. Again, when someone interrupted my Son with the message that his cousins and I had arrived, I was afraid that the multitude might shift their attention to me, and I asked him mentally to prevent such an outbreak.

He yielded and said, "My mother and my brethren are they who hear the word of God and act on it [Luke: 8, 21]." By these words, he did not deprive me of the honor due to me because of my holiness, but diverted the attention of the bystanders from me. On my part, I gained the object of seeing Jesus alone praised and acknowledged for his works. These events were quite common, for I often sought out my Son to beg favors of him regarding the conversion or cure of the sick or afflicted.

I did not practice humility just for myself, for I was a fervent teacher of humility for the Apostles and the disciples. This was necessary so that they would be well founded and rooted in this virtue in order to receive the gifts and to work the wonders, not only later on in the foundation of the Church, but even now, in the first beginnings of their duties as preachers of the word [Mark: 3, 14]. Jesus was to send before him these same Apostles and disciples, and he gave them power to expel demons from the possessed, cure the sick, and raise the dead. As Mistress of the humble, I counseled and exhorted them with the words of eternal life, and how they were to govern themselves in performing these miracles. By my teaching and intercession the spirit of wisdom and humility was deeply planted into their hearts, *so that they well understood how entirely these miracles are wrought by divine power and that all the glory of these works belonged to the Lord Jesus alone.*

The Scriptures mention only a select few of the miracles of my Son; it would take volumes to list them all; and that was not the intent of the Gospels. In addition to my Sons many cures, I also, by the power of God, brought about many miraculous conversions. I cured the blind, healed the sick and on some occasions I even called the dead back to life. These miracles were all hidden, in order that Jesus, in the eye of the public, remained the figure of power and miracles that he is. This was proper for many reasons. On the one hand, I was the Assistant in the principal work for which the Incarnate Word came into the world, namely in my Son's preaching and Redemption. On the other hand, as his mother, I was to resemble my Son in the working of miracles, increasing the glory of us both. In this way I accredited the dignity and doctrine of my Son and eminently and most efficaciously assisted my Son in his ministry. That these miracles should remain concealed was due both to the disposition of divine Providence and to my own earnest request. I performed all my miracles in secrecy. I had wrought the secret miracles in the name of the Redeemer, and thus he received all the glory.

Teaching in public, or at any prearranged time, was not incumbent upon women, therefore I refrained from doing so, leaving such things to the duly appointed teachers and ministers of the divine word. I contented myself with the assistance I could render by private instruction and conversation. In so doing, and with my added prayers, I secured more conversions than all the preachers of the world accomplished together. This will be better understood if you remember that besides the heavenly influence of my words that I also possessed a most intimate knowledge of the nature, disposition, inclinations and bad habits of all persons. I also knew the time and occasion best suited to bring all to the way of eternal life. To this was added the efficacy of my most fervent prayers. I rescued innumerable souls drawing them on and enlightening them. God denied none of my petitions and my results were exceedingly great. In all my actions, I preserved the quiet high-mindedness of a queen. Yet, at the same time, in imitation of Jesus, I joined with it a perfection of humility and sweetness. My Son and I treated all with great kindness and fullness of charity. We ate, spoke and conversed with the disciples and with the women that followed the Savior; observing all due moderation and reserve, so that no one found it strange, or doubted that the Savior was a true man, and my own natural and legitimate Son.

The principal lesson to be learned from my life is the profound humility that I was able to maintain throughout my life. Please remember that in being among the blessed in heaven, it is impossible for me to lie, or to be guilty of pride. Therefore, to properly instruct you, it is necessary for me to extol my own virtues, which I do only because it is the will of Almighty God. Neither angels nor men can understand my virtues in all their perfection. Because of my humility the Almighty looked upon me with pleasure and consequently all the nations have called me blessed [Luke: 1, 48]. In all my life, I never lost a single chance, occasion, time or place, for practicing all the acts of virtue possible, and none of my actions or virtues were ever found wanting in the least point of humility. This virtue raised me above all that was not God. Just as by humility I conquered all creatures, so, *in a certain sense,* by this same virtue I also overcame God himself. God never denied me any grace, either for myself or for others, because I was always so willing to please him. In my own home, I had won over my mother Anne and her servants to permit me to practice humility. Likewise in the temple, my companions had at last yielded to my self-abasement, and in matrimony, Joseph allowed me to perform the humblest services, although I was the Mother of God.

I alone, not having the touch of angels, gave way to my desire for lowly occupations, and the Apostles and Evangelists in turn respected my wishes and did not proclaim my praises to the world. By my humility, I was able to move the Father and the Holy Spirit, and even my most holy Son, to ordain that my dignity should remain concealed to the world. Jesus ordained that humankind would not praise me for Adam's guilt, nor was I to experience any of its foul and dangerous consequences. I alone fully understood the full extent of the position occupied by a mere creature. Consequently, I humiliated myself more than all the children of Adam did. Other persons, if they became humble, were first humiliated and had to confess, "Before I was humbled, I offended," or, "It is good for me that you have humbled me that I may learn your justification." However, guilt or passion had never degraded me, and therefore, I did not enter my humility by being humbled. The angels cannot be properly compared with men, being of a superior hierarchy and nature and free from passions or guilt or sin. Yet, these sovereign spirits could not attain the humility that I attained, although they did humble themselves before their Creator as his creatures. The angels could not use their higher spiritual nature to serve as a reason for abasing themselves as much as I was able. I also possessed the dignity of being the Mother of God and the Mistress of the angels and of all creation, and none of them could claim such a dignity and excellence which enhanced any act of humiliation on my part and made my humility surpass all perfection of this virtue ever attained by any other created being.

With knowledge comes wisdom. God's gift of this wisdom makes me not only understand but forces me to acknowledge the infinite greatness of our Creator, and to acknowledge how truly insignificant that I am as a human being when compared to such glory. Humility is an easy virtue when one can truly comprehend the mysteries of the infinite. If I did not abase myself, having been granted the gift of such wisdom, I would be the epitome of arrogance. Neither the knowledge that I am the Mother of God, nor the consideration of all the wonders that I wrought, or that were wrought by my divine Son, nor my position as the Keeper and Dispenser of all the divine treasures, as the most immaculate among all creatures and as the most powerful and most favored of all God's creatures, could ever cause my heart to forsake the place I have chosen in estimating myself the lowest of all the handiwork of the Most High.

With all my humility; however, I was never slow or ungrateful in the acknowledgment of all the favors lavished upon me. I rendered worthy thanks to the eternal Father for each one of them and thus filled the great void of ingratitude of the human race. I always sought to divert any attention or honors attributed to me by his followers.

I taught them that they themselves were merely the instruments that just as the brush does not deserve the glory attached to works of art, nor the sword that of victory, so that the honor and praise due their miracles belonged to the Lord and Master in whose name they performed them. The Holy Gospels do not mention the instructions I gave to the Apostles, which I believe is worthy to note. This fact was intentionally left out by those writing the Gospels, since it pertained to me and not to my Son. The Gospels were Jesus' message to the world; they were not about me. I made sure that the Gospel authors wrote only what was necessary about me. After Jesus sent the disciples out to preach and heal in his name, they returned full of exultation, because, in Jesus' name, the demons had been subject to them {Luke: 10, 17]. Jesus had to remind them that he had given them this power and that they should not be elated except in having their names recorded in heaven. So feeble was their humility that my Son was obliged to apply such corrections and antidotes in order to preserve it in his own disciples.

Afterwards, in order so that they might be worthy founders of the holy Church, the science of humility taught them by the Lord and I was still necessary. For then, they were to perform still greater miracles in the name of Christ and in confirmation of their faith and of their evangelical preaching.

The heathens, being accustomed blindly to give divine honors to anything great or strange, and seeing these miracles wrought by the Apostles, were only too ready to adore them as gods. In later years when the people saw Paul and Barnabas cure the man in Lycaonia who had been crippled from birth [Acts: 14, 9]; the people proclaimed the one Mercury and the other as Jupiter. Later, Paul survived the bite of a viper, while all the others bitten had died. Again, the people worshiped him as a god. In the fullness of my knowledge, I foresaw all of these miraculous events, as Jesus' assistant in the establishment of the law and grace. During the time of my Son's preaching, which was destined to last three years, Jesus celebrated the Pasch three times, and I accompanied him each time. I always conducted myself with heroic acts of virtue according to my condition and circumstances, and I regulated myself with sublime perfection, especially regarding the practice of my most ardent charity, which I derived from the Lord himself. Since I lived only in God and God in me, the charity of Jesus burned in my bosom and left me to seek the good of my fellow men with all the powers of my body and soul.

The miracles of Jesus and John the Baptist, and the beheading of John by Herod

My Son and I, with his new disciples, journeyed to Jerusalem and we traveled about in Judea for a short time and pursued the work of preaching and performing miracles. Jesus revisited Aenon, where John the Baptist had last baptized on the banks of the Jordan near the city of Salem. John had continued to baptize with water for repentance of sins, and proclaimed the coming of the Messiah until he was arrested, which was in fulfillment of John's own words that Christ must grow, while he must be diminished [John: 3, 22-30]. However, Jesus knew he had too many enemies in Judea to remain for long.

I was present in spirit in the baptisms by Jesus' disciples and I beheld all the great results of this regeneration in the favored souls. I felt as though I myself was receiving the benefits of the baptism. I was filled with gratitude, and. I gave thanks for them. I broke forth in canticles of praise and exercised heroic virtues as a thank-offering to the Author of them. Thus in these wonderful activities I gained for myself incomparable and unheard of merits.

We returned to Jerusalem, and for a few days I stayed with Mary, the mother of Mark, who was one of Jesus' new disciples. Then Jesus received a message from Lazarus, who lived nearby in Bethany. His sister, Mary the Silent, was gravely ill. She had always been absent in spirit, but I knew that in the silence of her own little world, she was very close and dear to her Creator. When Jesus was present, she recognized in him his gentleness and divinity, and she always came to him in her shy and silent manner and he often held her in his arms for extended lengths of time. Lazarus, and Martha his sister, had always treated her with the greatest solicitude and care in her infirmity. She was a fortunate, happily protected child of God.

Having anticipated our arrival, Lazarus came from his home in Bethany to meet us and embraced Jesus warmly. Lazarus was very upset over the illness of his sister, and the family had gathered at her side. He said to Jesus, "Master, would it be possible for you to heal her? She has led such a tragic life and now she is dying."

My Son replied, "It is not for me to interfere with God's plans for her, Lazarus. You are a very wealthy man and God has tested you and Martha with the malady of your sister. My Father is pleased with your compassion for her and for the sick and the poor. Mary will soon be called to the Bosom of Abraham, for her pilgrimage is soon to end."

Lazarus hung his head sadly and replied, "So be it, God's will be done."

Enroute, Lazarus spoke to Jesus of his concern for the soul of his youngest sister, Mary Magdalene, who was living a dissolute life. She had come to be with her dying sister. "Would you talk to her, Master? I am sure she will listen to you, but she has shunned all advice from Martha and me." With

Jesus' assurances in his ears, Lazarus made our entire group welcome, for there were many rooms at his large estate.

Jesus, after a warm greeting, asked Martha to take him to Mary the Silent. When he entered the room, she looked up. Seeing Jesus, she pushed away the protective hands of her nurses, rose to her feet, and walked to greet her Savior. She dropped to her knees at his feet, saying, "My Lord and my God." Jesus raised her to her feet, embraced her, and led her into the adjoining garden where he told her of his coming Passion. She now had the perfect use of her senses and knew that Jesus was to suffer frightfully. She was grief-stricken and our world, so new to her, seemed oppressive and filled with the ingratitude of men, which she foresaw in the prophecy of Jesus' sufferings. She was the tallest of the sisters and extraordinarily beautiful in an ethereal way. From her confinement, she was quite pale, but there was a special aura of light about her. Her hands, long and tapering, seemed to be made of exquisitely carved ivory. Afterwards, my Son led her back to her couch. There he blessed her and when he left, he kissed her on the forehead. As he departed, she rose and stood there like a finely carved statue mutely observing his departure, her heart-filled eyes brimmed over and spilled down her beautiful cheeks.

She was lying on her bed when I came in to see her. She held out her arms, for she recognized me as her spiritual mother. She was more lucid than I had ever seen her before. I realized that because she had suffered so much on earth, it was ordained that she should know who Jesus truly was, and how much he was to suffer for her and all men before he accomplished his Father's will. Mary had great compassion for Jesus' sufferings, and he allowed her to suffer for him, and she was soon to die.

Mary Magdalene was also present due to her sister's frail health. Her parent had also named her Mary, which was a common event in Israel. Mary; however, was living a very loose and immoral life in her estate in Magdalan, which I knew to be true because of my gift of intuition. She was perhaps the most beautiful woman that I had ever seen. Magdalene was slim and beautifully proportioned. God had graced her with a beautiful head of black hair and blessed her with fine, delicate, olive-toned features. There was a restless untapped energy in her that seemed to spill over into anything, which she ventured to do. Mary was exceptionally intelligent, gifted with grace, poise, and the ability to command and dominate an audience. However, much of her energy was directed inward, for she was a spoiled, self-indulgent person preoccupied only with her own selfish and often lustful pursuits.

However, quite out of character, she became quite reserved when she came into the presence of the Son of God. We had not seen her since she had moved to one of their huge estates at Magdalan with her own servants. Mary Magdalene appeared embarrassed and ill at ease but rather defiant in the presence of her Lord. Present at the dinner that night were many of our friends from Jerusalem. Veronica and her son were present as well as Susanna. John Marc, Simeon's sons, Joseph of Arimathea's nephews, and members of Nicodemus' and Joseph's family were also present, as well as some of John's disciples. Simon the Pharisee, a close friend of Lazarus was also there, and I knew that while he was not a bad person, he was still wavering in his beliefs. At dinner, Jesus spoke to them of the Kingdom of God, of his pending disciple's call, and even hinted at his own Passion.

That evening Jesus spoke to a large group of people who had assembled when the news of his approach had preceded him. Magdalene, subdued in Jesus presence, had turned down her brother's invitation for her to come and hear Jesus speak and remained in her room. However, when my Son spoke to huge crowds, every person distinctly heard his every word, even those on the fringes of the crowd. I knew that Magdalene, in spite of her seclusion in her private quarters, heard each word spoken by my Son. Later, drawn by my Son's words, I saw her hovering in the back of the crowd and I saw her humbly sink to her knees, for Jesus was speaking of sin, of life and death, and its just rewards and punishments.

Our Redeemer said, "Many of you have gathered here hoping to see miracles performed and you shall. You will be present when the soul of Mary, called the Silent, leaves her body this very night, for my Father is calling her home. To many of you Mary is a retarded and burdensome person; however, to her family and to my Father, she is a precious jewel and her reward in heaven was established the moment she was born without her full faculties. You have seen Mary go about for the past thirty years with her head raised to the heavens. You heard her speaking of heavenly things and you all presumed her mad. Be advised that her soul is not here in this world, but is in a different world where she sees and converses with heavenly creatures, for she was born without original sin. She has no understanding of this world, only of the next. She is totally happy and she knows no sin. When my mission is completed upon this earth, Mary will be taken by the angels into a special home in heaven that I will prepare for her."

Then Jesus began to speak of sin and its harm to the soul. He spoke of forgiveness and his intentions of removing the sins of the world, but he did not tell them how he intended to do so. That night Mary died perfectly lucid in the arms of her Savior. My Son and I witnessed the angels who came and carried her precious soul to limbo to be with the Patriarchs and the faithful departed until after my Son's Passion and Death. Her spirit was glorious to behold and she swooped down and prostrated herself at my Son's feet before the angels carried her off to her place of rest. Soothed by the words of my Son, the family of Lazarus was consoled in their grief, for their love for their sister knew no limits in spite of her condition.

Mary Magdalene was deeply moved by her sister's death. The words of my Son had greatly influenced her, and Jesus had removed seven demons from her soul when she came to him after Mary's funeral and fell sobbing at his feet. Jesus held her in his arms and her tears washed away the sins of her misspent life. She had wasted all her energy and enthusiasm over the years in vain pursuits. Mary now directed all her vigor and resourcefulness in pleasing her Lord and God. She became Jesus' most dedicated follower, and she and I become closer than the most devoted of mothers and daughters.

A month later, those of us who had purified ourselves from having handled a dead person accompanied Jesus when he returned to his Father's House in Jerusalem. There was a small group of disciples and ten women including me. My Son was terribly upset when he found ringed around the Court of the Suppliants, dealers engaged in the selling of herbs, birds and all kinds of eatables. However, in a kindly and friendly manner, he called their attention to the error of their ways, and instructed them to take their wares to the Court of the Gentiles where such merchandise was sold and did not desecrate the holy temple. Some of the merchants grumbled. However, when my Son and his disciples helped them, they made the move in a peaceable manner. The actions of my Son amazed the guards and the Pharisees. However, they were afraid to interfere, since the people applauded his actions.

At this time of my life, in God's eyes, which I will obediently describe at his request, I looked to be about thirty-three, was taller than most of my contemporaries and delicate, but firmly built. My face was slim and well molded, and my eyes were quite large, but true to my calling, I kept them downcast. In heavenly beauty, I stood out from amongst the other women although some of them were quite beautiful. As God had intended, I outshone them all because of my simplicity, modesty, sincerity, kindness and gentleness. The purity of my body and soul reflected in a marvelous way the image of God. The only person, I truly resembled in my bearing was my divine Son. The expression of my features revealed my innocence, gravity, wisdom, peace, and holiness. My whole appearance was one of true sanctity and nobility and yet I seemed too many like just an ordinary, but beautiful woman. I was usually serious and very quiet and when I wept; my grief did not spoil the loveliness of my features, for the tears just flowed gently down my face.

Soon after, I returned alone to our home in Capernaum. A few days later Jesus came home, but only remained overnight, for the next day, he and some of his disciples set out for Tyre and Sidon. I was unable to go, for I was not alone. An aged friend of my mother came seeking my help and I took her in. She was quite old and feeble, and was unable to manage for herself. I cared for her and tended to her needs. I spent much of my time in prayer and again took up my sewing, spinning, and weaving to support the needs of our home. I did my own housework, and instructed, and encouraged the other women of our rapidly growing group. In addition, various disciples dropped in frequently with news of my Son.

Upon his return from Tyre and Sidon my Son rejoined me, for the Sabbath began that evening. We walked up the hill to the Synagogue. The structure was built of beautifully wrought black basalt, and crowned the sloping hill upon which Capernaum stood. After the readings, Jesus sat on the hand-carved, black-basalt Moses Seat to preach to the large crowd who had come to hear him speak. Among the huge throng were some of his new followers, friends and family. His teaching was novel to these people for he used many parables, only a few of which are included in the Gospels. Jesus used them frequently to get his point across to these simple people, and he had various interpretations for the same parable. The parables were short examples and similitudes, which he used to explain his doctrine in terms with which they were familiar.

My Son explained the story of Elias and the rain cloud in terms of the coming of the Messiah bringing new life to all who were willing to accept his teaching. "Whoever was thirsty," he declared, "could now drink, and whoever had prepared his field could now receive refreshing rain. Jesus' words were so impressive that they moved us all to tears.

After the sermon they followed my Son to a small vale and assembled about him and he spoke about vocations and correspondence. Andrew was enthused about Jesus and told everyone about the wonders he had seen at Jesus' baptism and the miracles he had wrought. My Son called upon heaven to witness that they should behold still greater things and for the first time he spoke to them of his mission from his heavenly Father. He explained that they would all have to forsake everything when he called them. He said, "I will provide for you and you shall suffer no want until the Passover, for now I have to attend to other matters. In the meantime continue your customary occupations, but when I call you, you must come immediately."

His new disciples had questioned him as to how they should manage about their families. Peter stated, "At present I cannot leave my old step-father." It so happened that the step-father was also Phillips uncle."

Jesus responded, "I will not need you until after the Pasch, Peter. This will give all of you ample time toward freeing yourselves from your various vocations."

A week later, Jesus and about twenty of his followers were encamped on a little hill between where the Jordan flowed into the Sea of Galilee and the fishing village of Bethsaida. Below them on the sea, fishermen were busy at work. Nathanial exclaimed, "Lord, there is Peter's large boat manned by his crew, and there he is in a smaller boat. Look, there is James, and John, and their father Zebedee. Why don't we go down and invite them to join our group?" However, Jesus told them not to do so. Puzzled, Nathanial asked him, "How can these men be down there fishing after they have seen and heard what you have done?"

Jesus answered him, "They labor because I have not yet called them. Zebedee and Peter both carry on a large business for which many depend for their subsistence. I have told them to continue it and in the meantime prepare to make themselves available for my call. Until then, I have many things to do, and I have yet to go to Jerusalem for the Pasch."

* * *

By divine permission, Lucifer and his followers arose from their ruinous defeat, which they had suffered at the triumph of Jesus in the desert. Divine Providence ordained that while Lucifer and his forces would remain ignorant of the principal mystery connected with my Son, they would nevertheless see enough to lead to their great discomfort. God allowed them to perceive the great results of the preaching, miracles, and baptisms of Jesus' disciples. The demons were dismayed at the great number of souls that were lost to them. They had recognized the same results in the efforts of John, but remained ignorant of the essential differences between Jesus and John the Baptist, but they had no doubts about the final overthrow of their dominion, if these activities should continue.

The powers of heaven exerted against him by these two preachers left him powerless to resist. Therefore, he called another meeting of the princes of darkness and said to them, "Strange things are happening, and I fear lest the divine Word has come into the world according to the promise. I have searched the entire earth and have been unable to find him. In the meantime, these two men are preaching and deprive me every day of many souls and excite within me great misgivings. I could not overcome the one in the desert, and the other vanquished all of us, leaving us disheartened and crushed. If they continue as they have begun, all our triumphs will turn to confusion. They cannot both be the Messiah, and I cannot even be sure if either one of them is he. The one called John is now in prison; I cannot believe he would allow himself to be arrested if he were the Messiah. However, to draw so many souls from a life of sin is a work not equaled by anyone to this day. It supposes a new power, which we must investigate and trace to its source; and we must destroy these two men. Follow me and assist me with all your strength, astuteness and sagacity, because otherwise they will frustrate our intentions."

The evil hordes had no knowledge of the mysteries of the divine Wisdom, and their projects and resolves were vain and without firmness. They were badly misled and confused on the one hand, by so many miracles, and on the other hand by outward appearances entirely different from those which they had attributed to the Incarnate Word at his coming into the world. Consequently, Lucifer ordered meetings of the demons in which they were to communicate with each other what they had seen and understood concerning recent events. He ordered great rewards in his hellish dominion for good service. To throw them into still greater doubt and confusion, the Lord permitted the hellish fiends to imagine greater holiness in the life of John the Baptist. God also concealed some of the more extraordinary wonders performed by his Son, so that Lucifer remained in a state of confusion as to which was the true Messiah. "Both cannot be the Messias," Lucifer mused, "but be it as it may, they are my enemies and I must persecute them until I have undone them."

It was Lucifer, who incited the Jewish leaders in Jerusalem to send their priests and Levites to John to ascertain who he was. He did learn that John was of the tribe of Levi, and he knew by the Scriptures that the Messiah had to come from the tribe of Juda and from the House of David. John had stated that he was the "Voice" instead of the "Word" as the devil hoped to learn. Confused and angry, Lucifer remembered that John had reprimanded King Herod for his disgraceful and adulterous marriage to Herodias, who was not the wife of his half brother Philip as is so often reported, but was rather the wife of Herod's half brother Herod Boethus. King Herod was aware of the holiness of John. He had listened to his words with pleasure, yet whatever the force of truth and the light of reason exerted in Herod, it was easily perverted to evil by the malicious and boundless hatred of his wicked wife Herodias and her daughter Salome, who imitated her mother in morals. The adulterous Herodias, degraded by her passions and sensuality, lent herself readily as an instrument of demonic malice. The devil instigated the evil woman to obtain the death of John in various ways, and on many occasions she tried to persuade Herod to put him to death. The King, to stop her ceaseless diatribe, had had John arrested and chained him in his dungeon. Herodias had her servants scourge and maltreat John on six different occasions in her attempt to murder him. The devil incited these cruel henchmen to assail John with the vilest insults and cruel tortures, for they were the wickedest of men and easily misled.

* * *

When we had first learned of John's imprisonment, Jesus and I were both distraught, but we were fully aware that this was all part of God's plan. My Son and I favored John very much. Throughout John's life, I sent my holy angels to comfort him many times. When he was in need of food, I sent him nourishment. Jesus conferred on him many interior graces and favors. For this reason the demons gave no rest to Herodias, for they wished him dead.

During this time, Jesus stayed with Lazarus in Bethany just outside Jerusalem. After Jesus had moved the moneychangers from the holy temple, my friends warned me of the evil intentions of the Pharisees who were angered by the actions of my Son. For the next few days, I prayed for the safety of Jesus and his disciples. A week following the temple incident, a group of Pharisees and a contingent of temple guards pounded on our door in an attempt to arrest Jesus. They were rude and insulted, threatened, and ordered my friends and me to leave the city at once. That same night, we fled to the home of Lazarus, where his sisters took us in and gave us shelter from our enemies.

Jesus cured many sick strangers in Jerusalem this same day, chiefly among the poor and lame, working people, who dwelt in the area of the Cenacle on Mount Zion. The city of twenty-five thousand people contained within the three walls of the town was bursting at the seams, as was that part of the city that had grown outside Jerusalem's protective walls. The hillsides were dotted with an orderly encampment of huts and tents. The city elders had laid out long streets filled with market buildings. The merchants sold all manners of goods to the eager pilgrims, which included tents with all the accessories necessary to erect them. All manners of foodstuffs, especially Paschal lambs and doves for offerings were readily available. During the preceding weeks the roads had been repaired and the fords made passable for the hordes of pilgrim Hebrews that would be thronging Jerusalem from not only all over Israel, but from all parts of the known world. As many as a half-million Jews made their annual pilgrimage to Jerusalem to celebrate the Pasch every year.

The following day we returned to the temple and again Jesus found that the dealers, because of the huge crowds, had again pushed their way into the holy places and set up their wares for sale. Jesus ordered them to withdraw, some of the merchants became furious, he pushed the tables away, and with his hand outstretched, they were powerless against him. His disciples soon had the merchants removed to the Court of the Gentiles. Jesus then said to them, "I have warned you for the second time. If I find you inside the temple again I will deal with you more harshly."

One insolent merchant yelled at him, "What will the Galilean, the scholar of Nazareth dare to do? We are not afraid of you."

The devout Jews approved of his actions and some cried out in admiration, "The Prophet of Nazareth," and praised him in his absence. For his part, my Son chose to ignore their outbursts, I chose to pray for the angry Jews, and I encouraged the women of our group to do the same.

The Pharisees were ashamed and angry at what had occurred and warned the people to refrain from attaching themselves to Jesus during the feast or running after him. However, the more they talked and warned them, the more the people wanted to know about this forceful leader from Nazareth.

After the Pasch, we returned to our home near Capernaum preaching and instructing all those who came near. I knew it was now time for my Son to call the rest of his disciples, for it was time for him to make his public ministry fully known throughout Israel.

The next day we set out for Bethsaida. Before he left, Jesus took off his sandals, and of course, I emulated his every action, so I removed mine as well. My Son had foretold that during his public ministry that he would go barefooted in utter humility. It was a clear, beautiful spring day. A gentle breeze wafted and kissed the tops of the waves breaking on the sandy beach of the Sea of Galilee. There were about thirty of us in our group. We women followed the men, as was the custom. We came near where many fishermen were preparing and mending their nets. I entered the shallow water fully enjoying the cool refreshment of the cold water on my hot and aching feet. I stood there with my hands folded in prayer for the important event that was about to take place. People came running from every direction when they saw that it was Jesus. Jesus approached Simon and his brother Andrew, got into their boat and said,

"Put out a short distance from shore, "then he sat down and began to preach to the crowd that had assembled. After he had finished speaking, he said to Simon. "Put out into deep water and lower your nets for a catch."

Simon Peter replied, "Master, we have worked hard all night and have caught nothing, but at your command I will lower the nets." No sooner had they done so than they caught a great number of fish to the point that their nets were tearing. They signaled James and John, the sons of Zebedee, who were in another boat, and cried out excitedly, "Come help us, our boat is sinking." They came and filled both boats until they were all at the point of sinking. When Peter saw this he fell at the feet of his Savior and said, "Depart from me, Lord, for I am a sinful man."

However, Jesus replied, "Do not be afraid, Peter. Come with me, and I will make you fishers of men." Without a word, the four men dropped their nets and joined Jesus who proceeded on down the beach. They left Zebedee with only his hired men left. He had been prepared in advance for the calling of his sons to be the disciples of Jesus. Without wasting any time, Zebedee set his men to work on the sudden bonanza of fish.

The next day, our ranks swollen by Simon Peter, Andrew, James, and John, we left Peter's home, where we had spent the night. Peter, besides running a fishing business, was also engaged in agriculture and other ventures. Peter' home stood on the edge of Capernaum. A huge courtyard, with side buildings, silos and sheds surrounded the residence. The Brook of Capernaum flowed beside Peter' house; he had dammed the creek, which provided a large pond in which Peter maintained a large stock of fish. We moved on to Levi's, the tax collector's business, which was about fifteen minutes from Peter's home. All sorts of publicans and servants were busy at work in and about the building. When Levi saw my Son approaching him, he became confused and quite distraught, and withdrew to his private office. My Son waived us to remain behind, and when he drew near the customhouse, he called to him, "Levi, come out."

Levi hurried out, fell on his face before Jesus, and protested saying. "Lord, I am not worthy that you should be here."

My Son said to him, "Levi, arise and follow me."

Rising, Levi, with tears streaming down his face, said "I will instantly and joyfully abandon all things and follow you, Master." He followed Jesus back to the rest of his disciples. He was greeted joyfully by his half brothers, Thaddeus, Simon, and James the Less. Before their father Alphaeus married Mary Cleophas, he had sired Levi by his first wife who had died leaving him a widower with the one son. Levi insisted that they all remain for dinner, but Jesus told him that they would return for him in the morning. Inspired by Jesus, Levi had gone to the Jordan, and John the Baptist had baptized him. Levi had repented of his sins, and had made restitution to any persons that he had wronged. Overjoyed, he hurried to his home and informed his wife the good news and she and his four children rejoiced in his good fortune. He quickly arranged for a substitute to take his place being careful to pick a righteous man to replace him. He then arranged for a big breakfast for the following morning and sent out invitations. Levi was nearly as old as Peter Simon, and could have been mistaken for his half brother, Joses Barsabas. Levi was a big man; heavy boned, and had a dense black beard.

It was nearly noon the following day when our group returned to Levi's. The tax collector had invited many publicans; and overnight, several Pharisees and some of John's disciples had joined us. Seeing the publicans, the Pharisees at first would not enter the house, but remained in the gardens and complained to Jesus' disciples saying, "How can you tolerate your Master's making himself so familiar with sinners and publicans?"

Nathanael answered, "Why don't you ask him yourself why he does so?"

However, the Pharisee grumbled and replied, "One cannot speak with a man who always maintains that he is right."

Levi personally washed the feet of Jesus and his followers and introduced them to his wife and children, and Jesus blessed them. Then Levi's wife shooed the children off and returned to her duties to supervise the serving of the sumptuous repast that her husband had provided. Levi seated Jesus at the head of his table and he knelt before him. Jesus placed his hands on his head and said for all to hear. Your name is Levi, but I say to you, henceforth you shall be Matthew, meaning "Gift of Jehovah."

After speaking to the women in our party, I approached Matthew's wife and offered her our services to help serve the men at the huge banquet. At first, she demurred. However, I assured her it was our vocation to serve the disciples and tend to their daily needs. I told her that it would be a great favor if she allowed us to assist her. Matthew's wife gave in readily then, for she was dreadfully shorthanded for such a huge banquet on such a short notice. I was pleased with her decision, for it permitted us to serve others and to gain in humility.

A huge atrium dominated the center of Levi's house. The servants had arranged the tables in the shape of a cross. Jesus sat in the midst of the publicans, and during the course of the meal, they plied Jesus with questions. Throughout the meal, the disciples supplied food to poor travelers who were passing, for the house was on the road that led to the ferry, which lay just below them. The poor were also being fed and it was then the Pharisees and some of John's disciples entered the building determined to reproach Jesus for allowing his disciples to pluck fruit by the wayside for it was a day of fast.

Jesus asked them. "Is it proper for the guests to fast when the bridegroom is still with them? It is time enough when the bridegroom leaves, for them to fast [Luke: 6, 33-36]." They did not understand, and Jesus did not choose to enlighten them further. Since his arrival, crowds of people came pouring into Capernaum to see him, some of them friends, and others his enemies, but many of them were curious pagans, who were the followers of Zorobabel and other gods. Most of the residents of Capernaum were Jews, but many foreign merchants and transients passed through the town in a steady stream.

The next day we set out for the home of Simon Peter. Peter had received word that his mother in law was gravely ill and he asked Jesus to go see her. There were about twenty men in our group, including the Apostles, and ten women, including, Mary Magdalene, Mary Cleophas, and Salome. When we entered Peter's house Jesus went directly to the sick woman. She was burning with fever and was quite ill. He took her by the hand and said simply, "Be healed." She rose and joined Peter's wife who had began preparing a meal for our group. She insisted on serving Jesus personally [Luke: 5, 38-39].

Perhaps the most rewarding of my associations was my interaction with the disciples and especially my relationship with the Apostles. All of those whom my Son received into divine school; he infused into their hearts an especial reverence and devotion toward me. While this infused reverence was common to all, it was not equal in all the disciples. Jesus distributed these gifts according to the dispositions and in accordance with the duties and offices for which each was destined. God intended that by our conversation and familiar contact that their reverential love and devotion was to grow and increase. Because of my love for them and my personal instruction and prayers for each of them in their necessities, no one left my presence unreplenished by interior joy and consolation greater than that for which they had asked. Yet, the measure of good fruit derived from them was dependent upon the disposition of the heart of those that received these favors.

God ordained that the Apostles begin their contact with me in high admiration of my prudence, wisdom, holiness, and great majesty. God also made them aware of my humble and pleasing disposition. It was not timely for God to reveal me to the world, as his Mystic Ark of the New Testament. My Son constrained the holy Apostles and disciples into silence regarding this subject. However, they were allowed to vent their fervent feelings of intense love for my Son and me.

Because of my peerless insight, I knew the natural dispositions of each of the disciples, their measure of grace, their present condition of spirit and their future office. Equipped with this knowledge, I was able to direct my petitions, prayers, and conversations, in the best manner to support them in their individual vocations. This hidden Providence of the Lord received by the disciples at my intercession caused a divine harmony of action, hidden to men and manifest only to the heavenly spirits.

Especially signaled out for these sacramental favors were Simon Peter and John. Peter, because he was destined to be the Vicar of Christ and head of the Militant Church, and thus deserved my special reverence and love. John was destined to take the place of my Son after his Passion. He would care for me as he would have his own mother. Therefore, since the government and custody of the Mystic Church, namely myself, and the visible Militant Church, namely the faithful on earth, was to be divided between these two Apostles, it was proper that they be singularly favored by me their Queen.

My Son chose John to serve me and attain the dignity of an adopted son. John at once began to experience special urgings of grace and began to signalize himself in my service. Although all the Apostles excelled in their devotion to me beyond the power of human understanding, John penetrated deeper into the mysteries surrounding me and received through me such divine enlightenment as to excel all the other Apostles. John made this obvious himself in [John: 21, 21-20], and when my Son avoided telling Peter how John was to die, while he told the rest of the apostles that they were destined for a violent death. John gained the distinction of being called the "Beloved Disciple", because of his great love for me. All his love was reciprocated, and he became the most beloved disciple both of Jesus and me. Besides John's chastity and virginal purity, he was dear to me because of his virtues of dove-like simplicity and his gentleness and humility, which made him most meek and good. From the very beginning John became ever more anxious to serve me. He soon excelled all the others in piety toward me, and, as my most humble slave, tried to fulfill the least of my wishes. He sought in every manner to take upon himself some of my bodily labors connected with our nomadic life vying with my own angels for this privilege, which only made me more zealous to perform these works of humility myself.

John was most diligent in reporting to me all the works and miracles performed by the Christ when I was not present. He also brought to my attention each new disciple converted by the teaching of my Son. John always distinguished himself by the reverence with which he spoke of me. He always addressed me as "Lady" or my Mistress", and after Christ's death he often called me "Mother". In my absence he often referred to me as the "Mother of our Master Jesus." After the Ascension of the Lord, he was the first to call me "Mother of God and Mother of the Redeemer of the World. In my honor, he invented other titles calling me, "The Propitiation for Sin", and "The Mistress of Nations". In particular he invented the title "Mary of Jesus". The faithful often referred to me by this title in the early days of the Church. The other Apostles were well aware of the favor in which John stood with both Jesus and I, and they often asked him to be their messenger on their behalf for what they desired to say or ask of my Son or me.

Next to Peter and John, James was most beloved by me. He was John's brother and he obtained many favors from my hands. Andrew, the brother of Peter, was also specially favored, because of his great devotion to the cross of Jesus and of his being destined to die on it like his divine Master. Each Apostle had a special place in my heart, even Judas, whom Jesus and I both knew would one day betray him. Over the years, Jesus, by prayer and supernatural means, had groomed twelve men whom he would later name as his Apostles. They were Simon Peter, and his brother Andrew. There was also, James the son of Zebedee, and his brother John, whom Jesus named Boanerges the Sons of Thunder. In addition there were, Philip, Bartholomew, Thomas, and Levi the tax collector, whom Jesus renamed Matthew, also, James, the son of Alphaeus, Thaddeus, Simon, the Cananean, and the last to be called was Judas Iscariot [Mark:3, 14-19].

I will not dwell further on the merits of the Apostles for that subject would require volumes. However, I will speak of the wicked Apostle Judas, for it belongs in this history. Let his sad story and demise become a warning to the obstinate, and for those who stray from the straight path. Judas was attracted to the Teacher by his forceful doctrines. The same good intentions, which first moved the rest of the Apostles, also moved Judas. Powerfully drawn by these motives, he asked Jesus to admit him among his followers, and my Son received him as a loving Father. In the beginning Judas merited special favors and forged ahead of some of the other disciples, including some of those destined to be among the twelve Apostles. The Savior loved the soul of Judas as he did all sinners, but he especially loved the state of grace and the merits of the good works that Judas enjoyed at that time. By our infused knowledge, we were both aware of the perfidious treachery with which he was to end his Apostolate. Neither of us; however, denied him our maternal love or intercession, instead we applied ourselves more zealously to assist him in every manner possible, so that when his wickedness was put into action, he would not have the shadow of an excuse before men.

I took great care not to ignore any of the wants or the comforts of Judas. I began to treat him and to speak and listen to him more gently and lovingly than all the rest. From the beginning, I distinguished him by tokens of special love, and he, at the time, showed himself grateful for them. At this time, the Holy Spirit had not *confirmed* any of the disciples in virtue or grace, and of course, they were all guilty of some human failings. Judas, being imprudent, began to compliment himself on his perfections, and, at the same time, he began to find more faults with his brothers than he did with himself. Soon, he began to complain of these faults and sought to correct their weaknesses. Among those he singled out was John, and in his heart he accused him of ingratiating himself with the Master and me, forgetting all the favors he himself had received. To date, these were but venial sins and he had not lost his sanctifying grace. Unfortunately, he persevered in his faults and freely entertained a certain vain complacency in himself, which at once called into existence a certain amount of envy. This in turn, brought on a slanderous spirit and harshness in judging the faults of his brothers. These sins opened the way for greater sins; for when the fervor of his devotion decreased, his charity grew cold, and his interior light was lost and extinguished. Over the months and years that he was in our company, he gradually began to look upon the Apostles and me with disgust and found little pleasure in our company or in our heavenly activity.

Seeing his growing defection, I sought his recovery and salvation before he cast himself entirely into the death of sin. I spoke to him with sweetness and exhorted him to reform his life. Judas would change for awhile, yet it was only for a short time, and then his torment rose to disturb him anew. Toward the end of the ministry of Jesus, his obstinacy gave entrance to the devil in his heart, and in a furious rage he verbally lashed out at me. He sought to deny his sins and palliate them by alleging other reasons for his conduct. He eventually lost his interior reverence for me, and despising me, he reproached me for my admonitions. This act removed him from the state of grace, and my Son was highly incensed and he left him to his own evil counsels. Judas' resentment toward me soon spread to his Master, and he became unhappy and began to look upon the life of an Apostle as too burdensome.

In spite of all this, divine Providence did not abandon him, but continued to assist him. Although compared to his former mystical help, the help was more common and ordinary. They were; however, in themselves sufficient for his salvation if he had but made use of them. I continued to help him, offering to do penance for him if he would but humble himself and ask pardon of his divine Master. Judas dreaded this humiliation, which would have been to his credit, and he fell into still greater sins. In his pride, he rejected my counsels and chose to deny guilt. He protested with a lying tongue that he loved his Master and the rest of us, and that there was no occasion for him to amend his conduct.

Another cause of the ruin of Judas was his handling of the Apostles' purse. The need for a treasurer became apparent because of the amount of money received as alms. Jesus announced that he intended to appoint one of the Apostles to take charge of their finances. All the Apostles shunned this office, but Judas made it known that he wanted the job. He even humbled himself enough to ask John to intercede with me and ask me to arrange the matter with my Son. He also called upon Peter and the other Apostles to endorse his request, but Jesus, wishing to stay his ruin, avoided him.

However the ambition and avarice of Judas could not be stayed, and on the pretext of virtue, he presumed to come directly to me with his request saying, "Mistress, I have made my request for the position of purser through Peter and John with the sole desire of serving you and my divine Master. There are few qualified or desirous of this important function, and I beg of you to plead my cause with your Son."

I replied with all sincerity, "Consider well my dear, Judas, what you ask, and examine whether your intentions are upright. Your brother Apostles fear and refuse to accept this position unless Jesus orders them to do so. Do you deem it wise to seek that which all the rest shun? Jesus loves you more than you love yourself, and without a doubt knows best what will benefit you. I urge you to change your purpose, and seek instead to grow rich in humility and poverty. Rise from your fall, for I will extend you a helping hand and my Son will show you his loving mercy."

Judas just looked at me with fury in his eyes, but he prudently withheld his anger. He considered my well-meant advice as an insult. I pretended not to notice his obstinacy and said nothing more to him. Judas; however, could not rest, and casting aside all shame and modesty, he resolved to apply directly to his divine Master and Savior. Clothing himself in the proverbial garb of a sheep, he went to Jesus and said, "Master, I wish to fulfill your wishes and serve you as your purser and as the dispenser of the alms which we receive. I will look to the interests of the poor, fulfilling your doctrine that we should do unto others as we wish them to do unto us. I will see to it that the alms are distributed according to your wishes, and more profitably and orderly than before."

Jesus knew that he lied concealing his real intention, and in so doing showed his loss of infused faith, for he attempted to deceive Christ, his divine Master, by wearing the cloak of hypocrisy. If he truly believed that Jesus was true God and true man, who penetrated into the secrets of the heart, he would not have hoped to deceive him. Judas had lost belief in all these prerogatives, and to his other sins, he now added the sin of heresy. As it says in the first letter to Timothy, "For the desire for money is the root of all evils [1Tim: 6,10]

My Son said to him, "Do you know, Judas, what you seek and what you ask? Do not be so cruel to yourself as to solicit and seek to obtain the poison and the arms, which may cause your death."

Judas replied, "Master, I desire to serve you by employing my strength in the service of your faithful followers, and in this way I can do it better than in any other. I offer to fulfill all the duties of this office without fail."

Jesus, knowing he could not stop Judas in his evil, allowed him to take over the job of purser. We never ceased praying for Judas. I knew that he was not honest with his stewardship, but we hoped that our examples and prayers would divert him from his final act of treachery.

By the time of the Crucifixion, Judas had become highly incensed against me, because I distributed such generous alms among the poor. He likewise resented Jesus, because he would not accept large donations, and in turn loathed the Apostles, because they would not solicit them. A few months before the death of Jesus, he began to avoid the other Apostles and rejoined them only long enough to collect what donations he could. During these periods of absence, the demon inspired him with the thought of breaking entirely with the Master, and of delivering him over to the Jews.

After preaching and healing for several days in Capernaum, Jesus, accompanied by his disciples, boarded one of Peter's larger boats, there were about thirty of us, and we set sail for the territory of the Gadarenes. Jesus retired to the bow of the boat and fell asleep. A few hours later a violent storm came upon the sea, which threatened to swamp the boat. Mary Salome woke me and asked me to pray for us all. A short time later, James, usually so unshakeable, awakened Jesus and said, "Master, we are about to perish, help us."

Jesus sat up and said, "Why are you so terrified? Are you so little of faith?" He held his hand out over the smashing waves, rebuked them and said, "Be calm!" Instantly, a great calm settled over the wind, the rain, and the sea and everyone was amazed.

Thomas exclaimed in an awe-stricken voice, "What sort of man is this, whom even the winds and the sea obey?" I thanked God for this display of my Son's power, and led the group in hymns of praise to our Creator.

The next morning we landed on the shore of the Gadarenes, where most of the residents were pagans. Before we had advanced very far, two demoniacs coming down from the tombs met us. The violence of the men forced us to stop. The women huddled around me anxiously, but I assured them that they had nothing to fear. The men, long possessed by demons, wore no clothes, and they lived amidst the tombs of a cemetery. One cried out, "What have you to do with us, Son of God? Have you come to torment us before the appointed time?"

I began to pray for them, as did the rest of our party. Jesus said to the demons, "Depart from the man." Some distance away, a herd of about 2000 swine were feeding.

The demons pleaded with my Son, "If you drive us out, send us into the herd of swine."

Jesus asked the man, "What is your name?"

He replied, "Legion," because many demons had taken possession of him.

Jesus granted his wish saying, "Go then!"

The swine reacted wildly when the demons entered them. They stampeded down the hill into the lake and were all drowned. The swineherds, when they saw what had happened, ran away and reported the incident to their masters.

The people came out indignantly seeking the man who had drowned their swine, determined that he should make restitution. When they arrived, they found the possessed men sitting quietly at Jesus' feet, fully clothed and fully in their right minds. The villagers, when told what had happened, were filled with great fear and begged my Son to leave their area. The healed men begged their Savior to allow them to go with him, but Jesus replied, "Return home and recount what God has done for you." The men went off and proclaimed throughout the whole town what Christ had done for them. We then reentered the boats and set sail for Capernaum [Mark: 5, 1-20].

When we returned a great crowd had gathered; a man named Jairus, an official of the synagogue came forward. He threw himself at Jesus' feet and begged him to come to his house, for his only daughter, a girl of twelve was dying.

The crowd pressed in heavily all about Jesus. A woman afflicted with hemorrhages for twelve years, who had spent all her money on futile treatments by doctors, came up behind him and touched the tassel of his cloak thinking, "If I can but touch the tassel of his cloak, I will be healed." Immediately her bleeding stopped.

Jesus fully aware of what had happened asked, "Who touched me?"

While all were denying it, Peter exclaimed, "Master, the crowds are pressing in so tightly it would be impossible to determine who did so."

However Jesus insisted, "I know that someone has touched me, for power has gone out of me."

When the woman realized that she had not escaped notice, she came forward trembling. She fell at the Messiah's feet and explained what had happened. Jesus laid his hand on her head and said, "Daughter, your faith has saved you; go in peace [Mark: 6, 25-34]."

While he was speaking, someone from the synagogue official's house arrived and said to him, "Your daughter is dead; do not trouble the Teacher further."

Hearing this, Jesus told the father, "Do not be afraid; just have a little faith and she will be saved."

I began praying, and when we arrived at the house, my Son would not allow anyone to enter with him except Peter, James, John, and the child's parents. All were weeping and mourning for her, but Jesus said to them, "Do not weep any longer, for she is not dead, but sleeping."

From all around, people began murmuring and ridiculing him, because they had seen her and knew that she was indeed dead. Entering the room, Jesus took her by the hand and called to her, "Child, arise!" She began breathing and rose and stood by his side. He then told the parents "Give her something to eat." Everyone was astounded and he instructed them to tell no one what had happened Mark: 6, 35-43].

In quick succession Jesus healed two blind men, a mute person, and went around the neighboring towns and villages teaching in their synagogues and proclaiming the Gospel of the Kingdom of God. He cured their every disease and illness. The crowds of people were like sheep without a shepherd. Our hearts were moved with pity, and Jesus said to his disciples, "The harvest is abundant but the laborers are few, so ask the master of the harvest to send laborers for his harvest."

Reacting to his request, I led the women of our group in continuous prayer.

The next day Jesus summoned the twelve Apostles to him and sent them out two by two, "I want you to go out to all the neighboring towns and villages and tell the villagers that I will soon visit them. Tell them the Kingdom of God is at hand. I give you authority over unclean spirits, so that you can drive them out and cure every disease and every illness Take nothing with you; neither walking stick, nor sack, nor food, nor money, and let no one take a second tunic. When you enter a house, wish it peace. If the house is worthy, let your peace come upon it; if not, let your peace return to you. For those who do not welcome you or listen to your words, go outside that house or town and shake the dust from your feet in testimony against them. Amen, I say to you, it will be more tolerable for the land of Sodom and Gomorrah on the Day of Judgment than for that town [Mark: 6, 7-13]."

"Behold, I am sending you like sheep in the midst of wolves; so be shrewd as serpents and simple as doves. However beware of people, for they will turn you over to courts and scourge you in their synagogues. Governors and kings will have you led before them as a witness to me before them and the pagans. When they hand you over, do not worry about how you are to speak or what you are to say. For it will not be you who speak out, but the Spirit of your Father speaking through you. Many people will hate you because of my name. However I will save you, if you endure to the end. I say to you that you will not finish all the towns of Israel before the Son of Man comes. No disciple is above the teacher, no slave above his master. Do not be afraid of them. Nothing is concealed that will not be revealed, no secret that will not be known. Do not be afraid of those that kill the body, but cannot kill the soul."

So each Apostle went out two by two proclaiming the good news and as Jesus' representatives cured all the sick with whom they came in contact. Each was amazed and humbled with the results of the power given them by my Son.

Some of John the Baptist's disciples had joined Jesus, but others remained faithful to John still confused as to where their true loyalties should lie. John told those who visited him in prison to follow Jesus, for his own work was nearly done. Many hesitated; however, and so John sent them to Jesus hoping that his answers would convince them that he was indeed the Messiah. They asked my Son, "John has sent us to ask you, "Are you the one who is to come, or should we look for another?"

Jesus said to them in reply, "Go and tell John what you hear and see. The blind regain their sight, the lame walk, lepers are cleansed, the deaf hear, the dead are raised, and the poor have the good news proclaimed to them, and blessed is the one who takes no offense at me."

Then Jesus spoke to them and to the crowd that has assembled, "What did you go out into the desert to see? A reed swayed by the wind? Then what did you go out to see? Someone dressed in fine clothing? Those who wear fine clothing are in royal palaces. Then why did you go out, to see a Prophet? Yes, I tell you, and he is more than a Prophet is. This is the one about whom it is written, 'Behold, I am sending my messenger ahead of you; he will prepare your way before you. Amen, I say to you, among those born of women there has been none greater than John the Baptist; yet the least in the Kingdom of Heaven is greater than he. As ordained, the Kingdom of Heaven has suffered violence since John the Baptist began his ministry.'

It was not long after this that Lucifer eagerly seized the occasion of Herod's birthday celebration as the time to incite Herodias, her daughter Salome, and Herod to the heinous crime of murder. On Herod's birthday a great banquet was held for the king by all the magistrates and nobles of Galilee of which he was King. His degraded wife Herodias brought her beautiful daughter Salome to the feast in order to dance before the guests. Salome executed one of the dances long associated with the nomadic cultures of the Middle East. Salome performed an exotic dance bathed in subtle eroticism. She gave a performance of agility and grace.

The adulterous Herod was filled with drunken lust; he swore an oath to her, "Ask me for anything you wish, even half my Kingdom, and I will give it to you."

Salome, prompted by her mother, and both prompted by the Lucifer, answered firmly, "Bring me the head of John the Baptist on a platter."

Herod was distressed with her request, and he looked all about, for he knew his guests would expect him to keep his oath. It is an unbearable offense for a man to be called a woman, but it is a greater disgrace to be governed and led by a woman's whims, for he that obeys is inferior to the one that commands. Sincerely regretting his words, Herod gave the order for John's execution.

My most holy Son made me interiorly aware of this devilish plot through his interior will. I learned that the hour of John's martyrdom had arrived, and that he should give his life in testimony of the truths he had preached. That evening I prostrated myself at the feet of my Son and tearfully implored him to assist his servant and Precursor. I asked him to comfort and console John, and that his death might be so much more precious in his eyes in view of his suffering for the honor and defense of the truth.

Jesus responded with my request and we were miraculously and invisibly borne to John's dungeon cell where he lay fettered in chains and wounded in many parts of his body. Our presence filled the foul prison with celestial light. All the other parts of Herod's palace were infested with innumerable demons and sycophants more criminal than the state prisoners in their dungeons below. Our presence and our host of beautiful angels entirely sanctified the cell of John. John's chains fell miraculously from his limbs, and Jesus instantly healed him. With ineffable joy, John prostrated himself on the flagstone floor and in the deepest humility and admiration asked for our blessing. After the blessings, we remained for some time holding divine converse with our friend and servant, some of which I will repeat.

In the kindest tone and manner our Savior said, "John, my servant, how eagerly you press on to be persecuted, imprisoned, scourged, and to offer your life for the glory of the Father, even before I myself enter upon my suffering. Your desires are quickly approaching their fulfillment, since you are soon to enjoy the reward in my humanity. Thus, does the eternal Father reward the zeal with which you have fulfilled the office of being my Precursor. Let your loving anxieties now cease and offer your neck to the axe; for such is my wish, and thus you shall enjoy the happiness of suffering and dying for my name. I offer to the eternal Father your life, in order that mine be yet prolonged."

At first, John was overwhelmed so that he could not give an answer. Reinforced by divine grace; however, he dissolved in tears. John thanked my Son for the ineffable favor of our visit. He said, "My eternal God and Lord, I cannot ever merit pains or sufferings worthy of such a great consolation and privilege as that of enjoying your divine presence and that of your exalted mother, my Mistress. In order that your boundless mercy may be exalted, permit me, Lord, to die before you so that your holy name may be made more widely known, and look with favor on my desire to enduring the most painful and lingering death. Let Herod, and sin and hell itself triumph over me in my death, for I offer my life for you, my beloved, in the joy of my heart. Receive it, my God, as a pleasing sacrifice. In addition, Mary, mother of my Savior and my Mistress, turn your most loving eyes in clemency upon your servant and continue to show me the favor as a mother and as the cause of all blessing. I have despised vanities all my life. In addition, I love the Cross, which my Redeemer will sanctify. I have desired to sow in tears, but never could I have merited the delight of such a visit, which has sweetened all my sufferings, gladdened by bondage, and makes death itself more pleasing and acceptable than life."

Suddenly, the huge iron gates of the dungeon were thrown open. Three of Herod's servants entered, accompanied by an executioner, they were ready to rain upon John the implacable fury of the cruel adulterer. Bursting into John's cell, the guards were amazed to find him unshackled and in perfect health, for they could not see us. Overcoming their awe, they seized John, who, without a word, offered the officials his neck, and in a few seconds the foul deed was completed. Jesus, the High Priest, received in his arms the body of the saintly Precursor, while I held his head in my hands. Together we offered up this victim to the eternal Father on the altar of our sacred hands. John's soul soared up in incomprehensible beauty and immediately did homage to its Savior. While this went on, a dispute broke out among the attendants as to, which one of them would flatter the infamous dancer and her mother by bearing the head of John the Baptist to them. Finally, the largest guard grabbed up the coveted gift and the others followed. John was born six months before my Son and was taken from this life in 28 AD [Mark: 6, 21-29]

A multitude of angels escorted the sacred soul of John to limbo. Their arrival renewed the joy of the holy souls imprisoned there. My Son and I returned to our home in Capernaum. The blessed Precursor of Christ had received many great favors from our hands throughout his life, including his happy birth, his stay in the desert, and his preaching and holy death. God never wrought such wonders for any other man. John's disciples claimed John's body and they buried him. Then they came to my Son and me, and told us of his death. We grieved John, yet, at the same time, we rejoiced in his sacrifice. He gave his life for his Creator, and no greater gift is possible. Most of John's remaining disciples now requested permission to join Jesus. In addition to the twelve men that Jesus had named as Apostles, there were now a total of seventy-two disciples and many women, whose ranks fluctuated, with the needs of their families.

At the advent of John's death, Jesus retired with his main body of followers to a secluded spot. Once there he put out in one of Peter's boats and withdrew to mourn the death of his friend. However, news of his presence soon spread over the area and huge crowds gathered on foot from their towns and villages to hear him. When my Son disembarked and saw the vast crowd, his heart went out to them, and he cured their sick aided by his Apostles. In my own quite way, I managed to cure many a person without their being aware of the source.

That evening Peter approached Jesus and said, "Lord, this is a deserted place. There are over five-thousand men here along with their families. I suggest you dismiss them so they can go to the closest villages and purchase food for themselves.

However, my Son replied, "There is no need for them to go away; give them some food yourselves."

Andrew spoke up and said, "But, Master, we only have seven loaves of bread and two fish."

Jesus instructed them. "Have the people recline in groups and bring the food to me." Having done so, he placed his hands on the food and looking up to heaven; he said the blessing, broke the loaves and gave them to the disciples. His disciples took the food and as they distributed the food, they found that it multiplied in their hands and there was sufficient for all to eat their fill. When they were through, Jesus said, "Pick up the fragments so there will be no waste." When they had done so, they had twelve wicker baskets full. An awed hush settled over the crowd as they realized the significance of the event [Luke: 9, 10].

Then Jesus said to Peter, "Take the boats and precede me to the other side of the lake while I dismiss the crowd. In the meantime, the people began talking among themselves saying, "This is truly the Prophet, the one who is to come into the world." Knowing the people were going to come and carry him off to make him king, my Son dismissed the huge group of people, and withdrew alone on the mountain to pray for them and for his friend John. Meanwhile, a fierce wind began to whip up the Sea of Galilee. The disciples in the boats had been able to sail only a few miles from shore, because the wind was against them. During the fourth watch of the night, Jesus came walking across the water toward them. When the disciples saw him walking on top of the waves, many were terrified.

Bartholomew wailed, "It is a ghost," and everyone cried out in fear.

All except Thomas who snorted scornfully, "There aren't any such things as ghosts."

Seeing their state of mind, my Son called out, "Take courage, it is I, do not be afraid."

Overcoming his fear, Peter said, "Lord, if it is really you, command me to come to you on the water."

Jesus replied simply, "Come!"

Peter got out of the boat and began walking towards Jesus, who stopped and waited for him. The wind was blowing fiercely, and it frightened Peter, who began to sink, he cried out, "Lord, save me!"

Jesus stretched out his hand, caught him up, and he immediately rose to the surface. Jesus chided him gently saying, "Oh you of little faith, why did you doubt?" They entered the boat and the wind died down at once.

Everyone fell to their knees, and Peter exclaimed, "Truly, you are the Son of God." Within a short while we again landed on the shore below Capernaum [Mark: 6, 43-52].

Meanwhile the people from among the five thousand who had been fed came looking for Jesus, seeking to take him by force and make him king. They found Jesus in the Synagogue with many of his disciples and the leader came up to Jesus and said, "Rabbi, when did you get here?"

My Son knew what was in their hearts and replied, "Amen, amen, I say to you, you seek me, not because you have seen miracles, but because you did eat of the loaves and were filled. Do not labor for meat that perishes, but for that which endures for eternal life, which the Son of Man will give you. For on him the Father, God, has set his seal."

The man responded, "What can we do to accomplish the works of God?"

Jesus answered and said to them, "This is the work of God that you believe in him whom he has sent."

So, the leader asked, "What sign can you show that we may see, and may believe you? What can you do? Our ancestors ate manna in the desert, as it is written, 'He gave them bread from Heaven to eat.'"

My Son told them, "Amen, amen, I say to you; Moses gave you not bread from Heaven, but my Father gave you the true bread from Heaven. For the bread of God is that which comes down from Heaven, and gives life to the world."

The man eagerly replied, "Lord, give us this bread always."

Then my Son explained to them that which they could not see and that, which they would not accept, "I am the bread of life. He that comes to me shall not hunger, and he that believes in me shall never thirst. Although you have seen me, you still do not believe. Everything that the Father gives me will come to me, and I will not reject anyone who comes to me. I came down from Heaven, not to do my own will, but the will of the one who sent me. The one that sent me wills that I should not lose anything of what he gave me, but that I should raise it on the last day; for this is the will of my Father that everyone who sees the Son and believes in him may have eternal life, and I shall raise him up on the last day."

The leader turned to the people and they began murmuring among themselves saying, "Is this not Jesus, the son of Joseph" How can it be that he came down from heaven? Do we not know his mother and father? Then how can he say, 'I have come down from heaven?'"

Jesus said to them, "Stop your murmuring. No one can come to me unless the Father who sent me draws him, and I will raise him up on the last day. It is written in the prophets, 'They shall all be taught by God.' Everyone who listens to my Father and learns from him comes to me. No one has seen the Father except the one who is from God; he has seen the Father. Amen, amen, I say to you, whoever believes has eternal life. I am the bread of life. Your ancestors ate manna in the desert, but they died. This is the bread that comes down from heaven so that one may eat it and not die. I am the living bread that comes down from heaven; whoever eats this bread will live forever; and the bread that I will give is my flesh for the life of the world."

The group quarreled among themselves, saying, "How can this man give us his flesh to eat?"

Jesus said to them, "Amen, amen, I say to you, unless you eat the flesh of the Son of Man and drink his blood, you do not have life within you. Whoever eats my flesh and drinks my blood has eternal life, and I will raise him up on the last day, for my flesh is true food and my blood is true drink. Whoever eats my flesh and drinks my blood remains in me and me in him. Just as the living Father sent me and I have life because of the Father, so also the one who feeds on me will have life because of me. This is the bread that came down from heaven. Unlike your ancestors who ate and still died, whoever eats this bread will live forever."

Again, there was much murmuring and many of my Son's staunchest followers who were listening said, "This saying is most difficult, who can accept it?"

Jesus said to his disciples, "Does this shock you? What if you were to see the Son of Man ascending to where he was before? It is the spirit that gives life, while the flesh is of no avail. The words I have spoken to you are spirit and life. However, there are some of you who do not believe." My Son knew from the beginning the ones who would not believe, as had I. I had spent many nights on my knees praying for their acceptance and belief. Jesus said to them, "For this reason I have told you that no one can come to me unless it is granted him by my Father."

After much discussion, murmurs, and finally looks of anger and disgust, many of my Son's disciples, men and women, left us that day. Those that remained were badly shaken, but firm in their loyalties. Jesus turned to the twelve Apostles and asked them, "Do you also want to leave?"

Simon Peter looked around at the Apostles and answered for them, "Master, to whom shall we go? You have the words of eternal life. We have come to believe and are convinced that you are the Holy One of God."

In answer Jesus said, "Did I not choose you twelve? Yet, is not one of you a devil [John: 6, 22-71]?"

The twelve did not answer for they did not comprehend, and were afraid to ask the obvious question. My Son, of course, was referring to Judas, the son of Simon the Iscariot. It was he, who would betray my Son, one of the chosen twelve.

The next day many pagans as well as many of those that my Son had already cured had assembled to the mountain east of Bethsaida-Julius. For it was here, that Jesus intended to teach. Jesus had many of his remaining disciples remain in Capernaum to baptize those that had remained there. From there he instructed them to return to their fishing occupations in order to feed the vast multitudes of people who had gathered to hear Jesus speak. Before we left, he delivered to his disciples a comprehensive instruction. In it, he elaborated on the Eight Beatitudes, which he had decided to dwell on for a long time. He told them they were *the salt of the earth* destined to vivify and preserve others, and consequently they must not lose savor. He gave them numerous examples and parables, after which they set sail.

Peter, and the other fishermen, immediately began baptizing, and their first convert was Martial, the son of the widow Naim. They moved on down the beach baptizing as they went. I remained behind with the women to celebrate with the widow of Naim the repentance of her son. Baptizing alone; however, was simply not enough. In order to help those baptized persevere in faith; we had to teach the widow, her son, and the others about God.

Jesus spent fourteen days on the mountain teaching the Eight Beatitudes, He related examples, used parables, and spoke of the Messias, and especially of the conversion of the Gentiles. The disciples all referred to my Son as the Master and as such, he was truly the Master of public speaking. He held the people spellbound with his mellifluous voice painting word pictures that caught and held the ear of every person who ever heard him speak. Before the intervening Sabbath, he returned to Capernaum to again attend Synagogue with his disciples and me. We all assembled at the home of Peter. Soon a great crowd gathered in the hall and the courtyard, in which my Son usually sat and taught. He spoke of the Ten Commandments, and as he was speaking, a loud noise from the roof-edge of an atrium interrupted them.

Through the atrium opening, a paralytic was let down on a litter, and he cried out. "Lord, have pity on a poor sick man!"

His friends had tried in vain to get him near Jesus but failing in their attempt had seized upon this method of getting their friend to the attention of the Healer. The Pharisees that were present were irritated at this unheard of impertinence. My Son; however, was pleased at the faith of the poor people, and he stepped forward and addressed the paralytic, saying, "Be of good heart, my son, your sins are forgiven you!"

The Pharisees were outraged, and thought to themselves: That is blasphemy! Who but God can forgive sins?

Jesus knew their very thoughts and said to them, "Why do you have such thoughts of bitterness in your hearts? Which is easier to say to the paralytic, your sins are forgiven you; or to say, 'Arise, take up your bed, and walk?' However, so you may know that the Son of Man has power on earth to forgive sins, please observe:" Jesus then turned to the paralytic and said, "Arise! Take up your bed, and walk!"

Cured, the man arose, rolled up the coverlets of his bed, laid the laths and frame together, took them under his arm and accompanied by his friends, went off singing canticles of praise amid the shouts and praises of all those present. Shamed in front of the crowd, the Pharisees slipped off one by one. At that moment, the hazzan of the synagogue blew three blasts from the shofar, the ram's horn. It was the call announcing synagogue services, for the hour of the Sabbath was fast approaching. My Son and I followed by the crowd, repaired to the house of worship.

Jairus, the synagogue's rabbi was present. His twelve-year-old daughter Rachel, the one that Jesus had raised from the dead, was again near death. The terrible illness had fallen upon her in punishment of her sins. Her parent's sins had, in part, contributed to her punishment. She, her mother and sister, along with Jairus' mother, who lived with them, had all taken her miraculous healing in a very frivolous manner, without gratitude, and without in any way altering their sinful ways. Jairus was a weak man and was entirely under the control of his vain and beautiful wife. Their home was a theatre of female vanity. The women had purchased all the latest pagan styles of finery for their adornment. In addition, the women were gossips. Even after Jesus cured their child, they found fault with my Son, and ridiculed him. At first, the child retained her innocence, but finally she had followed their example. Some time later, a violent fever seized the girl, and she suffered a most extraordinary burning thirst. The girl now lay near death having been delirious for the past week. The parents suspected that they were to blame because of their frivolity, but they would not acknowledge it among themselves. At last, the mother ashamed and frightened, said to Jairus, "Do you think that Jesus will again have pity on us and spare our daughter?"

Jairus; however, was too embarrassed to ask Jesus for help once again in front of all the people. However, after the services, he managed to gather the courage to plead his case and he followed Jesus outside. There, he threw himself at his feet and exclaimed, Oh, Master, have pity on my daughter Rachel, for I have just left her in a dying state.

Filled with compassion, my Son promised to go with him. However, a messenger approached Jairus and told him that it was too late, his daughter was dead. Jesus comforted him and told him to have confidence. It was well past dark when we arrived. The mourners filled the courtyard; this time, they did not jeer at Jesus. Accompanied by Peter, James and John, Jesus entered the room and my Son asked that a small branch from the garden be brought to him along with a basin of water. The girl lay quite stiff and cold, there was no doubt that she was dead. Jesus blessed the water and then sprinkled some on the girl, prayed, then took her by the hand and said, "Little maid, I say to you, arise!"

The girl suddenly opened her eyes, obeyed the touch of her Savior, arose and stepped from the couch. Then Jesus turned to the parents and said sternly, "You must learn to receive the mercy of God thankfully. Turn away from vanity and worldly pleasure and embrace the penance that I have preached to you. Beware of compromising your daughter's life again. Your whole manner of living and the levity with which you received the first favor at the hand of God is reprehensible. The death of the soul is a more grievous death than the death of the body." Rachel was full of remorse and tearful, and Jesus told her, "Beware of the concupiscence of the eyes and the sins of the body. Live no longer according to the flesh, but eat of the Bread of Life." The parents and relatives were all filled with remorse and completely transformed; they all promised to break the bonds of their sins and to obey Jesus' orders. They all shed tears and gave thanks to Jesus. Jairus did change as he had promised, and gave a great part of his possessions to the poor. My Son and his disciples left by the back entrance to avoid he adulation of the crowd, and being aware of his departure, I returned to our home where I knew Jesus would soon return. There I prayed most of the night giving thanks to God for his many favors and praying that the family of Jairus would now persevere in the faith.

It was winter and we were again in Jerusalem, this time for the Feast of the Dedication. Jesus walked about with his disciples in the temple area on the recently constructed, beautiful Portico of Solomon. A determined group of priests and Pharisees approached and gathered about him and said, "How long are you going to keep us in suspense? If you are the Messiah, tell us plainly."

Jesus answered them, "I told you, and you do not believe, because you are not among my sheep. My sheep hear my voice; I know them, and they follow me. I give them eternal life, and they shall never perish. No one can take them out of my hand. My Father, who has given them to me is greater than all, and no one can take them out of the Father's hand. The Father and I are one." Outraged at this blasphemy, the Jews picked up rocks to stone him; however, Jesus continued to speak saying, "I have shown you many good works from my Father. For which of these are you going to stone me?"

Their leader answered, "We are not stoning you for good work but for blasphemy. You a man, are making yourself God."

Jesus replied, "Is it not written in your own law: 'You are gods' [Ps[s]: 82, 6]? If it calls them gods to whom the word of God came, and scripture cannot be set aside, how can you say that the one whom the Father has consecrated and sent into the world blasphemes, because I said, 'I am the Son of God'? If I do not perform my Father's works, do not believe me. However, if I perform them, even if you do not believe me, believe the works so that you may realize [and understand] that the Father is in me, and I am in the Father."

Enraged at his words they tried to arrest him; however, my Son simply clouded their minds and he walked through them unmolested. Knowing he was no longer safe in Jerusalem, Jesus took us back across the Jordan to the place where John had first baptized and there we remained for some time. Many people came to him and said, "John performed no sign, but everything John said about you was true." Consequently, numerous people came to believe in Jesus.

Time became a blur, as we traveled from town to town in Galilee spreading the Good News. Another Pasch had come and gone and we were fast approaching my Son's third and final Passover. I had mixed feelings. For the good of the world and the deliverance of souls, I looked forward to the final Passion of our Redeemer. However, as a mother, I also dreaded the coming event. The good my Son had already accomplished would more than compensate to satisfy the Creator for the Redemption of humanity. However, I knew that Jesus would never settle for half measures. Only by his death, could he truly compensate to his Father for all the sins of man, past, present, and future. My Son had again created a miracle, for again with just a few loaves of bread and a few fish, he fed four thousand men and their women and children.

The Pharisees were ever complaining of the disciples breaking the fast, and they were always demanding a sign. Jesus responded by teaching the disciples how to pray, and taught them the Paternoster. In addition, he taught them how to fast, how to give alms, and how to build up their treasures in heaven. My Son taught them to be dependent upon God, and to not judge others. "Ask," he said, "and it will be given to you." He taught them the Golden Rule, the danger of sin, and how small was the "Eye of the Needle". The Savior warned them of false prophets and how to be a true disciple. Jesus warned them of coming persecutions and told them to have courage in the face of that persecution.

At this time, we were near Caesarea Philippi, and we had stopped for the night. After we women had served the men their supper, we retired to one side to have our own meal, but remained within hearing distance so as not to miss a single word that came from the mouth of our Lord. Jesus said to his disciples, "Who do people say that the Son of Man is?"

Thomas replied, "Some say you are John the Baptist."

Andrew spoke up and said, "I have heard some say that you are Jeremiah or one of the Prophets."

Jesus then said to them, "But who do you say that I am?"

Simon Peter spoke up and stated emphatically, "You are the Messiah, the Son of the living God."

My Son said to him in reply, "Blessed are you, Simon, son of Jonah. For flesh and blood has not revealed this to you, but my heavenly Father. *Therefore, I say to you, you are Peter, and upon this rock I will build my Church, and the gates of hell shall not prevail against you. I will give you the keys to the kingdom of heaven. Whatever you bind on earth shall be bound in heaven; and whatever you loose on earth shall be loosed in heaven [Matt: 16, 17-20]."* Then he strictly ordered all of us to tell no one that he was the Messiah.

A short time later he said to his twelve Apostles. "Soon we will go to Jerusalem to celebrate the Passover. There I will suffer greatly from the elders, the chief priests, and the scribes. There, I will be killed, but on the third day I shall be raised up."

The Apostles were terribly distressed at this declaration. They had given up their own families, jobs, and fortunes to follow my Son, and now he was telling them that he was to die. The women and the other disciples were no less distressed. Greatly concerned, Peter took Jesus to one side and began to rebuke him, "God forbid, Lord! No such thing shall ever happen to you."

Jesus turned to Peter and said, "Get behind me, Satan! You are an obstacle to me. You are thinking not as God does, but as human beings do." Then my Son turned to all his followers and said, "Whoever wishes to come after me must deny himself, take up his cross, and follow me. For whoever wishes to save his life will lose it, but whoever loses his life for my sake will find it. What profit would there be for one to gain the whole world and forfeit his soul? Or, what can one give in exchange for his life; for the Son of Man will come with his angels in his Father's glory, and then he will repay everyone according to his conduct. Amen, I say to you, there are some standing here who will not taste death until they see the Son of Man coming in his kingdom."

From this point forward, my Son often spoke of his death in order to prepare his followers for that which was to follow. However, they had closed their minds. Few of them were prepared for the outrage, which was to happen all too soon to my Son, our Lord and Savior.

A week later we approached Mount Tabor in the center of Galilee. It was two leagues east of Nazareth and when we arrived Jesus instructed us to make camp at the foot of the mountain. I knew that it was my Son's intention to prepare and strengthen some of his Apostles for the scandal of his Passion, by manifesting to them beforehand in its glory that same body, which he was so soon to exhibit in the disfigurement of the Cross. After a day of prayer, Jesus took Peter, James, and John and led them up the mountain. Once there he led them in prayer and after awhile, as was so often the case, the Apostles, tired from their strenuous trek up the mountain fell asleep during the prayers. Jesus rose and spread his arms in the shape of a cross. God suddenly transfigured Jesus in all his glory. Peter, James and John awoke with a start, and they were stunned with the resplendent sight of the Transfigured Messiah. His face shone like the sun and his clothes became as white as light. All at once Moses and Elijah appeared to them and began conversing with Jesus about his coming Passion.

Just before the Transfiguration, my holy angels, at God's command, carried me to the top of Mt. Tabor; however, while I was present, I was not visible to the Apostles. An angel took my place within the camp. What was for the Apostles a gratuitous favor was considered a duty in my regards, for I was to be my Son's Companion and Co-partner in the works of the Redemption, even to the foot of the Cross. God granted me this vision of the transfiguration to fortify me for the coming crucifixion. I had previously been divinely fortified and enlightened when looking upon the Divinity. In addition, on other occasions, I had seen the body of my divine Son glorified. However, the sight of their glorified Master subjected the three Apostles to a terror and weakness of their senses. Because of my prior blessings, I was able to look fixedly upon his glorious body with no fear, only awe. The effects of the Transfiguration totally renewed and inflamed me. As long as I lived, I never lost the impression caused by the sight of such glory manifested in the humanity of my Son. Later this memory would greatly console me in the absence in my Son after his Death and Ascension. Yet, this experience also made me feel so much the more deeply the maltreatment experienced by Jesus in his Passion and Death.

When a lull opened in the conversation Peter said to Jesus, "Lord, it is good that we are here. If you wish, I will make three tents here, one for you, one for Moses, and one for Elijah."

While he was still speaking, a bright cloud suddenly cast a shadow over them, and then from the cloud came a voice that said, "This is my chosen Son, listen to him [Luke: 9, 35]."

The disciples fell prostrate, overcome with fear, when they heard this. However, Jesus touched them and said, "Rise and do not be afraid." Peter raised his eyes and was astounded, for he saw no one else but his friends and his Master. As they were coming down the mountain, my Son told them. "Do not tell the vision to anyone until the Son of man has been raised from the dead."

Then James asked him, "Why do the scribes say that Elijah must come first?"

Jesus replied, "Elijah will indeed come and restore all things; but I tell you that Elijah has already come, and they did not recognize him, but did to him whatever they pleased. So also will the Son of man suffer at their hands." It was then that the disciples understood that Jesus was speaking of John the Baptist.

After the Transfiguration, I began to ponder upon what I had seen and heard. I exalted and praised the omnipotent God, reflecting upon that bodily substance which I had carried within my womb, and nursed at my breast. I had heard with my own ears the voice of the eternal Father acknowledging Jesus as his own and appointing him as the Teacher of the human race. With my holy angels, I composed new canticles of praise to celebrate an event so full of festive joy for my soul and for the most sacred humanity of my Son.

Before he had time to speak of the event, Jesus asked him, "What is your opinion, Simon; from who do the kings of the earth take their tolls or census tax from, their subjects or from foreigners?" Peter replied, "From foreigners!" Jesus then said to him, "Then the subjects are exempt. However, in order not to offend them, go to the sea, drop in a hook, and take the first fish that comes up. Open its mouth and you will find a coin worth twice the temple tax. Give that to them for me and for you." Peter hurried to the lake and cast his hook into the water. He was overjoyed when he found the money in the mouth of the first fish he caught. He gave the money to the taxmen and told everyone of this marvelous event [Matt: 17, 24-27].

That evening after supper, we all gathered in the great hall to listen to Jesus, when James asked him, "Master, who is the greatest in the kingdom of God?" Jesus called a small child over and stood the child in their midst, and said, "Amen, I say to you, unless you turn and become like children, you will not enter the kingdom of heaven. Whoever humbles himself like this child is the greatest in the kingdom of heaven. Whoever receives one child such as this in my name receives me. Let all mankind take notice, whoever causes one of these little ones who believe in me to sin, it would be better for him to have a great millstone hung about his neck and to be drowned in the depths of the sea. Woe to the world because of things that cause sin! Such things must come, but woe to the one through whom they come!"

The next morning Jesus appointed seventy-two disciples whom he sent on ahead in pairs to announce his arrival to every town and place that he intended to visit. His instructions to them were much the same as those he had given previously to the twelve. In addition, he said to them, "Upon your return we will begin our final journey to Jerusalem. I send you out for the harvest is abundant but the laborers are few; so ask the master of the harvest to send out laborers for his harvest. I am sending you out like lambs among wolves. Tell all you see—the kingdom of God is at hand.

Two weeks later the seventy-two returned rejoicing saying, "Lord, even the demons are subject to us because of your name."

Jesus told them, "I have observed Satan fall like lightning from the sky. Behold, I have given you the power to tread upon serpents and scorpions and upon the full force of the enemy and nothing will harm you. Nevertheless, do not rejoice because the spirits are subject to you, but rejoice because your names are written in heaven [Luke: 10, 17-20]."

A few days later we prepared to leave our home in Capernaum, Jesus knew it would be for the last time. The night before, we prayed together long into the early morning. Part of his prayer to his eternal Father was as follows. "My eternal Father, in compliance with your will, I gladly hasten to satisfy your justice by suffering even unto death. My death will reconcile the children of Adam and pay all their debts. My sacrifice will reopen the gates of heaven, which you closed to them. I wish to vanquish hell and enhance the glories of the triumph over Lucifer, and over the vices, which he has sown into the world. I wish to satiate my heart with insults and affronts, which are so estimable in your eyes. I wish to humiliate myself even to death at the hands of my enemies. Our chosen friends, whenever they choose to humiliate themselves in suffering the same persecutions, may then be consoled in their tribulations and honored by high rewards. Oh beloved, Cross; soon you shall receive me in your arms? Oh sweet ignominies and affronts; you will bear me to overcome death through the sufferings of my entirely guiltless flesh? You, pains, affronts, ignominies, scourges, thorns, torments, and death, come to me for I wish to embrace you. Yield yourselves to my welcome, since I well understand your value. If the world abhors you, I long for you. If the world in its ignorance despises you, I, who am truth, wisdom and love embrace you. Come to me you pains and disappoint me not.

Heed not my Omnipotence, for I shall permit you to exert your full force upon my humanity. The deceitful fascination of the children of Adam in vainly judging as unhappy the poor and the afflicted of this world; shall now disappear. For if they see their true God, their Creator, Master, and brother, suffering horrible insults, scourging, and the ignominious torment and destitution of the cross, they will understand their error and esteem it as an honor to follow their crucified God."

I also prayed giving over to my personal feelings of grief and I prayed, "Today, my Lord and eternal Father, I leave my country and I joyfully follow my Son and Master in order to be present at the sacrifice of his life and of his human existence for mankind. There is no sorrow like my sorrow at seeing the Lamb, who takes away the sins of the world, delivered over to bloodthirsty wolves. I cannot bear to see my Son subjected to suffering, torment, and death. Jesus was engendered of your substance from all eternity and is your living image and figure. He is equal to you through all the ages, but now must be subjected to the insult and death of the Cross. He, whom I have given life in my womb, and I, who have basked in the beauty of that countenance for thirty-three years, which is the joy of my eyes and the delight of all the angels, must now see that beauty obscured by filth and wounds. Oh would it be possible that I receive the pains and sorrows, which awaits him, and that I might suffer death in order to save his life! Accept, heavenly Father, the sacrifice of my sorrowing affection, which I offer in unison with him. Oh how quickly flee the days and hours, which shall end in the night of my sorrow and bitterness! It will be a fortunate day for the children of men, but a night of affliction for my sorrow-laden heart, so soon to be deprived of its illuminating Sun. O children of Adam, so deeply lost in error and so forgetful of your souls. Awake at last from your heavy slumber and recognize the weight of your sins in the devastation they are about to cause your God and Creator! See their dire effects in my mortal sorrow and bitterness of my soul! Begin at last to take heed of the damage wrought by sin!"

The following morning, we began our final journey to Jerusalem. My heart was heavy with that which was soon to take place. Yet, paradoxically, the joy and wonder of Jesus' impending sacrifice filled my soul. I yearned to die with my Son, or better yet, die in his place. However, God had made it plain to me that this was not possible. Yet, a woman can only fret and act like a mother when it is her Son that is to suffer.

We slowly worked our way through Galilee, our destination the district of Judea across the Jordan. Great crowds followed Jesus and in these last few months of his life on this earth, he increased his miracles and cured all that came to him. In addition, the Apostles and the disciples also healed, instructed and prepared people for the baptism of penance. Mary Cleophas, Mary Salome, and I, along with about thirty other women were kept busy teaching and instructing the women, in addition to washing clothes, and preparing meals for the men of our party. Mary Magdalene had returned to Bethany to be with her family for she had received word that her brother Lazarus was ailing. Judas Iscariot had again absented himself from our midst in spite of my prayers and all that I could do to persuade him to amend his life. Now, he only showed up now long enough to collect as much money as he could to take care of his so-called alms. At this time, he was using the money primarily for his own use.

My Son and I parted company a few times in order to administer to the needs of people in different localities. On these excursions, Jesus assigned John to accompany me and to attend to my needs. From that time on I began to inform John of some of the great mysteries and hidden sacraments with which I had been blessed. On this last journey, I, like my Son, became more lavish in my blessed benefactions to the people. John and I brought many to the path of eternal life. We cured the sick, visited the poor, the afflicted, the destitute, and the infirm. I assisted the dying with my own hands, especially those that were the most forsaken and afflicted with greater suffering and pain. During these absences, my desire to return to the presence of Jesus increased a thousand fold. I had such a yearning desire to see him that I often swooned away in ecstasies of love and affection. Jesus, in turn, who knew all, that passed in my heart, faithfully corresponded with my feelings.

He spoke these words to me, "You have wounded my heart, my, Sister, my, Spouse; you have wounded my heart with one of your eyes."

I knew that my Son, in as far as he was man, could not have left my presence. Thus, it was natural that he should hasten to relieve and console me by his presence at every chance that he got. He explained to me, "The beauty of your most pure soul refreshes me and makes all my labors and hardships appear sweet. I look upon you as the choice and only fruit of all my exertions, and your mere presence repays me for all my bodily sufferings." These revelations only made me more humble before my Son, the Father, and the Holy Spirit, in an effort to make myself worthy of such love.

We wended our way toward Judea continuing to spread the word of God. As we neared Bethany, where Lazarus and his sister Martha lived, we received disturbing news. Martha and Mary Magdalene sent word that Lazarus was very ill, saying, "Master, the one you love is very ill and at the point of death." Of course, everyone expected that Jesus, in spite of the danger to him in Judea, would immediately move on to Bethany to cure Lazarus, for their close friendship was well known.

Instead; however, Jesus said, "This illness is not to end in death, but is for the glory of God that the Son of man may be glorified through it."

I, along with the rest of the women, began to pray for the quick recovery of Lazarus. Two days later my Son said to Peter, "We must go now to see Lazarus."

Peter; however, remonstrated with him saying, "Rabbi, the Jews of Judea intend to stone you, and you want to go back there?"

Jesus answered him, "Are there not twelve hours in a day? If one walks during the day, he does not stumble, because he sees the light of this world. But if one walks at night, he stumbles, because the light is not in him." Then he added, "Our friend Lazarus is asleep, but I am going to awaken him."

John pleaded with him, "Master, if he is asleep, he will be awakened"

Jesus; however, was speaking of death, while they were speaking of sleep. Therefore, my Son then said quite clearly, "Lazarus has died, and I am glad for you that I was not there, so that you may believe. Let us go to him."

Thomas, ever loyal, but usually pessimistic said to his fellow disciples. "Let us also go to die with him."

We arrived in Bethany four days later. Lazarus was indeed dead. His family had already buried him. Bethany was only two miles from Jerusalem, and many friends of Lazarus had gathered to console the family. When Martha heard that Jesus was coming she went to meet him, but Mary Magdalene remained at home. After greeting Jesus, she said to him, "Lord, if you had been here, my brother would not have died. But even now I know that whatever you ask of God, God will give you."

The Savior said to her, "Your brother will rise."

Martha replied, "I know he will rise in the resurrection on the last day."

Jesus told her, "I am the resurrection and the life; whoever believes in me, even if he dies, will live, and everyone who lives and believes in me will never die. Do you believe this?"

Martha replied, "Yes, Lord. I have come to believe that you are the Messiah, the Son of God, the one who was to come into the world." After saying this, she called her sister Mary Magdalene saying, "The Master is here and is asking for you." Upon hearing this, Magdalene rose quickly and went to him. When the friends and relatives saw Mary rush out they presumed that she was going to the tomb to grieve there and they followed her.

Mary came up to my Son and fell at his feet and said to him, "Lord, if you had been here, my brother would not have died."

When Jesus saw her and all her friends weeping, he became perturbed and deeply troubled, and said to them, "Where have you laid him?"

They replied, "Sir, come and see."

As our group fell in behind the mourners, my Son wept openly to which there was a mixed reaction. One person said, "See how he loved him."

However, another said, "Could not the one who opened the eyes of the blind man have done something so that this man would not have died?"

When we came to the tomb, Jesus, at the sight of the cave with its stone rolled across the front, was again visibly shaken and he said to them, "Take away the stone."

Martha, who had followed along protested, saying, "Lord, by now there will be a stench; he has been dead four days."

However, Jesus said to her, "Did I not tell you that if you believe you will see the glory of God?"

So the men took away the stone, and Jesus raised his eyes and said, "Father, I thank you for hearing me. I know that you always hear me; but because of the crowd here I have said this that they may believe that you sent me." After he said this, Jesus cried out in a loud voice, "Lazarus, come out!"

The dead man came out, tied hand and foot with burial bands, and his face was wrapped in a cloth. So my Son said to them, "Untie him and let him go." [John: 11, 17-44]

The people were amazed and consequently, many believed. However, some of them went to the Pharisees and told them what Jesus had done. Consequently, the Pharisees and the chief priests convened the Sanhedrin and asked, "What are we going to do? This man is performing many signs. If we do nothing, all will believe in him, and the Romans will come and take away our land and our nation."

However, Caiaphas, who was the high priest that year, said to them, "You know nothing, nor do you consider that it is better for you that one man should die instead of the people, so that the whole nation may not perish [John: 12, 49-50]."

God, as he often does, used his opponent to prophesy that Jesus was going to die for the nation, and not only for the nation, but also to gather into one the dispersed children of God. So it was that from that day on the Sanhedrin plotted to kill my Son. Prudently, Jesus no longer walked about in public among the Jews, but withdrew to a town near the desert called Ephraim, which was about twelve miles northeast of Jerusalem. There with a considerable following, we remained until it was time for the Passover. Many people went into Jerusalem early to purify themselves for the coming event. They looked for my Son and when he did not show up, they said, "What do you think? Do you believe that he will come to the feast?" They questioned whether he would show up, since the high priests and the Pharisees had given orders that if anyone knew where he was; he was to inform them, so that they might arrest him.

Six days before Passover, our group left for Bethany where Lazarus lived, the one my Son had raised from the dead. Judas had rejoined our group, for his own nefarious reasons, when he learned that Jesus intended to enter Jerusalem. During the journey, Jesus took the twelve Apostles aside by themselves, and said to them, "Behold, we are going up to Jerusalem, and the Son of Man will be handed over to the chief priests and Scribes, and they will condemn him to death. Then they will hand him over to the Gentiles to be mocked and scourged and crucified, and he will be raised up on the third day."

The Apostles still did not comprehend the message, for they would not allow themselves to believe that Jesus was to die, and in such an ignominious manner. As they were resting there the mother of the sons of Zebedee approached Jesus with her sons and did him homage, wishing to ask him for something. He said to her, "What do you wish?"

She said to him, "Command that these two sons of mine sit, one at your right, and the other at your left, in your kingdom."

Jesus replied, "You do not know what you are asking." Turning to the two men he asked, "Can you drink the cup that I am gong to drink?"

They said to him in unison, "We can."

Jesus said, "My cup you will indeed drink, but to sit at my right or at my left, is not mine to give, but it is for those for whom it has been prepared by my Father."

When the ten heard this, they became indignant at the two brothers, but Jesus called them to him and said, "You know that the rulers of the Gentiles lord it over them, and the great ones make their authority over them felt. However, it shall not be so among you. Rather, whoever wishes to be great among you shall be your servant; whoever wishes to be first among you shall be your slave. Just so, the Son of man did not come to be served but to serve and to give his life in ransom for many."

We left that place and as we entered Jericho a great crowd assembled about Jesus. Two blind men were sitting by the road and as he passed, they called out, "Lord, Son of David have pity on us?"

Jesus stopped and called out asking, "What do you want me to do for you?"

They answered him, "Lord, that our eyes might be opened."

Moved with pity, Jesus touched their eyes. They received their sight at once and began to follow him praising God.

When Lazarus learned of the impending visit, he arranged for a banquet for his distinguished guest. Lazarus seated my Son, and the twelve Apostles at the head table, and Martha insisted on serving them personally. Before the dinner was served, Mary Magdalene, inspired by the Holy Spirit and by her own burning love for Christ, the Redeemer, came up to Jesus who was reclined at the table. Taking an alabaster vase of costly perfumed oil made from genuine aromatic nard; she broke the vessel and anointed with the fragrant and precious liquid, the head and feet of her Master. Then she wiped his feet and dried them with her hair. This was the second time that she had done this for my Son. The fragrance of the oil filled the entire house.

Judas Iscariot, the one who was to later betray Jesus, began to criticize this mysterious anointing of his Master. Judas complained bitterly to the other Apostles. In his greed, Judas wanted such items given to him. Then he could sell them on the pretext of donating the money to charity. He whined, "The poor are being defrauded of their alms by the lavish expense and waste of so costly an article. Why was this oil not sold for three hundred days wages and given to those less fortunate?" He said this not because he cared about the poor but because he was a thief and intended the money for his own use.

However, Jesus said to him, "Leave her alone. Let her keep this for the day of my burial. It was by enlightenment of the Holy Spirit that she has done this thing. You always have the poor with you, but you do not always have me. Regard this act as a prophetic announcement of the mysterious unction that I am soon to undergo in the torments of my death and at my burial."

Judas did not take to heart anything that the Lord said, but on the contrary, he conceived a furious wrath against my Son because he had justified Magdalene's actions. Lucifer profited by this depravity, and incited Judas to new depths of avarice, anger, and a mortal hate against the Author of life. Consequently, Judas resolved to bring about the death of Jesus by betraying him to the Pharisees. Soon after, he slipped away to Jerusalem and told the Pharisees that his Master taught new laws contrary to those of Moses. He said Jesus was addicted to banquets, led a wicked life, was a friend of the depraved, and that this conduct should be stopped. The Pharisees were of the same mind, and instigated by the same prince of darkness, they readily accepted his advice and testimony. With them he agreed on a price for the betrayal of my Son, our Lord and Savior, Jesus Christ. All the thoughts of Judas lay open not only to the Lord, but also to me. Jesus said nothing to Judas regarding this matter, but continued to deal with him as a kind Father and tried to enlighten his obstinate heart. In turn, I redoubled my admonitions and gentle endeavors to withdraw Judas from the precipice, and on the night of the banquet, which preceded Palm Sunday, I called him aside to speak to him alone. With tears and my most persuasive words, I warned him of the terrible danger that threatened him if he should persist in his intentions. However, none of my efforts were to any avail, nor did any of my words soften his hardened heart and soul. On the contrary, as he could not find an answer and since my exhortations were so urgent, he lashed himself into a fury, and then exhibited his wrath by a sullen silence. I then left him and went to my Son and cast myself weeping at his feet, for the sins of Judas, like all sin, was that which would bring my Son to the Cross. I sought to bring him some consolation for the evil that Judas was about to do.

The Lord was now about to enter upon the greatest conflict of his career as man. While I was still with him, he offered himself anew to the eternal Father. Prostrate, with his face touching the ground, he confessed him and adored him with deepest resignation beseeching him to accept the insults and pains, ignominies and death of the Cross for his own glory and for the rescue of the human race. I retired to one side of his oratory, accompanying my beloved Son and my Lord in his prayers and shedding with him tears of inmost affection. On this occasion, before the hour of midnight, the eternal Father and the Holy Ghost appeared in visible form with multitudes of angels as witnesses. The eternal Father accepted the sacrifice of Christ; his most blessed Son, and formally consented that the rigor of his justice should be satisfied upon his Person for the pardon of the world.

Then the eternal Father said to me, "Mary, our daughter and spouse, I desire that you now again ratify this sacrifice of your Son, since I on my part am willing to deliver him up for the Redemption of man."

Most humbly and sincerely, I responded, "Oh Lord, I am but dust and ashes, unworthy that your Onlybegotten and the Redeemer of the world should also be my Son. I hold myself entirely subject to your ineffable condescension, which has given him *being* in my womb, and I offer him and myself entirely as a sacrifice to your divine pleasure. I beseech you, oh Lord God and Father, to permit me to suffer with your and my Son."

The eternal Father received my subjection as a pleasing sacrifice. He raised us to our feet and said, "This is the fruit of the blessed earth, which I have desired." Immediately thereupon he exalted the Humanity of Christ to the throne of his Majesty, and placed him on his right hand equal in authority and pre-eminence with himself. God entirely transformed and exalted me in wonderful splendor and jubilee of soul. On seeing Jesus seated at the right hand of his Father, I repeated the words from the one hundred and tenth Psalms, which had mysteriously prophesied this event,

"The Lord said unto my Lord, sit thou at my right hand."

I immediately composed a hymn of praise in honor of the Father and of the Incarnate Word. When I finished, the Father added all the rest of the Psalm, decreeing then and there by his immutable will that all the import of these mysterious and profound words should now be executed and fulfilled.

A large crowd had gathered for the feast at the house of Lazarus. They came to see Jesus, and also, to see Lazarus whom he had raised from the dead. The Sanhedrin was quickly informed and the chief priests plotted to not only kill Jesus, but to kill Lazarus as well, for he was a walking testimony of the Savior's powers. Learning that Jesus was coming to Jerusalem the following morning; the guests from the previous night and many others gathered palm branches and eagerly waited to greet him when he entered Jerusalem.

Early the following morning we all set out for Jerusalem accompanied by a huge following and, unseen by the multitude, we were preceded by a host of angels who sang hymns of praise at seeing their king so enamored of men and so solicitous for their eternal salvation. When we drew near Bethphage on the Mount of Olives, Jesus sent James and John ahead, saying to them, Go into the village opposite you, and you will find an ass tethered and a colt with her. Untie them and bring them to me. "If anyone should say anything to you reply, 'The Master has need of them.' Then he will send them at once." My Son did this so that what had been spoken through the Prophet might be fulfilled [Luke: 19, 30-34],

"Say to daughter Zion, "Behold your king comes to you, meek and riding on an ass, and on a colt, the foal of a beast of burden [Zec: 9, 9]."

James and John did as Jesus had ordered them. They found the animals just as Jesus had described. The big strong beast was a beautiful, pale-gray, Muscat ass. His coat was so light that it could be mistaken for white. Yet, it was still a beast contemptible in the sight of human vanity and pretension. The colt, never ridden by man, was a long legged, frolicsome copy of its mother. The Apostles brought them to Jesus and they laid their cloaks over both the beasts, for the Lord was to make use of both of them according to the prophecies of [Is: 62, 11] and [Zec: 9, 9]. The Prophets had foretold these particulars many years before, in order that the priests and scribes should not be able to allege ignorance as an excuse for not acknowledging Jesus as the Messiah. Many people spread their cloaks on the road, while others cut branches from the trees and strewed them on the road.

The crowds proceeding and those following him, joyfully waved their palms and cried out saying, "Hosanna to the Son of David; blessed is he who comes in the name of the Lord, hosanna in the highest."

All along the way the adults as well as the small children, hailed Jesus as the true Messias, the Son of David, the Savior of the world, and as their legitimate king. One cried out, "Peace be in heaven and glory in the highest, and blessed be he that comes as the king in the name of the Lord. Another said, "Hosanna to the Son of David. Save us, Son of David, and blessed be the kingdom which now has arrived, the kingdom of our forefather David."

When we entered Jerusalem the entire city was shaken and many pilgrims from the Diaspora asked, "Who is this man?"

The people replied, "This is Jesus the Prophet, from Nazareth in Galilee."

The crowds gave Jesus a king's reception and they greeted his disciples warmly. Judas was confused. Had he miscalculated? Was Jesus truly a king? He decided to stick close to his Master. Perhaps now, he was going to proclaim himself king? If so, it was not too late for him to change his mind. Jesus' timing to declare himself King, he thought, could not have been any better with thousands of Jewish pilgrims in Jerusalem to celebrate the Passover. I knew what Judas was thinking, and I asked my women friends to pray for him. What Judas could not know was that most of these people were enemies of my Son. God's divine power had interiorly motivated the masses of people. It would have been impossible to draw such a crowd even if they did admire Jesus for the miracles he had wrought. Many of them were heathens, and his declared enemies, who now, nevertheless, hailed him as the true Messiah, Savior, and king. They subjected themselves to a poor, despised and persecuted man. Jesus did not come in triumphal chariots, or on prancing steeds, or with an ostentatious display of riches, but instead he came without any arms or outward show of human power. Outwardly, all of this was wanting, as he thus entered seated on a beast contemptible in the sight of human vanity and pretension. The only signs of the dignity of Jesus were in his countenance, which showed forth the gravity and serene majesty of his soul, while all the rest fell far short and was opposed to what the world is inclined to applaud and celebrate. Hence, the outward happenings of this day proclaimed his divine power, which directly moved the hearts of men to acknowledge him as their Christ and Redeemer.

Jesus, by his divine light, moved the hearts of men in the city of Jerusalem to acknowledge him as Redeemer. Jesus did so to entirely fulfill the eternal Father's promises. All creatures felt the triumph of Jesus, especially those that were capable of reasoning. The archangel Michael announced these dramatic events to the holy Fathers and Prophets in limbo. God allowed them, by a special vision, to see these proceedings. Jesus moved those throughout the world, who knew him, to adore the Redeemer in spirit. In order that the triumph of our Savior over death might be more glorious, the Most High ordained that on that day *death* should have no power over any of the mortals. Ordinarily, in the natural course, many persons would have died on that day, but not one of the human race died within those twenty-four hours. To this triumph over death was added the triumph over hell, which, though it was more hidden, was even more glorious. As soon as the people began to proclaim and invoke Christ as their Savior, the demons felt the power of the right hand of God, and all of them, in whatever place they lurked in the world, were hurled into the dark caverns of the infernal abyss. During the short time of the march, not a demon remained upon the earth. All of them were trembling with wrath and terror in the depths of hell. They began to be filled with a dread that perhaps the Messiah was already in the world.

After the triumphal march of his Son, God suspended the divine influence, which had so readily disposed the people of Jerusalem in Jesus' favor. Although the just had been much benefited, and many had been justified, most of the people returned to their vices and imperfections. Although many had hailed and acknowledged Jesus as their king and Savior, not one tendered him hospitality or received him in their home. Each day, until the Passion, we walked back and forth to Bethany.

With the roar of the crowd in his ears, Jesus marched directly to the Temple of Jerusalem. When he entered the holy places, he found that the merchants had again set up their tables within the temple's holy precincts and were buying and selling as before. Taking a cluster of ropes, Jesus upset their tables, and using his whip drove them from the temple. He stormed at them, "My house shall be a house of prayer, but you are making it a den of thieves."

The blind and the lame approached him while he was in the temple area, and he cured them all. When the chief priests and the scribes saw the wondrous things he was doing, and heard the children in the temple area crying out, "Hosanna to the Son of David," they were indignant and complained to Jesus saying, "Do you hear what they are saying?"

Jesus replied, "Yes; and have you never read the text," 'Out of the mouths of infants and nurslings you have brought forth praise.'

Jesus left them then, and we all followed him back to the house of Lazarus and we all spent the night there.

While returning to the temple the following day, my Son became hungry. Seeing a fig tree, he went over to it but found that it was barren. He exclaimed, "May no fruit ever come from you again." Immediately the tree withered.

When everyone saw this they were amazed and Philip asked, "How was it that the fig tree withered?"

Jesus explained, "Amen, I say to you, if you have faith and do not waver, not only will you do what has been done to the fig tree, but even if you say to this mountain, 'Be lifted up and thrown into the sea,' it will be done. Whatever you ask for in prayer with faith, you will receive."

Jesus began preaching in the Court of the Gentiles and the rest of us spread out and began teaching and instructing the New Way. The chief priests approached Jesus as he was teaching and said, "By what authority are you doing these things? And who gave you this authority?"

The Messiah said to them in reply, "I shall ask you one question, and if you can answer it for me, then I shall tell you by what authority I do these things." So he asked them, "Where was John's baptism from? Was it of heavenly or of human origin?"

The elders discussed it among themselves and said, "If we say, 'of heavenly origin.' He will say to us, 'Then why did you not believe him?' But if we say, "Of human origin,' we fear the crowd, for they all regard John as a Prophet." So they said to Jesus in reply, "We do not know."

In reply, he stated, "Neither shall I tell you by what authority I do these things."

With this the elders turned away, and my Son continued to teach the people in parables. He taught the Parable of the Two Sons, the Parable of the Tenants, and the Parable of the Wedding Feast. Then the scribes came back trying again to entrap him in his answers. They said to him, "Teacher, you are a truthful man. We know that you teach the way of God in accordance with the truth, and that you are not concerned with anyone's opinion, for you do not regard a person's status. Tell us then, what is your opinion; is it lawful to pay the census tax to Caesar or not?"

Knowing their malice, Jesus said, "Why are you testing me, you hypocrites. Show me a coin that pays the census tax." Then they handed him a Roman coin. He said to them, "Whose image is this and whose inscription?"

They replied, "Caesar's"

At that he said to them, "Then repay to Caesar what belongs to Caesar and to God what belongs to God." When they heard this they went away amazed [Matt: 22, 15-22]

The next day when the Pharisees came again to question him, Jesus asked them, "What is your opinion about the Messiah? Whose Son is he?" They quickly replied, "He is David's son."

He said to them, "How then does David, inspired by the Spirit, call him 'Lord', saying, 'The Lord said to my Lord. Sit at my right hand until I place your enemies under your feet. If David calls him 'Lord,' how can he be his son?"

No one was able to answer him, and from that day forward, they were afraid to ask him any more questions [Matt: 22, 41-46].

The next day the Lord denounced the Scribes and the Pharisees, none; however, dared to give answer to him. Jesus lamented, "Jerusalem, Jerusalem, you who kill the Prophets and stone those sent to you, how many times I yearned to gather your children together, as a hen gathers her young under her wings, but you were unwilling. Behold, your house will be abandoned, desolate. I tell you, you will not see me again until you say, 'Blessed is he who comes in the name of the Lord.'"

We all left the temple area that evening, and as we were going away, the disciples were pointing out the various parts of the temple. Jesus stopped, turned, and pointing to the temple said, "You see all these things, do you not? I say to you, there will not be left here a stone upon another stone that will not be thrown down."

For two days, the demons lay shattered by the right hand of the Almighty manifesting their torment by their horrid and confused howls of despair. Even more confounded than the rest, Lucifer called into his presence all the devilish hosts and spoke to them as their leader,

"This Jesus who persecutes us and crushes my power has to be more than a mere Prophet. Moses, Elias and all our other enemies never vanquished us so completely, even though they also performed miracles, nor were any of them able to hide from me so many of their doings as does this one. Of his interior works, I can obtain little information. How can this mere man perform such works and manifest such supreme power over all creation, as are publicly ascribed to him. In celebrating his triumphal entry into Jerusalem, he has shown power over us and over the whole world. Even now I find that my strength for visiting destruction upon him vanishing away. In his present triumph, not only have his friends extolled and proclaimed him as blessed, but also many of those subject to me have done the same and have even called him the Messiah proclaimed in their law. He has drawn them all to venerate and adore him and this certainly seems to exceed mere human power. Never before has a mere man been able to partake of the divine power in such a degree. We have never experienced such ruinous defeat, since we were first cast down from heaven, nor have I ever encountered such overwhelming power before this man came into the world. If he should be the Incarnate Word, as I am now beginning to suspect, we must kill him before he, by his example and teaching, draw all mankind after him."

"In my hate, I have several times sought to bring about his death; but without success. In his own country, when I instigated his fellow citizens to cast him from the precipice, he contemptuously made his way through those, who were to execute the sentence. On another occasion, he simply made himself invisible to the Pharisees, whom I had incited to stone him."

"Now; however, with the help of Judas Iscariot, Jesus' own Apostle, matters seem to promise better success. I have so worked upon the mind of Judas that he is willing to sell and betray his Master to the Pharisees, whom I have also incited to furious envy. They are anxious to inflict upon him a most cruel death, and will no doubt do so. Judas, the priests, and the Pharisees are only waiting for an occasion, which I have planned and arranged for them. However, I now see in all my well-laid plans a great danger, which demands our closest attention. If this man is the Messiah, expected by his people, he will offer his death and all his sufferings for the Redemption of men, and thereby satisfy for their misdeeds and gain infinite merits for all of them. He will open the heavens and pave the way for mortals to the enjoyment of those rewards of which God has deprived us. Such an issue, if we do not prevent it, shall indeed be a terrible torment for us. Moreover this man will leave to the world a new example of patience in suffering and show its merit to all the rest of humanity, for Jesus is most meek and humble of heart and is never impatient or excited. He will teach all men these same virtues, which even to think of this taking place is an abomination to me. These traits are the virtues most offensive to me and to all those who follow my guidance. Hence, it is necessary to unite on a course of action about persecuting this holy man Jesus."

The princes of darkness lashed themselves to incredible fury, and held long consultations concerning this enterprise. The demons were greatly chagrined that God had led them into such a great error. In plotting the Redeemer's death, they had played right into his hands. They resolved to redouble their efforts to repair the damage done and do all they possibly could to hinder his death, for by this time they were all but convinced that Jesus, my Son, was indeed the Redeemer. Lucifer summed up their activities by saying, "Believe me, friends if this man is at the same time true God, he will by his Passion and Death, save all men, and we will be rendered powerless. God will then raise mortals to new happiness and dominion over us. We were greatly mistaken in seeking his death. Let us proceed at once to repair our damage."

Lucifer and his horde of demons poured into Jerusalem and its neighborhood and there, as is referred to in the Gospels, they exerted their influence with Pilate and his wife to prevent the death of the Lord. They beset Judas with new suggestions, trying to dissuade him from his intended treachery. Failing in this, Lucifer appeared to him as a man and reasoned with him not to continue with his plot to deliver Jesus over to the Pharisees. When this also failed, Lucifer, knowing of the avarice of Judas offered him great riches. However, while Judas had given himself up to following Satan's malice, he would not now follow his guidance away from it. Lucifer, not being God, was unable to call to his aid the force of divine grace, and was unable to convert the heart of this perfidious disciple. Jesus and his disciples had exposed Judas to a tremendous influence of good in his association with them. In spite of this blessing, Judas had hardened himself with demoniacal obstinacy. His hatred for my Son and me, made him incapable of seeking our mercy, for he was blind to all reason.

In despair, the demons turned their attention to the Pharisees. Lucifer's hordes attempted by many suggestions and arguments to dissuade them from persecuting Jesus, however like Judas, the demons could not divert the Jews from their wickedness. Unsuccessful in all their efforts, Lucifer called his minions of evil together and stated, "It is obvious we cannot stop that which we have started, therefore all we can hope for now is to induce the Pharisees and their executioners to heap the most atrocious cruelties upon this man. Perhaps we can overcome his invincible patience with the severity of their torture." The Lord allowed the devil's machinations, so that his triumph would be more complete. However, God did not allow the executioners to carry out some of the more indecent atrocities, to which the demons had incited them to do.

On the Wednesday, following my Son's triumphal entry into Jerusalem, we all remained in Bethany. On this day, the scribes and Pharisees met at the house of Caiaphas in order to plan the death of the Savior of the world [Mark: 14, 1]. The welcome with which my Son had been met from among the inhabitants of Jerusalem, following so soon the resurrection of Lazarus and the many other miracles that he had recently performed, had made the Pharisees more determined than ever to take my Son's life. In spite of Lucifer's efforts to the contrary, they had already decided to take away his life under the false pretext of the public good. Judas was now fully in the clutches of his avarice and hate, and altogether deprived of any saving grace. Judas attended the meeting fully determined to betray Jesus. He quickly consummated a deal to betray his Master for thirty pieces of silver. At this same time in Bethany, Jesus said to his disciples, "You know that after two days shall be the Pasch, and the Son of man shall be delivered up to be crucified."

Judas left the meeting of the Pharisees and immediately returned to Bethany seeking out the Apostles and began to inquire of them and of even of Jesus and me, as to what we intended to do on the following days. However, my Son and I were well aware of the reason for his feverish activity, for the holy angels had immediately reported to me the shameful contract into which Judas had entered. When he approached me, I merely said to him, "Who can penetrate, oh, Judas, the secret judgments of the Most High?"

Now certain of the irreparable ruin of Judas, and of the delivery of Jesus into the hands of his enemies, I no longer admonished him about his sins. In my grief, I turned to my angels and broke out into the tenderest lamentations, for they were the only ones with whom I could share my heartrending sorrow.

The three days before my Son's false arrest were in a way the sweetest and at the same time the bitterest of my life. Sweet because I was with my Son and bitter because I knew that I was to lose his physical presence so very soon. Jesus spent much of his time with me the first three days of the week, which followed the day the faithful, would forever after call Palm Sunday. During his last journeys into Jerusalem, Jesus instructed his Apostles and disciples more clearly and fully concerning the mysteries of his coming Passion and of human Redemption. Nevertheless, although they listened to the teachings and forewarnings of their God and Master, each person was affected thereby only in so far as his disposition allowed and according to the motives and sentiments of his heart. They were always tardy in their response and they fell short of their protestations of zealous love, as events afterwards would demonstrate.

Jesus explained the exalted sacraments and mysteries of the Redemption in such detail that many of them will remain hidden until they shall be revealed in the beatific vision. He instructed me in all that I was to do during his Passion and Death and enlightened me anew with divine light. In these conferences, he spoke to me with a new and kingly reserve, for now the tenderness and caresses of a Son and Spouse had temporarily ceased.

Thursday, the eve of the Passion and Death of our Savior, arrived all too quickly. At earliest dawn, the Lord called me to him and I prostrated myself at his feet. Raising me up, he spoke to me in words of soothing and tenderest love, "My, Mother, the hour decreed by the eternal wisdom of my Father has arrived. It is proper that again, we subject to him our will, as we have so often done before. Give me your permission to enter upon my suffering and death, and, as my true mother, consent that I deliver myself over to my enemies in obedience to my eternal Father. In this manner, you willingly co-operate with me in this work of salvation, since I have received from you in your virginal womb the form of a suffering and mortal man in which I will redeem the world and satisfy the divine justice. Just as you, of your own free will, did consent to my Incarnation, so I now desire you to give consent also to my passion and death of the Cross. To again sacrifice me of your own free will to the decree of my eternal Father shall be the return, which I ask of you for having made you my mother. For the Father has sent me in order that by the sufferings of my flesh, I might recover the lost sheep of his house, the children of Adam."

These words of my Son and Savior pierced my heart and cast me into the throes of sorrow greater than I had ever endured. For now had arrived that dreadful hour, from whence there was no issue for my pains, nor any appeal to the swift-fleeting time, or to any other tribunal. For now, as his most prudent mother, I looked upon him as my God, infinite in his attributes and perfections, and as the true God-man, in hypostatical union with the person of the Word, I beheld him sanctified and ineffably exalted by this union with the Godhead. Now I had to deliver him over into the hands of his enemies. My mind and my heart were numb with immeasurable sorrow, but I, as the Queen of heaven and of the earth, had to rise above my feelings as a mother, and I vanquished this invincible pain and prostrated myself at the feet of my divine Son.

In deepest reverence, I kissed his feet and answered him, "Lord and highest God, author of all that has being, though you are the Son of my womb, I am your handmaid. The condescension of your ineffable love alone has raised me from the dust to the dignity of being your mother. I offer myself and resign myself to his divine pleasure in order that in me, just as in you, my Son and Lord, his eternal and adorable will be fulfilled. I wish that I could die in your place. However, the inversion of our lot is not possible. My disappointment is the greatest sacrifice, which I can offer the Father; for to suffer in imitation of you and in your company would be a great relief for my pains, all torments would be sweet, if undergone in union with yours. That you should endure all these torments for the salvation of humanity shall be my only relief in my pains. Receive, oh my God, this sacrifice of my desire to die with you, and my still continuing to live, while you, the most innocent Lamb and figure of the substance of your eternal Father, undergo death. Receive also the agonies of my sorrow to see the inhuman cruelty of your enemies executed on your exalted person, because of the wickedness of human beings. I offer myself as a companion and Coadjutrix in your Passion and although most unworthy, I have but one request, which I desire from my inmost soul. I beseech you, if it is your pleasure, to make me a participant in the ineffable Sacrament of your body and blood. You have resolved to institute it as a pledge of your glory and I desire in receiving you sacramentally in my heart to share the effects of this new and admirable Sacrament. My perpetuating these merits through the same humanity, which you have received from my womb, creates for me a certain right. Let this right consist not so much in giving yourself to me in this Sacrament as in making me yours by this new possession. All my desires and exertions I have devoted to the worthy reception of this holy Communion from the moment in which you gave me knowledge of it and ever since it was your fixed decree to remain in the holy Church under the species of consecrated bread and wine. Do you then, my Lord and God, return to your first habitation which you did find in me, your beloved mother and your slave, whom you have prepared for your reception by exempting me from the common touch of sin. Then shall I receive within me the humanity, which I have communicated to you from my own blood, and thus shall we be united in a renewed and close embrace. This prospect enkindles my heart with most ardent love, and may I never be separated from you, who are the infinite good and the love of my soul."

My Son answered me, "My, Mother, it is my pleasure to grant your request. At the hour of its institution, you shall also receive the blessing of Holy Communion." Then he said to my angels, "Attend to her every need in visible forms. Serve and console her in her sorrow and loneliness." This, my angels were delighted to comply with. I had them join with me in canticles of praise, and I offered up my thanks with the deepest acts of devotion and acts of humility.

Jesus then said to me, "After I depart for Jerusalem with my disciples, I wish you to follow shortly after in the company of the holy women. Instruct and encourage them, in order that they might not be scandalized in seeing me suffer the great ignominies and torments of my frightful death on the Cross." He then gave me his personal blessing. The sorrow, which filled our hearts, passes all conception of man. This sorrow was in direct proportion to the love that we had for one another. This love was again proportional to the dignity and station of our lives. It is worthy of all believers to meditate upon our sorrow and follow us on my Son's sorrowful journey with the deepest compassion. God will consider you as hard-hearted ingrates, if you neglect to do so.

About midday, the following day, Jesus accompanied by his Apostles and disciples departed on his journey from Bethany to Jerusalem. Just before he left, my Son raised his eyes to heaven and prayed to his heavenly Father, "Eternal Father and my God, in compliance with your holy will I now go to suffer and die for the liberation of men, my brethren, and the creatures of your hands. As far as shall depend upon you and me, no soul shall be deprived of a salvation most abundant, and your inviolate equity shall stand justified in all those who despise this copious Redemption."

A short time later I followed my Son, accompanied by Mary Magdalene, and the other holy women. I instructed the holy women in the same manner as my Son had instructed the Apostles to prepare them for his Passion. Jesus instructed his disciples so that they would not desert him because of the ignominies that they were to witness, and the dangers of the temptations of Lucifer. Mary Magdalene's spiritual love for Jesus entirely consumed her in the flames of that love. She would distinguish herself at his crucifixion. She had a magnanimous, courageous, and energetic disposition, Magdalene was well educated and since her conversion was full of noble fidelity. She, before all the others of the Apostolate, had taken it upon herself to accompany me and attend upon me during the entire Passion, and this resolve she fulfilled as my most faithful friend. Jesus' prayer was imaged like a clear mirror in my soul, I was able to see all the works of my divine Son, and I was thus able to imitate him as closely as humanly possible. I ordered my angels, visible only to me, to give benediction, glory and honor to the Father, the Son and the Holy Ghost, and they eagerly fulfilled my wishes with the greatest enthusiasm.

On the journey to Jerusalem, Jesus again explained to his disciples all that was going to happen to him during his Passion. The various Apostles proposed their doubts, and difficulties. Jesus, as the Teacher of wisdom and as a loving Father, answered them in words, which sweetly penetrated into their very hearts. "After my Resurrection," he explained to them, "when I, as the Son of man, come into my glory, my angels will be with me, and I will be seated upon a glorious throne. I will separate the deceased souls, one from another, as a shepherd separates the sheep from the goats. I will place the sheep on my right and the goats on my left. Then I will say to those on my right, 'Come, you who are blessed by my Father, inherit the kingdom prepared for you from the foundation of the world. For I was hungry and you gave me food, and I was thirsty and you gave me drink, a stranger and you welcomed me, naked and you clothed me, ill and you cared for me'. Then the righteous will ask me, 'Lord when did we see you hungry and feed you, or thirsty and give you drink? When did we see you a stranger and welcome you, or naked and clothe you? When did we see you ill or in prison, and visit you?' Then I will tell them, 'Amen, I say to you, whatever you did for one of these least brothers of mine, you did for me.' Then I will say to those on my left, 'Depart from me you accursed, into the eternal fire prepared for the devil and his angels. For I was hungry and you gave me no food, I was thirsty and you gave me no drink, a stranger and you gave me no welcome, naked and you gave me no clothing, ill and in prison, and you did not care for me.' Then they will answer and say, 'Lord, when did we see you naked or ill or in prison, and not minister to your needs?' I will answer them, 'Amen, I say to you, what you did not do for one of these least ones, you did not do for me.' These will go off to eternal punishment, but the righteous shall receive eternal life [Matt: 26, 31-46]."

The disciples had no trouble in understanding this statement, but they were all confused and at odds with what the Lord had told them of his Passion. Their lack of understanding only made Jesus love them more. The knowledge of his impending Passion and the prospect of his great torment, did not hinder him in his manifestation of his love, first to those nearest him and then, to those who sought to kill him. Except for my Son and I, the rest of mortals are ordinarily roused to resentment by injury, or dismayed and disgusted by adversity, and they deem it a great thing not to revenge themselves on those who offend them. However, the impending ignominies of his Passion did not daunt the love of Jesus. The ignorance of his Apostles and their disloyalty, which he was so soon to experience, did not dampen his love either.

As they neared Jerusalem, James turned to Jesus and asked him, "Where do you wish us to celebrate the Passover supper?" For on Thursday night, all Jews were to partake of the lamb of the Pasch, a most notable and solemn national feast. This eating of the Paschal lamb was most prophetic and significant of the Messiah and the mysteries connected with him and his work. The Apostles of course were not yet aware of its intimate connection with Christ.

My Son said to Peter and John, "Go to Jerusalem and your feet will guide you to a house, where you will see a servant enter with a jug of water. Say to the master of the house, In the name of Jesus of Nazareth would you please prepare a room for his Last Supper with his disciples [Mark: 14, 12-16]?"

Jason was rich and influential, and was much devoted to Jesus and his teachings. My Son rewarded his great piety by choosing his house for the celebration of the great mystery. Thus was his home later consecrated as a temple for the faithful of the future. The heart of the householder was enlightened by special grace, and he readily offered them a very large hall, appropriately tapestried and adorned for the mysteries which, unknown to anyone, the Lord was to celebrate therein.

Later in the afternoon, Jesus, his Apostles and disciples, arrived at the banquet hall. The Upper Room was exceedingly large for the small city of Jerusalem. It easily held the one hundred and twenty faithful that were the close confidants of our Blessed Lord. The floor was paved with colorful mosaic tile and partitioned off with low cast-iron fences. Small staircases led from the main room to spacious side rooms. Several great pillars held up the vaulted ceiling. Ornate olive oil lamps hung from the high ceiling casting a cheerful but serene atmosphere to the entire room. The faithful would soon simply refer to the room, as the Upper Room or the Cenacle. A short time later, the holy women and I arrived. Upon entering, I prostrated myself at my Son's most holy feet, asked for his blessing, and what we were to do.

He answered. "My Mother, an adjoining room has been prepared for you and the holy women. I have made all the arrangements for the banquet. From your room, you will be able to see all that takes place according to the decrees of Providence. There you will console and instruct as far as is proper, the holy women of your company."

This we did and I exhorted them to persevere in faith and prayer. Knowing that the hour of my Holy Communion was at hand, I kept my interior vision riveted on the doings of my most holy Son and spiritually prepared myself for the worthy reception of his body and blood.

Jason, inspired by the Lord, had placed a large altar-like table at the head of the room for Jesus and his Apostles. Before the supper, Jesus arose from the table and prostrated himself before his eternal father and prayed silently, "Eternal Father and Creator of the universe, I am your image, the figure of your substance, and engendered by your intellect. I now desire to humiliate myself in the dust. By this humility of your Onlybegotten, I will confound the pride of Lucifer. I make this sacrifice to leave an example of humility to my Apostles and to my Church. The virtue of humility will be the secure foundation of my Church. I desire to wash the feet of my disciples, including Judas, the least of them all. I shall abase myself and offer him my friendship and salvation. Although he is my greatest enemy among the mortals, I shall not refuse him pardon for his treachery, nor deny him kindest treatment. Thus, if he declines to accept it, the entire world may know, that I have opened up to him the arms of my mercy, and that he repelled my advances with obstinate contempt."

Jesus then arose, and, his face beaming with peace and serenity, commanded his Apostles to be seated indicating that they were of a superior station, while he himself remained standing as if he were their servant. Laying aside his mantle, he girded himself with a large towel and hung it over one shoulder. Then he poured water into a basin, while his Apostles looked on in wonder. He first approached Peter, the head of the Apostles.

When my Son knelt at his feet, the excitable Peter who had acknowledged and proclaimed Jesus as the Son of God, overcome by his own humility exclaimed, "You shall never wash my feet!"

Jesus told him, "You do not know at present what I am doing, but later on you will understand it." I knew this was the same as my Son saying to him, 'First obey my command and will, and do not prefer your will to mine. Before all, you must yield and believe that what I do is proper. Then, having believed and obeyed, you will understand the hidden mysteries of my doings and to gain this knowledge you must first have obedience. Without obedience, you cannot be truly humble, but only presumptuous, nor can your humility take preference of mine. I humiliated myself unto death, and in order to thus humiliate me, I sought the way of obedience, but you, who are my disciple, do not follow my doctrine, by so dong you strip yourself of humility as well as obedience by following your own presumptuous judgment.'

Peter did not understand this doctrine, floundering in the errors of his indiscreet humility, he repeated his error and said, "I will never consent that you wash my feet."

The Lord then said severely, "If I do not wash your feet, you shall have no part of me."

According to human insight, Peter certainly had some excuse for being slow in permitting God to prostrate himself before the earthly and sinful man that he was and to allow him, who was God, to wash his feet. However, this opposition was not excusable in the eyes of the Savior, who could not err in what he wished to. Obedience must be blind and without evasion, if there is not an evident error in what is commanded. In this mystery, my Son wished to repair the disobedience of our first parents, Adam and Eve, by which sin entered into the world. Because of the similarity and relation between it and the disobedience of Peter, our Lord threatened him with a similar punishment, for disobedience would certainly deprive even the Apostle Peter of God's blessings.

The rebuke by Jesus chastened and instructed Peter. He immediately submitted from his whole heart and said, "Lord, not only my feet, but also my hands and my head." By this he acknowledged, 'I offer my feet in order to walk in obedience, my hands in order to exercise it, and my head in order to surrender all of my own judgment that may be contrary to its dictates.'

The Lord accepted this submission of Peter and replied, "He that is washed, needs only to wash his feet, but is clean wholly. And you are clean, *but not all of you*, for one of you will betray me." The doctrines of my Son had cleaned and justified all the disciples, except the unclean Judas to whom Jesus referred. The Apostles were clean of all sins except for some minor venial sins. They would have to purge these sins before they could receive Holy Communion worthily. For venial sins, distractions, and Luke warmness hinder all these benefits very much [John: 13, 1-11].

Jesus, in a last effort to convert Judas, had invited him to sit beside him during the Last Supper. Judas turned to him and asked, "Surely it is not I, Rabbi?" In a low voice that the others could not hear, for my Son still hoped for the soul of Judas, he replied, "You have said so." Then he said to them all, "The Son of man indeed goes, as it is written of him, but woe to the man by whom the Son of man is betrayed. It would be better for that man if he had not been born."

Thereupon my Son washed the feet of Peter and those of all the disciples, who in permitting were greatly astonished and humbled. Jesus washed their feet, and as he did so they were all reduced to tears. The Lord then filled each Apostle with new enlightenment and gifts of grace.

When my Son came to Judas, unknown to those watching, he manifested his special love toward Judas in two ways. First, by the kind and caressing manner in which he approached him, knelt at his feet, washed them, and pressed them to his bosom. Secondly, he sought to move his soul with inspirations proportionate to the dire depravity of his conscience. The assistance he offered to Judas was in itself much greater than that offered to the other Apostles. However, the disposition of Judas was most wicked. His vices were so deeply ingrained, that his understanding and his faculties were much disturbed and weakened. He had entirely forsaken God and given himself over to the devil. Since he had enthroned the evil spirit in his heart, he resisted the divine advances and inspirations connected with the washing of his feet.

During this final meeting with his friends and disciples, the outward appearance of Jesus was most exquisitely charming and attractive. The serene dignified countenance of the Lord was sweetly expressive and beautiful. Abundant waves of chestnut hair framed the face of Jesus, which grew freely after the manner of the Nazarenes. His frank and open eyes beamed forth grace and majesty. His mouth, nose and all the features of his face exhibited perfect proportions and his whole person was clothed in such entrancing loveliness, that he drew upon himself the loving veneration of all whom beheld him without malice in their hearts. Over and above all this, the mere sight of him caused in the beholders an interior joy and enlightenment, engendering heavenly thoughts and sentiments in the soul.

Judas now saw at his feet, this divine personage so lovable and venerable striving to please him by new tokens of affection and seeking to gain him by new impulses of love. However, so great was the perversity of Judas that nothing could move or soften his hardened heart. On the contrary, the gentleness of his Savior offended him, and he refused to look upon his face or take notice of his actions. From the time Judas lost his grace, he never again looked at my face or that of my Son

Greater, in certain respects, was the terror of Lucifer in the presence of Christ. Lucifer, having established himself in the heart of Judas, could not bear the humility of the divine Master toward his disciples, and he sought to escape from Judas and from the Cenacle. However, the Lord detained Lucifer in order to crush his pride.

When he finished washing the feet of his disciples, Jesus donned his mantle, sat down, and said to them, "Do you know what I have done for you? You call me Master and Lord, if then I, being your Lord and Master, have washed your feet; you also ought to wash one another's feet. For I have given you an example, that as I have done to you, so you do, also. Amen, amen, I say to you: the servant is not greater than his Lord is; neither is the Apostle greater than he that sent him is." Then the Lord proceeded to propound great mysteries and truths, and further enlightened those assembled in the mysteries of the most blessed Trinity and of the Incarnation and prepared them by new graces for the Holy Eucharist. He confirmed them in their understanding of the vast significance of his doctrines and miracles. Among them all, Peter and John were the most fully enlightened, but each Apostle and disciple received more or less insight according to his own disposition and according to the divine ordainment.

My Son forced Lucifer to remain in the upper room during his washing of the feet of the disciples, which caused him great anguish and pain. However, Lucifer had astutely conjectured that those assembled were about to receive some great blessing. He sought with implacable fury and pride to spy out these mysteries for the concoction of future malicious plans. To humble the devil, Jesus, allowed Lucifer's presence at the Last Supper, but he had no tolerance for him at the institution of the Holy Eucharist. God had placed the foiling of Lucifer's plans in my hands. To accomplish this, God gave new power to me, so that neither the rebellious Lucifer nor any of his hosts could resist. Inflamed by zeal, love, and the fury of a mother hen protecting her chick, I, as the sovereign Queen, cast the dragon and all his squadrons into the depths of hell. Fury filled the spirit of Lucifer. The demon's suspicions were newly aroused that this Jesus was most likely the true God.

By using the head table as his altar, my Son wished to put an end to legal suppers, and establish the new Supper of the law of grace, which a priest was to perform upon an altar. The first altars were similar to those in use today in the Roman Catholic Church. A rich cloth covered the altar. Servants placed a salver of bread in the center of the table along with a large chalice of wine. The master of the house had been inspired to offer these rich vessels. They were made of a precious emerald-like stone. The Apostles often used these sacred relics in later consecrations. The Lord then seated his Apostles at this table. I, from my retreat, beheld all that took place. The holy angels, invisible to the disciples, were present in bodily form. Other angels brought Enoch and Elias to the Cenacle from their place of abode, for my Son wished that these Fathers of the natural and of the written laws should be present at the establishment of the law of the Gospel, and that they should participate in its mysteries.

As they reclined at the table eating, Jesus said to them, "Amen, I say to you, one of you will betray me, one who is eating with me." They began to become distressed and to say to him, one by one, "Surely it is not I, Lord." He said in response to John's questioning him, "One of the Twelve, the one who dips with me into the dish. For the Son of Man indeed goes as it is written of him, but woe to that man by whom the Son of Man is betrayed. It would be better for that man if he had never been born."

Everyone present awaited full of wonder at his words. In addition, unseen by the disciples, God the Father, the Holy Ghost, and their heavenly court were present. God gave the privilege to a few of the disciples to witness a vision of some of these events. However, most of them only felt the divine presence. My Son had blessed John and Peter with an eagle-sight into the divine mysteries. While they were eating Jesus stood and all eyes were on the Son of God as he began the consecration of the bread and wine. He raised his eyes toward heaven with an expression of such sublime majesty, that he inspired the disciples, the angels and I with new and deepest reverence. He took the unleavened bread, blessed and broke it, and gave it to his disciples saying

"Take it and eat, this is my body."

Jesus then ate of the bread and then passed it on to Simon, who sat at his right. Then Jesus took the chalice of wine, again he gave thanks, and gave it to them saying,

"Drink from it, all of you, for this is my blood of the covenant, which will be shed on behalf of many for the forgiveness of sins. Do this in memory of me."

Jesus then drank and passed the cup to Simon. At the end of the consecration, I alone heard the voice of the eternal Father say, "This is my beloved Son, in whom I delight, and shall take my delight to the end of the world; and he shall be with men during all the time of their banishment."

Jesus then said, "I tell you, from now on I shall not drink this fruit of the vine until the day when I drink it with you in the kingdom of my Father."

I was aware of the great blessing contained therein for all men, and I foresaw the ingratitude of mortals concerning this ineffable Sacrament established for their benefit. I resolved to atone with all the powers of my being for the shameless and ungrateful behavior of mankind. I gave thanks to the eternal Father and to my divine Son for this extraordinary and wonderful benefit to the human race. Many times during my life, I shed tears of blood welling up from my pure heart in order to satisfy for such shameful behavior and torpid forgetfulness.

Before my Son began to distribute his body and blood to the Apostles, he handed a particle of the consecrated bread to the angel Gabriel who brought it to me in the next room. With tears of joy cascading down my face, I awaited the Holy Eucharist. The angels deposited the most Blessed Sacrament in my breast just above my heart as if it were a sacred tabernacle of the Most High. There it remained deposited until after the Resurrection, when Peter celebrated the first Mass and consecrated anew. My lady friends did not see this, but they could tell from my countenance that something wonderful was happening to me, and they joined me in canticles of praise to the Most High.

Jesus then distributed Holy Communion to his Apostles. When it came the turn of the perfidious Judas to receive communion, Jesus allowed him this last chance to atone for his sins, for the Eucharist, if accepted in faith and humility, could have changed him into a new man. However, by his accepting the Sacrament in bad faith, Judas added blasphemy to his list of crimes. After the institution of Holy Eucharist, Jesus and his twelve Apostles took their seats at the head table. In celebrating the feast of the Lamb, Jesus followed all the ceremonies of the Law as prescribed by himself through Moses. He gave the disciples an understanding of all the ceremonies of the figurative law, as observed by the Patriarchs and Prophets. He explained that how beneath it was hidden the *real truth*, namely, all that he himself was to accomplish as Redeemer of the world, for the Law of Moses and its figurative meaning would be made complete by his death on the Cross. The efficacy of the Sacraments of the new Law abrogates those of the old as being merely figurative and ineffectual. By celebrating this supper, he explained, he made an end to the rites and obligations of the old Law, which was only a preparation and a representation of what he was now about to accomplish, and hence having attained its end, would now become useless.

Jesus' instructions enlightened the Apostles concerning the deep mysteries of the Last Supper. The other disciples, that were present, did not understand these mysteries as well as the Apostles. Judas understood them least of all, actually not at all, for he was completely under the spell of his greed, thinking only of his prearranged treason and how he could execute it most secretly. My Son did not reveal his treachery, for it best served the designs and equity of his most high Providence. Moreover, he did not wish to exclude him from the Supper and from the other mysteries, leaving it to his own wickedness to bring about his exclusion. Jesus always treated him as his disciple, Apostle, and minister, and was careful of his honor. Thus, by example, he taught the children of the Church how they should venerate and treat his ministers and priests.

He taught them to guard, honor, and avoid speaking ill of any of his minister's sins and weaknesses, for they too are subject to human frailty in spite of their high office.

One after another the other Apostles swore to their loyalty to the death. The Apostles were deeply distressed at these revelations, especially at the thought of my Son's betrayal, which he had prophesied. As Jesus reseated himself, John, the beloved disciple, sat as close to him as possible. In order to prevent the treason, Peter was anxious to know, *who*, the traitor was that Jesus had referred to. He whispered to John, "Ask him who the traitor is?" The other disciples were also curious and were murmuring to one another, as to who it could be. John lay back against Jesus' bosom and asked him,

"Who is the one that will betray you?"

Jesus murmured quietly, "It is the one to whom I hand the morsel after I have dipped it." Jesus dipped a bitter herb into a bowl of salt water and handed it to Judas, son of Simon the Iscariot.

Jesus, having dispensed the Holy Eucharist, released the demons from the abyss, and Lucifer re-entered the soul of Judas. Then Jesus said to Judas, "What you are going to do, do quickly." None of those reclining at the table realized what had happened, and John kept the confidence of his Master until after his Passion. When Judas left, no one thought it unusual, for he handled the purse and Jesus often sent him off on errands.

After Judas left, Jesus said, "Now is the Son of Man glorified, and God is glorified in him. [If God is glorified in him} God will also glorify him in himself, and he will glorify him at once. My children, I will be with you only a little while longer. You will look for me, and as I told the Jews, "Where I go you cannot come, so now I say it to you. I give you a new commandment:

"Love one another, as I have loved you."

This is how all will know that you are my disciples, if you have love for one another. "

Simon Peter said, "Master, where are you going?"

Jesus replied, "Where I am going you cannot follow me now, though you will follow me later."

"Master, why can't I follow you now? I will lay down my life for you."

Jesus said to him sadly, "Amen, amen, I say to you, this very night before the cock crows, you will deny me three times [John: 14, 31-38]."

Then my Son prayed to his eternal Father. I must remind the reader, that my Son possessed two natures in one person, the divine and the human nature united in one divine person of the Word. The activities of the two natures are thus; rightly attributed to one and the same Person, just as the same Person is called both God and man. Consequently, when I say that the Incarnate Word spoke and prayed to the eternal Father, it must not be interpreted as meaning that he prayed or spoke in as far as he was divine. In divinity, Jesus was equal to the Father. However, as far as he was human, he was inferior and composed of body and soul as we ourselves are. It was in his human capacity that Jesus lived out his life and Passion on earth, and yet, he was still divine. Thus, in the human sense, yet knowing that he was God, Jesus confessed and extolled the immensity and infinitude of the eternal Father, praying for the whole human race.

He prayed, "My Father, and eternal God, I confess, praise, and exalt your infinite essence and incomprehensible Deity, in which I am one with you and the Holy Ghost, engendered from all eternity by your intellect, as the figure of your substance and the image of your individual nature. In the same nature, which I have assumed in the virginal womb of my mother, I wish to accomplish the Redemption of the human race with which you have charged me. My desire is to restore to this human nature the highest perfection and the plentitude of your divine complaisance. Then, I wish to pass from this world to your right hand, bearing with me all those whom you have given me without losing a single one of them for want of willingness on our part to help them."

"My delight is to be with the children of men, and in my absence they will be left orphans if I do not give them assistance. I wish, Father, to furnish them with a sure and unfailing token of my inextinguishable love and a pledge of the eternal rewards, which you hold in reserve for them. I desire that they find in my merits an easy and powerful remedy for the effects of sin, to which they are subject on account of the disobedience of the first man, and I wish to restore copiously their right to the eternal happiness for which they are created."

"However, since there will be few who will preserve themselves in this justice, they need other assistance. Impelled by my boundless love, Lord and Father, I have given of myself in the **Sacrament of the Holy Eucharist**. I ordain, that from now on men may reenter into your full friendship and grace through the **Sacrament of Baptism** of the **Holy Spirit**, and that they may do so at birth if their parents so dictate. Thus, they become heirs of your glory, freed from original sin and marked interiorly and indelibly as children of my Church. Let them receive the gifts of faith, hope and charity, by which they may perform the works of your children. Let this Sacrament be the portal of my Church and allow them to receive the virtues by which they restrain and govern disorderly inclinations and to be able to distinguish without fail, the good from the evil."

"I ordain they also receive the **Sacrament of Confirmation** by which they will be confirmed and rooted in the holy faith they have accepted. It will allow them to become courageous in its defense as soon as they arrive at the use of reason. As human frailty easily falls away from the observance of my law and since my charity will not allow them without an easy and opportune remedy, I wish to provide humanity with **the Sacrament of Penance**. Then I will reinstate contrite souls in justice and in the merits of the glory promised, if they acknowledge their faults and confess them with sorrow. Thus, Lucifer will be prevented from boasting of their having so soon been deprived of the advantages of baptism."

"By the justification of these Sacraments, men shall become fit to share in the highest token of my love, namely to receive me sacramentally. Under the species of bread and wine, they can receive my body and blood. In this heavenly nourishment, I will remain with them until the end of time. For the strengthening and defense of those, who approach the end of their lives, I appoint the **Sacrament of Extreme Unction**, which shall be at the same time a certain pledge of the bodily resurrection of those thus anointed."

"I institute the **Sacrament of Ordination** to distinguish and mark some of its members by a special degree of holiness and place them above the other faithful as fit ministers of the Sacraments and as my chosen priests. I wish that it should flow from me through one, who shall be my Vicar and the Chief, representing my person and act as my high priest. Into his keeping, I deposit the keys of heaven and all upon earth shall obey him. For the further protection of my Church, I also establish the last of the sacraments, the **Sacrament of Matrimony**, to sanctify the natural union of man and wife for the propagation of the human race. Thus, I shall enrich and adorn with my infinite merits all the levels of my Church. This, eternal Father, is my last will, whereby I make all the mortals inheritors of my merits in the great storehouse of grace, my new Church."

From my retreat, I saw and heard his prayer, I prostrated myself on the floor and I offered to the eternal Father the same petitions as my Son. Although I could not add anything to the merits of the works of Jesus, nevertheless, as on other occasions, I as his helpmate united my petitions with his, in order that by my faithful companionship, I might move the Father to so much the greater mercy. The Father looked down upon us in his infinite mercy and graciously accepted our prayers respectfully, for the salvation of men.

The Lord then rose to leave the hall; the Apostles remained with Jesus, while the rest of the disciples each went his own way. I left my room and met him face to face at the door. A sword of sorrow pierced our hearts inflicting a pang of grief beyond all human understanding. I threw myself at my Son's feet adoring him as my true God and Redeemer. He looked down upon me with majesty and at the same time with the overflowing love of a son, he spoke to me only these words, "I shall be with you in tribulation, Mother; let us accomplish the will of the eternal Father and the salvation of man."

I silently offered myself up as a sacrifice with my whole heart and asked his blessing. Having received this, Jason, the owner of the house, who was present at this meeting, moved by a divine impulse, offered his house and all that it contained to me saying, "Mistress, make use of my house and all that it contains during your stay in Jerusalem."

I accepted his offer with humble thanks. My thousand angels and a few women of my group remained with me. We retired to the room previously set aside for me. From there, by special favor of Jesus, I was able to see all that was to transpire concerning the Passion of my divine Son. Thus was I able to accompany him and co-operate in his Passion as far as devolved upon me.

I Am Mary

There are two things unknown to human wisdom. First, how pleasing to the highest Goodness is the service of those who with an ardent zeal for God's glory, devote their labor and solicitude toward removing the obstacles, which men place to their own justification and the communication of his favors. The satisfaction of the Most High, arising from this work in others, cannot be estimated in this mortal life. On this account, today's ministry of the Apostles, the prelates, the priests, and preachers of the divine word are highly exalted. Today's ministers succeed in office those who founded the Church and who labored in its preservation and extension. Each priest, prelate, and minister is to be co-operators and executors of the immense love of God for all souls created to be sharers in his divinity. Secondly, you must ponder the greatness and abundance of the gifts and favors, which the infinite power communicates to those souls, who do not hinder his most liberal bounty. The Lord manifested this truth immediately in the beginnings of the evangelical Church, when, to all those who were about to enter, he showed his bounty by such great prodigies and wonders. He frequently sent the Holy Ghost in a visible manner, working miracles in those who accepted the Creed, and showering forth other hidden favors on the faithful. His almighty power shone forth in the Apostles and Disciples, because in them there was no hindrance to his holy and eternal will, because they were true instruments and executors of the divine love, imitators and successors of Christ and followers of truth. Hence, they were elevated to an ineffable participation in the attributes of God, especially as regards his science, holiness and power, working for themselves and for the souls such great miracles that no man can ever sufficiently extol their virtues.

Leave aside at present the innumerable martyrs who shed their blood for Christ and gave their lives for the holy faith. Instead, let us consider the founders of religions, the great saints who flourished in them, the doctors, the bishops, the prelates, and apostolic men through whom the bounty and omnipotence of God has been so abundantly manifested. They are so great that others who are ministers of God for the welfare of souls and all the faithful, can have no excuse, even if God does not work similar miracles today in those he finds fit for his operations. There is great negligence among many of the ministers of today's modern Church. If they did not pervert the order of God's infinite wisdom, and if they lived up to the dignity to which God called and chose them before all others, they would find that the inclination of the highest Goodness to enrich souls has not changed since my term on earth.

God's love of his Church is always at its height. His mercy is just as much concerned at the innumerable miseries of men in modern times as it was in the beginning of the Church. The clamor of the sheep of Christ is louder than ever, and, in spite of a shortage of priests; their numbers are more numerous than ever before. If these facts are true, to what is attributed the loss of so many souls and the ruin of the Christian people? Why is it that the infidels not only do not enter the Church, but subject it so much affliction and sorrow? Why do the prelates and ministers not shine before the world, exhibiting the splendors of Christ, as in the ages gone by especially as in the primitive Church? Why do priests and bishops perform abominations before the Lord God, and lie and conceal their handiwork? The ministers have been assimilated by the people, and have sank to new lows, when, on the contrary, they should by their example raise people to the holiness, which is due to priesthood.

On June 18, 1965, I prophesized and warned the children of Garabandal, Spain that God's cup of wrath was filling up and was now overflowing. I told them that many bishops and many priests were on the road to perdition and taking many souls with them. Less and less importance was being given the Holy Eucharist. I pointed out that everyone must make more sacrifices and think often about the Passion of Jesus. Everyone must live good lives, for if people do not change, I warned them a great chastisement will befall humankind.

Too few priests heeded my warning, for not only have the priests submitted to the Secular Humanism of the modern-day world, but the sheep of the fold have also succumbed and have become slaves of the world, the flesh and the devil. Both priest and parishioner compromise the glory of Jesus Christ with their own selfish honor and vain esteem. They wander away from the pure and sincere doctrine and sometimes even in the Scriptures and according to which the holy teachers have explained them; they slime it over with their own ingenious subtleties seeking rather to seek the pleasures and admiration of their flock than their advancement. Do not be astonished, my children that divine justice has much forsaken the prelates, ministers and preachers of his word, or that the Catholic Church, having such an exalted position in its beginnings, should now be brought to such a low estate.

With those priests and the faithful that are not infected with these lamentable vices and are zealous, God is most liberal. However, they are few in numbers, as is evident from the ruin of the Christian people and from the contempt into which the priests and preachers of the Gospel have fallen. I assure you that without a doubt; sinners would reform and amend their lives if the number of the perfect and zealous workers were great. Many infidels would be converted; all would look upon and hear with reverence and fear such preachers, priests and prelates, they would rather respect them for their dignity and holiness, and not for their usurped authority and outward show, which induces a reverence too much like worldly applause and altogether without fruit. Bewail my, children, such a sad state, and invite heaven and earth to help in our weeping; for there are few who sorrow on account of it, and this is the greatest of all the injuries committed against the Lord by the children of the Church.

The Church owes much to its priests, in spite of so many of them being deceived by Lucifer and his demons; especially so when it comes to the Sacraments. I once asked this question, "If you were to meet a priest and an angel walking along together, who would you acknowledge and honor first?" The answer is quite simple, you honor the priest first, for it is only by his hands during Mass that the consecration of the Holy Eucharist can take place. Most Catholics are remiss in giving proper respect or acknowledgement to their parish priest or their bishop. If you gossip or complain about your priests then you are simply falling into the sin of judging others.

My Son said, "Stop judging that you may not be judged.

For as you judge, so will you be judged, and the measure with which you measure will be measured out to you. Why do you notice the splinter in your brother's eye, but do not perceive the wooden beam in your own eye? How can you say to your brother, 'Let me remove that splinter from your eye, while a wooden beam is in your eye? You hypocrite, remove the wooden beam from your eye first; then you will see clearly to remove the splinter from your brother's eye [Matt: 7, 1-5].'

Each parish should have a prayer for vocations at every Mass, or every service. Recently, Archbishop Edwin F. O'Brien stated succinctly,

"I tell you folks that unless we pray for priests we're not going to get them. Unless be pray for the priests we don't deserve them."

If you have no priests: Who will confess you?
Who will bless your marriage before Almighty God?
Who will baptize and confirm you in your faith.
Who will give you Extreme Unction as you lay dying in your sins?

You forget all too readily that your bishop; priest or deacon is just as human as you are. The priests are subject to many temptations to which the ordinary person is not subjected. He has made a vow of celibacy that few of you could or would make and keep. They gave up having a family and children, which few men are willing to do. Being human, they make mistakes just like you do. I hope that they will give better example than the ordinary Christian does. They need your daily prayers, *not your criticism.* Are you or your mother or father, or your husband or wife so perfect that no one ever finds fault with them? When was the last time you told your priest that he was doing a good job, or gave him comfort in times of his needs? It is imperative in God's plan that you pray for your priests and keep uppermost in your holy thoughts their welfare. You must guard, honor, and avoid speaking ill of any priest's sins and weaknesses, for you too are sinners and are subject to these same human frailties.

A good trend has recently begun where parishes across the United States have instituted chapels for the adoration of the Blessed Sacrament. This is most pleasing to the Holy Trinity, but likewise there has developed a careless attitude in some parishes for they are not maintaining the constant presence of two worshipers in the chapel at all times. This is most offensive to our Lord and is fraught with the danger of serious sin for those responsible. My Son looks forward to your visits. He died on the cross for each of us, and is most appreciative when you appear humbly, and share your loves, sorrows, and petitions with him in person. Your presence renders the Lord the proper reverence and respect due him as our Lord and Savior. If enough people in a diocese pray for priests at each Mass, fast, do penance, and honor the Holy Eucharist, there will be no shortage of priests.

Remember what Archbishop Edwin F. O'Brien says,

"UNLESS WE PRAY FOR PRIESTS WE'RE NOT GOING TO GET THEM. UNLESS WE PRAY *FOR* THE PRIESTS WE DON'T DESERVE THEM."

Pray for all religious

Mary

Chapter Nine

The Crucifixion of my Son, Jesus the Christ; true God and true Man

"My God, my God, why have you forsaken me?" [Matt: 27, 46]

From a darkened doorway, Judas watched Jesus leave the Cenacle and fell in behind him and his group of disciples. Jesus departed the city and crossed the Valley of Kidron to the Mt. of Olives. Judas had the information he needed. Jesus often went to the Garden of Gethsemane to pray. Judas sped off at a near run to report his findings to the Council of Priests Within him was the turmoil of sudden fear and anxiety, interior witnesses of the wicked deed that he was about to commit. Lucifer, perceiving the haste of Judas, and fearing that after all Jesus might be the true Messiah, took on the appearance of a wicked friend of Judas' and came toward him. He hailed Judas and stopped his hasty journey. They had previously discussed the selling of his Master, and now Lucifer tried to convince him that after thinking the matter over that perhaps it was not advisable to deliver Jesus over to the priests. Judas, in his agitation, could not be persuaded to change his mind.

The priests having heard that Jesus was in town, had gathered in Council to consult about the promised betrayal. Judas gained entrance and gasped excitedly, "My Master is on the way to Mt. Olivet where he intends to pray with his disciples. This is the most favorable time to take him; there are few people in the streets. Are your men ready?" The priests were overjoyed and busied themselves to put together an armed force to arrest the *trouble maker* as they referred to him.

If this stupendous struggle between good and evil began with the first man, it certainly reached its peak in the death of the Redeemer. Then, good and evil stood face to face and exerted their highest powers. Evil was represented by human malice in taking away the life and honor of the Redeemer. The goodness was Jesus' immense charity in freely sacrificing both for his love of mankind. In order for Jesus to find some object in creation in which his love could be recompensed, and thus warrant disregarding the dictates of his justice, it would seem, in human understanding that Jesus could only revert to me, his blessed mother. For in me alone could he expect to see his Passion and Death bring forth full fruit. In my immeasurable holiness, he found some compensation for human malice. In only my humility and constant charity could he deposit the treasures of his merits, so that afterwards, as the new Phoenix from the rekindled ashes, his Church might arise from his sacrifice. The consolation, which the humanity of my Son drew from the certainty of my holiness, gave him the strength, and new courage to conquer the malice of mortals. Jesus counted himself well recompensed for suffering such atrocious pains by the fact that I also belonged to humankind.

Upon leaving Jerusalem, Jesus led his eleven Apostles over the bridge that bridged the torrent of Cedron to the foot of Mount Olivet. Entering the Garden of Gethsemane, he said to his Apostles, "Sit here while I go over there and pray. Also pray that you do not fall into temptation." He said this to prepare them for all that they should see him suffer that night. For Satan would assail them to sift and stir them up by his false suggestions to doubt that their leader was truly the Son of God. Taking Peter, James, and John with him, Jesus led them further on into the garden. There he offered himself up anew to the eternal Father in satisfaction for his justice for the rescue of the human race. He gave consent that all the torments of his Passion and death be let loose over that part of his human being, which was capable of suffering. He did this so that his sufferings might reach the highest degree possible. At once, he began to feel the anguish of his coming trial.

He said to the three Apostles, "My soul is sorrowful even unto death. Remain here and pray with me." He went on alone into the deep shadows within the garden and fell prostrate in prayer. My Lord permitted this sorrow to reach the highest degree both naturally and miraculously possible in his sacred humanity. My perception of his actions allowed me to sense his massive grief and to emulate his every move.

Jesus prayed, "Father, if it is possible, let this cup pass from me; yet, not as I will, but as you will." In this prayer, Jesus besought his Father to let this chalice of dying for the reprobate pass from him. However, the Lord knew his death was not to be avoided. He now asked that not one soul, if possible, should be lost because of his sacrifice. He pleaded that as his Redemption would be superabundant for all that it should be applied to all in such a way as to make all, if possible, profit by it in an efficacious manner. "If this is not possible, he prayed, I resign myself to your divine will." Rising he returned to his three disciples, he found them asleep and waking them, and knowing the trials that his disciples would face he said to Peter, "Watch and pray that you may not undergo the test. The spirit is willing, but the flesh is weak." Withdrawing a second time, he prayed again, His agony grew in proportion to the greatness of his charity and the certainty of his knowledge that men would persist in neglecting to profit by his Passion and death. The mental anguish of Jesus was beyond human understanding. His grief created great drops of bloody sweat, which freely flowed onto the ground.

Then again, he prayed, "Father, if it is not possible that this cup pass without my drinking it, your will be done." He returned once more only to find his disciples asleep. The day had been long and hot, they were weary, and could not keep their eyes open. However, Jesus wanted his Apostles to learn what care and supervision they were to exercise over their flocks. He interrupted his most important prayers in order to teach them how they must postpone other enterprises and interests to the salvation of their subjects. Again he withdrew and prayed a third time, praying the same prayer. Then he returned to the sleeping three and stood there for a moment and wept over them, for he saw them oppressed and buried in this deathly shade of their own sloth and negligence.

He spoke to Peter, "Are you still sleeping and taking your rest? Could you not watch one hour with me? Jesus reprimanded Peter, not only because he had been placed at the head of the others, but also because he had loudly protested that he would not deny him and was ready to die for him. Peter deserved to be corrected and admonished, for he had freely made these protests from his whole heart. There is no doubt that the Lord chastises those whom he loves and is always pleased by our good resolutions even when we afterwards fall short in their execution.

Jesus then said to them, "Behold, the hour is at hand when the Son of man is to be handed over to sinners. Get up, let us go. Look, my betrayer is at hand." Startled, the Apostles all arose in a state of confusion and alarm, for coming in force was a large crowd of men and soldiers bearing torches and armed with clubs and swords.

When the Lord separated himself from the three Apostles in the garden, I was in my retreat in the Cenacle. I was privileged to clearly see all the mysteries and doings of my most holy Son in the Garden of Gethsemane. At this same time, I separated myself from the other women and went into my private room. As Jesus had done, I exhorted the women with me to pray and watch lest they enter into temptation. They did far better than the holy Apostles did, for they did not go to sleep. I took with me Mary Salome, Mary Cleophas, the mother of James and John, and Mary Magdalene the sister of Lazarus, whom Jesus had raised, from the dead. The three were the most holy of all the women, and I treated Mary Magdalene as the superior of the three. I secluded myself with my three confidants. I instructed them to assist me in my affliction and for this purpose; God endowed them with greater light and grace than the other women.

Like my Son, I began to feel unwonted sorrow and anguish and I said to them, "My soul is sorrowful because my beloved Son is about to suffer and die and it is not permitted me to suffer and die for him. Pray my friends, in order that you may not be overcome by the temptations that are to come."

Having said this, I went apart from them and emulated my Son's supplications and prayers. I begged the eternal Father to suspend in me all human alleviation and comfort, both in the sensitive and in the spiritual part of my being, so that nothing might hinder me from suffering to the highest degree in union with my divine Son. I prayed, "God, may I be permitted to suffer in my virginal body all the pains, wounds, and tortures about to be undergone by my Son?" The blessed Trinity granted me my petition. Consequently, I suffered all the torments of my most holy Son in exact duplications, as I will comment on as they happened. These pains were such that if the Almighty had not preserved me, they would have caused my death many times over. Yet, on the other hand, these sufferings, inflicted by God himself, were like a pledge and a new lease on life. For in my ardent love, I would have considered it incomparably more painful to see the suffering of Jesus and his death without being able to share in his torments.

Thus prepared, each time my Son went to his disciples, I went to my companions to exhort them, because I knew of the wrath of the demon against them. I was pleased that unlike the Apostles, they remained awake. In order to co-operate in all things, in my mental anguish, I also suffered a bloody sweat, similar to that of the Lord in the garden. Saint Michael visited and comforted my Son during his affliction. Afterwards, he also came to me. In turn, I sent a towel to Jesus by my angels and he allowed them to wipe his face to fulfill my motherly wishes. When my blessed Son was arrested, I informed my companions and we all bewailed this indignity with the most bitter of tears. Mary Magdalene was especially affected, for she signalized herself in tenderest love and piety for her Master.

Judas, who had been one of the chosen twelve, led the High Priest's men as they approached Jesus. On the one side was Christ our Lord; true God and true man. He was the Captain of the just, supported by his eleven Apostles, the chieftains and champions of his Church. In addition, there were innumerable, unseen, hosts of angelic spirits, all full of adoring wonder at this spectacle. On the other side was the renegade Judas, the originator of the treason. With him were many Jews and gentiles all intent on venting their malice with the greatest cruelty. Surrounding these were Lucifer and a multitude of demons inciting and prompting Judas and his helpers to boldly lay their sacrilegious hands upon their Creator. God did not allow the demons to see the holy angels that were present

Judas had told them, "The man I shall kiss is the one; arrest him." Judas went directly to Jesus and greeted him with a kiss saying, "God save you, Rabbi!"

Jesus answered him, "Friend, do what you have come for?"

My Son, even then, gave Judas another chance to repent. He inflamed his heart with a new and most clear light, by which Judas saw the atrocious malice of his treason, the punishment to follow, if he should not make it good by true repentance, and the merciful pardon still to be obtained from the divine clemency.

Then Jesus spoke to the soldiers, saying, "Whom do you seek?"

They answered, "Jesus of Nazareth."

Jesus replied, ***"I AM."***

By these inestimably precious and blessed words, Christ declared himself as our Redeemer and Savior. My Son's enemies did not understand the true meaning of these words, but my angels and I understood, as did, to some extent, the Apostles. Jesus spoke with divine power and his enemies could not stand before his majesty. When his words struck their ears, they all fell backwards to the ground [John: 18, 6]. Even the dogs and the horses, which the soldiers had brought with them, fell before his power; man and beast remained motionless like stones. God hurled Lucifer and his demons down with them; he deprived them of motion and they suffered new confusion and torture. They all remained motionless for eight minutes showing no more life than if they had died. Thus was the arrogance and vanity of the children of Babylon humbled, since only one word from the mouth of the Lord, spoken with meekness and humility, confounds, destroys, and annihilates all the pride and power of man and hell.

I prayed for their release and only then did the Lord release his hold upon them by saying, "Who are you looking for?"

They rose and again answered, "Jesus the Nazarean."

Jesus answered, "I have already told you, that **I AM**. If therefore you seek me, let these men go," and with a motion of his hand, he indicated his disciples. With these words, without the soldiers knowing it, my Son gave them permission to take him prisoner.

Malchus, a servant of the high priest stepped forward, and laid hands on Jesus to arrest him. Peter ever the rash one, and in spite of his fear, was roused with zeal to defend the honor and life of his divine Master. He drew his sword and slashed at the servant. Prompted by divine Providence, Malchus leaped to one side, and the blow only severed his ear. My Son would not allow any death but his own at his capture. His wounds, his blood, and his suffering alone, was to ransom the human race. Neither did he wish, according to his own teaching that his person be defended by the use of arms, nor did he want to leave such an example to his Church, as one to be imitated for her defense.

Jesus rebuked Peter saying, "Put your sword back into its sheath, for all who take the sword will perish by the sword." Stooping he picked up the ear and pulling the servant's hands away from the side of his head, my Son replaced the ear and said, "Be healed!" The man was instantly healed; the mob shrank back in awe.

Jesus admonished Simon saying, "Do you think that I cannot call upon my Father and he will not provide me at this moment with more than twelve legions of angels? But then how would the Scriptures be fulfilled, which say that it must come to pass in this manner?" Turning back to the dazed crowd, he said to them with great grandeur and majesty, "Have you come out against a robber with swords and clubs to seize me? Day after day, I sat teaching in the temple area, yet you did not arrest me. But all this has come to pass that the writings of the Prophets may be fulfilled."

With these words, the soldiers, overcoming their fear, fell upon the Lamb of God like fierce tigers. They bound him cruelly with ropes and chains, in order to lead him in disgrace to the house of the high priest. Utterly confused; the Apostles turned and fled. The priests had no love for them, either. The disciples knew the priests would also have them arrested, for they had performed many miracles. With his arrest, my Son's Passion was set into motion, which could only lead to his subsequent, ignoble death. Anguish wrung my heart, and tears flowed freely down my cheeks. We pitied and prayed for Judas, we sought to make recompense for his malice by adoring, confessing, praising and loving the Lord. We prayed for those who were planning and plotting the death of our Lord and

God. I enlightened my companions of all that was proper, reserving whatever they were not capable of understanding and we prayed all the long night.

When the servants of the high priest seized Jesus, I felt on my own hands and wrists the pains caused by the ropes and chains, as if I myself were being bound and fettered. In the same manner, I felt in my body the blows and torments that were further inflicted on the bound Lamb of God.

My Son's words to the soldiers that the Apostles should go free had the force of a divine decree. For Jesus did not intend that they be taken at this time. Lucifer immediately beset the fleeing men with various suggestions inciting them to flight. He did not wish that they witness the patience and virtues of my Son in his sufferings. Lucifer knew that the Apostles might be confirmed and fortified in their faith if they saw this new proof of his doctrine in his living example. Thus, they would resist the temptations, which he planned for them. He assailed them with rabid fury, filling them with strong doubts and suspicions against their Master, and he urged them to give him up and flee. They all yielded to his suggestions of flight, but they resisted many of his doubts against faith, although some failed more, some less, not all the Apostles being equally disturbed or scandalized.

Only Peter and John remained together and gathering up their courage, they determined to follow their Master and see the end of his misfortune. In the souls of each of the Apostles raged a battle of sorrow and grief, which wrung their hearts and left them without consolation or peace. On the one side battled reason, grace, faith, love and truth; on the other temptation, suspicion, fear, cowardice and sorrow. Reason and truth reproached them with their inconstancy and disloyalty in having forsaken their Master by cowardly flying from danger, even after Jesus had warned them of it, and after each of them had so recently pledged themselves to even die for him if necessary. They remembered their sloth in neglecting to pray and strengthen themselves against temptations, as my Son had advised them in the garden. Their conviction that he was the true God urged them to return and seek him, and even expose themselves to danger as faithful servants and disciples. They remembered me, and thought of my intense sorrow. Of course, in the meantime, my women friends and I were all praying for them. On the other hand was their timidity that exaggerated their fears of the Jews, their dread of death, and their shame and confusion.

Lucifer filled them with harassing doubts, suggesting that it would be suicide to give up, for if Jesus could not free himself, he certainly could not free them. Jesus would certainly be put to death, moreover, he suggested, it was a serious matter to follow a man, who was to be condemned to an infamous and frightful death. Only Peter and John resolved to follow Jesus at a safe distance. John was highly esteemed by the high priest Annas who with Caiaphas alternated in the office of high priest. In John, Annas saw a man of distinguished and noble lineage, well versed with courteous manners, and an amiable disposition. Trusting in this favorable circumstance, the two Apostles followed my noble Son with less fear. Deep in their hearts, they thought of me and they reflected on my bitter sorrow. Both desired to console me if possible, but neither one wished to face me. They feared that I might oblige them to return to their Master. In this pious and loving desire to console me, John excelled all the other disciples.

I clearly saw and understood not only all that my Son suffered, but also all that happened inwardly to the Apostles. I observed their tribulation and temptations, their thoughts and resolves, where each one was and what he did. Even knowing all this, I never allowed myself any feeling of indignation against the Apostles, nor did I ever reproach them for their disloyalty. On the contrary, I was the one that was instrumental in restoring them to a better frame of mind, as I will show later. The women of my group joined their prayers with mine to help the distraught disciples regain their faith and courage.

God, in divine justice, left Judas to his own counsel. Judas accompanied the band that seized Jesus. They went first to the house of Annas, and then on to the house of Caiaphas. When Judas saw his divine Master overwhelmed with blasphemies and injuries, and noted how he suffered with admirable silence, meekness, and patience, he began to reflect upon his own treachery and that he alone was responsible for the cruel injustice heaped upon his innocent benefactor. He recalled the miracles he had witnessed, the doctrines he had heard, and the benefits he had enjoyed at the hands of his Master. He remembered the kindness, meekness and charity, which I had ministered to him and the malice with which he had returned the benefits he had received from my Son and me.

Lucifer seized upon these facts and awakened in Judas contrition for his misdeeds. He then sought to convince him that the impossibility of his repairing the damage and to lead him to despair to which he at last yielded. He convinced Judas that the blood of the Just One would forever cry for vengeance against him. Filled with such thoughts roused by the demon, he became involved in confusion, darkness, and rabid rage against himself. He gnawed like a wild beast at the flesh of his own arms and hands, struck his head with fearful blows, tore out his hair, and began raving and ranting in his speech. He rushed away determined to throw himself from the highest roof, but without success.

Seeing him so distraught, Lucifer inspired him to hunt up the priests, confess his sin, and return the thirty pieces of silver that he had received from them for the betrayal of my Son. Judas hastened to the priests and shouted at them, "I have sinned, betraying innocent blood!"

The priests, hardened in their hearts answered him coldly, "What is this to us? You should have thought of that before."

The devil still hoped to hinder the death of Jesus, even though, he was still unsure of his identity. The repulse of the priests, so full of impious cruelty took away all hope from Judas, and filled with guilt and frustration; he hurled the thirty pieces of silver at the priests and dashed wildly from their presence. Lucifer seeing that Judas could of no further use to him, urged him, in order to avoid severer punishments, to end his own life. Thus the murderer of his own Creator became also his own murderer. Judas yielded to this terrible deceit, and rushing forth from the city, hung himself on a dried-out fig tree. This happened at twelve o'clock Friday, three hours before my Son was to die. This occurred well before the death of my Son, so as not to coincide too closely with his demise.

The demons immediately took possession of the soul of Judas and took it down to hell. His body, left hanging on the fig tree, suddenly burst open disgorging his entrails all about. Astonishment and dread filled the hearts of the people, when they saw this. The body remained hanging by the neck for three days, exposed for all to see. The authorities attempted to take down the body from the tree and bury it in secret. The sight caused great confusion to the Pharisees and priests, who could not refute this testimony of the wickedness of Judas. For three days, their efforts to remove the body from its position on the tree were futile. Then, Divine Justice allowed the demons to snatch the body from the tree and reunite it with his soul in hell. Thus, Judas will suffer eternal punishment in both body and soul in the profoundest abyss of hell.

The punishment of Judas is an object lesson. By divine command, I will reveal what my Son made known to me concerning it. Among the obscure caverns of the infernal prisons was a very large unoccupied one, arranged for more horrible chastisement than the others. The demons on occasion had attempted to use it, but had been unable to cast any soul into it since the time of Cain until the present day. All hell had remained astonished at the failure of these attempts, entirely ignorant of the mystery, until the arrival of the soul of Judas. This cavern is one of greater torments and fiercer fires of hell. God established it from the creation of the world. It was destined for those, who, after having received Baptism, would damn themselves by the neglect of the Sacraments, the doctrines, the Passion and Death of the Savior, and finally not turning to me for intercession. Being among the first to receive many Sacramental blessings, Judas fearfully misused them, and was the first to suffer the torments of this horrible place.

God commanded me to reveal this mystery as a dreadful warning to all Christians. It is a special warning to the priests, prelates and religious, who are accustomed to treat with familiarity the body and blood of Christ our Lord, and who, by their holy office and state are his closest friends. God allows the wrath, which the demons have conceived against my Son and I, to be taken out as far as is allowed them, on all those souls who imitate Judas in his contempt for evangelical law, the Sacraments, and the fruits of my Son's Redemption. May the children of the Church consider well this truth, for it cannot fail to move their hearts and induce them to avoid such a lamentable fate.

When Jesus stated to the soldiers, "I AM," Lucifer met with his demons and after conferring with them, said, "It seems without doubt that he is the one, who is God and at the same time man. If he is, and if he should die as we have planned, he will accomplish the Redemption of man and satisfy the justice of God. Then our sway will cease and all our intentions will be frustrated. We have erred in seeking his death. If now we cannot prevent his death, let us see how far his endurance will stretch. We will go and excite his enemies to torture him with most impious cruelty. Let us stir up their fury against him. We will motivate the Jews to inflict new insults, affronts, ignominies, and torments upon his person. Let us drive them to vent upon him their entire wrath in order to exhaust his patience and let us carefully study the results."

They were to find our; however that not all their devious plans would succeed. Jesus would not permit personal and private indignities to be inflicted upon his royal and divine person that was unbecoming. He did allow them free scope to their inhuman barbarities and savage fury. In addition, as the Queen of Heaven, I interfered in order to curb the insolent malice of Lucifer, for I was well aware of all the designs of the infernal dragon. I prevented some of the hellish suggestions made by Lucifer from reaching my Son's executioners both by prayer and by use of my holy angels, who, at my command, drove away and confused the persecutors of my Son. Yet, in all of this, I conformed to the just and hidden decrees of divine Providence.

In my clear vision of all that took place, I saw the soldiers bind my divine Son with a heavy iron chain that encircled the neck as well as the waist. They savagely bound his hands behind him. Fearing that he was a sorcerer, the soldiers took no chances and added two ropes. The one, they wound around his throat and tied it in heavy knots all about the body leaving two free ends so that the servants and soldiers might jerk him in different directions along the way. They used the second rope to bind his arms. They secured it around his waist, again leaving two loose ends by which his executioners could also jerk him around. To this injury, they added insulting blows accompanied with the vilest of language. Like venomous serpents, they shot forth their sacrilegious poison in abuse and blasphemy against him. They dragged Jesus from the Garden of Olives in the greatest of tumult and uproar. Some dragged him along by the ropes up front, and others retarded his steps from the rear by use of the other rope attached to his bound hands. In this manner, with unheard of violence, they sometimes forced him to run forward in haste, frequently causing him to fall. At the same time, others from the rear jerked him backwards, and then again, they yanked on him from side to side, satisfying their diabolical whims. Jesus fell to the ground many times. Then, the soldiers dragged him grievously wounding and lacerating his face and body. When he fell, they pounced on him like a pack of hungry wolves, inflicting blows and kicks, trampling upon his body, his head, and his face. The soldiers accompanied their violence with festive shouts and disgraceful insults.

Lucifer, while inciting these ministers of evil, watched closely the reactions of Jesus to this maltreatment. Even he was obliged to acknowledge the meekness, patience, and sweetness of my holy Son. The Lord's serene majesty was without change or expression amid all these injuries and suffering. The infernal dragon was enraged, and like one crazed by fury, he attempted to seize the ropes in order that he and his fellow demons might with superhuman force do great bodily harm to my Son. Divining his intentions, I made use of my power as sovereign Queen and commanded him to desist. All strength immediately left Lucifer and he could not proceed with his presumptuous intent. It was not becoming that the forces of evil should have any direct effect on the sufferings and death of the Redeemer. However, God allowed him to excite all his fellow-demons against the Lord. The Lord also gave the demons a free hand to incite my Son's mortal enemies among the Jews and Gentiles, since as humans they each had the use of free will.

Lucifer said to his cohorts, "What kind of man is this, who by his patience and his works so torments us and annihilates us? We have never from the time of Adam found such long-suffering or such humility and meekness. How can we rest when we see such a powerful example, drawing others to him? Evan if he is but a mere man, I cannot permit such an example for the rest of humankind. Make haste then my ministers; let us persecute him through his human foes, who obedient to my sway have conceived of me some of our own furious envy."

They dragged Jesus before Annas, who sat in a proud and arrogant state on the platform of the great hall. His servants thrust the Lord before Annas, and said, "At last, Master, we bring this wicked man, who by his sorceries and evil deeds has disturbed all Jerusalem and Judea. This time his magic art has not been able to save him." On the one hand, the angels of Jesus were confessing him and adoring him for his incomprehensible judgments of wisdom, on the other hand Lucifer and his evil minions were swarming all over the evil servants, and Lucifer was seated by Annas conjuring up the vilest of suggestions.

Tauntingly, the high priest said to Jesus, "Where are your disciples now, magician?"

When Jesus did not respond, Annas asked, "What doctrine are you preaching and teaching now?"

Jesus did not wish to give Annas a chance to misinterpret his answer so he replied, "I have spoken openly to the world. I have always taught in the synagogue and in the temple where all the Jews assemble, and in secret, I have spoken nothing. Why do you question me? Ask those, who have heard what I have spoken to them; they will know what I have said."

A servant of the high priest rushed up and struck Jesus in the face, snarling at him, "How dare you speak to the high priest like that?"

The Savior and I both prayed for the audacious servant, but so that the offender might not boast of his wickedness, Jesus replied, "If I have spoken evil, give testimony of the evil; if well, why strike me?" However, his words did not stay the malicious hands of those mistreating him.

At this time, John and Peter arrived at the house of Annas. The servants knew John well and they readily gave entrance to them. Peter, seeing a fire built by the soldiers near the portico, drew near to warm his hands, for the night was very cold. A servant maiden recognized him as one of Jesus' disciples and said to him contemptuously, "Are you not one of the disciples of this man Jesus?"

Peter, overcome with fear answered, "I am not his disciple," and he slipped away into the darkness and out of the compound to avoid further questioning.

The denial of Peter caused our Lord greater pain than all the blows that he had received. Peter's sin was directly opposed and abhorrent to the immense charity of Jesus, while pains and sufferings were sweet and welcome to him, since he could thereby atone for our sins. After this first denial of Peter, my Son prayed for him to his eternal Father and ordained that through my intercession pardon would be granted him after he had denied Jesus for the third time as prophesied.

Frustrated with the answers of his prisoner, Annas sent Jesus, still bound securely, to see the priest Caiaphas, his son in law, who that year officiated as the prince and high priest. With him were the scribes and distinguished men of the Jews, who had gathered in their Council to to urge the condemnation of the Lamb of God.

The invincible patience and meekness of the Lord astounded the demons. It filled them with the utmost confusion and fury. Unable to find a weakness in the armor of my Son's virtues, they redoubled their efforts to stir up the scribes and servants of the priests to vent their wickedness against Jesus. The soldiers dragged him before the priests, and they greeted him with loud derision and laughter. The Savior retaliated by offering up to the eternal Father the triumph, which his meekness and humility won over sin. He prayed for all those gathered to ridicule him, and my prayers echoed his.

At the end of the room, Caiaphas sat on his throne surrounded by Lucifer and his demons as they had Annas. Also in attendance were the angels of the Lord offering him honor, all unseen; however, by either man or demon. Caiaphas had arranged for false witnesses to testify against the Lord, but my Son remained mute and said not a word to their calumnies and lies. Caiaphas, provoked by the patient silence of the Lord, rose and said to him. "Why do you not answer to what all these witnesses say about you?" However, Jesus did not choose to answer. Wishing to use his words against him, the wicked priest was infuriated for it frustrated his evil purpose.

Urged on by Lucifer, Caiaphas, stirred up to the greatest wrath and haughtiness demanded, "I adjure you by the living God that you tell us if you are the Christ, the Son of God." My divine Son, out of reverence for the name of God, although appealed to by such sacrilegious lips answered, "You have said so. But I tell you: "From now on you will see the Son of man seated at the right hand of the Power, and coming on the clouds of heaven [Matt: 26, 64]."

Upon hearing this declaration, Lucifer could not bear it, but suddenly felt a superior force which hurled all the demons into the abyss and oppressed them by the truth that it contained. There, they would have remained if God had not allowed them to again doubt the identity of his Son. Consequently, Lucifer thought, had this man actually spoke the truth or had he lied to save his life? This uncertainty gave them new courage and they came forth once more to the battlefield. The high priest was furious, and he had the solution that he had sought.

In a false zeal to protect the honor of God, he tore his robes and cried out, "He has blasphemed! What further need do we have of witnesses? What is your opinion?"

The entire assembly exclaimed in a loud voice, "He is guilty of death, he deserves to die!" Roused by satanic fury, they all fell upon Jesus venting their wrath. They struck him in the face, kicked him and tore out his hair, some spat in his face, and others slapped and struck him on the neck, which was treatment reserved among the Jews only for the most abject and vile of criminals. They cursed him and piled frightful insults upon him and me, his mother, and our ancestors. Unable to bear the sight of his benign, benevolent face, in spite of all their abuse, they covered his face and struck him with their fists saying, "Prophesy for us, Messiah, who it is, that struck you?"

I heard, saw, and felt all these affronts, reproaches, and insults. They caused in me the same pains and wounds in the same parts of my body as those inflicted on my Jesus; the Almighty caused these pains in answer to my request to suffer the same pains and suffering as his Son. Strengthened by divine power, I survived their brutality. By these injuries and torments, and those that were to follow later, the Savior established for his perfect and chosen souls the beatitudes, which he promised and proposed to them some time before.

Peter followed the Lord Jesus from the house of Annas to that of Caiaphas; although he took great care to walk some distance behind the crowd for fear that the Jews might seize him. He had managed to partly repress his fear because of his great love for Jesus. When the large crowd arrived at the house of Caiaphas, it was not difficult for Peter to gain entry into the house. Again he tried to warm himself by a fire, but again a servant maid recognized him and went up to the soldiers who were also standing near the fire and stated boldly, "This man is one of those who were always in the company of Jesus of Nazareth."

One of the bystanders exclaimed, "There is no doubt that you are a Galilean and one of them."

Peter immediately denied it saying, "May you be cursed, for I am not one of them." He hurried away from the fire so as not to be recognized. Still concerned for his Master; however, he did not leave the compound, but kept moving about to avoid close scrutiny.

Then a relative of Malchus, whose ear Peter had severed, recognized him and he challenged him saying, "You are a Galilean and a disciple of Jesus, I saw you there with him in the garden when you cut off the ear of my cousin Malchus."

Upon discovery, Peter was overwhelmed with fear, and for the third time, he began to swear with oaths and imprecations that he did not know the man [Matt: 26, 74]. At that moment, a cock crowed fulfilling the prediction of my Son. Lucifer was anxious to destroy Peter. He had incited the two women to denounce Peter, for he could easily influence them, and had disturbed Peter with vivid imaginations of impending torture. Thus tempted, Peter simply denied the Lord at first, added an oath to the second denial, and curses and imprecations at the third. Hence, from one sin, he fell into another greater one, yielding to the cruel persecutions of the enemy. Upon hearing the rooster crow, Peter suddenly remembered the prediction of his Master, and he fled into the darkness crying with shame.

From my oratory in the Cenacle, I interceded with the Lord for Peter's sins. I threw myself upon the floor and tearfully interceded for him, alleging his frailty and appealing to the merits of my divine Son. The Lord himself moved the heart of Peter, and by means of the light sent to him, gently reproached him, as well as exhorting him to acknowledge his fault and deplore his sin. Bursting with sorrow, Peter ran from the house of the high priest, and broke into bitter tears over his weakness. To weep in full abandon he hid himself in a cave near Mount Calvary, even now called, the cave of the Crowing Cock. There he poured forth his sorrow and confusion in a flood of tears. At the end of three hours, he had obtained pardon for his sins. I sent one of my angels to him, who secretly consoled and excited in him the hope of forgiveness, so that he might not delay his full pardon by want of trust in the goodness of God. The angel did not appear to him visually, because Peter had so recently committed his sin. Peter was consoled and strengthened in his great sorrow by these inspirations and thus obtained full pardon through my intercession as ordained by my Son.

Herod's soldiers locked my son in a subterranean dungeon that night; a prison cell that had been set apart for robbers and criminals of the state. No one had cleaned the prison for many years. The filth and stench of offal, urine, and dead bodies permeated the dark pit. His jailers dragged him by his ropes causing him to stumble, and they kicked and hit him constantly with blasphemous imprecations. Once in the cell, they bound him to a huge stone in such a stooped position that he could neither sit, nor straighten up. Withdrawing, they left him alone in the dark with only the rats for company. Lucifer; however, was far from satisfied and he inspired the jailer to get his friends and entertain themselves with the helpless prisoner. Jesus' thousands of angels seeing him so destitute prostrated themselves before him, and showered him with praise and worship. They sang canticles of songs to him that I had written. They begged him to allow them to untie him and defend him, but he would not use his own infinite powers to alleviate himself.

He said to them, "Holy spirits of my eternal Father, I do not wish to accept any alleviation in my sufferings and at present I desire to undergo these torments and affronts in order to satiate my burning love for men and to leave to my chosen friends this example. At the same time I wish to justify my cause, so that on the day of my wrath, all may know how justly the reprobate shall be condemned for despising the most bitter sufferings by which I sought to save them. Tell my mother to console herself in this tribulation, since the day of rest and gladness shall come. Let her accompany me now in my works and sufferings for men; for her affectionate compassion and all her sacrifices afford me much pleasure and comfort."

When they came to me with these consoling words, I, of course, already knew of all that he had said. When they bound Jesus in this impossible position, I felt in my own pure body all the same pains and discomfort. Without authorization the guards untied their prisoner from the stone block and began to spit and rain blows on his body. They wished him to make some statement so that they could ridicule him the more, but Jesus opened not his mouth and never lost the serenity of his countenance. Again, they blindfolded and hit him and tried to get him to tell who had struck him. The meek Lamb silently bore this renewed flood of abuse. Lucifer was nearly frantic in his attempts to break Jesus and inspired the slaves to strip him of his clothes and do indecent things to his body. This: however, I would not allow. Using my powers as Queen, I commanded the faculties of these evil servants so they could not execute these indecencies. Some of these suggestions they forgot and others they could not follow up, because their limbs became as if they were frozen or paralyzed until they changed their intent. The Lord permitted them to practice any cruelty or indulge in any irreverence, if the act was not indecent. The slaves noticed these strange happenings but attributed them to the sorcery or magic of their victim. It was very late when they tired of their diabolical play and again fastened Jesus to the stone in his painful, stooped-over position.

It had been ordained that I safeguard the propriety and the decency due to my Son's person, which I did. My suffering did not seem to be much, nor my afflictions equal to those demanded by my affection, which was measured only by the love and dignity of my Son and the greatness of his sufferings. I did not reflect on the share, which I myself had in them. I deplored them only in so far as they outraged the divine Personality and caused damage to the aggressors. I prayed that the Most High might pardon them and grant them salvation from the evils of sin and enlightenment for gaining the fruits of Redemption. I felt every blow, and every insult inflicted upon his innocent body. *The same pains beset my Son and me, and the same sword pierced both our hearts; with this primary difference; that Jesus suffered as God-man and sole Redeemer of mankind, while I suffered as a mere creature and as a faithful helper of my most holy Son.*

At dawn Friday morning, the ancients, the chief priests and scribes, who according to the law were looked upon with greatest respect by the people came together to reach a decision concerning the death of the Redeemer. The Council met at the house of Caiaphas. They all wished the death of Jesus; however, they were anxious to preserve the semblance of justice before the people.

The guards came for him and as they untied him from the rock, they mocked him with great contempt saying, "Well now, Jesus of Nazareth, what good have your miracles done to save you? The power you bragged of being able to rebuild the temple in three days has failed. Now you shall pay for your arrogance and proud aspirations. The council is waiting to put an end to your imposition and deliver you over to Pilate, who will be your undoing."

The Lord was dirty from their spit, his blood, and dirt and filth from being dragged in the road, which had dried in streaks. Still bound, he was unable to clean himself, and yet, in spite of this veneer acquired of their hate, Jesus still stood before them calm and serene in his dignity. The Council was dreadfully surprised at how disfigured he was, but even that did not fill them with compassion.

Again, Caiaphas attempted to question Jesus. At first, he stood mute, for while he was willing to die for the truth he did not wish them to fabricate charges from what he might say. Therefore, he finally answered them in such a way that if they twisted his words it would be clear their words were wicked and lay not in his answer.

He said to them, "If I tell you that I am he of whom you ask, you will not believe what I say, and if I shall ask you, you will not answer, nor release me. But I tell you, that the Son of man, after this, shall seat himself at the right hand of the power of God [Luke: 22, 67]."

Caiphas asked him, "Then you are the Son of God?"

Jesus replied, "You say that I am."

By this inference, the priests cried out, "What need have we of further witnesses, since he himself asserts it by his own lips?"

They concluded that Jesus was worthy of death; however, the Jews could not condemn him to death. Pontius Pilate, who governed Judea, was the only person in Israel that could pass a death sentence. The Roman Senate, the emperor, or his representatives in the remote provinces, according to the laws of the Roman Empire, reserved the right to render Capital punishment in occupied countries. In these affairs of justice, the Roman people yielded to the requirements of natural reason more faithfully than any other nation. The priests were pleased with the prospect of having the sentence of death passed upon Christ by the heathen Pilate. Then, they could tell the people that the Roman governor condemned him and that this would certainly not have happened, if he were not guilty of death.

His persecutors took their bound victim through the crowded streets of Jerusalem. Great numbers of Jews from all over the Diaspora had gathered for celebration of the Pasch. As the rumor of Jesus' arrest spread throughout the city, people thronged to see him brought in chains through the streets.

They were divided in their opinion concerning the Messiah, some shouted as he passed, "Let him die, let him die, this wicked imposter who deceives the whole world."

Others replied, "His doctrines do not seem to be so bad, nor his works; for he has done well to many."

Still others, who believed in him, were much afflicted and wept; while the entire city was in confusion and uproar concerning my Son.

Lucifer was very attentive to all that happened. The patience and fortitude of Jesus stirred him to a fury, for such virtues could not be those of a mere human being. "If he were God," Lucifer reasoned to his demons, "he would never consent to such treatment, for the inherent power in his divine nature and communicated to the humanity, would certainly prevent such weakness."

The sun having risen, I left my quarters for the first time since my Son's arrest and going to the house of Caiaphas was in time to follow Jesus to the house of Pilate. As I left, John came to report to me all that had happened, for he did not know of my visions. John accompanied me and on the way he confessed to me his wickedness of his flight in the garden, and asked my pardon.

John deemed it wise to prepare me before I saw my Son in his pitiable condition and he said, "Oh my, Lady, our divine Master is in a deplorable state of suffering! The sight of your Son cannot but break your heart; for by the blows, the spittle, and his being dragged, his beautiful countenance is so disfigured and defiled, that you will scarcely recognize him with your own eyes."

Although I knew all of these facts, I could not help but break out into the bitterest of tears and heartrending sorrow. John's description filled my women friends with grief and terror.

I asked John to accompany us and said, "Let us hasten our steps, in order that my eyes may see the Son of the eternal Father, who took human form in my womb. You shall see, my, Friends, to what the love of mankind has driven my Lord and God, and what it costs him to redeem men from sin and death, and to open for them the Gates of Heaven."

I set forth through the streets of Jerusalem accompanied by John, the three Marys and Mary Heli, Martha, Johanna, Veronica, Susanna, Mary Marcus, and a few other holy and pious women, numbering sixteen, who remained with me throughout the ordeal. Also with me were my guardian angels, who opened a way for me to my divine Son. I heard different people about me expressing their different opinions concerning these sorrowful events. The most kindly lamented over his fate, but they were the fewest in number. In the midst of all this excitement, my group and I prayed for all the misguided people with whom we came in contact. I allowed no anger or indignation to mar my pious thoughts, for I loved them as sincerely as if I was receiving blessings and favors at their hands.

One lady recognizing me came up to me and said, "Oh sorrowful, Mother! What a misfortune has befallen you. Your heart must be wounded and lacerated with grief!"

Another said to me impiously, "Why did you permit him to introduce such novelties among the people? It would have been better to restrain and dissuade him: but it will be a warning for other mothers, and they will learn from your misfortunes, how to instruct their children."

Many women greeted me with these and other horrible sentiments. However, I met them all with burning charity, accepting the pity of the kind-hearted, and suffering the malice of the unbelievers. I was not surprised at the ingratitude of the unresponsive and ignorant, but implored the eternal Father to impart suitable blessings to all.

My angels conducted me through the swarming and confused crowds and making a sharp turn, I suddenly found myself face to face with my Son. I mentally prostrated myself before his sovereign person and adored him more fervently and with deeper and more ardent reverence than can ever be given by all the creatures. We looked at each other with ineffable tenderness and interiorly conversed with one another in abject sorrow. I stepped aside and then joined in with the faithful who followed closely behind him. We continued to communicate interiorly, and I showered him with my prayers. The image of my Savior, thus wounded, defiled and bound, would forever remain firmly fixed and imprinted in my soul as vividly as though he was present before me.

When the Jews presented themselves before Pilate, wishing to preserve themselves as clean before the law for the celebration of the Pasch and the unleavened bread, they excused themselves before Pilate for refusing to enter his court or the Praetorium. Their hypocrisy in wishing to remain ritually clean, while at the same time, they planned to murder the Savior of the world, was lost to them. Pilate, although a heathen, yielded to their ceremonious scruples, and went out to meet them in an open courtyard.

He eyed Jesus curiously, as he seated himself, and asked his jailers formally, "What accusation have you against this man?"

They answered rather defensively, "If he were not a criminal, we would not have brought him to you thus bound and fettered."

Pilate used to their evasive tactics pressed his inquiry and said, "What then are the misdeeds of which he has made himself guilty?"

They responded, "He is convicted of disturbing the commonwealth, he wishes to made himself our king and forbids paying tribute to Caesar [Luke: 23, 2]. He claims to be the Son of God, and has preached a new doctrine, commencing in Galilee, through all Judea and Jerusalem."

"Take him yourselves then," replied Pilate, "and judge him according to your laws. I do not find just cause for proceeding against him."

The Jews argued, "It is not permitted us to sentence anyone to death, nor to execute such a sentence."

My angels had cleared a path for John, the women, and I, and we were able to see and hear all that transpired. Shielded by my mantle, I wept tears of blood, pressed forth by the sorrow, which pierced my breaking heart. I asked the eternal Father to grant me the favor of not losing sight of my divine Son, as far as was naturally possible, until his death. God graciously conceded my request, except for the time that he was in prison. I also prayed that the lies of my Son's persecutors would not deceive Pilate. God granted my prayer, for Pilate clearly saw the truth. He was convinced of the innocence of Christ, and believed that he was the victim of the scribes and priest's envy. On my account, Jesus declared himself more openly to Pilate, although Pilate did not co-operate with the truth made known to him. It did serve him politically to convict the priests and Pharisees of their treachery. When the Jews perceived Pilate's hesitation to pronounce the sentence of death, they ferociously raised their voices, accusing Jesus repeatedly of revolting against the government of Judea and calling himself Christ, that is, an anointed one. Hebrew kings were anointed, and they insisted that Jesus in calling himself Christ intended to constitute himself as King of the Jews.

Pilate turned to Jesus and asked him, "What do you have to say in answer to the accusations which they bring against you?"

Jesus did not answer one word in the presence of his accusers, causing much wonder in Pilate at such silence and patience. However, desiring to question Jesus more closely, whether Jesus was truly a king, he withdrew into the Praetorium taking Jesus with him. There he asked him face to face, "Tell me, can it be that, you are a King of the Jews?" Since Jesus was not a reigning king, he wished to find out whether Jesus claimed or really possessed any right to the title of king.

Christ answered him, "Do you say this of me yourself, or have others told you about me?"

Pilate replied scornfully, "Am I a Jew? Your own nation and the chief priests have delivered you up to me. What have you done?"

Jesus answered him, "My kingdom is not of this world. If my kingdom were of this world, my servants would certainly strive that I be not delivered to the Jews; but my kingdom is not from here."

The judge partly believed this assertion of Jesus and therefore replied, "Are you a king then?"

Jesus answered, "You say that I am a king. For this, I was born and for this, I came into the world. Every one that is of the truth hears my voice."

Pilate wondered at this answer and commented dryly, "What is truth?" However, without waiting for an answer, he left Jesus in the Praetorium and going out, said to the Jews, "I find no fault in him. However, you have a custom of my releasing a prisoner to you each year at the Pasch. I ask you then, whom should I release, Jesus of Nazareth or Barabbas the murderer?"

All the Jews raised their voice crying out, "Release Barabbas, and crucify Jesus." They persisted in their demand that Pilate concede to their wishes.

The answers of Jesus and the obstinacy of the Jews greatly disturbed Pilate. However, he knew he could not please the Jews unless he satisfied their demands. On the other hand, he knew their claims were false and malicious and that they persecuted Jesus out of envy. He was satisfied by Christ's answers that he did not desire to make himself king. The humility and patient forbearance of our Savior toward his persecutors impressed the magistrate. By the light and grace that he had received, he became fully convinced that Jesus was truly innocent, although he never pierced the mystery of his divinity. He believed that there was indeed a great mystery connected with Jesus, and he desired to set him free; in this hope he decided to send him to King Herod. In not adjudicating the case then and there in the favor of Jesus, by allowing himself to be governed by the Jews and not by the dictates of justice, Pilate acted the part of the wicked judge, and yet his sin was far less than that of the vindictive Jews.

Pilate was not on good terms with Herod. Pilate ruled Judea and Herod ruled Galilee, the two principal provinces of Palestine. A short time before this distribution of Palestine, Pilate, in his zeal for the supremacy of the Roman Empire had murdered some Galileans during a public function in the temple. He mixed the blood of the insurgents with that of the holy sacrifices. Herod was highly incensed at this sacrilege. Pilate in order to afford him some satisfaction, and to rid himself of an odorous task, resolved to send to him Christ to be examined and judged as one of the subjects of Herod's jurisdiction. Pilate hoped that Herod would set Jesus free as being innocent and a victim of the malice and envy of the priests and scribes.

The soldiers hurried and dragged the bound Jesus through the crowded streets. The military savagely broke their way through the crowds, for they knew the priests and scribes were thirsting eagerly for the blood of my Son. Again, I was only able to keep up with the soldiers by ordering my angels to clear a path for us, which was done in a mystical manner so that the people were never inconvenienced. The people took out their frustrations against the soldiers by kicking, hitting and spitting on the innocent Lamb of God. When Herod heard the news, he was highly pleased. He knew that Jesus was a great friend of John the Baptist, whom he had ordered beheaded at the whim of his stepdaughter. Herod was most curious about Jesus, for he had heard many reports of his preaching and of his many miracles. He hoped to see Jesus perform some miracle for him and his court.

Loud laughter greeted Jesus as he entered the royal court, and the courtiers mocked him as an enchanter and conjurer. The priest and scribes made their usual accusations, but the Master of wisdom and prudence stood before the court, and, with humble reserve, did not answer Herod's questions—much to his disappointment. If Herod had been disposed to hear the words of life with reverence, my Son would have answered him. Instead, his vain curiosity thwarted, Herod resorted to mocking and ridiculing Jesus before his entire cohort of soldiers and the men and women of the court. Herod treated our Lord as a fool by dressing him in a white garment, which was a mark of an insane person and to be avoided as dangerous. However, by the divine Providence of the Most High, this dress signified the purity and innocence of the Savior. Thus, God used these ministers of wickedness to unwittingly give testimony of the truth.

Herod informed Pilate, that he found no cause in Jesus, but held him to be an ignorant person of no consequence whatever. By the secret judgments of divine wisdom, Herod and Pilate were reconciled on that day and thenceforward remained friends. The soldiers again dragged Jesus through the town on their return to Pilate. Worked up to a fever pitch by the priests, the people abused my Son terribly. Convinced by the priests of his unworthiness, the fickle people, who the day before had honored and venerated him as a king, now despised and condemned him to death. In the midst of all this confusion, the Lord passed along, repeating within himself words of unspeakable love, humility, and patience. The same words by which he had long ago spoken by the mouth of King David,

"I am a worm and no man, the reproach of man and the outcast of people. All they that saw me have laughed me to scorn. They have spoken with their lips and wagged the heads."

I was not with my Son inside the palace of the wicked Herod, but I knew all that took place. As he came forth from the hall, I met him and we looked at each other in reciprocal sorrow of our souls, each of us corresponded to the love between us as Son and mother. The sight of the white garment pierced my heart with new sorrow. However, I alone, of all humankind recognized the mystery of his purity and innocence indicated by this vestment. I adored him with the deepest respect and followed him back through the streets to the house of Pilate. Jesus fell frequently, because of the crush of people, and the guard's constant manipulation of the ropes. When he fell, because of his bonds, he could not easily rise to his feet. Consequently, the masses of people kicked and stepped on our Savior, and blood poured from the wounds caused by his persecutors. The guards only laughed at his plight. The soldiers, urged on by the demons, had become devoid of all human compassion, and were like so many wild beasts.

Dismayed by this cruelty, I ordered my angels to pick up all the blood that spilled from my Son's body, so that the feet of sinners would not dishonor it. I mentally appealed to Jesus to allow my angels to assist him when he fell; otherwise, the maddened crowd would trample him to death. This he did allow, and for the rest of this journey, my angels did not permit my Son to trip or fall. However, he did not allow them to curtail the blows and lashes of the guards and the people. John and the holy women, who accompanied me with ceaseless tears streaming down their faces, witnessed all of this. Mary Magdalene was especially affected, for they love most to whom the greater sins are forgiven [Luke: 8, 47].

The Jews again confronted Pilate with the bound Jesus, and they be-stormed him anew to condemn him to death. Pilate was annoyed at Herod's adept sidestepping of the issue, for he was convinced of the innocence of Christ and of the mortal envy of the Jews. He sought to placate the Jews in several ways. He privately interviewed some of the servants and friends of the high priests and scribes. He urged them to prevail upon their masters and friends, to accept Barabbas instead of Jesus, and to be satisfied with some other punishment he was willing to administer before setting him free.

However, none of his efforts bore fruit, and he said to the assembled Jews, "You have brought this man before me, accusing him of perverting the people by his doctrines. I have examined him in your presence, and I was not convinced of the truth of your charges. In addition, I sent him to Herod, King of the Galileans, to whom you repeated your accusations; he also refused to condemn him to death. It will be sufficient to correct and chastise him for the present that he may amend. Again I remind you, today I am to release a criminal for the feast of the Pasch, and I will release Christ, if you will have him freed, and punish Barabbas."

However, the multitude of Jews shouted angrily, "Enough, enough, release Barabbas to us, and crucify Jesus of Nazareth."

The Jews introduced the custom of giving freedom to an imprisoned criminal at the solemnity of the Pasch in grateful remembrance of the release of their ancestors from servitude to the Egyptians. The Almighty freed them from the power of Pharaoh by killing the first-born of all creatures of the Egyptians and afterwards his armies were annihilating in the waters of the Red Sea. Thus the Jews took great pride during the Pasch in releasing the greatest malefactor and pardoned him his crimes. In their treaties with the Romans, the Jews had been granted this privilege and it had been religiously maintained. By releasing Barabbas, instead of Jesus, they were breaking their own traditions and laws.

While Pilate was thus disputing with the Jews in the Praetorium, his wife, Pocola, sent him a message saying, "What have you to do with this man? Let him go free, for I have this very day had some visions in regard to him."

This warning originated through Lucifer and his demons. The more they saw of Jesus, the more confused they became, and at last, they determined that it was in their best interests to keep Jesus alive, in case that he was indeed the Messiah. Pilate received similar warnings in his mind from the crafty one.

Besieged by the obstinate hostility of the Jews against Jesus and unwilling to condemn him to death, for he knew him to be innocent, Pilate decided to have Jesus scourged to appease the anger of the Jews, hoping in this manner to spare his life. The guards dragged their innocent victim to an enclosure set apart for the punishment and torture of criminals. Columns that supported the roof surrounded the area. To one of these marble columns, they bound Jesus securely, for they still feared him and his magical powers. They tore off the white garment placed on him in the palace of Herod, but had to loosen the ropes and chains to remove his seamless tunic. Impatient with his efforts, they violently tore away his tunic leaving him naked except for a strip of cloth cinctured about his waist as an undergarment. However, while my Son stood ready to suffer every indignity, for my sake, he would not allow them to expose his nakedness. When his torturers attempted to take off his loincloth, their arms became paralyzed and stiff. All six of his guards separately made the attempt and suffered the same result. This miracle; however, did not soften or hinder them, for they attributed this to his sorcery and witchcraft.

The Lord stood nearly naked in the presence of a huge multitude and the six torturers brutally bound him to one of the columns. Then two at a time they began to scourge him with all the inhuman cruelty as was possible only in men possessed by Lucifer. I felt the first blow as assuredly as if they had struck my own flesh. I sank to my knees with a moan, but not because of the excruciating pain, but because my Son, the Onlybegotten Son of God, was being treated sacrilegiously. His torturers used hard, thick cords, full of rough knots, and in their demonic fury strained all the powers of their bodies to inflict the blows. This first scourging rose in the deified body of the Lord great welts and livid tumors, so that the sacred blood beneath his skin disfigured his entire body. The only part of his body spared the rod, was that beneath the skimpy loincloth. Although they tried repeatedly, they were unable to strike him there. The second two men took over from their exhausted companions. They used hardened leather thongs and leveled their strokes on the places already sore causing them to break open and bleed. The garments of the torturers were drenched with the Lord's blood from whence it ran down upon the flag-stoned floor. These two gave way to the third pair of tormentors. Their whips were made of leather thongs, which were tipped with sharp sheep bones. This wicked whip flayed the blessed Lord's flesh loose from his shoulder blades. The torturers of Jesus rendered him unrecognizable, for they did not spare one square inch of his body. His body seemed as one continuous bleeding wound. Their ceaseless blows had torn the immaculate and virginal flesh of Christ our Redeemer and scattered many pieces of it about the pavement. Large portions of Jesus' shoulder bones were uncovered, exposing both white bone and bloody bruised flesh. They beat him on the face, the feet and his hands, thus leaving unwounded only the private parts of his body that they could not violate.

All the while, they spat upon him continuously, and loaded him with insulting epithets. They lashed Jesus hundreds of times in just this one scourging. No other human being could have survived this savage beating. Thus was our Lord and Author of all creation, who, by his divine nature was incapable of suffering, was, in his human flesh and for our sake, reduced to a man of sorrows as prophesied. He was made to experience our infirmities, becoming the least of men, a man of sorrows, and the outcast of the people [Is: 53, 3-7].

Throughout my Son's trial, I had to endure vile, unheard of insults. Deeply affected by Jesus' injuries and the blasphemies heaped upon him, I retired with my little company of companions to the corner of the courtyard. There, assisted by my divine vision, I witnessed and felt all the scourging and torments of our Savior. Nothing was hidden from me, although, I did not see it physically with my eyes. It was as though I had been standing quite near. I felt in all parts of my virginal body, in the same intensity, as Christ felt them in his body. I shed no blood, except that which flowed from my eyes with my tears. However, my bodily pains so changed and disfigured my person that John and the holy women failed to find in me anything recognizable. In addition, I suffered ineffable sorrows of the soul in direct proportion to the immensity of my insight. My sorrows flowed not only from the natural love of a mother and a supreme love of Christ as my God, but it was proportionate to my power of judging more accurately than all creatures of the innocence of my Son. I alone was aware of the dignity of his divine Person, the atrocity of the insults coming from the perfidious Jews and the children of Adam, whom he was freeing from eternal death. I survived this horrible scourging only by the healing hand of God the Father.

Exhausted by having vented their physical faculties, the executioners freed Jesus from the column and ordered him to put on his garments. However, instigated by Lucifer, one of his tormentors had hidden his clothes to further embarrass the Lord by prolonging his nakedness. I knew of their evilness, and I, therefore, ordered Lucifer and all his demons to leave the area. My angels found the clothes and by their angelic power made his captors aware of where to look. My Son, during his nakedness had suffered greatly from the cold and his sacred blood had frozen, which did him the favor of congealing his wounds and stemming the great loss of his blood. However, his wounds became inflamed once he was dressed and added to his distress. There was no compassion from his executioners, or from among any of the Jews. However, I tearfully pitied him in the name of the whole human race.

Instead of compassion, the Jew's fury birthed an even more outrageous cruelty. They went to Pontius Pilate and complained, "This deceiver of the people, Jesus of Nazareth, in his boasting and vanity, has sought to be recognized by all as the king of the Jews. In order to humble his pride and humble his presumption, we desire your permission to place upon him the royal insignia merited by his fantastic pretensions." Pilate yielded yet again to the nagging demands of the envious Jews. The jailers took Jesus back to the Praetorium and again removed his clothes. They clothed him in a discarded mantle of purple and placed on his head a horrible, woven crown made from the branches of a thorn bush. They pounded the thorny crown onto his head with the flat of their swords driving the thorns deep into his flesh. Instead of a scepter, they placed into his hands a bundle of reeds. Next, they threw over his shoulders a scarlet cloak, discarded by a Roman soldier. For a throne, they seated him on a stool.

In this array of a mock king, the perfidious Jews decked him out, who by his divine nature was the King of kings and the Lord of lords. Then all the soldiers, in the presence of the priests and Pharisees, gathered around him and heaped upon him their mockery and derision. Some bent their knees and mockingly said to him, "God save you, King of the Jews."

Others hit him, and still others snatched the reeds from his hands and beat him with them. Others spit on him, and instigated by the furious demons, insulted him in every manner possible. Throughout it all, the Redeemer sat in dignified silence every bit the king he really was and is. Only the supreme will of Jesus kept him alive. Any ordinary person would have died from this senseless scourging.

The torturers brought Jesus to the lowest step that led up to Pontius Pilate. The governor, seeing the sad condition of Jesus, shuddered with compassion. Their victim was nearly unrecognizable because of the blood that filled his eyes and ran down into his beard and mouth from the cruel *crown of thorns* on his head. The face of Jesus was battered, and swollen, his nose flattened, his body was covered with hideous welts and wounds, and he was a mass of blood and filth. The gait of Jesus was hesitant and he tottered as he came to a halt, but, with a great effort of will, he squared his shoulders and looked up at the procreator without fear or rancor.

Pilate was standing with three of his officers, he leaned on one of his officers, and as the priests and the people kept up their shouts and mockery, he exclaimed, "If the devil were as cruel as the Jews, one could not live with him in hell!"

It seemed to Pilate that the spectacle of a man so maltreated as Jesus of Nazareth would move and fills with shame the hearts of that ungrateful people. He took him to an open window overlooking the courtyard where the unruly mob could see him crowned with thorns, disfigured by the scourging and the ignominious vesture of a mock king. Pilate pointed to Jesus and called out to them, "Behold, the man [John: 19, 5]!

The chief priests and scribes; however, were infuriated at the sight of Jesus and they yelled, "Away with him! Crucify him!"

Pilate called out, "Are you not yet satisfied? See the man you hold as your enemy. The torturers have handled him so roughly that he will never more want to be a king. I do not find any cause of death in him." What this judge said was certainly the truth. By his own words he condemned his own outrageous injustice, since knowing Jesus was innocent, he had had him tormented and punished in such a way that, according to reason, he should have been killed many times over.

When I saw Jesus thus exposed, I fell to my knees and openly adored him as the true God-man. John and the holy women quickly followed my example, knowing that not only me, but also God himself desired it so. I prayed that Pilate would act as a just judge and declare that Jesus was not guilty of death, or of any crime imputed to him by the Jews. Because of my prayers, Pilate felt great compassion for Jesus and when the Jews again demanded that Christ be crucified, he said to them, "Take him yourselves and crucify him, for I do not find any cause for doing it."

They replied angrily, "According to our law, he is guilty of death, for he claims to be the Son of God."

Pilate responded sarcastically, "If you have such a law, that a man like this one must die then may I never be a Jew!"

However, their attitude threw Pilate into greater consternation, for he conceived it might be true, that Jesus was the Son of God according to his heathen notions of the Divinity and it worked on his superstitions. What if this man should indeed be a god? Therefore he withdrew with Jesus into the Praetorium and with an oath; he demanded that Jesus defend himself. The Lord did not answer his question for Pilate was not in a state of mind to either understand or merit a reply.

Pilate insisted on an answer and said to him, "Why don't you speak to me? Don't you know that I have the power to crucify you and the power to dismiss you?" It seemed to Pilate that a man so tormented and in such a wretched state would gladly accept any favor from a judge.

However, the Master of Truth answered the Procreator without defending himself, but with unexpected dignity said, "You would not have any power against me, unless it was given you by my Father. Therefore, they that have delivered me to you, has the greater sin."

This answer by itself made Pilate's condemnation of Christ inexcusable since from what he had just said, neither he nor Caesar had any power of jurisdiction over Jesus. The Jews had unreasonably and unjustly delivered Christ over to Pilate's judgment. Judas and the priests had committed a greater sin than Pilate had in not releasing him and Pilate was guilty of the same crime, although to a lesser degree.

Pilate never divined the truth of my Son's statements, but nevertheless, he made still greater efforts to free him and taking Jesus, he went out on the balcony said to the people, "Behold! I bring him forth to you, that you may know that I find no cause in him!"

However, the priests, abundantly aware of his intentions, threatened him with the displeasure of the emperor, which he would incur, if he permitted Jesus to escape death. They cried out, "If you free this man, you are no friend of Caesar, since he who makes a king of himself rises up against his orders and commands."

Pilate knew if he released Jesus, the priests would condemn him before Rome, and this he could not afford, since he was not held in great favor by Caesar. However, his conscience reproached him. His own wife had said, "Jesus is holy." His superstition whispered, "He is an enemy of my gods," and his cowardice cried out, "He is himself a god, and he will avenge himself." However, intimidated and fearful of the maliciousness of the Jews, he seated himself in his tribunal at the sixth hour in order to pass sentence upon the Lord. Even then, he tried again to plead with the Jews saying, "See there is your King!"

All of them answered, "Away with him, away with him, crucify him."

Pilate replied, "Shall I crucify your King?"

They shouted unanimously, "We have no other king than Caesar."

Thereupon, Pilate asked for water and ordered the release of the murderer Barabbas. Then he washed his hands in the presence of all the people, saying, "I have no share in the death of this just man, whom you condemn. Look to yourselves in what you are doing, for I wash my hands in order that you may understand they are not sullied in the blood of the innocent."

Pilate thought that by this ceremony that he could excuse himself entirely and that thereby he could put its blame upon the princes and all those who had demanded the death of my Son. The wrath of the Jews was so blind and foolish that for the satisfaction of seeing Jesus crucified, they entered this agreement with Pilate and took upon themselves and upon their children the responsibility for their crime. Loudly proclaiming this terrible sentence and curse, they exclaimed; "His blood come upon us and upon our children [Matt: 27, 25]."

The words of the Jews pierced my sorrowful heart like a two-edged sword. I besought not revenge, but pardon for my Son's and my enemies, for they were depriving him of his life, and I was being deprived of the Onlybegotten of the Father and my only Son. I imitated all the actions of the most holy soul of Christ and accompanied him in his works of most exalted holiness and perfection. Pilate had faltered; he had allowed the obstinacy and the malice of the Jews to overcome his reason.

Jesus was again dressed in his own garments, for the simple reason that his face had been so disfigured that he could only be recognized by his clothes with which the common Jew was familiar. The priests deliberately circulated the news of Jesus' immediate execution over the entire city. The people flocked to the streets to see the spectacle. In the sight of all these multitudes, they brought forth our Savior, so disfigured by wounds, blood and spittle, that no one could recognize him. I sent my angels several times to remove the filth from my Son's face, but his enemies so persistently continued in their disgusting insults that his face ran with their vile expectorations. However, there was much division and confusion in the people's opinions of Jesus' guilt. Those who had been the beneficiaries of his healing hand and exposed to his kindness and inspiring doctrines showed their sympathy by their vocal support and their tears of anguish.

Of the eleven Apostles, only John was faithful and remained with me. However, my small but loyal group of holy women never left my side. They were so inspired that most of them conducted themselves with more courage than all the Apostles and the disciples. At the first sight of my Son, John's blood literally congealed in his veins and his face took on the appearance of death. The women with me fell into a prolonged swoon. I; however, remained unconquered, but my heart was overwhelmed by a grief beyond all human conception. As their Queen, I did not share the imperfections and weaknesses of the others, and in all my actions, I remained prudent and courageous. I comforted John and the pious women, and I gave special attention to Mary Magdalene, whose grief nearly rent her heart from her body. I besought the Lord to strengthen the women, which he granted. He did so in order that they might help and support me to the bitter end. Tears ran down my cheeks in a continuous stream, but I never lost my composure or dignity as the Queen of the heavens and of the earth.

Pilate ordered that the proper preparations be made for the pronouncement of the sentence. His servants brought his ceremonial robes to him, and they placed on his ahead a crown, in which a precious stone sparkled. Another servant placed a mantle about him, and he then carried a staff before him. With his officers, a guard complement, and a trumpeter leading the way, Pilate proceeded to the Forum. There, opposite the scourging place, was a tall, beautifully constructed judgment-seat. Only when delivered from that seat, did the sentence have full weight. On the day of Parasceve [day of preparation], seated amid his tribunal, which in Greek was called lithostratos, and in Hebrew gabbatha, Pontius Pilate pronounced the sentence of death against my Son, the Author of life. The priests circulated among the people urging them to silence, it was important to them that the death sentence be heard by all. A deathly calm fell over the multitude and the servants of Pilate read the sentence in a loud voice, with Jesus standing in full view as a criminal. Pilate had the sentence read throughout Jerusalem. At the crucifixion, a Centurion read the sentence again. It was afterwards published and posted throughout the city and read as follows:

Proclamation

"I Pontius Pilate, presiding over lower Galilee and governing Jerusalem, in fealty to the Roman Empire, and being within the executive mansion, judge, decide, and proclaim, that I condemn to death, Jesus, of the Nazarean people and a Galilean by birth, a man seditious and opposed to our laws, to our senate, and to the great emperor Tiberius Caesar. I decree that for the execution of this sentence that he suffer death upon a cross. The soldiers shall fasten him thereto with nails as is customary with criminals. He, in this very place, gathered around him every day many men, poor and rich, and has continued to raise tumults throughout Judea. He has proclaimed himself the Son of God, and King of Israel. At the same time, he threatened to ruin the temple of this renowned city of Jerusalem, and of the sacred Empire, and has refused tribute to Caesar. He dared to enter in triumph this city of Jerusalem and the Temple of Solomon, accompanied by a great multitude of the people carrying branches of palms. I command the first Centurion, called Quintus Cornelius, to lead him for his greater shame through the said city of Jerusalem, bound as he is, and scourged by my orders. So that all may know him, he shall wear his own garments and carry his own cross. Let him walk through the public streets with two other thieves, who are likewise condemned to death for their robberies and murders, so that this punishment be an example to all the people and to all malefactors."

I command that this malefactor be taken outside the city through the Pagora gate, now called the Antonian portal. Once there my herald, shall mention all the crimes pointed out in my sentence. The soldiers will then take him to the summit of the mountain called Calvary. There, the torturers will fasten and crucify him upon the cross placing him between the aforesaid thieves. Above the cross, that is, at its top, he shall have placed for him his name and title in three languages; in Hebrew, Greek and Latin; and in all and each of one of them shall be written: so that it will be understood by all and become universally known."

"THIS IS JESUS OF NAZARETH, KING OF THE JEWS'

At the same time I command, that no one, no matter of what condition, under pain of the loss of his goods and life, and under punishment for rebellion against the Roman Empire, presume audaciously to impede the execution of this just sentence ordered by me to be executed with all rigor according to the decrees and laws of the Romans and Hebrews.

Year of the creation of the world 5233, the twenty-fifth day of March."

Pontius Pilatus Judex at Gubernator Galilaeae inferioris pro Romano Imperio qui supra propria manu.

[Pontius Pilate, Judge and Governor of lower Galilee for the Roman Empire, who signed the above with his own hand.]

Two men came forward carrying the Lord's cross. The heavy timber taxed the strength of the two soldiers. My Son looked upon it with a countenance full of calm acceptance. In his heart he prayed, "Oh Cross, beloved of my soul, and now prepared and ready to still my longings. Come to me, that I may be received in your arms, and that, attached to them as on an altar, I may be accepted by the eternal Father as the sacrifice of his everlasting reconciliation with the human race. In order to die upon you, I have descended from heaven and assumed mortal and passible flesh; for you are to be the scepter with which I shall open the gates of heaven for all the predestined [Is: 22, 22]. I take upon my shoulders the wood for the sacrifices of my innocent and passible humanity and I accept it willingly for the salvation of men. Receive, eternal Father, this sacrifice as acceptable to your justice, in order that from today on they may no longer be servants, but sons and heirs of your kingdom together with me."

Four executioners accompanied my Son and they loosened his bonds sufficiently so that they could load the heavy patibulum, the crosspiece of the crucifix, onto his tender and mutilated shoulders. Jesus staggered under the unmerciful load and his torturers laughed as they jerked him forward with the ropes looped about his throat. The herald walked in front of the cavalcade proclaiming the sentence, followed by mounted Roman soldiers. Then came a contingent of foot soldiers and close behind them followed my Son, staggering under the burden of the heavy cross. His executioners surrounded him, and they jerked on his ropes constantly and were quick to flog him if he faltered in the slightest. Marching behind the three doomed men was another contingent of Roman soldiers.

I imitated my Son in his tokens of affections with which he received his cross, addressing it in the words suited to me as Coadjutrix of the Redeemer. In protest to the voice of the herald, I composed a canticle of praise and worship of the innocence and sinless ness of my all-holy Son and God. My angels joined in with me drowning out their voices between heaven and earth. When the weight of the patibulum crushed the shoulders of my Son, they crushed mine as well. I staggered under the weight, and John caught my arm and gave me support. I still felt my Son's pain, as if I were the one being punished, although I did not see all that he suffered. Of the dignity of the person of Christ our Redeemer, uniting within himself the divine and the human natures, of their perfections and attributes, I alone possessed the highest and intuitive knowledge outside of the Lord himself. On this account, I alone among all mere creatures attached sufficient importance to the Passion and Death of my Son. Of what he suffered, I not only was an eye witness, but I experienced it personally within myself, occasioning the holy envy not only of men, but of the angels themselves, who were not thus favored. When I did not witness his Passion, I felt his sufferings in my own body before my intelligence made me aware of them. Thus surprised, I would say, "Ah! What new martyrdom have they devised for my sweetest Lord and Master?"

Then I would receive the clear knowledge of what the Lord was enduring. I never permitted myself any easement either of my bodily pains, such as rest, or nourishment, or sleep; nor any relaxation of the spirit, such as consoling thoughts or considerations, except when I was visited from on high by divine influence. Then only would I humbly and thankfully accept relief, in order that I might recover strength to attend still more zealously to the object of my sorrows and to the cause of his sufferings.

The right hand of God wrought another hidden miracle through my instrumentality against the demons. The dragon and his evil minions, although they could not understand the humiliation of my Son, were most attentive to all that happened during the Passion. When he took upon himself the Cross, they all felt a new and mysterious tremor and weakness, which caused in them great consternation. Conscious of these unwanted feelings the prince of darkness feared that in the Passion and Death of the Christ, some dire and irreparable destruction of his reign was imminent. Fearfully, Lucifer decided to retire and flee with all his followers to the caverns of hell. However, when he sought to execute the resolve, I prevented him, for the Most High had enlightened me and advised me in what I was to do. At the same time, he invested me with his power. The demons could not resist my command for they all recognized and felt the divine power operating in me. God's power dragged the demons along behind Jesus like so many prisoners in chains. There, my Son had decreed he would triumph over them from the throne of the Cross. This punishment of the demons was in conformity with the maliciousness of their nature and proportional to the evil committed by Lucifer in introducing death and sin into the world. God himself was now undergoing death, in order to atone for all sin, past, present, and future.

Our Savior proceeded on the way to Calvary bearing upon his shoulders, according to the saying of, his own government and principality, which was none else than his Cross [Is: 9, 6]. From the Cross, Jesus was to subject and govern the world, meriting thereby that his name should be exalted above all other names and rescuing the human race from the tyrannical power of the demon over the sons of Adam. The executioners, bare of any human compassion, dragged my Son along by jerking him forward by the ropes and others yanked on them from behind. They caused Jesus to fall repeatedly opening great wounds and shredding his knees. The unsteadiness of the Cross added to his problems, and the guards and many bystanders insulted, spat on him, and threw dirt into his eyes. They dragged him in such haste that he could not catch his breath, his body having received so much abuse, was ready to yield up its life.

I followed my Son from the house of Pilate, accompanied by John, the holy women, and my angels. The surging crowds prevented me from getting close to Jesus, and I asked the eternal Father to permit me to stand at the foot of the Cross of my blessed Son. With the consent of the Father, I instructed my angels to manage things in such a manner as to make it possible for me to draw near my Son. The angels obeyed me with great reverence, and led me down some side streets in order to meet Jesus. Thus, it happened, as I turned a corner, that I came face to face with my Son, our Redeemer. We did not speak, for the cruel guards would have punished him even more severely. However, I honored him in silent communication. I interiorly besought my Son to inspire his executioners to enlist someone for his assistance, for I could tell by his condition and by my insight that so burdened, he would not live to reach Calvary. The power of God moved the Pharisees and the executioners to seek relief for my Son. A few did so out of natural compassion, and others did so in fear their victim would die before they reached the place of execution.

Thus, was Simon of Cyrene impressed to assist my Son to carry his cross. Simon was the father of the disciples Alexander and Rufus, and he most willingly leapt to obey the guards, as tears of compassion ran down his cheeks [Mark: 15, 21]. The face of my Son was a mass of blood, spittle, and dirt. As Jesus passed Veronica, who was a cousin of John the Baptist, and a relative of ours, she stepped forward boldly and wiped clean with her veil, the face of my Son. A Roman guard grabbed and threw her viciously into the crowd lining the road. She jumped up immediately clutching the veil to her bosom. Unknown to Veronica, my Son had imprinted his divine face on her veil for all posterity to see. Many other women followed the Savior in bitter tears and lamentations.

As he walked, he said to them, "Daughters of Jerusalem, weep not over me, but weep for yourselves and for your children. For behold, the days shall come, when they shall say, Blessed are the barren, and the wombs that have not borne, and the paps that have not given suck. Then shall they begin to say to the mountains; fall upon us, and to the hills, cover us. For if in the green wood they do these things, what shall be done in the dry?"

For daring to speak, the guards flogged him unmercifully until they tired of their sport.

I walked closely behind the guards, as near to Jesus as was possible. I had prayed for this privilege and the Father had granted it. I conformed myself in all the labors and torments of my Son according to his divine will. The bystanders sometimes vilified me when they recognized me, while others gave me comfort. However, I never allowed any sentiment or wish to arise interiorly or exteriorly, which could be interpreted as regret for the sacrifice I had made in offering my Son for the death of the Cross and its sufferings. My charity and love of men, and my grace and holiness were so great that I vanquished all the frail traits of my human nature.

The Jews considered Mount Calvary a place of defilement and ignominy. The Romans had reserved the hill for the chastisement of condemned criminals. Its common name was Golgotha, meaning the place of the skull, so named because the configuration of the hill was skull shaped. Above us on the summit, outlined by a turgid sky, were outlined three stiles, the upright sections of the cross, which had previously been embedded in the rocky-mount. My Son arrived at its summit so worn out, wounded, torn and disfigured that he seemed altogether transformed into an object of pain and sorrows. The power of the Divinity, which deified his most holy humanity by its hypostatical union, helped him, not to lighten his pains, but to strengthen him against death. In this manner, in order that our Redeemer might satiate his love fully, Jesus retained life until God permitted death to take it away on the Cross. I, too, was there, as were John and the three Marys, for they alone, through my intercession and the favor of the eternal Father, had obtained the privilege of remaining so constantly near to the Savior and to his cross.

The time for the Redemption of man was now at hand, for the executioners were about to strip my Son of his garments for the crucifixion. I turned in spirit to the eternal Father and prayed, "My Lord and my God, you are the Father of your Onlybegotten Son. He is engendered God of the true God, and as man he was born of my womb and received from me the human nature in which he now suffers. I have nursed and sustained him, and as the best of sons that can ever be born of any creature, I love him with a maternal love. As his mother, I have a natural right in the person of his most holy humanity and your Providence will never infringe upon any rights held by your creatures. This right as a mother I now yield to you, and once more, I place in your hands your and my Son as a sacrifice for the Redemption of man. Accept, my Lord, this pleasing offering, since this is more than I can ever offer by submitting my own self as a victim or to suffering. This sacrifice is greater, not only because my Son is the true God, and of your own substance, but because this sacrifice costs me a much greater sorrow and pain. For if the lots were changed and I should be permitted to die in order to preserve his most holy life, I would consider it a great relief and the fulfillment of my dearest wishes."

The eternal Father received my prayer with pleasure. As I finished my prayer, I could see that the impious ministers were preparing to give Jesus a drink of wine, myrrh and gall. The Jews were accustomed to give to those about to be executed a drink of strong and aromatic wine in order to raise their vital spirits and to help them to bear their torments with greater fortitude. However, the Pharisees perverted this custom by mixing in gall so that it would only torment his sense of taste by its bitterness. Aware of their intentions, I asked my Son interiorly not to drink it. Jesus in deference to my being his mother, refused to drink the mixture.

It was the sixth hour, noontime, and the executioners to further shame him, intended to crucify Jesus bereft of any clothing. There were six executioners. They were short, powerfully built men, filthy in appearance, and they were cruel and beastly looking in face and demeanor. They jerked the Lord's tunic up and over his head, which tore loose his crown of thorns, broke off many of them, reopened his wounds, and left the broken-off thorns still embedded in his flesh. With heartless cruelty they jammed it back on his head and again hammered it into his flesh with the flat of their swords. For the fourth time they took the clothes from Jesus, and this last time was the most painful for his wounds were more numerous and they broke open and bled profusely. In addition, cold blasts of wintry air added to the misery of his coming death struggle. Jesus Christ wished to die in great poverty, and he would gladly have submitted to being stripped completely naked. However, on my account, as a dutiful Son, he submitted in obedience to my wishes, and when the guards attempted to remove his loincloth, they were unable to do so.

Pilot pronounced the sentence of death at about ten in the morning, during which time a little hail had fallen at intervals. The sun came out during my Son's agonizing journey, but toward twelve, the sky became partially obscured by a menacing, reddish fog.

Jesus remained serene throughout his executioner's deviltry and their brutal treatment. He allowed no resentment to reflect interiorly or exteriorly throughout his ordeal. As his executioners prepared the cross, Jesus prayed, "Eternal Father, I offer my entire humanity that it has accomplished in descending from your bosom to assume passible and mortal flesh for the Redemption of men. I offer you myself, Father, and also my most loving mother. I offer you her perfect love, her exceptional works, her sorrows, her sufferings, her anxious and prudent solicitude in serving me and accompanying me unto death. I offer you my little flock of Apostles, the holy Church and the congregation of the faithful, such as it is now and as it shall be to the end of the world. With it, I also offer to you all the mortal children of Adam. All this I place in your hands as the true and almighty Lord and God. I wish to suffer and die for all mankind. Thus, may humankind pass from the slavery of the devil to be your children, my brethren and co-heirs of the grace merited by me. I beseech you, Father, to withhold your chastisement and not to raise the scourge of your justice over men, let them not be punished as they merit for their sins. Be their Father from now on, as you are my Father. I pray for and forgive those who are persecuting me. Above all do I ask you for the exaltation of your ineffable and most holy name."

God made this prayer known to me. Thus, I was able to imitate Jesus and made the same petitions to the eternal Father. I never forgot or disregarded the first words which I had heard from the mouth of my divine Son as an infant: "Become like unto me, my Beloved.

This I had done, because, like Jesus, I had felt in my own virginal body all the torments of my Son. Because of my conformity, I was also mentally and physically scourged, spat upon, buffeted, laden with the Cross and nailed upon it. Although I felt all these pains, I felt them in a different manner, yet I felt them with such conformity that I was altogether a faithful likeness of the sufferings of my Son. My Son stood to one side, as the Romans busied themselves with the cross and their equipment. I stepped forward and took his hand, adoring him and I kissed his hand. The guards allowed this for they thought the sight of his mother would cause him great affliction. However, they were ignorant, because the Lord during his Passion had no greater source of consolation and interior joy than to see in my soul the beautiful likeness of himself and the full fruits of his Passion and Death.

A callous guard brutally pushed Jesus down and he fell on the patibulum. One Roman grabbed his right arm and placing his knee in the middle of Jesus' chest held him in a prone position. Another guard stretched his left arm out flat on the patibulum and held his wrist flat on the board. Another put his knee on my Son's wrist and with a big hammer drove a huge iron nail through the palm of his hand into the patibulum. To his executioner's utter amazement, Jesus uttered not a word of pain or protest. The guard wrapped a leather thong around his victim's wrist and lashed it to the patibulum, so the weight of his victim would not rip the nail through the soft flesh of his hand. The first guard, holding onto Jesus' right arm sat down and dug his heels into the dirt and pulled and stretched Jesus until both sockets of his shoulders were dislocated. Then, holding him in this inhuman position, a guard tied Jesus' wrist to the patibulum and then drove another big spike through his palm and into the wood. In spite of the cold wind, sweat and blood ran from the body of the Redeemer and was seemingly sponged up greedily by the arid ground, but not a word of despair did he utter. Unseen, my angels caught up every essence of the blood of our Savior, leaving only an image of the blood where it had fallen.

God chained Lucifer and his demons to the scene. Having recognized their error that Jesus was indeed the Messiah; the demons had long ceased to incite the Redeemer's torturers in their barbaric treatment of the Savior. They were overwhelmed with pains and torments by the presence of the Savior and me, and in fear of impending ruin would have cast themselves into hell if it had been possible. In their frustration, they fell upon one another like sharks in a feeding frenzy. Lucifer was dismayed at the sight of the gibbet, for he knew his dream of setting his throne above the stars of heaven and drinking dry the waters of the Jordan had been put to shame.

The executioners, by the aid of a small derrick, then struggled and sweated to lift the patibulum with its precious burden to fit it into the notch prepared for it on the upper part of the stile. Then two executioners tied ropes to Jesus feet and pulled until his knees and hips were dislocated and then tied them to the stile. While this was taking place, the bystanders yelled at him, "He will not stretch himself out, but they will help him." Then the Romans attached the suppedaneum [a foot block] to the stile just beneath his feet. Taking a long nail the Roman soldier drove it through both of Jesus' feet, the suppedaneum, and on into the stile. The foot block would allow the crucified victim to push himself up a few inches in order to breathe. When the innocent Christ no longer had the strength to push up, he would die of suffocation.

The last nail driven, the torturers stepped back to admire their work. Jesus Christ, the Savior and Redeemer of the world hung suspended like a common criminal for all men to see. As the hammer grew silent, a moan of anguish rose from the followers of the Lord, amid the jeering shouts of the Pharisees. The torturers of Jesus had violently disjointed, distended, and pitifully stretched his body. The sacred and holy body of Christ hanging upon the Cross, in spite of his body's frightful disfigurement, appeared at once noble and touching. The body of the Son of God before his Passion began, was beautiful, holy, and pure. Now, in contrast we beheld the shattered body of the dying Paschal Lamb, laden with the sins of the whole human race, past, present, and future.

My Son had received his complexion from me, light olive tinged with ruddiness in his cheeks. Now his face was streaked with dirt, blood and spittle. His heavily tanned face was no longer recognizable. Jesus' chest was deep, broad, and relatively free of hair, which was impossible to distinguish and his chest heaved in labored contractions in an effort to breath. The thighs of Jesus were powerful with well-marked sinews, and his knees were large and strong, like those of a man that has traveled much by foot and knelt long in prayer. Now his legs hung slack, bloody and defiled and his muscles were only evident when he strained upwards to gasp for air. His perfect feet had been well developed from walking barefoot over rough roads; the soles were heavily callused and now pierced by a bloody nail from which the drops of Jesus' blood splattered upon the ground. The hands of Jesus, long, tapering, and well used to hard work, were now pierced and hung lifeless. His forehead was high and frank, his auburn hair, usually parted in the middle, was now plastered to his head with blood, dirt and spittle. His beard, rather short, and well trimmed, was also matted with blood and filth. The Jews had torn much of the hair from my Son's head. His body was open wound upon open wound. The torturers had crushed his chest, and there was a cavity visible below it. The soldiers brought up a ladder and a sign in three languages, as decreed by Pontius Pilate, was hung over Jesus' head. Adding the sign made the Cross of Jesus higher than the other two. The sign stated,

THIS IS JESUS OF NAZARETH, KING OF THE JEWS

The soldiers drove the last nail into my Son's flesh about noon. At that moment a flourish of trumpets sounded from the temple, the high priests had just slaughtered the Paschal Lamb. Even those hard of heart could not help but recall the words of John the Baptist, *"Behold the Lamb of God, who hath taken upon himself the sins of the world!"*

The Romans then crucified the two thieves and placed them one on Jesus right and one on his left. I recognized them as being from the family of thieves that had taken us in and had given us food and shelter, when Joseph and I had to flee to Egypt. Dismas, on Jesus' right, was the leprous boy whose mother had washed him using the same water in which I had bathed Jesus and he was instantly healed. As the executioners were drawing Dismas up on the Cross, he exclaimed in dire agony to his torturers,

"Had you treated us as grievously as the poor Galilean, this trouble would have been spared you." As they hauled Gestas up, he swore and screamed terrible oaths at his tormentors. The weight of their bodies brought them even more excruciating pain, and they yelled and shrieked in agony, their faces lived, and their lips purple from drink and confined blood. Their eyes were red, swollen, and bulging from their sockets. The wine they drank had acted as a stimulant and they suffered that much more.

I asked my companions to pray for their souls, and while praying I was enlightened as to their end. The Pharisees and priests paid no attention to the thieves but directed their wrath on their innocent victim. Wagging their heads in scorn and mockery, they threw stones and dirt at the crucified figure of Jesus, saying, "Fie on you liar, you who would destroy our temple and in three days rebuild it, save yourself. Others he had made whole, but himself, he cannot save. If this be the Son of God let him descend from the Cross, and we will believe in him." The soldiers joined in and mocked him and yelled, "If you are the King of the Jews, help yourself now [Matt: 27, 33-44]."

With the three Marys and John behind me, I boldly went up to the foot of the Cross and clasped the feet of my son in my arms. The guards started to remove me, but Centurion Cornelius stopped them saying. "Leave her be, she is his mother." Mary Magdalene fell at the foot of the Cross and hugged the rough log, and the blood of Jesus dripped on her consolingly. John and the four of us remained at the foot of the Cross, unopposed, the rest of the afternoon.

Seeing the Jews dishonor my Son, inflamed me with a new zeal I besought the eternal Father to see to the honor of his Onlybegotten and manifest it by evident signs so that the perfidy of the Jews might be confounded and their malice frustrated. Having gained approval of my petition to the Father, I, now with the authority as the Queen of the Universe, addressed all the irrational creatures and said,

"You insensible creatures created by the hand of God, I bid you to manifest your compassion to my Son, which is denied him by men incapable of reason. You heavens, you sun, moon, and you stars and planets, stop in your course and suspend your activity in regard to mortals. You elements, change your condition, earth lose your stability, and let your rocks and cliffs be rent asunder. You sepulchers and monuments of the dead, open and send forth your contents for the confusion of the living. You mystical and figurative veil of the temple, divide into two parts and by your separation threaten the unbelievers with chastisement. I bid you to give witness to the truth and to the glory of your Creator and Redeemer, which the Jews are trying to obscure."

In virtue of my prayer and of my commands, as the mother of the Crucified, the Omnipotence of God provided for all that was to happen at my Son's death. The Lord God enlightened and moved the hearts of many of the bystanders before the time of these events in order that they might confess Jesus crucified as holy, just, and as the true Son of God. Even Pilate was inspired to deny the Jews their demand to remove the sign over the head of Jesus proclaiming him, The King of the Jews. Pilate told them, "What I have written, I have written."

In obedience to my command, a benign calm settled over the earth and an eerie darkness stealthily enfolded the earth in its mysterious clutches. The executioners were so engrossed in their duties that at first, they did not notice the absence of the sun's light at midday, and there was not a cloud in the sky.

The Roman officer in charge, the first Centurion Quintus Cornelius, stood off to one side throughout the executions. His face was set in rigid lines as befitted an officer of the Roman Empire. However, interiorly, I knew that his thoughts were a riot of confusion. The more that he saw of my Son and all that were taking place the more confused he became. I instructed John and Mary Magdalene, Mary Cleophas, and Mary the mother of the younger James to join me in prayers for his soul. At this moment the centurion approached where we were standing to instruct the executioners that they now could divide the property of those whom they had crucified. The soldiers divided Jesus' outside cloak, or mantle, by cutting it into four pieces. However, by a mysterious decree of Providence, the soldiers did not cut the seamless garment. Instead, the soldiers cast lots for the garment fulfilling the prophecy in the twenty-first Psalm. Just as they finished, a messenger, sent by Nicodemus and Joseph of Arimathea, came running up. They told the guards that their master desired to purchase the clothes of Jesus. Thus, was it that the sacred relics of my Son came into the possession of the followers of Christ.

Jesus looked down on the guards with pity, and in perfect charity and perfection said, "Father, forgive them, for they know not what they do [Luke: 23, 34]!"

One of the crucified thieves, Gesmas, sneered at him and said, "They say you brought Lazarus back to life; if you are really the Son of God, save yourself and us."

Our small group was also praying for both of the thieves. Dismas had been receptive to our efforts. Gestas; however, was so steeped in evil that he would not accept our prayer. His companion; however, being assisted by our prayers was interiorly enlightened concerning my Son.

Dismas, by divine revelation, now remembered Jesus and me from our visit in Egypt, and moved by true sorrow and contrition for his sins, he turned to his friend and admonished him, "We are under the same sentence as this man, and yet you mock our God. We received our sentences justly, but this man has done no evil. How is it possible that you revile him when he is praying for you? He has kept silence and patience. He prays for you and you outrage him! He is a Prophet! He is our King! He is the Son of God! Looking at Jesus, he said, "Lord, remember me when you shall come into your kingdom [Luke: 23, 39-42]."

Dismas had lovingly corrected his brother, confessed his Creator, reprimanded those who blasphemed him, imitated him in patient suffering, asked him humbly, as his Redeemer, not to forget his miseries; and the Redeemer fulfilled his desires by saying to him, "Amen, I say to you, this very day you shall be with me in paradise."

At this unexpected reproof out of the mouth of the murderer hanging there in misery and my Son's forgiving words, a tumult arose among the scoffers. They picked up rocks to stone him on the cross. Centurion Cornelius; however, repulsed them harshly and restored order.

Lucifer and his demons were furious, at each forgiving word of Jesus. They realized that by his sacrifice and death that Jesus had earned forgiveness and heaven for all humankind. The human tongue cannot explain the demon's torment and confusion. It was so great; however, that Lucifer humiliated himself before me saying, "I beg you, Lady, cast us from your presence and into hell." This I could not allow, for the time had not yet arrived.

Jesus, having thus justified Dismas, the good thief, who had figuratively stolen heaven, next turned his compassionate gaze upon John and me, where we were standing at the foot of the cross. Speaking to us both, he first addressed me, saying, "Woman, behold your son!"

Then he said to John, "Behold your mother!"

By this word "woman", I understood him to say, Woman blessed among all women, the most prudent among all the daughters of Adam. Woman, strong and constant, unconquered by any fault of your own, unfailing in my service and most faithful in your love toward me, which even the mighty waters of my Passion could not extinguish or resist. I am going to my Father and cannot accompany you further. My beloved disciple John will attend upon you and serve you as his mother, and he will be your son.

The holy Apostle on his part received me as his own mother from that moment on; for he was enlightened anew in order to understand and appreciate the greatest treasure of the Divinity in the whole creation next to the humanity of Jesus my Son. In this light he reverenced and served me for the rest of my life, and I accepted John as my own son in humble subjection and obedience.

God answered all my prayers regarding the elements, and throughout the long afternoon, the elements went all awry. I saw the celestial bodies, the stars and the planets, circling in their orbits and passing one another. I saw the moon on the opposite side of the earth and then, by a sudden run, or bound, looking like a hanging globe of fire it flashed up full and pale above the Mount of Olives. Fog enveloped the sun, and the moon preceded it swept along out of the east. The sky became perfectly dark and the stars sparkled with a reddish gleam. Terror seized upon man and beast. The cattle bellowed and ran wildly about; the birds sought their hiding places and lighted in flocks on the hills around Mount Calvary. The strange phenomena silenced the scoffers, and the Pharisees tried desperately to explain away these signs as natural phenomena. However, they were not successful, and soon, they too were seized with terror. Many beat their breasts, wrung their hands and cried, "His blood be upon his murderers!" Others far and near fell on their knees and implored Jesus' forgiveness, and our Savior, in spite of his agony turned his head toward them in sympathy.

Fear and consternation filled Jerusalem. Red fog and gloomy darkness hung over the streets. Many hid in corners, and others stood on the roofs of their houses. They gazed up at the sky and uttered lamentations. Animals were bellowing and hiding, birds were confused, flying low and even falling to the ground. Pilate and Herod were no less terrified and consulted with one another and concluded that it did indeed have something to do with the crucifixion of Jesus. Pilate sent for some ancients and asked them what the darkness meant, as for him, he looked upon it as a sign of wrath and he consoled himself with the fact that he had washed his hands of the affair. The ancients, hardened in their hearts, explained it as a natural phenomenon not at all uncommon.

Many people in Jerusalem and on Mount Calvary were converted, and many of the same people, who in the morning had cried out, "Crucify him! Away with him!" now gathered in front of the Judgment Seat and cried, "Unjust judge! His blood be upon his murderers!" In fear for their lives, Pilate and Herod both surrounded themselves with guards.

Anxiety and terror reached its height in the temple. The slaughtering of the Paschal Lamb had just begun when the darkness of light suddenly fell upon Jerusalem. The events filled the people with consternation. The priests hurriedly lit candles and lamps making the sacred precincts as bright as day, but their dismay only became worse.

The ninth hour was fast approaching and darkness had enveloped all the land and the confusion of nature made it appear as a most chaotic night. At this time Jesus spoke again, saying, "My God, my God, why have you forsaken me?"

My Son spoke in Hebrew. However, many of the people did not understand him since his statement began with the words, "Eli, Eli."

The Jews thought he was calling upon Elias and a number of them mocked him, saying, "Let us see whether Elias shall come to free him from our hands?"

Jesus was in his death throes. His copious and superabundant Redemption, offered for the entire human race was sufficient to save all, but not the reprobate. Jesus had created and redeemed all souls to share eternal happiness with him. However, many souls would deny him because of their own free choice. Jesus' complaint only referred to those reprobates who God justly denied him.

In confirmation of this sorrow, the Lord added, "I thirst!"

Jesus' sufferings could easily have led to a natural thirst; however, my Son spoke because he was thirsting to see the captive children of Adam make use of the liberty, which he merited and offered to them, and which so many were abusing. He thirsted for the souls of the poor, the afflicted, the humble, the despised and the downtrodden, to approach him as their Savior and thus quench, at least in part, his thirst which they could not satisfy entirely. However, his executioners mockingly fastened a sponge soaked in gall and vinegar to a reed and raised it to his mouth, in order that he might drink of it. [Thus, was filled the prophecy of David.] And also, "In my thirst they gave me vinegar to drink [John: 19, 29]." Jesus tasted of it, but at my insistence, manifested interiorly, he desisted, because I, as the mother of grace, was to be the portal and Mediatrix of those who were to profit of the Passion and the Redemption of humankind.

At the ninth hour, Jesus raised himself up for the last time, and raising his eyes to heaven, he said in a loud and compelling voice, "It is consummated! Father, into your hands, I commend my spirit."

The head of the Redeemer fell forward, and I intuitively knew that my Son was dead. In order that I might participate until the very end as the Coadjutrix of his Passion, and just as I had felt in my body all the other torments of Jesus, although I remained alive, I felt and suffered the pangs and agony of his death. At his words, I fell prostrate on the ground and remained alive only because God miraculously preserved my life. This last pain was more intense and penetrating; and all that the martyrs and men sentenced to death have suffered from the beginning of the world cannot equal that which I suffered during the Passion.

Centurion Quintus Cornelius witnessed these extraordinary events, and at the last words of Jesus, he sank to his knees and said in awe, "Truly, this man was the Son of God!"

By the divine force of Jesus' last words Lucifer and his demons were hurled into the deepest caverns of hell, where they lay motionless unable to stir. Many legends sprang up over the years about Lucifer trying to imitate the Savior at his death and take his place in opening the Gates of Heaven. This cannot be so, for sin was defeated upon my Son's death. In addition, I immediately hurled Lucifer and his demons into hell by the powers given me by the Holy Trinity. Thence forward, neither death, nor the devil can attack men, unless they do not *avail themselves of the victory of Christ,* and again subject themselves to the vagaries of their own free will.

All the inanimate creatures, by divine will, obeyed my commands. The elements of the earth, from the noon hour until after the ninth hour, when my Son expired, made great changes on the earth and in the universe. For over three hours, the sun hid its light, and the planets showed great alterations. Just before the ninth hour, a tremendous earthquake struck Nicaea, which included Caesarea Philippi. Working its way south it passed through Galilee and the very moment my Son breathed his last, the very earth protested, and a severe quake struck Jerusalem. A great chasm opened on Mount Calvary, mountains were moved, and numerous graves ruptured.

History recorded numerous quakes throughout the world. In the fourth year of the 202nd Olympiad, Phlegon wrote, "A great darkness occurred all over Europe, which was inexplicable to the astronomers and that it engulfed Asia as well."

The historian Tertullian stated, "The Roman Senate was convening when the entire city was enveloped in total darkness, which threw the city into an instant turmoil."

Even further west, across the great unknown water bounding Hispania, a culture unknown during my Son's lifetime, left a written record of these traumatic events. The pagan Mayans, when their sun god mysteriously disappeared, were even more panic-stricken than the Romans. Their religious traditions stated that if the contract of living sacrifices was broken, the sky would darken and humanity would parish. Consequently, the Mayans offered up thousands of living sacrifices to appease the angry gods. The priests tore the live, beating hearts from the breasts of their victims in only fifteen seconds and then beheaded them. Thirty thousand victims perished during the dark of the sun. In their joy when it reappeared, the priests sacrificed even more hapless victims

In Jerusalem the earth convulsed angrily. Many walls fell and there was much general damage; however, no edifice was completely destroyed. Rocks were crushed, and graves opened and the known dead came forth and were seen walking and talking to people in the streets of Jerusalem and making dire warnings. The Jews of Jerusalem were dismayed and terror-stricken. However, their outrageous perfidy and malice made them unworthy of the truth and hindered them from accepting what all the insensible creatures were demonstrating to them. Lightening flashed in a cloudless sky and a sudden, short-lived squall of savage wind, beating rain and furious hail lashed the summit of Calvary. In the Holy Temple of Jerusalem, the mysterious finger of God tore the curtain shielding the Holy of Holies from top to bottom. Just as suddenly as it came, the earth became stable, and the rain, hail, and lightning stopped abruptly. Soon, the waning sun burned through; however, Jerusalem was still screened by the now dissipating, bizarre reddish fog.

My Son's murderers rose to their feet, stunned and shocked by the fury of the elements. Throughout the quake, my friends and I had kneeled and prayed. We also rose and in the distance, I saw a contingent of soldiers coming from Jerusalem. The Jews, in order to celebrate the Sabbath with unburdened minds, had asked Pilate for permission to break the bones of the three victims to hasten their deaths so they could be buried before nightfall. The victims could no longer raise themselves up by their legs to breathe once their legs were broken. The soldiers broke the legs of the two thieves, However, upon examining Jesus, they found that he was already dead and therefore did not break his bones, thus fulfilling the mysterious prophecy in [Ex: 12, 46]. "You shall not break any of its bones."

My Son's entire ministry was substantiated by all of the Messianic prophecies, including [Psalm: 22, 17-19];

"Indeed, many dogs surround me, a pack of evildoers closes in upon me.
They have pierced my hands and feet;
I can count all my bones;
They look on and gloat over me;
They divide my garments among them; and for my vesture, they cast lots."

A soldier by the name of Longinus stepped up, drove a spear through Jesus' side, and ruptured his heart. Blood and water gushed from his side as testified by {John: 19, 34], who was there with me.

Thus, was every drop of blood drained from our Savior's holy and divine body. My Son could now feel nothing. However, in his stead, God pierced my chaste bosom mystically by a sword, just as the priest Simeon had prophesied so many years ago.

Recovering, and moved by compassion, love and forgiveness, I said to Longinus, "May the Almighty look upon you with eyes of mercy for the pain you have caused my soul!"

Moved by my prayer of mercy and forgiveness, the Savior ordained that some of the blood and water from his sacred side should drop upon the face of Longinus and restore to him his eyesight, which was failing him. At the same time, the Lord gave him sight to his soul, so that he recognized in the crucified his Savior, whom he had so inhumanly mutilated. Through this enlightenment Longinus was converted. Weeping over his sins, and having washed them in the blood and water of the side of Christ, he openly acknowledged and confessed Jesus as the true God and Savior of the world. He proclaimed him as such in the presence of the Jews. The priests and scribes; however, confused and confounded by the forces of nature, were still blinded by the perfidy and hardness of their own hearts. Jesus, by his death; however, converted many other Jews as well as some of the Roman soldiers.

I needed to find a place to bury my Son before the Sabbath began. However, the Lord ordained that Joseph of Arimathea and Nicodemus should relieve my tribulations. He had inspired them with the need to bury their Master. From a distance, I could see a group of men coming toward us with ladders seemingly with the purpose of taking the bodies down from their crosses. I feared that the Jews might have devised more cruelty with which to discredit the Messiah.

I turned to John and said to him, "My Son, what may be the object of these people coming with all these instruments?"

The Apostle answered, "Do not be afraid, my Lady, for it is Joseph and Nicodemus with their servants and friends to help us."

Joseph, a leader of the Jews, had been a secret disciple of Jesus, but now he openly declared his allegiance to his Redeemer. He had gone boldly to Pilate and asked for the body of Jesus, in order to give him honorable burial before the Sabbath began. He openly maintained that Jesus was innocent and the true Son of God. Pilate was amazed that Jesus had died so quickly, for he had no measure of the severity of the scourging that Jesus had received. He dared not refuse the request of such a rich and powerful man as Joseph, and he granted him full permission to dispose of the dead body of Jesus as he saw fit.

Joseph called upon Nicodemus, a member of the Sanhedrin, also a secret follower of Jesus, to assist him with the burial. Joseph provided the winding sheets and donated his own newly hewn tomb, which was located in a garden near the execution site. Nicodemus brought a hundred pounds of spices, which the Jews used in the burial of distinguished men. Outraged at the sight of so painful a spectacle, they fell prostrate in sorrow and bitterness. All of the newly arrived group were weeping and sighing most bitterly, until I raised them up, whereupon they saluted and consoled me in humble compassion.

Joseph and Nicodemus removed their cloaks and they themselves set the ladders against the Cross. They first removed the Crown of Thorns revealing the gaping wounds on Jesus' head, and handed it down with great reverence amid abundant tears. Then, they drove the nails out of his hands and feet. I knelt at the foot of the Cross and held the burial cloth ready for my Son's body. John assisted by supporting the head and Mary Magdalene carried his feet all the while kissing and washing them with her tears. Seeing my son so wounded and all his beauty disfigured, the sorrows of my chaste heart were again renewed. I pressed him to my bosom. Holding the dead body of the Redeemer in my arms helped satiate my incomparable sorrow and love. I closed his mouth and his dead eyes and looked at him in adoration and worship. All those present joined me, but unseen by the others, the entire summit of Calvary was teeming with my angels and countless others from heaven all bowed with grief and pain of spirit. Gently, I washed the body of my Son, cleansing the wounds and adoring each one for their Redemptive value. Afterwards, I held at my breast the dead Jesus for so long that, as the evening was fast advancing, John and Joseph told me that I must now allow the final burial of my Son. Our Messiah, Jesus the Christ, was murdered during the celebration of the Jewish Passover. My Son died in 30AD during Passover and was only thirty-three years old.

A bier was prepared, and I swathed his body in a burial cloth, and covered his face. When they started to tie his hands in the Jewish custom, I stopped them from tying his hands and from sewing the burial clothe, for I knew that he would soon arise. Then, they laid my Son, the Savior of the world, on the bier. I embalmed the body with the spices, aromatic herbs, and ointments furnished by Nicodemus. The Romans had removed the bodies of the two thieves and were prepared to take them to a potter's field for burial. However, at my request, they gladly turned the bodies over to us. In Christian charity, we shared the aromatic herbs with them. Thus, we were able to bury these unfortunate men's bodies with some dignity. Joseph of Arimathea again came to our aid and provided an additional burial chamber for them. We buried the two thieves together. I called upon the angels of heaven to join our procession and many choirs of angels joined those of my personal guard. The Apostle John, Joseph of Arimathea, Nicodemus, and Centurion Quintus Cornelius, who had confessed Jesus as his Savior, carried the bier. Mary Heli, Mary Magdalene and I, followed close behind them. I managed to maintain my outward composure, while inside, I felt as though my heart was being torn from my body. At least I had the advantage of knowing positively, that on the third day, my Son would rise again. Jesus had told his followers many times that on the third day he would rise again. However, in their grief, they quite forgot my Son's words. Mary Magdalene wept with utter abandon, as though her grief alone could make up for all the sins of the world. Interiorly, I was devastated with the loss of my only Son. Yet, at the same time, I rejoiced, because I knew that my Son, Jesus the Christ, had earned Redemption for all humankind, past, present, and future.

The holy women and a large number of the faithful fell in behind us; some in awed silence and abject tears, and others were wailing their grief in good Jewish tradition. I noted that Longinus was also there. He was the first person miraculously healed and converted after the death of the Redeemer. The tomb was a new one, hewn into the rock. In this unblemished and blessed sepulcher, we placed the sacred body of Jesus. When Jesus was entombed two hearts were buried—not one. For is there not a saying, that where your treasure is, there also is your heart? Before we closed the tomb, we all adored our Redeemer, as did all the holy angels. Thereupon, the men closed off the tomb by rolling a huge, very heavy stone across its entrance. The mysterious graves, which God had opened at the death of the Christ, were at this moment, resealed. At my command, many angels remained to guard the sepulcher, where I also left my heart. From there, we returned to Calvary where we reverenced the holy Cross. Then John, the three Marys, the holy women from Galilee, and I took our leave. We left in all haste, for the beginning of the Sabbath was fast at hand and just as the trumpets blew from the Jewish Temple announcing the Sabbath, we entered the Cenacle.

The Pharisees, confused and disturbed by these events, learned from Jesus' followers that he was supposed to rise from the dead in three days. They hastened to see Pontius Pilate on the morning of the Jewish Sabbath. They asked him for soldiers to guard the sepulcher claiming that Jesus' followers would steal the body and claim he had risen. Again, Pilate yielded to their maliciousness. The posting of the Roman guards only made the subsequent Resurrection of my Son more public, and more fully confirmed. Pilate dispatched Roman Guards immediately and they sealed the tomb to prevent entrance. In the meantime, the fiends of hell were again plotting the destruction of humankind in spite of my Son's death on a Cross for the Redemption of men.

Lucifer's Devious Schemes

The rout of Lucifer and his angels from Calvary to the abyss of hell was far more violent and disastrous than had been their first expulsion from heaven. Though as Job says "That place is a land of darkness, covered with the shades of death, full of gloomy disorder, misery, torments and confusion [Job: 10, 21-22]. Yet, on this occasion, the chaos and disorder was a thousand fold increased. The demons, in their rabid fury, took out their frustrations by punishing the damned in a new and horrible fashion. However, it is certain that the demons cannot change the decree of divine justice and that any additional punishment had already been decreed by the Almighty.

Later, God removed his restraints, allowing the demons to continue their mischief. Lucifer began at once to devise new plans to assuage his pride. He called all his black angels together and from an elevated position spoke to them, saying, "To you, who have followed me for so many ages to help me avenge my wrongs, is known the injury which I have now sustained at the hands of this Messiah. For thirty-three-years he has deceived me, hiding his Divinity and concealing the operations of his soul. Now he has triumphed over us by the very death we arranged for him. Before he assumed flesh, I hated him. God cast us out of heaven because I would not acknowledge his Son as being greater than I am. He degraded us to this abominable condition so unworthy of my greatness and former beauty. From the birth of Adam, I have tirelessly sought to find and destroy the Messiah and his mother. If this is not possible, I at least wish to bring destruction upon all his creatures and induce them not to acknowledge him as their God, so that none of them should ever draw any benefit from his works. However, all of this has been in vain, for he has overcome me by his humility and poverty, crushed me by his patience, and at last has robbed me of the sovereignty of the world by his Passion and frightful death. Even if I succeed in hurling him from the right side of his Father, and if I should draw all the souls redeemed down into this hell, my wrath would not be satiated or my fury placated."

"Is it possible that the human nature, so inferior to my own, shall be exalted above all the creatures? Why are men so favored, gifted, and so ardently loved by their God, whom I abhor? How shall we now begin, oh my followers? How shall we recover our power over men? For now, if men are not senseless and ungrateful toward this God-man, who has redeemed them with so much love, it is clear that all of them will eagerly follow him, and none of them will then take note of our deceits. My, friends, we cannot allow the humans to follow Jesus. Our reign will be quite limited if they follow him, for they will all earn paradise. Now, all you demons who follow me, now is the time to give way to our wrath against God. Let us take counsel what we are to do; for I desire to hear your opinions."

The principal demons all agreed, after a full year of strategy that it was not possible to injure the person of Christ, or his mother. Nor was it possible to diminish the efficacy of the Sacraments, or to falsify or abolish the doctrine, which my Son had preached. The best plan, they determined, was to seek new ways of hindering and preventing the work of God by deceit and temptation. Lucifer told them, "It is true that men now have at their disposal a new and powerful doctrine, and new and efficacious Sacraments, as well as a powerful new Intercessor and Advocate in Mary, the holy Mother of God. However, the natural inclinations and the passions of the flesh remain just the same, for God did not change the nature of humankind. Let us begin a strenuous warfare against man by suggesting new attractions, exciting them to follow their passions and forgetting all else. Let us propagate idolatry in the world, so that man might not come to the knowledge of the true God and the Redemption. We will establish sects and heresies, for which we will select the most perverse and depraved of the human race as leaders and teachers of error. We will establish the false sects of Mahomet, Buddha, and the heresies of Arianism, Pelagianism, Nestorianism, and Monophysitism as a beginning and destroy the very foundation of man's rescue, namely divine faith.

We will form cells. One cell will pervert the inclinations of children at their conception and birth. Another will induce parents to be negligent in the education and instruction of their children. [This, I knew, would come to fruition in the twentieth century]. Another cell will plant discord and disharmony between parents and their children. Another will create hatred and mistrust between husbands and wives, especially by infidelity. We will plant discords of pride, vengeance, desire for riches and honors, and weaken the remembrance of Jesus' Passion and Death. We will especially create a lack of respect for the Holy Eucharist. One cell will tempt the successors of the Apostles with pride, ambition, power, and lust. [I knew this would find receptive souls in too many Popes and other religious throughout the ages] Lucifer finished his assignments and said to his demons,

"I am much beholden to you for your opinion, I have approved them all. It will be easy to put them into practice with those, who do not profess the law given by this Redeemer to men, though with those who accept and embrace these laws, it will be a difficult enterprise. However, against them all, I intend to direct all my wrath and I shall most bitterly persecute those who hear the doctrine of this Redeemer and become his disciples. Against them, we must press our most relentless battle to the end of the world. In this new Church, I must strive to sow my cockle, the ambitions, the avarice, the sensuality, and the deadly hatreds, with all the other vices, of which I am the head. Once these sins multiply and increase among the faithful, they will, with their attendant malice and ingratitude, irritate God and justly deprive men of the helps of grace left to them by the merits of the Redeemer. If once they have thus deprived themselves of these means of salvation, we shall have assured victory over them. We must also exert ourselves to weaken piety and all that is spiritual and divine; so that they do not realize the power of the Sacraments and receive them in mortal sin, or at least without fervor and devotion. For since these Sacraments are spiritual, it is necessary to receive them with a well-disposed will, in order to reap their fruits. If once they despise the medicine, they shall languish in their sickness and be less able to withstand our temptations. They will not see through our deceits, they will let the memory of their Redeemer and of the intercession of his mother slip from their minds. Thus will their foul gratitude make them unworthy of grace and so irritate their God and Savior, as to deprive them of his helps. In all this I wish that all of you strenuously assist me losing neither time nor occasion for executing my commands."

When I notified him of Lucifer's plans, John said, "Woe to the earth, for Satan is come down to you full of wrath and fury! Our enemy is astute, cruel, and watchful. We are sleepy, lukewarm, and careless. What wander that Lucifer has entrenched himself so firmly in the world, when so many listen to him, and accept and follow his deceits. Few resist him, and entirely forget the eternal death, which he so furiously and maliciously seeks to draw upon them? I beseech those that read this, not to forget this dreadful danger. They should be convinced of this danger through the evil condition of the world and through the evils each one experiences. If not; however, I pray that they will learn of this danger by the vast and powerful remedies and helps which the Savior thought it necessary to leave behind in his Church; for he would not have provided such antidotes if our ailment and danger of eternal death were not so great and formidable."

After the holy women of Galilee, the three Marys, blessed John and I returned to the Cenacle; I thanked them all with profound humility for persevering throughout the Passion of my Son. In his name, I promised them the reward due them for having followed him with so much constancy and devotion. "In addition, I said to them, "I offer myself to you all as a servant and as a friend." John acknowledged this favor, and kissed my hands and asked me for my blessing. They all begged me to take some rest and some bodily refreshments, but I answered them, "My rest and my consolation shall be to see my Son and Lord arisen from the dead. Do you, my dearest friends, satisfy your wants according to your necessities, while John and I retire to pray for my son."

Once alone, I fell to my knees before John and reminded him, "Do not forget the words my Son spoke to you on the Cross. He called you my son, and me your mother. You my, Master, are the priest of the Most High; and because of this dignity, it is proper that I obey you in all that I am to do. From this hour, I wish you to order and command me in all things, remembering that I shall always be your servant and that all my joy shall be to serve you as such until my death."

John replied, "My, Mistress and Mother of the Redeemer and Lord, I am the one who should be subject to your authority, for the name of a son implies devotion and subjection to his mother. He that has made me priest has made you his mother and was subject to your authority, though he was the Creator of the universe. It is reasonable that I should do likewise, and that I labor with all my powers to make myself worthy of the office he has conferred upon me. In order to serve you as your son, I would prefer to be an angel rather than a mere creature of the earth."

I answered him, "My son, John, my consolation shall be to obey you as my superior, since such you are. In this life, I must always have a superior to whom I can surrender my will in obedience. For this purpose you are the minister of the Most High; and as my son you owe me this as a consolation in my solitude."

John said humbly, "Let then your will be done, Mother, for in this lies my own security."

I nodded and said, "Would you please provide for some refreshment for the holy women, except for the Marys and me? It is our wish to persevere in our fast until we see the risen Lord." John went off to do as I had requested. For the first time, I was alone with my thoughts. I let loose the impetuous floods of tears that I had withheld in order to give the perfect example as the Queen of Heaven and Earth, and as the mother of the Son of God, our Lord and Redeemer. I reviewed in my mind my Son's frightful death, the mysteries of his life and his preaching and his miracles. In addition, I reviewed the infinite value of the Redemption and the new Church, which he had founded and adorned with the riches of the Sacraments and the treasures of Grace. I passed the whole night weeping, sighing and glorifying the works of our Savior. I prayed alone, and sometimes I conferred with my holy angels. On the following Sabbath morning, after four o'clock, John came seeking me to console me. I fell on my knees before him, and asked him for his priestly blessing. He in turn, with tears in his eyes, asked the same of me. Thus, we gave one another our blessings.

Afterwards, I said to John, "I beg of you to go and find Peter. He is looking for you now. You must receive and console him kindly, and bring him to me. Once you have found him, then please find the other Apostles and give them hope of pardon; then bring them here."

John hastened to do my bidding; he soon found Peter, who, full of shame and in tears, was timidly seeking to find me. Together, they found some of the others and came to me hoping for pardon. Peter entered first; alone in my presence he fell at my feet and exclaimed, "I have sinned before my God and I have offended my Master and you." He could not speak further, for he broke down uttering tearful sobs and sighs, which came from the depth of his oppressed soul.

I prudently realized the necessity for Peter to do penance for sins so recently committed. On the other hand, as the head of the Church; I did not deem it proper to prostrate myself before its leader, who had just denied his Master. My humility; however, would not allow me to withhold the reverence due his office. In order to conform my actions with both of these circumstances, I fell on my knees to do him reverence and said,

"Let us ask pardon for your guilt from my Son and our Redeemer." I prayed for him, reviving his hope by reminding him of the merciful behavior of the Lord concerning well known sinners. I pointed out to him his own obligation as head of the Apostolic College to give the example of constancy in the confession of the faith. By this and other arguments, I confirmed Peter in the hope of pardon. Then each of the other Apostles presented themselves before me each asking pardon for their cowardice in forsaking Jesus during his sufferings. They wept bitterly over their sin. I raised them up and promised them the pardon they sought and my intercession to help them obtain it. I succeeded in touching their hearts, and confirmed them in their faith to their Redeemer and Master; by arousing in them repentance and divine love.

I knew that my son intended to use the Holy Ghost to authorize each of the Apostles to forgive sins, so I asked Almighty God if I could use this medium to reestablish a state of grace in each of the fallen priests. Upon his approval, I informed Peter that he must make a good confession to John, for John was the only Apostle who had not abandoned my Son. John was the only priest still in a state of Grace. Afterwards, Peter as the head of the Church, was to hear the confession of the rest of the Apostles. Simon Peter and the other nine Apostles all felt an inward reverence for John, for he alone of the eleven had stood by the Lord at his crucifixion. At first, they were uncomfortable in his presence, but John showed them only love and consideration and their confusion soon passed. Once the confessions were heard each of the Apostles left the room with renewed fervor, and God justified them with new increases of grace and understanding they now possessed in the miraculous gift of Confession.

I retired that evening and contemplated the doings of the Most Holy Soul of my Son after it left his sacred body. I knew from the first that my Son had descended into Limbo in order to release the holy Fathers from the subterranean prison, where they had been detained since the death of the first just man that had died in expectance of the advent of a Redeemer. For your information, the hell of the damned is buried deep in the earth. This hell is a chaotic cavern, which contains many dark dwellings for diverse punishments, all of them dreadful and terrible. This horrible dungeon with all the damned shall be there for all eternity, as long as God is God; for in hell there is no redemption [Matt: 25, 41].

To one side of hell is purgatory. If the soul when it dies has not satisfied God for his faults in this life, the souls are purged to cleanse them of all stains of sin to prepare them to stand before the Beatific Vision. This cavern is also large, but not as large as hell; and though there are severe punishments in purgatory, they have no connection with those of hell. To the other side is limbo with two different divisions. The first was for the children, who die and are not baptized, tainted only with original sin, and without good or bad works of their own election. The second served as a retreat for the just, who had already satisfied for their sins. They could not enter heaven, nor enjoy the vision of God until Jesus redeemed man and opened the gates of heaven, which had been closed by the sin of Adam and Eve.

This cavern for the just is likewise smaller than hell. It has no connection with hell; nor are there in it the pains of the senses like in purgatory. For here, those already purged, remained in a state of grace until the death of the Redeemer. It was here that Christ's soul descended with the Divinity, and which we refer to in saying that he descended into hell. The word "hell" was used to signify any of the infernal regions.

The most holy soul of Christ, accompanied by innumerable angels, descended in full glory and majesty as a victorious and triumphant King. Jesus, as the Redeemer, threw open the ancient portals of this ancient prison. The drab cavern was converted into a heaven of wonderful splendor and to all the souls contained therein was imparted the clear vision of the Divinity. The souls broke into canticles of praise. Jesus also absolved the poor souls still detained in purgatory of all remaining punishment due their sins. He glorified them along with the just held in limbo.

For the damned in hell, this was a horribly bitter day. God made them see and feel the descent of the Redeemer into limbo, and all the holy Fathers witnessed the terror caused by this mystery to the demons and the damned. The demons, when they heard the voices of the angels advancing before their king were terrified anew. Like serpents pursued, they hid themselves and clung to the most remote caverns of hell. The damned were seized with confusion after confusion, becoming still more deeply conscience of their deviation and of the loss of salvation, now secured for the just. Judas and the unrepentant thief's torments were greater, and the demons were more highly incensed against them. The infernal spirits, as God intended, resolved to persecute and torment more grievously the Catholics, and chastise them more severely than those who deny or repudiate the Catholic faith do. The infidels had not yet heard the word of God, Therefore, the demons concluded by God's design that the Catholics merited greater punishment than the infidels did.

The Redeemer remained in limbo from half past three on Friday afternoon, until after three on Sunday morning, when Jesus was reunited with his body. I had instructed my angels to pick up and safeguard all the bits and pieces of my Son's body that had been so horrible mutilated. The Lord showed the Patriarchs and holy Fathers the cruelty of the Jews, by allowing them to see his wounded, lacerated and disfigured body. Thus did our first parents Adam and Eve witness the havoc wrought by their disobedience. They saw and understood the priceless remedy it necessitated and they and all the souls from limbo adored him and again confessed him as the Incarnate Word. Then in the presence of all those saints, my angels reunited to the sacred body all the relics, which the angels had gathered and held in reverence and awe. The soul of my Son then reunited with his body giving it immortal life and glory. Instead of winding-sheets and ointments, it was now clothed with the four gifts of glory, namely, with clearness, impassibility, agility and subtlety. The glory of the most holy soul of Christ, our Savior is incomprehensible and ineffable to man. The clear light inherent and shining forth from his body so far exceeds that of others, as the day does the night. Nothing else is comparable to it in all creation. With impassibility, his body became invincible to all created power, since no power can ever move or change him. Subtlety purified my Son's gross and earthly matter, so that it could now penetrate other matter, like a pure spirit. Accordingly, he penetrated through the rocks of the sepulcher without removing or displacing them, just as he had issued forth from my womb when he was born. Agility so freed him from the weight and slowness of matter that it exceeded the agility of the immaterial angels for he could move about more quickly than they could.

The sacred wounds now shone forth from his hands and feet so refulgent and brilliant that they added a most entrancing beauty and charm. In all his glory and heavenly adornment, my Son now arose from the grave; and in the presence of the saints, Patriarchs, and holy Fathers. said,

"I promise all of you and to all men, resurrection in your own flesh and body, and that moreover, as an effect of my own Resurrection, you shall be similarly glorified. I command that these souls on the Day of Judgment will be reunited with their bodies and rise up to immortal life."

A selected group was instantly reunited with their bodies [Matt: 27, 52]. Among them were Saint Joseph, Saint Anne and Saint Joachim and many others of the ancient Fathers and Patriarchs who had distinguished themselves in the faith and hope of the Incarnation. These marvelous events transformed me from sorrow to joy, from pain to delight and from grief to ineffable jubilation. It happened that John stepped in at that moment to visit and console me in my bitter solitude. Thus, in the midst of all my heavenly splendor and glory, he hardly recognized me for I was transfigured with supernatural exultation. He looked at me with wonder and reverence. I did not have to tell him that my Son and Redeemer had risen.

John left for I knew that my Son would soon visit me. I began to prepare myself for his presence, and I felt within myself a new kind of jubilation and celestial delight. Moreover, I perceived within myself another, a still more different effect implying new divine favors. I felt myself infused into my being the heavenly light heralding the advent of Beatific Vision and I received them to a more abundant degree, for now I had acquired the merits of this Passion. Hence, the consolations from the hands of Jesus corresponded to the multitude of my sorrows.

Thus prepared, my Son, risen and glorious, and in the company of all the Saints and Patriarchs, made his appearance. I prostrated myself and adored him, and Jesus, my Savior raised me up and drew me to himself. In this contact, far more intimate than the humanity and the wounds of my Son, I participated in an extraordinary favor, which, I alone, as exempt from sin, could merit. If my angels and the Lord himself had not previously strengthened me, my faculties would have failed. The glorious body of my Son so closely united itself to that of mine that he penetrated into it, or rather I into his. My body became like a crystal globe. For it takes up within itself the light of the sun and is saturated with the splendor and beauty of its light. Consequently, my spirit rose to the knowledge of the most hidden sacraments.

In the midst of them, I heard a voice saying to me, "My, Beloved, ascend higher!" By these words I was entirely transformed and saw the Divinity clearly and intuitively; wherein I found complete, though only temporary, rest and reward for all my sorrows and labors in this wonderful Beatific Vision. For several hours, I enjoyed the essence of God with my divine Son. By degrees I descended from this vision and found myself reclining on the right arm of my most holy Son. We talked concerning the mysteries of the Passion and of his glory. In this conference, I was again inebriated with the wine of love and charity, which I now drank unmeasured from the original fount. God conferred upon me on this occasion, all that a mere creature could receive. For in man's manner of conceiving such things, the divine equity wished to compensate my injuries, which I had undergone in suffering the same sorrows and torments of the Passion of my Son. As a reward, God inundated me with a proportionate joy and delight.

I was then allowed to converse with the Patriarchs, the holy Fathers and Adam and Eve. They joined with me in praising the Almighty. My greatest and special delight was in speaking with my parents, Saint Anne and Saint Joachim, my husband Joseph, and Saint John the Baptist. I spent most of my time conversing with them. I was in turn honored by all the Saints, for each one prostrated themselves before me acknowledging me as the Mother of the Redeemer and of the world, and as a cause of their rescue and as the Coadjutrix of their Redemption. The divine wisdom impelled them thus to venerate and honor me; however, I, as the Mistress of Humility, prostrated myself on the floor and reverenced the saints according to their due. This the Lord permitted, because, the saints, although they were inferior in grace, were superior in their state of blessedness, endowed with imperishable and eternal glory, in contrast I was yet a mortal and a pilgrim and had not as yet assumed the state of fruition. My Son remained with us throughout these festivities and I invited all the angels and saints, there present, to praise the victor over death, sin and hell. Whereupon, we all sang new songs, hymns of glory and magnificence honoring our Redeemer, until the hour arrived when it was necessary for the risen Savior to make his appearance in other places.

I was very happy, for from the time of my Son's Resurrection and until his Ascension, I remained at the Cenacle where my Son spent all of his time with me when he was not appearing to others. There I enjoyed the presence of the Redeemer of the world. In addition, the choir of Prophets and Saints attended us, as their King and Queen. Joseph of Arimathea, accompanied by some of the disciples and holy women left late that night after celebrating the Sabbath with our group in the Cenacle. Near Caiaphas' judgment hall a small band of pagan soldiers set upon them and imprisoned the good

Joseph in a tower in the city. All his companions fled in terror. The intention of Caiaphas was to let Joseph die of starvation and to keep his disappearance secret. Early Sunday morning, Joseph was praying, when suddenly his cell shone with a clear light, and Joseph heard his name called. Looking up he saw the roof of his cell lifted and an angelic figure let down a rope for him to climb up, which he did and then the figure closed up the roof. Descending the outside steps Joseph went directly to the Cenacle, where the disciples greeted him joyfully. He told them his story, and they gave him food and he left at once for Arimathea where he remained secure in his own castle until he learned that it was safe to return to Jerusalem.

Before the Sabbath, Mary Magdalene, Joanna, Mary Salome, and Mary, the mother of James and Joseph accompanied by some of the holy women of Galilee, purchased additional ointments and spices in order to return Sunday morning to the Sepulcher, and show their veneration by visiting and anointing the body once more. They had rested on the Sabbath, according to the Commandment. They were ignorant of the fact that the Romans had later sealed and placed the tomb under guard. On Sunday before dawn, and on the way, their only concern was how they could remove the large stone from in front of the tomb. In the meantime, a violent earthquake took place, and at the same time an angel of the Lord opened the sepulcher and cast aside the stone that covered the entrance. His appearance was like lightning and his clothing was white as snow. The Roman guards shaking with fear became like dead men. They did not see the Redeemer, for Jesus was risen and no longer in the tomb. The Marys, encouraged interiorly by the Lord, took heart and approached the tomb. Near the entrance, they saw the angel who had opened the tomb, seated upon the stone, refulgent in countenance and clothed in snow-white garments. The angels had neatly folded up the white shrouds of Jesus' and placed them at the end of the stone where he had laid.

The angel spoke to them saying, "Do not be afraid! I know that you are seeking Jesus the crucified. He is not here, for he has been raised just as he said. Come and see the place where he lay. Then go quickly and tell his disciples, he has been raised from the dead, and he is going before you to Galilee; there you shall see him [Matt: 28, 5-7]."

Mary Magdalene, still greatly upset and in tears, reentered the tomb. Although the Apostles had not seen the angels, she saw them and they asked her, "Woman, why do you weep?"

She answered them, "Because they have taken away my Lord; and I do not know where they have laid him."

She left the sepulcher, entered the garden, and met the Lord. However, she did not recognize him, thinking he was the gardener. Without further reflection she said to him, "Sir, if you have taken him away, tell me where you have laid him, and I will care for him."

Then the loving Master said, "Mary!" In speaking, he allowed himself to be recognized.

Mary aflame with joyous love, exclaimed, "Rabboni, Master."

Dropping to the ground, she grasped his feet to kiss them as was her custom, but the Lord stopped her saying, "Do not touch me, for I am not yet ascended to my Father from whence I came. Return and tell the Apostles that I am going to my Father and theirs."

Magdalene left, consoled and filled with jubilation, and shortly ran into the other women.

Scarcely had they heard what had happened to her and were yet conferring with each other in wonder and tears of joy, when Jesus appeared to them and said, "God save you!" They all recognized him and worshiped at his sacred feet, and he again commanded them to go to the Apostles and tell them that they had seen him and that they were to go to Galilee, where they would see him risen."

It was not until after this meeting that Jesus ascended to his Father in heaven. My Son appeared to the women first as their just reward for having remained constant during his Passion. Jesus then disappeared and the holy women hurried to the Cenacle to tell the Apostles all that had transpired.

Many of the Apostles were so shaken in their faith, and forgetful of his words that they thought the story of the holy women was a mere hallucination The women then came to tell me all that had happened, although I knew all that had taken place, I did not confirm their story. Instead, I took the occasion to confirm their faith in the mysteries and high sacraments of the Incarnation and in the passages of Holy Scriptures that pertained.

About this time, the guards at the grave awoke from their stupor and seeing the sepulcher empty; they fled and gave notice of the event to the princes and priests. Greatly concerned, the Pharisees called a meeting and concluded that they should pay the soldiers to induce them to say that while they slept, the disciples of Jesus had come and stolen his body from the grave. The priests assured the guards of immunity and protection, and therefore they spread this lie among the Jews.

Simon Peter and John departed in all haste to see for themselves, followed closely by many of the disciples. John arrived first, and seeing the folded burial sheets, stepped aside and waited for Peter. Peter entered, closely followed by John and they could see that the sacred body was not in the tomb. John had already begun to believe when he had seen the great change in me when I had learned of my Son's Resurrection. He boldly proclaimed his belief and they returned to the Cenacle to give an account of the wonder they had seen at the sepulcher. Peter, once he understood, sent disciples back to pick up the holy shroud of the Lord.

Simon Peter was alone in a side room of the Cenacle praying, tears running down his cheeks begging forgiveness for having denied Jesus, when suddenly, with a flash of marvelous light, Jesus, his Redeemer and Savior stood before him in all his majesty. Stunned and scared, Peter threw himself on his face before his Master, and with tears running down his cheeks, exclaimed, "Jesus, Master, forgive me for I denied you three times! I was a coward and I ran away. Depart from me for I am a weak, sinful man, and not worthy to lead your Church." Jesus raised him to his feet, and as he did so much of the aura of his Divinity left him and he stood before Peter as he had been seen by the holy women.

He said to him kindly, "Simon Peter, you did not pick me, I picked you. Your sorrow is your forgiveness, as well as your confession to John. In a short time, I will send the Holy Spirit to confirm you and the rest of the baptized in the faith I have given you. Even then, you must be strong and ever on the alert for Lucifer waits to sift you like flour if you waiver in your faith. Pray much and tell the other Apostles that they will see me soon." With that he disappeared, and after offering up prayers of thanksgiving, Peter came to me and excitedly told me all that had happened.

That afternoon Luke and Cleophas, disciples of Jesus, after they had heard the reports of the women, departed for Emmaus about four miles from Jerusalem They were reviewing all that had happened and Cleophas commented, "Jesus performed many miracles, gave sight to the blind, health to the sick, raised the dead, and spoke the most marvelous words. He also said that he would rise on the third day after his death, and this we do not fully understand." Luke pointed out, "What you say is true, he predicted his own death on a cross, and do not forget the story the women told us. Is it possible that he is raised?"

Before Cleophas could answer, Jesus came up to them in the habit of a pilgrim. He saluted them and asked, "Of what do you speak, for it seems to me that you are sad?"

Cleophas replied, "Are you the only stranger in Jerusalem that does not know of all that has happened during these past three days?"

The Lord asked, "What has happened then?"

The disciple then recounted all that had occurred over the past three days and finished by saying, "After the women told us they had seen the Master we were confused, and we are going home to Emmaus in order to await the drift of these events."

Then my Son told them, "Oh how foolish and slow of heart you are to believe, since you do not understand that what the women have told you is true." Then he explained to them the life and death of the Redeemer of the human race. He interpreted to them the Holy Scriptures that foretold all that had taken place. As they neared the castle of Emmaus, Jesus said, "I must part from you now to continue my journey." They both eagerly begged him to stay and have supper with them, as was the custom of our race. The Lord yielded and he sat and supped with the two men in the home of Luke. When seated, Jesus took the bread, blessed and broke it as usual and when he did, Jesus dropped the veil from their eyes and they recognized him. In the same instant, he disappeared. The two disciples were overjoyed and filled with wonder. Although it was already dark, they decided to return at once to Jerusalem. The disciples came directly to the Cenacle. John and I had taken up residence there. In addition, the Apostles and many of the male disciples had secreted themselves there as well. They feared to return to their homes, because they were afraid of the Jews.

They were discussing the testimony of the women, when Luke and Cleophas burst into the room and they exclaimed nearly in unison. "We have seen Jesus. He is truly risen."

They eagerly told the disciples the details of their visit from their Master. Peter joined in and told of his experience with the Redeemer.

Thomas, who was also there refused to believe them and stated categorically, "Unless I can see him for myself and put my fingers in his side and in his hands and feet, I will not believe." Saying this, Thomas left the room quite upset.

They locked the doors, still afraid of the Jews, and sat discussing the events when Jesus appeared through the locked door and appeared in their midst. He saluted them, saying, "Peace be with you. It is I; do not be afraid."

The disciples thought they were seeing a ghost and Jesus added, "Why are you troubled, and why do such thoughts arise in your hearts? See my hands and feet; see that it is I myself. Handle my hands and see; for a spirit has no flesh and bones, as you can readily see that I have."

The men were so excited and confused that although they saw him and touched the wounded hands of their Savior, they could not realize that it was truly Jesus to whom they spoke and whom they touched. My loving Son in order to reassure them still more, said to them, "Give me something to eat, if you have some on hand." Joyfully they offered him some fried fish and a comb of honey. He ate part of these and divided the rest among them, saying, "Do you not know, that all that has happened with me is the same that has been written by Moses and the Prophets in the Psalms and Holy Scriptures? All that was written had to be fulfilled in me as it was prophesized." At these words, he opened their minds, and they knew him, and understood the sayings of the Scriptures concerning his Passion, Death and Resurrection on the third day.

Having thus instructed them, he said again, "Peace be with you. As the Father has sent me, so I send you in order that you may teach the world the knowledge of the truth of God and of eternal life, preaching repentance for sins and forgiveness of them in my name."

He breathed on them and added, "Receive the Holy Ghost in order that the sins, which you forgive may be forgiven, and those, which you do not forgive, may not be forgiven. Preach to all nations beginning in Jerusalem."

Then Jesus, having consoled and confirmed them in faith and having given them and their successors the power to forgive sins, disappeared from their midst. Thomas returned soon after, but remained adamant in his disbelief. The other Apostles became indignant with his behavior and finally came to me and accused him of being an obstinate and stubborn transgressor, a man too dull to be enlightened. The Apostles, yet, were still imperfect. I explained to them to be patient with one another, for the judgments of the Lord were deeply hidden. I told them that the incredulity of

Thomas would occasion great benefits to others and bring much glory to God. I instructed them that they should wait and hope and not be disturbed so easily. In the meantime, I offered up many prayers for Thomas. Due to my efforts, Jesus hastened Thomas' understanding.

Thomas remained obstinate until the next day when Jesus returned appearing through the locked doors when all the Apostles were present. He saluted them as usual saying, "Peace be with you." Then he called Thomas to him and reprimanded him saying, "Come Thomas, and with your hands touch the openings of my hands and of my side, and do not be so incredulous, but convinced and believing."

Thomas touched the divine wounds and was interiorly enlightened to believe and to acknowledge his ignorance. Prostrating himself to the stone floor, he exclaimed, "My Lord and my God!"

The Lord replied, "Because you have seen me, you have believed; but blessed are they who do not see me and still believe." The Lord then disappeared, leaving the Apostles and Thomas filled with delight and joy. They came to me, in order to relate to me all that had happened, just as they had done after the first apparition of my Son. As I stated before, God had granted me great wisdom and knowledge; however, at this time, the Apostles were not yet able to comprehend these blessings. Therefore, I listened to them patiently and prudently as their loving mother and Queen. The Apostles and disciples then returned to Galilee, as Jesus had instructed them to do.

The Apostles, accompanied by many of the disciples and holy Galilee women, eagerly returned to Galilee as commanded, anxiously awaiting the return of my Son. I remained in the Cenacle for I was blessed with seeing my Son when he was not busy making his presence known to those five hundred fortunate souls who were to be personal witnesses to his Resurrection. While the Apostles waited Jesus' return, they returned to their trade as fishermen. Simon Peter and seven of the Apostles spent the night fishing and had caught nothing.

In the morning, Jesus appeared on the seashore without identifying himself. He was near the boat from which they were fishing and he called out to them, "Children, have you caught anything to eat?"

They answered, "We have caught nothing."

The Lord replied, "Throw out your net on the right side and you shall make a catch."

Out of respect for the person, they complied and their net became so filled that the boat was close to sinking. This miracle caused John to recognize the Lord, and he called out to Peter and said, "It is the Lord who speaks to us from the shore." Peter likewise recognized Jesus and always the impetuous one, he girded himself with his tunic, and cast himself into the sea, and walked ashore, while the rest rowed to shore in the boat. When they got there, they saw Jesus tending a charcoal fire with bread and fish already cooking.

Jesus said to them, "Bring along some of the fish you have just caught." Simon jumped to do as he was bid, and upon counting the fish, they learned that they had taken one hundred and fifty-three large fish and without breaking the net. The Apostles did not ask him who he was, for now they all recognized him in his newly Resurrected body. Jesus took the bread, blessed it, and gave it to them and in a like manner the fish. This was the third time my Son had appeared to the Apostles since his Resurrection.

After the meal Jesus said to Simon Peter, "Simon, son of John, do you love me more than these?"

Peter said to him, "Yes, Lord, you know that I love you."

Jesus replied, "Feed my lambs."

My Son then asked him the second time, "Simon, son of John, do you love me?"

Simon said, "Yes, Lord, you know that I love you."

Jesus responded, "Tend my sheep."

Yet a third time he asked, "Simon, son of John, do you love me?"

Peter was distressed with the repeated questioning and he replied, "Lord, you know everything; you know that I love you."

Again, Jesus said to him, "Feed my sheep." By these words, Jesus made Peter the sole head of his only and universal Church, and also gave him the supreme vicarious authority over all men.

Then he added, "Amen, amen, I say to you, when you were younger, you used to dress yourself and go where you wanted; but when you grow old, you will stretch out your hands and someone else will dress you and lead you to where you do not want to go." Peter then understood that he would glorify God by also dying on the cross.

Peter knew that Jesus deeply loved John. Genuinely concerned for him, he asked Jesus, "What will you do with the one that you so greatly love?"

My Son answered him rather abruptly, "Why do you need to know this? Follow me and do not concern yourself with what I desire to do with him." By his words, Jesus seemed to wish to conceal his will concerning the death of the Evangelist. Therefore, the Apostles believed that Jesus did not intend John to die a martyr's death. I had full intelligence of all these mysteries and apparitions of my Son. In addition, the Apostles and John constantly informed me of all that had happened to them.

I remained in retirement for forty days after the Resurrection and there enjoyed the sight of my divine Son and all the angels and saints who were to remain and give glory to the Redeemer until his Ascension into heaven, at which time they would join him. I had many wonderful hours of conversation with Saint Anne, Saint Joachim, and Saint Joseph, as well as Saint John the Baptist, his parents, and many of the great Patriarchs. Another wonderful thing happened during these forty days. All those who died in grace were also gathered at the Cenacle; however, those who were subject to purgatory were denied this privilege.

Jesus, as Teacher, spent many hours with his Apostles and disciples explaining the Gospels, how to establish his Church on earth, and answering their endless questions. The Eternal Father and the Holy Ghost appeared before me in the Cenacle a few days before the Ascension of the Lord. The Divine Persons sat upon a throne of ineffable splendor. Choirs of angels, saints, and other heavenly spirits attended them. Then my Son, the Incarnate Word, ascended the throne and seated himself with the other two. I was in a far corner prostrate in deepest reverence and adored the blessed Trinity. The Eternal Father commanded two of the highest angels to call me, which they did and advised me of the divine will, I arose from my dust in the most profound humility, modesty, and reverence. Accompanied by the angels, I approached the foot of the throne, meek and humble.

The Eternal Father spoke to me, saying, "Beloved, ascend higher!" Simultaneously the angels lifted me up and placed me on the throne of the royal Majesty with the three divine Persons. The saints were given to understand the sanctity and equity of the works of the Most High and they were filled with admiration to see a mere creature exalted to such dignity. The Father said, "My Daughter, I entrust to you the Church founded by my Onlybegotten Son, the new law of grace he established in the world, and the people he has redeemed; to you do I consign them all."

Then the Holy Spirit said, "My, Spouse, chosen from all creatures, I communicate to you my wisdom and grace together with which shall be deposited in your heart the mysteries, the words, the teachings, and all that the Incarnate Word has accomplished in the world."

Then Jesus said, "My most beloved Mother, I go to my Father and in my stead I shall leave you and I charge you with the care of my Church. To you I commend its children and my brethren, as the Father has consigned them to me." Then the three Divine Persons addressed the choir of holy angels and the other saints, and said, "This is the Queen of all created things in heaven and earth. She is the Protectress of the Church, the Mistress of Creatures, the Mother of Piety, the Intercessor of the Faithful, the Advocate of Sinners, the Mother of Beautiful Love and Holy Hope. She is mighty in drawing our will to mercy and clemency. In her shall be deposited the treasures of our grace and her most faithful heart shall be the tablet whereon shall be written and engraved our holy law. In her are contained the mysteries of our Omnipotence for the salvation of humankind. She is the perfect work of our hands, the plentitude of our desires. She shall communicate and satisfy the plentitude of our desires, without hindrance in the currents of our divine perfections. Whoever shall call upon her from their heart shall not perish. Whoever shall obtain her intercession shall secure eternal life. What she asks of us shall be granted, and we shall always hear her requests and prayers and fulfill her will; for she has consecrated herself perfectly to what pleases us."

When I heard myself so exalted, I humbled myself more deeply. In so doing, God raised me even higher. The right hand of the Most High then lifted me up above the entire human and angelic creatures. Considering myself the least of all, I adored the Lord and offered myself in the most prudent terms and in the most ardent love, to work as a faithful servant in the Church and to obey promptly all the desires of the divine will. From that day on I took upon myself anew the care of the Evangelical Church, as a most loving mother of all its children. I renewed all the petitions I had until then made, so that during the whole further course of my life they were most fervent and incessant, which I will discuss later. The favor the Trinity now conferred upon me elevated me to a participation in the being of my Son beyond all possibility of words sufficient to explain. He communicated to me his attributes and perfections in correspondence to my ministry as Instructress and Mother of the Church and as supplying his own ministry. He raised me to a new state of knowledge and power. For God now hid nothing from me either of the divine mysteries or of the inmost secrets of the human heart.

God taught me when and how; I was to use this communicated power of the Divinity in my dealings with men, with the demons, and with all creatures. In short all that could possibly be conferred upon a mere creature was given over in all its fullness and excellence to me as Queen of the World. The Trinity made John aware, to a certain extent, of the esteem in which they held me. From that day on, he venerated and served me with new solicitude and reverence, for that was the will of God.

When the pre-ordained time came for my Son to return to his Father, he gathered his disciples and Apostles in the Cenacle. They numbered one hundred and twenty men and women. He joined his eleven Apostles as they reclined at their supper. Jesus moderated the splendors of his beauty and glory so that all might look upon him. Having finished their meal, he said to the eleven,

"Know you, my disciples that my eternal Father has given me all power in heaven and earth, and I wish to communicate it to you in order that you may establish my new Church throughout the whole world. You have been slow and tardy in believing my Resurrection. However, it is time that as true and faithful disciples, you be the teachers of the faith to all men. Preaching my Gospel as you have heard it from my lips, you shall baptize all that believe, giving them baptism with water in the name of the Father, and of the Son, and of the Holy Ghost. The souls that believe and you baptize—I will save, those that do not believe—I will damn. Teach the believers to observe all that concerns my holy Law. In confirmation thereof, the faithful shall perform signs and wonders. They shall cast out demons from their habitations; they shall speak new tongues, and they shall cure the bites of serpents. If they drink anything poisonous, it shall not harm them, and they shall cure the sick by the laying on of hands."

Jesus then addressed all those disciples and holy women that he had summoned in his own unique way. "My sweetest, Children, you are among the five-hundred that I have appeared too, so that you may testify to the facts of my resurrection, I am about to ascend to my Father, from whose bosom I descended in order to rescue and save men. I leave with you in my stead my own mother as your Protectress, Consoler and Advocate, you are to hear and obey her in all things. Just as I have told you that he who sees me, sees my Father, and he who knows me, knows him. I now tell you, that he, who knows my mother, knows me. He, who honors her, honors me. All of you shall have her as your mother, as your Superior and Head, and so shall your successors. She shall answer your doubts, solve your difficulties; and in her those who seek me shall always find me; for I shall remain in her until the end of the world, and I am in her now, although you do not understand how."

What my Son meant was that he was actually Sacramentally present in my bosom. Jesus had preserved in me the sacred species, which I had received at the Last Supper. It was to be preserved in me until the consecration of the first Mass by the Apostles. The Lord added, "You will have Peter as the supreme head of the Church. I leave him as my Vicar; and you shall obey him as the chief high priest. You shall hold John as the son of my mother; for I have chosen and appointed him for this office from the Cross." My Son looked at me and I knew he wished to add to my honors by commanding them to reverence me in a manner suited to the dignity of the Mother of God, and of leaving this command under form of a precept for the whole Church. Interiorly; however, I begged him not to secure for me more honor than was absolutely necessary, for executing all that with which he had charged me. I desired to divert all the sacred worship of the Church immediately upon the Savior and to make the propagation of the Gospel redound entirely to the exaltation of his holy Cross. My Son honored my wish and reserved to himself the duty of spreading the knowledge of me at a more convenient and opportune time.

Jesus' instructions deeply moved the entire congregation. They remembered his words and his teachings of eternal life and how they had delighted in his company. These blessings were now about to be deprived them. Words of parting rose to their lips, but they could not bring themselves to utter them. How can we live without such a master, they thought? Who can ever speak to us such words of life and consolation as he? Who will receive us so lovingly and kindly? They begged him to take them with him, but he commanded them to remain in Jerusalem until he should send the Holy Spirit, the Consoler, as promised by the Father and as already foretold to the Apostles at the Last Supper.

It was now the most auspicious hour. The Onlybegotten Son of the eternal Father, after descending from heaven in order to assume human flesh, was to ascend by his own power, and in a most wonderful manner, to sit at the right hand of his Father. He was, in union with the Father, to send the Paraclete upon his Church after he himself should have ascended to heaven [John 16, 7]. My Son had chosen as his witnesses the same one hundred and twenty persons, including me that he had gathered in the Cenacle. The eleven Apostles were there, as was Mary Magdalene, Martha and Lazarus, Joseph of Arimathea, his nephews Aram and Themina, and Nicodemus, a prince of the Sanhedrin. Mary Salome, the mother of James and John, was present, along with Joanna, the wife of Herod Antipas' steward, Veronica, Mary Cleophas, Cleophas, Luke, and Centurion Quintis Cornelius. Also present were the seven disciples, who would later become the first deacons, including Stephen and Phillip, and many others who made up the seventy-two disciples mentioned in the Scriptures.

My Son, with me at his side, left the Cenacle and made his way through the streets of Jerusalem with Bethany our destination. Our guardian angels and the Saints from limbo followed us with songs of praise, which of course, only my Son and I could see, hear and appreciate. The news of the Resurrection of the Lord had spread throughout Jerusalem. In spite of the false testimony spread by the malicious princes and priests, many of the people would not accept their lies. Jesus led us triumphantly through the city. However, Jesus did not allow the inhabitants of Jerusalem to see him in our triumphant march.

We ascended the highest point of Mount Olivet and there formed three choirs, one of the angels, another of the Saints and a third of the Apostles and the faithful, which again divided into two bands all presided over by my divine Son. I prostrated myself at his feet, worshipped him with total humility, and asked for his blessing. He raised me up, blessed and embraced me and said tenderly "Emi" a Hebrew term of endearment for one's mother. My eyes brimmed with tears and I whispered "Tinoki" a mother's word of love for her son. As I stepped to his side, my fingers caressed his cheek fleetingly in a loving farewell. I stood beside my Son as each person came forward and worshipped and adored their Redeemer. To each, he had a word of comfort or advice and a blessing. All too soon, I knew that it was time for him to leave. In was then that I realized that I, unseen by the others, was to be taken up into heaven with my Son. To do so, the eternal Father gave me the power of bi-location, the ability to be in two places at the same time.

Just before he left, Phillip asked him, "Lord, it is good that we are gathered here with you, are you at this time going to restore the kingdom to Israel?"

Jesus answered him, "It is not for you to know the time or season that the Father has established by his own authority. But you will receive power when the Holy Spirit comes upon you, and you will be my witnesses in Jerusalem, throughout Judea and Samaria, and to the ends of the earth."

I asked Jesus to give us his final blessing, and we all kneeled humbly before him. The Messiah stepped up on a large rock and from there, he blessed us. Then, raising his right arm, he turned slowly toward the four points of the compass, and gave his blessing to the whole world.

No sooner had my Son done this, than a peaceful calm settled over the Mount of Olives more profound than the euphoria and awe, which enveloped me each time I entered the holy Temple of Jerusalem. Gradually a gentle breeze shattered the calm, and a delightful humming tickled my eardrums. I could feel vibrations that not only came from the souls of my feet, but it seemed to permeate the space about us. Then my ears were filled with a resounding chorus from the voices of millions of angels who formed the Angelic Choir singing praises to God the Father, God the Son, and God the Holy Spirit. The music saturated our minds, our bodies, and our very souls. I remembered the prophecy that my Son had made to Nathanael, when they first met when Jesus said to him [John: 1, 50-51], "Do you believe because I told you that I saw you under the fig tree? You will see greater things than this. Amen, amen, I say to you, you will see the sky opened and the angels of God ascending and descending on the Son of God."

Suddenly, a brilliant flash of light like unto the one at the creation of the angels revealed throughout the heavens a heavenly horde of angels pulsing with the reflected light of God enhancing their inherent beauty. Each angel's essence mirrored the thousands of beautiful graces endowed them by their Creator. They were all wonderful, all instinct, with supernatural holiness and spiritual magnificence.

I saw the Cherubs as innocent babies, or as ethereal children with gossamer wings. None appeared older than that of a very young teenager. They were exquisite of face and form. The Powers appeared as soldiers with long spears and magnificent white wings. The Archangels were awesome in their role as great warriors equipped with flaming swords of fire, who descended on their snowy white appendages, and hovered protectively as an honor guard over the head of the Redeemer. The nine choirs of angels were all present. The first hierarchy consisted of the Seraphim, the Cherubim, and the Thrones. The second hierarchy was made up of the Dominations, the Virtues, and the Powers. The last group consisted of the Principalities, the Archangels, and the Angels. From a cloudless sky, brilliant, snow-white, cumulus clouds boiled up out of nothingness and masked the sun, yet the heavens had never been so gloriously radiant. God, in his infinite love, presented his angels in forms that men's bodies could tolerate and their minds fathom. God privileged the disciples and Apostles to see this marvelous demonstration of God's love for his only Son, and for me, his mother.

Peter and the Apostles saw the magnificent display. Nathaniel remembered with awe the Lord's words to him when they first met. Stephen and the six others who would later be selected as deacons were so privileged, as were the holy women of Galilee, including Mary Magdalene, Joanna, Lazarus, Joseph of Arimathea, and Nicodemus. Longinus also saw the angels, as well as most of the one hundred and twenty souls assembled there by the Lord himself. Everyone saw the Lord ascend; however, a few were not privileged to see the heavenly welcome, for they were not in a full state of grace having committed certain venial sins that deprived them of this honor.

Our Savior's entire body became luminous, and a marvelous light enveloped him. Jesus' face beamed with peace and majesty. He joined his hands and by his power alone, he raised himself from the earth leaving on the rock the impression of his feet. Suddenly, I was rising with him. God granted them all the privilege to see the Son of God rise before them. However, only John, the beloved of Jesus, in a vision saw me rise with my Son, and later, he saw me when I descended. My Son and I arose amidst the nine choirs of angels all singing their praise and giving glory to Jesus Christ, the holy Son of God. Jesus drew after him all our guardian angels, except those who were to remain and guard my alter ego. The glorified Saints then came, led by Adam and Eve, followed by Abraham, Lot, Jacob, Isaac, Moses, Samuel, all the Prophets, King David, King Solomon, Joseph, and a long line of Joseph's and my ancestors, including Eliud and Ismeria, Anne and Joachim, Elizabeth and Zachariah, John the Baptist, and the many thousands of glorified souls who had waited in limbo for the gates of heaven to be opened as promised by Almighty God. Even Abel and Cain his brother were there, for Cain had many years on earth to repent that which he had done to my Son's satisfaction. Among those in the rear was Dismas, the good thief, who by his defense of the Savior had stolen heaven.

I remained in heaven for three days. They were glorious days and while there I enjoyed the perfect use of my powers and faculties, which God had given me. God kept the Apostles ignorant of this event, for they took great consolation in the fact that I was still with them, although my Son had ascended into heaven leaving them to carry on his work. As we approached the gates of heaven, the angels with us cried out to the angels, who had remained there, "Open your gates, let them be raised and opened up, and receive into his dwelling the great King of Glory, the Lord of Virtues, the Powerful in battle, the Strong and Invincible, who comes triumphant and victorious over all his enemies. Open the gates of the heavenly paradise, and let them remain open and free forever, since the new Adam is coming, the repairer of the whole human race, and rich in mercy, overflowing with the merits of his copious Redemption wrought by his death in the world. He has restored our loss and has raised human nature to the supreme dignity of his own immensity. He comes with the reign of the elect and the redeemed given him by his eternal Father. His liberal mercy gives to mortals the power of regaining in justice the right lost by sin, to merit by the observance of his law the gift of eternal life. He brings with him and at his side the Mother of Piety, who gave him his humanity and for overcoming the demon. She comes as our charming and beautiful Queen delighting all that behold her. Come forth, come forth, you heavenly courtiers, and you shall see our most beautiful King with the Crown given to him by his mother, and his mother crowned with the glory conferred upon her by her Son."

Between two rows of angels and saints, my Son and I made our entry into the empyrean heavens amidst hymns of praise in our honor. Then the eternal Father placed upon the throne of his Divinity at his right hand, the Incarnate Word, and in such glory and majesty that he filled with new admiration and reverential fear all the inhabitants of heaven. Seeing my Son so glorified, I prostrated myself at the footstool of the royal throne. I was annihilated in the consciousness of being a mere earthy creature and I adored the Father and broke out in new canticles of praise for the glory communicated to his Son. The angels and saints were filled with admiration and joy to see the prudent humility of their Queen, and they emulated my every move and prayer.

Then I heard the voice of the eternal Father say, "My, Daughter, ascend higher!"

Jesus also called me saying, "Mother, rise up and take possession of the place, which I owe you for having followed and imitated me."

The Holy Ghost said, "My, Spouse and, Beloved, come to my eternal embraces!"

The holy Trinity decreed that I was to sit at the right hand of my Son. No other human should ever again be so favored, for the honor was reserved to me as their Queen, which was to be my possession after my earthly life came to an end.

The angels then lifted me to the throne at the right hand side of my Son, and I, and the rest of the saints listened, as God said, "My, Daughter, as far as we are concerned, not only is this throne yours for all eternity, but if you choose you may remain here now without returning to earth."

God left it up to me to make my own choice. However, to assist me in my decision, God showed me anew the state of the Church upon earth. I beheld the plight of the orphaned and necessitous condition of the faithful. It was my choice to return to earth and assist them, or remain in heaven. This proceeding was made to allow me the occasion of going beyond, so to say, even of my own self in doing good and in obliging the human race with an act of tenderest love similar to that of my Son in assuming a passible state and in suspending the glory due to his body during and for our Redemption. Seeing clearly all the sacrifices included in this proposition, I willed to imitate the Incarnate Word.

I prostrated myself at the feet of the Trinity and said, "Eternal and Almighty, God, to accept this reward at once would secure my rest, but to benefit the children of Adam and the faithful of the Church, I feel I must return to the world and continue to labor in mortal life for the greater glory of your divine Persons. At present I renounce the joy of your holy Presence, although I well know what I now possess and receive, but I will sacrifice it to further the love you have for men. Accept, Lord and, Master of all my being, this sacrifice and let your divine strength govern me in this undertaking. Let faith in you be spread, and let your holy name be exalted. You have acquired your holy Church by the blood of your Onlybegotten and mine. I offer myself anew to labor for your glory, and for the conquest of the souls, as far as I am able. In addition, it would not be proper for me, a mere creature, to assume heaven without having first lived my normal life upon the earth, and then suffer the bitter pangs of death, even as my Son elected to do."

My sacrifice was pleasing to the Lord. He rewarded me by operating in me those purifications and enlightenments, which I have at other times mentioned as necessary to the Intuitive Vision of the Divinity. To date I had seen it only by the Abstractive Vision. Thus elevated, I partook of the Beatific Vision. God filled me with splendor and celestial gifts, altogether beyond the power of man to describe or conceive in mortal life. The Most High renewed in me all the gifts, which until now he had communicated to me. God confirmed and sealed them anew, in order to send me back as Mother and Instructress of holy Church. He confirmed all the titles he had conferred upon me as the Queen of all Creation, and as the Advocate and Mistress of all the Faithful. Just as wax receives the form of the seal, so I, by divine Omnipotence, became the image of the humanity of Christ, in order that I might thus return to the Militant Church and be the True Garden, locked and sealed to preserve the waters of grace.

They then lovingly permitted me to depart from the *Triumphant* to the *Militant Church* filled with ineffable treasures of grace. During my sojourn in Heaven, I had not forgotten my companions in the midst of my glory, for I had left them weeping and lost in grief as they stood absorbed in looking into the heavens where their beloved Redeemer and Master had disappeared. I besought my Son to console these, his children, whom he had left as orphans.

Moved by my prayer he sent down two angels in white resplendent garments who appeared to all the disciples and the faithful and they spoke to them saying, "You men of Galilee, do not look up to Heaven in so great astonishment, for this Lord Jesus, who departed from you has ascended into Heaven. He shall return again with the same glory and majesty in which you have just seen him ["Acts: 1, 11]. They consoled them with other words and instructed them to return to Jerusalem where they were to await the coming of the Holy Spirit as promised by my Son. The disciples just standing there was a useless and imperfect manner of seeking Jesus, for in order to obtain the presence and assistance of his grace, it was not necessary that they should see and converse with him corporally. That they did not understand this truth was a blamable defect in men so enlightened and perfected.

Nevertheless, this is the misfortune of our nature that in its dependence upon the senses and its satisfaction in exercising its lower faculties, it wishes to love and enjoy even the most divine spiritual blessings in a sensible manner. If their divine Master had not left them by ascending into heaven, they could not have separated from him without great bitterness and sorrow. Therefore, they would not have been as fit to preach the Gospel. For the disciples were to preach the Gospel throughout the world. They would do so at the cost of many labors and difficulties and at the risk of life itself.

The teaching of the Gospel could not be the work of small-minded men, but of men courageous and strong in love. Men who were not hampered or softened by the sensible delights, but men who clung to the spirit and were ready to go through abundance or want, infamy or renown, honors or dishonors, and sorrows or joys. The job would require men who could persevere in their love and zeal for the Lord with a magnanimous heart, and men who were superior to all prosperity and adversity. Thus, the disciples and faithful, accompanied by my alter ego, returned to the Cenacle, although most of them still feared for their lives. Once there, the one hundred and twenty souls, some fearful and some confused, persevered in prayer and waited in high expectation for the coming of the Holy Ghost.

I Am Mary

There is no excuse for the forgetfulness and negligence shown by the faithful of the Church regarding the spread and manifestation of the glory of their God by making known his holy name to all rational creatures. This negligence is much more blamable now since the Eternal Word became man in my womb, and taught and redeemed the world for this very purpose. With this end in view the Lord founded his Church, enriched it with blessings and spiritual treasures, assigned to it ministers and endowed it with temporal riches. God intended that these gifts were not only to preserve the Church in its present state, but also to extend it and draw others to the regeneration of the Catholic Faith.

Everyone should help to spread the fruits of the death of their Redeemer. Some can do it by prayer and urgent desires for the exaltation of his holy name; others by almsgiving, others by diligent preaching, and still others by fervent works of charity. However, if this remissness is perhaps less culpable in the ignorant and the poor, who have none to exhort them, it is very reprehensible in the rich and the powerful, especially so in the ministers and prelates of the Church, whose particular duty is the advancement of the Church of God. Many of them, forgetting the terrible account, which they will have to render, seek only their own vain honor, instead of Christ's. They waste the patrimony of the blood of the Redeemer in undertakings and aims not even fit to mention. Through their fault, they allow innumerable souls to perish. Proper exertions of the faithful could have gained these souls, for the holy Church. They also lose the merit of such exertions and deprive Christ of the glory of having such faithful ministers in his Church. The same responsibility rests upon the princes and the powerful of the world. These people receive from the hands of God honors, riches and temporal blessings for advancing the glory of the Deity, and yet think less of this obligation than of any other.

Grieve for all these evils and labor, as far as your strength will allow that the glory of the Most High be manifest, and that he be made known in all nations. Pray that the very stones generate sons of Abraham. Beseech him to send able workers and worthy ministers to his Church. Pray that he will draw men to the sweet yoke of the Gospel, for great and plentiful is the harvest, and few are the faithful laborers and zealous helpers for harvesting it. To those who obtain followers for my Son, I give my maternal and loving solicitude. I will preserve them in his doctrine and companionship. Never allow the flame of this charity to die out in your breast. Let my silence and modesty at the wedding feast be an example to you and your children.

In the secular world, it is no longer fashionable to be a leader or a spokes-person for the Church. Fifty years ago many Church dignitaries recognized the deplorable trend of decreasing vocations, not only to the priesthood, but to the various organizations of brothers and sisters as well. Any business executive, having recognized a potential shortfall of leaders, would have immediately mounted a campaign to supply their personnel requirements, or would have had to face the consequence of going out of business. The hierarchy and the faithful have been slow to react to the problem and to offer solutions.

When I became aware of Lucifer's plans after the death of my divine Son, I divined that in the sixth century that all the Bishoprics, except the Bishop of Rome, would succumb to heresy. Vigilius, a murderous heretic, when he became Pope, would also have remained heretical, except that as promised by my Son to Peter, "You are Peter, and upon this rock I will build my Church, and the Gates of Hell shall not prevail against it [Matt: 16, 18]." I was made to understand that Vigilius would be given sufficient grace by the Holy Spirit to enable him to stand firm against the wiles of the Empress Theodora. I also foresaw that the temptations of Lucifer's black angels would lead to the fall of a decadent Rome, which would lead the world into the dark ages.

Lucifer decided that one demonic cell would stir up hatred against the Jews in the hearts of Christians for having killed the Messiah. Lucifer's demons were quite successful, and, as a race, many Christians blamed my Son's death on all the Jews. Consequently, Christian nations constantly persecuted and killed the Jews, obviously forgetting the fact that my Son and I were Jewish as were the Apostles and all the first Christians. The persecution of the Hebrews climaxed in the twenty-first century with the murder of six million Jews. Even today, Satan's hordes still stir up hate throughout the world against the Catholics, the Jews, the blacks, or anyone that is different. Currently throughout Europe, a dangerous trend of anti-Semitism has again reared its ugly head. The black angels of hell are fanning this hate, and in consequence, many souls will be lost.

Another one of Lucifer's cells worked to prevent inventions that could lead men to a better life. In addition, Lucifer told his demons, "I assign one demonic cell to stir up priests and kings against the Church. [Among those to fall astray were Martin Luther and King Henry VIII who were the first to successfully divide the Church]. He created other cells to instill hatred and envy among nations. This caused ceaseless wars including, the Crusades, and the building of empires by the major nations of the world. All of which led to leaders like Napoleon of France, Kaiser Wilhelm and Hitler of Germany, Lenin and Stalin of Russia and Mao Tse Tung of China. These Godless leaders led the world into one heinous war after another including the Napoleonic Wars, WW I, WW II [atomic warfare], the cold war, Korea, Vietnam, Desert Storm, Iraq, Afghanistan and Libya, and worldwide terrorism spread by dissident Moslems, which could again lead to international warfare. Most of the wars in which you have been engaged you have been led into by your own Industrial Military Complex of which you have been warned by some of your Presidents. Wars are the result of sin.

My, children, the worst sect that Lucifer has yet devised in your times is called Secular Humanism. This is a system, which rejects any form of religious faith and worship. The sect denounces God and says that only man is responsible for his destiny. This has helped create the evils of an irresponsible media, and the moral breakdown of many faiths, which have given in to the demands of their worshipers to replace the laws of God with relaxed rules that allow them to satisfy their promiscuous behavior. All of this has led to countless mothers murdering their own children in their wombs. Many women now practice contraception, and men and women form promiscuous relationships, which causes the breakdown of families and leads to a drastic increase in crimes, such as: drugs, murder, rape, perversion, and children killing children. There are few families today, which the evil of secularism does not affect.

A few bishops in their dioceses have rallied to the needs of their flock and have overcome the problem of too few priests. However, this still leaves a huge gap, especially with the scandal of some priests violating their vows of celibacy and molesting children. My Son said, "Woe to those who abuse or cause these little ones to sin. It would be better for him to have a great millstone hung around his neck and to be drowned in the depths of the sea [Matt: 18-6]. While the Church has been derelict in leadership, the real fault lies within the hearts and souls of the faithful. Over ninety percent of Radio, Television and Hollywood films are sexually explicit and has become the toy of the devil to distribute pornography and graphic violence to a gullible public. The media in general has corrupted the morals of not only the faithful of the United States, but the entire world as well. Today sexually explicit sit-coms have become the norm, and because they make people laugh, they are acceptable in too many families. These programs are a subtle brainwashing of the family and have been one of Lucifer's greatest triumphs.

The Catholic Family is the backbone of the Church and prayer is the backbone of the family. Parents must pray with their children and by their example teach them how to pray and make sacrifices. Too few parents encourage their children to look up to the clergy and the brothers and sisters who sacrifice their own personal lives in order to serve others. Sacrifice has become an unwelcome word in the common vernacular and parents do not want their children to be the ones to make the sacrifice to serve others.

The full responsibility for the teaching of one's children lies with the parents. The Church will flounder, if parents refuse to shoulder that responsibility. Parents must live good lives, make many sacrifices, fast, pray the Rosary, and by their example inspire their children to greater levels of religious fervor in their efforts to emulate their parents. All members of the family should pray to Jesus, Mary and Joseph, and we will help you to avoid the snares, with which Lucifer and his demons intend to entrap you and your children's souls into hell.

Pray for the forgiveness of the sins of the world.
Pray for the forgiveness of the sins of the United States of America.

Your mother in heaven.

Mary

Chapter Ten

Life With Mary After Christ's Ascension

A VIRGIN BEFORE, DURING AND AFTER THE BIRTH OF GOD'S ONLYBEGOTTEN SON

THE CENACLE THE HUB OF EARLY CHRISTIANITY

My charity and humility would not allow me to remain in heaven when I knew that the children of Christ's Church needed me to assist and guide them in their pilgrim journey upon earth. I desired to gather into the faith many faithful followers by my solicitation and intercession and to imitate my Son and my brethren by dying upon the earth, although by my sinless ness, I owed no such tribute. I knew that it was much more precious to merit a reward and crown, than to possess them gratuitously in advance, even if the reward happens to be eternal glory. Now all heaven knew that the Father so loved the world as not only to give his Son for its Redemption, but also his daughter, for he sent me from glory to build up the Church, which Christ its Artificer had established.

Upon leaving Heaven, the Trinity enveloped me in a cloud of most resplendent light, which served as my couch upon which I was borne to earth by the seraphim. It was necessary for the Lord to hide my refulgence from those that saw me until the splendors of my reflected glory should have moderated. Saint John alone was privileged to see me as Queen in the full redundancy of the divine glory, which I had enjoyed in heaven. I arrived at the Cenacle as a substitute for my divine son in the new Evangelical Church. The gifts of grace that I had received for this ministry excited the wonder of the angels and the astonishment of the saints; for I was a living image of Christ, our Redeemer and Master. As I have pointed out before, the more one knows of God and the closer one comes to our Savior, the more they realize how truly insignificant we all are before the magnitude and goodness of God. Therefore, upon arrival, I prostrated myself to the dust of the floor and said to the Trinity,

"Most High, God, and my, Lord, behold this vile worm of the earth, acknowledging itself from it [Gen: 2, 7], and coming from this nothingness to this existence, which I hold through your most liberal clemency. I acknowledge oh highest, Father, without any merit of mine that your inexpressible condescension has raised me from the dust, to the dignity of being the mother of the Onlybegotten. In so favoring me, I praise and exalt your immense goodness. In gratitude, I offer myself to live and labor anew in this mortal life, according to all the decrees of your divine will. I consecrate myself as your faithful servant and as the servant of the children of the Church. All of them I present before your immense mercy and implore you, from my inmost heart to look upon them as their kindest God and Father. For them I offer up the sacrifice of being deprived of your glory and peace, and of having chosen of my own free will suffering rather than joy, denying myself the vision of you in order to perform what is so pleasing in your sight."

During the first three days upon my return, I remained much withdrawn from earthly things, still lingering in the overflow of joy of having been influenced by the Trinity. John was greatly confused after all that he had seen; on the third day, he came to me. When he looked upon my face he fell down prostrate for the splendors, which he saw reflected in my countenance were similar to those of the Lord when he was transfigured on Mount Tabor. I raised John up and fell to my knees before him and said, "My, Master and son, you already know that I am to be governed in all my actions by obedience to you, for you have taken the place of my divine Son, and are to command me in all that I am to do. I ask you to be solicitous in commanding me, because of the consolation I derive from obeying in all things."

John felt even more confusion, and again prostrated himself before me. He offered himself as my slave, and he begged me to command and govern him entirely. He remained adamant for some time until, overcome by my humility; he subjected himself to my will and agreed to command me as I wished. The vision of me as Queen of the angels in my state of glory was so deeply impressed upon the understanding and the interior faculties of the Evangelist that the image of it remained with him during his entire life. The intelligence he had received at the time of his vision was afterwards manifested in his writing of the Apocalypse.

It befitted the exalted dignity of Saint John, as the appointed guardian of the Mother of God that he should be the secretary of my ineffable sacraments and mysteries as the Queen of heaven and earth. For this reason, even before my excursion into heaven, many of my mysteries were revealed to him. In addition, he was made an eyewitness of my ascension with my Son, my enthronement at the right hand side of Jesus, and my subsequent descent from Heaven. These mysteries remained impressed in the memory of Saint John, as well as many others that I revealed to him over our years together as son and mother. In respect for my humility, he did not reveal any of these secrets during my lifetime. It was not until after my death that John, even then respectful of my humility, wrote the last book of the New Testament, In the Book of Revelation. John was instructed by the Holy Ghost to reveal my secrets in a deeply metaphorical and enigmatic language, which, as the Church itself confesses, is difficult to understand. This was done to prevent humankind from being misled into esteeming and adoring me as a God. In this danger, the ignorant could have fallen, and it could have confounded the Divinity of Christ the Redeemer and confused the fact that I am a mere creature and that only my Son is true God and true man.

John referred to me in Revelations when he says, "He saw the holy city of the New Jerusalem, prepared and adorned as a bride descending from heaven," etc. This metaphor of a city refers to me. It points out my descent after having first ascended to Heaven with my most blessed Son. John states, "And I saw a new Heaven and a new Earth. For the first Heaven and the first Earth were gone, and the sea is now no more." In this, he calls me and the sacred humanity of the Incarnate Word, 'a new Heaven and a new Earth' [Rev: 21, 1]. It is a new Heaven, because of the inhabitation of the Divinity in humanity, and a new Earth, because of the renovation of humankind. John also revealed, "And the wall of that city had twelve foundations and in them, the twelve names of the Apostles of the Lamb."

When I offered to come back to earth, my Son charged me especially with the care of the Apostles. He wrote their names in my bosom, including that of Mathias, although the Apostles had not yet appointed him. Their names are written in my heart, [the foundation of the Mystical City of Mary] for I was to be the mainstay of the Apostles and I was to lay the groundwork of the holy Church. By the doctrine taught me by Jesus, I taught the Apostles, and by the wisdom given me by the Trinity, I enlightened them. By my charity: I inflamed their hearts, by my patience, I bore with them, by my meekness, I drew them on, by my counsel, I governed them by my advice, I prepared them for their work, and by the dispensation of my heavenly powers, I delivered them from dangers. I rendered assistance to them all and never failed to protect them, and was present with them at all times and places. I defended and protected them without fail in all their necessities and labors. Through God, I obtained all the blessings and graces and gifts they needed to be fit ministers of the New Testament.

During my remaining stay on earth, I was blessed with an abstractive and continual vision of the Divinity. With it, I enjoyed another blessing in that the Holy Sacrament deposited in my bosom remained there continually as if in a tabernacle; whenever I received Holy Communion, the sacred species were not dissolved until I received them the next time. As long as I lived in the world after my descent from heaven, I bore within myself, without interruption, my divine Son and sacramental God. By a special vision I also saw him within myself and conversed with him without the necessity of seeking his royal presence anywhere outside myself. I bore him within my bosom and could say with the Spouse; "I hold him and will not let him go [Cant: 3, 4].

For three days, I was filled with the splendors of heaven perceived only by Saint John. Then, I came out of my retirement and joined with the Apostles and disciples. I enjoined them to join with me in prayers to hasten the times, when the feasts of the sacred mysteries should be celebrated on earth in the same manner in which they were celebrated in heaven. I persevered in these prayers until my return to heaven. I asked the Lord over the ages, to send men of exalted and distinguished holiness for the conversion of sinners, having at the same time a foreknowledge of their coming. When my prayers reached a fever pitch, Jesus would send one of his highest seraphim, who would promise me the fulfillment of my desires and petitions.

On the sixth day after I began my prayers with the Apostles, my Son descended personally to visit and to fill me with new gifts and indescribable consolation. I reclined on his chest nearly fainting with love and adoration. With his left arm of humanity, he consoled me and with his right arm of divinity, he illumined and enriched me with vivifying influences. Five hours later when he prepared to leave; I fell at his feet and asked for his blessing.

I spent much of my time after my return from Heaven to prepare the Apostles and disciples for the coming of the Holy Spirit. It was important that they should raise themselves above themselves and begin to live more by faith and love of God, than by sensual nature. I spent one hour each morning with them explaining the mysteries of the faith taught me by my divine Son. I exhorted them to spend another hour each day in discussing among themselves the admonitions, promises, doctrine, and teachings of their divine Master. I encouraged them to occupy themselves part of the day in reciting vocally the Our Father and some Psalms, while the rest of the day they were to spend in mental prayer. Towards evening, they were to eat of bread and fish and then indulge in moderate sleep. By these prayers, they were to dispose themselves for the advent and reception of the Holy Ghost. It was important that they prepare themselves properly for the Paraclete, but also by keeping busy, they were not plagued with fear of the Jews. In spite of all that they had been through, the thought of death and torture at the hands of the Pharisees still filled them with abject fear.

After my descent from heaven, I did instruct the Apostles; however, I never entered upon this duty without first being requested to do so by Peter or John. Through my prayers, I moved my Son to inspire them with these requests, in order that I might obey them as vicars and priests. Thus, all things happened as I arranged them, and in humility I obeyed them. I never made use of my sovereignty and dominion; instead, I conducted myself as an inferior. In this spirit, I then conferred with the Apostles and the other faithful.

During this time, I explained to them the mystery of the blessed Trinity in terms most exalted and mysterious, yet suited to the understanding of all. I also explained the mystery of the Hypostatic

Union and those of the Incarnation, as well as many others, which had already been taught them by Jesus. I explained that with the advent of the Holy Ghost that they would be enlightened for a deeper understanding of all these things. I taught them how to pray mentally, insisting on the excellence and necessity of that kind of prayer. I taught them how to thank the eternal Father for having given us his only Son for our Redemption. I exhorted them to give thanks to God for having singled them out as his Apostles, as his companions, and as the founders of his holy Church. I taught how to persevere in humble prostrations and other actions of worship and reverence in adoring the greatness and majesty of the Most High.

Every morning and evening I approached the Apostles to receive their benediction, first that of Saint Peter as their leader, then of Saint John, and then of the rest according to their age. At first, they all shrank from doing so, saying that as their Queen and as the Mother of God, I should bless them. However, I insisted that as ministers and priests of the Most High, the highest respect and reverence is due them, because of the dignity of their holy office. As this was a contest of humility, I had no choice and by sweet insistence and persuasion, I convinced them to accede to my wishes. I urged them on with heavenly force and enlightened them to practice the highest perfections of virtue and holiness. In a short time they perceived these wonderful effects upon themselves and rejoiced with one another giving full credit to me.

Peter said, "Truly in this pure Creature we have found again the teaching and consoling doctrine, of which we are deprived by the absence of her Son. Her words and doings, her counsels, her sweet and gentle conversation, teach us and draw us on in the same way as the conversation of the Lord, when he lived in our midst. The teachings and exhortations of this wonderful being inflame our hearts, as with those of Jesus our Savior. There is no doubt that he as the omnipotent God, has deposited in the Mother of the Onlybegotten, his own divine wisdom and grace."

The Lord God had decreed to me that before the Holy Ghost should descend upon the faithful that their number should be brought back to twelve. In one of my instructions, I advised the Apostles of this fact and all of them quickly acceded to the wisdom of this decision. They turned to me and asked me to choose one that I deemed worthy. I knew beforehand who was to be selected, but in my profound humility and wisdom, I knew that this important decision had to be made by Saint Peter, the first Pope of the Catholic Church. I was able to guide them to the decision that Peter, as the Vicar of Christ, should decide and announce his decision to the faithful. He decided to have an election and called the one hundred and twenty together. He reminded us of the treachery of Judas, and suggested that they select two candidates from the seventy-two disciples. The disciples selected Joseph, called the just, and Mathias. The one hundred and twenty then prayed that God would be the final judge. Then, between these two men, lots were drawn. In this fashion, God made the final selection picking Mathias as the replacement for Judas Iscariot. The Apostles embraced Mathias and each one blessed him by placing their hands on his head and blessing him in the Lord. I then asked him for his blessing, and imitating me, the rest of the faithful did the same. Then we continued with our fasting and prayers preparing ourselves for the coming of the Holy Ghost.

With constant prayer and fasting, the faithful in the Cenacle were well prepared for the coming of the Holy Ghost. In addition, they had also lost much of their fear of the Jews, although they still kept the door of the Cenacle locked. After the election of Mathias, there had been no discord, but only complete harmony among the faithful. Even the demons, which, since the death of the Savior had lain prostrate in hell, felt a new terrifying force emanating from the upper room.

As the Queen of Heaven and Earth, I knew that the Holy Ghost would appear on the fiftieth day after the Resurrection of my Son, and that day was at hand. I was aware of the final discussion between my Son and the Father. I had requested that the Holy Ghost appear in visible form so that the Evangelical Law might be honored before the entire world. In the Empyrean Heavens the persons of the Father and the Son, as the Principle, from which the Holy Ghost proceeded, decreed the active mission of the Holy Spirit. For to these two is attributed the sending of the third Person, because he proceeds from both. The third Person passively took this mission and consented to descend into the world.

Although all three divine Persons and their operations spring from the same infinite and eternal will without any inequality; yet the same powers, which is in all the Persons are indivisible and equal. Each has certain operations *ad intra* in each Person, which is not in the others. Thus, the understanding engenders in the Father, not in the Son, who is engendered; and the will breathes forth in the Father and the Son, and not in the Holy Ghost; who is breathed forth. Because of this reason, the Father and the Son, as the active Principle, are said to send the Holy Ghost *ad extra,* while to the latter is attributed the being sent, as if in a passive manner.

The Militant Church is Established.

On Pentecost morning I exhorted the Apostles, the disciples, men and women, numbering one hundred and twenty, to pray more fervently, since the hour was at hand in which they were to be visited by the divine Spirit from on high. At the third hour [nine o'clock], when they were gathered in a semi-circle about me and engaged in fervent prayer, there resounded a tremendous thunder and the blowing of a violent wind mixed with the brightness of lightning, all centering inside the Cenacle. The house was enveloped in light and divine fire was poured out over the holy gathering. A tongue of fire appeared over the head of each person filling them with divine influences and heavenly gifts [Acts: 2, 2].

My spouse, the Holy Spirit entered my soul; I was transformed and exalted in God. For a short time, I intuitively and clearly saw the Holy Ghost, and for a short time enjoyed the Beatific Vision of the Divinity. My glory for that space of time exceeded that of the angels and of the blessed in heaven. The Holy Trinity was so pleased with my conduct on this occasion that it considered itself fully repaid and compensated for having created the world. In me were renewed all the gifts and graces of the Holy Spirit, creating new effects and operations altogether beyond man's capacity to understand.

The Apostles were also replenished and filled with the Holy Ghost; for they received a wonderful increase of justifying grace of a most exalted degree. They were confirmed in this sanctifying grace and were never to lose it. In each of them, according to their merit, were infused the habits of the seven gifts; Wisdom, Understanding, Science, Piety, Counsel, Fortitude and Fear. In this magnificent blessing, the twelve Apostles were created fit ministers of the New Testament and founders of the Evangelical Church for the entire world. This new grace communicated to them a divine strength most efficacious and sweet, which inclined them to practice the most heroic virtue and the highest sanctity. Thus strengthened, they prayed, they labored willingly and accomplished the most difficult and arduous tasks, and did so with the greatest joy and alacrity.

In the rest of the faithful, the Most High wrought proportionally and respectively the same effects, except that they were not confirmed in grace like the Apostles. According to the disposition of each, the gifts of grace were communicated in greater or less abundance in view of the ministry; they were to hold in the Catholic Church. The same proportion was maintained in regard to the Apostles; yet Peter and John were more singularly favored because of the high offices assigned to them; the one to govern the Church, and the other to attend upon me, the mother of Jesus. In addition, the Holy Ghost overflowed the Cenacle and caused diverse and various effects among the inhabitants of

Jerusalem. Those who had shown compassion toward Jesus during his Passion were interiorly visited with new light and grace, which disposed them afterwards to accept the doctrine of the Apostles. Those that were converted by the first sermon of Peter, were mainly those, whose compassion for Jesus had merited them such a great blessing.

By the dreadful thunder and lightning, and the violent commotion of the atmosphere, the Holy Ghost, the Holy Finger of God, terrified the enemies of the Lord in Jerusalem each one according to his own malice and perfidy. The chastisement was particularly evident against those who were actively involved in the death of Christ, and who had signalized themselves in their rabid fury against him. All these fell to the ground on their faces and remained thus for three hours. Others were punished with intense pains and abominable sicknesses. None of these events; however, were so important that any of the faithful recorded them. Even the demons were seized with new confusion and oppression for three days, and Lucifer and his demons broke forth in fearful howling.

Jerusalem was crowded with foreigners, for it was the Feast of Weeks, or Shavuot, celebrated annually by the Jews. The inhabitants and the visitors were filled with wonder over the visible and open signs by which the Holy Ghost descended on the faithful in the Cenacle. All Jerusalem was gathering at our doors and Peter came to me, out of courtesy, and requested permission to preach to the people. Glowing with my blessings, the faithful left the Cenacle and Peter began to preach to the people while they were still filled with amazement, for already the Pharisees, who had become even more obstinate and rebellious, were spreading lies about the miraculous events. Peter spoke to them loudly and boldly, for the gifts of the Holy Ghost had made him utterly fearless. While he spoke, the rest of the Apostles and disciples spread throughout Jerusalem and began preaching with unhesitating boldness; they poured forth burning words that like a flashing fire penetrated to the souls of their audiences.

Peter said in response to the dissenters, "You men of Judea, and all you that dwell in Jerusalem, be this known to you and with your ears receive my words. We are not drunk as you suppose, but we are intoxicated with the seven gifts of the Holy Spirit. For this is that which was spoken of by the Prophet Joel;"

"And it shall come to pass, in the last days; I will pour out my Spirit upon all flesh: and your sons and your daughters shall prophesy, and your young ones shall see visions, and your old men shall dream dreams. And upon my servants indeed and upon my handmaids I will pour out my Spirit, and they shall prophesy. I will show wonders in the heavens, and on the earth there will be blood, fire, vapor, and smoke. The sun shall be turned into darkness, and the moon into blood, before the great and manifest day of the Lord arrives; and it shall come to pass, that whoever shall call upon the name of the Lord, shall be saved [Joel:18-27]."

"You men of Israel hear these words: Jesus of Nazareth, a virtuous man approved of by God performed many miracles, wonders, and signs among you, as you well know. This same Being was crucified and slain at the hands of wicked men. However, as prophesied by David, God raised him from the dead, and we ourselves are witnesses as having seen him raised and ascending into heaven by his own power, where he was seated at the right hand of the Father. Let the unbelievers understand these words of truth, which they wish to deny in the perfidy of their malice. For against them stand the wonders of the Most High, which wrought in us as witnesses to the doctrine of Christ, and to his admirable Resurrection. Let the whole house of Israel understand that God has made this Jesus, whom you crucified, his anointed, the Lord of all, and that he raised him from the dead on the third day [Acts: 2, 14-15]."

As Peter was speaking, the people were filled with wonder at these events. They looked at one another in consternation and asked each other, saying, "What is this that we witness? Are not all of the men that spoke Galileans? How then do we hear them speaking in the language in which we were born? We Jews and Proselytes, Romans, Greeks, Cretans, Arabs, Parthians, Medes and all the rest of us from different parts of the world, hear them speak and we understand them in our own languages? Oh greatness of God! How admirable is he in all his works!"

I wish to make it clear that although the Apostles were speaking in Aramaic, everyone understood them in their own language. In addition, the Holy Spirit had blessed them with the ability to speak in any language, for they were to spread the Word to the four-corners of the earth. This miracle the Lord wrought at the time in order that they might be understood and believed by the different nationalities, and so that Peter would not have to repeat his homily in all the different languages of those present. Those that listened piously received a deep understanding of the Divinity and of the Redemption of man, now so eloquently and fervently put forward to them. They were moved to learn the truth. The Lord filled them with compunction and sorrow for their sins and interiorly filled them with the desire for divine mercy and forgiveness. With tears in their eyes they called out, "What must we do to gain eternal life [Acts: 2, 37]?"

Others; however, hardened their hearts, and were untouched by the divine truths preached to them. They became indignant with the Apostles, and called them innovators and adventurers. Many Jews, steeped in their perfidy, insisted they were drunk and insane. Among those were some of the men who had fallen to the ground for three hours and upon rising were more obstinate and rebellious than before. These were the very men that Peter was trying the hardest to reach. He answered the question and said to them, "Do penance and be baptized every one of you in the name of Jesus Christ, for the remission of sins; and you shall receive the gift of the Holy Ghost; for the promise is to you and to your children, and to all that are far off. Whosoever the Lord our God shall call makes use of the remedy, and save you from this perverse and incredulous generation."

The perfidious Jews were confounded and when they could not come up with any rebuttal to the questions of the Apostles, they withdrew. Three thousand people were converted that day. There were many cures and healings and even the holy women of Galilee were healing people and teaching them the tenets of the New Way. The Apostles, to the great consternation and fear of all Jerusalem, baptized the converts, and the wonders and prodigies performed by the elect filled them with terror and dismay.

That evening, the Apostles retired to the Cenacle, where I had remained praying for their success. With them were a great number of converts, all wishing to meet and venerate the mother of the Messiah. Of course, I was well aware of all that had transpired; I had remained prostrate on the stone floor all day praying and had sent many of my angels to inspire and encourage the holy Apostles throughout the day. I received them joyfully with all the sweetness I could muster as a loving and true mother.

Peter turned to his converts and said, "My brethren and servants of the Most High, this is the mother of our Redeemer and Master, Jesus Christ, whose faith you have received in acknowledging him as true God and true man. *She gave him human form, conceived him in her womb, and bore him, and remained a virgin before, during and after his birth.* Receive her as your mother, as your refuge and intercessor, for through her you shall receive light, direction, and release from your sins and miseries."

I filled the new adherents of faith with admirable light and consolation. The privilege of conferring great interior blessings and of giving light to those who looked upon me with pious veneration was renewed and extended in me when I was seated at the right-hand of my divine Son in heaven. The converts prostrated themselves at my feet and with tears begged for my assistance and blessing. However, I demurred for I was in the presence of Saint Peter, the Vicar of Christ, and the other priestly Apostles.

Seeing this, Saint Peter said to me, "Lady, do not refuse these faithful when they so piously ask you for the consolation of their souls."

Once ordered, I was delighted to comply with the wishes of the head of the Church. In the humble serenity of a Queen, I gave my blessing to those newly converted. The love that filled their hearts made them desire to hear some words of consolation from me; however, they were too humble and reverent to ask for this favor.

Instead they asked Peter to intercede for them and he considered this favor most proper and was fully aware that I knew what must be done, and he said to me, "Lady, listen to the petitions of your children."

In willing response, I said to them, "My dearest brethren in the Lord give thanks and praise with your whole hearts to almighty God. From among all men, he has called you to the sure path of eternal life in Jesus your Redeemer. Be firm in the confession of your new faith, and believe all that the Law of Grace contains as preached and ordained by its true Teacher, Jesus, my Son, and your Savior. Be eager to hear and obey his Apostles who teach and instruct you, so that you may be signed and marked by baptism in the character of children of the Most High. I offer myself as your handmaid to assist you in all that serves toward your consolation, and I shall ask my Son to look upon you as a kind Father and to manifest to you the true joy of his countenance, and to also communicate to you his grace."

The Apostles and disciples from that day on continued without interruption their preaching and their miracles. Through the entire octave they instructed not only the three thousand, who had been converted on Pentecost day, but multitudes of others, who came from all parts of the world. They conversed and spoke with each person in their own language, for as I said above, the Apostles spoke in various languages from that time on. This grace was not only given the Apostles, but to the disciples as well, including the holy women from Galilee. This was quite necessary when you consider the great number of people from all parts of the world being converted and baptized so quickly. Although all of the men and most of the women came to the Apostles, yet many, after having heard them, went to Mary Magdalene and her companions, who catechized, instructed and converted them and many others. The gift of healing was also given to the women, who, by the imposition of hands cured the sick, gave sight to the blind, tongue to the mute, motion to the lame, and even life to many of the dead. The Apostles principally worked these and other wonders; nevertheless, both their miracles and those of the women excited the wonder and astonishment of all Jerusalem. Nothing else was being talked about except the prodigies and the preaching of the Apostles.

The fame of these events soon extended throughout most of the known world for no one that sought help was left uncured. Once cured bodily, the word of the Lord healed their souls, hence the number of the faithful increased daily. Their fervor and faith was so ardent that the converts began to imitate the poverty of my Son and me. They despised riches and property and laid all their possessions at the feet of the Apostles without reserving anything for themselves [Acts: 2, 45]. They wished to possess all things in common and thus free themselves from the dangers of riches. They preferred to live in poverty, humility, and continual prayer without any other care than that of eternal life. All of them considered themselves as brethren and children of one Father in heaven [Matt: 23, 9]. Faith, hope, charity, and the sacraments were the common blessing of all, and as they were all seeking the same grace and eternal life, inequality in other things seemed dangerous to these early Christians. It seemed inappropriate that having such a union in essential things that some should be rich and others poor, for all gifts are from the one and the same Father for all his children.

This was the happy beginning and the *golden age* of the Evangelical Church. Here the rushing of the stream rejoiced the city of God and the current of grace and the gifts of the Holy Spirit fertilized this new paradise so recently planted by the hands of my Son Jesus, while I, Mary, stood in its midst like the tree of life. Then, were faith alive, hope firm, charity ardent, sincerity pure, humility true, and justice most equitable. This was the time when the faithful neither knew avarice nor followed vanity, when they trod under-foot vain pomp, and were free from covetousness, pride, and ambition. They avoided the vices, which later prevailed among the faithful, who, while confessing themselves as followers of Christ, then denied him in their works

It is not my intent to relate all the doings of the Apostles, or to record all that they did after my Son's Ascension. For one thing, I was seldom present after the Apostles began their evangelizing throughout the known world. I certainly knew all that passed and to do them justice it would take volumes to record their good works. I will select the salient points from the Acts of the Apostles written by the Evangelist and fill in those parts concerning myself, which was left out of his writings. It was not his purpose, nor proper for him to write about me at that time. It is sufficient to say that I did not rest or lose one moment or occasion of conferring some singular favor either upon the whole Church or some of its members. I consumed myself either in praying and beseeching my divine Son, without ever experiencing a refusal; or in exhorting, instructing, counseling, and, as treasurer and dispenser of the divine favors, distributing graces in diverse manners among the children of the Gospel. I can tell you that in these first ages, during which I lived in the holy Church, the number of the damned was proportionately very small; and that comparatively in those few years, a greater number were saved than in succeeding ages.

I devoted much of my time and attention to the Apostles. With the rapid sequence of events and the rapid escalation of the Church, I fixed their attention on the prodigious manifestation of the divine power, by which my Son was nurturing the faith of his Church. I also pointed out the virtue, which the Holy Ghost had communicated to them in order to make them fit ministers, and the ever-present assistance of the divine right hand. I exhorted them to acknowledge and praise the author of all these wonderful works and to render him humble thanks for them all. I encouraged them to follow up in secure confidence their preaching and exaltation of the name of the Lord, in order that he might be known, extolled and loved by all the faithful. I taught and practiced prostration and humiliation before the Most High, and often broke forth into canticles of praise and exaltation. I performed these duties faithfully and never failed to give thanks and to offer fervent prayers to the eternal Father for those persons converted, for each person remained distinctly present in my mind.

I personally received all those that wished to speak with me, and inspired them with words of light and life. Many of them conversed with me in private, and confessed to me their inmost thoughts. As I told you before, I was given divine knowledge and insight of all men's secrets. I knew the hearts of all their affections, inclinations and conditions, which enabled me, by use of this divine knowledge and wisdom, to accommodate myself to their needs and to render them assistance.

I instructed and catechized many into the holy faith, and not one of them was lost, for as long as they lived I offered up special prayers for them. To insure their being written into the book of life, I prayed to my Son, "My Lord and life of my soul, according to your will and pleasure, I have returned to the world in order to be the mother of your children. Please do not allow my heart to be torn by seeing the fruit of your priceless blood fail in any one of these that seek my intercession. Do not allow them to reap unhappiness from their having sought my help to obtain your clemency. Admit them my, Son, into the number of your friends predestined for your glory."

To these prayers, my Son instantly responded promising that what I asked for would be done. This still happens to this day to any person that merits my intercession, and who ask for it with sincere hearts, Be assured that any time I go to my Son with similar petitions, he will not deny me that which I ask.

Many of the new faithful whom I helped, highly impressed, returned to present me with jewels and rich gifts, especially the women who despoiled themselves of their fineries to lay them at my feet. I could not permit such gifts. At times; however, I did secretly inspire them to give their gifts to the Apostles, in order that they might be justly distributed among the poor and needy. I gratefully acknowledged such gifts as if they had been given to me. The poor and the sick I received with kindness, and I cured many of them of long-standing illnesses. Through the hands of Saint John, I supplied many secret wants, never omitting the least point of virtue. As the Apostles and disciples were engaged all day in preaching the faith and in converting those that came, I busied myself in preparing their food and attending to their comfort. At times I served them on my knees and humbly and reverently asked to kiss their hands. For only these hands, the hands of the priests, by the miracle of transubstantiation, change the whole substance of bread and wine into the real body and blood of Jesus Christ, with only the accidents of bread and wine remaining. Sometimes in vision, I saw the Apostles clothed in great splendor, which elicited from me increased reverence and veneration.

The Apostles continued their preaching and wonders in Jerusalem and by the seventh day, the number of faithful had risen to five thousand. The disciples were kept busy catechizing newcomers in preparation for baptism, for the Apostles were busily preaching and converting in spite of some heated controversies with the Pharisees and Sadducees. In my oratory, I also was busy. Considering that our little flock was increasing so rapidly, I prostrated myself on the floor and after adoring the Lord, I asked him, "Most high and eternal God, as a vile worm of earth, I wish to praise and exalt you for the immense love you have manifested for the human race. You show the mercy of a Father by calling so many to the knowledge and faith of your divine Son, which glorifies and spreads the honor of your name throughout the world. I beseech you oh, Lord, to enlighten and instruct your Apostles, my Masters, to dispose and order all that concerns the government, amplification and preservation of your holy Church."

I was caught up at once in a vision; the Lord was very pleased and said, "Mary, my spouse, what do you wish, my will is inclined toward your petitions?"

I answered him, "My, Lord and my, God, my wishes and desires are not unknown to your infinite wisdom. I seek your greater glory and the exaltation of your name in the Church. I present to you these new children whom you have called, and I desire that they now receive holy baptism, since they have already been instructed in the faith. If it is according to your will and service, I desire that the Apostles begin to consecrate the body and blood of our Son in the holy sacrifice of the "Breaking of the Bread.". By this new and admirable sacrifice, you will be given thanks and praise for the blessing of the Redemption, and through it all the favors you have conferred upon the world. In addition, according to your will, the children of the Church in partaking of the Holy Eucharist will receive the nourishment of eternal life. I am but dust and ashes, the least handmaid of your faithful. I am a woman; and I hesitate in proposing this to your priests and Apostles; will you inspire oh, Lord, the heart of your Vicar Saint Peter to ordain what you wish?"

The Lord answered me, saying, "My beloved, dove, let what you wish be done. My Apostles, through Saint Peter and John, shall speak to you and you may tell them what you wish to be done."

Inspired by God, the Apostles came to me at once. I received them as usual by reverently falling to my knees before them and asked for their blessing. This Saint Peter imparted, and then he said, "My, Lady, the new converts should now receive baptism, and be marked as the children of Christ, and be admitted to the bosom of the Church. Please tell us the order to be followed as most appropriate and pleasing to the Most High?"

I answered him tactfully, "My, master, you are the head of the Church and the Vicar of my Divine Son. All that shall be ordained must be done in the name of Jesus; and shall be approved by him; your will with that of my Son, is my will."

Peter then ordained that baptism would be given to all those converted on the following Sunday, which corresponds to the Sunday of the most holy Trinity. This arrangement was fully satisfactory to the rest of the Apostles. However, the question arose as to which baptism was to be used that of John the Baptist, or the baptism of Christ our Savior. Some said that the baptism of John, which was one of penance, should be given to them and through it to be admitted to the Church. Others, on the contrary, contended that with the baptism and the death of Christ, the baptism of John had expired. John's baptism, they argued, served merely to prepare the souls for the reception of Christ as the Redeemer. The baptism of the Lord; however, gave grace sufficient for justifying the souls and for washing away all sins of those properly disposed. Peter and John deemed it necessary to introduce the Baptism of Christ into the Church, and it was so ordered by Peter. I then confirmed their decision.

All then agreed that natural water was the proper matter to be used, and that the form should be that which my divine Son had instituted, "I baptize you in the name of the Father, and of the Son, and of the Holy Ghost. Whenever in the Acts of the Apostles it is said that they baptized in the name of Jesus, this saying does not refer to the form, but to the author of baptism, Jesus Christ.

Then as instructed by the Lord, I asked permission from Peter to address the congregation, and said to them, "My, masters, the Redeemer of the world, the true God and my Son, out of the love which he had for men, offered to the eternal Father the sacrifice of his sacred body and blood. He consecrated himself under the species of bread and wine. Under these appearances, he resolved to remain in his Church in order that its children shall have in it the sacrifice and food of eternal life, as intended by their Savior. Through this sacrifice, which embodies the mystery of the life and death of the Son, the Father is to be placated; and in it, and through it, the Church shall give the thanks and praise which it owes to him as its God and benefactor. At present each family is celebrating the Breaking of the Bread in their homes, which has proved satisfactory until now. However in time it is possible that it will lose the respect due our blessed Lord, and people might change the procedure to suit their own interpretation of the divine service. You are the priests and ministers, and you alone are the ones that should offer it to the people. It is my desire, if such is your will that you begin to offer the unbloody sacrifice of the "Breaking of the Bread," I wish that you consecrate the body and blood of my divine Son, in order that we may render fit thanks for the benefit of his Redemption, and the sending of the Holy Ghost into the Church. Initiate a service of the Breaking of the Bread, in order that the faithful, by receiving this holy Sacrament, may begin to enjoy the bread of life in all its divine effects. All those may partake of the sacred body, who have received baptism, and who have remained in a state of grace; but baptism is the prerequisite for its reception."

The Apostles thanked me and it was resolved that on the following day, after the baptism of the catechumens that the "Breaking of the Bread" would be celebrated by Saint Peter. Before he dismissed them, Peter said, "My dearest brethren, you already know that our Redeemer, the Lord Jesus by his example, and by his doctrines and commands ordained and taught the virtues of poverty [Matt: 6, 20]. He desires that we should live, abhorring and shunning the cares entailed by riches and possessions, and neither desiring nor amassing wealth in this life. We also have the formidable example of Judas, who was an Apostle, and by his avarice and covetousness went astray and fell into the abyss of wickedness and eternal damnation. So that we may avoid this danger, we must arrange some sort of administration to control the gifts and alms brought to us each day, and I am open to your suggestions."

There were many ideas, but they all fell upon delegating one person to handle the situation. At last, recognizing the diversity of opinion, Peter asked me to show them the right way that would be pleasing to my Son. I answered, "Since we are following the footsteps of our true Master, it is necessary that we all embrace poverty and that we honor and revere it, as the mother of all virtues and holiness,. I am of the opinion that we should detach our hearts from the love of money and riches and that all of us should refuse to handle it or to accept valuable and precious gifts. Therefore contemplate the appointment of seven persons of established virtue, who are to receive the alms and whatever else the faithful wish to deposit in their desire to live more securely and to follow Christ without the embarrassment of possessions. All of this must be given in the form of alms, not as rents, income, or capital. All of it should be used for supplying the needs of the community and our brethren, the poor, the needy, and the infirm. Let none of the community consider any of these goods as belonging to themselves any more than to any of the brethren. If the alms given are not sufficient for our needs let those that are appointed for these works ask for more in the name of God. We must all understand that our lives depend upon the Most High Providence of my Divine Son and not upon the solicitude for acquiring money, or under the pretext of providing for our sustenance."

This kind of poverty flourished afterwards for many years. Later, through human frailty and through human malice of the enemy, it decayed in many Christians, and finally came to be restricted to the ecclesiastical state. From this, God raised up the religious communities, where, with some diversity, the primitive poverty was renewed and kept alive in its entirety or in its main intent. Let everyone understand that the first step in the imitation and following of Christ is voluntary poverty; and those that pursue it more closely, can so much the more freely rejoice in sharing with Christ its advantages and perfections.

In preparation for celebrating the "Breaking of the Bread", I asked the owner of the Cenacle to furnish it the same way as it had been for the Last Supper. He deferred to my wishes with sincere courtesy and reverence. I prepared the wine and the unleavened bread necessary for the consecration, together with the paten and chalice used at the Last Supper. For the baptisms, I provided pure water and basins for administering the solemn ritual. With the assistance of my angels and the three Marys we cleansed and scrubbed the entire hall. Then we arranged the seats and tables, and adorned them with the necessary accouterments.

I then retired and spent the night in fervent aspirations, prostrations, thanksgivings and other exercises of exalted prayer. I offered to the eternal Father all that I, in my God-granted wisdom, knew would help to worthily prepare myself and the faithful for the worthy administration of baptism and the worthy participation in the first "Breaking of the Bread" offered by the Apostles.

Early the next day, which was the octave of the coming of the Holy Ghost, all the faithful and the catechumens gathered with the Apostles and disciples in the house of the Cenacle. Saint Peter instructed them in the nature and excellence of baptism; the need in which they stood of it, and its divine effects. He explained how they would through it, be made members of the mystical body of the Church, receive an interior character; be regenerated to a new existence as children of God and inheritors of his glory through the remission of sins and the gain of sanctifying grace. He exhorted them to the observance of the divine law, to which they subjected themselves by their own free will. He urged them to give humble thanksgiving for this benefit and for all the others, which they received from the hands of the Most High. He told them about the mysterious and sacred truth of the Holy Eucharist, which was to be celebrated in the consecration of the true body and blood of Jesus Christ, and he gave special instructions to all those who were to receive Holy Communion after their baptism.

All the converts were inspired by his sermon with additional fervor; for their dispositions were altogether sincere, the words of the Apostles full of life and penetration, and their interior grace most abundant. Then the Apostles began to baptize amid the most devout and orderly attention to the others. The catechumens entered one door of the Cenacle and after being baptized, they passed out through another, while the disciples and others of the faithful acted as ushers. I stood to one side of the hall and was able to recognize the effects of baptism in each one, according to the greater or less degree of virtues infused in their souls and I prayed for each one. I beheld them renewed and washed in the blood of the Lamb, and their souls restored to a divine purity and spotlessness. God, wishing to authenticate the first beginnings of this Sacrament in his holy Church, *created a clear light that was visible to all*, which descended upon each catechumen as he was baptized.

Baptisms continued all day, and at day's end five thousand persons had been baptized. As each person received his baptism, they gave praise and thanksgiving for this admirable blessing. Once finished, the Apostles and all those present prostrated themselves on the floor or on the streets of the city, wherever they happened to be to prepare themselves to worthily attend the first "Breaking of the Bread Ceremony and receive Holy Communion. Up till now the individual Apostles and disciples had been practicing the "Breaking of the Bread," as they ate their supper at night. It was important that the Church set up a formal Church Rite for this ceremony if they hoped to establish an authentic Church.

In preparation they recited the same prayers and Psalms, which my Son had recited before consecrating the bread and wine, faithfully imitating that sacred function just as they had seen it performed by their divine Master. Saint Peter took in his hands the unleavened bread, and looking up to heaven with admirable devotion, he pronounced over the bread the words of consecration of the most holy body of Christ, as had been done before by the Lord Jesus. The Cenacle was filled with the *visible* splendor of innumerable angels. This light converged in a most singular manner on me, as the Queen of Heaven and Earth and was seen by all those present. Then Saint Peter consecrated the chalice and performed all the ceremonies, which Christ had observed with his consecrated body and blood, raising them up for the adoration of all the faithful. Peter ate and drank of the Sacrament and communicated it to the eleven Apostles, as I had instructed him to do. I approached the holy Altar and as I neared the holy priest, I made three profound prostrations, and touched the stone floor each time with my face. Thereupon, Peter served me the Body of Christ on my tongue, and then I drank the Blood of Christ from the chalice, while all the celestial spirits present attended with ineffable reverence. I returned to my place and, as I returned, I was entirely transformed and elevated, completely absorbed in this divine conflagration of the love of my most holy Son, whom I had just received bodily. I remained in a trance elevated from the floor; but my holy angels, at my request, shielded me so as not to draw attention to myself, because of the obvious divine effects apparent in me [Acts: 2, 42-47].

The most ardent love my Son and I had for humankind had induced me to return to earth in order to help establish the Church. My Son, in order to recompense me for the privation of his presence, to a certain extent, decided to continue his sacramental presence in my pure heart. After Jesus took his seat in heaven, the Holy Eucharist remained in my bosom. In this manner, he partially compensated me for being denied his physical presence after having been the core of my life for thirty-three years.

The disciples distributed Holy Communion first to the one hundred and twenty who had been believers before the Ascension. Each of us received both the body and blood of our Lord Jesus Christ. Then the body of Christ was distributed to another thousand of the faithful, for not all those baptized had been properly prepared for the reception of the Holy Eucharist. From this early beginning, the Church chose to distribute Holy Communion only in the species of bread, reserving the reception of both body and blood to the priests and religious. This difference was not made because the new faithful were less worthy of the one species than of the other. The Holy Fathers knew that in each species a person received the same object in its entirety, namely the sacramental God; and that there was no precept, and likewise no necessity that a person receives both species. Only in modern times has this tradition been revised. Today, in the wisdom of Holy Mother Church, the faithful, if in a state of grace, may receive both the body and the blood of our blessed Lord, but only at the celebration of the Holy Mass.

In the beginning there was no way in which to store or preserve the Holy Eucharist, so only enough was consecrated to serve the needs of those present, just as it is done today with the wine. However, during these first years when there was no designated Church or tabernacle, I was the only sanctuary and temple, in which for some years the most Blessed Sacrament was preserved. This was done so that the Church of Christ might not be deprived even for one moment of the Word made Flesh, from the time when he ascended into heaven until the end of the world. He was not present in the tabernacle of my bosom for the use of the faithful, yet he was there for their benefit and for other glorious ends, since I offered up my prayers and intercessions for all Christians in the temple of my heart. I adored the sacramental Christ in the name of the entire Church; while by his indwelling, Christ was present and united to the mystical body of the faithful. Because of this fact, the people of that age were supremely fortunate, for my Son was sheltered within my bosom, just as he is today harbored within the sanctuaries and tabernacles. I continually adored and reverenced him, and he was never offended, as he is now in many of our Churches. By indwelling in my bosom, Jesus satisfied his love for me and I for him, while I continued my sojourn on earth.

After all the converts had received Holy Communion, Saint Peter ended the ceremony by reciting some psalms and prayers, which he and the other Apostles offered up in thanksgiving. This was the new Church's first effort to celebrate a Mass and it was quite simple. Over the early years, the Apostles successor's, formalized the basic rites and ceremonies of the Catholic Mass, which incorporated the writings of the early leaders of the Church, and the Gospel of our Lord Jesus Christ, which, at that time, had not yet been put down on paper.

I had been elevated to the highest degree of grace and holiness possible in a mere creature, and I saw with eyes of divine knowledge the little flock of the Church increasing each day. As a good shepherd, I watched with the deepest insight lest any assault or attack from the ravenous wolves of hell threatened the sheep of my fold.

A few days after the coming of the Holy Ghost, while at my prayers, I spoke to my Son, "My, Lord, the God of true love, I know that the little flock of your Church, of which you have made me the mother and defender, is of no less price to you than your own life and blood, by which you redeemed it from the powers of darkness. It is therefore reasonable that I also offer my life and all my being for the preservation and increase of what is so highly esteemed by you. Let me die my, God, if it is necessary for the enhancement of your name and for the spread of your glory throughout the world. Look kindly upon your faithful; govern your vicar Peter that he may rightly direct your sheep. Watch over all your Apostles and your ministers; bless and guide all of us, so that we all may execute your perfect and holy will."

My blessed Son answered me, "My, spouse and, beloved, I am attentive to your petitions. However, you already know that my Church is to follow in my footsteps and my teachings. The Church is to imitate me in the way of my suffering and the Cross. The Apostles and disciples and all my intimate friends and followers are to embrace the Cross and suffering; for they cannot be my friends without this condition of labor and sufferings [Matt: 10, 37-39]. It is also necessary that my

Church should bear the ballast of persecutions, by which it will pass securely through the prosperity of the world and its dangers. Such is my high Providence regarding the faithful and the predestined. Attend therefore, and behold the manner in which this is to be brought about."

In a vision, I saw Lucifer and a great multitude of hellish followers rising from out of the depths of the infernal caverns, where they had lain oppressed since the time they had been vanquished on Mount Calvary and hurled into hell. I saw the dragon with seven heads coming up from the depths of the sea, followed by hordes of demons. He came forth much weakened, but in his pride he lashed himself into implacable fury and arrogance, having experienced passions in him greater than his power. Lucifer quickly reconnoitered the entire earth, then he hastened to Jerusalem in order to persecute with all his fury the sheep of Christ. From afar, he studied the multitude of faithful. He noted how the Apostles continued to preach and perform miracles daily. He was frustrated with the way the new converts renounced and abhorred riches, and how the holy Church was founded with all the principles of invincible sanctity. He then sought to approach nearer to the congregation, but found he could not, because they were all united in perfect charity. This virtue, together with faith, hope and humility, rose like an impenetrable shield against Lucifer's ministers of evil. He schemed and plotted to attract some of them to give him an opportunity of entering the fortress of virtue. Everywhere he found his entrance forestalled by the vigilance of the Apostles and by my personal protection.

Seeing such an army of demons rising up against the evangelical Church, my heart was filled with compassion and sorrow, for I knew well the ignorance and weakness of men and the malicious and cunning hatred of the ancient serpent. In order to restrain and check his pride, I turned on them and said, "Who is like God that dwells in the highest? Oh foolish and vainglorious enemy of the Omnipotent! Jesus vanquished you on the Cross and crushed your arrogance. He redeemed the human race from your cruel tyranny; his power annihilates you, his wisdom confounds you, and hurls you back to hell. In his name, I now do this, so as to deprive you of the power to hinder the exaltation and glory due to him from all men as their God and Redeemer."

Then I spoke to the Lord; "Supreme, God and, Father, if your power does not restrain and quench the fury, which I see in the infernal dragon and his hosts, I doubt not that he will cover the whole face of the earth with ruin of its inhabitants. Do not allow oh, Lord that this venomous serpent be allowed to pour its poison upon the souls redeemed and washed in the blood of the lamb. Oh that the wrath of this dragon be turned upon me alone, and that your redeemed be placed in safety. Let me eternal, Lord, fight the battles against your enemies? Clothe me with your power in order that I may humiliate them and crush their pride and haughtiness?"

In virtue of my prayer, Lucifer was struck with a great fear and for the time being he did not dare to approach any of the congregations of the faithful. Instead, he turned his efforts to enlist the aid of the scribes and Pharisees in their obstinate perfidy. With his suggestions, he filled them with envy and hatred against the Apostles. Fearing that they would spread the glory of the name of Jesus, the Jews held many meetings to decide a course of action against them. They decided to wait for some act done by the Apostles by which they could arrest them.

Their opportunity came quickly, for the next day as Peter and John were going up to the temple area for the three o'clock hour of prayer, a man crippled from birth was sitting before the Beautiful Gate begging for alms, as he had for many years. He stretched out his arm to them and called out, "Alms, for the love of God, alms."

Peter stopped and looked intently at him and said, "Look at us. "The man paid attention to them expecting to receive alms in return. Instead, Peter said, "I have neither silver nor gold, but what I do have I give you in the name of Jesus Christ the Nazarene, 'Rise and walk'. Then Peter took him by the right hand and raised him up. The man's feet and ankles grew strong, and he walked and leaped about praising God. The people who knew him were amazed at his miraculous cure.

At Solomon's Portico, a huge crowd gathered about them, and Peter addressed the people, "You Israelites, why are you amazed, and why do you look so intently at us as if we had made him walk by our own power or piety? The God of Abraham has glorified his servant Jesus whom you handed over and denied in Pilate's presence. You denied the Holy and Righteous One and asked that a murderer be released to you. You put the author of life to death, but God raised him from the dead and of this, we are witnesses. By faith in his name, this man whom you see and know has been cured. My, brothers, I know that you acted out of ignorance just as your leaders did. However, God has brought to a fulfillment what he had announced beforehand through the mouth of all the prophets that his Messiah should suffer. Repent, therefore, and be converted that your sins may be wiped away."

While they were still speaking to the people, the Captain of the temple guard, accompanied by several priests and Sadducees, arrested them for teaching the people about Jesus and his resurrection. It was now evening and they were held in jail overnight.

The next day, they were brought before the Sanhedrin with Annas, the high priest presiding over the elders, the scribes, and the Sadducees and Pharisees. Annas said to the Apostles, "By what power or by what name have you done this thing?"

Then Peter filled with the Holy Ghost answered, "Leaders of the people and elders, if we are being examined today about a good deed done to a cripple, then, by what means was he saved? All of you and all the people of Israel should know that it was done in the name of Jesus Christ the Nazarene, whom you crucified and whom God then raised from the dead. In his name, this man stands before you healed. Jesus is the stone rejected by you, the builders, which has become the cornerstone. There is no salvation through anyone else, nor is there any other name under Heaven given to the human race by which we are to be saved."

Annas had Peter and John taken outside and then he said to the assembled leaders, "We know these men, and we know that they were the disciples of Jesus. What are we going to do with them? Everyone in Jerusalem knows that the cripple was cured through them and we cannot deny it. However, so that it may not spread any further among the people, let us give them a stern warning never again to speak to anyone using his name."

Peter and John were called back and ordered not to speak or teach again in the name of Jesus. However, Peter replied, "Whether it is right in the sight of God for us to obey you rather than God, you are the judges. It is impossible for us not to speak about what we have seen and heard."

Annas, knowing of no way to punish them, because all Jerusalem was talking about the miracle, released them after a stern warning. The two Apostles immediately came to see me at the Cenacle, in order to report their experience. I, by a special vision, had seen all that had happened, which I did not reveal to them, and I joined with them in a most exalted prayer, in which the Holy Ghost again came upon all of us with visible signs.

The community of believers was of one heart and mind, and no one claimed that any of his possessions was his own, for they held everything in common. Then came that which I feared the most, Lucifer tempted a young couple and they committed a great sin against God and the Community. When I detected Lucifer's intent, I prayed to Jesus to not allow this terrible thing to happen.

My Son replied, "My beloved, Mother, let not your heart, in which I reside be affected; for I shall draw much good out of this evil for my Church. It is for this end that my Providence shall permit it. In chastising these sins, I shall teach the rest of the faithful by a visible example, to fear such sins in the Church and thus shall caution them against the deceit and the covetousness of money."

The young couple in question was a man named Ananias and his wife Sapphira, who had recently joined our group. They were rather well off and money meant a great deal to them. However, in keeping with the custom of the community, Ananias, with the knowledge of his wife, sold a piece of property and retained some of the money for themselves. He laid the difference at Peter's feet and lied, claiming it was the price obtained for the property. Peter said to him, "Ananias, why has Satan filled your heart so that you have lied to the Holy Ghost and retained part of the price of the land? While it remained unsold, did it not remain yours? When it was sold was it still not under your control? Why did you contrive this deed? You have lied not to human beings, but to God."

When Ananias heard these words, he fell dead at the feet of the Apostle. The disciples came, wrapped him up, and carried him out and buried him. After an interval of three hours, his wife came in, unaware of what had happened. Peter said to her, "Tell me, did you sell the land for this amount?" She answered, "Yes, for that amount." Then Peter said to her, "Why did you agree to test the Spirit of the Lord? Listen, the footsteps of those who have buried your husband are at the door, and now they will carry you out." Sapphira fell at his feet and breathed her last. The young men came in, carried her out, and buried her with her husband. Great fear came upon the whole Church and upon all those who heard of these things.

I was upset over this apostasy and could see the handiwork of Lucifer, and fearing lest the conversion of other souls be prevented, I took up their cause and said to the cruel tyrant, "Enemy of the Most High, how do you dare to rise up against God's creatures, when by the Passion and death of my son, you have been completely vanquished, subjected and despoiled of your tyrannous empire. Do you not know that you are subjected to his infinite power and that you cannot resist his invincible will? He commands you, and in his name I command you to descend into hell with all your hordes from which you may not rise to persecute the children of the Church."

Lucifer could not resist my mandate, for Jesus allowed them to see my Son Sacramentally present in my bosom. Lucifer and his demons were hurled into the depths of hell, and for some time, they remained there powerless, lashing themselves into a fury. Lucifer said to his cohorts, "Advise me what I can do against my enemy, who torments and overwhelms me? She battles against me more strenuously than all the creatures together. Shall I give up persecuting her in order that she may not succeed in destroying me? She vanquishes me in each battle, and she continually diminishes my powers. Where is my exalted sovereignty? I dare not present battle with her, so let us seek to overthrow some of her followers, so that in some measure my confusion may be allayed and my revenge satisfied."

Later, the Lord permitted the dragon and his hordes to return and tempt the faithful for their probation. However, when the demons became acquainted with the state of their souls and the great virtues with which they were adorned, they found no approach open, nor any of the faithful that would listen to their insane deceits and illusions.

The signs and wonders of the Apostles drew many people to Solomon's Portico, where the Apostles often assembled. The people carried the sick and those with unclean spirits and placed them in rows near where Peter walked in hopes his shadow would pass over them and that they would be healed. They came from near and far and Peter and his ministers healed them all. The high priests were filled with jealousy and had Peter and John arrested and placed in the public jail.

From their cell, the Apostles prayed to their God and to me to intercede for them. When I, by divine enlightenment, became aware of their condition, I prostrated myself in the shape of a cross and made the following petition, "My supreme, Lord, I know your Apostles must follow your doctrine of patience in labor and adverse situations that come from men. I pray that if possible that Peter and John your servants be granted their freedom and their life in order to found the Church, preach your holy name, and bring the world to the true faith. I beg you my, Lord, to permit me to favor your vicar Peter and my son, your beloved disciple John, and all those who by the cunning of Lucifer are imprisoned. Do not allow your enemy to gloat in having triumphed over your servants. Crush his haughtiness my, Lord, and let him be confounded in your presence."

The Most High answered, "My, Spouse, let what you desire be done, for this is also my will. Send your angels to undo the work of Lucifer, for my power is with you."

With this approval, I sent one of my angels, of a very high hierarchy, to the prison to free the two Apostles of their fetters and release them from the dungeon. The angel appeared to them full of light and glory and said to them, "I have been sent by my Queen to liberate you from this prison. Go and take your place in the temple area, and tell the people everything about this life." They did as instructed, and the following morning when the guards went to the prison to take them before the Sanhedrin, they found the prison locked, but the prisoners were gone. Hearing the Apostles were again teaching in the temple, the Sanhedrin sent the temple guard to bring them before them, but without the use of force, for they were afraid the people would stone them. When the Apostles stood before him, Annas said to them, "I gave you strict orders to stop teaching in that name. Yet you have filled Jerusalem with your teaching and want to bring this man's blood upon us."

Peter said in reply, "We must obey God rather than men. The God of our ancestors raised Jesus, though you had him killed by hanging him on a tree. God exalted him at his right hand, as leader and Savior to grant Israel repentance and forgiveness for sins. We are witnesses of these things, as is the Holy Spirit that God has given to those who obey him [Acts: 4, 29-32]."

Hearing this, the Sadducees wished to put them to death; however, I sent other angels to drive Lucifer and his demons from the presence of the members of the Sanhedrin. I instructed them to inspire the Jews and to instill in them a fear of injuring the Apostles, or hinder their preaching. They did their mission so well that a Pharisee in the Sanhedrin named Gamaliel, a teacher of the law and respected by all the people, stood up, ordered the Apostles to be put outside for a short time and said to his colleagues, "Fellow, Israelites, be careful what you are about to do to these men. Some time ago, Theudas appeared, claiming to be someone important, and about four hundred men joined him, but he was killed and all those who were loyal to him were disbanded and came to nothing. After him came Judas the Galilean at the time of the census. He also drew people after him, but he too perished and all those loyal to him were scattered. So now I tell you, have nothing to do with these men and let them go. For if this endeavor or this activity is of human origin, it will destroy itself. But if it comes from God, you will not be able to destroy them; you may even find yourselves fighting against God [Acts: 5, 33-39]."

Annas was persuaded by Gamaliel to release them, and after recalling the Apostles, he had them flogged, ordered them to stop speaking in the name of Jesus, and then dismissed them. The Apostles immediately came to me and recounted all their adventures and glorying in the fact that they were worthy to suffer in the same manner as the Lord. When they were finished, I knelt at their feet and said to them, "Now my, masters, you appear to me true imitators and disciples of your Master. Since you suffer affronts and injury for his name and with a joyous heart help him to bear his cross, you become his worthy ministers and assistants in applying the fruit of the blood he has shed for the salvation of men. May his right hand bless you and strengthen you with divine virtue." I then kissed their hands and administered to their needs.

I loved all the Apostles dearly, and served them with incredible affection and reverence, both because of their great holiness and because of their dignity as priests, and as ministers, preachers, and founders of the Gospel. With the rapid increase of the Church, they were soon obliged to go outside Jerusalem in order to baptize and admit to the faith many of the inhabitants of the neighboring villages. During their journeys, Lucifer sought to hinder the spread of the divine word, by rousing the unbelievers to many contradictions and altercations with the Apostles. When I was not present, the enemy imagined the Apostles disarmed and at his mercy, for the furious pride of the dragon, as is written in Job, esteems the toughest steel as weak straw, and the hardest bronze as a stick of rotten wood. He does not fear the dart, or the sling, but he feared me and waited to tempt the Apostles when I was not present.

However, my protection failed them not, for from the watchtower of my exalted knowledge, I reached out in every direction. Like a vigilant sentinel, I discovered the assaults of Lucifer and hastened to the relief of my sons and ministers of the Lord. Since I could not talk to the Apostles in any of their afflictions, I sent my holy angels to their assistance in order to encourage, forewarn and console them, and sometimes to drive away the assaulting demons. At times, the angels did their job secretly by inspirations and interior consultations, at others and more frequently, they manifested themselves visibly, assuming most beautiful and refulgent bodies and informing the Apostles of what was proper for the occasion, or what I had ordered. This happened quite often because of the purity and holiness of the Apostles, and because of the necessity of favoring them with an abundance of consolation and encouragement.

With all the other faithful, I proportionately exhibited the same care for all the converts in Jerusalem and in Palestine. I remembered them all in their necessities and tribulations. I thought not only of the need of their souls, but of those of the body. Many I cured of grievous illnesses. Others, whom I knew were not to be cured miraculously, I visited in person. Of the poor, I took the greatest care. I administered to them with my own hand on their sick bed and saw that they were kept clean. I refused no service or lowliest ministry to the faithful. I filled each one with joy and consolation and lightened all their labors. For those that I could not personally attend, I assisted secretly through my holy angels or by my prayers and petitions.

I was especially attentive to those who were in the agony of death. I attended many of them and did not leave them until they had secured their eternal salvation. For those who went to purgatory, I offered up most fervent prayers and even performed works of penance, such as prostrations in the form of a cross, and genuflections by which I satisfied for their faults. Then I would send one of my angels to draw them from purgatory and deliver the soul to my Son in heaven as his own, and as the fruits of his blood and Redemption. To those, even to this day, who are disposed properly for meriting my presence, this favor is not denied them.

I will relate the story of one young girl who was among the first five thousand converts in Jerusalem and who had received baptism. She was from a poor and humble parentage. While busying herself with her household duties, she took ill and the sickness lingered for many days. She had fallen from her first religious fervor and had in neglect committed some sins endangering her baptismal grace. Lucifer, ever watchful, attacked her with fiercest cruelty. The demon appeared to her in the form of another woman, and with much cajolery, told her to withdraw from the people who were preaching the Crucifixion, and not to believe anything they said, because it was all a lie. The priests and judges, who crucified the teacher of that false religion, the woman said, will punish you if you do not follow my advice. However if you obey, the demon promised, you will live peacefully and free from danger.

The girl replied, "I will do what you say, but what will I do in regard to that Lady, whom I have seen with these men and women, and who appears to be so kind and peaceful? I desire her goodwill very much."

The demon answered, "This one whom you have mentioned, is worse than all the rest, and you should shun her most of all. It is important that you withdraw from her snare."

Infested with the deadly poison of the ancient serpent, the soul of this simple child was brought near to eternal death and her body, instead of being relieved dropped into even more serious illness and was in danger of a premature end. One of the seventy-two disciples, who visited the faithful, was informed of her dangerous illness, but when he called on her she would not speak to him. He zealously sought to exhort and instruct her, but she hid and stopped up her ears. Seeing the eminent peril of this soul, the disciple sought help from Saint John. John, however, was treated in the same manner, and in his concern he came to me for help.

I turned my interior vision upon the sick one and recognized the unhappy and dangerous state of her soul. Prostrate on the floor, I prayed for her rescue, but my Son did not answer me, not because my cause was not pleasing to him, but because he was pleased with my clamors pretending deafness in order to hear them so much longer. He also wished to teach the faithful the prudence and charity of his mother on these occasions. In spite of his silence, I increased my prayers and when he did not answer, I could not be remiss in my duties to my children. I prudently dispatched one of my angels to bring aid to the soul by defending it against the devil, and by exhorting her with holy inspirations to forsake the devil's deceits and return to God. However, even my angel could not overcome the girl's obstinacy in clinging to her illusions.

My angel returned and said to me, "My, Mistress, I unhappily return, for the soul's hardness of heart is such, that she will not listen to anything I say. I have fought against the demon in her defense, but they resisted standing on the rights which this soul has freely yielded and continues to yield to them. I cannot my, lady, give you the consolation you expected. Again I prayed, but again my prayers were unanswered. I therefore decided that if the angel and the Apostle were not powerful enough to awaken the girl from sin, then I myself must go and heal her in person.

The home of the young girl was some distance from the Cenacle and I had no sooner taken my first steps than my holy angels, at the command of my Son, approached to take me to the house in their arms. As God had not manifested his intentions to me, I asked them, "Why do you detain me?"

They answered evasively, "There is no reason why we should consent to your walking through the city, when we can bear you along with greater propriety." They placed me on a throne of resplendent clouds, bore me along, and placed me in the sick room. The dying girl, being poor and now unable to speak had been forsaken by all; many demons surrounded her waiting eagerly to snatch off her soul. At my appearance, the evil spirits vanished like flashes of light. I commanded them to descend into hell and remain there until I should permit them to come forth. I approached the sick girl and taking her by the hand, I called her by name. Instantly a complete change came over the girl, and she began to breathe more freely and recover herself.

Then she said to me, "My, lady, a woman came to me, who persuaded me to believe that the disciples of Jesus were deceiving me, and that I had better separate myself from them and from you; otherwise, if I did not accept their way of life, I should fall into great misfortune."

I said to her, "My, daughter, she who seemed to you to be a woman, was Lucifer your enemy. I come in the name of the Most High to give you eternal life. Return then to the true faith of Jesus, which you have received, and confess him with all your heart as your God and Redeemer. Jesus died upon the Cross for your salvation and that of the entire world, Adore and call upon him, and asks him for the pardon of your sins."

She replied, "All this I have believed before, but they told me it was very bad, and that they would punish me if I should confess it."

I consoled her, "My, friend, do not fear this deceit, but remember that the chastisement and pains which are really to be feared are those in hell, to which the demons wish to bring you. You are now very near death and you can avail yourself of the remedy I now offer you, if you will only believe me. If you believe, you will free yourself of the eternal fire which threatens you, because of your mistake?"

Through my exhortations and the graces I extended to her, she was moved to tears of compunction and implored me to further assist her, declaring herself ready to obey all my commands. Guided by me, she openly professed her faith in my Son and made a good act of contrition in preparation for confession. I then sent for Saint John to come and administer the Sacraments to her. After her confession, the girl repeated the acts of contrition and love. I remained with her for two hours in order to prevent the demons from renewing their assault. Then, invoking the name of Jesus and my name, the girl happily expired in my arms. By my prayers, I was able to deliver her soul from all guilt and punishment. I sent her directly to Heaven accompanied by some of the twelve angels that bore on their breasts the sign of the Redemption.

After this miracle, Lucifer was allowed to return with his host of demons in order to test the constancy of the faithful; for in this manner the just and the predestined must gain their crowns. They came forth filled with even more wrath, and began to seek entrance into the hearts of the faithful by searching out the evil inclinations of each one, as he does even now. Out of the multitude of converts, it had to be expected that the fervor of charity would begin to cool in some. Among the faithful Saint John had found two men, who were beset with evil inclinations and habits before their conversion and who sought favor and alliance with some of the Jewish princes in the hope of worldly gain and honor. Infected by covetousness [which is the root of all evils], they temporized with the powerful and flattered them in order to retain their friendship.

Because of these dealings, the demons judged them weak in their faith and virtue. The serpent suggested to the priests many ways of reprehending and intimidating the two converts for having accepted the faith in Jesus Christ and being baptized. The anger of those in authority is apt to frighten weak subjects, and the priest expressed much anger with the two men. The men's faith weakened and soon proceeded from weakness to apostasy from the faith of my Son. As their association with the priests grew, the two men soon ceased attending the preaching and the other holy exercises presented for the converts, which made apparent their falling away.

The Apostles were much aggrieved at the ruin of these converts. They conferred as to whether they should notify me, John told them that I knew of all the affairs of the Church and that this incident could not have escaped my attention. They came to me and gave me an account of the two apostates, whom they had exhorted and tried to lead them back to the faith with no success. I did not hide my sorrow from them, for it was important that they learn from my sorrow, how they must esteem the children of the Church, and with what zeal they were to preserve them in the faith and bring them to eternal life.

When they left, I prostrated myself on the floor as usual and poured out a fervent prayer for the two apostates, shedding bloody tears for them. In order to lessen my grief by the knowledge of his hidden judgments; the Lord spoke to me, "My, Spouse, chosen among all creatures, I wish you to understand my just decrees concerning those two souls for whom you pray, and concerning others who are to enter my Church. These two having apostatized from my true faith could do more harm than good among the other faithful if they continue their association with them. They have depraved habits and have become even harder of heart in their evil inclinations. Hence, in my infinite knowledge, I foresee that they will be reprobates, and that it will be better to separate them from the flock of the faithful and cut them off from the mystical body of the Church. Thus, they shall be prevented from infecting others by their contagion. However, my beloved One, in conformity with my most high Providence, of all those that join my Church; some by their sins shall incur damnation, and others, through my grace, will save themselves by the faith I have given them and by their subsequent good works. My teachings and my Gospel are to be as the net which gathers in all kinds of fish, good and bad, the wise and the foolish. The enemy is to sow his cockle among the pure grain of truth, in order that the just may justify themselves so much the more, and the impure if so they choose in their malice, may defile themselves still more."

At the same time that I received the answer to my prayer, my Son renewed within me participation in his knowledge, so that I might understand the equity of the Most High in condemning those unworthy of his friendship and glory. I alone, of all God's creatures, understood fully what it meant to lose God eternally and to be condemned to eternal torments. I am sure you are aware that the angels and the saints of heaven, who share this mystery in God, cannot feel sorrow or pain, because that would be inappropriate to their happy state. The sorrow and pain for the perdition of souls is impossible to the saints in heaven. However, I felt this pain so much the greater because I exceeded them in wisdom and charity, and since I was still in a state of pilgrimage.

When I saw these two souls and an almost infinite number of others in the Church, who were to draw upon themselves eternal damnation, I lamented, "Is it possible that any soul, of its own free will, should ever deprive itself eternally of seeing the face of God, and should choose rather to look upon so many demons in hell?"

While I was thus retired in my affliction, Saint John entered to visit me and to inquire to my needs. When he saw me so afflicted, he asked permission to speak saying, "My Lady and mother of my Lord, since our Master died I have never seen such grief on your countenance, and your eyes filled with blood. Tell me, lady, if possible, the cause of this new affliction, and whether I can alleviate it even at the cost of my life."

I answered him, "I weep when I see that after my Son's supreme sacrifice that some are seeking to crucify him anew by their sins; their apostasy, and by the abuse of the fruits of his most precious blood. I know that in his most ardent love for men, he has suffered for the salvation of each one in particular whatever he suffered for all together. I see his immense love so little requited and so many souls lost who should know him that I cannot constrain my sorrow. Oh children of Adam formed according to the image of my Son and Lord, what are you thinking of? Where is your justification for thus incurring the calamity of losing God forever?"

Saint John replied, "My, mother, if your sorrow is occasioned by those two apostates, you must know that among so many there must be unfaithful servants. Even in our Apostolate itself was numbered Judas, a disciple in the school of our Redeemer."

I responded, "Oh, John, if God himself wished the perdition of some souls, I should be able to restrain my sorrow, but though he permits the damnation of the reprobate since they themselves seek it, this is not the absolute will of the divine goodness. He wishes all to attain salvation, if only by their own free will they do not resist. My Son sweated blood for those who will not benefit themselves of the blood shed for them. If now he could be aggrieved for a soul that damns itself, he would doubtlessly be more aggrieved than if he again had to suffer for it. Hence, I, who know this truth and am still living in the flesh, rightfully feel what my Son desires to feel if it were possible."

John was moved to tears with my grief and he joined me in prayers lamenting the folly of humankind.

The office of Mother and Teacher of the holy Church, which my Son had conferred upon me, was necessarily accompanied by knowledge and light proportionate to these high offices. For I was to know all the members of this mystical body, which I was to govern, so that I might apply my teachings and ministrations according to each one's station, condition and necessity. I knew all the faithful that had joined the Church beginning with the one hundred and twenty souls in the Cenacle. I was informed of their natural inclinations, of the degree of virtue and grace they possessed, the merits of their works from beginning to end. I was ignorant of nothing pertaining to the Church, except when sometimes my Son concealed from me some affair, which afterwards was made known to me at its conclusion. I gave neither more or less than was proper according to the desserts of love and estimation due to each one. I conducted myself as a loving mother, without niggardliness or forgetfulness. I carefully avoided showing favoritism to avoid rousing jealousy or envy among my charges. I taught them all not to exalt themselves in vain presumption, or deem themselves worthy of great honors, or of being favored more highly, especially by God, the Apostles or me. I was careful not to fail in the veneration and honor due the dignity of the office of the Apostles or the other faithful. In spite of all this, I was still human and I had special feelings for Peter and John, for both were so loved by my Son, and also for the rest of the Apostles, the disciples, the family of Lazarus, especially Mary Magdalene, and the holy women from Galilee.

Stephen: Deacon and Martyr

There were others of our original group that were quite dear to me. Shortly after Peter had organized and set up our community, the converts of Greek origin, called Hellenists, complained against the Hebrews, saying that their widows were being neglected in the daily distribution of food. Peter called the Apostles and disciples together and said to them, "It is not right for us to neglect the word of God to serve at table. Brothers, select from among you seven reputable men filled with wisdom and the Holy Spirit. We will appoint them to this task, while we shall devote ourselves to prayer and to the ministry of the word."

The proposal was readily accepted, and so they chose Stephen, a Greek from Alexandria, filled with faith and the Holy Spirit. They also chose Philip, Prochorus, Nicanor, Timon, Parmenas, and Nicholas of Antioch, a convert to Judaism. They presented these men to the Apostles, who prayed and laid hands on them and designated them as the first deacons of the new Church. The word of God continued to spread and the number of disciples in Jerusalem increased greatly, even a large group of Jewish priests became obedient to the faith [Acts: 6, 1-7].

I was deeply impressed with the choice of the seven deacons. Of course they were already known to me, personally and interiorly. Of the seven, Stephen was the first and the outstanding choice. From the very beginning, I had looked on him with an especial love, placing him first, or among the first, in my estimation. I knew that Jesus had chosen Stephen, for the defense of his honor and his holy name, and that in the future he was to give up his life for him. Stephen was born of a rich and noble family in Alexandria, and he had given up a prestigious and luxurious life to join my Son. He was as fair as the sun with the body and face of an Adonis and his head was crowned with golden curls. This courageous saint was of a sweet, humble, and peaceful disposition, and he was rendered much more amiable and docile to all holiness by the workings of God's grace. When I found such persons of a peaceful and meek character, I found that they resembled my divine Son and they were very special to me. I loved him tenderly, obtained many blessings for him, and thanked the Lord for having created, called, and chosen such a one for the first fruits of his martyrs. In consideration of his coming martyrdom, revealed to me by my Son, my heart was filled with additional affection for this great saint.

The decision to appoint the seven deacons was a wise one, and the community was filled with harmony and the love of God. Months and years rolled by and the Church grew with leaps and bounds. A large Christian community was established outside the gates of Jerusalem. There, all the faithful shared equally in the fruits of the labors of the Church members. The Apostles went further a field each day and many small communities of the New Way were established in other villages and towns. Our success was a thorn in the side of the priests and scribes and many meetings were held to discuss how they could rid themselves of the menace they felt we posed to the established Law of Moses. The Synagogue of Roman Freedmen in Jerusalem was extremely vociferous in their outrage with the New Way and they continually attacked our way of life. While Peter and John were the recognized leaders, who debated fiercely with the Jews, in time, the brilliant oratory of Deacon Stephen outshone them all.

Stephen was very wise, full of the Holy Spirit and faith. He was always asking me for information on many mysterious matters. I answered all his inquiries, encouraged and exhorted him zealously to work for the honor of Christ. However, Stephen's success was fermenting a great deal of anger and discord within the ranks of the stiff-necked Jews. I knew that in a very short time the Jews would vengefully lash out at him. It was time for me to help prepare him for his coming ordeal.

In order to confirm him more fully in his strong faith, I forewarned him of his coming martyrdom and said, "Stephen, you shall be the first-born of the martyrs engendered by my divine Son and Lord by the example of his death. You shall follow his example, like a privileged disciple, his master, and like a courageous soldier, his captain. At the head of an army of martyrs, you shall carry Jesus' banner of the Cross. Hence, arm yourself with fortitude under the shield of faith, and be assured that the strength of the Most High shall be with you in your final conflict."

This warning inflamed the heart of Stephen with an actual desire of martyrdom. From the beginning Stephen had been filled with grace and fortitude and had wrought great wonders in Jerusalem. He had debated with the great teacher, Gamaliel, and even with Saul, a violent, dedicated, defender of the Jewish faith. The Synagogue of Roman Freedmen; however, was his nemesis. They were a Jewish religious group of Cyrenians, Alexandrines, and people from Cilicia and Asia. Rabbi Agamemnon was their leader and had debated Stephen several times. Stephen's wisdom was so great that he not only won every debate, but at each discussion, he converted some of Agamemnon's followers, which infuriated the vengeful Rabbi. Over the years, they had been unable to overcome his wisdom in public, and failing to murder him at night, Agamemnon resorted to seeking false testimony against him. He accused Stephen of blasphemy against God and against Moses by verbally attacking the Holy Temple and the Law, and of asserting that Jesus would destroy as well the one, as the other.

The false witnesses loudly proclaimed their slander and many people were being aroused by their falsehoods. Agamemnon sought the aid of the Sanhedrin and he plotted with the priests against Stephen. He sought out Stephen and engaged him in debate, hoping to get him to repeat the predictions of Jesus regarding the destruction of the Temple of Jerusalem.

I was informed of what was to happen. To prepare Stephen for his ordeal, I sent one of my angels to him before their debate began. Through the holy angel, Stephen sent me his reply, "I go with joy to confess my Master and with unflinching heart I give my life for him, as I have always desired. I beg you, from your retirement to send me your blessing. That is my only regret, since I have not been able to obtain your parting benediction."

In the meantime, Stephen replied to the Roman Freedmen, "In the one case, Jesus' prophesy was not about the Temple of Jerusalem being rebuilt in three days, but rather the temple of his own body. Jesus prophesied that you Jews would kill him, yet in three days he would rise again from the dead. In the other instance, he prophesied that at some future date the Temple of Jerusalem would not have one stone left upon another for it will be destroyed, because of the sins of the Jews."

Agamemnon roared with anger, "He blasphemes, let us take him to the Sanhedrin." The ugly crowd grabbed Stephen and dragged him before the Sadducees, the Pharisees, the scribes, and the judges of the Sanhedrin. The presiding judge took the deposition of Saint Stephen before the court.

The false witnesses testified and said, "This man never stops saying things against this holy place and the Law. We have heard him claim that this Jesus, the Nazarian, will destroy this place and change the customs of Moses handed down to us."

From the time he was seized, Stephen had a benign look about him and he had been oblivious to their rough handling and physical abuse. All eyes were on him and his handsome face was like the face of an angel [Acts: 6, 8-15].

The judge asked him, "Is this testimony so?"

Stephen stood, looked about him, composed and serene. The charge that Jesus had changed the Law of Moses was not true. Jesus had made his position clear when he said, "I did not come to change the law, but to fulfill it." Stephen had perceived the fuller implications of the teachings of Jesus. Consequently, Stephen's preaching was the first to show the many differences between Judaism and Christianity. To make his position clear on this subject, Stephen was willing to face the wrath of the rabbis and priests of the Pharisees and the Sadducees.

The Deacon was willing to give up his life for the honor and defense of my Son, our Redeemer. I was so moved by Stephen's request for my blessing that I desired to attend upon him in person. I hesitated to go out; the streets were packed with people, and I would have little chance of approaching Stephen to talk to him. I prostrated myself in prayer and asked my Son for his divine favor at this late hour. Jesus sent a multitude of angels, and with those of my own angelic guard, they carried me on a refulgent cloud to where Stephen was being interrogated by the Sanhedrin. The vision of my appearance in the temple was hidden from all except Stephen. He saw me supported in the air by the holy angels in a cloud of heavenly splendor and glory. This extraordinary favor inflamed anew the divine love and the ardent zeal of this champion of the honor of God. In addition to his joy of seeing me, my splendors shone upon his countenance so that it gleamed with wonderful beauty and light. The people seeing this watched and listened to him with rapt attention.

When Stephen spoke he began at the beginning of the Bible. In a long discourse he proved that Jesus had complied with all the words of the prophets concerning the coming of the Messiah, and that the Jews had killed their own Messiah by nailing him to a tree. He then summed up, with his eyes flashing with indignation, "You stiff-necked people, uncircumcised in heart and ears, you always oppose the Holy Spirit; you are just like your ancestors. Which of the Prophets did your ancestors not persecute? They put to death those who foretold the coming of the righteous one, whose betrayers and murderers you have now become. You received the law as transmitted by angels, but you did not observe it [Acts: 7, 51-53]."

The Sanhedrin and the men of the Roman Synagogue were infuriated at his words. They ground their teeth and held their hands over their ears to stop his blasphemous words. Looking up at me, Stephen beheld the heavens behind me open up. He saw the glory of God and Jesus standing at the right hand of God, and he called out, his face radiant with the glory he beheld, "Behold, I see the heavens opened and the Son of Man standing at the right hand of God."

Like enraged beasts the Jews cried out, some holding their hands over their ears and dragged him out of the city to the stoning pit. Stoning was a capital punishment; it was the typical Hebrew execution. It was of great antiquity, and is often mentioned in the Bible. In Deuteronomy it clearly states that it is the punishment to be inflicted by the entire community. The persecuting witnesses and he accusers were to throw the first stones. The tractate Sanhedrin states, which make this punishment, seem a little less barbaric that the condemned person was to be taken to a cliff, the height of two men, and one of the accusers would threw him off the cliff backwards. The fall was intended to stun or even to break the person's back to make the ordeal less painful. It was only then that the first stone could be thrown, and it had to be aimed at his heart. The Law required a posted guard who could call off the execution if the judicial authorities changed their mind. Also at all executions each condemned person was to be given a strong drink made of incense or myrrh dissolved in wine or vinegar. There was even a community of religious women, who made sure that this hypnotic drink was given to the victim.

The furious Jews pushed the religious women aside, and instead of casting him off the edge backwards so that he might fall and stun himself, simply pushed him into the pit. Stephen got to his feet, turned, and fearlessly faced his executioners, displaying invincible courage and his countenance continued to shine like that of an angel. A man by the name of Saul of Tarsus, a vindictive and tireless Pharisee who was persecuting the New Way, stood at the edge of the pit and guarded the coats of the executioners as they piled them at his feet. Stephen had debated Saul to a standstill on several instances, and Saul's heart was steadfastly set against the followers of Christ.

With Stephen standing serenely in the pit, I gave him my final benediction and spoke words to him of encouragement and endearment. I charged my angels with orders to present his soul to my Son in heaven as soon as his ordeal was over.

Thus, from my retirement, by a special vision, I saw all that happened in the martyrdom of Saint Stephen. The Jews were shouting that he was a blasphemer worthy of death. People from all corners of Jerusalem quickly assembled to see what was happening and many of them called out in horror, as Agamemnon picked up a huge stone and threw it with unerring aim to strike Stephen directly in the heart as was required by Hebrew Law. His face blanched and he staggered back from the force of the blow. Then a shower of stones of all sizes rained down upon their innocent victim amid the cries of enraged, bestial men, who were beyond all reason or compassion. Several of the smaller stones imbedded themselves in his skull and Stephen with a benign smile on his face sank to his knees. Blood stained all of his garments and he was bleeding profusely from his face, arms, and chest.

Great and tender was my compassion as I witnessed his cruel martyrdom. However, I was thrilled at seeing Stephen meeting it so calmly and gloriously. I prayed for him constantly and tearfully. When the invincible Stephen saw that he was near death, since the deadly hail of stones never let up for a second, he prayed a silent prayer for Saul, for he was made aware of God's designs for him. Then in a clear, resonant voice, in imitation of his Master, he said, "Lord, receive my Spirit."

Still on his knees, he exclaimed aloud, "Lord, do not hold this sin against them."

In these prayers, I fully supported him. I was filled with incredible joy to see the faithful disciple, the first deacon of the Catholic Church, so closely imitating his divine Master by praying for his enemies and persecutors and commending his spirit into the hands of his Creator and Redeemer.

With this final word, Stephen expired and he fell forward still resting on his knees, for the multitude of rocks thrown fastened him there. Immediately my angels and I bore his pure spirit to the presence of God so that he might be crowned with eternal honor and glory. Stephen was born the same date as my son and likewise died on the same date [Acts: 7, 54-60].

Jesus received him with these words, "Friend, ascend higher; come to me, you faithful servant; for, since you have been faithful in small things, I shall reward you with abundance and I shall confess you before my Father as my faithful servant and friend just as you confessed me before men."

All the angels, Patriarchs, Prophets and all the Saints were filled with a special joy and welcomed the invincible martyr as the first fruits of the Passion of the Lord and as the example of all those that should follow him in martyrdom. Stephen was placed very high in glory and close to the most sacred humanity of Christ our Savior.

I was allowed to participate in all that took place by a special vision. In praise of the Most High, I composed hymns and canticles with my angels. Stephen's feast day is the twenty-sixth day of December. The disciples secured the body of Stephen and buried it with great honor and loud mourning, for the handsome, leader of the new faith was highly loved and respected by many in Jerusalem.

The prayers said by Stephen and me for Saul of Tarsus that day merited his conversion, as I will explain later. However, from this day on Saul signalized and took upon himself the task of persecuting and destroying the Church of God. The wrath of the Jews was highly inflamed with the death of Saint Stephen. The Pharisee scribes unleashed a concerted persecution against the new believers. With the blessing of the Sanhedrin, Saul, in his jealous defense of the Law of Moses accompanied by temple guards broke into the homes of the faithful, arrested, and put them in prison where they were badly abused. They were taken before the magistrates and denounced. If the Christians renounced their new faith they were released, if they refused, they were executed [Acts: 8, 1-3].

Dispersion of the Disciples

Fear gripped the City of God and Christians fled the town and hid among their friends and relatives. The twelve Apostles and I were not arrested, because the Pharisees feared the wrath of the people. We were highly respected and in daily attendance at Temple Services. In spite of the persecution, we fearlessly attended to our daily business. However, the remaining six deacons and many of the disciples were forced to flee the city. There was also a secret cause for the severity of these attacks.

The secret cause was the dismay of Lucifer and his demons; they were much perturbed by the death of Stephen. They began to stir up and excite themselves to diabolical wrath against the faithful, especially against the Church and me. To confuse them even more, the Lord had permitted the demons to see how the angels had carried me to the site of Saint Stephen's persecution and death. Lucifer concluded that I would do the same with other martyrs, who were to die for Christ. They presumed that I would at least aid and encourage them to despise torments or death and meet such persecutions with invincible courage. Lucifer had set his hopes that men loved life so much and had a fear of death and were especially fearful of a painful and violent death that they would fall away from the faith rather than encounter such a fate.

When Lucifer saw Stephen die so fearlessly and gloriously, he called his demons together and said to them, "I am much disturbed by the death of this disciple and by the favors he has received at the hands of the woman our enemy. If she assists the other disciples and followers of her Son, we shall not be able to overcome or mislead any of them by the threat of torments or death. They, on the contrary, will be animated by mutual example to suffer and die like their Master, and instead of succeeding in destroying them, we ourselves shall be overcome and humbled. We shall destroy ourselves by following our present course. We must persuade others to give up their lives in support of my fallacies, just as they do for God. All men will not merit the protection of this invincible woman, or be so courageous as to undergo such inhuman torments as I shall devise. Let us go and excite our friends amidst the Jews, so that they may destroy this cult and blot out from the face of the earth the name of Jesus.

It was not difficult for Lucifer and his demons to sow this cockle in the hearts of the princes and magistrates of the Jews, so many of whom were already so perfidious and ravaged by sins. They filled them with ungoverned fury and envy against the followers of Christ. By his deceitful suggestions, Lucifer inflamed them with a false zeal for the Law of Moses and the ancient traditions. The authorities decided to banish some of the disciples from Jerusalem, others from Palestine, and still others were killed or were forced to flee for their lives. Greedily, they decided to dispossess the believers of their possessions before they could dispose of them and give them to the Apostles. Many disciples fled from Jerusalem. They scattered throughout Judea and Samaria, but began to preach throughout all the land with unfaltering courage.

Deacon Phillip went directly to the city of Sebaste in Samaria. There he proclaimed the message of the Messiah to them. He cleansed many people of unclean spirits and many paralyzed and crippled people were cured. When the news reached Jerusalem that Phillip had baptized hundreds of converts, Simon and John hurried to Sebaste to confirm them in the faith [Acts: 8, 4-23].

Thirty-five and thirty-six AD were perilous times for the Church. When I saw the Church so disturbed, persecuted and afflicted by the fury of the demons and the wrath of the men instigated by them, I turned upon the originators of this evil and imperiously commanded Lucifer and his ministers to descend into hell. They fell howling into the abyss without any power of resistance. There, they remained bound and imprisoned for eight days, until the Lord, according to his own divine plan permitted them to rise. Before the disciples left Jerusalem, I gave them my blessing. In their labors, I comforted and assisted them through my holy angels. I inspired them with courage and had them taken to different localities, whenever necessary. Thus was the case of Phillip. He left Sebaste taking the road to Gaza, and enroute he was called upon by God to baptize an Ethiopian eunuch, a court official of Queen Candace, ruler of the Ethiopians. When he was finished, by the command of God, one of my angels snatched Phillip away from the eunuch and set him on the road to Azotus. Along the way he continued proclaiming the Good News until he reached his objective, the great port city of Caesarea built by Herod the Great [Acts: 8, 26-40].

The cares and labors of the Apostles in this persecution were much greater than those of the other faithful. As the founders and leaders of the Church, it was necessary to extend their care to all inside the city as well at those outside Jerusalem. Although they were full of knowledge and of the gifts of the Holy Ghost, yet the work was arduous and the opposition so powerful that without my counsel and direction they would often have felt dejected and oppressed. Consequently, they frequently consulted me, and I often called them to meetings and conferences, which I arranged for to, transact the necessary business. I alone fully understood the present affairs and foresaw clearly those of the future. I had written in my heart the Evangelical Law and stamped therein the image of the Church. I deeply pondered within myself all that concerned it; and the trials and tribulations of its members. In my conferences with the Lord, I sought to dispose and order all its affairs with heavenly knowledge and insight according to the holy will of the Most High. In all things, I was a faithful copy of my divine Son.

The Assignments of the Apostles

In order to consult the will of God in the Assignments of the kingdoms and provinces in which each Apostle was to preach, the Apostles, upon my advice, resolved to fast and pray for ten successive days. This practice to fast and pray for ten days had been observed right after the Ascension for disposing themselves for the coming of the Holy Ghost and would be continued for the more important decisions to be made. Then Peter held a Church Service and after partaking of the body and blood of our Redeemer, we ardently invoked the assistance of the Holy Ghost for the manifestations of his will in this matter.

Then the twelve Apostles uttered aloud the following prayer, "Most high and eternal God, we are your least and insignificant servants, whom the Lord Jesus Christ condescended to choose as his ministers, to act as founders of his holy Church, and to preach his holy doctrine and law. With one heart and soul, we offer ourselves to suffer and die for the confession and spread of the holy faith in the world, according to the commands of our Lord and Master Jesus Christ. We wish to be spared no labors, difficulties or tribulations in the performance of this work, even unto death. However, distrusting our weakness, we beseech you, Lord God most high, send your divine Spirit to govern and direct our footsteps in the imitation of our Master and to visit us with his strength. Do you manifest and instruct us to which kingdoms and provinces each of us shall depart according to your good pleasure for the preaching of your holy name?"

Suddenly a wonderful light descended upon the Cenacle surrounding them all and a voice was heard saying, "My Vicar Peter shall point out the province which falls to each one. I shall govern and direct him by my light and spirit."

The appointments were left to Peter in order to confirm anew his power as head and universal pastor of the Church. The Apostles thoroughly understood that it was by the will of the Almighty, that the Church was to be founded throughout the world under the direction of Saint Peter and his successors, to whom they were to be subject as the Vicars of Christ. Saint Peter in obedience proceeded to partition out the provinces.

He began with himself, and said, "I, my Lord, offer myself to suffer and die in imitation of my Lord and Redeemer. I will preach the faith at present in Jerusalem, and afterwards in Pontus, Galatia, Bythinia, Cappadocia, and provinces of Asia. I shall take up my residence at first in Antioch and afterwards in Rome, where I will establish my seat, and found the Cathedra of Christ our Redeemer and Master. There, the head of the Church shall have his residence."

Peter spoke these words in obedience to a positive command of the Lord, pointing out that Rome was to be the center of the Universal Church. Peter then continued, "Andrew, the servant of Christ, will follow his Master preaching his faith in the Scythian provinces of Europe, Epirus, and Thrace. He will govern all of that province and others of his lot from the city of Patras in Achaia."

"The servant of Christ, our dearest brother James [the greater], will follow his Master preaching the faith in Judea, in Samaria, and in Spain. From there he shall return to Jerusalem to preach the doctrine of our Lord Jesus Christ."

"John, our most dear brother, shall obey the will of our Savior as made known to him from the Cross, discharging the duties of a son toward our great Mother and Mistress. He shall serve her and assist her with filial reverence and fidelity. He shall administer to her the sacred mysteries of the Eucharist and in addition take care of the faithful in Jerusalem during our absence. When our Lord and Master shall have taken his most blessed mother into heaven, he shall follow his Master in the preaching of the faith in Asia Minor. He shall govern the Churches established from the Island of Patmos; whither he shall retire on account of persecution."

"The servant of Christ, our dearest brother Thomas, will follow his Master preaching in India, in Persia and among the Parthians, Medes, Hircanians, Brahmans, and Bactians. He shall baptize the three Magi Kings and as they shall be attracted by the rumor of his preaching and his miracles, he shall instruct them fully in all things according to their expectations."

"Our dearest brother James [the less], the servant of Christ, shall follow his Master in his office as pastor and bishop of Jerusalem, where he shall preach to all the Jews and shall assist John in the attendance and service of the great mother of our Savior."

"The servant of Christ, our dearest brother Philip, shall follow his Master preaching and teaching in the provinces of Phrygia and Scythia of Asia and in the city called Hieropolis in Phyrgia."

"Our dearest brother Bartholomew shall follow his Master preaching in Lycaonia, part of Cappadocia in Asia; and he shall go to far off India and afterwards to Armenia Minor."

"The servant of Christ, our dearest brother Matthew, shall first teach the Hebrews, and then shall follow his Master, preaching in Egypt and Ethiopia."

"The servant of Christ, our dearest brother Simon, shall follow his Master, preaching in Babylon, Persia and also in the kingdom of Ethiopia."

"Our dearest brother Judas Thaddeus, the servant of Christ, shall follow his Master, preaching in Mesopotamia, and afterwards shall join Simon to preach in Babylon and in Persia."

"The servant of Christ, our dearest brother Mathias, shall follow our Master, preaching his holy faith in the interior of Ethiopia and in Arabia, and afterwards he shall return to Palestine. And may the Spirit of God accompany us all, govern and assist us, so that in all places we fulfill his holy and perfect will, and may he give us his benediction, in whose name I now give it to all."

When Peter finished speaking a roll of loud thunder was heard and the Cenacle was filled with splendor and refulgence in witness of the presence of the Holy Ghost. From the midst of this splendor was heard a sweet and soft voice saying,

"Let each one accept his allotment."

The Apostles and I prostrated ourselves upon the ground and with one voice said, "Most High, Lord, your word and the word of your Vicar we obey with a prompt and joyous heart and our souls rejoice and are filled with sweetness in the abundance of your wonderful works."

This entire and ready obedience of the Apostles to the Vicar of Christ our Savior, since it was the effect of their ardent and loving desire to die for his holy faith, disposed them on that occasion for the grace of once more receiving the Holy Ghost. He confirmed and augmented the favors they had already received. They were all filled with a new light and knowledge concerning the peoples and provinces assigned to them by Saint Peter. Each one recognized the conditions, nature and customs of the kingdoms singled out for him, being furnished interiorly with the most distinct and abundant information, concerning each assignment. The Most High gave them new fortitude to encounter labors, and agility for overcoming distances. They were frequently assisted by my holy angels; and the fire of divine love, so that they became inflamed like seraphim lifted far beyond the condition and sphere of mere human creatures.

I experienced more of the divine influences than all of the Apostles put together. I was exalted supereminently above all creatures, so the increase of my gifts was in like proportion, transcending immeasurably those of the others. The Most High renewed in me the infused knowledge concerning all creatures, and especially concerning the kingdoms and nations assigned to the Apostles. I received a personal and individual knowledge of each person to whom the faith of Christ was to be preached. At the same time, I was made just as familiar with all the earth and its inhabitants, as I was with my own oratory and all those that entered therein. My knowledge was that of supreme Mistress, Mother, Governess and Sovereign of the Church, which the Almighty had placed in my hands. I was to take care of them all, from the highest to the lowest of the saints, as well as all the sinners of the children of Eve. Since Jesus had decreed that no one was to receive any blessing or favor from the hands of my Son except through my own hands, it was necessary that I should know all of my family, whom I was to guard as a mother. I not only had the infused images and knowledge of all this, but I actually experienced it accordingly, as the disciples and Apostles proceeded in their work of preaching. Before me lay, like an open book, all their labors and dangers, and the attacks of the demons against them. I heard all the petitions and prayers of the faithful, so that I was able to support them with my own prayers or aid them through my angels or by myself in person.

Besides the knowledge derived from infused images, I had another knowledge obtained from my Abstractive Vision, by which I continually saw the Divinity. However, there was a difference between these two different kinds of knowledge. When I saw in God the labors of the Apostles and of all the faithful of the Church, enjoying at the same time through this vision a certain participation of the Eternal Beatitude, I was not affected with the sensible sorrow and compassion, which filled me when perceiving these tribulations themselves through earthly images. In the images, I felt and bewailed them with maternal compassion. At the same time, I had absolute command of my faculties, so that I admitted no images or ideas except those that were necessary for sustaining life, or for some work of charity or perfection.

On this occasion, I offered a profound prayer for the perseverance and courage of the Apostles in their preaching throughout the world. The Lord promised me that he would guard and assist them to manifest the glory of his name and that he would at the end worthily reward them for their labors and merits. I was bursting with happiness, and I exhorted the Apostles to give themselves up to this work with all their hearts, to set out joyfully and confidently for the conversion of the world. I congratulated each of them on my knees in the name of my divine Son for the obedience they had shown, and I thanked them for the zeal they had manifested for the honor of the Lord and for the blessings they had brought to souls by their sacrifice. I kissed the hands of each of the Apostles, offering them my prayers and services, and asked for their blessing, which they, as priests of God, gave me. A few days after the partition of the earth among the Apostles, they began to leave.

Jerusalem, especially those that were allotted the provinces of Palestine and first among them was Saint James the greater. Others stayed longer in Jerusalem, because the Lord wished the faith to be preached there more abundantly and the Jews to be called before all the others, if they chose to come and accept the invitation of the marriage-feast of the Gospel. In the blessings of the Redemption, this people, although more ungrateful than the heathen, was especially favored. Afterwards all the Apostles gradually departed for the regions assigned to them. For each of the twelve, I made a woven tunic of a color between brown and ash-gray, similar to that of my Son. In order to weave these garments, I called my holy angels to aid me, and I gave each of the Apostles a garment. In addition I had twelve crosses made of the same height and size of each of the Apostles and gave one to each, so that, as a witness of their doctrine and for their consolation, they might carry it along in the wanderings and their preaching. Each of the Apostles preserved and carried this cross with him to his death. Some were so loud in its praise that some tyrants made use of this same type of instrument to torment them happily to death.

In addition, I furnished each one of them with a small silver case, in which I placed three of the thorns from the crown of my divine Son. I included some pieces of the cloths in which I had wrapped the infant Savior, and of the linen with which I had wiped and caught the most precious blood of the circumcision and Passion of the Lord. The Apostles received them with tears of consolation and joy. They then prostrated themselves before the sacred relics and thanked me for these favors.

The Apostles were to preach not only in the areas assigned them, but in many other neighboring and more remote regions. This is not difficult to understand, because many times they were carried from one country to another by the angels, not only in order to preach, but in order to consult with each other, especially with Peter, the Vicar of Christ. Even more frequently, they were brought into my presence, for they needed my sympathy and counsel in the arduous enterprise of planting the faith in so many different and barbarous nations. If, in order to bring nourishment to Daniel, the angel took Habbacuc to Babylon [Dan: 14, 35-39], it is nothing strange that such miracles, through God, should be performed by the Apostles. The miracles attracted the people, so that the Apostles and disciples might preach Christ, make known the Divinity, and plant the Universal Church for the salvation of the human race. Above, I mentioned the angel who carried Phillip, one of the seven original deacons, from the road to Gaza to Azotus, as related by Saint Luke [Acts: 8, 40]. All these miracles and innumerable others, unknown to you, were necessary to these men, because they were sent to so many kingdoms, provinces, and peoples yet in possession of the devil. These places were full of idolatries; errors, and abominations, which was the condition of the world at the time the Incarnate Word came to save the human race.

The Conversion of Paul

I was once a blasphemer and a persecutor and an arrogant man, but I have been mercifully treated because I acted out of ignorance in my unbelief [Tim: 1, 13].

Saul of Tarsus was distinguished in Judaism for two reasons. The one was his own character, and the other was the diligence of the demon in availing himself of his naturally good qualities. Saint Paul was of a disposition generous, magnanimous, most noble, kind, active, courageous and constant. He had acquired many of the moral virtues. He glorified in being a staunch professor of the Law of Moses, and in being studious and learned in it. Although in truth, he was ignorant of its essence, as he himself confesses to Timothy, because all his learning was human and terrestrial. Like many Jews, he knew the Law merely from the outside, without its spirit and without the divine insight, which was necessary to understand it rightly and to penetrate its mysteries. However, as his ignorance seemed to him real knowledge, and as he was gifted with a retentive memory and keen understanding, he was a great zealot for the traditions of the rabbis. He judged it an outrage and absurdity, that a new law, invented by a man crucified as a criminal, should be published in opposition to the Law of Moses, a Law given by God himself and received by Moses on Mount Sinai. Hence, Saul conceived a great hatred and contempt for Christ, his law, and his disciples. Steeped in this error he called into activity all his moral virtues [if that can be called virtue which was devoid of true charity], and prided himself much in combating the errors of others. This is a common fault with the children of Adam that they please themselves in some good work without making the much more important effort to reform some of their own vices.

In this self-deception lived and acted Saul, deeply convinced that he was zealously promoting the honor of God in upholding the ancient Law of Moses and its divine ordainments. It appeared to him that in acting thus, he was defending God's honor. For Saul had not really understood this law, which in its ceremonies and figures was but temporal and not eternal and as Moses himself foretold [Deut: 18, 15], was to be abrogated by a more wise and powerful legislator. Thus, as I stated before, Saul, with the blessings and help of the Sanhedrin, persecuted the followers of my Son throughout Jerusalem. The deacons and the disciples were among the first to flee, for they were high on the list of those 'most wanted' by the Jews. Saul was like a man possessed in his zeal to exterminate the cult of Christ and no baptized person was safe from his wrath. Many were arrested, tried, and some were even executed when they refused to denounce the Christ.

This indiscreet zeal and vehemence of Saul was fanned by the malice of Lucifer and his demons, which irritated and roused him to even greater hatred against the Law of our Savior Jesus Christ. In the course of this history, I have many times mentioned the malicious attempts and infernal schemes of the dragon against the holy Church. Among the demons was an anxious search for men who would serve as apt and efficient instruments and executors of their malice. Lucifer and his demons, although they are able to tempt men singly, are unable to rise up their rebellious banners in public or become leaders in any sect or sedition against God, unless it is through the assistance of some human being in leading on the blind and unenlightened. Lucifer recognized the inclinations of Saul, his habits and the state of his interior, and all seemed to harmonize well with his own designs of destroying the Church of Christ through the willing hands of unbelievers.

Lucifer consulted with the other demons concerning this wicked plan in a meeting held especially for this purpose. With common accord, they resolved to ceaselessly urge Saul by stirring up his anger against the Apostles and the followers of my Son. They represented his indignation as a virtue to be gloried in. Although Saul was dissatisfied and opposed to the teaching of my Son even before his death on the Cross; yet he had not then declared himself so zealous a defender of the Law of Moses and adversary of the Lord. It was only at the death of Saint Stephen that he showed the wrath, which the infernal dragon had roused against the followers of Christ. Emboldened by his success with Saul, Lucifer tried to induce him to single-handedly take the life of all the Apostles and even to take my own life. However, the disposition of Saul was most noble and generous, and therefore it appeared to him beneath his dignity and honor to stoop to such crimes and act the part of an assassin. It seemed to him to him to be more proper to destroy the Law of Christ by the power of reasoning and open justice. He felt a greater horror at the thought of killing me, on account of his regard for me as a woman, and because he had seen me composed and constant in the labors and in the Passion of my Son. He considered me a magnanimous woman and worthy of veneration. I had won his respect together with some compassion for my sorrows and afflictions; the magnitude of which had become public knowledge. His compassion for me, and his natural resistance to the thoughts of the demons, hastened his conversion. Rejecting all the wicked thoughts of the demons, Saul resolved to incite all the Jews to persecute the Church until it should be destroyed together with the name of my Son.

With all their evil, the demons were unable to hinder the work of grace, when God so wished it. The demons never suspected that Saul would ever accept the faith of Christ, and that the life, which they were trying to preserve and lengthen, was to rebound to their own ruin and torment. Such events were provided by the wisdom of the Most High, in order that the devil, being deceived by his evil counsels, might fall into his own pits and snares. Such were the decrees of the Highest Wisdom in order that the conversion of Saul might be more wonderful and glorious. With this intention, God permitted Saul to go to the chief priest with fierce threats against the Disciples of Christ, who had left Jerusalem, and to solicit permission for bringing them back as prisoners. For this enterprise, Saul offered his person and possessions, and even his life; at his own cost and without salary. The Sanhedrin immediately gave Saul a commission to go to Damascus, where, according to report, some of the disciples were preaching. He prepared for the journey, hiring officers of justice and some soldiers to accompany him. However, his most numerous escorts were the legions of demons, who in order to assist him in this enterprise poured forth from hell. The demons hoped through Saul, they might be able to make an end of the Church, and entirely devastate it through blood and fire. With great determination and misplaced zeal, Saul, with his entourage of evil, set out for Damascus.

The Apostles kept me well informed of these events, and of course by my gift of vision, I knew all that was to transpire. Saul was to become a powerful Apostle of my Son, and a man wonderful and distinguished in the Church. However, Saul's persistent persecution had discouraged many of the disciples. I was filled with great sorrow; concerned for the welfare of the Church and for the conversion of Saul.

I prostrated myself before my Son, and I poured forth the following prayer, "Most high, Lord, Son of the eternal Father, how shall I your slave, live, if the persecution of the beloved Church you have commended to my care shall prevail and be not put down? How shall my heart behold the fruit of your precious blood despised and trodden under foot? You my, Lord, have given to me the children begotten by you in the Church. If I am to love them and look upon them as a mother, how shall I be consoled when I see them thus oppressed and destroyed for confessing your holy name and loving you with a sincere heart? My, Son, confound the pride of this ancient serpent, which in its pride again rises up to vent its fury against the simple sheep of your flock. Behold how Lucifer has drawn into his deceits Saul, whom you have chosen and set apart as your Apostle. It is time, oh my, God that you show your Omnipotence and save this soul, through whom and in whom your name is to be so highly exalted and so much good to be secured for the world."

In his infinite wisdom, my Son had foreseen my meditation. He descended from Heaven and said to me, "My beloved, mother, in whom I find the fulfillment of all my will and pleasure, what are your requests?"

As usual I lay prostrate in the presence of my divine Son, and adored him as the true God, and then replied, "My highest, Lord, far in advance do you know the hearts and the thoughts of your creatures, and my desires are open to your eyes. I ask oh my, Son that you look upon the affliction of your Church, and that like a loving Father you hasten the relief of your children engendered by your most precious blood. You did choose Paul as your Apostle and I do not ask anything that you yourself have not resolved beforehand. However, I grieve my, Son that any further delay to his conversion would be a hindrance to the glory of your name; to the joy of your angels and saints, to the consolation of the just, and to the confusion of your enemies."

My Son delighted in hearing me ask for his favors and he acted as if he were ignorant of what I desired and asked me many questions. Finally, I said to him, "Do not then my, Son and Lord, despise the prayers of your mother. Let your divine decrees be executed and let me see your name magnified; for the time and occasion are opportune and my heart cannot suffer such a blessing to be delayed."

As I made my appeal for charity, my bosom broke into such a flame that without a doubt it would have taken my natural life, if the Lord had not preserved me by his miraculous power. He permitted me to suffer the pangs of love in order to enjoy my excessive love for him. I went into a swoon; he then consoled and restored me, and granted my request saying, "My, mother, chosen from among all creatures, let your will be done without delay. I will do with Saul as you ask. It will so change him that from this moment he will be a defender of the Church, which he persecutes, and he will be a great preacher in my name and glory. I shall now proceed to receive him into my friendship and grace."

Thereupon Jesus disappeared from my presence, and I continued my prayers with a clear insight of what was to happen. Saul was well on his way to Damascus when my Son appeared to him as a resplendent cloud. At the same time, Saul was flooded with divine light without and within. His heart and senses were overwhelmed beyond power of resistance. He was suddenly struck from his horse and at the same time, he heard a voice from on high saying,

"Saul, Saul, why do you persecute me?"

Full of fear and consternation he answered, "Who are you, Sir?"

The voice replied, "I am Jesus whom you are persecuting."

Saul replied with greater fear and trembling, "Lord, what do you desire of me?"

The Lord answered, "Get up and go into the city and you will be told what you must do."

Saul's companions saw the splendor surrounding Saul and heard the voice, and they were filled with dread and astonishment [Acts: 9, 3-9].

This miraculous event was far more reaching than what could be taken in by the senses. For Saul was prostrated in body, and was blinded and bereft of his strength. He would have expired if the divine power had not sustained him; Saul suffered more of a change interiorly than when he passed from nothingness into existence at his conception. For Saul was changed from an image of the demon to that of one of the highest and most ardent seraphim. God, through his divine Wisdom and Omnipotence, had especially held in reserve this triumph over Lucifer and his demons.

Thus, it happened that in the same short time, in which Lucifer through pride was changed from an angel to a devil, the power of Christ changed Saul from a demon into an angel. Losing grace, Lucifer, as the enemy of God plunged from heaven into the deepest abyss of the earth. Saul, given grace, ascended as a friend of God from the Earth to the highest Heaven. The Lord gave Saul more than Lucifer had lost, making his triumph more glorious. For Lucifer, although he fell from that exceedingly high grace, which he had received, had never possessed Beatific Vision, nor had he made himself worthy of it; hence, he could not lose what he did not possess. However, Saul on disposing himself for justification and on gaining grace, began to partake of glory and clearly saw the Divinity, though this vision was gradual.

During the time in which Saul lay prostrate upon the earth, he was entirely renewed by sanctifying grace and other infused gifts, restored and illumined proportionately in all his interior faculties, and thus, he was prepared to be elevated to the Empyrean Heaven, which is called the third heaven. There, by more than ordinary vision, though in a transient manner, he saw the Divinity clearly and intuitively. He recognized the mystery of the Incarnation and Redemption, and all the secrets of the law of grace and of the state of the Church. He saw the peerless blessing of his justification and of the prayer of Saint Stephen for him. Still more clearly, he was made aware of how his conversion had been hastened by my prayers; and my merits had made him acceptable in the sight of God.

From that hour on he was filled with gratitude and with deepest veneration and devotion to me, as the Queen of Heaven. At the same time he recognized the office of Apostle to which he was called, and that in it he was to labor, suffer and die. In conjunction with these mysteries were revealed to him many others, of which he himself says that they are not to be disclosed. He offered himself in sacrifice to the will of God in all things, as he later demonstrated repeatedly in the course of his life. The most blessed Trinity accepted this sacrifice and offering of his lips, and in the presence of the whole court of Heaven named him Paul and designated him as the preacher and teacher of the Gentiles to carry the name of the Most High throughout the world.

Saul came out of his rapture changed into Paul; rising from the ground he found that he was blind and could not even see the light of the sun. His companions brought him to Damascus to the house of his acquaintances and there to the admiration of all, he remained three days without eating or drinking engaged in earnest prayer saying,

"Woe is me, in what darkness and blindness have I lived, and how far have I hastened on the way of eternal perdition? Oh infinite sweetness of the eternal bounty, who, oh my, Lord and God has induced you to act thus toward me, the vile worm of the earth, your enemy and blasphemer, except yourself and your mother. In blindness and darkness I persecuted you, my most kind Lord, you came to meet me while I was busy shedding innocent blood, which shall always cry out against me. You, the God of mercies, did wash and purify me and make me a partaker of your ineffable Divinity. How shall I praise eternally such unheard of mercies? How shall I sufficiently bewail a life so hateful in your eyes? I shall preach your holy name and shall defend it in the midst of your enemies."

On the third day after the conversion of Saul, the Lord spoke in a vision to Ananias, one of his disciples who lived in Damascus. The Lord directed him to the house of a man named Judas and there he found Saul of Tarsus engaged in prayer. Saul also had a vision and knew that Ananias was to come and restore his sight. Ananias not knowing of Saul's conversion said to the Lord, "Lord, I have information of this man having persecuted your saints and caused a great slaughter of them in Jerusalem. Not satisfied with that, he has now come bearing warrants from the high priests in order to seize whomever he can find invoking your holy name. Do you then send a simple sheep like me to go in search of the wolf that desires to devour it?"

The Lord replied, "Go, for the one you judge to be your enemy, is for me a trumpet that will herald my name before Gentiles, kings, and Israelites. I shall assign to him what he is to suffer for my name." The Lord then told him all that had taken place. Trusting in the Lord, Ananias obeyed and went to the house of Judas.

He found Saul in prayer as the Lord had said and he said to him, "Brother Saul, our Lord Jesus, who appeared to you on your journey, has sent me in order that you may receive your sight and be filled with the Holy Ghost."

Saul was baptized and received Holy Communion at the hands of Ananias and was strengthened and made whole, giving thanks to the author of all these blessings. Then Saul ate for he had not eaten in three days. He remained for some time in Damascus, conferring and conversing with the disciples in that city. He prostrated himself at their feet and asked for their forgiveness and to receive him as their servant and brother. At their approval and counsel, he went forth publicly to preach Christ as the Messiah and Redeemer of the world. He spoke with such fervor, wisdom and zeal that he brought confusion to the unbelieving Jews in the numerous synagogues of Damascus. All wondered at this unexpected change, and the Jews plotted to take away his life [Acts: 9, 10-19].

All that happened to Saul, now to be called Paul, was known to me. This, according to my Son, was only proper and due to me, because I was the mother of the Lord and of his holy Church. It was proper that this important event be celebrated by the whole human race. I invited all my holy angels and many others from heaven, who formed into alternate choirs, to sing with me the canticles I composed of praise in exaltation of the power, wisdom and liberal mercy of the Almighty toward Paul.

Paul in the meantime, not knowing that I was aware of all that took place, began to be concerned about what I might think of him. 'She must think of me as an enemy and persecutor if her most holy Son and his disciples intent on the destruction of the Church,' he thought. Paul was now a humble man; through my Son he had developed a sincere veneration for me as the mother of Jesus. With his newly acquired knowledge, he recognized in me a most kind helper in his conversion and salvation. Yet, the wickedness of his past life humiliated and somewhat frightened him, as one unworthy of such a favor. It seemed to him that for the pardoning of his grave sins an infinite mercy was necessary, and I was a mere creature. On the other hand, he reasoned, I had in imitation of my Son, pardoned his executioners. The disciples also told him that I was kind and sweet to all sinners. Paul was suddenly inflamed with the ardent desire of seeing me; he resolved in his mind to throw himself at my feet and kiss the ground I walked upon. However, he was overcome with shame at the thought of appearing before me, the mother of Jesus.

Amid these disquieting thoughts, the Lord permitted Paul to suffer a harrowing, yet sweet sorrow. Paul finally said to himself, "Take heart vile and sinful man, for without a doubt she will receive and pardon me. She will act as the mother of her Son, and both of them are all mercy and kindness, she will not despise a contrite and humble heart."

These thoughts were not hidden from me, but I also knew that Paul would not find an occasion to see me for a long time. I did not wish his consolation to be postponed for so long a time. Therefore I instructed one of my angels saying, "Heavenly Spirit, I beg you, go to Damascus and console and comfort Paul in his fears. Congratulate him on his good fortune and remind him of the thanks he owes eternally to my Son. Advise him that never has such mercy been shown to any man, as to him. Tell him for me that I shall aid him as a mother in all his labors and serve him as the handmaid of all the Apostles and ministers of the name and doctrine of my Son. Give him my blessing in the name of my son.

The holy angel appeared before Saint Paul the day after his baptism. The angel manifested himself in human form, wonderfully beautiful and resplendent, and fulfilled all my requests. Paul listened with incomparable humility and replied, "Minister of the omnipotent and eternal God, I am the most vile of men, and I beseech you to give thanks and praise to the Lord for having so undeservedly marked me with the character and divine light of his children. The more I flew from his immense bounty, the more he followed me and advanced to meet me. When I delivered myself over to death, he gave me life; when I persecuted him as an enemy, he raised me to his grace and friendship. He recompensed the greatest injuries with the most extraordinary blessings. No one ever rendered himself as hateful and abominable as I; yet no one was so freely pardoned and favored, help me to be eternally grateful. Please tell the Mother of Mercy that I lie prostrate at her feet adoring the ground on which they tread. With a contrite heart, I ask her pardon for having so daringly sought to destroy the honor and name of her Son and Lord. I am deserving of chastisement and retribution for so many sins, and I am prepared to suffer all. I am aware of her clemency of heart, and I desire her favor and protection. Let her accept me as a child of the Church, which she loves so much. All the days of my life, I shall devote myself entirely to its increase and defense. I pledge to serve her, whom I recognize as my salvation and as the Mother of Grace."

When the holy angel reported to me Paul's answer, I heard it with especial joy and again gave thanks and praise to the Most High. I thanked him for the works of his divine right hand in the new Apostle Saint Paul, and for the benefits which would result to his holy Church and the faithful. God then showed me in a vision, the coming sufferings of its early saints and martyrs. The Lord explained to me that it was not possible to grant my request, in spite of my prayers and my intense desire to take upon my shoulders all that the first Christians would suffer. In the plan of the Divine Providence, it was necessary that those holy martyrs should have such opportunities to earn their eternal reward and to advance the cause of the Church by their example.

I was given to understand that through my own compassion and sorrow at seeing the sufferings of the Apostles and followers of Christ, I would compensate myself for not being allowed to take upon myself their sufferings as I had desired. To afford me an opportunity for this kind of suffering, I was informed of the near death of Saint James and the imprisonment of Saint Peter. I understood also that the Lord portioned out to the Apostles and the faithful that kind of suffering or martyrdom, which corresponded with each one's grace and strength of soul. Later, I described to Peter and John the conversion of Saul, and at the same time I warned them that all the followers of Jesus Christ would soon have to suffer cruel persecution at the hands of the enemies of his Church.

Saint James was farther away than the other Apostles. He was the first of the twelve to leave Jerusalem, after having preached some days in Judea, he had then departed for Spain. Five months before the conversion of Saul, James had sailed from Joppa, which is now called Jaffa, touched down at Sardinia, and shortly afterwards arrived in Spain. He disembarked at Carthaginian, and guided by the spirit of the Lord, made his way to Granada. There he found the harvest of souls bountiful and the opportune occasion for beginning his labors for his Master.

Before I go farther, I must tell you that James was one of the most intimate and beloved disciples of mine. James was related to me, as was Saint John, his brother. I never expressed my feelings for him, for I was most prudent and impartial in all my dealings with the Apostles. Since John had been named as my son, the entire Apostolic College knew that the Lord had appointed him; therefore, I was not under any restrictions in regard to exterior tokens of love with Saint John, as I was with the rest of the Apostles. Interiorly I loved Saint James with special tenderness, and I manifested this love in extraordinary favors conferred upon him during his life until his martyrdom. He deserved these favors, because of his special piety and affection toward me, as the Mother of God. His love distinguished him above all the rest. He needed my protection. James had a magnanimous heart and a most fervent spirit, because of which, he volunteered for difficult and dangerous assignments. Hence, he was the first one to go forth preaching the faith, and the first of all the Apostles to be martyred. While on his missionary journeys, he was like the 'Son of Thunder,' as he was called by his fellow Apostles.

During his labors in Spain, the demons raised up incredible persecutions through the unbelieving Jews, as they also did in Italy and Asia Minor and all the distant countries in which he traveled in the few years before his martyrdom. I watched over him with an especial love, and through my angels, I defended and rescued him from many dangers. I consoled and comforted him, sending him information and advice that he needed more often than the other Apostles during his short life. Many times my Son sent his angels from Heaven to defend his great Apostle and to carry him from one region to another during his missionary travels. I personally visited James twice, once in Granada and once in Saragossa.

While in Granada, the Jews had established some synagogues, maintained since the time of their first coming from Palestine to Spain. The people there were aware of Christ, and although some of them were sympathetic to his doctrine, the majority influenced by the demons, did not believe and would not permit him to speak with the Jews or the heathens. They accused James of being an adventurer, a deceiver, the author of false sects, and a legerdemain and enchanter. James brought twelve disciples with him, in imitation of his Master. When they preached the Gospel, the Jews wished to kill them all and later did kill one of the disciples. The disciples did not fear the Jews and their followers increased rapidly. The Jews seized them all, and bound and led them beyond the city walls. Once there they chained their feet, for they considered them sorcerers who might otherwise escape.

As their enemies prepared to decapitate them, James called upon the Most High and me, praying as follows, "Most holy, Mary, mother of my Lord and Redeemer Jesus Christ, extend your favor in this hour to your humble servant. Pray for us, sweetest and kindest of mothers. If it is the will of the Most High that we die here, do you ask oh, lady that my soul may be received in his presence. Receive in sacrifice my resignation to my misfortune of not seeing you. If this is to be the last day of my life, Oh, Mary! Oh, Mary!"

With my gift of vision, I saw and heard all, and I was moved with compassion. I did not ask the Lord to take me to where the disciples were, because my prudence and humility prevented me from making such a petition. In asking for such miracles, as long as I lived in the flesh, I exercised the highest discretion and restraint, always subjecting my desires to the will of God. However, my Son, knowing my every thought, commanded the thousand angels of my guard to assist me. They all manifested themselves to me in human form and placing me on a throne made of a beautiful cloud, they carried me to the field in Spain where the disciples were being held. James alone was privileged to see me in the sky, and I spoke to him in most endearing terms saying,

"James my, son and dearest friend of my Lord Jesus Christ, be of good heart and be blessed eternally by him who called and brought you to his divine light. Rise then, faithful servant of the Most High, and be free of your bonds."

The fetters of James and his disciples fell away. God struck the Jewish guards to the earth, where, deprived of their senses, they remained for some hours. The demons, who had accompanied them and stirred them up, were hurled into the profound abyss, thus leaving James and his disciples free of their demonic deviltry. James informed his disciples of the miracle that had taken place, so they could give proper thanks. They gave thanks and sang praises to God and me for this blessing.

During this period, 37 AD, Pontius Pilate was relieved of his duties, because he suppressed a supposed armed uprising by a group of Samaritans who had assembled at their shrine on Mount Gerizim. They had gathered to search for the holy vessels of Moses, reputedly buried there. At the time, there was much unrest and turmoil throughout Judea and Samaria. Pilate ordered the pilgrims ambushed, and many were killed and others were later executed. There was an outcry against Pontius Pilate to the legate of Syria, who suspended Pilot from his office. In 39 AD the new Caesar, Caligula, exiled him to Vienna-on-Rhone. There he committed suicide, as was the custom among Roman aristocrats convicted of a crime.

Having freed James with God's blessings, I ordered him to continue his journeys, for I wished all Spain to benefit from his preaching and instruction. I commanded hundreds of my angels to accompany him and show him the way from one place to another. They defended him and his disciples from all dangers, and they toured many parts of Andalusia. Then he went to Toledo, Portugal, Galicia and Asturia. From there he arrived at Rioja, thence passing through Lograno and Tudela. Thus, after having traveled all the provinces of Spain, I ordered, my angels take him back to Saragossa. James had left some of his disciples in Granada, who afterwards suffered martyrdom. During his missionary journey, James left disciples as bishops in the different cities of Spain, planting the faith and divine worship. So great and prodigious were the miracles he performed in this kingdom that those of which you know would not appear extraordinary in comparison. The fruit of Jame's preaching in Spain was immense in proportion to the shortness of his stay. In all the places reached by him, he established the faith and ordained many bishops for the government of the children he produced for Christ in this kingdom.

My Journey to Ephesus and some events reported out of Continuity.

Lucifer, after the death of Saint Stephen, incited his demons against the Church forcing the disciples to flee Jerusalem, which began the spread of the Word of my Son. Later, after the conversion of Saint Paul, I plunged the demons back into hell. But according to God's plan, the demons were again unleashed to tempt and try men's souls. Divine Providence at times gives the demons this permission, and at other times he withdraws it. Consequently, the primitive Church sometimes enjoyed peace and tranquility, at other times, when the truce was again broken, it was molested and afflicted; and this has become the lot of the Church in all ages.

When Lucifer returned from Hell, he was in a raging fury. He brought two thirds of his demons with him, leaving the rest to torture the damned spirits. The Most High has never permitted full sway to the demon's envy, for in one moment they would overturn and destroy the whole world. However, he gave them limited freedom, in order that by affliction the Church might root itself in the blood and the merits of the saints. Through persecution and torments, the Holy One wisely directed his little ship the Church. Upon resurfacing, Lucifer commanded his black spirits to scour the entire Earth and found that the Apostles and the disciples were concentrating their main efforts in Jerusalem. It was God's intention, as he had promised that the chosen people of God were to be the ones first called. Satan set up his seat of authority in Jerusalem in order to direct the operations against the very stronghold of faith.

In Jerusalem, the dragon and his associates avoided the spots consecrated by the blood of the Lord during his Passion. I assigned an angel to each Station of the Cross, to guard and defend them. I charged each guard to resist Lucifer and his demons, lest they destroy or profane by irreverence those sacred spots, as they intended to do through the unbelieving Jews. I told them to drive away by holy inspirations the bad thoughts and diabolical suggestions, by which the infernal dragon sought to excite the Jews and other mortals to blot out the memory of Christ in these holy places. I assigned them this duty until the end of man's tenure on Earth, since the wrath of the evil spirits against the places and the works of the Redemption will endure through all the ages.

Saint John attended upon me with the watchful devotion of a son. The slightest change in my appearance could not remain concealed for long from his discerning eye. Noting that I seemed forsaken and alone, he became quite concerned and prayed to my Son,

"My, Lord and, God, I acknowledge my indebtedness to you for having given me your mother as my own. Through this blessing, I am made rich and prosperous in the possession of the greatest treasure of Heaven and Earth. However, without your royal presence, my mistress is sad and distressed, and for it neither men nor angels can compensate, much less me a lowly worm and a slave. I desire to console her and alleviate her grief, but I find myself incapable of doing it. Reason and love urge me on; but reverence and my frailty prohibit it. Give me oh, Lord, light and spirit for doing what will please you and serve your mother."

Three times John approached my door, but three times he was withheld by his reverence for me. Out of respect for him as a priest, I rose from my prayers and sought him out, saying to him, "Master, tell me what you ask of your servant."

Encouraged by my statement, John was strengthened and answered, "My, lady, my office and desire of serving you has caused me to notice your sorrow, and I am troubled at your suffering, which I am anxious to alleviate."

I turned to my Son in prayer and prayed, "My, God and, Son, you have wished your servant John to take your place as my companion and attendant. I have received him as my prelate and superior. I wish to obey his will and desire, as soon as they become known to me, so that I may live and be governed by your obedience. Give me permission to tell him of my anxiety according to his wish."

I felt my Son's sanction at once, and I fell on my knees at the feet of John, kissed his hands, and asked for his blessing. He blessed me, and having asked him for permission to speak I replied, "My, master, the sorrow of my heart is well founded, for the Most High has shown to me the tribulations that are to come over the Church. He has advised me of the persecutions, which all its children, especially the Apostles, shall suffer. I have seen the infernal dragon with his hosts of evil all filled with implacable wrath for the destruction of the Church. This city of Jerusalem will bear the fury of their assault. In it, one of the Apostles will meet his death, and others will be imprisoned and afflicted at the instigation of the demon. My heart is filled with compassion and sorrow at the opposition of these enemies to the exaltation of the holy name of God and to the salvation of souls."

John was likewise aggrieved at this news, but in the strength of divine grace he responded saying, "My, mother, your wisdom cannot ignore that the Most High will draw great fruits for his Church and for his faithful children from the trials and tribulations of the Apostles, and that he will assist them in their affliction. We Apostles are prepared to sacrifice our lives for the Lord, who has offered his own life for the entire human race. We have received great blessings and it is not just that they remain idle and useless. When we were little ones in the school of our Teacher and Lord, we behaved like children. However, since he has enriched us with the Holy Ghost and enkindled in us the fire of love, we have lost our cowardice and desire to walk the way of the Cross, which he taught us by his doctrine and example. We know that the Church is to be established and preserved by the blood of its ministers and children. Pray for us my, lady that by the divine power and your protection we gain the victory over our enemies, and that for the glory of the Most High we triumph over them all. However, if this city of Jerusalem is to bear the brunt of the persecution, it seems to me my, lady that you should not stay here, lest the fury of Hell, by inciting the malice of men, attempt some indignity to the tabernacle of God."

In my love for the Apostles and all the faithful, I spurned all fear. I would rather have stayed in Jerusalem, in order to visit, console, and encourage all of them in their impending tribulation. However, I did not make known to John this preference, though properly holy, For as it was the choice of my heart, I preferred to disregard it and yield in humble obedience to the wishes of the Apostle, whom I held as my prelate and superior. I gave him no direct answer, but simply replied, "Thank you, John, my son, for your courageous desire to suffer and die for Christ. As for my departing from Jerusalem, you are merely to command and dispose of me as you see fit. I will obey you in all as your subject, and I will ask the Lord to guide you by his divine light and according to his light and pleasure."

John answered saying, "My, lady, let us leave Jerusalem and labor for the exaltation of the name of the Most High. It seems best for us to retire to the city of Ephesus where you can bring forth the fruits of faith, which are not to be expected in Jerusalem. If only I were one of the angels, who assist at the throne of the blessed Trinity, so as to serve you more worthily in this journey, but I am but a vile worm of the Earth. The Lord; however, will be with us and you shall have your God and your Son as a propitious helper."

I retired to my room and John proceeded to give the proper notice to the other Apostles and the faithful of our intended journey. In my oratory, I prayed as follows, "Most High and eternal, God, this humble handmaid prostrates herself before your royal presence and from my inmost heart I beseech you to direct and guide me in your greater pleasure and good will. I will make this journey in obedience to your servant John, whose will shall be as your own. It is not just that I should take any step, which is not for the greater glory and exaltation of your holy name. Attend oh, Lord, to my desires and prayers, in order that I may act most appropriately and justly."

Then the Lord said, "My, Dove and dearest, Spouse, I have ordained this journey for my greater pleasure. Obey John, and go to Ephesus; for there in due time, I wish to manifest my clemency to some souls through your meditation and presence."

I was consoled in the knowledge of God's divine will, and I asked him for his blessing and for permission to prepare for my departure at the time set by John. God's wishes filled me with the fire of charity and I was inflamed with the desire of promoting the good of souls in Ephesus. I had no knowledge of how long I would be gone, so I arranged many things by myself and through my angels, so as to provide all that seemed proper for the needs of the Church. I knew the most effective service I could render to the faithful was by my continual prayer to secure the assistance of the infinite power of my divine Son for the defense of the Apostles and the faithful against the proud and vaunting schemes of Lucifer's wickedness. Knowing that James was to be the first to be martyred of the Apostles, I offered up special prayers for him, more at the time than for the other Apostles.

A few days before we were to leave for Ephesus, I felt in my heart new and sweet affections, as was usual when I was about to receive some signal favor. I responded to them by saying, "Lord, tell me your wishes for me? Speak oh, Lord, for your handmaid listens."

I was delighted to see my divine Son descend in person to visit me. He was seated upon a throne of ineffable majesty and accompanied by a host of heavenly angels from the heavenly choirs and hierarchies. I worshiped him with the deepest respect and the Lord said to me, "My most beloved, Mother, I am attentive to your petitions and holy desires, and they are pleasing to me. I shall defend my Apostles and my Church; I am their Father and Protector, and it will not be overcome, nor shall the gates of hell prevail against it. As you already know, it is necessary for my glory that the Apostles labor with my grace, and that at the end they must follow me to the Cross and to the death I suffered for the whole human race. The first one to imitate me is to be my faithful servant James; he is to suffer his martyrdom in this city of Jerusalem. In order for him to come here, I wish you to visit him in Spain where he is preaching my name. Go to Saragossa where he is and command him to return to Jerusalem. However, before he leaves the city he is to build a temple in your name and title, and place therein a pillar and a marble image of you. You shall be venerated and invoked for the welfare of that country, for my glory and pleasure and that of the most blessed Trinity."

With sincerest gratitude I answered, "My, Lord and true God, let your holy will be done and let all the creatures praise you for the admirable works of kindness done to your servants. Grant me, my, Son that in the temple you command to be built by James that I may be permitted to promise the special protection of your almighty arm. May this sacred place be part of my inheritance for the use of all those that call with devotion upon your holy name and ask me to intercede for them with your clemency?"

My Son answered me, "My, Mother in whom I am well pleased, I give you my royal word that I shall look with especial clemency and fill with blessings all those who, with devotion and humility, call upon me through your intercession in that temple. As my mother, who holds my place and power, you can signalize that place by depositing therein your riches and promising in it your favors; for all will be fulfilled according to your will."

Again, I thanked my Son, and by command of my Lord, I departed with a great entourage of angels, who formed a royal throne for my use from a most resplendent cloud. Borne by the hands of the seraphim, I departed body and soul for Saragossa in Spain.

Although this journey could have been completed in the shortest possible time, the Lord ordered the angels to move along slowly singing hymns of praise and jubilee to me as their Queen. Some of them sang the "Ave Maria," others the "Salve sancta Parens" and "Salve Regina"; and others sang the "Regina coeli laetare". They sang songs not yet written, but well known in Heaven.The choirs of angels sang in a harmony and concord of sounds that no human art could ever attain. I responded, humbled and grateful, by singing "Holy, holy, holy, Lord God Sabaoth have pity on the poor children of Eve," and many other songs glorifying almighty God.

James was encamped with his disciples outside the wall running along the banks of the Ebro River. He was praying alone some distance from his disciples. Some of the disciples had fallen asleep and others were absorbed in prayer. The procession of angels spread out and sang still louder so that James and all his disciples could hear them. They were all filled with interior sweetness and wonder, and they shed tears of joy. The disciples saw in the sky a most brilliant light, brighter than that of the sun, but it was not diffused beyond a certain space and seemed like a large luminous globe. However, while the disciples could see the light and hear the beautiful music, they were not privileged to see me, or the holy angels, but they were among the first to see the marble image of me that the angels had fashioned at God's command. The holy angels placed my throne within sight of James. Though still engaged in most exalted prayer, he clearly heard, and saw all that transpired.

The angels bore with them a small column hewn of marble: and a small image of me their Queen. The angels carried the image with great veneration, for during the night they had fashioned it for the occasion. I appeared before James, and God showered me in glorious splendor that far outshone the beauty of the angels. James prostrated himself upon the earth and in deepest reverence venerated me as the Mother of God. He was shown at the same time the image and the pillar carried by the angels.

I gave him my blessing in the name of my divine Son and said, "James, servant of the Most High, you are blest by his right hand. May he raise you up and show you the light of his divine countenance."

All the angels responded, "Amen!"

I continued, "My son, James, the most high and omnipotent God of Heaven has destined that this place be consecrated by you for the erection of a temple and house of prayer. He wishes to be glorified and magnified here, under my patronage and name. The treasures of his right hand shall be distributed from this temple, and, if the faithful ask in true faith and sincere piety, all his ancient mercies shall be opened up through my intercession. I promise them great favors, blessings, and assistance in the name of the Almighty, for this is to be my house and temple, my inheritance and possession. This column, with my image placed upon it, shall be a pledge of this truth and of my promise. It shall be preserved until the end of the world in the temple you shall build for me. You shall begin to build this temple of God, and after you have completed it, you shall depart for Jerusalem; for my divine Son wishes you to offer the sacrifice of your life in the same place where he offered his for the salvation of the human race."

At my orders, the holy angels then set up the column and upon it placed my image, as God had ordained. The angels, the Apostle, and his disciples recognized the spot as holy ground, consecrated as a temple to the glory of the Most High with me, his mother, as the Mediatrix for the human race. This was the happy origin of the sanctuary of our Lady of the Pillar in Saragossa. It has been justly called the Angelic Chamber, the House of God, and of me, the Mother of God. It is worthy of the veneration of the entire world and it is a secure and earnest pledge of God's favors and benefits, *if not prevented by the sins of humankind.* As witness of this fact James and his disciples prostrated themselves on the ground, and, in union with the holy angels celebrated the dedication of the first Catholic temple in Spain. God honored me by dedicating the first Church in my name with the title, "The Lady of the Pillar."

James gave most humble thanks to me, and asked me for the special protection of the Spanish Kingdom and especially of this place they had just consecrated to my devotion and name. I granted all his requests, and was carried back to Jerusalem borne on my angel's wings. At my request, the Most High appointed an angel with the care and defense of this sanctuary, and from that day until now he has fulfilled this office and will continue it as long as the sacred image and column shall remain there. Remember, while my Son and I seem to absolutely guarantee to preserve this temple, yet our words contain an implicit condition, as is the case with many other promises of Holy Scripture regarding particular blessings of divine grace. The implicit condition is that you, on your part, must conduct yourselves in such a way as *not* to oblige God to deprive you of this merciful privilege.

Another reason is that Lucifer and his demons, since they know of these blessings, have attempted and are still attempting to introduce into Saragossa a more refined malice than elsewhere. The intent of the serpent is to induce the inhabitants of Saragossa to offend God, as to cause him to abolish the sanctuary. If that fails, they then try to hinder souls from showing proper reverence and devotion to the sacred temple and to the great blessings that I have been able to promise through God's good grace.

As I faded away from Saint James's sight, he called his disciples together and revealed to them God's intention to build on this site a Church dedicated to me. They began at once to build a little Chapel around the pillar and image, and with the assistance of my angels the job was soon completed and the Church consecrated to God and to me as its patron. There was an immediate devotion by the faithful to me as the Mother of God, all, beseeching and asking me to plead their case before by Son. This, I prayerfully did, and God's mercies were immediately apparent. Later generations erected a magnificent church which was completed about 400 AD. For more than sixteen-hundred years faithful Catholics have been able to see with their own eyes, the wonderful preservation of this sanctuary containing a column bearing an image of my likeness. It has remained intact and uninjured amid all the perfidy of the Jews, the idolatry of the Romans, the heresy of the Arians, and the savage fury of the Moors and pagans. In addition, it has survived the numberless plots and schemes, which Hell has fabricated throughout the ages by arousing the Infidel Nations for the destruction of this sanctuary.

I did not tell John of these events, for they did not concern the faith of the universal Church. However, later, when James visited me in Ephesus, James related to him all of his efforts in Spain, and told him of the two visions that he had had of me. John used the information to help confirm the converts in Jerusalem in their faith and devotion to me, and to awaken in them the confidence of my protection. Over the years, Spain would build many temples in my honor, and as God had planned, I was publicly venerated throughout Spain.

My angels then returned me to Jerusalem; I humbled myself and gave thanks to God for all his benefits. This new debt that I owed the Lord seemed so great that I felt obliged to aspire to new and more exalted degrees of holiness in recompense. This I did, and I arrived at a degree of wisdom and humility beyond all your capacity to conceive, none of which I was fully aware of as a human being. I spent the better part of four days in my prayers, and while I prayed, John made ready for our journey by ship. I asked John for permission to visit all the holy places of the Redemption before I left. I made the stations with John with humble devotion and tears of reverent love, and John was no less affected.

When we returned to the Cenacle, I went into my oratory and asked permission of the Lord to depart Jerusalem, and then I proceeded to take leave of the owner of the house and its inhabitants. It was a sorrowful parting, they begged me to return, and I consoled them by expressing my own humble love for them. I then dropped to my knees before John and asked him to bless me for the journey. I rode to the port on an unpretentious donkey, and I recollected all the journeys and pilgrimages that I had made with my Son and Joseph my husband. In order to comfort me, my holy angels made themselves visible to me in corporal forms surrounding and protecting me in their midst.

My Sea Voyage to Ephesus

We came to the harbor of Jaffa and in a very short time embarked on the ship with other passengers. This was my first time upon the sea, and with my Interior Vision I saw and comprehended with clearness the vast ocean called the Great Sea, now called the Mediterranean. I knew its every secret, even to how many men had drowned and perished in voyaging it. My knowledge extended to all these things not only as they are in themselves and without deceit, but far beyond the sphere of angelic knowledge. With compassion, I prayed to the Almighty for all those that trusted their lives to the indomitable fury of the sea in navigating over its waters. I fervently besought God to protect from its dangers all, who should call upon my name and ask for my intercession. The Lord granted my petition and promised that anyone sailing the sea, and who carried some image of me, and sincerely looked upon this image for help from the peril of the sea, would receive his favor.

Accordingly, let it be understood that if the faithful encounter ill success and perish in navigating the ocean, it is because they ignore the favors to be obtained from me as the Queen of Angels. If because of their sins, they forget to remember me in the raging storms, or fail to seek my favors with sincere faith and devotion, then they deny the Lord and me the opportunity to come to their aid, for the word of the Lord can never fail.

The second day I was greeted with all the fish of the sea and other maritime animals. I gave them my blessing, and commanded them to acknowledge and praise their Creator in the manner they were capable of. It was wonderful to see all the fish obeying my command, for with incredible swiftness they placed themselves in front of the ship. All the species of the sea were represented and they soon surrounded the ship and were so densely packed that they impeded the progress of the ship. They showed their heads above the water and acknowledged me as the Queen and Mistress of all creatures. This strange event astonished all the passengers, and they gazed upon this spectacle and wonderingly discussed it. Only Saint John understood the miracle and he could not restrain his tears of devoted joy. John came to me and asked me to give the fish my blessing and my permission to depart. I did so and they all left with great splashing, and they all complied.

My trip to Ephesus is interrupted while I explain Paul's conversion, the death of James, the imprisoning of Peter, and the death of Herod Agrippa I.

While traveling I had laid out my plans to assist all of the faithful. I called my angels and sent some of them to aid the Apostles and disciples, whom I knew to be hard-pressed in the persecutions, raised by the demons through infidel men. In these days, Saint Paul fled from Damascus where he had preached for three years before the attacks of the Jews forced him to flee. In the dead of night, he was let down from the walls of the city in a basket. To defend him on his way to Jerusalem, I sent angels to be his guard, for the wrath and fury of Hell was roused against Saint Paul more than against any of the other Apostles. Paul entered Jerusalem a month after I had departed for Ephesus.

Paul was met with a certain amount of fear and suspicion, in spite of all the good reports that the Apostles had received concerning his good works. When Paul was presented to Peter, he fell at his feet and kissed them in acknowledgment of his errors and sins. He begged to be admitted as one of his subjects and as a follower of his Master, whose holy name and faith he desired to preach at the cost of his blood. Peter was reassured of Paul's good intentions when he prostrated himself before him. He, and the other disciples, received him with great joy of soul. Paul was commissioned to preach in Jerusalem. This he gladly did, to the astonishment of all the Jews who knew him. His words were like burning arrows that penetrated into the hearts of all that heard him. In two days all Jerusalem was roused by the news of his arrival and preaching and they flocked to see with their own eyes.

Upon Paul's arrival, the torment of the demons was increased, because the divine power was so strong in him that it oppressed and paralyzed the infernal dragon. They were roused to a fury against him and Lucifer called together many legions of black angels to assail and destroy Paul in any manner possible. They excited Herod and the Jews against Paul hoping to have him executed as they had done with Saint Stephen.

Aware of their intentions, I increased my prayers and concerns for Paul and the Lord answered my call saying, "My, dove, I have heard your petitions and I assure you that Paul will be protected from this danger and assault of Lucifer."

Soon after, while Paul was praying in the temple, the Lord commanded him to leave Jerusalem. Paul informed Saint Peter, as the head of the apostolic college, and after only fifteen days in Jerusalem, he was sent secretly to Caesarea and Tarsus. After giving proper thanks to the Lord, I turned my attention to James, for I still entertained the hope that through the assistance of the divine Providence, I might be able to save the life of my cousin James, who was very dear to me. James was still in Saragossa protected by my one hundred angels that I had assigned to him in Granada. Through my angels, James had learned that I was on a ship bound for Ephesus, and when he had brought the Chapel of the Pillar to a sufficient state of completion, he consigned it to the care of the bishop and the disciples appointed by him as he had in other cities of Spain. He departed from Spain for Italy without further delay. He pursued his journey overland always preaching until he again embarked for Asia Minor, for he ardently desired to see me again.

After my arrival in Ephesus, James visited me and he prostrated himself at my feet shedding copious tears of joy and veneration. He thanked me from his inmost heart for the peerless favors obtained from my hands through the Most High. I raised him from the ground and said to him, "My, Master, remember you are the anointed of the Lord and his minister, and that I am a most unworthy servant."

I fell to my knees before him and asked for his blessing, which he did with great joy and veneration. James spent several days with John and I, and we had many conferences of which I will record this one. In order to prepare James for his leave-taking, I said to him, "James, my son, these will be the last days of your life. You know how deeply I love you in the Lord, and how I desire to raise you to his intimate love and eternal friendship, for which he has created, redeemed and called you. In these few days that still remain of your life, I desire to demonstrate to you my love and by the divine grace, I offer you all that I can as a true mother."

James replied with deep veneration, "My, Mistress and mother of my God and Redeemer, from the bottom of my soul I thank you for this new benefit, possible only to your unbounded charity. My, lady, I beseech you give me your blessing that I may suffer martyrdom for your Son, my true God and Savior. If it is for his will and for his glory, I beseech you from my soul, not to forsake me in the sacrifice of my life. I pray that I may see you with my own eyes in passage and that you offer me as an acceptable victim in his divine presence."

I promised to present his petition to the Lord and told him I would fulfill it, if the Divine Will should so permit. I comforted him and added, "My son, James, what torments or suffering shall ever seem great at the prospect of entering the eternal joys of the Lord? The most bitter shall seem sweet and the most terrible welcome and desirable to him who knows the infinite and Highest Good, which he shall possess in return for a momentary sorrow. I congratulate you, my Master, for your most happy lot and that you are so soon to leave the tribulations of this mortal life in order to enjoy the infinite Good as a comprehensor in the gladness of his divine countenance. In this, my heart is lightened that you shall soon obtain what my soul desires for you, and that you give your temporal life for the unending possession of eternal rest. I give you the blessing of the Father, of the Son, and of the Holy Ghost, in order that all three persons, in the oneness of their essence, assist you in tribulation and lead you to the desired end. My own blessing shall be with you in your glorious martyrdom."

Taking leave of me, James said, "My, Mistress, blessed among women, your life and intercession is the prop on which the holy Church, now and during the ages in which it is to exist, shall rest securely in the midst of the persecutions and temptations of the enemies of the Lord. Keep in mind always, as our sweetest mother, the Kingdom of Spain, where the holy Church and the faith, of your divine Son and Redeemer have been planted. Receive it under your special protection, and preserve in it your sacred temple and the faith, which I have so unworthily preached; and give me your holy blessing."

I promised to fulfill his petition and desires, and when we parted, I again bestowed upon him my heartfelt blessing. James also took leave of his brother John, and knowing his mission, they shed abundant tears, but not of sorrow but of joy. James came to the city of Jerusalem at a time when the authorities were very much incensed against the disciples and followers of my Son. This new fury had been stirred up by the recent preaching of Saint Paul, which the demons had seized upon and used to whip up the Jews zeal for the old Law and their jealousy of the New Way. They were relieved when Paul left the city, although he had only been there for fifteen days. However, they were again thrown into consternation by the speedy arrival of Saint James, who showed no less zeal and heavenly wisdom in proclaiming the name of Christ the Redeemer.

Lucifer seized upon this new means of exciting the spleen and rousing the wrath of the high priests and scribes. Saint James began to preach most fervently the name of the Crucified, and his mysterious Death and Resurrection. In the first few days, he debated with Hermogenes and Philetus, both were magicians and sorcerers, and they had a pact with the devil. Hermogenes was deeply versed in magic and Philetus was his disciple. The Jews engaged the services of these two in order to overcome Saint James in dispute, or if that was impossible, to take away his life by magic.

Philetus first began the debate with Saint James, so that if he should gain no advantage, Hermogenes, as the more skilled master in the black arts, might enter the contest. Philetus brought forward his sophistical and false arguments, but the holy Apostle spoke with such wisdom and force that all his sophism yielded as the darkness before the light. The magician's disciple was overwhelmed and converted to the truth of Christ, and became a defender of the Apostle and his new faith. However, he feared the diabolical power of his former master and sought the protection of Saint James. The holy Apostle gave the man a piece of cloth, which James had received from me. With this relic, Philetus was able to protect himself against the power of the magician.

Although Hermogenes now feared Saint James, he could not evade the meeting, because he had pledged himself to the Jews. Accordingly, he tried to enforce his errors by using more cogent arguments than his disciple had done. However, he could not prevail against the heavenly force and wisdom of Saint James, who brought him to silence with the validity of his arguments. He obliged Hermogenes to confess his belief, just as he done with Philetus. The demons were aroused to a fury against Hermogenes and through the power they had acquired over him, began to maltreat him. The convert, knowing how Philetus had defended himself, besought Saint James to help him, also. James gave him a scarf, and he was able to put the demons to flight and make them powerless against him.

From my retreat in Ephesus, I had hastened these conversions and others with my prayers. Unfortunately Hermogenes and Philetus persevered for only a short time, for later, while in Asia where they had joined Saint Paul, they found that the evil and perverse inclinations of their vices still remained, which drew them away from the faith [Second epistle to Timothy].

When the Jews saw their hopes frustrated with these conversions, they were filled with new anger against Saint James. They determined to put him to death. For this purpose, they bribed Democritus and Lysias, centurions of the Roman militia, to furnish them with soldiers for the arrest of the Apostle. To hide their treachery, they feigned a disturbance where James was preaching, and thus had a reason to arrest him. The execution of this wicked plan was left to Abiator, the high priest of that year, and to Josias a scribe. While James was preaching, Abiator gave the signal to Josias; backed by the Roman soldiers, he threw a rope around the neck of Saint James and proclaimed him a disturber of the people, and the author of a new religion in opposition to the Roman Empire. Democritus and Lysias, thereupon, rushed up with their soldiers and brought the bound Apostle to Herod. He had been stirred up by the Jews and the demons, for they left him no peace. He ordered James to be beheaded, as the Jews had asked.

James was filled with joy at being seized and bound like his Master. He went willingly to the place where he was to pass from this mortal life, as a martyr. He offered most humble thanks for this benefit and publicly recited the Apostles Creed. Remembering his request, he called upon me to be present at his death. I favored him with my most ardent prayers. During my prayer, I saw a great multitude of angels and heavenly spirits of all hierarchies descending from heaven, part of them surrounding the Apostle in Jerusalem as he was led to the place of execution, while other angels approached me in Ephesus.

One of these addressed me saying, "Empress of Heaven and our lady, the most high Lord and God bids you to hasten to Jerusalem to console his great servant James, to assist him in his death and to grant all his holy and loving desires."

This favor I joyfully and gratefully acknowledged. I praised the Most High for the protection granted to those who trust in his mercy and put their lives in his hands. In the meantime, James was led to execution and on the way, he wrought great miracles upon the sick and ailing, and on some possessed by the demons. There were a great number of petitioners, because the news of his execution by Herod had spread quickly and many of the unfortunates hastened to receive his last ministrations. The great Apostle healed all that appealed to him for help.

In the meantime, I had been placed upon a most refulgent throne, as the angels had done on other occasions, and I was whisked to Jerusalem to the place of execution. The holy priest fell upon his knees in order to offer his life to the Most High in sacrifice, and when he raised his eyes to Heaven, he saw me hovering above him. God had clothed me in divine splendor surrounded me by hosts of angels.

At this heavenly spectacle, the soul of James was seized with the ardor of divine love. He wished to proclaim my presence, but one of the sovereign spirits restrained him in this fervent desire and said, "James, servant of our Creator, restrain within your bosom these precious sentiments and do not manifest to the Jews the presence and assistance of our Queen; for they are not worthy or capable of knowing her, but instead of reverencing her, they will only harden themselves in their hatred."

Thus advised, the Apostle moving his lips in silence spoke to me, "Mother of my Lord Jesus Christ, my Mistress and Protectress, bestow upon me your so much desired blessing. Offer for me to your Son and Redeemer of the world, the sacrifice of my life, since I am burning with desire to be a holocaust for the glory of his name. Let your pure and spotless hands be the altar of my sacrifice in order that it may be more acceptable in his eyes. Into your hands and through them into the hands of my Creator, I commend my spirit.'

With his eyes fixed on me, the executioners completed their task and beheaded the most holy James. I received the soul of the beloved James, and with him beside me on my throne, the angels took us directly before the throne of my Son. There, in an Abstractive Vision, I presented to him the unblemished soul of the Apostle James. The holy court greeted us with hymns of praise, and my Son received the soul of James and placed it in eminent glory among the princes of his people. Prostrate before the throne of God, I composed a song of praise and thanksgiving for the triumphal martyrdom first gained by one of my Son's Apostles. I was then returned to my oratory in Ephesus, where an angel had taken my place. I fell flat on my face and gave thanks to almighty God [Acts: 12, 2].

The disciples of Saint James during the following night secured the sacred body of Saint James and secretly brought it to the port of Jaffa, where, inspired by divine inspiration, they embarked with it for Galicia in Spain. I sent an angel to guide and accompany them to the port in Spain. Although they did not see the angel, they could sense his holy presence. Saint James died in the year 41 of our Lord, on the twenty-fifth of March, five years and seven months after setting out to preach in Spain. The Jews rejoiced at the news of the death of Saint James and emboldened by their praise, King Herod imprisoned Saint Peter with the full intention of having him beheaded after the coming Pasch. James' feast day is not celebrated on the day of his death, as is the case with most martyrs since it fell on the same day as the Incarnation. Instead, it was transferred to the twenty-fifth of July, which is the day on which the body of James was brought to Spain.

Goaded by Lucifer the Jews hoped to put an end to all the Christians by killing their leader, Saint Peter. The prelate was bound in heavy chains, and the entire body of the Church of Jerusalem was filled with anxiety and all the disciples and faithful were greatly afflicted at the news. In their affliction, the faithful multiplied their prayers and petitions to the Lord for the preservation of Saint Peter, whose death threatened the whole Church with great havoc and tribulations. They also invoked my protection and powerful intercession. In my visions, I saw all that had transpired and I increased my ardent requests, with sighs, prostrations and bloody tears, supplicating the Lord for the liberation of Saint Peter and the protection of the holy Church. My prayers penetrated the Heavens and wounded the heart of my Son Jesus. In response, the Lord descended in person to my oratory where I lay prostrate in the shape of a cross with my face buried in the dust. Our sovereign King entered and raised me lovingly from the ground saying, "My, Mother, moderate your sorrow and ask whatever you wish, for I shall grant it all and you shall find grace in my eyes to obtain it."

I was consoled with the loving caress of my Son and I renewed my petition, "My, Son, you know the tribulations of your holy Church and her clamors sound in your ears, while they penetrate my most afflicted heart. Your enemies are resolved to take away the life of your Vicar, and if you, my Lord, permit it now, they will scatter your little flock and the infernal wolves will triumph over your name in seeing their wishes fulfilled. If it be to your glory and according to your will let these tribulations come over me. Allow me to suffer for your faithful children and be the aid of your right arm, so that I may battle with the invisible enemies in the defense of your holy Church."

My Son answered, "I desire that you act according to your wishes, using the powers I have given you. Do or undo whatever if necessary for the welfare of my Church, and you may be sure that all the fury of the demons will be turned against you."

I replied in all humility, "High, Lord, although I am but useless dust, I fear not the infernal dragon. Since you wish me to dispose and act for the welfare of the Church, I now command Lucifer and all his ministers of wickedness, who are disturbing the Church, to descend to the abyss. There, they shall be silenced until it shall please your Providence to permit their return to surface of the Earth."

This command was so powerful that all the demons in Jerusalem were precipitated into hell. Lucifer and his demons knew that it was I that had chastised them, and they remained there until the Lord saw fit for them to continue the battle against me. In Hell they plotted their revenge when they were again released, which they believed would soon happen. I then asked Jesus, "Now my, Son and Lord, if it is your will, let one of your holy angels be sent to deliver your servant Peter from prison."

Jesus approved my request and we dispatched an angel to liberate Peter from his prison in Jerusalem. The angels found Peter securely bound with two chains with a guard to each side of him and a number of soldiers at the entrance to the prison. The Pasch had already been celebrated and Peter was to be executed the next day. In spite of this, Peter was sleeping with no concern as to his fate. The angel when he arrived was forced to shake him awake and while Peter was still drowsy, said to him, "Get up quickly, and the chains fell from his wrists. The angel said to him, "Put on your belt and your sandals." He did so. Then he said to Peter, "Take up your cloak and follow me."

Saint Peter found himself freed from the chains, and without fully understanding what was happening to him, followed the angel believing he was having a vision. They passed one guard and then the second and came to the iron-gate leading out to the city, which mysteriously opened for them. Having conducted Peter through some streets, the angel told him, "The Almighty has freed you from prison through the intercession of the Blessed Virgin Mary." Thereupon, the angel disappeared. Saint Peter coming to himself understood the mystery and gave thanks to the Lord and to me his benefactor.

Peter thought it best to first give an account of his liberation and consult with James the Less and others of the faithful before taking safety in flight. Hastening his steps he came to the house of Mary, the mother of John, who was also called Mark. This was the house of the Cenacle, where many of the disciples had gathered in their affliction. Peter called to them from the street, and a servant-maid, by the name of Rhode, descended to see who was calling. Upon recognizing the voice of Peter, instead of opening the gate, she left him standing outside the door and fled excitedly to the disciples telling them that it was Peter. They thought she was mistaken, but she stoutly maintained that it was Peter, but even then, they thought it might be his angel. In the meantime, Peter was in the street clamoring at the door, until they opened it and saw, with incredible joy, that it was indeed the Vicar of Christ [Acts: 12, 3-19]].

The prelate then gave them a detailed account of what had happened to him, and dispatched them in strict secrecy to notify James the Less and the rest of the brethren. Foreseeing that Herod would search for him with great diligence, they unanimously decided that he should depart from Jerusalem that very night and not return. The next day, Herod instituted a search in vain, and ordered the guards tried and executed, and was roused to even greater fury against the disciples. However, because of his pride and impious designs, God cut short his activity by a severe punishment, of which I shall now speak.

The Death of Herod Agrippa I

Only the Infinite Wisdom could fathom my love for my fellow men, for if all the love of the holy angels and of men could be united into one person, it would be less than that which I retained in my heart. Therefore, you can understand that there could be no other mastery, no movement or liberty other than that of my loving supremely the highest Good. Thus my charity filled at the same time with the most ardent desires of seeing the face of God, who was absent, and assisting the holy Church, which was present to me, was consumed by two opposite tendencies. However, I governed them with such prudence that no conflict arose, nor did I give myself up to the one to the neglect of the other. With the Church left in my charge, with the grace of God, Peter had been freed and had fled Jerusalem.

The Divine Wisdom ordained that I should at that time have a very intimate knowledge of the evil disposition of King Herod. I perceived the abominable ugliness of that most unfortunate soul brought on by his boundless vices and oft-repeated crimes, which had aroused the wrath of the just and almighty judge. I was made aware of how enraged Herod and the Jews were against my Son and his disciples after the escape of Peter. I saw how the seed of rage sown by the demons in the hearts of Herod and the Jews had grown, and how furious their hatred against Jesus our Redeemer and his disciples had become. Herod had decided to exterminate all the faithful within the confines of Judea and Galilee.

I was horrified at this ghastly state of affairs, I said to Xnoir, one of my angels, "My solicitude for the holy Church strongly urges me to seek its welfare and progress. I beseech you to ascend to the throne of the Most High, and ask him in my name that I may be permitted to suffer instead of his faithful servants and that Herod is prevented from executing his designs for the destruction of the Church."

While I remained in prayer, the angel conveyed my message to the Lord. He returned at once with the Lord's answer, "Princess of heaven, the Lord of hosts says that you are the Mother and Mistress and the Governess of the Church, and that you hold his power while you are upon earth. He desires that you, as Queen and Mistress of the Heavens and Earth, execute sentence upon Herod."

In my humility, I was somewhat disturbed by this answer, and urged by my charity, I replied to the angel, "Am I then to pronounce sentence against a creature that is the image of the Lord? Since I come forth from his hands, I have known many reprobates among men and I have never called for vengeance against them. I have always desired their salvation if possible and never hastened their punishment. Return to the Lord, my angel, and tell him that my tribunal and power is inferior to and dependent upon his. I cannot sentence any one to death without consulting my Superior. If it is possible to bring Herod to the way of salvation, I am willing to suffer all the travails of the world according to the disposition of his divine Providence in order that this soul may not be lost."

Again, my Lord sent back his answer, and Xnoir said, "Our, Mistress and Queen, the Most High says that Herod is of the number of the foreknown. He is obstinate in his malice, and takes no admonition or instruction. He will not co-operate with the helps given to him; nor will he avail himself of the fruits of the Redemption, or of the intercession of the saints, or of your own efforts in his behalf, oh Queen and lady."

For the third time, I dispatched the heavenly prince with still another message for my Son, telling him, "If Herod must die, in order to stop him from persecuting the Church, do you, Xnoir, represent to the Most High, how in his charity he has granted me in mortal life to be the refuge of the children of Adam, and the advocate and intercessor of sinners. Therefore, my tribunal should be that of kindness and clemency, for the refuge and assistance of all that seek my intercession. All should leave my refuge with the assurance of pardon in the name of my divine Son. If I am to be the loving mother to men, who are the creatures of his hands, and the price of his life-blood, how can I now be a severe judge against one of them? Never was I charged with dealing out justice, always mercy, to which all my heart inclines. Now it is troubled by this conflict of love with obedience to rigorous justice. Present anew, oh angel, my anxiety to the Lord, and learn whether it is not his pleasure that Herod die without my condemning him."

Xnoir ascended the third time, and the blessed Trinity listened to his message with pleasure at my pity for the tyrant Herod. Returning, the angel informed me, "Our, Queen, Mother of our Creator, and my lady, the almighty Majesty says that your mercy is for those who wish to avail themselves of your powerful intercession, and not for those who despise and abhor it like King Herod. You are the Mistress of the Church invested with all the divine power, and therefore it is proper that you use it. Herod must die; and it shall be through your sentence and according to your order."

I answered most humbly, "Just is the Lord, and equitable are his judgments. Many times would I suffer death to rescue this soul of Herod, if he himself did not make it impossible. By the use of his own free will, he makes himself unworthy of mercy and instead chooses perdition. Herod is a work of the Most High, formed according to his own image and likeness. The blood of the Lamb, which takes away the sins of the world, redeemed him; however, I set aside all this. I must consider only his having become an obstinate enemy of God, unworthy of his eternal friendship. By the most equitable justice of God, I condemn him to the death he has merited in order that he may not incur greater torments by executing the evil he has planned."

My Son had previously stated, "The Son cannot do anything that the Father does not. However, he does the same because the Father loves him. If the Father raises the dead, the Son may also raise whom he pleases. The Father has ordained that the Son is to judge everyone, in order that just as all honors the father; they may also honor the Son; for no one can honor the Father without honoring the Son." He then added, "The Father has given me the power of judging, because I am the Son of man, which I am through my most blessed mother. Because of the likeness of my heavenly mother to me, the relation or proportion of my mother with me in this power of judgment must be transferred to my mother in the same manner as that from my Father to me."

I am the Mother of Mercy and Clemency to all the children of Adam that call upon me. In addition, the Almighty wishes it to be understood that I possess full power of judging all men and that all should honor me, just as they honor my Son and true God. As my Son's true mother, *he has given me the same power with him in* **the degree and proportion** *due to me as his mother and a mere creature.*

Making use of this power, I sent my princely angel to Caesarea, where Herod was staying, to take away his life as the minister of divine justice. Herod had long been angry with the people of Tyre and Sidon. However, they now came to him in a body suing for peace, because their country was supplied with food from the king's territory. On an appointed day, King Herod, attired in royal robes, and seated on the rostrum, addressed them publicly.

The assembled crowd cried out, "This is the voice of a god, not of a man."

Herod, in foolish vanity, instead of ascribing the honor to God, was pleased with the adulation of the crowd, My angel chose this precise moment to strike Herod interiorly, and from it sprang a vile corruption of worms, with which, the proud king was being eaten alive. He died a hideous and lingering death for his numerous crimes, among them his persecution of the Apostles, mocking the Lord during his Passion, the beheading of John the Baptist and the Apostle James, as well as living in sin with his sister in law, Herodias [Acts: 12, 20-24].

Upon his death, Xnoir reported the fact to me, and I wept over the loss of this soul. However, I praised the just judgments of the Lord and gave him thanks for the benefit, which the Church would derive from his chastisement, for as Saint Luke says [Acts: 12, 24]; the Church grew and increased by the word of God. This was true not only in Galilee and Judea, from where the persecutor Herod was removed, but also in Ephesus. There, due to the previous efforts of Saint James and the current effort of Jame's disciples, and Saint John and I, the Church was taking firm root, as I will now relate.

I Am Mary

Have mercy on me, oh God in your goodness; in the greatness of your compassion wipe out my offense. Thoroughly wash me from my guilt and of my sin cleanse me [Ps[s]: 51, 3-4].

In order that I might enlighten my Son's Church in the first age, my son sent me, and made me known to the first children of his holy Church. In the course of ages, he has continued to manifest my holiness and greatness by the wonders he has had me perform as Queen, such as the innumerable favors and blessings that have flowed from my hands upon humankind. In the last ages, which are the present, he will spread my glory and make me known in new splendor, because of the Church's great need for my intercession and of my help against the world, the demon, and the flesh. Lucifer, through men's own fault, as we see even today, will assume greater sway and strength to hinder the working of grace in men and to make them more unworthy of glory.

God, without any obligation on his part, and without any merit on the part of humankind, seeks to draw them to the secure path of the Passion and Death of my divine Son. Remember, everyone who is now in a state of grace, could have been born in other times and ages before God made himself known to the world. Moreover, any person could have been born among pagans, idolaters, heretics, or other infidels, where his eternal damnation would be unavoidable. Without any merit on their part, God has called such persons to his holy faith, giving them knowledge of the certain truth; justifying them in baptism, putting at their disposal the Sacraments, the priests, the teachings and knowledge of eternal life. He has placed them upon the sure path, granted them his assistance, pardoned them their sins, raised them by his mercy, and rewarded them for their repentance, invited them by his mercy, and rewarded them with a liberal hand. He defended them through his holy angels, gave them himself as a pledge and as the food of eternal life. Thus, he accumulated so many blessings upon them that they are without measure or number. There is neither a day nor an hour pass without increasing their indebtedness.

I desire to help those Catholics who seek my aid in accordance with the command s of God and my own maternal affection. The saints, especially Saint John, rejoiced when they learned that the revelations concerning my ascension with my Son and Lord would be disclosed. It is now time for the children of the Church to know and understand more fully the blessings to which the Omnipotent has raised me. Thereby you can enliven yourselves and make yourselves more capable of the favors I can and will bestow upon you. I am the loving mother, filled with pity at seeing you so deceived and oppressed by the tyranny of Satan to whom you have blindly submitted.

However, I will not wait until you pursue me, for I will hasten to assist you. I will be the leaven of mercy inducing the Most High to grant it. I will be your Portal of Heaven, which will open through my intercession and prayers, for nothing defiled or deceitful may enter. I am never roused to indignation or hatred against men, for in me there is no deceit, no fault or defect. I cannot fail in anything that you may need for your salvation. You have no excuse or pretext for not coming to me with humble acknowledgment; since I, being pure and spotless, will purify and cleanse you. I hold the keys to the fountains from which, as Isaiah says, you may draw the waters of the Redeemer. My intercession in response to your petitions will turn these keys, so that the waters will gush forth to wash you and make you worthy of my blessed company and that of my divine Son for all the eternities.

In ancient times, the Holy Ghost came upon the faithful in the Cenacle in visible form. However, in your times, he still comes to many just souls, although not with such open manifestations, because it is neither necessary nor proper. However,: God allowed the guardian angel of the author of this book to advise him in 1982 that his mother and father had just entered Heaven together from Purgatory on that very day. The really significant issue is that his parents were divorced in a nasty two-year long court trail when he was eight years old. God also allowed his guardian angel when asked, to reveal his name to him, and when the Author asked me for permission to write this story, I gave him a sign.

What is surprising is that on Pentecost with all the outward preaching, and the fact that all who heard the Word received interior inspirations in order to help them make the transition; only three thousand people were converted that first day in Jerusalem. It is even more surprising that in our times so few are converted to the way of eternal life. Today, the Gospel is more widespread with the written word, radio, television, its ministers more numerous, preaching prolific, and the light of the Church clearer and the knowledge of the divine mysteries are more definite. With all this, men are blinder; their hearts more hardened, pride more inflated, avarice more bold, and all the vices are practiced without fear of God and without consideration of the penalties involved. Forgetfulness among men is very blameworthy and deserves a fearful chastisement.

Many priests and bishops today have convinced themselves that it is no longer popular to preach on controversial subjects. They worry about their popularity and the loss of income if people become offended over such subjects as the *real presence,* of the body and blood of Jesus Christ, abortion, contraception, premarital sex, monthly confession, homosexuality, immodesty, and endless number of unmarried young people living together. Many teachers of the RCIA program of instruction in today's Church, either gloss over these subjects, or treat them so lightly that few of those accepted into the Church have the slightest idea whether they are committing a sin or not. Consequently, they seldom have recourse to Confession. First: Perhaps confession has never been properly explained to them. Secondly: Because too many mainline Catholics today do not believe in the importance of the Sacrament of Confession. Since Vatican II, nearly everyone receives communion at the Sunday Masses. Instead of the Eucharist being exalted; as was intended by Vatican II, it has been downgraded by the negligence and the lack of respect for the Holy Eucharist. Many recipients of Communion today are adding blasphemy to their sins, because of their casual attitude toward confession and their selective process of practicing only those rules of the Church that are convenient to them and their lifestyles.

Pope John Paul II pointed out graphically that many Catholics today have an idea of sin, which is not based on the Gospel, but instead have one that is socially acceptable with their peers. They have the mentality, 'What one does in one's own bedroom is their own business.' They refuse to take responsibility for their own actions, because "everyone does it". Is there any wonder that God does not visit his people as often as he did in the beginning? Wars are a punishment for the sins of mankind. Can anyone remember when there was not a war raging during the twentieth century? Is there any wonder why there are so many natural and manmade chastisements afflicting the world today?

The Catholic Church and all its children, by the abundant testimony of Holy Scriptures and later, the teaching of the holy doctors and masters of the spiritual life, are informed of the malice and most vigilant cruelty of Lucifer seeking to draw all men to the eternal torments. From the same sources, we also know how the infinite power of God defends us. Thus, if we wish to obtain for ourselves God's invincible friendship and protection, and if on our part make ourselves worthy of the merits of Christ our Savior, you must walk securely on the path of eternal salvation. As Saint Paul said, "Be sober and watch, because your adversary the devil goes about like a roaring lion, seeking whom he may devour."

Men live in a false sense of security, they ignore the inhuman and hidden cruelty with which the devils solicit and draw them to perdition and therein succeed. Men are also ignorant of the divine protection by which they are surrounded and defended. "Woe is to the Earth," says Saint John in the Apocalypse, "because Satan has come down to you with great indignation of his wrath." The saints in Heaven, while they cannot feel sorrow, pity you for this danger. The fiend is a pure spirit and is never fatigued or ever in need of rest. He begins his combat from the very first instant of our existence in our mother's wombs, and he does not abate his fury against the soul until it leaves the body. The saying of Job is verified,

"The life of man on Earth is warfare."

The angels use the sacraments and blessings of the Church as well as the virtues of alms giving, being kind, the practice of devotions or good works as powerful arms to ward off the devils and defend their charges. The angels often repeat the words, "Who is like unto God?" They also draw on my Son and me, saying, "Who is equal to Christ, the true God and true man, who died for the human race? And also, "Who is to be compared with the most holy Mary, our Queen, who was exempt from all sin, and gave flesh and bodily form to the Eternal Word in her womb, a virgin before, during, and forever."

Whenever the soul justifies themselves through the Sacraments, especially by virtue of a truly sorrowful confession, it often happens that the devils for a long time dare not appear before the penitent, nor for many hours even presume to look at him. The soul must not encourage the demons by losing the divine favor and returning again to the dangers and occasions of sin; for then the demons quickly cast off their fear inspired by true penitence and justification. See that you always approach the sacrament of Confession with fervor, esteem and veneration, and with a heartfelt sorrow for your sins. This Sacrament inspires the dragon with great terror and he exerts himself diligently to hinder souls by his deceits, in order to cause them to receive this Sacrament lukewarmly, out of mere habit, without sorrow, and without proper disposition.

I will close this chapter with the message for the world that I recently gave the children in Medjugorje: "Dear children, I have been with you nine years to tell you that God your Father is the only way, truth and life. To show you the way that you can reach eternal life, give good example to your children and to those who do not believe. You will not have heavenly happiness on this Earth; neither will you come to Heaven if you do not have a pure and humble heart, and if you do not fulfill the laws of God. I am asking you for your help to join me in praying for those who do not believe. <u>You are helping me very little</u>. You do not have enough charity or love for

your neighbors. God gave you love and showed you how you should forgive and love others. For that reason, reconcile, and purify your soul by going to confession. Take your rosary and pray. Take all your suffering patiently. You should remember how patiently Jesus suffered for you. Do not impose your faith on unbelievers. Show it to them by your example and pray for them my children. Please pray for them. I am your mother in Heaven. Call on me and I will answer you. Say the family Rosary daily for the forgiveness of the sins of the world and for the poor souls in Purgatory.

Remember: If a thing is worth praying for, it must be prayed for every day.

I will be with you when you say each Rosary."

I LOVE YOU

MARY

Chapter Eleven

Ephesus

"Why did the gentiles rage and the peoples entertain folly? The kings of the earth took their stand and the princes gathered together against the Lord and against his anointed [Acts: 4, 26]"

The Sea Voyage to Ephesus was a delight. The sheer size and magnificence of the Great Sea made me appreciate my Lord and my God even more. John and I converted the passengers and the most of the crew, and we had catechized them by the time we reached Greece, and John baptized them before we set foot on Greek soil.

The splendid Aegean port of Ephesus in Asia Minor had experienced many renowned events throughout the years. However, Christianity, ushered in by Saint James and his disciples was to eclipse all these events. Ephesus, by pagan standards, was a beautiful city of a quarter-million people. Architecturally the city was magnificent, and had the most splendid main street of the Roman Empire. From the port, we traveled along this main thoroughfare. The street featured an ornate roofed colonnade, thirty-six feet wide, and a third of a mile long. The cities' most famous landmark was the ancient Temple of Artemis, which was almost as long as a modern football field and was four times as large as the Parthenon in Athens. The Nobility, in building the temple, had constructed one-hundred-columns, each six-foot in diameter, and more than fifty-feet high. The Temple of Artemis was one of the Seven Wonders of the World. My heart went out to these people. People who could construct such beauty, and yet whose souls were so hideous.

We had pursued our course from Jaffa and days later we reached Greece and sailed up the River Cayster to the Aegean port of Ephesus. A few Christians from Jerusalem had fled to Ephesus during the persecution following Saint Stephen's death. When the Christians learned of our arrival, they had hastened to greet us and offered us their dwellings and possessions for our use. I did not require much for myself and chose to stay in the home of a poor woman named Mary. She shared her home with four widowed companions. They generously placed their home at our disposal. It was a large residence, the remnant of a former large estate. They selected a secluded room for me and another for Saint John, and here we remained for some time.

The Apostle John and I were to firmly establish the faith in this pagan city. At present the city was dominated by its ancient abominations of the pagan worship of the goddess Diana, and was famed throughout the world for its magicians and its mammoth pagan sanctuary. From the port, I had offered up special prayers, asking my divine Son to pour out over its inhabitants his blessings and as a kind father to, illumine and bring it to the knowledge of the true faith. Jesus informed me that I was free to do as I pleased, but he suggested that I should take notice of obstacles, which this city placed in the way of the divine clemency by its ancient and existing abominations.

My Son told me, "The inhabitants have locked the gates of mercy and merited the rigors of justice, which would have already been executed upon them, if I had not ordained that you, my mother, live among them. For, at this time, their wickedness has reached the highest point and calls the loudest for punishment."

I perceived by this answer that the divine justice would consent for the destruction of the idolatrous people of Ephesus and its neighborhood, if I so ordered. My heart was much afflicted, but my charity was not intimidated, and I multiplied my prayers.

I answered him, "Most, High, just and merciful King, do not exclude your mercy, or the rigor of your justice will be executed. To gain your mercy, any motive found by your wisdom is sufficient, although the inducement presented on the part of sinners may be small. Consider therefore oh, Lord, how this city has afforded me a dwelling according to your will and how its inhabitants have helped me and offered your servant John and I their goods. Temper your rigor my God, and exercise it on me, for I am willing to suffer for the salvation of these unfortunates. In your infinite goodness, let not my eyes behold the destruction of so many souls, for they are the works of your hands and have been purchased by your blood."

The Lord replied, "My, mother, I desire that you see for yourself the cause of my just indignation and how much these men, for whom you plead, have merited it. Attend, and you shall see."

I saw a meeting Lucifer had held with his demons well before the Incarnation. He said to his minions, "From the delights of my former state in heaven, I know God shall be beholden to men and women for abstaining from certain vices, which I however, desire to maintain upon the world. These vices are those connected with the delights of the flesh, the pleasures of possession and avarice. For love of him, God wishes humankind to renounce that, which he allows. In order that they may so be induced, he shall furnish them with many spiritual benefits. He desires that they may be chaste and poor of their own accord, and subject their free will to that of others. If through these virtues, they overcome us, they will merit great reward before God. If they succeed, my plans will be seriously frustrated; therefore we must take measures to counteract this damage. If the Divine Word is to assume human flesh, as I have been given to understand, he will be very chaste and pure, and he will teach this chastity to others, not only men, but women, who though they are weaker, yet usually are more tenacious. I desire your counsel, and with your diligent help we must begin now to hinder men from attaining such great benefits."

This plotting of Hell against evangelical perfection was far in advance of its profession in the religious orders. Lucifer appointed hellish legions to tempt those desirous of living a life of chastity, poverty and obedience. In derision of chastity, they decided to institute a sort of false and apparent state of virginity, in which counterfeit and hypocritical virgins were to consecrate themselves to Lucifer and his demons. They resolved to found this false religion upon man's weakness for the flesh, and his greed for possessions and power. In secret, those interested agreed to establish pagan temples and to live licentiously under the name of chastity in honor of false gods.

Lucifer said to his demons, "It would be a great pleasure to me to have real virgins consecrated and dedicated to my worship and adoration in the same way as God wishes them. Yet, chastity and purity of the body so offends me, that I cannot endure this virtue, even if practiced entirely in honor of my greatness. Therefore, we must see to it that these virgins are the objective of our basest attempts. If any of them should remain chaste in body, we shall fill her with bad thoughts and desires, so that in reality none of them will be chaste, though some of them may strive to contain themselves out of vain pride. As they are impure in their thoughts, we will seek to maintain in the vainglorious conceit of their virginity."

The demons scoured the earth, seeking women suitable to start these false religious orders. They first instigated the building of a temple to Artemis, who was an ancient, many breasted fertility goddess by the same name. Later, when Lucifer decided to have his own following of vestal virgins, they decided upon a group from Scythia in Asia Minor, who called themselves Amazons. In their arrogance and pride, the Amazons covered up their feminine weakness by force of arms. They conquered extended provinces and constituted Ephesus as the center of their power. For many years, they governed themselves, disdaining subjugation to men and life in their company, for they considered such a life as slavery or servitude. Since these Amazons were proud, vainglorious and averse to men, Lucifer found them predisposed toward his counterfeit virginity. He filled them with vain hopes of gaining great veneration and renown in the world by being known as pledged to virginity and stirred them up with the desire of becoming famous and admired of men and perhaps of one of them reaching a position and worship of a goddess. In this vain hope they gathered around them many Amazons, both true and counterfeit virgins, and instituted their spurious congregation of virgins in the Temple of Artemis in Ephesus, the place of their origin.

The cult grew rapidly, and the pagan world greatly admired and applauded them. Among the virgins, one stood out and became celebrated for her great beauty, nobility, high intellect, chastity and other allurements. Her name was Diana, and fame and admiration of her became widespread. Diana gradually gained the worship and title of goddess among the blind multitude. The wily princes soon had the rich and sumptuous temple dedicated to her. Soon, the people commonly referred to the temple as the Temple of Diana. The pagans in other parts of the world, in imitation of it, built many other temples dedicated to Diana. In order to spread her renown, Lucifer communicated with her and filled her with diabolical illusions. Lucifer surrounded her with a false splendor and manifested to her secrets, which she promulgated. He taught her some of the ceremonies and forms of worship similar to those of the people of God, by which she and the people might worship the devil. The other virgins venerated Diana as a goddess, which the virgins from other heathen temples soon emulated.

Many years later, the neighboring kingdoms waged a war against the Amazons. They defeated them, and assumed control of Ephesus. The kings; however, preserved the Temple of Ephesus as something sacred and divine, and they permitted the continuance of that gathering of foolish virgins. Later, some of the outraged citizens of Ephesus destroyed the wicked temple. However, the city and government authorities quickly rebuilt it. All of this happened about thirty years before the Redemption of the human race. Hence, when John and I arrived, the kings had already rebuilt the second temple. The virgins now occupied separate apartments in the new temple, and idolatry was firmly established. The vestal virgins had now degenerated to one of the lowest forms of humanity. Nearly all of them had held abominable intercourse with the demons. In connection therewith, they committed many loathsome crimes. They deceived the world by their humbugging wicked prophecies, with which, the devil had filled both them and their dupes.

I was aware of these events before I arrived in Ephesus; however, once there I was struck with a sorrow so devastating that it would have been fatal if I had not been preserved by my Lord. Having seen that Lucifer had appropriated the statue of Diana as a throne of his wickedness, I prostrated myself before my Lord and said, "Lord, God Most High, it is proper that these abominations, which have lasted so many ages should cease. My heart cannot bear to see that such a sinful and abominable woman should receive the worship due to the true God. How can I endure to see the name of chastity so profaned and prostituted in honor of the demons? You have made me the guide and mother of virgins, which is the most noble part of your Church, and it has become the precious fruit of your Redemption most pleasing to you. Will you consecrate the title of chastity in the souls, which shall be my children? I cannot bear to leave it any longer to these adulterous women. I make complaint against Lucifer and against Hell, for their presumption in unjustly appropriating such a right. I beseech you, my Son, to chastise them by rescuing these souls from his tyranny and conferring on these souls the liberty of your faith and true light."

The Lord answered, "My Mother, I grant your petition, for it is not just that this virtue of chastity, which was ennobled in you and is so pleasing to me, should be ascribed to my enemies. However, many of these counterfeit virgins are foreknown as reprobates because of their abominations and their obstinacy. Most of them will refuse to embrace the way of eternal life; however, a few of them will accept the faith, which you shall teach them."

At this moment, John came to my oratory, but he did not know that I was engaged in a vision with my Son. I wished that John be allowed to join his prayers with mine, and I secretly asked my Son for permission to speak to him, and upon his nod of approval, I said to John, "John, my son, my heart is grieved on account of the abominable crimes committed against the Most High in the Temple of Diana and my soul desires to see them ended and atoned."

The holy Apostle replied, "My, lady, I have seen something of what passes in that abominable place. I cannot restrain my sorrow and my tears, because the demon is there, venerated and worshipped as is due to God alone. No one can put a stop to such great evils, unless you my, mother, will take this matter in hand." I then asked John to pray with me for a remedy of these evils. John retired to his chamber to pray, and I remained in the oratory with my Son. With burning fervor and in agonizing sorrow, I appealed to my divine Son for comfort and consolation. I received the following response to my petitions.

"My, Mother and my, dove, let what you ask be done without delay. Give your orders and commands according to your heart's wishes as the powerful Mistress." As Queen, I regally ordered all the demons in the temple of Diana to leave at once, and to descend to their proper place in Hell. Untold legions of them had inhabited the temple for generations, deceiving men by their superstitions and profaning their souls. At my command, the power of God hurled all of them into the deepest caverns of hell. So great was the terror by which I struck them down that as soon as I opened my lips to pronounce the first word they waited not for the second. Even the swiftness of an angel, proper to them as pure spirits, appeared slow to them in their haste to flee from me as the Queen of Heaven and Earth. There the demons remained until the Omnipotent One again released them in accordance with his divine will.

With my Son's approval, I then ordered my angel Azora to destroy the Temple of Artemis without leaving one stone upon the other. Of all the women that dwelt there, the angel was to save only the nine designated by me, the rest were reprobates and condemned by God to die. Consequently, the temple debris crushed them. Even that was an act of mercy, for Jesus took them before they could increase their just punishments by more sins. He buried them in Hell with the demons, whom they had obeyed and worshipped. I will speak later of the nine women saved. The sudden destruction of the temple roused astonishment and great fear in the inhabitants of Ephesus. The authorities of the city could not find anyone upon whom to place the blame for this calamitous event.

Saint John took advantage of their confusion to preach with even greater fervor the divine truth to free the Ephesians from the deceits and errors of the demons. Together, John and I gave thanks to the Most High for this triumph over Lucifer and over idolatry. Sadly, after I left Ephesus the kings rebuilt the temple. This evilness was again deceiving the people, when Saint Paul visited Ephesus in later years.

John baptized many of those he converted and confirmed their faith by great miracles and prodigies, such as had never before been witnessed by the Gentiles. The Greek schools in this area turned out many philosophers and learned men in the human sciences, notwithstanding an admixture of many errors. The blessed Apostle convincingly taught them the true science, making use not only of miracles and signs, but also of argumentation for the credibility of the Christian faith. He sent all his catechumens to me and I instructed many of them, having the advantage of knowing the interior inclinations of each person. I spoke to the heart of each one and filled it with heavenly delight. I wrought prodigies and miracles for the benefit of the unfortunate. I cured the possessed, the infirm, and succored the poor and the needy, and by the labor of my own hands, I gave assistance to the sick and attending upon them in person.

The kindly women of Ephesus, who had shared their home with us, were our first converts. Consequently, they graciously accepted the nine virgins from the Temple of Diana into their home. John realized that space was now a problem and he was the only male amidst so many women and he did not feel comfortable and he came to me and said. "My, mother, with your permission I deem it advisable for me to find new quarters for you, for our hosts have stretched their hospitality thin with the additional nine holy women they have taken into their home."

I readily agreed with John, for the cramped quarters threatened my need for privacy, prayer, and meditation. The area he selected was three hours distance from Ephesus. It stood on a height to where several Christian families from Judea had fled seeking sanctuary from the Jewish persecution after Stephen's death. Two of the women were distant relatives of mine. Between this height and Ephesus, a small stream wound and led a path down the slope to the city. From the southeast, I could see the city lying before me at the foot of a mountain. Narrow footpaths led up to this mountain retreat from a solitary but fertile plain covered with wide spreading trees and containing many clean rocky caves. By means of light thatch work, early Christian settlers from Jerusalem had converted the caves into hermitages after having fled there for refuge. Not far from the Christian settlement rose a castle whose occupant was a disposed king. John often visited him, and with the aid of my prayers, he was finally converted. At a later period, this place became a bishopric.

Before John brought me to this settlement, he had built for me a small dwelling of stone, similar to my home in Nazareth. A fireplace in the center divided the house into two apartments, and the house was nestled amidst a fine stand of trees. The fire was on the earth opposite the entrance, in a kind of furnace, formed by the wall, which rose-up on either side like steps to the roof of the house. The smoke escaped through a tube that protruded above the flat roof. Wicker screens, placed on either side of the fireplace, separated the front from the back. Similar screens rested against the walls right and left the whole length of the house. The screens were used to form little cubicles when various holy women came to visit me, for it was a simple matter to set up separate sleeping areas. To the right and left of the fireplace light doors opened through the wicker partitions into the two back rooms whose end walls were rounded and very pleasing to the eye, covered as they were with neatly wrought woodwork. In the most remote space of the rounded end, I had my oratory, before which hung a curtain. John had erected a small tabernacle for me in a niche in the wall. I could open or close it, as I needed. In it was the cross which the angels had made for me, and which I always kept in my oratory. At the foot of this cross, I had stored the holy relics, which I had taken with me from the crucifixion of my divine Son.

In my house, I stored a supply of clothes donated by kind souls. Thus, I was able to clothe many of the poor, forsaken by their fellowmen. Many people found their way to my door, and I helped them all with their physical and spiritual needs. John and I spent much time in the city of Ephesus, and when there I lodged with our good friend, Mary the elder, who had first given us lodgings in that wicked city. I helped many persons in the hour of their death, and gained these souls in their last agony bringing them safely through all the assaults of the demon to their Creator. There were too many to be recorded, except in the books of heaven, for no day passed in which I did not increase the possessions of the Lord by a copious and abundant fruit of saved souls.

After so many defeats at my hands, Lucifer arrogantly resolved to make a complaint against me to the Lord himself. The demons cannot present themselves before the Lord in person, for they are entirely incapable of such action. However, Jesus permitted them to speak to him from time to time. To prepare himself, Lucifer said to his demons, "If we do not vanquish this woman, our enemy, I fear that without a doubt, she will destroy my sovereignty. We all find in her strength more than human, which annihilates and oppresses us, whenever and in whatsoever manner she pleases to exercise it. This is what makes her intolerable to me. We all know that God has the infinite power to destroy us. However, this woman, though she is the Mother of God of the Incarnate Word, is not God. She is a mere creature of a nature inferior to ours. Yet, she treats me in an imperious manner, which I cannot endure. Let us all go forth to destroy her and let us make our complaint to the Omnipotent as to what we have now concluded to do."

Lucifer, in reliance upon his pretended rights, alleged that God, instead of leaving me in my humble condition exposed to the persecutions and temptations of the demons, had by his graces and gifts unjustly raised me above him, though I was but the dust of the earth, while he was an angel of superior essence. The Almighty gave Lucifer permission to go forth in battle against me. However, the conditions asked by Satan were unjust, and therefore many of them were not conceded. The divine Wisdom furnished those weapons, which were appropriate to each combatant, in order that the victory of me, his mother, might be so much the more glorious and crush the head of this ancient and poisonous serpent.

The battle was mysterious, no less than its triumphant issue, as I will discuss later. Its mysterious character is plainly evident in the twelfth chapter of the Apocalypse. I wish only to state here that the divine Providence foreordained all this, not only for my greater glory, but also in order to bring relief to the Church from the persecutions roused against it by the demons. He also wished to bind himself with some show of justice to the bestowal of the infinite favors and blessings, which I alone could merit for the whole Church. The Lord continually works in this manner in his Church; preparing and fortifying some chosen souls, against which, as members and parts of his holy Church, the dragon may exert all his wrath and fury. If they overcome him by the help of divine grace, their victories redound to the benefit of the whole mystical body of the faithful. God allowed Lucifer to have certain rights and power over humankind. However in turn, the Lord allowed the victories of the faithful to diminish the power of Lucifer. Jesus has rewarded many of his staunchest defenders, who successfully resisted the advances of Satan, to be canonized as saints through his Church for the greater glory of God.

Having destroyed the Temple of Diana, I conceived still greater desires of laboring for the exaltation of the name of Christ, and for the spread of his Holy Church, so that the triumphs gained over his enemies might bring its proper fruit. While I was thus meditating, God's holy angels manifested themselves to me, saying, "Our, Queen and, Mistress, the great God of celestial hosts commands us to bring you to Heaven before his royal throne to which he calls you."

I responded, "Behold the handmaid of the Lord; let his holy will be done."

The angels received me on a throne of light, and bore me up to the Empyrean Heavens before the throne of God by an Abstractive Vision. I prostrated myself before the sovereign throne and adored the Trinity in profound humility and reverence.

The eternal Father spoke to me and said, "My, daughter and meekest, dove, the cries of your inflamed heart for the exaltation of my holy name have come to my ears. Your petitions for the holy Church are acceptable in my eyes, inclining me to mercy and clemency. In response to your love,

I wish to renew in you my power, in order that you may defend my honor and glory, and triumph over my enemies and their ancient pride. I wish you to bind and crush their necks, so that through your victories you may assist my Church and acquire new blessings and favor for its members your brethren."

I replied, "Behold oh, Lord, I am the least of your creatures. My heart is prepared for all that shall be your pleasure and for all that shall promote the exaltation of your ineffable name and your greater glory; let your divine will be done in me."

The eternal Father added, "Let all my courtiers of Heaven understand, that I appoint Mary as the chief and leader of all my hosts, and as the conqueror of all my enemies to gloriously triumph over them." The other two divine Persons, the Son and the Holy Ghost added their approval.

The blessed with the angels answered, "Your holy will be done oh, Lord in Heaven and on Earth."

Thereupon, the Lord ordered eighteen of the highest Seraphim to adorn, strengthen, and arm me, their Queen, for battle against the infernal dragon. On this occasion were mysteriously fulfilled the promise in the Book of Wisdom that the Lord armed the creatures for vengeance upon his enemies and the other sayings recorded there [Wisdom 5, 18]. Six Seraphim adorned me with a sort of light like that of an impenetrable armor, which at the same time manifested my holiness and justice as Queen. This light made me invincible and impenetrable to the demons. Thus, in an ineffable manner, the Trinity made me God-like in strength. For this wonder the Seraphim, the Saints and I gave thanks to God.

Another six of the Seraphim approached and furnished me with another new enlightenment. It was a sort of reflection of the Divinity on my countenance, unbearable in the eyes of the demons. In virtue of this gift, the enemies who later came to tempt me, could not look upon my saint-like face, not being deemed worthy of this privilege by the Lord. Then came the last six Seraphim and at the command of the Lord, they furnished me with offensive weapons, since I was to take upon myself the defense of the Divinity and its honor. In pursuance of their divine commission, the angels added to all my faculties, new qualities of divine virtue, corresponding to the gifts with which the Most High had endowed me. In virtue of this privilege, I received the power to impede, restrain and counteract at my will the most secret schemes and attempts of all the demons. Thus, all of them became subject to my will and mandate, and without the liberty to hinder my decrees. Later, I made use of this power frequently in favor of the faithful and of my clients. The Holy Trinity conferred upon me these gifts corresponding to each of their divine attributes. The Trinity then told me to return to the Church and use these attributes to triumph over the enemies of the Lord.

Upon returning to my oratory, I conferred within myself for some time, in order to prepare for my conflict with the demons. While I was thus meditating, I saw issue from the earth, as from the abyss, a fearful red dragon with seven heads. From each head came forth the smoke and fire of vast fury, while many other demons followed him in a variety of hideous shapes. This vision was so horrible that no other living creature could have looked upon it without losing their life. I could now see the necessity for the Lord to prepare me for such an onslaught. They gathered around me furiously howling, and began to vaunt their threats, saying, "Come, come, let us destroy our enemy. We have the permission of the Almighty to tempt her and make war upon her. This time we shall make an end of her. We shall take vengeance for the injuries she has continually inflicted on us and for the destruction of our Temple of Diana. Let us destroy her likewise; she is but a woman, a mere creature whereas we are knowledgeable, astute and powerful spirits. We need not fear this earthly creature."

The entire host of infernal dragons advanced on me, Lucifer leading them on and challenged me to battle. The most deadly poison of the serpent is his pride, by which he usually instills his vices for the destruction of innumerable souls. It seemed to him proper to begin with this vice, outwardly concealing it in accordance with the state of sanctity, which he attributed to me. For this purpose the dragon and his followers transformed themselves into angels of light and thus manifested themselves to me, imagining that I had not yet seen and recognized them as demons and dragons of Hell.

They began with flattery and praise, saying, "Powerful are you, Mary, great and valorous among women. The entire world honors and celebrates you for the virtues it sees in you and for the prodigies and wonders you perform among them. You are worthy of glory, since no one equals you in holiness. We know this better than all the rest, and therefore we proclaim it and sing it to you in festive joy at your doings."

By this counterfeit acknowledgement, Lucifer sought to excite in my mind haughty thoughts of pride and presumption. However, instead of moving me to any pleasure or consent in them, they were instead like living darts of pain that transfixed my heart. Not all the torments of the martyrs were as painful to me as these diabolical flatteries. In order to confound them, I performed acts of humility, annihilating and debasing myself in such an admirable and resistless manner, that all Hell could not bear it, nor remain longer in my presence. For the Lord had ordained that Lucifer and his ministers should recognize and feel these acts of humility. All the devils fled emitting dreadful howls, screaming, "Let us flee to the abyss, for less painful to us is the confusion of that place than the humility of this invincible woman."

They left me then and I most prudently and with great humility gave thanks to the Almighty for this first victory of the spiritual war allowed by our Lord.

After the unhappy death of the tyrant Herod, the primitive Church of Jerusalem enjoyed some measure of quiet and tranquility for a considerable time. The Lord felt that I merited this favor for my maternal care and solicitude. During this time, Saint Barnaby and Saint Paul preached with wonderful success in the cities of Asia Minor, Antioch, Lystra, Perge and others. Saint Peter had fled to Asia Minor beyond the domain of the Herod's authority and from there; he governed the Christians in Palestine and Asia Minor. All of them acknowledged and obeyed him as the Vicar of Jesus Christ and head of the Church. The faithful believed that all Peter ordained and enacted upon Earth, God confirmed in Heaven. With this firm faith, they went to him with all their doubts and difficulties, as their supreme pontiff.

Among other matters, they asked him to decide the questions raised by some of the Jews concerning the doings and teachings of Saint Paul and Barnaby that were in opposition to the circumcision proscribed by the Law of Moses. Consequently, the Apostles and disciples of Jerusalem begged Peter to return to the holy city in order to settle these controversies and establish order. Since the death of Herod, the Pharisees and priests had no one to assist them in their persecutions, and therefore the faithful assured Peter that it was safe for him to return. They also asked him to invite me to return, for all the faithful longed to see me again. Because of these appeals, Peter decided to return to Jerusalem, and he sat down and wrote me a letter inviting me to join him in Jerusalem.

When the messenger brought me the letter advising me it was from Peter, I received it on my knees in reverence for the Vicar of Christ, and I kissed the letter. However, I did not open the message, and when John asked me the contents, I replied in humility and obedience,

"Do you, my master, read the letter first and then tell me what it contains."

John opened the letter, read it to me, and then asked me what he should do. However, in this also I did not wish to give the appearance of being his equal or superior, preferring to obey. Therefore, I answered him saying, "My, Son and, Master please arrange whatever is proper, for I as your servant, will obey."

John replied, "I would deem it best to return to Jerusalem at once.

It is right and proper to obey the head of the Church." I replied, "Let us prepare to leave at once."

John called together our friends from our Christian hamlet and bid a tearful farewell to them. With John's permission, I turned the house over to a poverty stricken widow with several children. A woman I had taught to weave and support her young family by the use of her own hands, as I had been doing off and on for so many years. It was a lovely home, a lovely setting, and peopled with many lovely Christians, and while I was tearful, I did not look back. It had not been my wish to leave Jerusalem, but subject to obedience I had not protested nor complained. My years were long and when I died, I sincerely wished to die in the holy city of Jerusalem. The Church had firmly established its roots there, roots which the feet and blood of my Son had made holy. I named these steps of Christ's Passion, the Stations of the Cross. Before I left Mary the elder, and the Commune of Sisters, I set up the fourteen Stations of the Cross to allow all Catholics, wherever they were, the privilege of walking the Passion of the Cross with their Lord and Redeemer. Wherever I went, I always practiced this worthy rite, and found great consolation and gained many favors for the Church by meditating on the Passion of Christ.

Early the following morning, John and I set off for Ephesus, and upon arrival, he left me with Mary the elder, while he went to arrange our passage. At John's request, I called together my women acquaintances and disciples, in order to take proper leave and instruct them in what they must do to persevere in their faith. There were seventy-three of them, and many were virgins, among whom were the nine virgins saved from the temple of Diana. These and many others I had converted and catechized in the faith. I had formed of them a *Community* in the home of our former host. Through the worthy works and prayers of this congregation of women, humankind had begun to atone for the sins and abominations, perpetrated in the Temple of Artemis for so many ages. I had established the observance of chastity in community life in the very city of Ephesus where the devil had profaned the virtue of virginity. Only John and I knew that I had destroyed the Temple of Diana. In this manner, the devil could not stir up retaliation against any of the Christians.

I said to my charges, "My, daughters, the will of the Almighty calls me back to Jerusalem. In my absence keep in mind the doctrine, which you have received from me, and which I heard from the mouth of the Redeemer of the world. Look upon him always as your Lord and Master, and as the spouse of your souls, serving him and loving him with all your heart. Keep the Commandments of his Holy Law, in which the disciples and priests will fully instruct you. Reverence and obey them in humility, without ever accepting other teachers, who are not Disciples of Christ. I shall always see that his ministers assist and protect you, and I shall never forget you or cease to commend you to the Lord. In my place, I leave you Mary, the elder. Obey her in all things with great respect, and she will care for you with the same love and solicitude as I have done. You will observe inviolate retirement and recollection in this house, and no man shall ever enter it. If it is necessary to speak to anyone, it shall be in the portal, in the presence of three of your number. Your prayers shall be uninterrupted and private. Recite and sing the ones I have left you in my chamber. Observe silence and meekness and treat your neighbors, as you would wish to be treated. Speak always the truth, and be ever mindful of Christ crucified in all your thoughts, words, and actions. Adore him and confess him as the Creator and Redeemer of the world. In his name, I give you his blessing, and I ask him to live in your hearts."

I left them written copies of the, Our Father, the Ten Commandments, and the Magnificat together with other prayers which they were to recite vocally. I had my angels make them a large cross, which was set up in my old oratory. I distributed among them all the personal things I had in my possession, which had little value; nevertheless, they were rich to them as being pledges and proofs of my maternal love. Thus, did I establish the first of many religious convents that in time would become prevalent throughout the world. When I took leave of them two days later, they all prostrated themselves at my feet amidst great wailing and abundant tears. However, I watched over them carefully, and I am happy to say that all seventy-three persevered in the fear of God and the faith of Christ our Lord. Yet, the demon rose up violent persecutions against them and against the inhabitants of Ephesus. Foreseeing this, I fervently prayed for them before leaving and I asked my divine Son to guard and preserve them, and to appoint some angels for the defense of this small flock. All this, my Son granted me, and afterwards I was able to console them by sending exhortations from Jerusalem, and by charging the disciples and Apostles at Ephesus to watch over these virgins and retired women. I continued this care throughout my life on earth, and throughout their lives, without the loss of a single soul.

The Subjugation of the Demons

As we left I asked John for his blessing and we departed Ephesus after living there for two and one half years. On leaving, my angels manifested themselves to me in visible forms. They formed into squadrons, armed for battle. In this manner, the angels forewarned me that I was to be prepared to continue my conflict with the great dragon and his allies. Before reaching the sea, I saw a great multitude of the infernal legions challenging me in various dreadful and horrible shapes. In their midst came a dragon with seven heads, he was larger than a huge ship, and as fierce and abominable as to cause torment by its mere glance. I repeated the words of Psalms and the sayings from the mouth of my most holy Son; thus, I fortified myself by my most firm faith and fervent love. I ordered my holy angels to assist me, for these monstrous creatures did inspire with some human dread and horror. No human creature can look upon such abominations and not be visible shaken for the evil they represent against humankind. John saw nothing of this, until I later informed him of the dangers facing him and all humankind.

We had no sooner set sail than the demons, using the power God allowed them, stirred up the sea by a tempest such as had not been seen before that time or until now. In allowing this, the Lord God wished to exalt the power of his arm and my holiness. The waves rose with terrific roaring, piling themselves upon the winds and apparently even upon the very clouds. The waves created towering mountains of water and foam, as if the demons were preparing to burst the bounds of the abyss that imprisoned the ocean. The waves lashed and battered the ship too and fro, and it seemed a miracle that it was not shattered to splinters at each shock. Sometimes the waves hurled the ship up into the clouds, and then plunged it down as though to plow up the sand of the oceans' abyss. The furious hurricane buried the ships' sails and masts in the foaming waves, forcing my angels to hold the ship up in the air in order to save it from some of the vaster billows, which would inevitably have overwhelmed and sent it to the bottom.

The mariners and passengers perceived the effects of this assistance, but remained ignorant of the cause. In their distress, they were beside themselves, bewailing their destruction, which they deemed inevitable. The demons added to their fears, for they assumed human shapes and pretending to be from neighboring ships, they called the mariners urging them to forsake the ship and to save themselves and others. For while all ships traveling these seas greatly suffered in this storm, yet the wrath of the demons and their power of doing harm were confined principally to the ship upon which John and I rode. The mariners, deceived by the demons', gave up caring for their own vessel and hoped another ship would help them. However, when this happened, my angels took their places, and directed and steered the ship during their moments of despair.

During all this chaos, I preserved my tranquility, although I experienced the same dangers of navigation subjected to all humans traveling upon the high seas. I was moved to great compassion for all voyagers at sea and renewed all my former prayers and petitions that I had made on my previous voyage. I admired the indomitable forces of the ocean. This insensible creature, the sea well represented the wrath of divine justice. I suffered much physical discomfort and inconvenience the same as the rest of the passengers; however because the demons were attacking me, my fellow passengers were forced to suffer the same persecution and tribulation on my account, and this caused me greater suffering than my personal discomfort did.

I offered up the extreme hardships of this voyage, and prayed the most ardent prayers for the conversion of the world and the increase of the Church. John suffered the most, because of his deep solicitude for his responsibility to protect me, the Mother of God. Added to this was his suffering, and his sincere efforts to console, assist, and comfort me. Although the trip from Ephesus to Palestine usually lasted only about six days, this one lasted fifteen, of which fourteen were tempestuous.

One day Saint John was very much disheartened at the continuance of this measureless hardship and no longer able to control his composure said, "My, lady, what is this? Are we to perish at sea? Beseech your divine Son to look upon us with the eyes of a Father and to defend us in this tribulation."

I answered him, "Do not be disturbed my, son: for we must now fight the battles of the Lord and overcome his enemies by fortitude and patience. I shall beg of him that no one who is with us shall perish, and that he sleeps not, who watches over Israel. The strong ones of his court assist us and defend us. Let us suffer for him who placed himself upon the Cross for the salvation of all." These words bolstered John's courage, and he joined me in heartfelt prayer for those terrified souls on board the ship, and for the forgiveness of the sins of the world.

Lucifer and his horde of demons, with increasing fury threatened me by saying that I would perish in the sea. These threats were like so many spent arrows, I despised them, heeding not their words, and did not look upon them, nor did I speak a single word to them. For their part, they could not even bare to glance on my face, because the virtue of the Most High shone from my countenance. The more they tried to overcome this virtue, the weaker they became, and the more the offensive weapons, with which the Lord had clothed me, tormented them. However during this prolonged conflict on the high seas, my Son withdrew from me leaving me to fight my own battles. He not only concealed his purpose from me, but he never once showed himself to me during the sea voyage.

At the end of fourteen days my, Son appeared before me on the sea, saying, "My dearest, mother, I am with you in tribulation."

Help is always more welcome in necessity, and I adored my Son and God and answered, "My, God and only good of my soul, whom the winds and the sea obey. Behold my, Son our affliction, let not the works of your hands perish."

The Lord said to me, "My, mother and my, dove, from you I have received human form, therefore I desire that all creatures obey your orders; command them as the Mistress of all, for they are subject to your will."

I had desired my Son to command the waves, as he had done before on the Sea of Galilee, but the occasion was different, since at that time there was no one else but he to command the winds and the sea. I therefore obeyed, and in the name of my Son, I first commanded Lucifer and his hosts to instantly leave the Mediterranean. The demons fled in the direction of Palestine, for I had not ordered them into Hell, not wishing to put an end to the battle. Once the demons retired, I commanded the water and the winds to subside. They immediately obeyed, becoming tranquil and serene in the shortest space of time to the great astonishment of the passengers, who had no idea of the miracles taking place. Thus on the fifteenth day, we disembarked happily at the port of Jaffa. John and I gave thanks to our Redeemer and benefactor; then we both set out for Jerusalem.

My holy angels accompanied me in battle array for the demons were awaiting my arrival resolved to continue the conflict as soon as I reached the shore. With incredible fury, they led an assault by suggesting various temptations against all the virtues, but all their darts fell back upon themselves. Before entering my house in Jerusalem, I yearned to visit the sacred spots consecrated by the Redemption, which was the last thing I had done when I left the city. However it was not proper that I cater to my own private devotions, but to show proper veneration and respect for the Vicar of Christ. I found Peter at the Cenacle, where he was staying, and once there I fell on my knees before him. I asked for his blessings and begged his pardon for not having complied sooner with his command. I kissed his hand as the high priest of God. I did not lay the blame for my delay to the storm, and I offered no other circumstance or excuse.

The vicar of our Savior and all his disciples and faithful of Jerusalem received me with indescribable joy, reverence and love, which I returned with all my heart. They prostrated themselves at my feet and thanked me for having come to fill them with gladness and consolation, and to live where they could see and serve me. This made me most uncomfortable, yet, being the Mother of God, it was proper that I accept their accolades, but I did so with the utmost humility. Peter did not find out about the storm, until later, when John gave him a detailed account of our journey.

After I complied obediently with the will of Peter, and with John's permission, I again visited the sacred spots of our Redemption. John and I left the Cenacle to visit the sacred places, my angels, again assembled in battle formation, and we met Lucifer's forces ready to do battle. However, as I approached each holy spot, the demons fell back, repelled by divine power. Lucifer, urged on by the temerity of his pride, attempted to come nearer, for with his permission to tempt and persecute me; he was over-anxious to gain some great victory over me. Thus, the very exercises that he attempted to disturb became a sword that overcame him. As I worshipped my divine Son at each Station of the Cross, I renewed the grateful remembrance of the Passion. It caused such terror to the demons that they could not tolerate it, and they felt a force so oppressive and tormenting proceeding from me that they were obliged to recede even further from my presence.

They broke out into horrible shrieks, audible to me alone, and they exclaimed, "Let us fly from this woman, our enemy who so confounds and oppresses us by her virtues. We seek to blot out the remembrance and the veneration of these places. The Lord redeemed humankind here, and here, he despoiled our dominion. This woman, a mere creature, hinders our designs and renews the triumphs gained by her Son upon the Cross."

After completing the Stations, I proceeded to Mt. Olivet, where my Son had ascended into heaven. Suddenly, the Lord himself, in majestic beauty and glory, surrounded by angels, descended from his throne to visit and console me. He manifested himself to me with the affection and bounty of a Son, yet as the infinite and powerful God. I perceived that these favors were part of my reward for my humility and obedience toward Saint Peter. He promised me anew his assistance in my battle against the demons; in fulfillment of this promise, the Lord ordained that Lucifer and his hosts should become convinced of a power in me such as they had not experienced before.

I returned to the Cenacle and the demons again sought to renew their temptations. My humility hurled them back with greater force than that with which they had assaulted me, and they rebounded like rubber balls. They broke out in still more furious howling, and were driven to confess certain truths. God often uses his enemies to make certain facts known, or for them to even make prophetic statements. Much to their own dismay they said, "Oh unhappy ones, who are obliged to look upon such happiness of the human nature. What great excellence and dignity man has now attained in this pure creature. How ungrateful shall men be, and how foolish, if they do not profit by the blessings bestowed upon them in this daughter of Adam. She is truly its salvation and our destruction. Great things her Son does for her, but she is worthy of them. A cruel punishment is this that we must confess all these truths. Oh would that God conceal from us this woman, who adds such torments to our envy. How shall we vanquish her, if the mere sight of her is insufferable to us? Let us console ourselves in the fact that men lose so much of that which this woman merits for them, and for which they foolishly despise her. In them we shall avenge our injuries through them we shall exercise our fury filling them with illusions and errors. If men paid attention to her example, all of them would profit by this woman and follow her virtues."

"However, Lucifer added, "This is not enough to console me, for this woman, his mother, can please God more than all the sins we can lead men into to displease him. Even if this were not so, my position does not permit me to remain indifferent at seeing human nature so highly exalted in a mere weak woman. This wrong is unbearable; let us return to persecute her; let us give vent to the fury of our envy even in spite of the torment. Though we all suffer by it, let our pride be not dismayed, for possibly some triumph may yet be gained over this woman."

I heard all these threats, but as the Queen of Virtues, I despised them all. With no outward sign, I retired to my oratory in order to prudently meditate concerning the mysteries of this conflict, and also concerning the difficult business now before the Church in seeking to end circumcision and the ancient law. I labored on these problems for several days in continual prayers, petitions, tears and prostrations. I asked the Lord to stretch out his almighty arm against Lucifer and grant me the victory over him and the demons. I knew that God was on my side and would not desert me in my tribulations. I prayed as if I was the weakest of creatures in the time of my temptations. By my example, I have taught what each soul must do when tempted. I prayed for the holy Church and asked the Lord to grant to it his Evangelical Law, pure, unsullied without wrinkle, and unhampered by the ancient ceremonies.

I prayed with burning fervor, for I knew that Lucifer and all Hell sought through the Jews to unite circumcision with baptism, and the rites of Moses with the truths of the Gospel. The admission of these fallacies would help to maintain the Jews in their stubborn adhesion to the old Law during the coming ages. In the meantime, I knew that Saint Paul and Saint Barnabas were hastening from Antioch to Jerusalem in order to confer with Saint Peter in order to solve these difficulties raised by the Jews.

Paul and Barnabas were aware that I had returned to Jerusalem, and upon their return, in their ardent desire to see me, they sought my presence at the Cenacle. They cast themselves at my feet, shedding abundant tears of joy. My joy was no less at meeting these holy men, toward whom I bore an especial love in the Lord, because of their zealous labors for the exultation of God's holy name and the spread of the faith. I, of course, desired them to first present themselves to Peter, but in God's eyes they preserved the proper order in their reverence and love believing that none on earth should be preferred before me, who was the Mother of God. As they entered, I prostrated myself at their feet, kissed their hands and asked for their blessings. On this occasion, Saint Paul was favored with a wonderful Ecstatic Abstraction, in which were revealed to him great mysteries and prerogatives of me, and he saw me as it were completely invested with the Divinity.

This vision filled Saint Paul with admiration and with incomparable love and veneration for me as the Mother of God. Somewhat recovering himself he said, "Mother of all piety and clemency, pardon this vile and sinful man for having persecuted your divine Son, my Lord and his holy Church."

I answered him, "Paul, servant of the Most High, if he who created you to his friendship and made you a vessel of election, how can I, his slave, refuse to pardon you. My soul magnifies and exalts him, because he wished to manifest himself so powerful, liberal, and holy in you."

Paul thanked me for the benefits of his conversion, and the other favors I had conferred upon him in saving him from so many dangers. Barnabas echoed Paul's thanks, and they both asked for my protection and help, which I readily agreed to do.

The Council of Jerusalem

Peter, as Christ's Vicar, convoked the first Council of the Church. He included all the Apostles, and those disciples and presbyters working in and near Jerusalem. In order that I would not in my profound humility absent myself from this meeting, Peter ordered me to appear by his authority as vicar. When we were all gathered he said, "My brethren and children in Christ our Savior, it was necessary that we meet in order to define the affairs, which our most beloved brethren Paul and Barnabas have brought to our attention. We must also determine other matters touching the increase of holy faith and the definition of the precepts of our faith. It is proper that we obtain the assistance of the Holy Trinity; to do so we shall prepare ourselves by observing a ten-day period of fasting and prayer. We shall celebrate a daily sacrifice of the Breaking of the Bread, by which we shall dispose our hearts to receive the divine light."

In order to celebrate the Breaking of the Bread during the ten-days; I prepared the upper room of the Cenacle, cleaning and decorating it with my own hands and holding all things in readiness. The owner had humbly donated the upstairs room to the Apostles, and it was here that several years before, Peter had celebrated the first official Breaking of the Bread Ceremony, after the Ascension of our Blessed Lord. James the less had later converted several large estates that the faithful had donated to them, to observe the Breaking of the Bread for the many converts. In addition to the daily Breaking of Bread, many of the faithful were also attending the Jewish services at the holy temple. This is not so strange, when you consider the Jewish background of most of the converts. This double observance of God's old and God's new Covenant would not cease entirely until the Jewish Holy Temple was destroyed by the Roman Titus in 70 AD. Even the Apostles and I attended services there, but we avoided offering up burnt sacrifices, for God wanted love, not holocausts.

The next day Saint Peter, as high priest, officiated in the rites and ceremonies of the Breaking of the Bread. All the disciples and Apostles received the Holy Eucharist at the hands of Peter, before I, in abject humility, received my Son's Body and Blood. Many angels descended to the Cenacle, and God allowed some of the disciples present to see them. God filled the Cenacle with a wonderful light and fragrance when Peter consecrated the bread and wine. At the consecration, the Holy Spirit wrought wonderful effects on the souls of all those present. Having celebrated the eating of the Holy Eucharist, they then agreed upon certain hours in which they were to persevere together in daily prayer, without neglecting the necessary ministry of souls and their necessity to work to pay their own way.

I retired to my oratory for the entire ten days without eating or speaking to anyone, except to receive Holy Communion. During this time, I experienced such hidden mysteries as to move the angels to astonishment. The first day, I prostrated myself to pray after Holy Communion, and at the command of the Lord, my angels lifted me up. They took me, body and soul, to the high heavens. An angel again took my shape so that the Apostles in the Cenacle might not become aware of my absence. They bore me up in splendor and magnificence described by me on other occasions, and this time it was even greater because of the designs of the Lord.

When I arrived in a region of space far removed from the earth, the almighty Lord commanded Lucifer and all his hellish hosts to come and attend me as their Queen. All the demons from Hell assembled before me. I knew them all by name and God made known to me, the condition of their spirits. The sight was most painful for me. The demons' spirits were abominable and disgusting to look upon. However, God had armed me with divine virtue, and this horrible and execrable sight could not harm me. Not so for the demons; however, for the Lord gave them to understand by an especial insight the greatness and superiority of their Queen, a mere woman, whom they were persecuting as their enemy. The Lord made them perceive how foolishly presumptuous they had been in their attempts against me. To their still greater terror, they saw that I carried in my bosom the sacramental Christ. They realized then that the Divinity had enveloped me in its Omnipotence for their humiliation, overthrow and destruction.

The demons heard a voice proceeding from the Deity itself, saying, "With this shield of my powerful arm, invincible and strong, I shall always defend my Church. This woman shall crush the head of the ancient serpent, and shall forever triumph over its haughty pride for the glory of my holy name."

The reprobates perceived and understood all this and other mysteries relating to me as their Queen. So great was the despair and crushing pain they felt that they, with loudest clamors, exclaimed, "May the power of the Almighty cast us immediately into Hell; do not keep us in the presence of this woman, who torments us more than the fire. Oh invincible and strong woman, recede from us since we ourselves cannot fly from your presence, where we are bound by the chains of the Almighty. Why do you torment us before our time? You alone of all human nature are the instrument of the Omnipotent against us; and through you, men can acquire the eternal blessings we have lost. Those that have sunk into despair of ever seeing God eternally are now rewarded for the accredited good works of their Redeemer by the vision of you, which in our hate is to us a torment and chastisement. Please release us, almighty, Lord and, God! Let this new punishment in which you renew that of our fall from heaven cease. For in it, you execute the punishment you have threatened us with in this wonder of your powerful arms."

God bound the demons in my presence, during their lamentations of despair. The black angels made valiant efforts to fly from my presence. However, God did not permit them to do so, even as their fury urged them on. In order that the terror of their Queen might strike them so much the deeper and become the more notorious, the Lord ordained that I should use my own authority as Mistress and Queen in permitting them to leave. I did so, and they all cast themselves, with the swiftness of light, from the upper regions into the abyss.

The demons emitted dreadful howls, and terrorized all the damned souls with new punishments. They were full of dismay and torments in not being able to deny their defeat. The Lord forced them to proclaim in the presence of the damned souls, the power of Jesus, their King, and of me his holy mother, their Queen. My Son then triumphantly escorted me to the Empyrean Heaven, where the angels and saints received me with new and admirable jubilee, and I remained there for twenty-four hours.

Upon arriving I prostrated myself before the throne of the blessed Trinity and adored it in the unity of its undivided nature and majesty. I prayed for the Church, in order that the Apostles might understand and resolve what was proper for the establishment of the Evangelical Law and the termination of the Law of Moses. In answer to these petitions, I heard a voice from the throne, by which the three divine Persons, one after the other, and each one for himself, promised to assist the Apostles and disciples in declaring and establishing the divine truth. They assured me that the Father would direct its establishment by his Omnipotence. The Son, as head of the Church, would assist it by his Wisdom, the Holy Ghost, as its spouse, by his love and his enlightening gifts. Then I saw the most holy humanity of my Son present to the Father, the prayers and petitions, which I myself had offered for the Church. The Father approved of them, and he stated, "I desire that the faith of the

Gospel and my Son's entire holy law might be established in the world in accordance with the decrees of the divine will and mind."

In execution of this will and proposal of Christ our Savior, I saw issuing forth from the Divinity, the form of a church, beautiful, clear and resplendent, as if built of diamond or of sparkling crystal, adorned with many enamels and bas-reliefs to enhance its beauty. The angels and saints saw it and in astonishment exclaimed; "Holy! Holy! Holy! And powerful are you, Lord, in all your works."

The blessed Trinity placed the Church in the most holy humanity of my Son, and he then united it with himself, in a manner in which I cannot describe in words. Thereupon, Jesus turned the Church over to me, and the Lord filled me with new splendor, as soon as I received it. I annihilated myself within myself, and then saw the Divinity, clearly and intuitively by Eminent and Beatific Vision. I remained in this joy for many hours. What I experienced and received there surpasses all created thought or capacity to understand. In effect, I was directed with new fervor toward the Church consigned to me. Enriched by these favors, the angels transported me back to the Cenacle. In my hands, I held the mystical Church that I had received from my divine Son. I remained in prayer the remaining nine days without motion and without interruption. During this time, I distributed the treasures of the Redemption among the children of the Church. I began with the Apostles and going through the different ages, I applied them separately to the just and the saints according to the secret disposition of eternal predestination.

On the last day, Peter celebrated the Breaking of the Bread, and we all received Holy Communion. Then Peter convened the first Council of the Church, the Council of Jerusalem. After invoking the Holy Ghost, he began to consult with the Apostles and disciples about the solution of the difficulties that had arisen in the Church. The first to stand up and speak were a group of Pharisees who had become believers, and they stated, "It is necessary for us to circumcise the Gentiles first and then direct them to observe the Mosaic Law."

Peter then addressed them, saying, "My brothers, you are well aware that from early days God made his choice among you that through my mouth the Gentiles would hear the word of the Gospel and believe. God, who knows the heart, bore witness by granting them faith. Only by faith can a soul gain salvation. God makes no distinction between them and us; for by faith, he purified their hearts. Why are you then putting God to the test by placing on the shoulders of the disciples the yoke of the Mosaic Law that neither our ancestors nor we have been able to bear? On the contrary, we believe that we are saved the same way as the Gentiles are."

The whole assembly then listened while Paul and Barnabas described the signs and wonders God had worked among the Gentiles through them. James [the less], the bishop of Jerusalem, then said, "My brothers, it is my judgment that we ought to stop troubling the Gentiles who turn to God. We should tell them by letter; however, to avoid pollution from idols, unlawful marriage, eating the meat of strangled animals, and blood. At the close of the first council, Peter, the Vicar of Christ, ruled, "Only through baptism and faith in Christ can a soul gain eternal salvation. A soul does not gain salvation through the Law of Moses, and therefore the Gentiles do not have to be circumcised."

The Council of Jerusalem rendered other decisions, which defined certain matters concerning the government and the ceremonies of the Church. The indiscreet piety of some of the faithful had introduced certain abuses, and the Council defined these matters of faith [Acts: 15, 1-35].

The Creed

Before the convening of the Council of Jerusalem, the disciples having dispersed to preach the name and faith of Christ, had not been furnished an express creed to uniformly guide themselves and teach the faithful. This was necessary so that all Christians might believe the same express truths. I knew the Apostles and disciples would soon have to go far a field to spread and establish the Church throughout the world. It was proper that they should be united in their doctrine, upon which was to be founded all the perfections of a Christian life. I wished to see the divine mysteries, which the Apostles were to preach and the faithful to believe, reduced to a short formula. I prayed to the Lord, "Most High and eternal God, Creator, and Ruler of the entire universe, look with favor on the new children, which the blood of Christ has engendered for you, and on those who Jesus will engender for you in the Church during the future ages. Please send the Holy Spirit to inspire your Vicar Peter, and the Apostles, to produce the truths of the Church in a simple Creed. This must be done so that its children may know what to believe, without differences in opinion."

My Son descended from Heaven in all his glory to answer my prayers in person. He said, "My beloved, mother, be relieved of your anxiety. It is in my power to fulfill your wishes and you are the one to oblige me to do so, since I will deny nothing you desire.

I was prostrate, and my Son raised me to my feet and filled my heart with joy, as he gave me his benediction. Before he left, he promised to send me great gifts and favors for the Church. He told me the very wording of the articles, of which the Creed was to be composed. Now the time had come for the executing what had been intended so long before. Jesus wished to renew it in my pure heart, in order that the fundamental truths of the Church might flow from the lips of Christ himself.

Thus it was that during the First Council of Jerusalem, Jesus inspired Peter and the other Apostles to set up a symbol of the universal faith of the Church. Peter spoke to the Apostles as follows, "My dear brethren, the Divine Mercy, in its infinite goodness and through the merits of our Savior, have favored his holy Church by gloriously multiplying its children, as we have seen and experienced since our first Pentecost. For this purpose, the Almighty has multiplied miracles and prodigies daily, having chosen us, though unworthy, as the instruments of his divine will. Together with these favors, he has sent us tribulations and the persecutions of the devil and of the world, in order that we may imitate our Savior and Redeemer. The disciples have evaded the wrath of the high priest and have spread throughout the neighboring cities, preaching the faith of Christ. For several years, as Jesus intended, we have concentrated our efforts in Israel, to first spread the word to God's chosen people. We Apostles must soon depart and preach throughout the world, according to the command of the Lord before he ascended into Heaven. Just as there is one baptism in which men are to receive this faith, so there must be but one doctrine, which the faithful are to believe. We firmly hope that he will now assist us with his divine Spirit to understand and define, in his name and by an unchangeable decree, the articles to be established in his holy Church as long as it shall last, to the end of the world."

The Apostles all agreed to this proposal of Saint Peter. We then prostrated ourselves in prayer calling upon the Holy Ghost to assist us. After we had prayed for some time, we heard the sound of a fierce wind, as on the first coming of the Holy Ghost. Suddenly, light and splendor filled the Cenacle, and the Holy Spirit enlightened us. Peter then asked each Apostle to define a mystery, according as how the divine Spirit should inspire them. Thereupon Saint Peter began, and was followed by each Apostle in the following order:

Saint Peter	**I believe in God, the Father almighty, Creator of Heaven and Earth,**
Saint Andrew:	**and in Jesus Christ, his only Son, and our Lord.**
Saint James [G]:	**Who was conceived by the Holy Ghost, and born of the Virgin Mary.**
Saint John:	**He suffered under Pontius Pilate, was crucified, died and was buried.**
Saint Thomas:	**He descended into Hell, and arose from the dead on the third day.**

Saint James [L]:	**He ascended into Heaven, and is seated at the right hand of God the. Father Almighty,**
Saint Philip:	**from thence he shall come to judge the living and the dead.**
Saint Bartholomew:	**I believe in the Holy Ghost,**
Saint Matthew:	**the holy Catholic Church, the Communion of Saints.**
Saint Simon:	**the forgiveness of sins,**
Saint Thaddeus:	**the resurrection of the body,**
Saint Mathias:	**and life everlasting. Amen.**

As soon as the Apostles had finished pronouncing this Creed, the Holy Ghost approved of it by saying out loud, "You have decided well!"

We gave thanks to the Most High, and I thanked the Apostles for having merited the assistance of the divine Spirit. Inspired by my Son, I fell at the feet of Saint Peter, and in full voice, proclaimed the Apostle's Creed in the name of all the faithful. I then said to him, "My lord, whom I recognize as the Vicar of my most holy Son, in your hands, in my name, and in the name of all the faithful of the Church, I confess and proclaim all that you have set down as the divine and infallible truth of the Catholic Church. In it, I bless and exalt the Most High, from whom it precedes."

Thus, after the Apostles formulated the Creed of the Catholic faith, God gave me the privilege to be the first to profess it publicly.

As soon as the symbol of the faith was established, I wasted no time in providing innumerable copies of the Creed to all the disciples. With the aid of my angels, I prepared several copies for each to distribute. I informed those disciples not present of the Creed. In addition, the Apostles ordered that all the faithful should accept and verbally profess the Creed. To those close by, I sent the copies by members of the faithful, for those far away; I sent them by my staff of angels. Most of the disciples were able to see the angels, but to some, the papers were placed in their hands, and at the same time their hearts were interiorly moved. We distributed many copies in Jerusalem and instructed the faithful on how the Lord had sent the Holy Ghost in inspire and approve it in such a signal manner.

The Holy Ghost, who had ordained this Creed for the security of the Church, began to confirm it by new miracles and prodigies; it was operating not only through the hands of the disciples and Apostles, but also through many of the believers. Many, who received it with special veneration and love, were suddenly enveloped in divine splendor, filled with heavenly science and celestial manifestations of the Holy Ghost. By these miracles, others were in their turn moved to a desire of possessing and reverencing these documents. Others restored the sick to health, raised the dead, or expelled the demons from the possessed by merely placing the Credo upon the person. Among other marvels, it happened one day that a Jew, who was roused to anger at hearing a Christian devoutly reading the Creed, was about to tear it from his hands, he fell dead before he could do so. From this time on, those that were baptized, being adults, were required to profess the faith according to the Apostolic Creed; and while they professed it, the Holy Ghost visibly appeared above them in tongues of fire.

The gift of tongues likewise continued; for the Holy Ghost gave it not only on the day of Pentecost, but to many of the faithful afterwards, who assisted in preaching or in giving instructions to the new believers. Wherever they spoke to a group of many nationalities, they were understood by each nationality, although they spoke only in the Aramaic language. In a like manner, they were able to speak in other languages, when they happened upon a gathering of people all speaking the same foreign language. Besides these miracles, the Apostles wrought many others and whenever they laid hands upon believers, or confirmed them, the divine Spirit descended. There were too many miracles to all be set down and recorded. Saint Luke adds in his writings, in a general way that they were very numerous, and therefore could not be included in his short history.

I was greatly astonished but not surprised at the liberal bounty of the Almighty. There were two reasons for this liberality; First: God ardently desired men to participate in his Divinity by sharing his eternal happiness and glory. Therefore, he induced the Eternal Word to appear in this world in visible and passible flesh. In addition, the Third Person descended many times in visible and appropriate form upon his Church, in order to establish and confirm it by the demonstration of his omnipotence and love. Secondly, in the beginnings of the Church, the merits of the passion and death of Christ, together with my prayers and intercession, were in a certain sense more acceptable and therefore [according to your way of understanding] more powerful with the eternal Father. At that time, the children of the Church had not yet introduced the many and grievous sins, which have been committed since then and which have placed such great obstacles to the benefits of the Lord and to his Holy Spirit. Hence, he does not now manifest himself so familiarly to men, as he did in the primitive Church.

James [the less] notified the faithful of Palestine of the changes, and Peter had letters sent by Paul and Barnabas, who were accompanied by Judas and Silas to Antioch and to other cities announcing these decisions. When the bishops and priests read these letters to the faithful, the Holy Ghost descended in visible fire. He did so to console the faithful and confirm them in this Catholic truth. I gave thanks to the Lord for the blessings upon the Church. When Peter returned Paul, Barnabas, and the rest of the disciples, to their labors, I gave them relics of the clothes of my Son and some objects still left of the Passion. I offered them my protection and prayer for the labors and persecution still awaiting them. During the days of the council, Lucifer, because of the terror I had inspired in him, could not come near the Cenacle, yet they persisted in prowling around from a distance but were unable to execute any of their malice against its members [Acts: 13, 1-3].

In spite of his continual prowling, Lucifer saw that he could gain no advantage himself, so he resorted to engaging some sorcerers with whom he had an express pact. He persuaded these women to make an attempt on my life by magic means. His unhappy dupes tried in several different ways, but their enchantments were of no avail. Several times, they placed themselves directly in my path, and for their trouble, the Lord struck them dumb and motionless. Filled with compassion, I tried to undeceive them and convert them by kind words and deeds. However, out of the four that Lucifer sent, I was only able to convert one and she happily received holy baptism. When all his attempts failed, Lucifer was so confused and enraged that if his pride had allowed him, he would have given up trying to tempt me.

Although Lucifer and his demons had already been punished in their first rebellion by the eternal loss of the beatific vision and hurled into Hell, they were now punished anew in this second battle by additional accidental torments corresponding to their evil desires and attempts against me, their Queen. Having desired my defeat so vehemently, it was an inconceivable torment for the infernal dragons to find themselves again vanquished and foiled in the desperate desires and hopes entertained by them for so many ages.

Because the Lord has ordained it, I will tell you of some of these mysteries. In the Beatific Vision, I cannot brag, boast, or lie; I may only perform God's holy will. In overthrowing the ancient serpent, I gained a most joyful triumph. For the state which I was to enjoy during the rest of my life, my Son held in readiness so many and such great blessings as surpass all human and angelic capacity. The reader must understand that because of your limited powers and capacity, you are constrained to use for the most exalted mysteries the same terms and words as you use for the more ordinary ones. Yet, in what I am to speak of now, there is an infinite latitude and extent of mystery. In this, the Almighty can raise the creature from one state which seems to you the highest, to one more exalted and from this, repeatedly, to an even higher and more excellent state. For God destined and confirmed me in a world of graces, gifts, and favors. After reaching all that is not God's essence, I embraced within myself a vastness of excellence so great that of its own self, it constitutes a new hierarchy greater and more exalted than all the rest of the creatures angelic and human.

When I hurled the demons down from the Heavens into Hell, and later, when Lucifer tried to have me killed, and failed, it was not God's intention that that he, and his horde of demons, should be completely subjugated. Lucifer; however, fearing in his malice that he might have little time left for his temptations and persecutions, wished to make up for the shortness of time by an increase in his fury and temerity. Hence, Lucifer resorted to the use of sorcerers. Lucifer had especially instructed these men in black magic and witchcraft. He gave these sorcerers special and minute directions on how to take away my life. These ministers of evil attempted to fulfill their mission many times, making use of very powerful and pernicious charms. None of them; however, could, in any way, harm either my health or my life. The effects of sin exerted no influence over me, for I was sinless. The Lord had made me exempt and superior to all natural causes. Seeing his plans frustrated, the Evil One visited upon these sorcerers, fierce and cruel punishments. The Lord permitted this, because they had merited chastisement for their temerity, and in order that they might know what kind of master they had elected to serve.

Full of fury, Lucifer convened all the princes of darkness and reminded them of the many reasons they had since their fall from grace to cast down the woman, their enemy. They now clearly recognized me as the one shown to them at that time. They all agreed with him and resolved to unite and again pursue their vendetta against me. They assumed that on some occasion or another they would find me less prepared and bereft of defense. I was alone in my oratory when Lucifer emptied Hell and advanced upon me in united multitudes. This battle was the greatest fought with a mere creature. In order to estimate the fury of the demons, one must consider their torments. They hated the Divine Power that emanated from me, and hated the memory of how often God had vanquished and oppressed them, through me. It was as if they were throwing themselves on pikes and swords to avenge themselves upon me. However, not to make the effort, was even a greater torment.

The demons first assault consisted of terrific howling and confused clamors. The whole world seemed on the point of destruction. To make this look more real, they assumed diverse visible shapes, of horrid and various kinds of demons, others appeared as angels of light. They staged a dark and formidable battle, and I could hear the terrible noise of a great battle between the two forces. Their best efforts produced no fear or disturbance in my soul. In truth, they would have struck terror in any other person, and no one could have encountered them without losing their life, for this onset lasted for twelve hours.

Observing no changes in me, they then proceeded to tempt my interior faculties. They poured out their diabolical malice more than I can describe. The entire hellish multitude exhausted the full measure of their devilish astuteness. They concocted false revelations and suggestions, and by their promises and threats, they attempted to infect each of my virtues by their temptations. It is not necessary to enumerate each of these trials; however, I was able to perform acts of contrary virtues, which reached an excellence fully in proportion to the impulse and force of my then acquired state of grace, gifts and perfections. I prayed on that occasion for all that are afflicted and tempted by the demon. In return the Lord granted me the power of extending my protection to all those who are tempted and who invoke my intercession. The demons persisted in this battle until they had tried every kind of malice against me. Only then did I call upon the divine justice. I asked God to rise-up, judge his cause, and put to flight those who abhorred his presence.

To fulfill his judgment, the Incarnate Word descended from heaven to my oratory in the Cenacle. He appeared to me as my most sweet and loving Son, and to his enemies as the severe Judge on the throne of his supreme majesty. Innumerable angels accompanied him, as well as many of the ancient saints, including Adam and Eve, many patriarchs and prophets, and Saint Anne and Saint Joachim. I prostrated myself in deepest veneration and worship, and adored my Son and true God. The Lord did not reveal himself to the demons. However, they were fully aware of his royal presence and they tried to fly from his imminent punishment. The divine power detained them, fettering them in the manner in which their spirit nature permitted. The Lord then passed the ends of their fetters into my hands.

Then a voice issued from the throne, saying, "Today comes upon you the wrath of the Almighty, and the first sentence, fulminated against the ancient serpent from on high and afterwards in paradise, shall be executed. A woman descended from Adam and Eve shall crush your head, because in your disobedience and pride, you have despised the humanity of the Word in the virginal womb."

The six Seraphim, nearest the throne of God, raised me from the Earth. God enveloped me in a refulgent cloud, and placed me at the side of the throne of my divine Son. From the Lord's own essence and Divinity there issued a glorious splendor, in which a woman was enveloped and surrounded like the globe of the sun. Beneath her feet appeared the moon, indicating that she was to subject to her all that was inferior, earthly and changeable symbolized by the concavity of the moon. Over her head was placed a crown of twelve stars, as an emblem of the divine perfections. The woman appeared as though pregnant, and she gave forth a wail of sorrow for the birth of what she had conceived. [Because of Eve's sin, the woman gives birth in distress and pain] The woman spoken of here symbolizes God's people in the Old and New Testament. The Israel of old gave birth to the Messiah and then becomes the New Israel, the Church, which suffers persecution by the dragon.

God conceived this sign in the Divine Mind, and he showed it to Lucifer in heaven in all its grandeur. Lucifer was present as the great red dragon with seven heads crowned with seven diadems and ten horns. In this horrid shape, he represented himself as the author of the seven capital sins. He attempted to crown these sins with his invented heresies as diadems, and armed by his astuteness and strength as with ten horns, he sought to overthrow the Divine Law contained in the Ten Commandments. In a like manner, he had encircled with his tail and drawn into Hell with him a third part of the stars of Heaven. He not only seduced the myriads of angels, who followed him in disobedience, but also in denying Heaven to many of the believers of the Church, who seemed to have risen above the stars either in dignity or sanctity.

Lucifer took on a horrid, bestial form, and with him were many other demons of various abominable shapes arranged in battle array against the woman of the vision who was about to bring forth in spiritual birth the perpetual existence and enrichment of the holy Church. The dragon was envious that a mere woman, a creature inferior to him, should be so powerful in establishing and spreading the Church, and that I, by my own merits, example, and intercession could enrich it with so many graces and raise myriads of men to their predestined eternal happiness. He stood by in readiness to devour if possible that which the woman was about to bring forth and in so doing, destroy this new Church. In spite of his envy, the woman brought forth a male-child, who was to govern all the nations with a strong rod of iron. This Man-Child was the most righteous and strong spirit of the Church, which in the righteousness of Christ, our God holds sway over all the nations in justice. It likewise signified that the Apostles, who in the same righteous spirit are to judge with the iron rod of divine justice. All of this I brought forth, not only, because I gave birth to Jesus, but also because through my merits and diligence I brought forth the Church in holiness and rectitude. I nourished it during the time I lived in it, and even now and forever, I preserve it in the manly spirit in which it was born, maintaining the uprightness of the Catholic truth, against which the gates of Hell shall not prevail.

John then states, this Man-Child was taken up to the throne of God, and the woman, fled to her destined place in the desert in order that she might be nourished there for one thousand two-hundred and sixty days. The solitude to which God carried me was a most exalted and mysterious state, which he raised me after my personal battle with Lucifer. I alone of all creatures was in the state of solitude and no other person would ever attain it. I lived in this state for the prescribed time before passing on to another.

The confidence of the demons was taken away with their knowledge of my destiny, which, for more than five thousand years, had inspired the dragon with the hope of someday being able to vanquish the woman who was the mother of the Incarnate Word. To a certain extent, you can imagine the despair and torment of Lucifer and his evil companions. They now saw themselves overcome and held bound by the very woman, whom they had with insane fury sought to cast down from grace and deprive of the merits and fruits of the Church.

The dragon in agonizing efforts to escape, begged me, "Oh woman, give me leave to hurl myself into Hell, for I cannot bear your presence. I will never again venture to come before you, as long as you live upon this world. You have conquered me, oh woman. You have conquered, and I acknowledge your power in him who has made you his mother. Omnipotent God, chastise us yourself, since we cannot resist you, but do not send your punishment through a woman of a nature so inferior to ours. Her charity consumes us, her humility crushes us, and she is in all things a living manifestation of your mercy for men. This is a torment surpassing many others. Assist me, you demons! But alas, what can our united efforts avail us against this woman, since all our power cannot ever deliver us from her presence until she herself casts us forth? Oh foolish children of Adam, who follow me, you forsake life for the sake of death, truth, or falsehood? What absurdity and insanity is yours, [even in my despair God makes me confess] since you have in your midst and belonging to your own nature the Incarnate Word and this woman? Greater is your ingratitude than mine is, and this woman forces me to confess the truths, which I abhor with all my heart. Cursed be my resolve to persecute this daughter of Adam, who so torments and crushes me."

While the dragon thus gave vent to his despair, Saint Michael, the prince of the heavenly hosts, and his angels appeared to defend the human cause of the Incarnate Word and me. They engaged the enemy in another battle. Saint Michael and his forces hurled the convincing arguments of old at them, reproaching them for their pride and disobedience in heaven. They also charged them with their temerity in persecuting and tempting the Incarnate Word and me, and for contending with us in whom they had no right whatsoever, since they could accuse us of no sin, injustice, or imperfection. Saint Michael justified the works of divine justice, declaring them most righteous and just chastisements for the disobedience and apostasy of Lucifer and his demons. They again anathematized them and confirmed the sentence of their damnation, confessing the Almighty as holy and just in all his works. The demon and his angels, on the other hand, likewise tried to defend their rebellion and the audacity of their pride. However, all their defenses were false, vain, and full of diabolical presumption and error.

A silence ensued after this altercation, and the Lord of Hosts spoke to me, "My beloved, Mother, chosen from the creatures by my eternal wisdom for my habitation and holy temple! You have given me human form and restored the human race. You have followed me, imitated me, and merited the graces and gifts communicated to you above all my creatures. You have never permitted them to be unprofitable in you. You are the worthy object of my infinite love, the protection of my Church, its Queen, Mistress, and Governess. I commissioned my power to you, and as the Almighty God, I place it in your most faithful disposal. In virtue of it, command the infernal dragon that as long as you shall live in the Church, he shall not sow the seed of error and heresy which he holds in readiness. Cut off his hardened neck, crush his head; for during the remaining days of your life, I desire that the Church shall derive this advantage from your presence."

I enjoined the infernal dragons to become mute and powerless to spread their false doctrines among the faithful, and that as long as I lived upon the earth, none of them were to presume to deceive mortals by their heretical tenets and doctrines. The demon had planned to pour out his wrath and vengeance against the Church, but the Lord, for his love of me, hindered it during my remaining days upon earth. After my glorious Assumption, God again gave permission to the demon to spread his heresies because the sins of men subjected them to the just judgments of the Lord.

I cast forth the great dragon, the ancient serpent, called devil, upon my decree, and with his demons, he was banished from my presence. God lengthened their chains and the demons fell upon the earth, where God permitted them to remain. The voice of the archangel was heard in the Cenacle, saying, "The accuser of our brethren is cast forth, who accused them before our God day and night. Now is come the salvation, and the strength, and the Kingdom of God, and the power of Christ, because they overcame him by the blood of the Lamb, and by the word of the testimony, and they loved not their lives unto death. Therefore, rejoice oh Heaven and you that dwell therein. Woe to the earth and to the sea, because the devil is come down unto you, having great wrath, knowing that he has but a short time."

When Lucifer saw himself cast upon the earth, he again attempted to persecute me, but mystically to me had been given two wings as of a great eagle, in order that I might fly into the solitude or desert, where I was nourished hidden away from the serpent. The serpent then cast after me a great river, but I was safe in my solitude. As you can see the dragon's word is meaningless, he never allows his envy to slumber, his pride to weaken, or his malice to sleep in tempting me anew, as he had the power and permission; but they were taken from him in regards to myself, and, thus, it is said that two wings were given me to flee into the desert, where I was nourished during the stated times. These wings were the divine power of ascending to the vision of the Deity given to me, and of descending to distribute the treasures of grace to men, as I shall describe later.

The solid and firm set earth, which is the immutability of the Church, and the imperishable Catholic truth, helps me, because I open my mouth and swallow and absorb the flood poured out against me by the serpent. Thus, it happens in reality, since the holy Church, which is the organ and the mouthpiece of the Holy Ghost, has condemned and overthrown all the errors, the false sects and doctrines by her definitions, by Holy Scriptures, by the decrees of her councils, by the teachings of her doctors, instructors and preachers of the Gospel.

God had cast Lucifer to earth in chains. My Son now willed that I was to hurl Satan and his hosts into the infernal caverns in order to end the conflict. Fortified and strengthened by God, I released them from their bonds and commanded them to depart for Hell. As soon as I pronounced the word, all the demons fell into the most distant caverns of Hell, where they remained until my death giving forth terrible and despairing howls.

Then the holy angels sang new hymns to the Incarnate Word and me, because of our victories. Adam and Eve gave thanks to God, because he chose me, their daughter for his mother and thus repaired the ruin they had caused to their posterity. The Patriarchs also gave thanks, because their great expectations and prophecies were so happily and gloriously fulfilled. Saints Joachim, Ann and Joseph, with still greater jubilee, glorified the Almighty for their daughter and spouse. All of them together sang the glory and praise of the Most High, so holy and admirable in his counsels. I prostrated myself before the royal throne, adored the Incarnate Word, and offered myself again to labor for the Church, and I asked for their blessing, which I received with admirable effects. I asked for the blessing of my parents and my spouse Joseph, recommending the holy Church and all the faithful to their prayers. Thereupon the entire celestial gathering took their leave and returned to Heaven in a glorious display of pageantry.

The Continual Abstractive Vision

God then raised me in the sphere of holiness beyond all human thought. The devouring flame of my celestial love grew into a conflagration, which excited the astonishment of all the angels and courtiers of heaven. I desired God to annihilate me entirely in the essence of his Divinity. The miraculous influence of God sustained me, or my love would have consumed me. My love also drew me toward men by my maternal charity, for they depended upon me, just as the plants of earth depend upon the sun that vivifies and nourishes them. I lived in a state of violent longing to unite both the objects of my love in my bosom.

I felt impelled to withdraw from all the sensible things, on the one hand, in order to wing my flight to the continual and supreme union with the Divinity in imitation of the state of my divine Son on Earth. I wished to free myself from all hindrance of creatures in order to enjoy all that my Son enjoyed outside of what belonged to him in virtue of the hypostatic union. This later of course was not possible, yet the height of my sanctity and love seemed to demand all that was next below the state of eternal happiness in heaven. The Most High had permitted me this sort of solicitude in order that the favor of a new state, held in readiness for me by his omnipotence, might be that much more opportune.

God spoke to me and said, "My, Spouse and my, Beloved, the anxious aspirations of your most ardent love have wounded my heart and by the power of my right hand I wish to operate in you what I have not done to any of the creatures; nor ever shall do. I have chosen you for my delights. For you alone I have prepared a state and condition, in which I shall nourish you with my Divinity as one of the blessed, yet in a different manner. In it, you shall continually enjoy my sight and my embraces, my peace and my tranquility, without being embarrassed by created things, or by your condition as a pilgrim. In this habitation you shall wing your flight freely and without bonds through the infinite regions required by your love; and from it you shall also fly to the aid of the holy Church, of which you are the mother. Charged with my treasures, you shall distribute them among your brethren according to your pleasure in their necessities and labors, so that through you they may all be relieved."

This is the same favor, which I mentioned in the last chapter. It is not easy to understand; for it contains many supernatural effects, which have no counterpart in any other of God's creatures, and are wonders reserved by God exclusively to my faculties. Since faith teaches us that we cannot measure or comprehend the power of the Almighty, it is proper to confess that he can operate in me much more than you can comprehend. This vision was not new to me, for I had enjoyed this type of vision off and on throughout my life. As you may remember, I had my first Abstractive Vision at my Conception. However, from now on it was permanent and continual, enduring until my death, when I passed into the Beatific Vision. In addition, it now continued to increase in intensity day by day and thus reached a degree more exalted, more admirable and excellent than before, and beyond all created thought and measure.

For this purpose, God touched all my faculties by the fire of the sanctuary, causing new effects of the Divinity, illuminating and exalting me above the ordinary. This state was to be a participation of that held by the blessed, yet at the same time, different from theirs. The likeness consisted in my seeing the same object of the Divinity and the same attributes which they enjoyed by secure possession; however, I understood them more deeply than they did. The differences consisted in three points; first, the blessed see God face to face and by Intuitive Vision. However, I saw him by an Abstractive Vision as described before. Secondly, the Beatific Vision of the saints in the Fatherland and their essential fruition, in which the glory of the understanding and the will consists, cannot increase, whereas the Abstractive Vision seen by me in my pilgrimage had no limit or restriction.

My knowledge of the infinite attributes and the divine essence increased every day; and for this I was given my two mystical wings of an eagle; by which I was able to soar continually in this limitless ocean of the Divinity, comprehending ever more and more of its infinity. The third difference was that the saints neither suffer or merit for this is incompatible with their state. On my part, I could still accumulate suffering and merit in my state of vision, since I was still on pilgrimage. This state of grace and holiness was of a most inestimable value and price to all humankind. As the Queen and Mistress, I had the power to dispense and distribute the treasures of grace, and at the same time, to add to them by my own merits. Although I was not a Comprehensor, as are the saints in Heaven; yet in my state of pilgrimage I held a place so near to my Son and so like to his on Earth that, if compared with him, I was indeed a pilgrim in body and soul. However, compared to the other pilgrims on Earth, I seemed a Comprehensor and one of the blessed.

At the beginning of my story, I told you that I never looked upon any images or species, ever keeping my eyes cast down discreetly, saving my eyes for the image of my Son and that of the Trinity. The only exceptions were those that were necessary for my exercise of charity and other virtues. Now even these, in as far as they were terrestrial, and in as far as they partook of the sensitive in entering my understanding, the Lord abolished, purging and distilling them of all that they yet contained of their origin in the senses. In place of the images and impressions, which I could receive through the natural activity of my sensitive and intellectual faculties, the Lord infused into my mind other species, more pure and immaterial, and by means of these, my perception and understanding was raised to a more exalted level.

We obtain certain impressions of objects as they are encountered, when we call into action the five bodily senses, by which we hear, see, taste, touch, and smell. The brain passes these impressions on to another interior and corporeal faculty called the general or common sense. This creates an imaginative or estimative fantasy. Here, all the impressions of the exterior senses are united and perceived or felt and are deposited and kept in reserve, as in a storehouse of the five senses. Humankind in their understanding calls upon the five senses to create a fantasy, from which it speculates in order to understand according to the natural routine of our acting faculties. The soul and the body are united, and the soul depends upon the five senses in its operations.

After entering my new state; however, this mode of procedure was not entirely preserved. The Lord had miraculously supplied for my intellect another mode of action, independent of the fantasy and the general sense. In place of the species, which my understanding was naturally to draw from the impressions of exterior objects through the senses, God had infused into my senses other kinds of images. These images represented exterior objects in a more exalted manner. These images enhanced the data stored by the five senses, for God had furnished me with a supernatural set of senses. These my understanding made use of in its activity, while at the same time those received and stored in the general fantasy served me for the feeling of pain and sensible afflictions.

Thus, God hewed and polished in the lower sensitive faculties of my soul, the building blocks of my virtues. From the common senses, I offered up my hardships, sorrows, and pains, which I bore for the faithful in the Church. In the Holy of Holies of my intellect and my will, I offered up the perfume of my contemplation and vision of the Divinity, and the fire of my incomparable love. Since the species of my senses represented objects in an earthier manner, and with the turmoil natural to them, they were not appropriate. Therefore, the divine power excluded them altogether and replaced them with other images of the same objects. These were infused, supernatural and purer, capable of nourishing the abstractive contemplation of the Divinity and more appropriate to my knowledge of God, whom I increasingly looked upon and loved in the inviolable peace, tranquility and serenity of my soul.

These infused species God founded upon his own essence. They represented all things to my understanding in the same way as a mirror represents objects to our eyes and makes them known to us without obliging us to inspect them directly. In this manner, I was aware, in all things, of whatever was for the good of the children of the Church. I knew what I was to do for them in their labors and difficulties and of the manner in which I was to promote the fulfillment of the divine will in heaven and on earth. Favored by this kind of vision, God enabled me to make my petitions in such a way as to have them all granted. From this type of insight, the Lord exempted in me the works, which I was to perform in obedience to the commands of Saints Peter and John, and those sometimes requested by the other Apostles. I had asked for this exemption, because I did not wish to interrupt my practice of obedience, which I loved so much. I also wished to make it plain that through obedience the will of God is known with such certainty that the obedient person needs no other means or byways of finding the will of God than this obedience to the command of responsible superiors; for this obedience is, without a doubt, what God wishes and commands and it is therefore right.

In all other doings my understanding did not depend upon my exchange with sensible creatures, nor on the images of the senses, except that which pertained to obedience and Communion. For them, I remained independent and undisturbed. I enjoyed the Abstractive Vision of the Divinity without interruption. It did not matter whether I was awake or asleep, working, or at rest. There was no need of forethought or reasoning about what was perfect, or more agreeable to the Lord, about the necessities of the Church, or the time and manner of my coming to its aid. All of this was present in my mind in the vision of the Divinity, just like to the blessed through the Beatific Vision. Just as the least important of the knowledge of the blessed is that concerning the creatures; so also [besides what I knew concerning the state of the Church, its government and of all the souls], the principal object of my knowledge was the incomprehensible mysteries of the Divinity. I comprehended these more deeply than the highest Seraphim and saints. I was sustained, in the *solitude* the Lord prepared for me, with this heavenly bread and nourishment

In it I was solicitous for the Church without being disturbed, busily employed without inquietude, attentive without distraction, and in all things I was full of God within and without. I was clothed with the purest gold of the Divinity, immersed and absorbed in this incomprehensible sea. Yet at the same time, I was attentive to all my children and their welfare, finding no rest except in the ministrations of my maternal charity.

You can better understand the happiness of this age by some examples of my prayers and interventions. I rendered assistance to a well-known man living in Jerusalem. This man held a prominent position. God had endowed him with more than an ordinary mind, and he upheld some moral virtues. As for the rest, he was a zealous upholder of the ancient law like Saint Paul had been, and he was a bitter opponent of the teachings and the law of my Son. Because of his good standing in the opinion of some disciples, I desired very much to convert him. Before I had entered my new state of being, I had made every effort to find a means of converting this soul, but I had not come up with the proper answer. However, this kind of study was no longer necessary, for now I needed only to attend to the Lord, where at my request; all that I had to do for his conversion was made clearly manifest to me.

I clearly saw that this man was to come to me through the preaching of Saint John and that I need only tell John to preach where this Jew would hear him. The Evangelist obeyed my request; and at the same time, the guardian angel of the man inspired him with the desire of seeing me, the mother of the crucified. Many persons he knew had praised me as a loving, modest and pious woman. The Jew did not foresee at that time any possible spiritual good to result from this visit. However, out of calculating curiosity, he came to visit me. When he came into my presence and looked upon me, he saw and heard that which my Son intended. The Holy Spirit changed him into an entirely new man, and he prostrated himself at my feet when I spoke to him. He stated, "Your Son is the Savior of the world, and I wish to be baptized." Saint John baptized the man at once. As John pronounced the words of baptism, the Holy Ghost descended in visible form upon this man. Thenceforward, he was distinguished for his holy life. I sang a hymn of thanksgiving for this great and wonderful favor.

Another inhabitant of Jerusalem, deceived by her cousin who was versed in witchcraft, apostatized from the faith. Since I knew all things in the Lord, I was aware of her fall. Distressed, I applied myself to tearful prayers and exercises of atonement for the return of this woman. I knew that it would be most difficult for her to find her way back alone. My prayers paved the way for the salvation of this soul deceived by the serpent. I sent Saint John to warn and exhort this woman, to make her aware of her evil deed, consequently, the woman confessed her sin, and was restored to grace. Afterwards, I exhorted her to persevere and resist the demon.

Lucifer and his cohorts dared not disturb the Church in Jerusalem while I was present. Instead, they sought to make conquests among the baptized of those ports of Asia, where Saint Paul and the other Apostles were preaching. They succeeded in perverting some to apostasy and managed to cause disturbance in the preaching of the Gospel. I knew of his devious schemes and I asked the Lord for assistance, if it should be proper under the circumstances.

My Son answered me, "You have found grace in the eyes of the Most High and you may act as the Mother, and as the Queen and Mistress of all creation."

Thus encouraged, I clothed myself with invincible strength. Armed with the divine power, I rose up against the dragon, snatched the prey from his maw, wounded him with the power of my virtues, and commanded him to again plunge into the abyss. Perhaps these examples will help you to understand how I spent much of my time.

The Writing of the Gospel

As far as God has permitted, I have tried to explain the exalted state in which the blessed Trinity placed me. I will now describe the call of the Evangelists to undertake the writing of the Gospels. As I stated before, I had positive knowledge of all the mysteries of grace, of the Gospels and other holy writings, which were to serve for the confirmation of the new Law. Knowing this, I often prostrated myself in prayer before the Lord, asking him to send his divine light upon the Apostles and holy writers and to order them to write the Gospels, when the opportune time came. It was after my return from Heaven, when God put me in charge of the Church that the Lord made it known that the time had come to begin writing the holy Gospels. He instructed me, as the Mistress and Instructress of the Church to proceed. In my profound humility; however, I knew that the Lord intended for Peter, his Vicar, and the head of the Church to take care of this function. I suggested that God especially assist him by divine enlightenment for a matter of such importance. All of this was granted by the Most High, and Peter, during the meeting when the Apostles settled the doubts about circumcision, proposed to them the necessity of recording in writing the mysteries of the life of my Son. Only by a divinely inspired set of documents could the Word of God be preached to all the faithful in the Church without variation or difference, thus establishing the New Covenant in writing for the enrichment of the world.

After Peter had consulted with me, and all the council had approved of his proposal, they called upon the Holy Ghost to point out the Apostles and disciples who should write the life of the Savior. A light was seen descending upon Saint Peter and a voice was heard to say:

"The Vicar of God shall assign four men for the recording of works and the teachings of the Savior of the world."

All present lay prostrate before the Lord and gave thanks for the favor. When they had again all risen, Peter spoke, "John Mark, our beloved cousin of Barnabas, shall immediately begin to write his Gospel in the name of the Father, the Son, and the Holy Ghost. Matthew shall be the second, who shall likewise write the Gospel in the name of the Father, the Son, and the Holy Ghost. Young Luke, our beloved Physician, shall write the third, in the name of the Father, the Son, and the Holy Ghost. Our beloved brother John, son of Zebedee shall be the fourth and last to write the mysteries of our Savior and Teacher in the name of the Father, the Son, and the Holy Ghost."

This decision the Lord confirmed by permitting the heavenly light to remain until these words were repeated and formally accepted by all those appointed.

Within a few days, Matthew set about writing his Gospel. While he was praying in a quiet room of the Cenacle, and asking to be enlightened for the inception of his history, God sent me to him. I appeared before him seated on a throne of great majesty and splendor, the doors of the room remaining closed. I told him to rise, which he did, and he asked me for my benediction.

I replied, "Matthew, my servant, the Almighty sends me with his blessing, in order that with it you begin the writing of the Gospel with which you have the good fortune to be entrusted. In this, you shall have the assistance of the Holy Ghost, and I shall beg it for you with all my heart. Be advised; however, that concerning myself, it is not proper that you write anything except what is absolutely necessary for manifesting the Incarnation and other mysteries of the Word made Man, and for establishing his faith in the world as the foundation of his Church. The Gospel is to be of Jesus the Christ, our Savior and Redeemer. The Gospel message is not about me, his mother, for I am but a poor and humble creature like you. There will be a time when God will use me in his divine plan. The Almighty will find other means, when the time comes, to reveal to the faithful the mysteries and blessings wrought by his powerful arm in me."

Saint Matthew signified his willingness to obey my mandate, and while he conferred with me about composing his Gospel, the Holy Ghost came down upon him in visible form. In our presence, Matthew began to write the words as they are found today in his Gospel. However, his Gospel was not finished until after my death.

The Evangelist Mark and Matthew compared notes while writing their Gospels. Matthew made this obvious by his references to Mark's Gospel. Before beginning his Gospel, Mark asked his guardian angel to notify me of his intention and to implore my assistance for obtaining the divine enlightenment for what he was about to write. I heard his prayer and the Lord commanded the angels to carry me with the usual splendor and ceremony to the Evangelist, who was engaged in prayer. The Lord presented me to him seated on a most beautiful and resplendent throne.

He prostrated himself before me and said, "Mother of the Savior of the world, and Mistress of all creation, I am unworthy of this favor, though I am the servant of your divine Son and of yourself."

I answered him, "The Most High, whom you serve and love, sends me to assure you that your prayers are heard, and that his Holy Spirit shall direct you in the writing of the Gospel, with which he has charged you."

I then told him, as I had Matthew, not to write of the mysteries pertaining to me. The Holy Ghost, in visible and most refulgent shape, descended upon Saint Mark, enveloping him in light and filling him with interior enlightenment. In my presence, he began to write his Gospel. Saint Jerome later said that Saint Mark wrote his Gospel in Rome, at the instance of the faithful residing there. However, I would like to call attention to the fact that this was a translation or copy of the one he had written in Palestine; for the Christians in Rome possessed neither his nor any other Gospel, and therefore he set about writing one in the Roman or Latin language.

Two years later, Luke began to write his Gospel with many names translated into the Greek language. To him also, as I had with the others, I appeared when he was about to begin writing. He pleaded that in order to manifest the Incarnation and life of my divine Son; it was necessary to touch upon the manner of the actual conception of the Word made man and upon other things concerning my dignity as the natural mother of Christ. Thus, Saint Luke obtained my permission to write somewhat more freely of me in his Gospel. The Holy Ghost descended upon him and in my presence, he began to write his Gospel, drawing his information principally by direct inspiration from me. Thereafter, Saint Luke retained in his mind the image of me seated on my throne of majesty, and in this manner, he lived continually in my presence. Saint Luke was in Achaia, when this event occurred, and there he wrote his Gospel.

The last of the four Evangelists, to write his Gospel, was Saint John. John wrote his Gospel in the Greek language during his stay in Asia Minor after my glorious transition and Assumption. After my Assumption, Lucifer and his demons immediately began to sow heresies, and Saint John directed his Gospel against these errors. Since Lucifer had been humiliated by the mystery of the Incarnation, he at once directed the onslaught of heresy against it. For this reason, Saint John wrote sublimely and adduced many arguments for the true and undoubted Divinity of Christ our Savior, which far surpassed the other Evangelists in this regard.

When John was ready to begin his Gospel, I descended from Heaven in person, resplendent with ineffable glory and majesty and surrounded by thousands of angels of all choirs and hierarchies. Appearing to Saint John I said, "John, my son and servant of the Most High, now is the proper time for writing the life and mysteries of my divine Son, so that all mortals may know him as the Son of the eternal Father, as true God and at the same time as true man. However, it is not yet the opportune time for recording the mysteries and secrets, which you know of me. They shall not be manifested to a world so accustomed to idolatry, lest Lucifer abuse them for disturbing those who are to receive the faith in their Redeemer and in the blessed Trinity. The Holy Ghost will assist you and I desire you to begin writing in my presence."

John venerated me, and God filled him with the divine Spirit as he had done with the other writers of the Gospels. Assisted by me, he set about writing his Gospel. Before I departed to the right hand of my Son, I gave him my benediction and promised him my protection for all the rest of his life. Such were the beginnings of the sacred Gospels. As the Mother of the Church, I initiated the writing of the four Gospels. Today's historians express doubts about, who wrote the Gospels and when, completely ignoring tradition. Some disciples strayed from the teachings of Jesus Christ, which necessitated the early writing of the Gospels as inspired by my Son. Even Paul complained in his letters of many heresies, which were the result of the work of Lucifer and his demons. I will now return to my story.

My Favors to the Apostles

As a true mother and teacher, I lavished my special attention upon the Apostles, whose names and whose welfare I bore written in my heart. After the Council of Jerusalem, the Apostles, with the exception of James the less the Bishop of Jerusalem, and Saint John my son, left Jerusalem for the field of their labors. I was deeply concerned at the thought of the hardships and difficulties connected with their evangelism. It was truly necessary that in order for me to attend to and take care of so many matters throughout the holy Church that God raise me to the state, which I now held.

In addition to my knowledge and solicitude for the whole Church, I again charged my angels to take care of the Apostles and the disciples. They were to console them in all their tribulations, and to hasten to their aid in all their difficulties. The angels, by the subtlety of their spiritual natures could attend to all this without losing sight of the face of God and enjoying the Beatific Vision. I instructed them to inform me of all that the Apostles and disciples were doing, and especially when they were in need of clothing. All of them were clothed similar to those clothes worn by my Son. Assisted by the holy angels, I wove with my own hands the tunics for this purpose and sent them through the angels to the Apostles on their journeys. However, as regards the other necessities of life, such as food, I left them to beg and to labor with their hands, the same as my Son and I had done.

In obedience my angels frequently assisted the Apostles in their travels, their tribulations, and those dangers caused by the demons, who constantly stirred the people up against them. The angels often visited them in visible shapes, conversing with them and consoling them in my name, and the name of my divine Son. Sometimes they performed the same services without manifesting themselves. The angels often freed the Apostles from prison. In addition, they warned them of dangers and snares, sometimes they accompanied them or carried them from one place to another. They also informed them of what they were to do according to the circumstances peculiar to certain places or peoples. The angels kept me informed of all of these things. It is not possible for me to enumerate all the cares, solicitudes and diligent things I did for the Apostles, for not a day or night passed, in which I did not perform many miracles for the Apostles and for the Church. In addition, I wrote to them frequently, animating them with heavenly exhortations, and filling them with consolation and strength.

Whenever they were in serious tribulation or necessity and called upon me, I often appeared to them myself. I will only mention my apparitions to Saint Peter, who as head of the Church stood in greater need of my counsels and assistance. Hence, I sent my angels to him more frequently. Peter wrote and communicated with me more often than did the other Apostles. Soon after the Jerusalem Council, Peter went to Antioch, where he first established his pontifical see. He met many difficulties and he was downcast and afflicted. I well knew of his trouble and how much he stood in need of my favor.

Therefore, I had my angels take me to Peter and I appeared to him seated on a splendid throne. When I appeared before him so resplendent, he prostrated himself before me, with fervor and bathed in tears said to me, "Why does the mother of my Redeemer come to me a sinner?"

I descended from my throne and most humbly knelt before him, for he was the high priest of the Church, and I asked for his blessing. When I came in an apparition, I only did this with Peter, although when I conversed with the Apostles personally, I always asked for their blessing from upon my knees. With Peter, I descended from my throne, and as a member of the Church, I rendered him proper reverence. We conferred on such weighty matters as the advisability of beginning to celebrate some of the feasts of the Lord. Once decided, I returned to Jerusalem. Some time later, Saint Peter, under obedience to my Son, had gone to Rome with the intention of transferring the Apostolic See to that city, and I appeared to him again. Peter ordained that the Roman Catholic

Church should thenceforth celebrate the Nativity of my divine Son. In addition, Christians were to celebrate the Passion of my Son by emulating his sufferings during a special Lenten season. Much later, he also instituted the celebration of the most holy Sacrament on Holy Thursday. Later, the Church established the Feast of Corpus Christi on the first Thursday after the octave of Pentecost. However, after counsel with me, Saint Peter instituted the first Feast of the Blessed Sacrament on Holy Thursday. He also introduced the Feast of the Resurrection. He established Sunday as the weekly day of worship, and fixed the Feast day of the Ascension and other observances of the Roman Church. After this, Peter went to Spain and visited some of the churches founded by Saint James, and established other Churches before returning to Rome.

Peter while at Rome, was greatly distressed and concerned when confronted with a dispute among the Christians. Peter grieved deeply that he did not have my counsel and assistance. I knew the sincere fervor and humility of Saint Peter, and I commanded my angels to bring him to Jerusalem. Peter suddenly found himself before me in the Cenacle, and he prostrated himself before me overwhelmed with tears of joy. I commanded him to rise, and I fell before him on my face, saying, "My, Master, give your servant your blessing as the Vicar of Christ."

Saint Peter obeyed and gave me his blessing. Although I knew of his problems, I listened patiently as he explained them to me. I advised him of all that he needed to know in order to allay the trouble and restore peace in the Church of Rome. He was overwhelmed in his admiration and joy, and he gave humble thanks for the favor. I instructed him on many things for establishing the Church in Rome. I then asked for his blessing and my angels whisked him back to Rome. I remained prostrate on the ground in the form of a cross, and asked my Son to quiet the disturbance in Rome. He heard my prayer, upon arriving in Rome, Saint Peter found matters in a better state, and soon, using my suggestions, the faithful returned to the peaceful worship of our Lord and Redeemer.

The Religious Exercises I practiced in my Twilight Years

In spite of the many privileges I had received throughout my life, I constantly kept fresh in my memory the doings and mysteries of the life of my divine Son. For besides the Abstractive Vision in my final years, I saw the Divinity and knew all things, because the Lord had from my Conception conceded to me the privilege of never forgetting what I once had known or understood. In this regard, I enjoyed the privilege of an angel, as I stated much earlier. In the second part, if you remember, I told you that I felt in my body and soul all the pains and torments of my Son Jesus. In addition, at my request, the Lord imprinted in my interior all the images or impressions of the Passion just as I had received them, and consequently, they were never blotted out. Rather, through the Vision of the Divinity, Jesus made the images more vivid in order that I might miraculously rejoice in my compassion, and at the same time suffer those sorrows. This was my desire during the time I was to live in mortal flesh, and to this exercise I devoted my natural willpower. As exquisite as my favors were, they nevertheless were all pledges and tokens of the reciprocal love of my divine Son. He in your way of thinking could not contain himself or refrain from dealing with me his mother, as the God of Love, and as the Omnipotent infinitely rich in mercies. However, I did not ask for these gifts or seek them. My sole desire was to be crucified with our Redeemer, to continue interiorly his sorrows, renew his Passion, and without this it seemed useless and idle to live in passible flesh.

Therefore I arranged all my duties in such a manner that I might at all times preserve in my heart the image of Jesus Christ, afflicted, outraged, wounded, and disfigured by the torments of his Passion. Within myself, I beheld this image as in a very clear mirror. I could see the injuries, outrages, affronts and blasphemies against him, with all the circumstances of time and place, and I beheld the whole Passion as in one living and penetrating vista. Throughout the day this sorrowful vision excited me to the most heroic acts of virtue and stirred my sorrow and compassion, but even then my love did not allow me to content myself with just these exercises. I engaged in exercises with my angels, especially those that carried the torture instruments of the Passion, and I used them in the following exercises as well.

For each kind of wound and suffering, I recited several prayers, in order to give them special adoration and worship. For each of the contemptuous and insulting words of the Jews, and his other enemies, I composed several hymns of veneration and honor to make up for their attempts to diminish it. For the insulting gestures, mockeries and personal injuries, I practiced profound humiliations, genuflections and prostrations, and in this manner I sought continually to make up for the affronts and injuries heaped upon the Lord in his life and his passion. Thus, I confessed his Divinity, his humanity, his holiness, his miracles, his works and his doctrines. For all, I gave him glory and magnificence, and all my holy angels joined me.

The force of my love was equal to martyrdom many times over, and I would have died in them many times, if the divine power had not sustained my life. Do not allow your own meditations to be half-hearted and lukewarm. The effects of my meditations were often astounding. Many times, I wept tears of blood, which covered my entire face and body, which ran off onto the floor. The violence of my grief sometimes wrenched my heart from its natural position in my breast. When I was in such extremes, my divine Son would come down from heaven, and furnish me with new strength and life to soothe my sorrow and heal the wounds caused by my love of him. I was then able to continue my exercises of compassion.

However, Jesus wished me to lay aside these sorrowful sentiments and affections on the days when I commemorated the mystery of his Resurrection. I obtained the consent of Saint John that I be allowed from my oratory each Friday to celebrate the death and burial of my divine Son. Thereafter, John remained in the Cenacle to receive those who called upon me, and to allow no one to disturb me. If he could not be there, he arranged for someone else to perform this duty. I retired for this exercise at five o'clock on Thursday and did not reappear until noon of Sunday. I did not wish to neglect important matters during these three days, so I appointed one of my angels to take my place. Thus, the affairs of charity that concerned my children and domestics suffered no delay.

To truly comprehend what transpired during these exercises is not possible until you view the Beatific Vision; I will describe the ritual I observed. I began with the washing of feet and commemorated all the mysteries up to that of the Resurrection; and in each hour and moment I renewed in myself all the movements, actions, works and sufferings, as they had happened to my divine Son. I repeated the same prayers and petitions, as he himself had made, and as you have seen, described in their place. In doing so, I felt in my virginal body all the pains endured by Christ our Savior. I carried the Cross and placed myself upon it. I renewed Christ's entire Passion every week, as long as I lived. Through this exercise, I gained great favors and blessings for those who devoutly bear in mind the Lord's Passion. To all such souls, I promise especial assistance and participation in the treasures of the Passion. I desire from my inmost heart that the Church shall continue and preserve its commemoration. In virtue of my wishes and prayers, the Lord ordained that afterwards many persons in the holy Church would indeed follow these exercises of the Passion in imitation of me.

In these exercises, I sought especially to celebrate the institution of the most Blessed Sacrament with hymns of praise and thanksgiving. Though I was worthy of preserving within myself the Holy Eucharist as a tabernacle, I was most solicitous in preparing myself anew by the most fervid exercises and devotions every time I was to again receive Holy Communion. I received Holy Communion nearly every day with few exceptions. I prepared myself with prostrations in the shape of a cross, and with many genuflections, prayers, and adorations of the immutable essence of God. I asked permission of the Lord to speak to him and to permit me, in spite of my earthly lowliness to partake of my Son in the Holy Sacrament. I appealed to his infinite bounty and to his love toward the Church in thus remaining sacramentally present, as a reason that I should be favored with this blessing. I offered to him his own Passion and Death, and all his works from the moment of his Conception in my virginal womb. I also offered to him all the virtues of angelic nature and its works, and of all the just in the past, present, and future times.

I then made intense acts of humility, professing that I was but dust and ashes in comparison with the infinite being of God, to which the highest creatures are inferior and unequal. I was so deeply moved, when I contemplated what I was to receive sacramentally, it is impossible to describe it in words. I called upon my guardian angels, humbly asking them to supplicate the Lord to dispose and prepare me for receiving him worthily. They assisted me and accompanied me in these petitions in which I persevered for the greater part of the night preceding my Holy Communion.

To my prayers and petitions, Jesus often responded by a personal visit, in which he would tell me with what pleasure he came to dwell sacramentally in my heart, and he would renew the pledges of his infinite love. When the hour of my Communion arrived, I first heard the prayers usually celebrated by Saint John. In these celebrations, since the Epistles and Gospels were not yet written, they were not part of the early ceremonies. However, the consecration was always the same as now, and to it were added other rites and ceremonies with many psalms and orations. At the serving of Communion, I approached the altar and made three profound genuflections, all inflamed with my love. I received my Son in the Sacrament, welcoming in my pure bosom and heart that same God to whom I had given the sacred humanity in my virginal womb. After I received Communion, I retired to my oracle, unless some very urgent need of my fellowmen demanded otherwise, there I remained for three hours. My Son often allowed John the privilege of witnessing rays of light darting forth from my body as from the sun during this period.

I provided ornate and mysterious vestments, different from those they wore in ordinary life for the Apostles and priests to wear during the celebration of the Breaking of the Bread. Accordingly, with my own hands; I provided ornaments and sacerdotal vestments for its celebration, thus originating the ceremonious observances picked up later in the Church. Although these vestments were not quite of the same form as nowadays; yet they were not materially different in appearance from those, which in the course of time came into common use in the Roman Catholic Church.

Converts from many kingdoms and provinces came to Jerusalem in order to visit and converse with me, as the Mother of God. Among them were four sovereign princes, royal governors of provinces, who visited me and brought with them many valuable presents, which they placed at my disposal for my own use and for the Apostles and disciples.

I told them, "Alas, my, masters, I am but a poor person like my Son. The Apostles and disciples are also poor in imitation of Jesus. Hence, these riches are not appropriate to the life we profess."

The princes begged me to console them by accepting the gifts for the poor, or for divine worship. Because of their persistence, I accepted part of what they offered and from the rich silks; I made some ornaments for the altar. The rest I distributed among the indigent and the infirmaries. I was accustomed to visit such places and often served and washed the poor with my own hands, performing such services as well as distributing alms on my knees. Whenever possible, I consoled the needy and assisted the dying in their last agony. I never rested from the works of charity, either actually engaging in them, or pleading and praying for others from my oratory.

During their visit, I gave constructive advice to the princes admonishing them and instructing them regarding the good government of their provinces. I charged them to watch over the equitable administration of justice without acceptation of persons. I admonished them to remember that they themselves were as mortal as the rest of men. The Lord, I told them, would judge each one according to his faith and his own works. Above all, I instructed them to exalt the name of Christ, and firmly propagate and secure the holy faith in their own kingdoms. Without faith, I explained, government is but a lamentable and disastrous slavery of the demons, which is permitted by the hidden judgments of God for the punishment of both those that govern and that are governed. Some of them were not yet believers, but when they left they loudly proclaimed their belief in the true God; for they were unable to restrain the interior forces awakened by being in the presence of the Mother of God. After they left, I discussed with James the less the need to assign disciples to take up the mission of properly catechizing the citizens of these countries.

During these last years, I ate and slept but little and this only because John asked me to rest for at least a small portion of the night, which of course I did in obedience. However, this sleep was only a sight suspension of the senses, lasting no longer than a half-hour, during which, I never lost the Vision of the Divinity. I ate only a few mouthfuls of ordinary bread, and sometimes a little fish, taken at John's request and in order to keep him company during his meals, which I prepared and served to him. I partook of this bit of food and sleep, not as a matter of necessity, but only so I could practice obedience and humility. The Holy Eucharist within the tabernacle of my bosom was like your modern day atomic furnace furnishing me with unlimited energy and enthusiasm to please the Lord.

I had begun to suffer a ceaseless martyrdom caused by the violence of my love in the final years of my life. Philosophers profess that in the corporal world: "The nearer a moving object approaches its center of attraction; the more powerfully it is drawn to that center." In my spiritual life, I can testify that this theory is even more pronounced. I had approached so near the infinite and highest Good that only the grating or partition of mortality divided me from it. This fact did not suffice to impede our reciprocal vision and love, for between us was only the vast force of love, impatient of all hindrances to complete the union. My Son's desires were held back only by his reluctance to deprive his Church of me as its teacher. This was also my desire, and although I restrained myself from asking for a natural death, I could not restrain the forces of my love and thus felt the violence of the constraint of mortal life and the fetters that hindered my flight.

Yet, as long as the conditions predetermined by the eternal Wisdom had not arrived, I continued to suffer the pains of that love, which is strong as death. Through them, I called upon my beloved, who came from his retreat from the mountains to dwell in the village of the plains. By the darts of my eyes and of my desires, I wounded the heart of the Lord and drew him from the heights into my presence. Thus, the ardor of my love grew to such proportions that I was languishing with love. I pined away because of the impetus of my Immaculate Heart being drawn toward the Sacred Heart of my divine Son, in order that just as he was the cause of my ailment, he might also be its glorious medicine and cure. I conjured my angels to tell Jesus that I was languishing with love. He came in visible form and supported me in his arms because of the pains of love that overcame me.

My Son, surrounded by myriads of resplendent angels refreshed and comforted me and said, "My, mother, most beloved and chosen for our delight, the clamors and sighs of your loving soul have wounded my heart. Come my, dove; come to my celestial fatherland, where your sorrow shall be turned to delight, your tears into gladness, and where you shall rest from your sufferings."

My angels placed me on the throne beside my Son and we all ascended to the Empyrean Heaven. I fell in adoration at the throne of the most holy Trinity. Jesus presented me, and spoke to the eternal Father, saying, "My, Father, and eternal God, this is the woman that gave me my human form in her virginal womb. She nourished me at her breast and sustained labors for me that shared in my hardships and co-operated with me in the works of the Redemption. This is she who was always most faithful and fulfilled our will according to our entire pleasure. She, pure and immaculate as my mother, through her own works, has reached the summit of sanctity according to the measure of the gifts we have communicated to her. When she had merited her reward and could have enjoyed it forever, she deprived herself of it for our glory and returned to attend to the establishment and instruction of the Church Militant. We, in order that she might live in it for the succor of the faithful, deferred her eternal rest, which she has merited repeatedly. It is just that in our Providence we should remunerate my mother for her works of love beyond all other creatures. Toward her, the common law of the other mortals should not apply. If I have merited for all the infinite merits and boundless graces, it is proper that my mother should partake of them above all the others who are so inferior. In her conduct, she corresponds to our liberality and puts no hindrance or obstacle to our infinite power of communicating our treasures and participating in them as the Queen and Mistress of all that is created."

The eternal Father replied to his holy Son, "My most beloved, Son, in whom I am filled with pleasure; you are the First-born and the Head of all the predestined and in your hands, I have placed all things in order that you may judge with equity all the nations and generations, and all my creatures. Distribute my infinite treasures and communicate them, as you desire to your beloved, who clothed you in passible flesh. Reward her according to her dignity and merit, which are so pleasing in our eyes."

My divine Son said to me in the presence of all the angels and saints, "My pure and virginal, Mother, in union with the pleasure of my eternal Father, I decree that henceforth, for so long as you live in mortal flesh, you shall on every Sunday after finishing your exercises of the Passion, be brought by the holy angels to the Empyrean Heaven. There, in the presence of the Most High, you will celebrate in body and soul the joys of the Resurrection. When you receive *daily* Holy Communion, I will manifest in you my most sacred humanity united to the Divinity in a new and wonderful manner, different from that which you have enjoyed until now. This is to serve as a pledge and a foretaste of the glory, which I have reserved for you, my most holy mother in eternity."

The residents of the Empyrean Heavens, rejoiced at his words, and all of them sang new canticles of praise and glory to the Lord. Then Christ, my Son and God, turned to me and added,

"My most loving, Mother, I shall remain with you always as long as your mortal life shall last, and I shall be with you in a new manner, as wonderful as neither men nor angels have known until now. In my presence you shall not feel lonely, and where I am there shall be my reign, in me you shall rest from your anxieties. I shall be your recompense in the narrowed space of your exile, for you the fetters of your mortal body shall not be irksome and soon you shall be free of them. Until that day comes, I shall be the end of your afflictions, and I shall release the barriers still opposing your loving desires. In all this do I give you my royal promise."

While my Son lavished his gifts upon me, I immersed myself in abject humility, praising, magnifying, and thanking the Omnipotent for his beneficent liberality and annihilated myself in my own estimation. For to know the depth of the eternal Trinity as I did, I alone of all humanity realized how fully insignificant I was and am. The more I received, the more humble I had to become. On one hand God was freely proclaiming that I, his mother, was worthy of assuming the highest place in the estimation of his infinite wisdom, while I, in rivalry with the Infinite Power, humiliated, abased, and annihilated myself, although I merited the exaltation that I received.

Besides all this, I was enlightened and renewed in all my faculties for the Beatific Vision. When I was thus prepared, the veil fell, and for some hours, wrapped in the Intuitive Vision of God, I enjoyed the essential fruition and glory in a manner far above that of the saints. I drank the waters of life from their own fount. I satiated my most burning desires. I reached my center and rested from that swift motion, which I was again to assume as soon as I was to return from my vision. After this vision, I gave thanks to the most blessed Trinity and again interceded for the Church. Then entirely refreshed and comforted, the holy angels brought me back to my oratory. For as long as I lived, my Son fulfilled his word. On every Sunday, after my exercises of the Passion at the hour of the Resurrection, all my angels raised me on a cloud-throne to the Empyrean Heaven, where Christ, my most holy Son, came forth to meet and unite me with himself. The Divinity did not always manifest itself to me intuitively; but aside from this, the effects and participation of this visit were glorious beyond human capacity to comprehend. On these visits, I consulted with the Lord about the arduous affairs of the Church, prayed for it, particularly for the Apostles, and returned to the earth laden with riches like that ship of the merchant of which Solomon speaks in the thirty-first chapter of the Proverbs.

For two reasons, my Son felt that I deserved my Sunday visitations; First, because I voluntarily deprived myself of the joys of the Beatific Vision by remaining upon the Earth. Consequently, because of my ardor of love and of seeing God, I many times suffered the agonies of death. Secondly, in renewing every week the memory of the Passion of my divine Son, it was as if I suffered it in my own person and died with the Lord. Consequently, it was deemed proper that since he was already glorified in heaven, it was reasonable that I should through his presence, be made a participant in the joy of his Resurrection, and thus reaps the fruits of the sorrows and tears I had sown.

Regarding Holy Communion, which my Son promised me, I had, up to this time omitted Holy Communion on some days. For instance, I did not receive Holy Communion during the journey to Ephesus and the return, and on some instances during the absence of Saint John, and on a few other occasions. I had submitted to these omissions without complaint in obedience to the Apostles, for in all things it was and is my job to teach perfection by the use of self-denial, and also in such things as appear most holy and proper. Thus, Jesus willed that I was to receive daily Communion. However, since all things had to be executed in obedience to Saint John, I could not order him, even if I recognized it to be the will of God.

It happened one day that John was very much absorbed in his preaching and allowed the hour for Communion to pass. I conferred with my holy angels, asking for their advice. They answered saying, "My Lady, the command of your divine Son must be fulfilled, and we will inform John and advise him of this order of his Master." Then one of the angels manifested himself to John where he was preaching and said, "John, the Most High wishes that his mother, our Queen, receive him *Sacramentally* every day during her life upon earth."

Thus reminded, the Evangelist immediately returned to the Cenacle, where I was waiting for Holy Communion and said to me, "My, mother and, lady, the angel has told me of the command of the Lord that I administer his Sacramental Body to you each day without exception."

I answered him, "And you, sir, what do you command in regard to this?"

Saint John replied, "Behold me ready to obey in all things as your servant."

From then on, I received Holy Communion daily, including the Fridays and Saturdays, the days of my exercises of the Passion. On Sunday; however, instead of my receiving Holy Communion, Jesus raised me to the Empyrean Heavens to be with the divine Trinity, the angels and the blessed saints. When I received in my heart Holy Communion, the sacred humanity of Christ manifested itself in the manner he had when he instituted the Blessed Sacrament. The Divinity manifested itself to me habitually by the Abstractive Vision. Now, my Son manifested himself to me more gloriously, resplendent and wonderful than at his Transfiguration on Mount Tabor. This vision I enjoyed for three consecutive hours each time I received Holy Communion. I cannot describe the vision's effect upon me in words. This was the second reward offered to me to recompense me somewhat for the eternal glory, which my Son had delayed at my own request. In addition, the Lord wished to recompense himself and counteract beforehand the ingratitude, the lukewarmness and evil disposition with which the children of Adam were to receive and handle the sacred mystery of the Eucharist during the ages of the Church. If I had not made up for these shortcomings of creatures, the Lord would have earned no sufficient thanks from his creatures, nor could he have been satisfied with the returns made by men for the institution of this sacrament.

Establishment and Celebration of Feast Days

All the offices and titles and honors, which I held in the Church that of Queen, Mistress, Mother, Governess and Teacher, and all the rest, were given me by the Omnipotent One. They were not empty and fruitless names, for God communicated to each a superabundance of grace, which is proper and fitting. This abundance of grace consisted in this that as Queen; I knew all that concerned my reign and its extent. As Mistress, I knew the measure of my power. As Mother, I knew all the children and dependents of my household without excepting anyone through all the ages of the Church until the end. As Governess, I knew all that were subject to me; and as Teacher, I possessed the wisdom and science through which the holy Church, by my intercession, was to be instructed and guided while enjoying the presence and influence of the Holy Ghost until the end of the world.

Hence, I had a clear knowledge not only of all the saints that preceded or followed me in the Church, but also of their lives, their works, their deaths, and subsequent rewards in heaven. I also knew of all the rites, ceremonies, decisions, and festivities of the Church in the course of the ages. I knew all the reasons, motives, necessities and opportunities, in and for which they were established with the assistance of the Holy Ghost; for he gives us our spiritual nourishment in proper time for the glory of the Lord, and the increase of the holy Church. From my full knowledge and my corresponding holiness, there arose within me a certain thankful eagerness to introduce into the Church Militant the worship, veneration and festivities observed by the holy angels in the triumphant Jerusalem. I wished to initiate, as far as possible, what I had so often seen done in Heaven for the praise and glory of the Most High.

In this seraphic spirit, I began to practice by myself many of the ceremonies, rites and exercises, which the Holy Spirit later introduced in the Church. I also inculcated and impressed these upon the Apostles, in order that they might introduce them as far as the circumstances then allowed. As stated before, I devised the exercises of the Passion, as well as many other customs and ceremonies which were later received in the Church, and by its congregations. The next mysteries that I celebrated were those of my Immaculate Conception and the Nativity. I imagined that I was altogether incapable of ever acknowledging them properly with sufficient gratitude. I began my exercises on the evening before on December seventh, and spent the whole night in devotions, shedding tears of joy, making acts of humility, prostrating, genuflecting, and singing praises of the Lord. I reflected deeply that according to the common order of nature, I, too, had descended from Adam. Yet, God had preserved and exempted me from the weight of Adam's guilt. He had conceived me with abundant gifts and grace only because I was set apart and snatched from the rest by the Almighty. I invited my angels to help me return proper thanks and in union with them, I alternated new songs of praise. Consequently, I became so inflamed with my love for God that my natural life force was nearly consumed, and the Lord was obliged to strengthen me

The Feast of the Immaculate Conception:

On the eighth day of December of each year after the Incarnation, I celebrated my Immaculate Conception with a jubilee and gratitude beyond all human words, for this privilege was for me of the greatest importance and value. After my all night marathon of prayers, my Son descended from Heaven and the angels raised me to his royal throne in Heaven, where the celebration of the feast was continued with new glory and praise from all the residents of the Empyrean Heavens. I prostrated myself and adored the Holy Trinity, again giving thanks for the benefit of my immunity from original sin by my Immaculate Conception. Then I took my place at the right hand of Christ my Son. He acknowledged the goodness of the eternal Father in having given him a mother so worthy and so full of grace, exempt from the common guilt of Adam.

The Father spoke, and said to me, "Beautiful are your footsteps oh prince's, daughter, conceived without sin."

The Son then said, "Altogether pure and without guilt is my mother, who gave me human form to redeem man."

Then the Holy Ghost added, "All fair are you my, Spouse, all fair are you and without stain of the universal guilt." In between, the choirs of angels and saints sang in sweetest harmony,

"Most holy Mary conceived without original sin."

In answer to these honors, I answered with thanksgiving, worship and praise of the Most High, rendered with profound humility. God then raised me to the Intuitive and Beatific Vision of the most holy Trinity. The angels returned me to the Cenacle after I had enjoyed this glory for some hours.

The Feast of my Nativity:

I began this celebration the night before, as I had with the Immaculate Conception. I began with the same prostrations and canticles of praise. I gave thanks for having been born to life into the light of this world. I also gave thanks that God had raised me to Heaven at my birth and allowed me to look intuitively upon the Divinity. I resolved anew to spend my whole life in fulfilling the pleasure of the Lord, and acknowledged that God had given me my life for this purpose. Although I had advanced far in merit, I resolved now, in my twilight years, to begin to labor anew as if I was just beginning the practice of virtue. I asked the Lord for his help and to govern me in my actions and lead me to the highest end proposed for his glory.

Instead of being raised to Heaven the following morning, my divine Son chose to come to the Cenacle with many choirs of angels, with the Patriarchs and Prophets, and with my parents, Saints Joachim and Anne, and also my spouse Saint Joseph. With this company, the Christ descended in order to celebrate my birthday with me. As usual, I adored the Lord with great reverence and worship. I gave him thanks for having placed me upon the earth, and for all the benefits connected therewith. Then the angels sang, "Nativitas tua, Dei Genetrix Virgo," etc. Thy birth, oh Mother of God, announced to the entire universe a great joy; for of you was born the Sun of Justice, Christ our God. The patriarchs and prophets sang their hymns of glory and thanksgiving. Adam and Eve joined them, because in me was born the Restorer of man's ruin. In addition, my parents and Joseph were there, because they had been blessed with such a daughter and spouse. Then the Lord himself raised me from the floor on which I lay prostrate, and placed me at his right hand. Straightaway God manifested new mysteries of the Divinity in me. However, this vision was abstractive, afforded me a still deeper insight and participation in the Divinity.

By these ineffable favors, God transformed, inflamed and spiritualized me to the likeness of my divine Son in a new and special manner, as if for a new beginning. On these occasions, the Evangelist Saint John merited some measure of participation in the feast. God not only allowed John to hear some of the music of the angels, but also privileged him to share the Breaking of the Bread, while the Lord and the angels were present in the oratory. He gave me Holy Communion, which I received sacramentally with Jesus, my Son, at my side. After Communion, my Son remained with me in the sacramental form, while he, in his glorious and natural form, ascended to Heaven with his entire court.

The Feast of the Presentation

As was my custom, I commenced the night before and spent the entire night in spiritual exercises of thanksgiving, as described before for the Conception and Nativity. In addition, I reviewed in my memory the teachings and instructions given to me in the holy Temple by the priests and my teachers. With loving solicitude, I preserved in my memory the teachings of my holy parents Joachim and Anne, and those of the temple priests. I rehearsed them all and practiced with greater perfection as I advanced in years. Although the teachings of my divine Son were eminently sufficient for all my doings, yet I recalled those received from all the others. I never ceased the practice of humility and obedience, and I never permitted these virtues to become obscure or to remain idle. In celebrating this feast, I did feel some natural regret for the quiet retirement of the holy Temple of my youth. Notwithstanding that, I had promptly obeyed the Lord in forsaking it and in resigning myself to the exalted ends, for which he had withdrawn me. However, he did not fail to requite me by some special favors on this feast.

On this day, the Lord descended from Heaven in great magnificence and in the company of angels and addressed me in my oratory, "My, Mother and, dove, come to me your God and your Son. I wish to afford you a temple and a habitation, more exalted, more secure and god-like, one that is within my own being. Come, my most beloved, to your legitimate dwelling."

With these sweet words, the seraphim raised me from the ground where I lay prostrate, and with heavenly music placed me at the right hand of the Lord. I felt myself filled at once with the Divinity as a temple with his glory and bathed, surrounded, and contained as a fish in the sea, experiencing by this union or contact with the Divinity new and unspeakable effects. Thereby, I attained a possession of the Divinity, which is impossible to describe, but which afforded me a great delight and joy, additional to that of seeing God face to face. I called this favor my exalted refuge and dwelling, and the feast itself I called, "The Feast of the Being of God. I thanked the Almighty for having created the ancient patriarchs and prophets, including all from Adam to my natural parents in whom my lineage ended. I turned to my parents Joachim and Anne and thanked them for having presented me so young to God in the holy Temple of Jerusalem, and asked them to give my thanks to the Omnipotent God for having exempted me from original sin and having chosen me as his mother.

Feasts of Saints Joachim and Anne

I celebrated these Feast Days almost with the same ceremonies as that of my presentation. On this occasion, both Saints descended with my Son to my oratory with a multitude of angels. I gave thanks to God for having provided me with parents so holy and conformable to the divine will, and for the glory he had conferred upon them. My angels and those from on high divided into choirs, some explaining to the Queen the attributes or perfections of the Divinity, and others of the

Incarnate Word. These gave my parents and me great joy. Before they returned to Heaven, I asked for and received their and my divine Son's blessing.

Feast of Saint Joseph

I celebrated my espousal to this most chaste and holy man, in whom the Lord had given me a most faithful companion. Joseph concealed the mysteries of the Incarnation of the Word, and executed with high wisdom the secret works of the Redemption of man. I recorded all these events in my heart, I held them in worthy contemplation, and commemorated them with ineffable joy and thanksgiving. On this feast, Saint Joseph came in the splendor of glory and with myriads of angels, in order to solemnize the feast with joyful music. They sang the new hymns and canticles, which I composed in thanksgiving for the blessings my holy spouse and I received at the hands of the Most High.

I spent many hours that day conversing with my spouse about the perfection and attributes of God, for in my Son's absence, I delighted in such discourses and conferences. On making leave of Joseph, I begged him to pray for me in the presence of the Divinity, and to praise him in my name. I recommended to his prayers also the necessities of the holy Church, and of the Apostles. When my Son still lived upon the earth, when I celebrated this feast and he happened to be present, he was accustomed to show himself Transfigured as he was on Mount Tabor. On most of these feasts, it was my custom to give food to the poor. I prepared the food myself and served them with my own hands and on my knees. For this purpose, I directed Saint John to gather in the most needy and destitute. I also had more costly food sent to the poor sick and I often visited them in person to console and heal them by my presence.

Feast of the Incarnation.

I began this solemnity on the evening of the sixteenth of March in the evening and during the next nine days until the twenty-fifth of March. I remained in retirement without eating or sleeping. Saint John was the only one who came to me, and then only to administer holy communion to me. The Almighty renewed all the favors and blessings, which he had conferred upon me during those days before the Incarnation. There was one difference; however, for now my Son and our Redeemer added new ones. For, as he was already born of me, he took it upon himself to assist, regale and favor me in this feast. On the first six days of this novena, after I had passed some hours of the night in my accustomed exercises, the Incarnate Word descended from Heaven refulgent in glory and majesty. He was accompanied by myriads of angels; and he entered my oratory and showed himself to me. I prostrated myself and adored my Lord, my God, and my Son. Again, Jesus placed me on the throne and I felt within myself an intimate and ineffable union with the humanity and the Divinity. I was transformed and filled with glory and new divine influences not comprehensible to man. In this condition, the Lord renewed in me the marvels of the nine days before the Incarnation in the order in which they had then occurred. To these, he added other favors and admirable effects to the state attained since then by both him and me.

On the **first** of these nine days, he showed me that God on the first day created Heaven and the Earth, and gave the world day and night. I saw the creation of the angels, their perfections, their perseverance in grace, and the obedient and disobedient and the fall of the apostates. I likewise recognized the intentions of the Almighty in the creation of all things; lest the renewal of this knowledge be fruitless in me [Gen: 1, 1-5].

My divine Son said to me, My, mother and my, dove, I gave you knowledge of all these works of my infinite power, in order to manifest to my greatness before assuming flesh in your virginal womb, and I renew it in you now. Thus, I confirm in you your possession and dominion over the angels, the Heavens, the Earth, the light, and the darkness, all of which shall serve and obey you as my mother. This affords you a worthy occasion to thank and praise the eternal Father for the blessings of creation, which men do not know how to appreciate."

I responded to the will of the Lord and satisfied for the indebtedness of humankind in its entirety, giving thanks in my own name, and in that of all men, for these incomparable blessings. On the **second** day at midnight, the Lord again descended in the same manner and recalled in me the knowledge of the works of the second day of creation. From the midst of the waters was formed the firmament, dividing the one from the other, the number of the heavens, their harmonious arrangement, nature and character, their greatness and beauty. All of this I knew with infallible certainty [Gen: 1, 6-8].

On the **third** day, Jesus refreshed my knowledge of the Scriptures. The Lord congregated the waters upon the earth and formed the sea, the dry land, and upon the command of its Creator, the dry land immediately produced plants, herbs, trees and other things for its beauty and adornment. I knew the nature and qualities of all these plants and the manner in which they are useful or hurtful to man [Gen: 1, 9-13].

On the **fourth** day, I recognized particularly the formation of the sun, the moon and the stars of heaven, their material, their form, properties, influences and all their movements, dividing them into seasons, days and years [Gen: 1, 14-19].

On the **fifth** day, the Lord explained to me how God had first formed the birds of the air and the fishes of the sea from the waters. I learned how God then reproduced and propagated these animals, how many species there were, and the conditions and faculties of the animal of the land and the sea [Gen:1, 20-23].

On the **sixth** day, I received new enlightenment and insight into the creation of man, as the terminus of all the material creatures, and in understanding his exquisite and harmonious nature as a recapitulation of all the rest of the world of creatures. I comprehended also the mystery of the Incarnation, which was the end and purpose of his creation, and I possessed the other secrets of the divine Wisdom hidden in this and the other works, testifying to his infinite greatness and majesty [Gen: 1, 24-31].

On each of these days, I composed special hymns of praise to the Creator for the works performed on the corresponding day of creation and for the mysteries made known to me. Then I prayed for all men, especially for the faithful, asking for their reconciliation to God and their enlightenment concerning the Divinity and his works, in order that they might thereby be helped to know, love, and praise the Almighty. For the unbelievers, who would not come to the knowledge and belief of the true faith, I performed heroic and admirable works in compensation for these defects of the children of Adam. Because I so faithfully responded, my Son raised me to a new participation in the gifts of his Divinity and attributes, accumulating upon me all that the rest of mortals lost by their ungrateful forgetfulness. Over all the works that day, he confirmed upon me anew, full possession and dominion, in order that all might acknowledge me and serve me as the Mother of their Creator and the supreme queen over all creatures in Heaven and on Earth.

On the **seventh** day, since God was finished with the work he had been doing, he rested on the seventh day from all the work that he had undertaken. God blessed the seventh day and made it holy [Gen: 2, 1-3].

My divine Son did not descend from Heaven in the last three days; but instead I was raised up to him in correspondence with what had happened on the three days before the Incarnation. The angels carried me up to the Empyrean Heaven, where, while I was adoring the Immutable Being of God, the supreme seraphim clothed me in a vestment more pure and white than the snow and more refulgent than the sun. They girded me with a girdle of jewels so rich and beautiful that there are none in nature with which to compare them. Then they added bracelets, necklaces, and other adornments befitting me whom they adorned. Each of them in its own way signified a new participation and communication of the Divinity. Not only did the adornments signify this, but also the six seraphim likewise represented mysteries contained in their ministry.

Six other seraphim succeeded the first, and adorned me by retouching my faculties and giving them subtlety, beauty, and grace unspeakable in human words. Still another six seraphim furnished the celestial light by which my understanding and will was made capable of the Beatific Vision and fruition. The eighteen seraphim raised me to the throne of the blessed Trinity and placed me at the right hand of the Onlybegotten, our Savior and my Son.

The Trinity then asked me, "Our, Daughter, what is your petition and desire?"

I answered, "I ask mercy for my people oh, Lord; and in their name and mine, I desire to thank your Almighty clemency for giving human form to the Eternal Word in my womb for their salvation." I added other petitions of love and wisdom, supplicating for the entire human race, and especially for the holy Church.

Then my divine Son spoke to the eternal Father and said, "I confess and praise you my, Father, and I offer to you this creature, the daughter of Adam, pleasing in the eyes as the one chosen for my mother from all the creatures and as a testimony to our infinite attributes. She alone knows worthily and fully to estimate and thankfully to acknowledge the favor I have shown to men in vesting myself in their nature for the purpose of teaching them the way of eternal life and saving them from death. We have chosen her in order that she might appease our indignation at the ingratitude and small return we receive from mortals. She makes up for what the others are either unable or unwilling to give; and we cannot despise the prayers, which our beloved offers for them in plentitude of her holiness and entirely to our pleasure."

I repeated all of these prayers on each of the last three days of the novena. On the last day, which was the twenty-fifth of March, at the hour of the Incarnation, the Divinity manifested itself to me intuitively, and with a greater glory than to all the blessed. The saints in Heaven received an addition to their accidental joy on all these days. However, the last one was one of greater festivity and of extraordinary jubilee for the whole of Jerusalem triumphant. The favors I received far exceed all human thought. All my privileges, graces and gifts were on that last day ratified and increased by the Almighty in an ineffable manner. As I was still a pilgrim, and knew all the conditions of the holy Church in the present and the future ages, I asked and merited great blessings for all times. To say it more briefly, I obtained all the blessings, which the divine power wrought for men from the beginning and shall work unto the end of the world.

On all the feasts that I celebrated, I obtained the conversion of innumerable souls, which at that time, and at succeeding times, were to come to the Catholic faith. On the Feast of the Incarnation; however, God made this privilege even more extensive. On this day, I merited for many kingdoms, provinces and nations, God's blessings and favors they later received in being called to the holy Church. On the day, I celebrated the Incarnation; God gave me the privilege to liberate all the souls from Purgatory. From Heaven, I was able to send the angels to bring all these souls to me in order that I might offer them as the fruit of the Incarnation to the eternal Father. From there, I returned to Earth, where I continued my thanksgivings with even greater humility.

I began my exercises at the same hour as the other feasts. The Incarnate Word descended to my oratory with the same majesty accompanied with his angels and saints. Since this mystery consisted in my Son beginning to shed his blood for men and in subjecting himself to the law of sinners, as if he were one of them, my acts in commemoration of that great condescension and clemency were ineffable. I humiliated myself to the lowest depths; I lovingly sympathized with the sufferings of the Child-God at such a tender age. I thanked him for this blessing conferred upon all the children of Adam. I bewailed the universal forgetfulness and want of appreciation of the blood shed for the rescue of all.

I felt ashamed in the presence of my Savior for not having paid my debts. I offered my own life and my own blood in satisfaction and in imitation of my Master's example. Yet, although the Lord accepted my offerings, he felt it was not befitting to let me actually pay all the sacrifices of my inflamed love. Therefore, I added other inventions of my charity toward the mortals. I besought my Son to divide his gifts, caresses and favors among all the children of men. I begged that God would allow me to suffer for his love, so that all persons should share in the reward, and that they should taste the sweetness of the divine Spirit. I prayed that all might be induced to enter the path of eternal life, and none be lost in eternal death, since their God himself became man and suffered for the very purpose of drawing all men to him.

Then I offered the blood to the eternal Father in Heaven, which Jesus, in his sinlessness, shed in his Circumcision and the humility he demonstrated in submitting his flesh to the knife. My divine Son gave me his blessing and returned to the right hand of his eternal Father in Heaven, after I had thus exercised acts of adoration of him as true God and true man.

Feast of the Magi

To prepare for this feast, I began my devotions some days in advance, in order, as it were, to get ready some presents to offer to the Incarnate Word. My principal offering was the souls brought to a state of grace and called by me, the *gold.* To obtain this gift of gold, I used the services of my angels, ordering them to lead numerous souls to the knowledge and belief of the true God by special and powerful inspirations. This was brought about by their ministry and much more by my own prayers and petitions, so that I drew many from sin, brought others to the faith and to baptism, and snatched others from the talons of the infernal dragon at the hour of their death.

To this gift, I then added the gift of *myrrh,* which were my prostrations in the form of a cross, my humiliations, and other exercises of penance, by which I prepared to present my own self as myrrh before my God. My third offering was the incense of my inflamed love, my words and ejaculations, and I delivered them as full of wisdom and sweetness as I could manage.

Our Redeemer, on the hour and day of the mystery, descended with innumerable angels and saints in order to receive these offerings. I invited all the courtiers of heaven to assist me, and I made my offering, accompanying it with adoration, worship and love; and with it, I combined a fervent prayer for all the mortals. Then God's angels took me up to the throne of my Son to share the glory of his sacred humanity in an ineffable manner. God divinely united me in his glory, and its splendors and translucency transfigured me. A few times, in order to moderate the conflagration of my love, the Lord embraced me and permitted me to recline upon his arms. These favors as such cannot be described in words worthy of the blessing. Again at his feet, I supplicated the Lord for mercy upon humankind, and concluded my petitions with canticles of praise in the name of all, and I asked the saints to accompany me in all this. At the end of this feast, I asked all the patriarchs and saints present to intercede for me with the Almighty that he might assist and govern me in all his works. For this purpose I went to each soul and repeated my request, and I humbly kissed their hands. Jesus, ineffably pleased, permitted me to exercise my humility before my parents, the patriarchs, and the prophets related to me. The angels of course were not included, because they were my ministers and not in the same relations with me as my holy forebears.

The Feast of the Baptism of Christ

I celebrated the baptism of my Son with magnificent thanksgiving for his submitting himself and subsequently establishing this Sacrament. After offering my prayers for the Church, I withdrew in order to fast for the following forty days to commemorate the fast of the Lord and of myself after his baptism.

The Forty Days of Lent

Unless some great necessity of the Church demanded my presence, I did not sleep, eat, or leave my retreat during these forty days. Saint John interrupted my Lenten fast only when he served me daily Communion, or when I was obliged to dispatch some business for the Church. John seldom left the Cenacle in order to give me support; for, in my absence, he attended to the numerous persons who came seeking my help in their necessities, and he often cured the sick by applying to them some article of my clothing. Many demons fled, as the possessed approached my dwelling place, for they could not abide my presence. When John touched one of the possessed with one of my veils or cloaks, even obstinate demons cast themselves into the abyss. However, the Evangelist did call upon me if any of the demons persisted; and, at my presence, they fled without waiting for my command.

At the end of lent, Jesus regaled me with a banquet similar to the one brought by the angels to him at the end of his fast, as I described previously. This one was even more splendid, since the glorified Savior was present. He was full of majesty and accompanied by myriads of angels, some of them serving, others singing in divine and celestial harmonies, and the Lord himself furnished what I ate. This day was very delightful to me, more on account of the presence of my divine Son and his tokens of love, than on account of the exquisite nectars and manna of Heaven. In thanksgiving, I prostrated myself and asked for his benediction, all the while adoring him. After he had done so, he returned to his celestial regions.

The Feast of the Purification and Presentation

In order that I might make this offering, and that God might accept it, the most blessed Trinity appeared in my oratory with his heavenly court. To prepare me for offering up the Incarnate Word, the angels vested and adorned me with the same garments and jewels, as I described for the Feast of the Incarnation. Then I offered up a comprehensive prayer in which I supplicated for the whole human race and especially for the Church. The reward for this prayer and for my humility, with which I subjected myself to the law of purification as well as for my other exercises, was a new increase of grace. I received new gifts and favors for myself, and for many others, great wonders and blessings.

The memory of the Passion, the institution of the Blessed Sacrament, and the Resurrection

Each year, I observed Holy Week in the same manner as is now done in the Church. In addition, in commemoration of the crucifixion on Good Friday, I placed myself upon a cross and remained there for three hours. I renewed all the prayers of the Lord, which included his sorrows and mysteries of that day. On the following Sunday, which corresponds to the Resurrection, I was raised by the holy angels to the Empyrean Heavens. There, I enjoyed the Beatific Vision, while on the ordinary Sundays my vision of the Godhead was abstractive.

Feast of the Ascension

After solemnizing the Resurrection, I prepared myself for this great festival. During this time, I renewed the memory of the favors and blessings I had received from my divine Son and of the glorious company of the ancient patriarchs and saints delivered from limbo. I also reviewed all that transpired day after day during those forty days, giving thanks with new hymns and devotions, as if they were again transpiring before me, for all of these events were indelibly impressed upon my memory. During this preparation, I received incomparable favors and experienced new influences of the Divinity, by which I was prepared for the extraordinary favors I was to receive on the feast itself.

On the day of the Feast of the Ascension, Jesus came down in person to my oratory. The Patriarchs and Saints he had originally taken up with him into Heaven accompanied him. I awaited his visit prostrate on the floor in the utmost self-debasement of my ineffable humility; yet, at the same time, being elevated above all human and angelic thought to the highest pinnacle of love possible to a mere creature. My divine Son manifested himself amidst the choirs of saints, and renewed in me the sweetness of his blessings. He commanded the angels to raise me from the floor and place me at his right hand.

Thereupon he asked me, for my request and my desire. I answered him, "My, Son and eternal, God, I desire the glory and exaltation of your holy name. In it I wish to render you thanks for the whole human race, and acknowledge the blessings of having on this day, through the almighty power, raised our nature to eternal glory and felicity. I beg that all men may know, praise, and magnify your divinity and most sacred humanity."

The Lord replied, "Mother, you are the dove, chosen from amongst all creatures for my habitation, come with me to my celestial country. There your desires shall be fulfilled, your petitions granted, and you may enjoy the solemnity of this day, not among the mortal children of Adam, but among my courtiers and among my inhabitants of Heaven."

The entire court, with me at my Son's right hand traversed the empty regions of the sky to the Empyrean Heavens. Upon arriving, the whole celestial company arranged themselves in choirs, and not only they and all Heaven, but the Holy of the Holies, himself, were so to say, wrapped in a new kind of silence and attention. I then asked permission of the Lord to descend from the throne and, prostrate myself before the footstool of the most Blessed Trinity. With permission granted, I sang a song of praise. In it, I included the mysteries of the Incarnation and Redemption with all the triumphs and victories of my divine Son up to his glorious Ascension to the right hand of his eternal Father.

The Most High manifested his pleasure and all the saints responded with songs of glory, extolling the Omnipotent for having created me and making me their queen. Then, again at the right hand of my Son, and having been illumined and adorned, as on other occasions, I looked upon the Divinity in glorious and Intuitive Vision. I spent part of the day in this Beatific Vision, and during it, the Lord again confirmed upon me the possession of that place, which from all eternity he had destined for me, and which was mentioned on the day of the Ascension. Each year on that same date, the Lord himself asked me, whether I would prefer to remain in that eternal joy forever, or return again to Earth for the benefit of the Church; the decision being thus left entirely in my hands.

I answered each time, "If it be the will of the Almighty, I shall return to labor for men, who were the fruit of the Redemption and of the death of the Son of God."

Thus, many times did I deprive myself of the eternal Beatific Vision, in order to direct the Church and enrich it with my prayers and sacrifices. While there, I added my prayers for the exaltation of God's name, for the propagation of the Church, for the conversion of the world and the victories over the devil. All my petitions were granted and successfully executed in their time, and will be executed in all the ages of the Church. These favors would be greater, if the sinners of the world would not hinder them and make mortals unworthy of receiving them. The angels brought me back to my oratory amid celestial music and harmony, and I prostrated myself in deepest humility to give thanks for these new favors. John did have some knowledge of these mysteries and participated in their effects; for after these journeys to Heaven, he usually saw me so refulgent with heavenly light that he could not look upon my face. My glorification often filled Saint John with reverential fear and disquiet, but mixed with a wonderful joy and incitement to holiness. In spite of this, I always humbled myself by knelling at John's feet, in order to ask him for his consent for various projects.

The Feast of Pentecost

I availed myself of the effects and blessings of the festivity of the Ascension in order to celebrate more solemnly the coming of the Holy Ghost fully preparing myself during the nine days that intervened. Each year the Holy Ghost descended upon me at the same hour in which he had descended upon the one hundred and twenty disciples, which included me in the upper room. This Holy Spirit's coming was not less solemn than the first. He came in the form of visible fire of a wonderful brightness and with a mysterious noise, yet these signs were not manifest to all, as had happened at the first coming. At the first coming, God felt a visible presence was necessary, but afterwards it was seldom granted that anyone, except me, and to a certain extent, Saint John, should share in this miracle.

Myriads of angels attended upon me at such times, singing the canticles of the Lord in sweet harmony; and the Holy Ghost entirely inflamed and renewed in me superabundant gifts and increase of the blessings, which I already possessed. I gave humble thanks, not only for this favor, but because he had filled the Apostles with wisdom and charismatic gifts to make them worthy ministers of the Lord, and founders of his holy Church. Through his coming, he had sealed the works of the human Redemption. In a prolonged prayer, I then asked the divine Spirit to continue the influences of his graces and wisdom through the present and the future ages, and not to suspend it because of the sins and unworthiness of men at any time. All these petitions the Holy Ghost granted to me, and the holy Church is now reaping the fruit of them, and shall enjoy them until the end of the world.

Feast of the Holy Angels

I added this feast to honor the angels, and for several days I prepared myself, as I have mentioned before. When the day for the feast arrived, I invited them all. Many thousands of the celestial choirs and orders descended and manifested themselves in wonderful beauty and glory in my oratory. Then forming two choirs, I made up one, and the other was comprised of all the supernal spirits. We sang songs of celestial harmony in alternate verses during that entire day. If I could describe these canticles to you, they would no doubt be counted among the miracles of the Lord and astonish all the mortals. This day was one of admirable joy and jubilee to me, and of unplanned joy to the angels, especially to the thousand angels of my ordinary guard, for they also participated in the glory given them by their queen. On neither one side nor the other, was there an obstacle of ignorance, or any want of the appreciation of the mystery rehearsed. This interchange of heavenly songs was full of incomparable reverence, as it shall be with you when you shall experience it in the Lord.

The Feast of the Saints

For this feast, I also prepared myself with many prayers and exercises of devotion as on the other festivals. All the patriarchs, prophets and the rest of the saints, including those that had died after the Resurrection, came from Heaven on the day designated, to celebrate with me as their Reparatrix this joyful day. I composed new canticles of thanksgiving for the glory of the saints and efficacy of the death of my divine Son. Great was my happiness and joy on this occasion, because I knew the secret of their predestination, and because, in spite of the dangers of mortal life, they had now attained secure and eternal felicity. For this blessing, I extolled the Lord and Father of mercies and rehearsed in my thanksgiving the favors, graces and benefits, which each one of the saints had received at his hands. I asked them to intercede for the Church, and for all those who were fighting its battles and were still encountering the danger of losing the crown. I also gave thanks for the victories and triumphs; I myself had attained through the divine power over the demons. Finally, I added new canticles of humble and fervent thanksgiving for me, and for all the souls, God was to snatch from the powers of darkness.

In these last years of my life, my activity increased to such an extent that there was no cessation or relaxation in my operation, and it exceeds all powers of ordinary comprehension. Because of my special gifts, the mortality and weight of human nature no longer hindered me. I operated like the indefatigable spirits, and accomplished more than all of them together. I became one devouring flame and conflagration of immense activity. All my days seemed short, all occasions too few, and all my exercises seemed limited, because my divine love continually tended to exceed all bounds of what I was doing, although that was without limit. There is an abyss or infinite distance between what I actually did, and what you are capable of understanding. I can only beseech you to give to God all that you have to give, lest you make yourselves unworthy of the light, which awaits you in Heaven.

I Am Mary

Have mercy on me, oh God, in your goodness
In the greatness of your compassion wipe out my offense.
Thoroughly wash me from my guilt and of my sin cleanse me [Psalm: 51, 3-4].

In order that I might enlighten my Son's Church in the first age, my son sent me, and made me known to the first children of his holy Church. In the course of ages, he has continued to manifest my holiness and greatness by the wonders he has had me perform as queen, such as the innumerable favors and blessings, which have flowed from my hands upon humankind. In the last ages, which are the present, he will spread my glory and make me known in new splendor, because of the Church's great need for my intercession and of my help against the world, the demon, and the flesh. For these, through men's own fault, as we see even today, will assume greater sway and strength to hinder the working of grace in men and to make them more unworthy of glory

Against the malice of Lucifer and his demons, the Lord wishes by my merits, intercession, and example to defeat him. I am to be the refuge and sanctuary of sinners, and the straight and secure way full of splendor for all that wish to walk upon it. The kings, princes and leaders of the world should walk in my light, and seek their honor and glory in me, the Mother of God. If they employed the greatness, power, and riches of their states in advancing the honor of my most holy Son and me, then they could rest assured that they would govern their states with great success. For this reason, Jesus has given me the title of Patroness, Protectress, and Advocate of these countries. Through this singular blessing, the Most High has resolved to remedy the calamities and difficulties, which the Christians, because of their sins are to endure and suffer, each in their own times, sorrowfully and tearfully. The infernal dragon has poured out his fury against the holy Church, because he sees the carelessness of its heads and members, and because he sees so many men in love with vanity and delusive pleasures.

I desire to help the Catholics who seek my aid in accordance with the commands of God and my own maternal affection. The saints, especially Saint John, rejoiced when they learned that God was going to reveal the facts concerning my ascension with my Son and Lord. It is now time for the children of the Church to know and understand more fully the blessings to which the Omnipotent has raised me. Thereby you can enliven yourselves and make yourselves more capable of the favors I can and will bestow upon you. I am the loving mother, filled with pity at seeing you so deceived and oppressed by the tyranny of Satan, to whom you have blindly submitted.

In this prudent alertness, you will understand how closely you must imitate me in living faith, confident hope, fervent love, profound humility, and in the worship and reverence due to the infinite greatness of the Lord. I warn you again of the cunning vigilance of the serpent, who seeks to induce mortals to neglect the veneration and worship due to God and presumptuously to despise this virtue and what it implies. Into the minds of the worldly and of the vicious, he instills a foolish forgetfulness of the Catholic truths, and thus, he succeeds in making them no better than the heathens, who do not know the true God.

Without further delay gather for yourselves the fruits of all that I have revealed to you. However, at the same time, humiliate yourself to the very earth and shrink to the very last place among creatures, for you can call nothing yours except misery and want. Consider well within yourself how great the kindness is and condescension of the Most High about yourselves and what thanks that you owe him. If the one who pays his debts, even entirely, cannot take special credit; then it is just that you who cannot satisfy your debt should remain humble. Although you labor ever so much and utilize all your powers, you shall nevertheless remain a debtor. What shall then be your indebtedness, if you remain remiss and negligent?

I love you

Mary

Chapter Twelve

My Transition-Assumption-and Coronation

"Death is swallowed up in victory. Where, O death is your victory? Where, O death is your sting?" [1 Cor: 15, 55]

For sixty-seven years, I labored for the Lord. Yet I did not look to be more than thirty-three, nor did I feel any different than I had then, except for the fact that I had continued to grow in the love of the blessed Trinity. My overwhelming desire to unite with the Divinity had attained the summit of power in me. The earth itself, made unworthy by the sins of mortals to contain me, could no longer bear the strain of withholding me from my true Lord. In return, the eternal Father desired his only and true daughter; my Son desired his beloved and loving mother, and the Holy Spirit desired the embraces of his most beautiful spouse. The holy angels longed for their queen, and all the heavens mutely awaited the presence of their empress who would fill them with delight. All that could be alleged in favor of my still remaining in the world and in the Church, was the need for such a mother and mistress and the love, which God himself had for the miserable children of Adam.

The Almighty therefore resolved to give me a definite notice of the term remaining of my life on Earth. For this purpose, the angel Gabriel with many others of the celestial hierarchies came to acquaint me with these facts. The holy prince descended with the rest of his court to the Cenacle and entered my oratory, where they found me prostrate on the floor in the form of a cross, asking mercy for sinners. Hearing the sound of the music and then seeing them, I rose to my knees in order to show proper respect for God's Ambassador, and to hear the message I knew they had for me. They came in white and refulgent garments and surrounded me with wonderful delight and reverence. All of them came with crowns and palms in their hands to confer upon me, each one different, and each represented the diverse premiums and rewards of inestimable beauty and value.

Gabriel saluted me with the Ave Maria, and added thereto, "Our, empress and, lady, the Omnipotent and the Holy of Holies send us from his heavenly court to announce to you in his name the happiest end of your pilgrimage and banishment upon Earth in mortal life. Soon oh, lady is that day and hour approaching, in which, according to your longing desires, you shall pass through death to the possession of the eternal and immortal life, which awaits you in the glory and at the right hand of your divine Son our God. Exactly three years from today, you shall be taken up and received into the everlasting joy of the Lord, where all its inhabitants await you, longing for your presence."

I received this message with a singing heart, and again prostrated myself upon the ground; I answered Gabriel with the same words as at the Incarnation of the Lord, "Behold the handmaid of the Lord, be it done according to your word."

Then I asked the holy angels and the ministers of the Most High to help me to give proper thanks for this welcome and joyful news. For two hours, we exchanged canticles of praise and thanksgiving. I then begged the supernal spirits to beseech the Lord to prepare me for my passage from mortal to eternal life, and to ask all the other angels and saints in heaven to pray for the same favor. They offered to obey me in all things, and therewith they took their leave and returned to the Empyrean Heavens.

I prostrated myself upon the floor and prayed, "Earth, I give you thanks as I should, because you have sustained me for sixty-seven years without any merit on my part. I ask you to help me during the rest of my dwelling upon you. I thank you heavens, planets, stars and elements, created by the powerful hands of my beloved, for the preservation of my life. You are faithful witnesses and announcers of his greatness and beauty. May I begin anew with your help to perfect my life during the time left of my career. Thus, may I show I am thankful to our Creator.

Inflamed with the fires of divine love, I multiplied my exercises of devotion. I wished to make up for any relaxation or negligence in my fervor up to that time. I was urged on by the loving desires of the eternal order, as the traveler hastens his footsteps when a great part of his ways is still before him as the day declines, and as the laborer redoubles his exertions when evening overtakes him before the completion of his task. Consequently, I wrote the Apostles and disciples more frequently than before to encourage them in their labors for the conversion of the world, and urged them to greater efforts. My behavior was that of one who begins to prepare for their departure, and yet desires to leave their friends rich and prosperous, and filled with celestial benedictions.

Saint John; however, was different. I regarded him as my own son, and he in return attended upon me and cared for my every need, physical and spiritual. I asked for and received permission from my Lord and Son to inform John of my approaching death. Approaching John, I asked him for his blessing and for permission to speak to him.

This he gave me with delight and I said to him, "You already know, my son that among the creatures of the Most High that I am the most indebted of all and under the greatest obligations to submit to his holy will. God, in his condescending mercy, has revealed to me that I have but three more years until my passage into eternal life. I beseech you my son, to aid me in giving thanks to the Most High and render him some return for the immense blessings and love that I have received. I beseech you from the bottom of my heart, pray for me."

My words tore the heart of Saint John. Unable to restrain his sorrow and his tears he answered, "My, mother, I am bound to obey your will and that of the Most High, although my merits are far below what they ought to be and what I desire. Will you my most loving, mother, help your poor child, who is to be left an orphan deprived of your most desirable company?"

John could say no more, overcome by his tears and sighs of sorrow. In spite of my encouragement and consolation, the heart of the Apostle was pierced by a dart of pain and grief. It struck him down and caused him to wither like a flower snipped from its stem. In fear that he might lose his life in this affliction, I came to his relief by my loving promises, assuring him that I would be his mother and advocate with my divine Son. In turn, John felt it necessary to inform James the less, who, as bishop of Jerusalem, and according to the previous orders of Saint Peter, assisted John in my service. From that time on, the two Apostles were even more solicitous in attending upon me. This was especially true of the Evangelist, who seldom left my presence.

During the course of these three years, the divine power permitted a certain hidden and sweet force to throw all nature into mourning and sorrow at my prospective death, for by my life I had beautified and perfected all creation. The rest of the holy Apostles, although they were scattered over the Earth, began to feel new anxiety and misgivings regarding the time when they should be deprived of my presence and help. Already the divine light intimated to them that this event could not be far off. Others of the faithful living in Palestine began secretly to feel that their treasure and joy should not be theirs much longer. The heavens, the stars and planets lost much of their brightness and beauty, like the day at the approach of night. The birds of the air fell into singular demonstrations of sorrow during these last years. A great multitude of them ordinarily gathered wherever I happened to be. They surrounded my oratory in unusual flight and motions, they uttered, instead of their natural songs, sorrowful notes as if they were lamenting and groaning in their grief, until I ordered them again to praise the Creator in their natural and musical tones. A few days before my transition innumerable hosts of little birds gathered, laying their heads and beaks upon the ground. They picked at their breasts in groans, like some one taking farewell and asking for the last benediction.

One day, I went to visit the holy places of the Redemption, as was my custom. When I arrived on Mount Calvary, I found that many wild beasts had come from the surrounding mountains to wait for me. Some of them prostrated themselves upon the ground, others bowed their necks, and they all uttered sorrowful sounds, and thus for some hours, they manifested their grief at my impending departure, for they recognized me as their queen. The moon and the stars and the light of the sun was diminished on this day of general mourning, and at my death, the sun and moon were eclipsed as at the death of the Redeemer. Many wise and thoughtful men noticed these unwonted changes in the celestial orbs, but all were ignorant of its cause.

The Evangelist, before all the others, shared in the sorrow of the creatures, and he was unable to conceal it from the more familiar inmates of the house. Two daughters of the master of the house, who were much in attendance upon me, and some other very devout persons, chanced to see him shedding many tears in his sorrow. Knowing him so well, they urged him to tell them the cause of this unusual sorrow in order to relieve him if possible. The Apostle suppressed his grief for a long time, but finally with divine approval, he told them that my happy transition was soon to take place.

Thus, the great mercy and Providence of the Lord, timely forewarned many faithful of the Church of my impending death. Their tears and sorrow obliged me, during the remainder of my life, to favor and enrich them with the treasures of divine grace, which I, as their mistress, could confer upon them in my departure. The tears of the faithful moved my heart. During my last days, I obtained from my divine Son new mercies and blessings of the Divinity for them and for all the Church. At no time was anyone ever disappointed who trusted in me. I helped and relieved all that did not resist my loving advances. No one during the last three years of my life could ever count or estimate the wonders and benefits I wrought upon all the mortals that flocked in multitudes around me. I healed all the sick that presented themselves before me in both body and soul. I converted many to the evangelical truth. I drew innumerable souls from sin to the state of grace. I relieved the great miseries of the poor. I confirmed all in the fear of God, in faith and obedience to the Church. As mistress and treasurer of the riches of the Divinity, obtained by the life and death of my divine Son, I wished to dispense his mercy before my death to enrich all my children in the holy Church. Above all, I consoled them and encouraged them by my promise that I would continue throughout history to favor, from the right hand of my divine Son, all the children of the Church.

I was more certain of eternal reward than any other rational creature. Yet, not withstanding this certainty, and having received notice of my death three years in advance, I disposed and prepared myself for the hour of death with the holy fear proper to a mortal and earth-born creature. In this, I acted as a creature subject to death, and as the Teacher of the Church, I gave example to the rest of the faithful of what they were to do as mortals for avoiding eternal damnation. If in your wickedness, you incur the guilt of commission or omission of sin, do not allow the sun go down without having sorrowed for it, or confessed it. If you cannot immediately confess your sin, make an act of contrition and commence to work with new fervor and solicitude to overcome your weaknesses.

Upon learning that I was soon to depart for Heaven, I soon found it near impossible to constrain the impetus of my heart, nor seemed able to master my interior activities or hold dominion over them. I had yielded all my liberty to the sway of love, and to my desire of possessing the highest Good, in whom I lived transformed and forgetful of earthly mortality. It happened many times during these last days that I had to abate the excesses of my love, in order to prevent my bosom from being torn asunder.

I broke the silence of my retreat and spoke to God, "My sweetest, Love, highest, Good and, Treasure of my soul, draw me now after the sweetness of your ointments, which you have permitted your handmaid and mother to taste in this world. My will always found its rest entirely in you, the highest truth and my true good. I have never known any other love than the love of you. Please, my only hope and glory, let not my course be prolonged, let not the beginning of that much desired freedom be postponed. Solve now the chains of that mortal existence, which still detains me. Do you pity this stranger among the children of Adam, captive in the bonds of mortal flesh? Present to my Lord the cause of my sorrow, of which he is not ignorant. Tell him that for his sake I embrace suffering in my banishment. I so desire it, but I cannot desire to live in my own self. Love it is, which gives me life and at the same time deprives me of it. Life cannot live without love; hence, how can I live without the life, which alone I love? In this sweet violence I am perishing, tell me if possible of the qualities of my beloved, for amid such aromatic flowers the swooning of my impatient love shall find recovery."

My angels addressed me as follows, "Our, queen and, lady, we will speak to you of the tokens of your beloved. Consider that he is beauty itself, and that he contains within himself all the perfections beyond all desire. He is amiable without defect, delightful beyond comparison, and pleasing without the least flaw. In wisdom, his is inestimable, in goodness, without measure, in power, boundless, in greatness, immeasurable, and in essence, infinite. In his judgments, he is terrible, his counsels, inscrutable, in his justice, most equitable, in his thoughts, unsearchable, in his words, true, in his works, holy and rich in mercies. God never fails in his wisdom nor does he change in his will. Space cannot overreach him, narrowness cannot confine him, sorrow cannot disturb him, and joy cannot cause any change in him. God has no need of anything, for he participates in and causes all things. God exalts all his friends, and at last, glorifies them by his Eternal Vision, for those who love and extol him are blessed and are happy. This, our Lady, is the good which you love, and whose embraces, you shall shortly enjoy without intermission through all eternities."

Such discussions took place frequently between my angels and I. During the last days of my life, I not only enjoyed the favors mentioned above, namely those of the feast days and the Sundays, and too many others to enumerate. However, in order to sustain and nourish me in my anguishes of love, my divine Son visited me more frequently than ever before. During these visits, he recreated and comforted me with wonderful favors and caresses. He assured me again and again that my banishment would now be short that he would bear me up to his right hand, where I would be placed on the royal throne by the Father and the Holy Ghost and be absorbed in the abyss of the Divinity.

Among the wonders the Lord wrought for me during these final years, years which blended together in a blur, there was one which was manifest not only to John, but also too many of the faithful. When I received Holy Communion, I shone for some hours afterwards with a translucency so wonderful that I seemed transfigured and gifted with glory. As my time drew near for my final transition, I resolved to take leave of all the holy places before my departure to Heaven. Having obtained the permission of Saint John, I left the house with him and the thousand angels of my guard. While they were always with me, on these special occasions, they manifested themselves to me in far greater beauty and refulgence, as if they felt a special joy in seeing themselves already at the beginning of my last journey into Heaven. I visited each memorable place of the Redemption, marking each with a sweet abundance of my tears, in recalling the sorrowful memories of what my divine Son had to suffer there. I fervently renewed its effects by my most fervent acts of love, and petitions of all the faithful. On Calvary, I remained a longer time, asking my divine Son the full effects of his redeeming Death for all the multitudes of souls snatched from destruction. My ardor and ineffable charity during this prayer would have destroyed me if my divine Son had not relieved me. Thereupon, my Son descended in person and appeared to me at this place of his death.

Answering my petitions he said, "My, mother and my, dove, coadjutrix in the work of human Redemption, I have heard your petitions and they have touched my heart. I promise you that I shall be most lenient with men. I shall dispense to them continually my graces and favors, in order that with their own free will, they will merit the glory earned for them by my blood, if they do not of their own accord despise this happiness. In Heaven, you shall be their *Mediatrix and Advocate.* All those that obtain your intercession, I shall fill with my treasures and infinite mercies."

Prostrate at his feet, I begged him by his most precious and bloody death, to give me his final benediction. The Lord did so, and then returned to the right hand side of his Father. Comforted in my loving anguish, I pursued my devotions; kissed and worshipped the ground of Calvary saying, "Oh holy, Earth and consecrated spot, from Heaven I shall look down on you with reverence, bathed in that light, which manifests all in its fount and origin, and from where came forth the divine Word to enrich you in his immortal flesh."

I again charged the holy angels to assist me in the custody of these sacred places, to inspire with holy thoughts all the faithful who should visit them with devotion, so that they might know and esteem properly the admirable blessing of the Redemption wrought thereon. I also charged them with the defense of these sanctuaries. If the crimes of men had not voided this favor, without a doubt the holy angels would have warded off the sacrilege of the heathens and the infidels. Even as it is, they defend them in many ways to the present day. I asked the angels assigned to the sanctuaries and the Evangelist to give me their final blessing in this last leave-taking. I then returned to my oratory shedding tears of tenderest affection for what I loved so much upon this Earth. I prostrated myself on the floor, and poured forth-another long and most fervent prayer for the Church. I persevered in it, until in an Abstractive Vision of the Divinity, the Lord assured me that he had heard and conceded my petitions at the throne of his mercy.

In order to give the last touch of holiness, I asked permission of the Lord to take leave of the holy Church saying, "Exalted and most high, God, Redeemer of the world, head of the saints and the predestined, Justifier and Glorifier of souls, I am a child of the holy Church, planted and acquired by your blood. Give me oh, Lord, permission to take leave of such a holy, loving mother Church, and of all my brethren, your children belonging to it."

I was made aware of the consent of the Lord, and therefore turned to the mystical body of the Church, addressing it in sweet tears as follows, "Holy Catholic Church, which in the coming ages shall be called the Roman, my mother and mistress, true treasure of my soul; you have been the only consolation of my banishment. You have been the refuge and ease of my labors, my recreation, my joy, and my hope. You have sustained me in my course. In you, I have lived as a pilgrim to the Fatherland, and you have nourished me after I had received in you my existence in grace through Jesus Christ, my Son and my Lord. In you are the treasures and the riches of his infinite merits. You shall be, for his faithful children, the secure way to the Promised Land, and you shall safeguard them on their dangerous and difficult pilgrimage. My happy, mother, Church Militant, you are rich and abundant in treasures. For you, I have always reserved my heart and my solicitude; but now is the time come to part from you and leave your sweet companionship in order to reach the end of my course. At the cost of my life, a thousand times would I bring to you all the nations and tribes of mortals that they might enjoy your treasures. I am about to leave you in mortal life, but in the eternal life, I will find you joyful in an existence, which includes all good. From that place, I shall look upon you with love, and pray always for your increase, your prosperity, and your progress."

My time was near, and I prepared to make my last will and testament. When I made this prudent wish known to my Lord, he deigned to approve of it by his own royal presence. For this purpose, the Blessed Trinity, attended with a myriad of angels and saints, descended to my oratory in the Cenacle. I adored the Trinity, and I heard a voice speaking to me, "Our chosen, spouse, make your last will as you desire, for we shall confirm it and execute it entirely by our infinite power." For some time, I remained lost in profound humility, seeking to know first the will of the Most High, before I should be so brash as to manifest my own.

The Lord, who knows all thoughts, responded to my modest desires, and the person of the Father said to me, "My, daughter, your will shall be pleasing and acceptable to me; for you are not wanting in merits of good works in parting from this mortal life that I should not satisfy your desires."

Both my Son and the Holy Ghost then gave me this same encouragement; and I made my will as follows. "Highest, Lord and eternal, God, I, who am but dust and ashes, confess and adore you with all the reverence of my inmost soul as the Father, the Son, and the Holy Ghost. You are three persons distinct in one undivided and eternal essence, one substance, and one in infinite majesty of attributes and perfection. I confess you as the one true Creator and preserver of all that has being.

In your kingly presence, I declare and say that my last will is this:" "I possess none of the goods of mortal life that I can leave, because I have never possessed or loved anything beside you, who are my good and only possession. To the heavens, the stars, the planets, and to all the elements, and to all creatures in them, I give thanks. Because, according to your will, they have sustained me without my merit, and lovingly I desire and ask them to serve and praise you in the offices and ministries assigned to them, and that they continue to sustain and benefit my brethren and fellow-men. In order that you do it so much the better, I renounce and assign to mankind the possession and as far as possible, the dominion of them, which your Majesty has given me over these irrational creatures, so that they may now serve and sustain my fellowmen. My cloak, which served to cover me, I leave to John for his disposal, since I hold him as a son. My body I ask the earth to receive again for your service, since it is the common mother and serves you as your creature. My soul, despoiled of its body and of all visible things, oh my, God, I resign into your hands, in order that it may love and magnify you through all the eternities. My merits and all the treasures, which, with your grace, and through my works and exertions, I have acquired, I leave to the holy Church, my mother and my mistress, as my residuary heiress, and with your permission I there deposit them wishing them to be much greater. And I desire that before all else they redound to the exaltation of your holy name and procure the fulfillment of your will on earth, as it is done in heaven, and that all the nations come to acknowledge, love, and venerate you, the one and true God."

"In the second place, I offer these merits for my masters, the Apostles and priests of the present and of the future ages. So that in view of them, your ineffable clemency may make them apt ministers, worthy of their office and state, filled with wisdom, virtue, and holiness, by which they may edify and sanctify the souls redeemed by your blood. In the third place, I offer them for the spiritual good of my devoted servants, who invoke and call upon me in order that they may receive your protection and grace, and afterwards eternal life. In the fourth place, I desire that my services and labors may move your mercy toward all the sinning children of Adam, in order that they may withdraw from their sinful state. From this hour on, I propose and desire to continue my prayers for them in your divine presence, as long as the world shall last. This, Lord, and my, God, is my last will, always subject to your own."

When I finished, the Blessed Trinity approved and confirmed it; and Christ the Redeemer, as if authorizing it all, witnessed it by writing in my heart these words, "Let it be done as you wish and ordain."

When I had made my testament, I gave thanks to the Almighty and asked permission to add another petition, saying, "Most clement, Lord and, Father of mercies, I desire that, with your permission, all the Apostles and the disciples be present at the departure of my soul, so they may pray for and bless me at my transition from this life to eternal life."

To this my divine Son answered, "My most beloved, mother, the Apostles are already on the way to come to you, and those that are near shall shortly arrive. Those that are far off shall be carried by my angels, because for my greater glory, it is my will that all assist at your glorious departure for the eternal mansions, so that you and they may be consoled."

For this new favor, I gave thanks prostrate upon the stone floor, and therewith the divine Persons returned to the Empyrean Heavens.

My Transition

God gathered the Apostles and disciples in Jerusalem, three days before my most happy and prophesied death. Saint Peter was the first to arrive. He was in Rome, an angel told of my imminent death, and that God had ordered him to be present at the event. The angel then transported Peter from Rome directly to the Cenacle. I lay there somewhat weakened in body by the force of my divine love; for since I was so near to the end, I was subjected more completely to love's effects. Born without original sin, I was not subject to death by some debilitating disease, but rather from the burning fire of my *all-consuming* love for my Creator. I met Saint Peter at the entrance of my oratory, and I knelt at his feet and asked for his pontifical blessing.

He complied with tears running down his cheeks and I said to him, "I give thanks and praise to the Almighty that he has brought to me the Holy Father, for assisting me in the hour of my death."

Then Saint Paul came; to whom I showed the same reverence and similar tokens of my pleasure at seeing him again. One by one, the Apostles saluted me as the Mother of God, and as their queen and mistress of all creation, but they all demonstrated a deep sorrow equal to their reverence. After the Apostles, the disciples came and others who had also witnessed the crucifixion. I received them with profound humility, reverence, and love, asking each one to bless me. All of them complied and saluted me with admirable reverence. Saint John and James the less, by my orders, saw that they were all hospitably entertained and accommodated. All appeared before me, except Thomas, whose presence had been delayed by the Lord for his own intentions.

Saint Peter, as the head of the Church, called them all together to tell them the cause of their coming and said to them, "My dearest, children and, brethren, the Lord has called and brought us to Jerusalem from remote regions with a cause most urgent and sorrowful to us. The Most High wishes now to raise up to the throne of eternal glory his most blessed mother, our mistress, our consolation, and our protection. His divine decree is that we all be present at her most happy and glorious transition. When our Master and Redeemer ascended to the right hand of his Father, although he left us orphaned of his most delightful presence, we still retained his most blessed mother. As our light now leaves us, what shall we do? What help or hopes have we to encourage us on our pilgrimage? I find none except the hope that we all shall follow her in due time."

Peter could speak no further because of his uncontrollable tears and deep sighs, nor could the rest of them find words, because of their overwhelming grief. After awhile, Peter recovered himself and added, "My, children, let us seek the presence of our mother and lady. Let us spend the time left of her life in her company and ask her to bless us."

With John's permission, they all presented themselves to me in my oratory, where I was knelling upon my couch. They saw me full of God's beauty and celestial light, surrounded by the thousand angels of my guard. The natural condition and appearance of my virginal body were the same as at my thirty-third year, for as I have stated before, from that age onward my body experienced no change. It was not affected by the passing years, showing no signs of age, no wrinkles in my face or body, nor did it give any signs of weakening or fading, as in other children of Adam. This unchangeableness was my privilege alone, as well because it consorted with the stability of my pure soul, as because it was the natural consequence of my immunity from the sin of Adam, the effects of which in this regard touched neither my sacred body nor my pure soul.

The Apostles, and the disciples, including Mary of Magdala, Martha, Joanna, Susanna, Veronica, and many others, occupied my chamber. I knew that Jesus had made known to Mary Magdalene that she was to live concealed in the wilderness. Mary Magdalene, after my death, retired to a cave and devoted her life to solitude and prayer for the forgiveness of the sins of the world. I also knew that my Son had assigned Martha the task of establishing a holy community of women, which she did quite successfully. Saint Peter and Saint John then placed themselves at the foot of my couch.

I met them in my accustomed modesty and reverence with my head bowed humbly, and spoke to them, saying, "My dearest, children, please give permission to your servant to speak in your presence and to disclose my humble desires."

Peter answered that all listened with attention, and would obey me in all things, and he begged me to seat myself upon the couch, while speaking to them. I was exhausted for having knelt for so long and it was proper that as their queen that I seat myself. As the teacher of humility and obedience unto death, I practiced both of these virtues in that last hour in obedience to Saint Peter.

Later, with Peter's permission, I left the couch and kneeling before him said, "My, friend, I beseech you, as the universal pastor and head of the holy Church, to pardon me your handmaid for the smallness of the service I have rendered in my life. Grant that John disposes of my two tunics, giving them to the two poor maidens, Maria and Debra, who have always obliged me by their charity."

I then prostrated myself; kissed the feet of Saint Peter as the Vicar of Christ, and washed them by my abundant tears. From Saint Peter, I went to Saint John, and kneeling at his feet I said, "Pardon me my, son and my, master, for my not having fulfilled toward you the duties of a mother as I ought and as the Lord had commanded me, when from the Cross, he appointed you as my son and me as your mother. I humbly, and from my heart, thank you for the kindness, which you have shown me as a son. Please give me your benediction for entering into the vision and company of him who created me."

I then proceeded in my leave taking, speaking to each of the Apostles in particular, and to some of the disciples, and then all the assembly together, for there was a great number present. I missed many faces of those already called to their reward. I rose to my feet, and addressed them all saying, "Dearest, children and my, masters, I have always kept you in my soul and written in my heart. My Son gave me his tender love and charity, with which I have loved you and see in each of you. I now go to the eternal mansions in obedience to his holy and eternal will, where I promise you as a mother, I will look upon you by the clearest light of the Divinity, the vision of which my soul hopes and desires in security. I commend unto you my Mother, the Church, the exaltation of the name of the Most High, and the spread of the Evangelical Law. I charge you with the honor and veneration for the words of my divine Son, the memory of his Passion and Death, and the practice of his doctrine. My, children, love the Church and love one another with that bond of charity, which your master always inculcated upon you. To you, Peter, holy Pontiff, I commend my son John and all the rest."

My friends, seized with irreparable sorrow, cast themselves upon the stone floor dissolved in streams of tears, sighs, and groans sufficient to move to compassion the very earth. They all wept, and I wept with them, for I could not resist this bitter and well-founded sorrow of my children. After some time, I asked them to pray with me and for me in silence, which they obligingly did. During this quietness, the Incarnate Word descended from heaven on a throne of ineffable glory, accompanied by all the saints, and innumerable angels. The house of the Cenacle was filled with glory. I adored my Lord and kissed his feet. Prostrate before him, I made the last and most profound act of faith and humility in my mortal life. On this occasion, I shrank within myself and lowered myself to the earth more profoundly than all humankind together ever have or ever will humiliate themselves for all their sins.

My divine Son gave me his blessing, and in the presence of the courtiers of Heaven, spoke to me these words, "My dearest, mother, whom I have chosen for my dwelling place, the hour is come in which you are to pass from this world into the glory of the Blessed Trinity. There you shall possess the throne at my right hand prepared for you from before Creation, and you shall enjoy it through all eternity. Since, by my power, I have caused you to enter this world, as my mother free and exempt from all sin, death, if you wish not to pass through it, shall have no right or permission to touch you at your exit from this world. Come with me now to partake of my glory, which you alone of all souls, have merited."

I prostrated myself at his feet, my face glorious with happiness and replied, "My, Son and my, Lord, I beseech you, please allow your mother and your servant to enter into eternal life by the common portal of natural death, like the other children of Adam. You, who are my true God, have suffered death without being obliged to do so. It is proper that as I have followed you in life, so I follow you also in death."

My Son approved of my decision and my sacrifice, and consented to its fulfillment. Then all the angels began to sing in celestial harmony some of the verses from the Canticles of Solomon and many other new ones. Only Saint Peter, Saint John, and a selected few of the other Apostles were enlightened as to the presence of Christ the Savior. Yet, many others felt in their interior its divine and powerful effects. The music; however, was heard by all the Apostles and the disciples, and by many others of the faithful there present. A divine fragrance spread about, which penetrated even to the street. The house of the Cenacle was filled with glorious effulgence, visible to all, and the Lord ordained that the multitudes of the people gathered in the streets of Jerusalem were to witness this new miracle.

The angels began their music and I reclined on my couch, my tunic folded about my virginal body. I was entirely inflamed with the fire of divine love, for it was no longer necessary for me to hold my love in check. I joined my hands and fixed my eyes upon my divine Son. The angels intoned the second chapter of the Canticles singing, "Surge, propera, amica mea," that is to say: "Arise, haste my, beloved, my, dove, my beautiful, one, and come, the winter has passed," etc.

I looked into my Son's eyes, and in imitation of my Son's last words at his crucifixion, I said, "Into your hands, oh, Lord, I commend my spirit." I simply closed my eyes and my Lord, my Son, my Redeemer; my Savior received my last breath. The sickness that took my life was love, without any other weakness or accidental intervention of whatever kind. God withdrew his miraculous assistance, my love consumed the life-humors of my heart, and I breathed my last.

My pure soul passed from my stainless, virginal body, and the angels joyfully placed me on the throne at the right hand side of my divine Son, The music seemed to fade off into the upper air, as our procession of angels and saints escorted their King and Queen to the Empyrean Heavens. My sacred body, the temple and sanctuary of God in life, shone with an effulgent light, and breathed forth a wonderful and unheard of fragrance. My thousand angels, remaining behind, and stood watch over their treasure, my virginal body.

The Apostles and disciples, amid the tears and the joy of the wonders they had seen, were absorbed in admiration for some time. Then they sang many hymns and psalms in my honor, now departed from their midst. This glorious *Transition* took place in the hour in which my divine Son had died, at three o'clock on a Friday, the thirteenth day of August. I had attained the age of seventy years, plus the days numbered between the thirteenth of August, the day of my death, and the fifth of August, the day of my birth.

Great wonders and prodigies happened at my death, since I was their queen. The sun was eclipsed, and its light hidden in sorrow for some hours. Many birds of different kinds gathered around the Cenacle. By their sorrowful clamors and groans, they, for a while, caused bystanders themselves to weep. All Jerusalem was in commotion, and many of the inhabitants collected in astonished crowds, confessing loudly the power of God, and the greatness of his works. The Apostles and disciples, with others of the faithful, broke forth in tears and sighs. Many of the sick of Jerusalem were cured. The angels and saints in heaven were overjoyed, when the Lord released all the souls from purgatory to join in their joyful celebration.

At the moment of my death, three men and two women, residing near the Cenacle also died. They died in sin, were impenitent, and were subject to eternal damnation. God restored them to life when I appeared before the Lord's tribunal and interceded for them. They died in a state of grace at their eventual deaths, having amended their lives.

The Apostles, the disciples, and many other extremely devoted members of the faithful grieved to the point of death. The divine power, by especial providence, consoled them in their incomparable affliction, thereby sparing their lives. The thought of the lack of my protection and company, left them, as it were, without a breath of life. However, the Lord, knowing all things, secretly upheld them by his encouragement, and so they began preparing at once for my burial, which was the custom of the time.

John, and the holy Apostles, justly inherited this duty. John, because he had been delegated by Jesus as my son, and the Apostles, the designated leaders of the Church of which I was their queen. They selected a new sepulcher prepared mysteriously by the providence of my divine Son, for my tomb. Accordingly, to prepare me for burial, they called the two maidens, Maria and Debra, the daughters of Jason, the owner of the Cenacle, who had assisted me during my stay in Jerusalem, and whom I had designated as the beneficiaries of my tunics.

Peter instructed the girls, "Anoint her body with the greatest reverence and modesty and wrap it in the winding sheets so that it can be placed in the casket."

The two maidens entered my oratory with great reverence and fear. However, the glorious lights emanating from my body barred and blinded them in such a manner that they could neither see nor touch my body, nor even ascertain in what exact place that I lay.

The maidens scurried from the room, their reverence greater than on their entrance. In great excitement and wonder, they related to the Apostles what had happened. Saint Peter and Saint John then entered my oratory and perceived the effulgence, and at the same time, they heard the celestial music of the angels, who were singing: "Hail Mary, full of grace, the Lord is with thee." Others responded; "A virgin before childbirth, in childbirth, and after childbirth."

From that time on, many of the faithful would express their devotion toward me with these same words of praise given them by heaven, and were to be often repeated with the approbation of the holy Church.

The two Apostles were lost in admiration at what they saw and heard of me their queen. In order to decide what to do, they sank on their knees beseeching the Lord to make it known. Then they heard a voice saying, "No one touch or uncover the sacred body."

Peter and John approached the couch, the effulgence receded, and with their own hands, they reverently took hold of my tunic at both ends. Thus, without changing the posture of my body, they raised their sacred and virginal treasure and placed it on the bier in the same position as I had taken when I lay upon the couch. They could easily do this, for they felt no more weight than that of my tunic. On the bier, the former effulgence of my body moderated even more, and those present, by disposition of the Lord, and for their consolation, could now see and study the natural beauty of my virginal hands and countenance. However, as for the rest of my body, God protected this, his *heavenly dwelling* from prying eyes. God had ordained that neither in life nor in death should anyone behold any other part of my body, except what is common in ordinary conversation, mainly my continence. My face, and my hands, with which I had labored for them, was all that any man had seen of my body, for my tunic flowed to the ground concealing my feet.

My Son made me like unto himself with my Immaculate Conception. Likewise at birth, he preserved me from impure temptations and thoughts. However, he was a man and the Redeemer of the world through his Passion and death, he permitted with his own body, what he would not allow with the body of his mother. I had asked my Son that no one should be permitted to look upon my body in death, and therefore, the Lord kept my virginal body entirely concealed.

The Apostles then had many candles lighted and placed about my bier. The multitudes of people in Jerusalem followed suit. The candles burned miraculously for two days without being consumed or wasted. In order that this and many other miracles wrought by the power of God on this occasion might become better known to the world, the Lord himself inspired all the inhabitants of Jerusalem to be present at my burial.

The Apostles became my pallbearers, and as priests of the evangelical law, they bore my bier. They proceeded in an orderly procession from the Cenacle in mid city to the valley of Josaphat, located near the Garden of Gethsemane. Visibly, I was accompanied by the faithful and the dwellers of Jerusalem, and invisibly there was another multitude that of the courtiers of Heaven. The thousand angels of my personal guard continued singing their celestial songs for three days. The Apostles and disciples, as well as by many others, heard these songs. In addition to these, many spirits had descended from Heaven. Many thousands of legions of angels accompanied by the ancient Patriarchs and Prophets were among the heavenly hosts. Included were my parents Saint Joachim and Saint Anne, Saint Joseph my spouse, Saint Elizabeth and Saint Zachariah accompanied by their holy son, John the Baptist, as well as many other saints who were sent by my Son Jesus to assist at my funeral rites and burial.

I do not have the space to describe all the miracles that took place along the way. All the sick along the route were entirely cured. Many evil spirits, unable to bear my approach, fled freeing many possessed persons. Many conversions were wrought among the Jews and Gentiles, as my bier passed through their midst, for I was the treasure house of the divine mercy. Many souls came to the knowledge of the Christ, and they loudly confessed him as the true God and Redeemer, and began demanding baptism. After the funeral, the Apostles and disciples, spent many days catechizing and baptizing those who had been converted to the holy faith

The Apostles in carrying my sacred body felt wonderful effects of divine light and consolation, in which the disciples shared according to their measure of faith. All the multitudes of people were astonished at the fragrance diffused about, the sweet music, and the other prodigies. The multitude proclaimed God great and powerful in me, his creature, and in acknowledgment, they struck their breasts in sorrow and compunction.

As the procession neared the sepulcher, innumerable birds gathered in the air. Many wild animals rushed from the mountains towards the sepulcher, the birds caroled sorrowfully, and the domesticated beasts emitted groans and doleful sounds. All of them were showing grief in their actions, mourning over the common loss. Only a few unbelieving Jews, more hardened than the rocks and more impious than the wild beasts failed to show sorrow at my death, as they had failed to do also at the death of their Redeemer and Master.

When the procession came to my final resting-place, Peter and John with sorrowful reverence placed the bier in the holy crypt and covered me over with a white linen cloth. They then closed off the sepulcher with a huge stone, as was the custom. The celestial courtiers returned to Heaven, while my thousand angels mounted guard over my sacred body. The people gradually drifted away, as did the birds and the beasts. The Apostles and disciples dissolved in tender tears, and returned as a group to the Cenacle. An exquisite fragrance wafted from both the tomb and the Cenacle. Its fragrance remained in my oratory for some years. People, burdened with sickness and difficulties, soon found the Cenacle a place of refuge. There, they found miraculous assistance in all their needs. These miracles continued for several years. However, in time, the sins of Jerusalem and of its inhabitants drew down the wrath of God, and he allowed the Romans to purge the city of its sins. Their greatest loss; however, was that of being deprived of the miraculous blessings of their queen.

Having gathered at the Cenacle, the Apostles and disciples determined that some of them should keep watch at my grave, as long as they should hear the celestial music. Peter assigned the Apostles and disciples to the task of catechizing and baptizing the new converts. However, whenever possible, they all stole off to the tomb. Peter and John were more zealous in their attendance, coming only a few times to the Cenacle, and then returned quickly to where was laid the treasure of their hearts.

The Assumption

Upon my death, my Son gathered my soul and conducted me to the Empyrean Heavens escorted by countless angels and saints, all singing, praising, and glorifying the holy Trinity. I alone, of all mortals, deserved exemption from particular judgment. There was no account asked or demanded of me for what I received. The Holy Trinity chose me as the Queen of all Creation, and in doing so; they exempted me from the common guilt. Therefore, God will not judge me with the rest of humanity. Instead, seated at the right hand of the Judge, I will judge all the creatures with him.

God, at my Conception, had rendered me brilliant from the rays of his Divinity, even brighter than the most exalted seraphim. The hypostatic Word, who derived his humanity from my pure substance, illumined me still further at the first contact of the hypostatic Word. It necessarily follows that if I was to be his companion throughout eternity, that I possess a likeness to him, a likeness greater than possible between any other creature and God.

In this effulgent light the Redeemer himself presented me before the throne of the Divinity and uttered these words, "Eternal, Father, my most beloved mother, your beloved daughter, and the cherished spouse of the Holy Ghost, now comes to take possession of the crown and glory, which we have prepared as a reward for her merit. She is the one who was born as the rose among thorns, untouched, pure and beautiful, worthy of being embraced by us and of being placed upon a throne to which none of our creatures can ever attain, and to which those conceived in sin cannot aspire. This is our chosen and our only one, distinguished above all else. To her, we communicated our grace and our perfections beyond the measure accorded to other creatures. In her, we have deposited the treasure of our incomprehensible Divinity and its gifts. She has most faithfully preserved and made fruitful the talents, which we gave her. Our chosen one never swerved from our will, and she found grace and pleasure in our eyes."

"My Father, most equitable is the tribunal of our justice and mercy, we repay our friends in the most superabundant manner. Throughout her whole life and in all her works she was as like to me as much as possible for a creature to become. Therefore, let her also be as like to me in glory and on the throne of our Majesty, so that where holiness is in essence, there it may also be found in its highest participation."

The Father and the Holy Ghost approved this decree of the Incarnate Word. My Son placed my soul on the royal throne of the most holy Trinity. No other man, angel, or seraphim will ever attain such an honor for all eternity. Thus, I was designated Empress, and it was my privilege to be seated on the throne with the three divine Persons. All the rest of humanity will act as servants and ministers to the highest King. To the eminence and majesty of this position, inaccessible to all other creatures, I enjoy more than all others that infinite Object, which the other blessed also enjoy in an endless variety of degrees. I know and understand the eternal Essence much deeper than any creature. In this life, no one can describe, nor can it be understood, my likeness to Christ. *However, there is, and there will always be an infinite distance between the Divinity and me.*

Then the eternal Father declared, "In the glory of our beloved daughter all the pleasure of our holy will is fulfilled to our entire satisfaction. To all the creatures, we have given existence, creating them out of nothing, in order that they may participate in our infinite goods and treasures according to the inclination and pleasure of our immense bounty. The very ones, who we made capable of our grace and glory, have abused this blessing. Our cherished daughter alone had no part in the disobedience and prevarication of the rest. She has earned what the unworthy children of perdition have despised; and our heart has not been disappointed in her at any time or moment. The rewards belong to her, which according to our conditional decree, we had prepared for the disobedient angels and for their followers among man, if they had been faithful to their grace and vocation. Mary has recompensed us for their falling away by her subjection and obedience. She has pleased us in all her operations and has merited a seat on the throne of our Majesty"

On the third day, after I had taken possession of my throne never to leave it, the Lord manifested to the saints his divine will. He ordained that I should return to the world, resuscitate my sacred body and unite myself with it, so that I, in body and soul, am again raised to the right hand of my divine Son without waiting for the general resurrection of the dead. When the time for this wonder came, my Son descended from Heaven with me at his right hand and accompanied by many legions of angels, patriarchs and ancient prophets. We came to the sepulcher in the valley of Josaphat, and the Lord said to us, "My mother was conceived without stain of sin, in order that from her virginal substance I might without stain clothe myself in the humanity in which I came to the world and redeemed it from sin. My flesh is her flesh. She cooperated with me in the works of the Redemption, hence I must raise her, just as I rose from the dead, and this shall be done at the same time and hour, for I wish to make her like me in all things."

All the ancient saints of the human race then gave thanks for this new favor in songs of praise and glory to the Lord. Those that especially distinguished themselves in their thanksgiving were our first parents Adam and Eve, and Saint Anne, Saint Joachim, and Saint Joseph, as being the more close partakers in this miracle of his Omnipotence. Then, at the command of my Lord, I reentered my virginal body, reanimated it and raised it up, giving to it a new life of immortality, glory, and communication, and the four gifts of clearness, impassibility, agility, and subtlety. Endowed with these gifts, I passed through the walls of the tomb without disturbing the position of the stone, or the tunic and mantle that had enveloped my sacred body. It is impossible to put into human words the beauty and glory given me by my Son. It is sufficient to say that I, in my womb, had given my divine Son the form of a man, pure, unstained and sinless. Therefore, in return, the Lord through my resurrection and new regeneration gave me a glory and beauty similar to his own. In this mysterious and divine interchange, each of us did what was possible; I had engendered Christ, assimilating him as much as possible to myself, and Christ resuscitated me, communicating to me his own glory as far as I, a mere human creature, was capable of receiving.

The Lord then started a most solemn procession, moving with celestial music, through the regions of the air toward the Empyrean Heaven. This took place just after midnight, at which time the Lord had also risen from the grave; and therefore, not all of the Apostles were a witness to this prodigy. The disciples, guarding the tomb; however, were honored to see this majestic spectacle. The saints and angels entered Heaven in the order in which they had started, and in the last place came my Son with me at his right hand, bathed in the gold of variety. The heavenly court turned to me and blessed me with new jubilee and songs of praise. Thus were heard those mysterious eulogies recorded by Solomon:

"Come, daughters of Zion, to see your Queen, who is praised by the morning stars and celebrated by the sons of the Most High."

"Who is she that comes from the desert, like a column of all the aromatic perfumes?"

"Who is she that comes up from the desert resting upon her beloved and spreading forth abundant delights?"

"Who is she in whom the Deity itself finds so much pleasure and delight above all other creatures, and whom he exalts above them all in heaven; oh novelty worthy of the infinite Wisdom, oh prodigy of his Omnipotence, which so magnifies and exalts her!" Amid this glorious celebration, I arrived, body and soul, at the feet of the most Blessed Trinity.

The Coronation

All the divine Persons received me with an embrace eternally indissoluble. The eternal Father said to me, "Ascend higher, my, daughter and my, dove."

The Incarnate Word spoke, saying, "My, Mother, of whom I have received human being and full return of my work in your perfect imitation, receive now from my hand the reward you have merited."

The Holy Ghost said, "My most beloved, spouse, enter into the eternal joy, which corresponds to the most faithful love. Do you now enjoy your love without solicitude, for past is the winter of suffering for you have arrived at our eternal embraces."

My soul was absorbed in the contemplation of the three divine Persons, and the saints stood by in wonder. When my Son, the Savior, left his Apostles in order to commence his suffering, he told them not to be disturbed in their hearts because of things he had revealed to them. He told them, "In the house of my Father, which is eternal happiness, there are many mansions. There is room and just reward for all, although your merits and your good works will be varied. In the house of God there are many grades and many dwellings, and perhaps you will see others more favored or advanced than you. In spite of this just distribution of my Father's favors, no will be disturbed in his own peace and just reward, for each soul shall be content with what shall belong to him without envy; for this is one of the great blessings of that eternal felicity. *The soul can never be unhappy while basking in the Beatific Vision, even if their loved ones are in grave sin or have been condemned to Hell.*

I have stated that God assigned me to the supreme position and state on the throne of the most blessed Trinity. I have expressed myself in these terms many times in order to point out great sacraments and similar terms are used by the saints and by the sacred Scriptures themselves. No other argument is necessary. Nevertheless, for those who have not such a deep insight, I will say that God, as he is the purest Spirit and at the same time infinite, immense, and incomprehensible, has no need of a material throne or seat; for God fills all creation and is present in all creatures. He is comprehended or circumscribed by none, but he himself comprehends and encompasses all things. The saints do not see God with corporal eyes, but with those of the soul. However, to describe how they see him [in order for you to understand] I say that God is upon the royal throne of the most blessed Trinity, though in reality he had his glory within himself and communicates it to his saints. However, the most sacred humanity of Christ and I, hold a place supereminent over all the saints. Among the blessed that are in Heaven with body and soul, there is an order in relative position nearer or farther from Christ our Lord and from me your queen. However, here is not the place to inquire into the manner into which this arrangement shall be made in heaven.

The Holy Trinity manifests itself to the saints as the principal cause of their glory, and as the infinite eternal God, independent of all things, and on whose will all creatures depend. Jesus manifests himself as the Lord, the King, the Judge, and the Master of all that is in existence. This dignity, Christ the Redeemer possesses, in as far as he is God, essentially, and as far as he is man through the hypostatic-union, by which he communicates his Godhead to humanity. Hence in Heaven, he is the King, Lord, and supreme Judge. The saints, though their glory exceeds all human calculation, are as servants and inferiors of this inaccessible Majesty. In this hierarchy, I participate in an inferior degree, and in a manner indescribable but proportionate to a mere creature so closely related to the God-man. Therefore, I assist forever at the right hand of my Son as Queen, Lady, and Mistress of all Creation, and my dominion extends as far as that of my divine Son, although in a different manner.

After placing me on this exalted and super eminent throne, God the Father declared to the courtiers of Heaven, "Our daughter Mary was chosen according to our pleasure from amongst all creatures, the first one to delight us, and who never fell from the title and position of a true daughter such as we had given her in our divine mind. She has a claim on our dominion, which we shall recognize by crowning her as the legitimate and peerless Lady and Sovereign."

The Incarnate Word said, "To my true and natural mother belong all the creatures which were created and redeemed by me; and of all things over which I am King. She too shall be the legitimate and supreme Queen."

The Holy Ghost said, "Since she is called my beloved and chosen spouse, she deserves to be crowned as Queen for all eternity."

Having thus spoken, the three divine Persons placed upon my head a crown of such splendor and value that the like has never been seen before or after by any mere creature. At the same time, a voice sounded from the throne saying, "My, beloved, chosen among the creatures, our kingdom is yours. You shall be the Lady and the Sovereign of the seraphim, the ministering spirits, the angels, and of the entire universe of creatures. Attend, proceed, and govern prosperously over them, for in our supreme consistory, we give you power, majesty, and sovereignty. Filled with grace, you humiliated yourself beyond all the rest to the lowest place. Receive now the supreme dignity you deserve, for from your royal throne to the center of the Earth you shall reign; and by the power we now give you, you shall subject Hell with all its demons and inhabitants. Let all of them fear you as the supreme Empress and Mistress of those caverns and dwelling-places of our enemies. In your hands and at your pleasure, we place the influences and forces of the Heavens, the moisture of the clouds, and the growths of the Earth. You shall distribute all of them according to your will, and our own will shall be at your disposal for the execution of your wishes."

You shall be the Empress and Mistress of the Militant Church, its Protectress, its Advocate, its Mother and Teacher. You shall be the special Patroness of the Catholic countries, and whenever they, or the faithful, or any of the children of Adam call upon you from their heart, serve or oblige you, you shall relieve and help them in their labors and necessities. You shall be the Friend and Defender and the Chieftain of all the just and of our friends. You shall comfort, console and fill all of them with blessings according to their devotion to you. In view of all this, we make you the Depository of our Riches, the Treasurer of our Goods. We place into your hands for distribution the helps and blessings of our grace. We wish that anything given to the world should be through your hands. We deny nothing to you, which you wish to concede to men. Angels and men shall obey you everywhere, because whatever is ours shall be yours, just as you have always been ours, and you shall reign with us forever."

The Almighty commanded all the courtiers of Heaven, angels and men, to show me obedience and recognize me as their Queen and Lady. Throughout my pilgrimage I had humbled myself before my God and all mankind, sincerely seeking and finding the lowest place even though I knew that I was the Mother of God, full of grace and holiness even above the angels and the saints. Yet, now that I was in possession of the kingdom, God ordained that I be venerated, worshiped and extolled by all creatures. Both the angelic spirits and the blessed souls, while first rendering their adoration to the Lord with fear and worshipful reverence, rendered a like homage in its proportion to me as the Queen of Heaven. The angels and saints prostrated themselves and gave bodily signs of their veneration. It was a day of festivity, and those that partook more especially were my loyal one thousand guardian angels, my devoted spouse Saint Joseph, my parents Saints Anne and Joachim, and their parents Eliud and Ismeria. In addition, present were their parents Emorun and Stolanus, all the women had been *Vessels of the Promise*, with the *Mark of the Promise* indelibly marked on their stomachs. All generations had been heroically faithful helping to create the holy, genealogical ancestry of my family tree. I was the only one born without the Mark of the Promise, for I was the Holy Vessel of the Promise.

Within my body, visible to the saints of Heaven, was a small globe or monstrance of singular beauty and splendor given me by the Holy Trinity. It was a reward given me for having given the Sacramental Word an acceptable resting-place and sanctuary. It was also a reward for my having received Holy Communion so worthily, purely and sacredly without any defect or imperfection, and with devotion, love and reverence attained by none of the other saints.

As stated before my transition happened on the thirteenth of August, while my Resurrection and Assumption and Coronation happened on the Sunday the fifteenth, the day that it is celebrated in the Church. My body remained in the sepulcher thirty-six hours, just as the body of my divine Son had, for my death and Resurrection took place in the same hours of the day as that of my Son.

I now take you back to Earth where the Apostles and disciples were keeping watch at my tomb for the third day. Saint Thomas, delivered by an angel from India, had just joined Saint Peter. Both Saint John and Peter were still in tears, when Thomas approached and threw himself down and kissed the feet of Peter and wailed aloud, "Alas holy, Father, I am too late for the passing over and burial of our most holy queen."

Peter consoled the distraught Apostle, and said, "Thomas, listen to the heavenly music that fills the air." Soothed and consoled by the angelic choir Thomas said to Peter, "Is it not possible that I may enter the tomb to bid one last farewell to my queen and mother?"

At that moment the celestial music ceased. Dismayed, the Apostles were enlightened by the Holy Ghost, and they conjectured among themselves, 'Had I been raised from the dead and entered Heaven body and soul?' They conferred about this matter and concluded that it must be so. Urged on by Saint Thomas, Saint Peter, as head of the Church, decided that such a wonderful fact should be ascertained as far as possible and made known to those who had witnessed my death and burial. Peter called all the Apostles and disciples to come to the sepulcher. He gave them his reasons for verifying what would be a wonderful truth and wonder to the Church. They all approved his decision, and at his order, they removed the stone, which sealed the tomb. Peter allowed the grief-stricken, but eager, Apostle Thomas, to enter the tomb first.

"Our holy Mother is gone," he exclaimed with wonder."

Saint John ran from the tomb and called out excitedly, "Our Lady's body has been assumed into Heaven, come and see."

When the Apostles crowded into the small space, they all witnessed that the grave was empty, and a heavenly scent of roses and other flowers saturated their senses. The body of their queen had been assumed into Heaven to join her immortal soul. They found my tunic, surrounded by heaps of fresh, fragrant roses, which had replaced the burial herbs and spices. My tunic was in the same position as when it had covered my body. It dramatically demonstrated that my body must have passed through the tunic and the stone of the sepulcher without disturbing any part of them. Saint Peter took the tunic and mantle and they all venerated it. They were now certain of my Resurrection and Assumption. Peter encouraged each person to take a rose with them. With mixed joy and sorrow, they wept sweet tears at this prodigy and sang psalms and hymns of praise and glory to the Lord and to me, his blessed mother. Peter then ordered the tomb sealed for the last time.

My Transition, Assumption, and subsequent Coronation; however, was not the important message that the Apostles and the faithful were to preach. As I later told Saint Bridgette of Sweden, "After my death, the Lord willed that at first my Assumption was not to be made known to many persons, in order that faith in Christ's Ascension might first of all be firmly established in the hearts of men. Humankind was not yet prepared to believe in his Ascension, especially if my Assumption had been announced in the beginning."

In their affectionate wonder the Apostles and the faithful remained looking at the tomb, spellbound, until an angel of the Lord descended and manifested himself to them, saying, "You men of Galilee, why are you astounded and tarry here? Your and our queen now lives body and soul in Heaven and reigns in it forever with Christ her Son. She sends me to confirm you in this truth, and in her name. I tell you that she recommends to you anew the Church, the conversion of souls, and the spread of the Gospel. She desires me to tell you that each of you must now return to your ministry, with which you were charged, and that from her throne, she will take care of you."

The angel's message consoled the Apostles. They experienced my protection in their wanderings over the years, and much more in the hour of their martyrdom. I appeared to each of them in that hour to present their souls to the Lord personally and I wish to do the same for each of you.

I implore all of you to wear my Brown Scapular in good faith and I will be there at your death to personally present your soul to my divine Son. Live good lives! Pray, pray, pray! Say the Rosary daily, fast, and make many sacrifices. God loves you and wishes you to be with him throughout all eternity.

I Am Mary

"Do you think I have come to establish peace on the earth? No, I tell you, but rather division. From now on, a household of five will be divided three against two and two against three. A father will be divided against his son and a son against his father, a mother against her daughter and a daughter against her mother, a mother–in-law against her daughter-in-law, and a daughter-in-law against her mother-in-law." [Luke: 12, 51-53]

I related to you my decision when the Lord offered me the choice of the Beatific Vision either with or without passing through the portals of death. If I had preferred not to die, the Most High would have conceded this favor, because sin had no part in me, and hence I was not subject to its punishment, which is death. Thus, it would also have been with my divine Son, and with a greater right, if he had not taken upon himself the satisfaction of divine justice for men through his Passion and Death. Hence, I freely chose death in order to imitate and follow Jesus, the same as I did during his grievous passion. Since I had seen my Son and true God die, I would not have satisfied the love I owed him, if I had refused death. I would have left a great gap in my conformity to, and my imitation of my Lord the God-man. He wished me to bear a great likeness to him in his most sacred humanity. As I would thereafter never be able to make up for such a defect, my soul would not have enjoyed the delight of having died as did my Lord and God.

Hence, my choosing to die was so pleasing to him, and my prudent love therein obliged him to such an extent that in return he conceded to me a singular favor for the benefit of the children of the Church and conformable to my wishes. It was this,

Those devoted to me shall be under my special protection, if they should call upon me at the hour of their death, thus constituting me as their advocate in memory of my happy Transition and of my desiring to imitate Jesus in death. I shall intercede and present them before the tribunal of his mercy, and they shall have me as a defense against the demons.

In consequence, the Lord gave me a new power and commission, he promised to dispense his grace for a good death, and for a purer life on all those who in veneration of this mystery of my precious transition should invoke my aid.

I want you to keep in your inmost hearts a devout and loving memory of this mystery, and because God wrought such sacred miracles for me and for all mortals, bless, praise, and magnify his Omnipotence, By this concern and act of faith, you will oblige the Lord and me to come to your aid in that last hour.

As your mother, I have appeared countless times to my children throughout the history of the Church. The Church lists 400 of these during the last forty years. The history of Venerable Anne Catherine Emmerick, a stigmatist, Saint Bridgette of Sweden, and Saint Mary of Agreda are the major themes of this book. To recount a few others, I appeared to Saint Dominic [1170-1221] when the great heresy of Albigensian was rampant in the land. They preached that all matter was evil, and therefore Jesus was only divine, not human. I appeared to Saint Dominic and during a five-year civil war and gave him the Rosary with which to defeat this evil threat.

I appeared on Dec. 9, 1531 to Blessed Juan Diego, an Indian farmer near what is now Mexico City. I said to Juan, "My dear son, whom I love tenderly, know that I am the Virgin Mary, Mother of the True God; the giver and maintainer of life: Creator of all things: Lord of Heaven and Earth, who is in all places. I wish a temple to be erected here, where I can manifest the compassion I have for the natives and for ***all,*** who solicit my help."

Juan's bishop did not believe him, until I instructed Juan to pick the roses miraculously growing in barren stony ground in the middle of winter. He gathered them in his cloak [tilma] and when he opened the cloak before the Bishop they found an image of me imprinted on his cloak. The Mexicans honor me today, as the Lady of Guadalupe. The Basilica in Mexico City, Mexico and the faithful in Mexico also honor Juan's cloak as a religious relic. Consequently, when over eight million Mexicans were converted to Catholicism; I presented a new Catholic nation to my dear Son.

I gave the world the Miraculous Medal in Paris, France [1830]. In 1846, I appeared at LaSallette, France to two children. I told them of God's displeasure at the people not keeping holy the Sabbath, the men taking the name of the Lord in vain, the poor manner in which the people observed Lent, and that they did not abstain from meat on Fridays.

In 1858, during a period of apostasy, I appeared to Saint Bernadette at Lourdes, France as the Immaculate Conception.

I appeared to three children at Fatima, Portugal in 1917. The world was then enmeshed in World War I. I warned the world of the coming of an even greater evil than World War I. I told them, "I have come to ask for consecration of Russia to my Immaculate Heart and the Communion of Reparation of five First Saturdays of each month. If my requests are granted, Russia will be converted and there will be peace. Otherwise, Russia will spread her errors throughout the world provoking wars and persecution of the Church. Many will be martyred; the Holy Father will have much to suffer, several nations will be annihilated. In the end my Immaculate Heart with triumph and a period of peace will be granted the world."

I appeared again in Beauraing, Belgium in 1932-33 and in Banneux, Belgium in 1933. Again, I appeared 2000 times to four children in Garabandal, Spain during the period of 1961-1965 to warn the world of the wrath of God because of the evil of humankind. My first message was, "October 18, 1961. We must make many sacrifices, perform much penance, and visit the Blessed Sacrament frequently. However, first, we must lead good lives. If we do not, a chastisement will befall us. The cup is already filling up, and if we do not change, a very great chastisement will come upon us."

My message on June 18, 1965 was, "As my message of Oct. 18th has not been complied with and has not been made known to the world. I am advising you that this is the last one. Before the cup was filling-up; now it is flowing over. Many cardinals, many bishops and many priests are on the road to perdition and are taking many souls with them. Less and less importance is being given to the Eucharist. You should turn the wrath of God away from yourselves by your efforts. If you ask his forgiveness with sincere hearts, he will pardon you. I, your mother, through the intercession of Saint Michael the Archangel, ask you to amend your lives. You are now receiving the last warnings. I love you very much and do not want your condemnation. Pray to us with sincerity and we will grant your requests. You should make many sacrifices. Think about the passion of Jesus."

I appeared many times to Padre Pio, a stigmatist for fifty years, who died in 1968. There have been numerous other appearances such as the recent one in Florida. Each time I call for my children to come back to their faith and to my Son, for God is grievously offended and time is running out for humankind.

I keep my promises, and Pope John Paul II's Collegial Consecration of March 25, 1984, fulfilled my requests. Consequently, the Lord God has given the world many beneficent blessings. Two months after my Consecration for the conversion of Russia, on May 13, 1984, the 67th Anniversary of the first apparition at Fatima, an explosion in the Soviet Union destroyed 80% of the Soviet's main munitions in a storage depot.

In Siberia, on Dec. 13, 1984, another explosion destroyed the Soviet's largest ammunition depot.

Marshal Ustinov, the Soviet Union's Minister of Defense, died on Dec. 19, 1984.

The new Minister of Defense, Marshal Sodolov, died three days later.

The President of the Soviet Union, Chernenko, died just one year after the Consecration of March 1985. The new President, Mikhail Gorbachev, instituted *glasnost and perestroika* [freedom of the press and religion], this in turn led to the downfall of Communism in the USSR.

During the period of the Solemnity of the Assumption, Aug. 15, 1989, Poland made their move for a government led by non-communists.

On the Feast of the Holy Rosary, Oct. 7, 1989, The Hungarian Communist Party voted to adopt a European democratic socialism.

The Berlin Wall tumbled down on Nov. 9, 1989, which symbolized and foretold the fall of the Iron Curtain.

Gorbachev met with Pope John Paul II on Dec. 1, 1989 and promised to grant the Russian people religious freedom. The Pope said that this was "Divine Providence."

Consequently on Mar. 15, 1990, the Vatican established diplomatic relations with Russia.

Bishop Amaral of Leiria-Fatama remarked, "Everything leads us to think that the consecration requested by our Lady has been done. A short time later, on July 13, 1990, Cardinal Paskai of Hungary said, "Profound changes have begun in the countries of Central and Eastern Europe. The events that happened cannot be explained by purely human factors. Politicians who are believers also acknowledge the hand of God can be seen in these changes. We are certain that the promise of Our Lady is fulfilled, and that these changes are a result of her intercession."

The first religious services since the Communist Revolution of 1917, was held at the Cathedral of the Assumption inside the Kremlin, on Oct. 13, 1990. Before this, the Cathedral was used as a museum of atheism, and before that it was used as a stable.

Pope John Paul II was congratulated on Nov. 11, 1990 for Poland having been freed from Communism, but the Pope said emphatically, "No, not me, but by the works of the Blessed Virgin, in line with her affirmations at Fatima."

In a last desperate move, the Communists tried to overthrow Gorbechev on Aug. 19, 1991. A few days later, on Aug. 22nd, on my Feast of the Queenship of Mary, the Reds were defeated.

For the first time in years, Russian pilgrims came to Fatima on Oct. 13, 1991, the 74th Anniversary of the 6th Apparition of Fatima.

On the Feast of the Immaculate Conception, Dec. 8, 1991 the Commonwealth of Republics was begun, which marked the end of the Soviet Union. The new President of Russia, Boris Yeltsin, met with the Pope in Rome.

On Christmas Day, 1991, The Communist flag was lowered for the last time over Russia. On December 30th, their fifteen Republics were freed from Soviet domination as the Warsaw Pact was dissolved.

The Berlin Wall fell and the beginning of the Conversion of Russia has begun. It will take many prayers and sacrifices on the part of the world; however, to bring about their full conversion. In the meantime the faithful of the United States and throughout the world have their hands full to pray, and sacrifice to make to overcome the trend of too few priests and clergy to satisfy the needs of over one billion Catholics throughout the world.

I am now making an appearance at Medjugorje, Yugoslavia. I have been appearing regularly to six children since March 1, 1984. Again, I have come in the name of the Eternal Father, to warn the world of impending chastisements.

I have given two of the children ten secrets, chastisements that will plague the world unless humankind changes its ways. Mirjana, one of the children, will announce the first two events to Father Peter Ljubicic, O.F.M., who is the Franciscan friar in residence at Saint James Parish in Medjugorje.

Mirjana will advise Father Peter ten days before each chastisement is to begin. Father Ljubicic will pray and fast for seven days and he will then announce the event to the world. The advance warning will serve as a proof of the authenticity of the apparitions at Medjugorje and a final call to the world for conversion. After the first secret has taken place, *the power of Satin will be broken* and that is why he is so aggressive now. I have shown the children **Heaven**, and **Hell**, and **Purgatory**, so that they can **witness** to you that such places do exist. Please listen to what they have to say.

I told my children at Medjugorje to tell you, "My children, you have forgotten that prayer and fasting will stop war. *It will even change the natural law.* The world must find salvation while there is time. Pray with fervor, and may it have the spirit of faith."

Have faith; the Rosary will protect all whom pray it with their hearts. Mass and the Eucharist are armor, for those able to attend Mass and receive Holy Communion. Each person that comes into the world does so with the covenant of God's love in his heart, and each person is able to hear God in the silence of his own heart. Some people hear clearer than others, because they listen more attentively. The knowledge of good and evil is inherent in every person. Just think, if Catholics lived their faith by example, the whole world could become Catholic.

I would like to point out the role God established for me from before the beginning of time. By God's design, the hierarchy of the Roman Catholic Church has promulgated very little about my role in the end times. My time is just beginning. God has opened-wide his arms of Mercy to all his people, as he has never done before.

Fr. Roman Hoppe said,

"The greatest outpouring of God's mercy is reserved for mankind in the twentieth century."

We are in the final times, as revealed by my Son to St. Margaret Mary Alacoque [1647-1690] when he stated to her, "The end of the world is slowly approaching."

I told the children at Medjugorje, "The first two promises of chastisement will be realized during your lifetime."

The prayers of the faithful have for many years withheld the just punishments of the world. I am not predicting the end of the world. Your prayers can change these predictions and even the prediction that I gave to Akita in Japan in 1973,

"The heavenly father is ready to [allow] a great chastisement on the whole of mankind. If humankind does not repent and amend its lives, the Heavenly Father will [permit] a supreme chastisement, worse than the deluge. Fire will plunge from the sky, and a great part of humanity will be annihilated. The good will die with the bad. Those who survive will suffer so much that they will envy the dead."

However, be of good heart. In these end times, God's Mercy is Infinite, and to emphasize this Jesus appeared to three religious sisters to establish his plan called the Two Divine Promises. He appeared as follows.

Sister Benigna [1885-1916]. Jesus' message was, "The reminder of God's Mercy"
Sister Josefa [1890-1923]; Jesus' message was, "The depth of God's Mercy."
Saint Faustina Kowalska [1905-1938]; Jesus' message was, "The trust in God's Mercy"
In 1954, Jesus revealed to Saint Faustina, "The realization of God's Mercy"

In 1938, Jesus told Saint Faustina Kowalski; "Write, secretary of my Mercy, speak of My Great Mercy, for the dreadful day of my Justice is slowly approaching." He added; however, I cannot punish even the most hardened sinner, if he sincerely appeals to my Mercy. He is immediately granted pardon through my incomprehensible and unfathomable Mercy." And also; "Satan has acknowledged to me that a thousand souls do him less harm than you do when you speak of Almighty God's great Mercy. He states, "Hardened sinners gain confidence and return to God, while I," says the devil, "lose all, and by this I am personally persecuted."

Jesus told Faustina; "From Poland will come the spark that will ignite the whole world and prepare it for my final coming." In 1954, the Lord revealed the Two Divine Promises to Saint Faustina Kowalska, saying; "Each individual who will receive Holy Communion worthily for thirty [30] consecutive days, and will recite one Our Father and one Hail Mary for the welfare of the Catholic Church, will **receive** for **himself** and **one other soul** selected by him, the assurance of **Eternal Salvation**."

To make a thirty-day novena for the salvation of the soul of your loved ones is the greatest gift one can give. God has offered his infinite mercy to everyone in the strife-ridden years that loom ahead. Great warnings of severe chastisements and wonderful signs have been given three times in this past century by our Lord Jesus Christ in a final effort to have his people turn to him and to turn away from sin.

I want all people on earth to form prayer groups, because I know what lies ahead. There will often be divisions and sometimes infighting in such groups. Which fact adequately demonstrates Satan's hatred for prayer cells, as well as bringing to mind the prophetic words of Jesus as reported by [Luke: 12, 51-53]. [As seen at the beginning of this section] Remember, prayer without fasting in like a soldier without a leg. I point out to you the success of your prayers, which helped to topple the Berlin Wall and the collapse of the Iron Curtain. However, the conversion of the Russian people has just begun. It will take many more prayers to effect this conversion. To give validity to my message at Medjugorje, I told the visionary Marija Pavlovic on August 25, 1991, before the event, that the military power of the Soviet Union was collapsing. In October of 1981, I also told the children this about Russia.

*"It is the place where God will be most glorified. The **West** has made civilization progress but **without God**, as if they were their own creators"*

You are too concerned about non-Christians. Before God created the world, he knew each one of us. He personally has named each person with a free will on the planet. He breathed us out of the love in his heart into our mother's wombs. This is a special time of grace; your prayers really matter. I ask all of my faithful children to pray and fast for unbelievers that they, too, may come to the kingdom of heaven. Fasting is a type of purification. It is also a type of discipline. It allows you to experience the value of your free will over yourselves and the requirements of your bodies. I am calling all of God's children, for my Son sees no difference in race, color or creed. Your prayers and fasting will help spare the souls of those that need your help. Without prayer; however, you will not be able to fast. Take your rosary and pray. Accept all your suffering patiently. You should remember how patiently Jesus suffered for you. *Do not impose your faith on the unbelievers,* show it to them with your example and pray for them my children while there is still time. Remember that a flower's life is very beautiful while it lasts, but it is so short, like your human life on earth. I am too humble to ever impose myself upon you. I only come to you when I am invited.

People have divided themselves on earth. I want you to know that the Moslems and the Orthodox, the same as Catholics; are equal before my Son and me. Every person is equally created is a child of God. Certainly all religions are not equal; however, 'All men are equal before God.' You do not have to be Catholic to be saved; however, it is necessary to respect and obey the Commandments of God in following one's conscience. All people are destined in the end to live in the house of God our Father. Salvation is available to everyone without exception. My Son Jesus redeemed *all* people on earth, not just a select few. Only the humans who deliberately refuse to accept God as their Creator and Savior are condemned. God will expect little from a person who has been given little, but to whoever has been given much [Catholics, Christians, who know] very much will be required. God alone in his infinite justice will determine the degree of responsibility and render judgment.

I showed the children purgatory and asked them to tell the world to pray for those souls who have died and have no one to pray for them. Those who die no longer have a free will and it is not possible for them to make up for the things that they did when they had their body. On July 24, 1982, I told Mirjana, "We go to heaven in full conscience; with that which we have now. At death, we are conscious of the separation of the body and soul. It is false to teach people that we are reborn many times, and that we pass to different bodies. One is born only once. The body, drawn from the earth, decomposes after death. It never comes back to life again. Man receives a transfigured body at the last Judgment. Whoever has done very much evil during his life can go straight to heaven if he confesses, is [truly] sorry for what he had done, and receives Communion at the end of his life."

At the death of the body, the soul is given the "light" to see its whole life from the moment it is breathed out of the heart of God into its mother's womb until the moment when its freedom of choice is ended at biological death. In this "light" the soul knows where it belongs. The soul happily enters heaven if its choices have been totally compatible with God's will. If the soul has not made full reparation for his sins before he dies, he will gratefully accept purgatory, a place of reparation, instead of the alternative of the eternal fires of hell. Here a soul must wait until someone from among the people still on earth corrects, through God's graciousness, all the deliberate violations that the soul has caused to God's loving plan. The soul's guardian angel remains with him, until his debt is paid, and I often visit and console these poor souls. Woe to those souls whose religion does not believe in purgatory, for there will be no one to pray for them.

In purgatory, there are different levels: The lowest is close to hell and the highest gradually draws near to heaven. It is not on All Soul's Day, but at Christmas, that the greatest number of souls leaves purgatory. There are in purgatory, souls who pray ardently to God, but for whom no relative or friend prays on earth. However, God does allow them to benefit from the prayers of other people. It happens that God permits them to manifest themselves in different ways to their relatives or friends on earth in order to remind people of the existence of purgatory and to solicit their prayers to come close to God, who is just, but total goodness.

The majority of people go to purgatory. Many go to hell.
A small number go directly to heaven.

Your prayers soften and melt hearts of stone and great love is then possible on earth. When you pray for your loved ones by name, *they can see you here on earth.* Many religions do not believe in purgatory, and consequently they do not pray for their loved ones after their death. Many souls languish in purgatory awaiting the prayers of the faithful for their early release from their place of punishment.

The sufferings of humankind will increase, as is made evident by the news media decrying the acts of evil persons. However, if you pray you will have the strength to endure whatever comes. Those that do not pray, of their own choosing, will have much to suffer. Let those who have ears to hear, listen; let those who have eyes, see, for God's kingdom lives now in the hearts of those who love God. The fire of love in my faithful children's hearts shall consume the world, as you know it. Rest entirely in God's love and rely totally on God's power, for to enjoy his providence, is to never fear for anything.

God in his infinite mercy has named and assigned a guardian angel to each person before he made the world. God named each of the angels as well, and they will communicate their names to you as well as many more things, if you but ask. They always see God and may see the plan God has for each of us. The plan is the path we must each walk to get home to heaven, and your angels will help you if you respond to the help the angel gives. When you sin, your guardian angel prods you to get back on the path to heaven by repenting your sins.

I am extremely concerned about the youth of the world, because I am the mother of all humankind. I pray for each person on earth by name and I know all the traps that confront today's youth. Today's permissive, hedonistic, and materialistic society victimizes children from the moment of their birth. The constant assault on people's modesty and morality has dulled the awareness of good and evil. Blatant sex, sexual innuendoes, and excessive violence are the lure of many of today's sitcoms, soap operas, books, and movies. Anyone suggesting these things as being wrong is frowned upon as being prudes or religious fanatics, because the human mind and conscience has been deceived and dulled to apathy, No shame is associated today with young couples that choose to live together instead of making an honest commitment in marriage, and many writers make the sanctity of the home a laughing stock. All, of which, is completely contrary to the Ten Commandants as dictated by God.

The only answer is prayer, fasting and setting the example of a proper Christian life. Families must pray together and parents must provide a loving environment of respect for the children to grow up in. When there is little love between the husband and wife, there is often very little respect one for the other. When this happens, the spirit of the children is sickened. This gives Satan immense power over the family. Parents must set God-given standards of conduct for their families based on the Ten Commandments. Praying the rosary daily is the best protection against the evil one and his minions. Divorce is the product of sin. Sin is the result of strong temptation. Sin is the result of weakness. At least one party in a marriage has to sin to destroy a sacramental union. Wherever there is sin there is Satin. Once Satin has divided the family he then returns and goes after the children one by one.

Sacramental confession is a remedy for the materialism of the West, because of its power of grace. If each family would pray and fast as a family, there would be peace in the world. If parents would pray, bless, and sacrifice more for their children, the children would thrive. If children would pray for their families, especially the safety of their parent's marriage, and love and obey their parents, family life would be a source of great love and peace on earth. God's abundance would fill the homes. Where there is no prayer and sacrifice, God is absent. A place without God is a place of great danger and pain. Family prayer and penance will bring peace in people, peace in the Church, and peace in the world.

The only way you can help is through family prayer. God respects the family so much that when my Son took human form, he chose to live in a family. The disease of materialism now greatly threatens the family. Often both parents must work; therefore, they claim to have no time to pray together. This is an excuse, and a great lie and most people are living this lie. I promise that for those of you who pray together there will be harmony and unity. Prayer must begin when children are babies. It is a process. By the time children are in their teens it is very hard to erase the bad habits they have acquired. However, it is never too late to begin, for God's mercy is infinite. Remember, as I told you in Chapter Six,

"That which is daily required must be asked for every day."

The authority of parents is a regime of love. Ask yourself; what kind of freedom do you give your children? Do you really help Satan by neglecting your duties or your authority? Parents must restrict their own freedom in the service of their children, just as children must obey and love their parents. Sacrificial love brings great blessings for parents and children. Three generations in one family is most pleasing to God.

I am your devoted mother in heaven and I do not wish your condemnation. God loves each soul that he has created equally without any reservations as to who you are or what you are. Remember God loves you no matter what you have done, or what you have not done. God created each person to spend eternity in heaven with him, if the soul will but live good lives. He has left that choice up to each person concerned. For this reason, he gives each soul a ***free will.*** He invites you to spend eternity in paradise with him, but he will never force you to accept him, the choice is yours.

The transition of the soul is the beginning of eternity!

The decision of Heaven or Hell is yours and yours alone!

What will your decision be?

Thank you for reading my story.

I love you!

Your Spiritual Mother in Heaven

MARY